PART ONE

Also by Frank Schätzing

Death and the Devil

FRANK SCHÄTZING

[LIMIT]

PART ONE

TRANSLATED BY

Shaun Whiteside,

Jamie Lee Searle
and
Samuel Willcocks

Jo Fletcher
BOOKS

First published in the German language as *Limit* by Frank Schätzing

First published in Great Britain in 2013 by Jo Fletcher Books
This edition published in two parts, this part in 2015 by

Jo Fletcher Books
an imprint of
Quercus Publishing Ltd
Carmelite House
50 Victoria Embankment
London EC4Y 0DZ

An Hachette UK company

A CIP catalogue record for this book is available
from the British Library

PART 1 PB ISBN 978 1 84916 517 4
PART 2 PB ISBN 978 1 78429 420 5
EBOOK ISBN 978 0 85738 540 6

10 9 8 7 6 5 4 3 2 1

Typeset by Jouve (UK), Milton Keynes
Printed and bound in Great Britain by Clays Ltd, St Ives plc

For Brigitte and Rolf
who gave me life in the world

For Christine and Clive
who gave me a piece of the moon

2 August 2024

PROLOGUE

EVA

I want to wake up in a city that doesn't sleep—

Good old Frankie-boy. Untroubled by urban transformation, as long as there was a stiff drink waiting for you when you woke up.

Vic Thorn rubbed his eyes.

In thirty minutes the automatic alarm signal would rouse the early shift from their beds. Strictly speaking he couldn't have cared less. As a short-term visitor he was largely free to decide how he was going to spend the day, except that even guests had to adapt to a certain formal framework. Which didn't necessarily mean getting up early, but they woke you anyway.

If I can make it there,

I'll make it anywhere—

Thorn started unfastening his belt. Because he thought staying too long in bed was degrading, he didn't trust anyone else's automatic devices to allow him to spend as little time of his life as possible asleep. Particularly since he liked to decide for himself who or what summoned him back to consciousness. Thorn loved turning his music systems up to the max. And he preferred to entrust his wake-up call to the Rat Pack, Frank Sinatra, Dean Martin, Joey Bishop, Sammy Davis Junior, the disreputable heroes of times past, for whom he felt an almost romantic affection. And up here nothing, nothing at all, was conducive to the habits of the Rat Pack. Even Dean Martin's now famous observation that 'You're not drunk if you can lie on the floor without holding on' was physically invalidated, and nor would the inveterate toper have been able to indulge his predilection for falling off his bar-stool and tottering out into the street. At 35,786 kilometres above the Earth's surface there were no prostitutes waiting for you outside the door, just lethal, airless space.

King of the hill, top of the heap—

Thorn hummed along with the tune, mumbling a wonky-sounding *New York, New York*. With a faint twitch, he pushed himself away and floated off his bunk, drifted to the small, round porthole of his cabin and looked outside.

In the city that never slept, Huros-ED-4 was on the way to his next assignment.

He wasn't bothered by the cold of space or the total lack of atmosphere. The sequence of day and night which, at such a vast distance from the Earth, was in any case based more on general agreement than on sensory experience, held no validity for him. His alarm call was made in the language of the programmers. Huros-ED stood for *Humanoid Robotic System for Extravehicular Demands*, the 4 placed him along with another nineteen of his kind, each one two metres tall, torso and head entirely humanoid, while their exaggeratedly long arms in their resting state recalled the raptorial claws of a praying mantis. When required, they unfolded with admirable agility, and with hands that were able to perform extremely difficult operations. A second, smaller pair of arms emerged from the broad chest, packed with electronics, and these were used to provide assistance. The legs, however, were completely absent. Admittedly the Huros-ED had a waist and a pelvis, but where the hips would have been in a human being there sprouted flexible grippers with devices that allowed him to fasten himself on wherever he happened to be needed. During the breaks he looked for a sheltered niche, connected his batteries to the mains supply, topped up the tanks of his navigation nozzles with fuel and settled down to a spot of mechanical contemplation.

By now the last break was eight hours ago. Since then Huros-ED-4 had been working away industriously in the most diverse spots of the gigantic space station. In the outer zone of the roof, as the part turned towards the zenith was called, he had helped to swap ageing solar panels for new ones, in the wharf he had adjusted the floodlights for Dock 2, where one of the spaceships for the planned Mars mission was currently under construction. Then he had been dispatched a hundred metres lower to the scientific payloads fastened along the cantilevers, to remove the defective platinum parts from a measuring instrument designed to scan the surface of the Pacific Ocean off the coast of Ecuador. After this reconditioning had been successfully completed, his task was to go back inside the spaceport to investigate one of the manipulator arms that had ceased to function in the middle of a loading process.

The spaceport: that meant descending a bit further along the outside of the station, to a ring 180 metres in diameter, with eight berths for incoming and outgoing moon shuttles, and a further eight for evacuation pods. Leaving aside the fact that the ships anchored there were passing through a vacuum rather than through water, what went on around the ring was not much different from what happened in Hamburg or Rotterdam, the big terrestrial seaports, meaning that it too had cranes, huge robot arms on rails, called manipulators. One of these had packed in halfway through the loading process of a freight and passenger shuttle that was to start its journey to the Moon in only a few hours' time. The arm should have been working, but with mechanical stubbornness it absolutely refused to move, and instead hung, effectors spread, half inside the shuttle's loading area and half outside, which meant that the ship's opened body couldn't be closed.

On stipulated flight-paths, Huros-ED-4 passed alongside docked shuttles, airlocks and connecting tunnels, spherical tanks, containers and masts until he reached the defective arm that glinted coldly in the unfiltered sunlight. The cameras behind the visor on his head and the ends of limbs sent pictures to the control centre as he passed close by the construction and subjected every square centimetre to detailed analysis. The control constantly compared these pictures with the images located in his data storage system, until it had found the reason for the failure.

The control instructed him to clean the arm.

He stopped. Someone in his central steering module said, 'Fucking shit!', prompting a query from Huros-ED-4. Although programmed to respond to the human voice, he could detect no meaningful order in the exclamation. The control room neglected to repeat the words, so at first he did nothing but examine the damage. Tiny splinters were wedged into the joint of the manipulator. A long, deep gash ran diagonally across the top of the joint's structure, gaping like a wound. At first sight the electronics seemed to be intact, meaning that the damage was purely material although serious enough to have caused the manipulator to switch off.

The control room issued an instruction to clean the joint.

Huros-ED-4 paused.

Had he been a human being, his behaviour might have been described as indecisive. At length he requested further information, thus indicating in his own vague way that the task was beyond his capabilities. Revolutionary a piece of engineering though he was – sensor-based steering, sensory impression feedback, flexible and autonomous operation – robots were still machines that thought in templates. He probably knew they were there, but he didn't know *what* they were. Likewise, he recorded the tear, but was unable to match it with familiar information. As a result the defective places did not exist for him. Consequently it was hard to tell exactly what he was supposed to be cleaning, so he didn't clean anything at all.

A smattering of consciousness, and robots would have realised that their lives were mercifully free of anxiety.

But everyone else was anxious enough to be going on with. Vic Thorn had had a long shower, listened to 'My Way', put on a T-shirt, trainers and shorts, and had just decided to spend the day in the fitness studio when the call came from headquarters.

'You could be useful to us in solving a problem,' said Ed Haskin, under whose responsibility the spaceport and the systems attached to it fell.

'Right now?' Thorn hesitated. 'I was planning to spend a bit of time on the treadmill.'

'Right now would be better.'

'What's up?'

'It looks as if there are problems with your spaceship.'

Thorn bit his lower lip. A thousand alarm bells went off in his head at the idea that his take-off might be delayed. Bad, very bad! The ship was supposed to leave the port at about midday, with him and another seven astronauts on board, to relieve the crew of the American moon base who, after six months of selenic exile, were succumbing to hallucinations of tarmac roads, carpeted flats, sausages, meadows and a sky full of colour, clouds and rain. On top of that, Thorn was scheduled to be one of the two pilots for the two-and-a-half-day flight and, to cap it all, to be leader of the crew, which explained why they were talking to him rather than anyone else. And there was another reason why any hesitation struck him as more than inopportune—

'What's up with the crate?' he asked, with deliberate indifference. 'Doesn't it want to fly?'

'Oh, it wants to fly all right, but it can't. There was a glitch during loading. The manipulator broke down and blocked the hatches. We can't shut the freight area.'

'I see.' Relief flooded through Thorn. A defective manipulator could be dealt with.

'And you know why it broke down? *Debris*. A heavy fall.'

Thorn sighed. Space debris, whose unwelcome omnipresence was down to an unparalleled orbital congestion, begun in the 1950s by the Soviets with their Sputnik launches. Since then, the remnants of thousands of missions had circulated at every altitude: burnt-out propulsion stages, decommissioned and forgotten satellites, wreckage from countless explosions and collisions, from complete reactors to tiny fragments of shrapnel, drops of frozen coolant, screws and wires, bits of plastic and metal, scraps of gold foil and vestiges of flaked-off paint. The constant fracturing of the splinters with each fresh collision meant that they were breeding like rodents. By now the number of objects larger than one centimetre was estimated at 900,000. Barely three per cent of these were constantly monitored, and the ominous remainder, along with billions of smaller particles and micrometeorites, was on its way elsewhere – in case of doubt, with the inevitability with which insects ended up on windscreens, towards wherever you happened to be.

The problem was, a wasp hurtling at a luxury limousine with the momentum of an identically sized fragment of space debris would have developed the kinetic energy of a hand-grenade and written off the

vehicle in an instant. The speeds of objects moving in opposite directions became extreme in space. Even particles only micrometres across
had a destructive effect in the long term: they ground away at solar
panels, they destroyed the surfaces of satellites and roughened the outer
shells of spaceships. Near-Earth debris burned up sooner or later in the
upper layers of the atmosphere, but only to be replaced by new debris.
With increasing altitude its lifetime extended, and it could theoretically
have survived for all eternity at the level at which the space station was
orbiting. The fact that several of the dangerous objects were known
and their flight-paths could be calculated weeks and months in advance
provided a certain consolation, because it allowed the astronauts just to
steer the whole station out of the way. The thing that had crashed into
the manipulator plainly hadn't been one of those.

'And what can I do about it?' asked Thorn.

'I know, crew time.' Haskin laughed irritably. 'Tightness of resources.
The robot can't sort it out all by itself. Two of us will have to go out,
but at the moment I've only got one staff member available. Would you
jump in?'

Thorn didn't think for long. It was very important for him to get out
of there on time, and besides, he liked space-walks.

'That's fine,' he said.

'You'll be going out with Karina Spektor.'

Even better. He'd met Spektor the previous evening in the crew canteen, an expert in robotics, of Russian origin, with high cheekbones
and cat-green eyes, who had responded to his attempts at flirtation with
seeming willingness to engage in further international understanding.

'I'm on my way!' he said.

—*in a city that never sleeps*—

Cities tended to generate noise. Streets in which the air seethed with
acoustic activity. People drawing attention to themselves by beeping,
calling, whistling, chatting, laughing, complaining, shouting. Noise as
social putty, coded into cacophony. Guitarists, singers, sax players in
house doorways and subway tunnels. Disgruntled crows, barking dogs.

The reverberation of construction machinery, thundering jackhammers, metal on metal. Unexpected, familiar, wheedling, shrill, sharp, dark, mysterious, noises that rose and fell, that approached and fled, some that spread like a gas, others that caught you right in the pit of the stomach and the auditory canal. Background noises of traffic. The flashy bass baritone of heavy limousines vying with dainty mopeds, with the purr of electro-mobiles, the grandiloquence of sports cars, souped-up motorbikes, the thumping get-to-the-side of the buses. Music from boutiques, footstep concerts in pedestrian precincts, strolling, shuffling, strutting, rushing, the sky vibrating with the thunder of distant aeroplane turbines, the whole city one great bell.

Outside the space city:

None of that.

Familiar as the sounds might have been inside the living modules, laboratories, control rooms, connecting tunnels, leisure areas and restaurants distributed across an overall height of 280 metres, there was a ghostly feeling the first time you left the station for EVA, 'Extravehicular Activity', the external maintenance service. Suddenly, without transition, you were out there, really out there, more out there than anywhere else. Beyond the airlocks all sound stopped. Of course you didn't go entirely deaf. You could hear yourself very clearly, and you could hear the rush of the air-conditioning unit built into the spacesuit, and of course the walkie-talkie, but it was all being played out inside your own portable spaceship.

All around you, in the vacuum, perfect silence reigned. You saw the mighty structure of the station, peered through illuminated windows, saw the icy radiance of the floodlight batteries high above, where enormous spaceships were being assembled, spaceships that would never land on a planet and only existed in weightless suspension, you were aware of industrial activity, the turning and stretching of the cranes on the outer ring and the shuttles from the inner zone, you observed robots in free fall, so like living creatures that you felt like asking them the way – and intuitively, overwhelmed by the beauty of the architecture, the far-away Earth and the coldly staring stars, their light undispersed by the atmosphere, you expected to hear mysterious or dramatic music. But space stayed mute, its sublimity orchestrated only by your own breath.

In the company of Karina Spektor, Thorn floated through the emptiness and silence towards the defective manipulator. Their suits, fitted with steering nozzles, enabled them to navigate precisely. They slipped across the docks of the vast spaceport embraced by the tower-like construction of the space station, wide as a freeway. Three moon shuttles were currently anchored on the ring – two of them fixed to airlocks, Thorn's spaceship in the parking position – and also the eight plane-like evacuation pods. Basically the whole ring was one great switching yard, around which the spaceships constantly changed location to keep the symmetrically constructed station in balance.

Thorn and Spektor had left Torus-2, the distributor module in the centre of the port, and headed for one of the external locks not far from the shuttle. White and massive, with opened loading hatches, it rested in the sunlight. The frozen arm of the manipulator loomed high above them, bent abruptly at the elbow and disappearing into the cargo zone. Huros-ED-4 hung motionless by its anchor platform. With his gaze fixed on the blocked joint, there was something unsettling about his posture. Only at the very last moment did he move slightly to the side so that they could get a glimpse of the damage. Of course his behaviour was not the result of cybernetic peevishness, as a Huros doesn't even have the beginning of a notion of selfhood, but his images were now surplus to requirements. From now on what mattered were the impressions that the helmet-cameras sent to the control room.

'So?' Haskin asked. 'What do you think?'

'Bad.' Spektor gripped the frame of the manipulator and drew herself closer to it. Thorn followed her.

'Odd,' he said. 'It looks to me as if something's brushed against the arm and torn this gaping hole, but the electronics seem to be undamaged.'

'Then it should move,' Haskin objected.

'Not necessarily,' said Spektor. She spoke English with a Slavic smoothness, rather erotic, Thorn thought. A shame, in fact, that he couldn't stay another day. 'The impact must have released lot of micro-debris. Perhaps our friend is suffering from constipation. Did the Huros perform an environmental analysis?'

'Slight contamination. What about the splinters? Could they have caused the blockage?'

'It's possible. They probably come from the arm itself. Perhaps something's got twisted, and it's under tension.' The astronaut studied the joint carefully. 'On the other hand, this is a manipulator, not a pastry fork. The object would have been seven or eight millimetres long at the most. I mean it wasn't an actual collision, it should really be able to cope with something like that.'

'You certainly know your way around these things,' Thorn said appreciatively.

'Party trick,' she laughed. 'I hardly deal with anything else. Space debris is our biggest problem up here.'

'And what about this?' He leaned forward and pointed to a spot where a tiny, bright shard protruded. 'Could that come from a meteorite?'

Spektor followed his outstretched index finger.

'At any rate it comes from the thing that hit the arm. The analyses will tell you more.'

'Exactly,' said Haskin. 'So get a move on. I suggest you get the thing out with the ethanol blower.'

'Have we got one of those?' Thorn asked.

'The Huros does,' Spektor replied. 'We can use his left arm, there are tanks inside and nozzles on the effectors. But it'll take two of us, Vic. Have you ever worked with a Huros?'

'Not directly.'

'I'll show you. We'll have to turn him off partially if we want to use him as a tool. That means one of us will have to help stabilise him, while the other—'

At that moment the manipulator stirred into life.

The huge arm stretched out of the loading-space, pushed backwards, swivelled, grabbed the Huros-ED and shoved it away as if it had had enough of its company. Thorn automatically pushed his companion downwards and out of the collision zone, but couldn't keep the robot from striking her shoulder and whirling her around. At the last second Spektor managed to cling on to the frame, then the manipulator crashed into Thorn, dragged him away from her and from the ring and catapulted him into space.

Back! He had to get back!

Fingers flying, he tried to regain control over his steering nozzles. He was followed by the pirouetting torso of the Huros-ED, which was getting closer and closer, as Haskin and Spektor's shouts rang in his ear. The robot's abdomen hit his helmet. Thorn somersaulted and started circling helplessly as he was slung over the edge of the ring-level and hurtled from the space station at terrifying speed. He realised with horror that in attempting to protect his companion he had lost his only chance of saving himself. In wild panic he reached around him, found the switches for the steering nozzles, turned them on to stabilise his flight-path with short blasts, to slow his circling trajectory, found he couldn't breathe, realised that his suit had been damaged, that it was all over, waved his arms around, tried to scream—

His scream froze.

Vic Thorn's body was carried out into the silent, endless night, and everything changed in the seconds of his death, everything.

19 May 2025

THE ISLAND

Isla de las Estrellas, Pacific Ocean

The island wasn't much more than a rocky outcrop, set on the equator like a pearl on a string. Compared with other nearby islands, its charms were rather modest. In the west a quite impressive cliff rose from the sea, crowned by tropical rainforest, which clung dark and impenetrable to jagged volcanic slopes, and was inhabited almost exclusively by insects, spiders and an unusually ugly species of bat. Streams had dug cracks and gorges, collected into waterfalls and poured thundering into the ocean. On the eastern side, the landscape fell in terraces, intermingled with rocky elevations and largely bare. You would have looked in vain for palm-lined beaches. Black basalt sand marked the few bays that gave access to the interior. Rainbow-coloured lizards sunned themselves on stone pillars amidst the crashing waves. Their day consisted of catapulting themselves several metres into the air and snapping for insects, the meagre climax of an otherwise unclimactic repertoire of natural spectacles. Overall, the Isla had hardly anything to offer that didn't exist in more beautiful, bigger and higher forms elsewhere.

On the other hand its geographical location was impeccable.

It actually lay exactly at the middle of the Earth, where the northern and southern hemispheres met, 550 kilometres west of Ecuador and thus far from any air routes. There were no storms in this part of the world. Major accumulations of cloud were a rarity, lightning never flashed. During the first half of the year it sometimes rained, violently and for hours at a time, without the air growing particularly cooler. Temperatures hardly ever fell below twenty-two degrees Celsius, and usually they were significantly higher than that. Because the island was uninhabited and economically useless, the Ecuadorian parliament had been more than happy to lease it, for the next forty years in return for an invigorating boost to the state economy, to new tenants whose first job was to rename Isla Leona as Isla de las Estrellas: Stellar Island: island of the stars.

Subsequently part of the eastern slope disappeared under an accumulation of glass and steel that promptly united the fury of all animal conservationists. But the building had no effect on the island's ecology. Flocks of noisy seabirds, unperturbed by the evidence of human presence, daubed cliff and architecture alike with their guano. The creatures were untroubled by ideas of beauty, and the humans had their minds on higher things than swallow-tailed gulls and ringed plovers. In any case, not many people had set foot on the island for a long time, and everything indicated that it would remain a rather exclusive place in future as well.

At the same time, nothing fired the imagination of the whole of humanity as much as this island.

It might have been a rough pile of bird-shit, but at the same time it was considered the most extraordinary, perhaps the most hopeful place in the world. In fact the actual magic emanated from an object about two nautical miles off the coast, a gigantic platform resting on five house-sized pontoons. If you approached it on misty days, at first you couldn't see what was so special about it. You saw flat structures, generating plants and tanks, a helicopter landing pad, a terminal with a tower, aerials and radio telescopes. The whole thing looked like an airport, except that there was no runway to be seen. Instead, a massive cylindrical construction grew from the centre, a gleaming colossus with bundles of pipes meandering up its sides. Only by narrowing your eyes could you make out the black line that emerged from the cylinder and soared steeply upwards. If the clouds were low, they engulfed it after a few hundred metres, and you found yourself wondering what you would see if the sky cleared. Even people who knew better – in principle, then, anyone who had managed to get through the high-security area – expected to see something where the line ended, a fixed point on which the overstretched imagination could settle.

But there was nothing.

Even in bright sunshine, when the sky was deep blue, you couldn't see the end of the line. It became thinner and thinner until it seemed to dematerialise in the atmosphere. Through field-glasses it just disappeared a little higher up. You stared until your neck ached, with Julian Orley's now legendary observation in your ears, that the Isla de las Estrellas was the ground floor of eternity – and you started to sense what he had meant by it.

Carl Hanna strained his neck too, craning from the seat of the helicopter to look up stupidly into the blue, while below him two finback whales ploughed the azure of the Pacific. Hanna didn't waste a glance on them. When the pilot pointed out the rare animals yet again, he heard himself murmuring that there was nothing less interesting than the sea.

The helicopter curved round and roared towards the platform. The line blurred briefly in front of Hanna's eyes, seemed to dissolve, and then it was clearly visible in the sky again, as straight as if drawn by a ruler.

A moment later it had doubled.

'There are two of them,' observed Mukesh Nair.

The Indian brushed the thick black hair off his forehead. His dark face glowed with delight, the nostrils of his cucumber-shaped nose flared as if to inhale the moment.

'Of course there are two.' Sushma, his wife, held up her index and middle fingers as if explaining something to a child in reception class. 'Two cabins, two cables.'

'I know that, I know!' Nair waved her impatiently away. His mouth twisted into a smile. He looked at Hanna. 'How amazing! Do you know how wide those cables are?'

'Just over a metre, I think.' Hanna smiled back.

'For a moment they were gone.' Nair looked out, shaking his head. 'They simply disappeared.'

'That's true.'

'You saw that too? And you, Sushma? They flickered like a mirage. Did you see—'

'Yes, Mukesh, I saw it too.'

'I thought I was imagining it.'

'No, you weren't,' Sushma said benignly and rested a small, paddle-shaped hand on his knee. Hanna thought the two of them looked as if they'd been created by the painter Fernando Botero. The same rounded physiques, the same short, inflated-looking extremities.

He looked out of the window again.

The helicopter stayed an appropriate distance from the cables as it drifted past the platform. Only authorised pilots from NASA or Orley Enterprises were allowed to fly this route when they brought guests to the Isla de las Estrellas. Hanna tried to catch a glimpse of the inside of the cylinder, where the cables disappeared, but they were too far away. A moment later they had left the platform behind, and were swinging in towards the Isla. Below them, the shadow of the helicopter darted across deep blue waves.

'That cable must be really thin if you can't see it from the side,' Nair reflected. 'Which means it must actually be flat. Are they cables at all?' He laughed and wrung his hands. 'They're more like tapes, really, aren't they? I've probably got it all wrong. My God, what can I say? I grew up in a field. In a field!'

Hanna nodded. They had fallen into conversation on the flight here from Quito, but even so he knew that Mukesh Nair had a very close relationship with fields. A modest farmer's son from Hoshiarpur in Punjab, who liked eating well but preferred a street stall to any three-star restaurant, who thought more highly of the concerns and opinions of simple people than of small-talk at receptions and gallery openings, who preferred to fly Economy Class and who craved expensive clothes as much as a Tibetan bear craves a tie. At the same time Mukesh Nair, with an estimated private fortune of 46 billion dollars, was one of the wealthiest people in the world, and his way of thinking was anything but rustic. He had studied agriculture in Ludhiana and economics at Bombay University, he was a holder of the Padma Vibhushan, the second-highest Indian order for civilian merits, and an unchallenged market leader when it came to supplying the world with Indian fruit and vegetables. Hanna was intimately acquainted with the CV of Mr Tomato, as Nair was generally known, having studied the careers of all the guests who were travelling in for the meeting.

'Now look, just look at that!' shouted Nair. 'That's not bad, is it?'

Hanna craned his neck. The helicopter hovered along the eastern slope of the island so that they could enjoy a perfect view of the Stellar Island Hotel. Like a stranded ocean steamer it lay on the slopes, seven receding storeys piled up on top of one another, overlooking a prow with a huge swimming-pool. Each room had its own sun terrace. The highest point of the building formed a circular terrace, half covered by a huge glass dome. Hanna could make out tables and chairs, loungers, a buffet, a bar. Amidships lay a part that had been left level, plainly the lobby, bounded to the north by the stern-shaped construction of a helicopter landing pad. Architecture alternated with sections of rough stone, as if the architects had been trying to beam up a cruise-ship right in front of the island, and had miscalculated by a few hundred metres towards the centre. It seemed to Hanna that parts of the hotel grounds must have been blown into the mountain with explosives. A footpath, interrupted by flights of steps, wound its way down, crossed a green plateau whose design looked too harmonious to be of natural origin, then led further down and opened up into a path running along the coast.

'A golf course,' Nair murmured in delight. 'How wonderful.'

'I'm sorry, but I thought you liked things simple.' And when the Indian looked at him in amazement, Hanna added, 'According to yourself. Plain restaurants. Simple people. Third-class travel.'

'You're getting things muddled.'

'If the media are to be trusted, you're surprisingly modest for a public figure.'

'Such nonsense! I try to keep out of public life. You can count the number of interviews that I've given over the past few years on one hand. If Tomato gets a good press, I'm happy. The main thing is that no one tries to get me in front of a camera or a microphone.' Nair frowned. 'By the way, you're right. Luxury isn't something I need to live. I come from a tiny village. The amount of money you have is irrelevant. Deep down, I'm still living in that village, it's just got a bit bigger.'

'By a few continents on either side of the Indian Ocean,' Hanna teased. 'Got you.'

'So?' Nair grinned. 'As I said, you're getting things muddled.'

'What?'

'Look, it's quite simple. The platform we just flew over – things like that occupy my heart. The fate of the entire human race may hang on those cables. But this hotel fascinates me the way theatre might fascinate you. It's fun, so you go there from time to time. Except that most people, as soon as they get some money, start thinking theatre is real life. Ideally they'd like to live on stage, dress up again every day and play a part. That makes me think; you know the joke about the psychologist who wants to catch a lion?'

'No.'

'Quite easy. He goes into the desert, sets up a cage, gets in and decides that inside is outside.'

Hanna grinned. Nair shook with laughter.

'You see, I have no interest in that, it was never my thing. I don't want to sit in a cage or live out my life on a stage. Nonetheless, I shall enjoy the next two weeks, you can bet on that. Before it gets going tomorrow, I'll play a round of golf down there and love it! But once the fourteen days are over I'll go back home to where you laugh at a joke because it's good and not because a rich person's telling it. I'll eat things that taste good, not things that are expensive. I'll talk to people because I like them, not because they're important. Many of those people don't have the money to·go to my restaurants, so I'll go to theirs.'

'Got it,' said Hanna.

Nair rubbed his nose. 'At the risk of depressing you – I don't actually know anything about you at all.'

'Because you've spent the whole flight talking about yourself,' Sushma observed reproachfully.

'Have I? You must excuse my need to communicate.'

'That's fine,' Hanna said with a wave of his hand. 'There isn't so much to say about me. I tend to work in silence.'

'Investment?'

'Exactly.'

'Interesting.' Nair pursed his lips. 'What fields?'

'Mostly energy. And a bit of everything.' Hanna hesitated. 'It might interest you to know that I was born in New Delhi.'

The helicopter lowered itself towards the heliport. The landing pad had room for three helicopters that size and was marked with a fluorescent symbol, a silvery O with a stylised orange moon around it: the company logo of Orley Enterprises. At the edge of the heliport Hanna spotted people in uniform, taking reception of passengers and luggage. A slim woman in a light-coloured trouser suit broke away from the group. The wind in the rotor-blades tugged at her clothes, her hair glistened in the sun.

'You come from New Delhi?' Sushma Nair, visibly taken with Hanna's unexpected revelation, edged closer. 'How long did you live there?'

The helicopter came gently to rest. The door swung aside and a step-ladder unfolded.

'Let's talk about it by the pool,' Hanna said, putting her off for the time being, then let them walk ahead of him and followed them without any great haste. Nair's smile revealed more tooth enamel. He beamed at the staff, the surroundings and life, he drew the island air into his nostrils, said, 'Ah!' and 'Incredible!' As soon as he caught sight of the woman in the trouser suit he started praising the grounds in the most effulgent terms. Sushma added indifferent noises of appreciation. The slim woman thanked them. Nair went on talking, without drawing breath. How wonderful everything was. How successful. Hanna practised being patient as he appreciated her appearance. Late thirties, neat ash-blonde hair, well groomed and displaying that natural grace that is never entirely aware of itself, she could have played the glamorous lead in an advertisement for a credit company or a range of cosmetics. In fact she was in charge of Orley Travel, Orley's tourism department, which made her the second most important person in the biggest business empire in the world.

'Carl.' She smiled and extended her hand. Hanna looked into sea-blue eyes, impossibly intense, the iris dark-rimmed. Her father's eyes. 'Nice to have you here as our guest!'

'Thanks for the invitation.' He returned her handshake and lowered his voice. 'You know, I'd prepared a few nice remarks about the hotel, but I'm afraid my predecessor pre-empted everything I had to say.'

'Haha! Ha!' Nair clapped him on the shoulder. 'I'm sorry, my friend, but we have Bollywood! Your old-school charm couldn't possibly match so much poetry and pathos.'

'Don't listen to him,' said Lynn, without turning her eyes away. 'I'm very susceptible to Canadian charm. Even its non-verbal variant.'

'Then I won't allow myself to be discouraged,' Hanna promised.

'I would be most offended if you did.'

All around them, willing hands were busy unloading mountains of battered-looking luggage. Hanna assumed it belonged to the Nairs. Solidly built things that had been in use since Old Testament times. He himself had brought only a small suitcase and a valise.

'Come on,' Lynn said cordially. 'I'll show you to your rooms.'

From the terrace, Tim saw his sister leaving the heliport with an Indian-looking couple and an athletically built man, and walking to the reception building. He and Amber lived in a corner room on the fifth floor, with a perfect panoramic view. Some distance away, glinting in the sunlight, was the platform that they would be going to the following morning. Another helicopter was approaching the island, its arrival heralded by the clattering noise of the rotors.

He threw his head back.

A day of rare, crystal clarity.

The sky stretched across the sea like a deep-blue dome. A single ragged cloud hung there like an ornament or a landmark, apparently motionless. It made Tim think of an old film that he'd seen years ago, a tragicomedy in which a man grew up in a small town without ever leaving it. He'd gone to school there, got married, taken a job, met up with friends he'd known since childhood – and then, in his mid-thirties, he discovered that he was the involuntary star of a television show and the town was one huge, colossal fake, stuffed full of cameras, fake walls and stage lighting. All the inhabitants apart from him were actors with lifetime contracts, *his* lifetime, of course, and consistently enough the sky proved to be a huge, blue-painted dome.

Tim Orley narrowed one eye and held up his right index finger in such a way that the tip seemed to touch the lower edge of the cloud. It balanced on it like a piece of cotton wool.

'Do you want something to drink?' Amber called from inside.

He didn't reply, but wrapped his left hand around his wrist and tried to keep his finger as still as possible. At first nothing happened. Then, extremely slowly, the tiny cloud drifted eastwards.

'The bar is full to the brim. I'll take a bitter lemon. What would you like?'

It was moving. It would drift on. For some unfathomable reason it reassured Tim to know that the cloud up there wasn't nailed on or painted up.

'What?' he asked.

'I asked what you'd like to drink.'

'Yes.'

'So, what?'

'No idea.'

'Goodness me. I'll take a look and see if they've got any.'

He returned his attention to Lynn. Amber came across the terrace towards him, swinging an open bottle of Coca-Cola seductively between thumb and forefinger. Tim mechanically accepted it, put it to his lips and drank without noticing what he was pouring down his throat. His wife watched him. Then she looked down to where Tim's sister and her little entourage were just disappearing into the lobby.

'Oh, I see,' she remarked.

He said nothing.

'You're still worried?'

'You know me.'

'What for? Lynn's looking good.' Amber leaned against the railing and sucked noisily on her lemonade. 'Really good, in fact, if you ask me.'

'That's exactly what I'm worried about.'

'That she looks good?'

'You know exactly what I mean. She's trying to be more perfect than perfect, all over again.'

'Oh, Tim—'

'You've dealt with her before, haven't you?'

'More than anything I've experienced her having everything under control here.'

'Everything here has *Lynn* under control!'

'Fine, so what should she do, in your opinion? Julian's invited a crowd of filthy-rich eccentrics that she's got to look after. He's promised them two weeks in the most exclusive hotels of all time, and Lynn's responsible for them all. Should she start letting herself go, and walk around the place looking all unwashed and with her hair in a mess, neglect her guests, just to prove that she's a human being?'

'Of course not.'

'This is a circus, Tim! She's the ringmaster. She *has* to be perfect, or else the lions will eat her.'

'I know that,' Tim said impatiently. 'That's not the issue. It's just that I can see that she's starting to get agitated again.'

'She didn't seem specially agitated to me.'

'That's because she deceives you. Because she deceives everybody. You know how well her personal diplomacy works.'

'I'm sorry, but isn't it possible that you're dramatising everything just a little bit?'

'I'm not dramatising anything at all. I'm really not. Let's leave aside the question of whether it was a brilliant idea to join in all this nonsense in the first place, but fine, nothing to be done. You and Julian, you—'

'Hey!' A warning light flashed in Amber's eyes. 'Don't go saying we twisted your arm again.'

'What else?'

'No one twisted your arm.'

'Oh, come on! You insisted like mad.'

'So? How old are you? Five or something? If you really hadn't wanted—'

'I didn't. I'm here because of Lynn.' Tim sighed and rubbed his eyes. 'Okay, okay! She *looks* fantastic! She seems to be stable. But still.'

'Tim. She *built* this hotel!'

'Sure.' He nodded. 'Yes, sure. And it's great! Really.'

'I'm taking you seriously. I just don't want you to start blaming Lynn simply because you can't sort things out with your father.'

Tim tasted the bitterness of the insult. He turned to face her and shook his head.

'That's unfair,' he said quietly.

Amber turned her lemonade bottle between her fingers. Silence fell for a while. Then she put her arms around his neck and kissed him.

'I'm sorry.'

'It's fine.'

'Have you talked to Julian about it?'

'Yes, and I'll give you three guesses. He insists she's doing brilliantly. You say she looks as if she's in the pink. So I'm the idiot.'

'Of course you are. The most lovable idiot who's ever got on anyone's nerves.'

Tim grinned crookedly. He pressed Amber to him, but his gaze was fixed beyond the parapet. The helicopter that had brought the athlete and the Indian couple here hummed its way out to the open sea. The next one was hovering above the heliport and preparing to land. Below it, Lynn was leaving the lobby to welcome the new guests. Tim's eyes drifted across the steep terrain between the hotel and the cliffs, the abandoned golf course, then followed the walkway down to the coastal path. Dips and gorges had required the construction of several small bridges, with the result that you could comfortably stroll along the whole of the eastern side of the Isla de las Estrellas. He saw someone ambling along the path. A slender form came darting up from the opposite direction, its body gleaming bright in the sun.

Bright as ivory.

Finn O'Keefe saw her and stopped. The woman was running at an athletic pace. She was a curious creature, with willowy limbs, almost on the edge of anorexia, but still shapely. Her skin was snow-white, as was her long, flowing hair. She wore a skimpy mother-of-pearl-coloured bathing suit and trainers of the same colour, and moved as nimbly as a gazelle. Someone who belonged on the front pages.

'Hello,' he said.

The woman stopped running and approached him in springy steps.

'Hi! And who are you?'

'Finn.'

'Oh, of course. Finn O'Keefe. You look somehow different on screen.'

'I always look somehow different.'

He held out his hand. Her fingers, long and delicate, gave a surprisingly firm handshake. Now that she was standing right in front of him he could see that her eyebrows and eyelids were the same shimmering white as her hair, while her irises were almost violet. Below her narrow, straight nose, a sensuously curving mouth arched with almost colourless lips. To Finn O'Keefe she looked like an attractive alien whose firm skin was starting to crease in places. He guessed that she was just past forty.

'And who are you?'

'I'm Heidrun,' she said. 'Are you part of the tour group?'

Her English sounded as if it ran on crunchy gears. He tried to guess her accent. Germans generally spoke a kind of saw-toothed English, the Scandinavian version was soft and melodious. Heidrun, he decided, wasn't German, but she wasn't Danish or Swedish either.

'Yes,' he said. 'I'm part of it.'

'And? Fed up?'

He laughed. She didn't seem even slightly impressed to find herself bumping into him here. Exposed as he was to the wearying and universal admiration of women who would happily have ditched their husbands just to go to bed with him, not to mention the men who fancied him too, he was constantly on the run.

'Quite honestly, yes. A bit.'

'Whatever. Me too.'

She brushed her sweat-drenched mane from her brow, turned round, spread the thumbs and index fingers of both hands into right angles, brought the tips together and studied the platform in the sea through the frame she had created. You could only make out the vertical black line if you looked very carefully.

'And what does he want from you?' she asked suddenly.

'Who?'

'Julian Orley.' Heidrun lowered her hands and directed her violet gaze at him. 'He wants something from each of us, after all.'

'Really?'

'Oh, come on. Otherwise we wouldn't be here, would we?'

'Hmm.'

'Are you rich?'

'I get by.'

'Silly question. God, you must be rich! You're Mr Royalties, aren't you? If you haven't somehow screwed everything up, you must be worth a few hundred million dollars.' She laid her head curiously on one side. 'And? Are you?'

'And you?'

'Me?' Heidrun laughed. 'Forget it. I'm a photographer. With what I own he couldn't even have the platform repainted. Let's say I'm part of a job lot. It's Walo that he's after. Walo.'

'Sorry, who's that?'

'Walo?' She pointed up to the hotel. 'My husband. Walo Ögi.'

'Doesn't ring a bell.'

'I'm not surprised. Artists are incapable of thinking about money, and he doesn't do anything else.' She smiled. 'But he does have a lot of good ideas on how you can spend it once you've got it. You'll like him. Do you know who else is here?'

'Who's that?'

'Evelyn Chambers.' Heidrun's smile assumed a mischievous quality. 'Darling, she'll put you through the wringer. You can run away from her down here, but up there—'

'I have no problem talking to her.'

'Let's bet you do?'

Heidrun turned her back on him and started climbing the path back up to the hotel. O'Keefe came after her. In fact he did have a brontosaurus-sized problem talking to Evelyn Chambers, America's number one talk-show host. He avoided those shows more than anything else in the world. A thousand times, perhaps more, she'd invited him onto *Chambers*, her high-rating spiritual striptease that millions of socially depraved Americans gathered in front of their screens to watch every Friday evening. On every occasion he'd declined. Here, now, without the bars between them, he was the fillet steak and she was the lion.

Appalling!

They passed by the golf course.

'You're an albino,' he said.

'Clever Finn.'

'Not scared of burning? Because of – what do you call it—'

'My pronounced melanin disorder and my light-sensitive eyes,' she chanted the answer down at him. 'Nope, not a problem. I wear highly filtered contact lenses.'

'And your skin?'

'How flattering,' she said mockingly. 'Finn O'Keefe is interested in my skin.'

'Nonsense. I really am interested.'

'Of course it's entirely free of pigment. Without sun protection I'd go up in flames. So I use Moving Mirrors.'

'Moving Mirrors?'

'It's a gel with microscopic mirrors that adjust themselves according to the heat of the sun. It means I can stay in the open for a few hours, but of course it shouldn't become a habit. So, sporty guy, fancy a swim?'

After she'd spent most of the day accompanying guests from the heliport to the hotel and going back to wait for the next helicopter to arrive, back and forth, back and forth, Lynn Orley was surprised she hadn't worn a groove in the ground ages ago.

Of course she'd done other things as well. Andrew Norrington, deputy head of security at Orley Enterprises, had turned the Isla de las Estrellas into the kind of high-security zone that made you think you were in the Hotel California: 'You can check out any time you like, but you can never leave!' Lynn's own idea of security included protection, but not its visible display, while Norrington argued that you couldn't hide the guards in the bushes like garden gnomes. She mentioned that it had been difficult enough to persuade the new arrivals against having their own bodyguards with them at all times, and referred to Oleg Rogachev, who had only reluctantly left at home the half-dozen heavies he usually arrived with, and pointed out that half of the service staff were highly trained sharp-shooters. No one, when they were out jogging or playing golf, wanted to be constantly bumping into dark figures with the word Emergency prac-tically stamped on their foreheads. Besides, she rather liked gun-toting gnomes who looked after you without tripping you up all the time.

After a stubborn battle Norrington had finally retrained his brigades and found ways of adapting them to their surroundings. Lynn knew she was making his life difficult, but he had to deal with it. Norrington was excellent at his job, highly organised and dependable, but he was also a victim of that infectious paranoia that gripped all bodyguards sooner or later.

'Interesting,' she said.

Beside her, Warren Locatelli snorted like a horse.

'Yes, but you wanted to lower the price! My God, I lost it at that point. I said hang on. Hang *on* . . . ! Do you know exactly whom you're dealing with here? Pimps! Monkey-brains! I didn't just climb down from the trees, you get me? You don't lure me out of the jungle with bananas. Either you play by my rules or I'll . . .'

And so on and so forth.

Lynn nodded sympathetically as she walked the new arrivals to recep-tion. Warren Locatelli was such a jerk! And Momoka Omura, that silly tart beside him, not one bit better. But as long as Julian thought it was important, she would have to pay attention even to a talking dung-beetle. You didn't necessarily have to understand it to have a conversation with it. It was enough to react to tone, tempo and accompanying noises like grunts, growls or laughter. If the torrent of words raining down on you ended in merriment, then you joined in with the laughter. If it rattled down furiously, you were always on the safe side with an 'Unbelievable!' or a 'No really?' If the situation called for contextual understanding, you just listened. Mockery was legitimate, it was just important not to get caught out.

In Locatelli's case autopilot was sufficient. As long as he wasn't talking shop, his main topic of conversation was the state of his own awesomeness, and the fact that everyone else was a bunch of assholes. Or pimps and monkey-brains. Depending.

Who would arrive next?

Chuck and Aileen Donoghue.

Chucky, the hotel mogul. He was okay, even though he told terrible jokes. Aileen would probably turn to the kitchen first thing to see if they were cutting the meat thickly enough.

Aileen: 'Chucky likes fat steaks! They've got to be fat.'

Chucky: 'Yes, fat! What Europeans call steaks aren't steaks at all. Hey, you know what I call European steaks? You want to know? You do? Okay – carpaccio!'

But Chuck was okay.

To Lynn's regret, on Julian's chessboard Locatelli was the queen, or at least a rook. He had managed to do something that had driven generations of physicists to despair, namely developing solar cells that converted over sixty per cent of sunlight into electricity. With those, and because he was also a brilliant businessman, Locatelli's company Lightyears had become market leader in the solar energy sector and made its owner so rich that Forbes put him at number five among the world's billionaires. Momoka Omura strutted indifferently along beside him, let her eye wander over the grounds and managed a grudging 'nice'. Lynn imagined hitting her between the eyes with her clenched fists, but instead took her arm and complimented her on her hair.

'I knew you'd like it,' Momoka replied with the faintest of smiles.

No, it looks lousy, Lynn thought. Complete disaster.

'Nice to have you both here,' she said.

At the same time Evelyn Chambers, sunning herself on her sixth-floor terrace, was calling up her knowledge of Russian and pricking up her ears. She was the high-society seismographer. Every tremor, however small, registered as news value on her personal Richter scale, and there had just been a big one.

The Rogachevs were in the room next door. The terraces were separated by sound-absorbing barriers, but she could still hear Olympiada Rogacheva's breathless sobs, now close by, now further away. She was obviously pacing back and forth on the sun-deck, clutching a full glass, as usual.

'Why?' she wailed. 'Why again?'

Oleg Rogachev's answer came dully and incomprehensibly from inside the room. Whatever he had said made Olympiada explode in a volcanic eruption.

'You complete bastard!' she yelled. 'Right in front of my eyes!' Muffled sounds, gasps. 'You didn't even bother to do it in secret!'

Rogachev stepped outside.

'You want me to have secrets? Then fine.'

His voice was calm, uninterested and designed to bring the surrounding temperature down a few degrees. Evelyn pictured him in front of her. A middle-sized, inconspicuous man with thin, blond hair and a foxy face, eyes set in it like little icy mountain lakes. Evelyn had interviewed Oleg Alexeyevich Rogachev the previous year, shortly after he had become majority shareholder of the Daimler company, and met a polite, quiet businessman who had willingly answered all her questions while at the same time appearing as impenetrable as a piece of armour plating.

She recapitulated what she knew about Rogachev. His father had run a Soviet steel firm, which had been privatised as a consequence of Perestroika. The usual model at the time was to give the workers voucher share certificates. For a short time, the multicellular organism of the proletariat had assumed command, except that shares in a steel-works didn't get families through the winter. So most workers had quickly been willing to turn their certificates into money, selling them to finance companies or their superiors, and receiving, on the eat-or-be-eaten principle, just a fraction of their actual value. Gradually the former state companies of the fragmented Soviet Union had fallen into the hands of investment firms and speculators. Old Rogachev had also turned up and bought enough of his workers' share certificates to purchase the company himself, which brought him into the firing line of a competing Mafia clan, unfortunately in the literal sense of that phrase: two bullets hit him in the chest, a third drilled its way into his brain. The fourth had been intended for his son, but missed. Oleg, who had until that point been more inclined towards student distractions, had immediately interrupted his studies and established an allegiance against the murderers with a clan close to the government, that led to a shoot-out about which no further documentation was available. At this point Oleg was demonstrably living abroad, but after his return he was suddenly appointed chairman of the management committee and a welcome guest at the Kremlin.

He had simply sided with the right people.

In the years that followed Rogachev set about modernising the company, raked in considerable profits and swallowed up a German and an English steel giant in quick succession. He invested in aluminium, signed contracts with the government relating to the extension of the Russian railway network, acquired shares in European and Asian car companies and made a fortune in China, with its hunger for raw materials. At the same time he was painfully aware that he had to take the interests of the powerful men in Moscow into account. In return the sun shone for him: Vladimir Putin assured him of his high esteem, Dmitri Medvedev invited him to his table as an advisor. When the world market leader Arcelor Mittal was plunged into a crisis, Rogachev took over the ailing steel giant and put himself, with Rogamittal, at the top of his field.

At around this time Maxim Ginsburg, Medvedev's successor, had so permanently abolished the boundaries between private business and politics – which were eroding in any case – that the press dubbed him the 'CEO of Russia PLC'. Rogachev paid homage to Ginsburg in his own way. One very drunken evening, in fact, it turned out that Ginsburg had a daughter, Olympiada, taciturn and of no apparent charm, whom the president was anxious to see married, if possible to someone of a wealthy background. Somehow Olympiada had managed to complete a course of studies in politics and economics. Now she was a Member of Parliament, expressed her love of her father in referendums and faded away without having blossomed. Rogachev did Ginsburg the favour. The marriage of these two great fortunes passed off with much pomp, except that on the wedding night Rogachev shunned her bed and went elsewhere. From then on he was, in fact, constantly elsewhere, even when Olympiada gave birth to their only son, who was entrusted to a private school and from that point onwards seldom seen. Ginsburg's daughter got lonely. She didn't know how to respond to her husband's enthusiasm for martial arts, guns and football, even less to his constant affairs. She complained to her father. Ginsburg thought of the 56 billion dollars that his son-in-law put on the scales, and advised Olympiada to take a lover. She did exactly that. His name was Jim Beam, and he had the advantage of being there whenever you needed him.

How on earth was the poor woman going to survive the next fourteen days?

Evelyn Chambers stretched her Latin physique. Not bad for forty-five, she thought, everything still firm, even though the inevitable muscular fatty degeneration was beginning, and signs of cellulite were appearing on her bottom and thighs. She squinted into the sun. The cry of seabirds filled the air. Only now did it strike her that there was just one single cloud in the whole of the sky, as if it had strayed there, a cloud-child. It seemed to be floating very high up, but then what was height? She would be travelling far above the point where clouds dwelt.

Up, down. All a matter of perspective.

In her mind she ran through the members of the travelling party, assessing them for their media usefulness. Eight couples and five singles, including her. Some of those present would not welcome her participation. Finn O'Keefe, for example, who refused to go on talk-shows. Or the Donoghues: hard-line Republicans who didn't much care for the fact that America's powerful talk-show queen supported the Democrat camp. Admittedly Evelyn's only active excursion into politics, in 2017, when she had fought for the office of governor of New York, had begun in triumph and ended in disaster, but her stranglehold on public opinion remained unbroken.

Mukesh Nair? Another one who didn't like going on talk-shows.

Warren Locatelli and his Japanese wife, on the other hand, had entertainment value in spades. Locatelli was vain and coarse, but he was also brilliant. There was a biography of him entitled *What if Locatelli had Created the World?*, which accurately captured his vision of the world. He sailed, and had won the America's Cup the previous year, but his chief enthusiasm was racing. Umura had for a long time appeared as an actress in indigestible big-screen experiments before enjoying a *succès d'estime* with *Black Lotus*. She was snooty and – as far as Evelyn could tell – free from any kind of empathy.

Who else? Walo Ögi, Swiss investor, art collector. Involved in every imaginable area from property, insurance, airlines and cars via Pepsi-Cola to tropical wood and ready meals. According to rumour, he planned to build a second Monaco on behalf of that country's prince, but Evelyn was more interested in Heidrun Ögi, his third wife, who was said to have financed her photographic studies as a stripper and an actress in porn films. Also part of the group was Marc Edwards, who owed his popularity to the development of quantum chips so tiny that they were switched on and off with a single atom, and Mimi Parker, creator of intelligent fashion, whose fabrics were woven with Edwards' chips. Fun people, sporty and socially committed, moderately exciting. The Tautous might have more to give. Bernard Tautou had political ambitions and had earned billions in the water business, a subject that preoccupied the human rights organisations with monotonous regularity.

The eighth couple, finally, came from Germany. Eva Borelius was seen as the uncrowned queen of stem-cell research; her companion, Karla Kramp, worked as a surgeon. Flagship lesbians. And then there was Miranda Winter, ex-model and squeaky-voiced widow of an industrialist, as well as Rebecca Hsu, Taiwan's Coco Chanel. All four of them had already opened their hearts to Evelyn, but she didn't know the slightest thing about Carl Hanna.

She thoughtfully rubbed her belly with suntan oil.

Hanna was strange. A Canadian private investor, born in 1981 as the son of a wealthy British diplomat in New Delhi, who had moved at the age of ten with his family to British Columbia, where he later studied business. Apprentice years in India, death of his parents in an accident, return to Vancouver. He had clearly invested his inheritance cleverly enough never to have to lift a finger ever again: according to rumour he planned to invest in India's space trip, and that was that. The CV of a speculator. Of course, not everybody had to be a bighead like Locatelli. But Donoghue boxed, for example. Rogachev was trained in all kinds of martial arts and had bought Bayern Munich a few years previously. Edwards and Mimi dived, Borelius rode, Karla played chess, O'Keefe had a scandalous drugs career behind him and had lived with Irish gypsies. Everyone had something that identified them as a person of flesh and blood.

Hanna owned yachts.

Originally, Gerald Palstein had been scheduled to fly instead of him: the director of strategy of EMCO, the third-largest mineral company in the world, was a free spirit who had, years before, thought out loud about the end of the fossil-fuel years. Evelyn would have liked to meet him, but the previous month Palstein had been victim of an attempted assassination, and injured so badly that he had had to cancel, and Hanna had stepped in.

Who was this guy?

Evelyn decided to find out, swung her legs over her lounger and walked to the balustrade of her terrace. Deep below her glittered the enormous pool of the Stellar Island Hotel. Some people were already diving into the turquoise-coloured water, and Heidrun Ögi and Finn O'Keefe were arriving at that very moment. Evelyn wondered whether she should go down and join them, but suddenly the very thought of conversation made her feel ill, and she turned away.

That was happening to her more and more often. A talk-show queen who was allergic to talking. She fetched herself a drink and waited for the attack to pass. O'Keefe followed Heidrun to the pool bar, where a stout man of about sixty was explaining something, waving his arms around as he did so. He was enjoying the attention of a sporty-looking couple who were listening agog, laughing comfortably as one, saying 'Good heavens!' at the same time and looking like the kind of people who rode around on tandems.

'It was extreme, of course,' the older man said, and laughed. 'Completely over the top. And that's exactly why it was good!'

There was something craggily sublime about his features, powerful Roman nose, chiselled chin. His wiry dark hair, run through with silver, was greased back, his tousled moustache matched his finger-thick eyebrows.

'What was over the top?' Heidrun asked, giving him a kiss.

'The musical,' the man said, and looked at O'Keefe. 'And who is this, *mein Schatz?*'

Unlike Heidrun he spoke smooth, almost unaccented English. The odd thing was that he said 'my darling' in German. Heidrun came and stood next to him and rested her head on his shoulder.

'Don't you ever go to the cinema?' she said. 'This is Finn O'Keefe.'

'Finn – O'Keefe—' The wrinkles on his high forehead formed into question marks. 'Sorry, but I—'

'He played Kurt Cobain.'

'Oh! Ah! Brilliant! Great to meet you. I'm Walo. Heidrun's seen all your films. I haven't, but I remember *Hyperactive*. Incredible achievement!'

'I'm delighted.' O'Keefe smiled. He had no particular problems meeting people, except that he always found the rigmarole of mutual introductions horribly tiring. Shaking hands. Telling someone you'd never seen before how brilliant it was to meet them here. Ögi introduced the blonde at his side as Mimi Parker, a tanned all-American girl with dark eyebrows and perfect teeth. Presumably Californian, O'Keefe thought. California seemed to have registered a patent on this kind of girl who smelled of the sun.

'Mimi designs incredible clothes,' Ögi raved. 'If you wear one of her pullovers you'll never need to see a doctor again.'

'Really! How come?'

'Very simple.' Mimi was about to say something, but Ögi talked over her. 'It measures your bodily functions! Let's say you have a heart attack, it sends your medical records to the nearest hospital and calls the ambulance.'

'But it can't perform the operation itself?'

'It has transistors woven into it,' Mimi explained seriously. 'The item of clothing is effectively a computer with a million sensors. They form connections with the wearer's body, but they can also be connected to any external system.'

'Sounds scratchy.'

'We weave Marc's quantum chips into them. They don't scratch at all.'

'May I take the opportunity,' the fair-haired man said and held out his right hand. 'Marc Edwards.'

'Pleased to meet you.'

'Look.' Mimi pointed to her bathing costume. 'Even in this there are about two million sensors. Among other things they absorb my body heat and turn it into electricity. Of course you only get very small amounts of usable energy from a human power station, but it's enough to warm the costume up if necessary. The sensors react to the temperature of the air and water.'

'Interesting.'

'I've seen *Hyperactive*, by the way,' Heidrun said in a bored voice. 'Finn grew up with guitars and pianos. He even has his own band.'

'I had.' O'Keefe raised his hands. 'I *had* a band. We don't meet up that much these days.'

'I thought the film was great,' said Edwards. 'You're one of my favourite actors.'

'Thanks.'

'Your singing was great in it. What was your band called again?'

'The Black Sheep.'

Edwards pulled a face as if he was inches away from remembering the Black Sheep and all their hits. O'Keefe smiled.

'Believe me, you've never heard of us.'

'He hasn't either.' Ögi put his arm around his shoulders and lowered his voice. 'Between ourselves, young man, they're all kids. Bet you they don't even know who Kurt Cobain *was*.'

Mimi Parker looked uncertainly from one to the other.

'To be quite honest—'

'You mean he really existed?' Edwards said in amazement.

'A historical figure.' Ögi took out a cigar, cut it and set the tip thoughtfully alight. 'Tragic hero of a generation infatuated with suicide. A romantic in nihilist's clothing. *Weltschmerz*, a latent longing for death, nothing you wouldn't find in Schubert and Schumann as well. Brilliant exit. How did you prepare for the part, Finn?'

'Well—'

'Did you try to be *him*?'

'He'd have had to pump himself full of drugs,' said Edwards. 'That guy Cobain was permanently stoned.'

'Perhaps he did,' said Ögi. 'Did you?'

O'Keefe shook his head with a laugh. How could he explain in a few words to a pool party how you played Kurt Cobain? Or anyone else?

'Isn't that called method acting?' Mimi asked. 'The actor gives up his identity for his character in the film, weeks and months before filming. He basically subjects himself to a kind of brainwashing.'

'No, it's not quite like that. I have a different way of working.'

'How's that?'

'More mundanely. It's a job, you understand. Just a job.'

Mimi looked disappointed. O'Keefe felt Heidrun's violet gaze settling on him. He began to feel uncomfortable. Everyone was staring at him.

'You were talking about a musical,' he said to Ögi, to creep away from the focus of interest. 'Which one would that be?'

'*Nine Eleven*,' said Ögi. 'We saw it in New York last week. You?'

'Not yet.'

'We're thinking of going,' said Edwards.

'Do that.' Ögi gave off swirls of smoke. 'As I said, extreme stuff! They could have let it drown in piety, but of course the material needs a powerful production.'

'The set's supposed to be amazing,' Mimi raved.

'Holographic. You think you're sitting in the middle of it.'

'I like the tune with the cop and the girl. It's always on the radio. "Into Death, My Child" . . .'

She started humming a tune. O'Keefe hoped he wouldn't have to express an opinion on the matter. He hadn't seen *Nine Eleven*, and had no intention of doing so.

'The slushy numbers on their own don't justify a visit,' Ögi snorted.

'Yes, Jimeno and McLoughlin are constantly busy, and so are their wives, but it's mostly worth it for the effects. When the planes come, you can't believe it! And the guy who sings Osama bin Laden. He's really OTT.'

'Bass?'

'Baritone.'

'I'm going swimming,' said Heidrun. 'Who's coming? Finn?'

Thanks, he thought.

He went to his room and got undressed. Ten minutes later they were competing at the crawl in the pool. Heidrun left him behind twice in a row, and it was only the third time that they reached the edge of the pool at the same time. She pulled herself up. Walo blew her a Havana-smoke kiss, before carrying on with a story accompanied by vigorous hand gestures. At that moment an athlete and a woman with a curvy figure and a fire-red ponytail arrived near the pool.

'Do you know that guy?' he asked.

'Nope.' Heidrun folded her arms on the edge of the pool. 'They must just have arrived. Maybe it's that Canadian investor. Something with an H, Henna or Hanson. I've seen the redhead before, I think. But I can't remember where.'

'Oh, yeah! Wasn't she a murder suspect at some point?'

'For a while, yes.' O'Keefe shrugged. 'She's quite witty, once you've got used to the fact that she has names for her breasts and that she's squandering an inheritance of thirteen billion dollars pretty much at random. No idea if there was anything to those accusations. It was in all the papers. She got off in the end.'

'Where do you meet such characters? At parties?'

'I don't go to parties.'

Heidrun slipped lower into the water and lay on her back. Her hair spread into a faded flower. O'Keefe couldn't help thinking of stories about mermaids, seductive creatures who had risen from the depths and dragged mariners underwater to steal their breath with a kiss.

'That's right. You hate being at the centre of things, don't you?'

He thought for a moment. 'I don't really, no.'

'Exactly. It only annoys you when there isn't at least a screen or a barrier between you and the people who see your films. You enjoy the cult that's organised around you, but even more than that you enjoy making people think you couldn't care less.'

He stared at her in amazement. 'Is that your impression?'

'When *People* magazine voted you sexiest man alive, you pulled your cap over your forehead and claimed you really couldn't understand why women cried at the sight of you.'

'I don't get it,' O'Keefe said. 'I really don't.'

Heidrun laughed. 'Me neither.'

She plunged under the surface of the water. Her outline fragmented into Cubist vectors as she darted away. O'Keefe wondered for a moment whether he liked her answer. The hammering of rotors reached him. He looked into the sky and found himself confronted with a single white cloud.

Lonely little cloud. Lonely little Finn.

We understand each other, you and I, he thought with amusement.

The rump of a helicopter entered his field of vision, crossed the pool and came down.

'There are people in the water,' Karla Kramp observed. She said it with analytical coolness, as if referring to the appearance of microbes under warm and damp conditions. It didn't sound as if she wanted to join them. Eva Borelius looked out of the helicopter window and saw a pale-skinned woman gliding against a turquoise-coloured background.

'Perhaps it's finally time for you to learn to swim.'

'I've already learned to ride for you,' Karla replied expressionlessly.

'I know.' Borelius leaned back and stretched her bony limbs. 'You never stop learning, my jewel.'

Facing her, Bernard Tautou was dozing with his head leaning back and his mouth half open. After spending the first half-hour of the flight giving an account of his exhausting everyday life, which seemed to play out between remote desert springs and intimate dinners at the Élysée Palace, he had fallen asleep, and was now giving them a view of his nasal cavities. He was short and slim, with wavy, probably dyed hair that was starting to lighten at the temples. His eyes, beneath their heavy lids, had something weary about them, which was further accentuated into melancholy by the long shape of his face. The impression vanished as soon as he laughed and his eyebrows rose clownishly, and Tautou laughed often. He delivered compliments and acted interested, just to use his interlocutor's statements as a springboard for self-reflection. Every second sentence that he directed at his wife ended in a challenging *n'est-ce pas?*, Paulette's sole function being to confirm what he had said. Only after he had gone to sleep did she become more lively, talked about his friendship and hers with the French president, the country's first female head of state, and how important it was to grant humanity access to the most precious of all scarce resources. She talked about how, as head of the French water company Suez Environnement, he had contrived to take over Thames Water, which had made the resulting company a leader in global water supply and saved the world, which as good as meant her husband had saved the world. In her account plucky Bernard was tirelessly laying pipelines to the areas where the poor and wretched lived, a guardian angel in the battle against thirst.

'Isn't water a free human resource?' Karla had asked.

'Of course.'

'So it can't be privatised?'

Paulette's expression had remained unfathomable. With her hooded eyelids she looked like the young Charlotte Rampling, although without the actress's class. The question just asked had been put to people in the water business with great regularity for decades.

'Oh, you know, that debate is passing out of fashion, thank God. Without privatisation there would have been no supply networks, no treatment plants. What's the use of free access to a resource if you have no chance of accessing it?'

Karla had nodded thoughtfully.

'Could you actually privatise the air that we breathe?'

'Sorry? Of course not.'

'I'm just trying to understand. So Suez is building supply installations, for example in—'

'Namibia.'

'Namibia. Exactly. And are such planned constructions subsidised by development aid?'

'Yes, of course.'

'And the plant operates on a profitable basis?'

'Yes, it has to.'

'That means that Suez is privately registering profits that have been subsidised by development aid?'

At that point Paulette Tautou had assumed a tortured expression, and Borelius had said quietly, 'Enough, Karla.' Right now she didn't feel like getting involved in disasters as she usually did when Karla deployed the scalpel of her curiosity. After that they had exchanged harmless pleasantries and admired the platform in the sea. More precisely, her gaze and Karla's had hung spellbound on that endless line, while Paulette eyed them rather suspiciously and made no move to shake her husband awake.

'Aren't you going to wake him?' Borelius had asked. 'I'm sure he'd love to see this.'

'Oh, no, I'm happy for him to get some sleep. You can't imagine how hard he works.'

'We'll be there in a minute. Then you'll have to wake him anyway.'

'He needs every second. You know, I'd only wake him for something really *important*.'

Something really important, Borelius thought. Okay . . .

Now that the helicopter was lowering itself onto the landing platform, Paulette forced herself to say 'Bernard' several times in a quiet voice, until he opened his eyes in confusion and blinked.

'Are we there already?'

'We're landing.'

'What?' He jerked upright. 'Where's the platform? I thought we were going to see the platform.'

'You were asleep.'

'Oh! *Merde!* Why didn't you wake me, *chérie*? I'd have loved to see the platform!'

Borelius forebore from commenting. Before they got out, she caught a glimpse of a stately, snow-white yacht far out on the sea. Then the skids touched the ground, and the side door of the helicopter swung open.

On the yacht Rebecca Hsu left her study, crossed the huge, marble-covered drawing-room and stepped out onto the deck, while she phoned her headquarters in Taipei.

'I don't give a damn what the French sales manager wants,' she said harshly. 'We're talking about a perfume for twelve-year-old girls. *They* have to like it, not *him*. If *he* starts liking the stuff, we've made a mistake.'

Wild arguments came crackling down the line. Rebecca walked quickly to the stern, where the first officer, the captain and the speed-boat were waiting for her.

'It's already clear to me that you want your own campaign,' she said. 'I'm not stupid, after all. You always want something of your own. These Europeans are terribly complicated. We've put the perfume on the market in Germany, Italy and Spain, without giving anyone special treatment, and we've been successful every time. I don't see why France of all places— What? He said *what*?'

The information was repeated.

'Nonsense, I love France!' she yelled furiously. 'Even the French! I'm just fed up with all that constant rebellion. They will have to learn to live with the fact that I've bought their beloved luxury company. I'll leave them in peace as far as Dior and so on are concerned, but for our own creations I expect unconditional cooperation.'

She looked irritably across to the Isla de las Estrellas, which rose from the Pacific like a humpbacked sea serpent. No breeze stirred the air. The sea stretched like dark aluminium foil from horizon to horizon. She ended the conversation and turned to the two liveried men.

'And? Did you ask again?'

'I'm extraordinarily sorry, madame.' The captain shook his head. 'No permit.'

'I'm absolutely mystified about what's going on.'

'The Isla de las Estrellas and the platform can't be approached by private ships. The same applies to air-space. The whole area is one single high-security zone. If it wasn't you, we would even have to wait for their helicopter. Unusually, they have given us permission to ferry you across in our own speedboat.'

Rebecca sighed. She was used to rules not applying to her. On the other hand the prospect of a trip on the speedboat was too much fun for her to insist.

'Is the luggage on board?'

'Of course, madame. I hope you have a pleasant holiday.'

'Thank you. How do I look?'

'Perfect, as ever.'

That would be lovely, she thought. Since she had turned fifty, she had been fighting a losing battle. It was played out on various piece of fitness equipment, in swimming-pools with cross-current features, on private jogging paths and her 140-metre yacht, which she had had built in such a way that you could perform a circuit of it unimpeded. Since leaving Taiwan she ran there every day. With iron discipline she had even managed to get her extreme hunger under control, but still her body went on expanding. At least the dress emphasised what was left of her waist, and was appropriately extravagant. Her trademark bird's-nest hairdo was characteristically chaotic, and her make-up was impeccable.

As soon as the speedboat cast off, she was back on the phone again.

'Rebecca Hsu is heading this way,' Norrington said on the walkie-talkie.

Lynn left the kitchen of Stellar Island Hotel, gave the canapés a quick examination, issued instructions to her little group of waiters and waitresses and stepped out into the sunlight.

'Has she brought bodyguards?' she asked.

'No. On the other hand she has checked several times to ask if we seriously intend to refuse her docking permission.'

'Excuse me? Rebecca wants to park her *damned yacht* here?'

'Calm down. We refused to budge. Now she's coming in the speedboat.'

'That's okay. When does she get here?'

'In about ten minutes. As long as she doesn't fall overboard on the way.' An idea that Norrington seemed to find cheering. 'There must be some pretty good sharks around here, don't you think? When I last saw our little darling she was fit for a banquet.'

'If Rebecca Hsu gets eaten, you're dessert.'

'Funny and relaxed as ever,' Norrington sighed and ended the conversation.

She followed the coastal path at a walking pace, as her mind split into pieces and thousands of concerned and disembodied Lynns haunted the hotel grounds. Was there something she'd overlooked? Each of the booked suites gleamed immaculately. Even in terms of furniture the personal preferences of the guests had been taken into account: lilies, mountains of lychees and passion fruit for Rebecca Hsu, Momoka Omura's favourite champagne, a luxury volume about the history of car-racing on Warren Locatelli's pillow, reproductions of Asian and Russian art on the Ögis' walls, old tin toys for Marc Edwards, the biography of Muhammad Ali with photographs never before published for the edification of good old Chucky, chocolate-scented bath oils for Miranda Winter. Even the menu reflected likes and dislikes. Lynn's worried ghosts sighed in the saunas and jacuzzis of the spa area, prowled icily over the golf course, streamed damply into Stellar Island Dome, the underground multimedia centre, and found nothing to complain about.

Everything that was supposed to work, worked.

And besides, no one would *see* that they hadn't been ready in time. Unless the guests opened doors they had no business opening.

Tools were still lying around in most of the rooms, bags of cement were stacked up, the paintwork was only half finished. In the knowledge that she couldn't keep the official opening deadline, Lynn had put all her energy into getting the booked suites ready. Only part of the kitchen was operational, enough to spoil the group, but certainly not the three hundred visitors for whom the hotel had actually been conceived.

She stopped for a moment and looked at the gleaming ocean steamer that grew out of the basalt. As if her pause were a signal, hundreds of seabirds scattered from a nearby cliff and formed a swarming cloud that drifted inland. Lynn gave a start. She imagined the creatures swooping

down on the hotel grounds, shitting all over it, hacking and scratching it
to pieces and chasing the few people into the sea. She saw bodies drifting
in the pool, blood mixing with water. The survivors ran up to her and
screamed at her for not preventing the attack. Loudest of all was Julian.

The hotel staff were frozen. Their eyes wandered back and forth
between Lynn and the hotel, visibly unsettled, since their boss suddenly
gave every appearance of witnessing the Day of Judgement.

After a minute of complete stillness she pulled herself together and
continued down the coastal path to the harbour.

Andrew Norrington saw her walking on. From the hill above the pool
where he had taken up his post, he could look out over large sections of
the eastern shore. In the harbour, a natural inlet extended by blasting,
several small ships lay at anchor, most of them patrol boats and some
Zodiacs, marked with the familiar O of Orley Enterprises. He could have
provided plenty of room for Rebecca Hsu's yacht, but not even in his
wildest dreams did Norrington imagine giving the Taiwanese woman
special treatment. All the others had, as agreed, flown in on Orley's company helicopters, why not her? Rebecca could be glad that she'd been
allowed to travel in by water at all.

As he walked down to the pool, he thought about Julian's daughter.
Even though he didn't particularly like Lynn, he respected her authority
and competence. Even at a young age she had had to shoulder a huge
amount of responsibility, and in spite of all the naysayers she had put
Orley Travel at the top of all tourist companies. Without a doubt, Stellar
Island Hotel was one of her *pièces de résistance*, even though there was
still much to be done, but it paled into insignificance next to the OSS
Grand and the Gaia! No one had ever built anything comparable. In her
late thirties, Lynn was a star in the company, and those two hotels *had*
been finished.

Norrington threw his head back and blinked into the sun. He absently
flicked a saucer-sized spider from his shoulder, entered the pool landscape via a path overgrown with ferns and conifers, and gazed forensically
around the area. By now the whole travelling party had met up by the

pool. Drinks and snacks were being handed out, people were noisily introducing themselves. Julian had selected the participants very cleverly. The diverse group there was worth several hundred billion dollars: world-improvers like Mukesh Nair, oligarchs along the lines of Rogachev, and people like Miranda Winter, who had, for the first time, found her pea-brain faced with the task of spending money sensibly. Orley planned to relieve them all of part of their fortunes. At that moment Evelyn Chambers joined them, and smiled radiantly around. Still remarkably good-looking, Norrington thought. Perhaps she'd become a bit plump over time, but nothing compared to the progressive spherification of Rebecca Hsu.

He walked on, ready for anything.

'Mimi! Marc! How lovely to see you.'

Evelyn had overcome her revulsion, and was once again capable of communicating. She was almost on friendly terms with Mimi Parker, and Marc was a nice guy. She waved to Momoka Omura and exchanged kisses on the cheek with Miranda Winter, who greeted every new arrival with a 'Wooouuuuhhw' that sounded like a burglar alarm, followed by a saucy, 'Oh yeah!' Evelyn had last seen Winter with long, steel-blue hair, and now she wore it short and bright red, which made you think of fire alarms. The ex-model's forehead was decorated with a filigree pattern. Her breasts squeezed themselves reluctantly into a dress that only just covered the planetary curve of her bottom and was so tight at the waist that it made one fear that Ms Miranda might at any moment split in two. The youngest here, at the age of twenty-eight, she had undergone so many surgical interventions that the mere documentation of her operations kept hundreds of society reporters in employment, not to mention her extravagances, her excesses and the aftershocks of her trial.

Evelyn pointed at the pattern on her brow.

'Pretty,' she said, trying frantically to escape the massive double constellation of the Miranda cleavage, which seemed to be drawing her gaze powerfully downwards. Everyone knew that Evelyn's sexual appetite was equally divided between men and women. The revelation of her private life, namely the fact that she lived with her husband and her lover in a *ménage à trois*, had cost her the candidacy in New York.

'It's Indian,' Miranda replied gleefully. 'Because India is in the stars, you know?'

'Really?'

'Yes! Just imagine! The stars say we're heading for an Indian age. Quite wonderful. The transformation will begin in India. Humanity will change. First India, then the whole world. There will never be war again.'

'Who says that, darling?'

'Olinda Brannigan.'

Olinda Brannigan was an ancient, dried-up Hollywood actress from Beverly Hills who looked like a codfish. Miranda went to her to have her cards read and her future predicted.

'And what else does Olinda have to say?'

'You shouldn't buy anything Chinese. China's going to go under.'

'Because of the trade deficit?'

'Because of Jupiter.'

'And what sort of dress are you wearing?'

'This? Cute, isn't it? Dolce & Gabbana.'

'You should take it off.'

'What, here?' Miranda looked furtively around and lowered her voice. 'Now?'

'It's Chinese.'

'Oh, stop! They're Italians, they—'

'It's Chinese, darling,' Evelyn repeated with relish. 'Rebecca Hsu bought Dolce & Gabbana last year.'

'Does she have to buy everything?' For a moment Miranda looked frankly hurt. Then the sun came out once again. 'Never mind. Maybe Olinda made a mistake.' She spread her fingers and shook herself. 'Anyway, I'm *reaaally* looking forward to the trip! I'm going to squeal the whole time!'

Evelyn didn't doubt for a moment the serious intent behind this threat. She glanced around and saw the Nairs, the Tautous and the Locatellis in conversation. Olympiada joined the group, while Oleg Rogachev studied her, nodded to her and went to the bar. He immediately came over with a glass of champagne, handed it to her and assumed his familiar, sphinx-like smile.

'So we're going to be exposed to your judgement in space,' he said in a strong Slavic accent. 'We'll all have to be very careful what we say.'

'I'm here as a private individual.' She winked at him. 'But if you really want to tell me anything—'

Rogachev laughed quietly, without losing his icy expression.

'I'm sure I will, not least for the pleasure of your company.' He looked out to the platform. By now the sun was low over the volcano, and bathed the artificial island in warm colours. 'Have you been through preparatory training? Weightlessness isn't everyone's cup of tea.'

'In Orley Space Centre.' Evelyn took a sip. 'Zero-gravity flights, simulation in the immersion tank, the whole caboodle. You?'

'A few sub-orbital flights.'

'Are you excited?'

'Thrilled.'

'You do know what Julian is trying to do by organising this event?'

The remark hovered in the room, waiting to be picked up. Rogachev turned to look at her.

'And now you're interested to find out my opinion on the matter.'

'And you wouldn't be here if you weren't thinking seriously about it.'

'And you?'

Evelyn laughed.

'Forget it. In this company I'm the church mouse. He can hardly have had his beady eyes on my savings.'

'If all church mice had to reveal the state of their finances, Evelyn, mice would run the world.'

'Wealth is relative, Oleg, I don't have to tell you that. Julian and I are old friends. I'd love to convince myself that it was that that persuaded him to make me a member of the group, but of course I realise that I manage capital that's more important than money.'

'Public opinion.' Rogachev nodded. 'In his place I'd have invited you too.'

'You, on the other hand, *are* rich! Almost everybody here is rich, *really* rich. If each of you throws only a tenth of his wealth into the jackpot, Julian can build a second lift and a second OSS.'

'Orley won't allow a shareholder to influence the fate of his company to any great extent. I'm a Russian. We have our own programmes. Why should I support American space travel?'

'Do you really mean that?'

'You tell me.'

'Because you're a businessman. Nation states may have interests, but what good is that if you lack money and know-how? Julian Orley dusted off American state space travel and at the same time sealed its fate. He's the boss now. Worth mentioning to the extent that space travel programmes are now almost exclusively in private hands, and Julian's lead in the sector is astronomical. Even in Moscow people are supposed to have been saying that he doesn't give a fig for the interests of nation states. He just looks for people who think the same way as he does.'

'You might say he doesn't give a fig for loyalty either.'

'Julian's loyalty is to ideals, believe it or not. The fact is that he could get on perfectly well with NASA, but NASA couldn't cope with him. Last year he presented the White House with a plan for how a second lift could be financed by the Americans, and that would have meant that he was putting himself in a highly dependent position as a supplier of know-how. But rather than using the opportunity to involve him, Congress hesitated and expressed concern. America still hasn't worked out that for Julian it's just an investor.'

'And because this investor seems to lack a certain potency at the moment, he's extending the circle of his possible partners.'

'Correct. He couldn't care less whether you're a Russian or a Martian.'

'Even so. Why shouldn't I invest in *my* country's space travel?'

'Because you have to ask yourself whether you want to entrust your money to a state which, while it might be your homeland, is hopelessly underperforming in technological terms.'

'Russian space travel is just as privatised and efficient as the American version.'

'But you haven't got a Julian Orley. And there isn't one on the horizon, either. Not in Russia, not in India, not in China. Not even the French and the Germans have one. Japan is running on the spot. If you invest your money in the attempt to invent something that other people invented ages ago, just for the sake of national pride, you're not being loyal, you're being sentimental.' Evelyn looked at him. 'And you aren't inclined towards sentimentality. You're sticking to the rules of the game in Russia, that's all. And you feel no more connected to your country than Julian feels to anybody.'

'You think you know so much about me.'

Evelyn shrugged. 'I just know that Julian would never pay for anyone to take the most expensive trip in the world simply out of love for his fellow man.'

'And you?' Rogachev asked an athletically built man who had joined them in the course of the conversation. 'What brings you here?'

'An accident.' The man came closer and held out his hand to Evelyn. 'Carl Hanna.'

'Evelyn Chambers. You're referring to the attempt on Palstein's life?'

'He should have been flying instead of me. I know I shouldn't be pleased in the circumstances—'

'But you've been promoted and you're pleased anyway. That's completely understandable.'

'Nice to meet you anyway. I watch *Chambers* whenever I can.' His eyes turned to the sky. 'Will you be making a programme up there?'

'Don't worry, we'll keep it private. Julian wants to shoot a commercial with me, in which I praise the beauties of the universe. To stimulate space tourism. Do you happen to know Oleg Alexeyevich Rogachev?'

'Rogamittal.' Hanna smiled. 'Of course. I think we even share a passion.'

'And that would be?' Rogachev asked carefully.

'Football.'

'You like football?'

The Russian's impenetrable, foxy face grew animated. *Aha*, Evelyn thought. *First clue about Hanna*. She looked with interest at the Canadian, whose whole body seemed to consist of muscle, although without the awkwardness that bodybuilders so often had. With his close-shaven hair and beard, his thick eyebrows and the little cleft in his chin, he could easily have played the lead in a war movie.

Rogachev was usually a little frosty with strangers, but the mention of football made him seem suddenly almost euphoric. Straight away they were discussing things that Evelyn didn't understand, so she took her leave and moved on. At the bar she ran into Lynn Orley, who introduced her to the Nairs, the Tautous and Walo Ögi. She at once took a liking to the swaggering Swiss. Complacent, and with a parodic tendency to overdramatise things, he immediately proved to be open and attentive. In general, no one was talking about anything but the imminent trip. To her delight, Evelyn didn't have to try to attract Heidrun Ögi's attention, as she cheerfully waved her over to introduce her, with furtive delight, to the tormented-looking Finn O'Keefe. Over the next five minutes Evelyn didn't manage to ask him a single question, and said she presumed it would stay that way.

'For ever?' O'Keefe asked slyly.

'For the next fortnight,' she confessed. 'Then I'll give it another go.'

Not staring at Heidrun was a far more hopeless task than escaping the gravitational pull of Miranda Winter's breasts – undulating landscapes of promised delight, but nothing in the end to lose your head over. Miranda, by and large, was a simple design. Sex with her, Evelyn guessed, would be like licking out a honey-pot, sweet and enticing, a bit ordinary after a while, eventually boring and possibly making you feel a bit sick afterwards. Heidrun's pigment-free, anorexic body, on the other hand, her white hair, snow-white all over, promised an intense erotic experience.

Evelyn sighed inwardly. She couldn't afford any kind of adventure with this lot, particularly since everything about Heidrun shouted that she wasn't interested in women.

At least not that way.

A little way off she spotted Chuck Donoghue's barrel shape, with its complete lack of a neck. His chin jutted bossily forwards, his thinning, reddish hair blown into a sculpture on his head. He had just launched into a noisy diatribe directed at two women, one tall and bony, with strawberry-blonde hair, the other dark and delicate, looking as if she had emerged from a painting by Modigliani. Eva Borelius and Karla Kramp. At regular intervals Chuck's lecture was counterpointed by Aileen Donoghue's maternal falsetto. With her rosy cheeks and silver hair, you might have expected to see her flitting off at any moment to serve homemade apple pie, which according to rumours she did with great enthusiasm when she wasn't helping Chuck run their hotel empire. To talk to Borelius, Evelyn would have had to put up with Chuck's teasing, so instead she went in search of Lynn, and found her in conversation with a man who looked uncannily like her. The same ash-blond hair, sea-blue eyes, Orley DNA. Lynn was saying, 'Don't worry, Tim, I've never been better,' as Evelyn walked in.

The man turned his head and looked at her reproachfully.

'Excuse me. Didn't mean to interrupt.' She made as if to go.

'Not at all.' Lynn held her back by the arm. 'Do you know my brother?'

'Great to meet you. We hadn't had the pleasure.'

'I'm not part of the company,' Tim said stiffly.

Evelyn remembered that Julian's son had turned his back on the firm years before. The siblings were close, but there were problems between Tim and his father that had started when Tim's mother had died, in a state of total insanity, it was rumoured. Lynn had never revealed any more than that, except that Amber, Tim's wife, didn't share her husband's dislike of Julian.

'You wouldn't happen to know where Rebecca is?' said Evelyn.

'Rebecca?' Lynn frowned. 'She should be down at any moment. I just dropped her off at her suite.'

In point of fact Evelyn couldn't have cared less where Rebecca Hsu had got to. She just had a distinct feeling of being about as welcome as a case of shingles, and tried to find a reason to slope quietly off again.

'And otherwise? Do you like it?'

'Brilliant! – I heard that Julian's not getting here until the day after tomorrow?'

'He's stuck in Houston. Our American partners are causing a few problems.'

'I know. Word gets around.'

'But he'll be there for the show.' Lynn grinned. 'You know him. He loves making the big entrance.'

'But it should be you in the limelight,' said Evelyn. 'You've sorted everything out fantastically well, Lynn. Congratulations! Tim, you should be proud of your sister.'

'Thanks, Evie! Many thanks for that.'

Tim Orley nodded. Evelyn felt more unwelcome than ever. Curious, she thought, he's not a nasty guy. What's his problem? Is he pissed off with me for some reason? What did I burst in on?

'Are you flying with us?' she asked.

'I'm, er . . . Of course, this is Lynn's big moment.' He forced a smile, put his arm around his sister's shoulder and drew her to him. 'Believe me, I'm *incredibly* proud of her.'

There was so much warmth in his words that Evelyn had every reason to feel touched. But the undertone in Tim's voice said, *clear off, Evelyn.*

She went back to the party, slightly flummoxed.

The twilight phase was brief but dreamlike. The sun adorned itself in blood-red and pink before drowning itself in the Pacific. Darkness fell within a few minutes. Because of the Stellar Island Hotel's location on the eastern slope, for most of those present the sun didn't disappear into the sea but slipped behind the volcanic peaks; only O'Keefe and the Ögis were able to enjoy its big farewell. They had left the party and driven up to the crystal dome, from where you had a view of the whole island including its inaccessible, jungle-covered western side.

'My goodness,' said Heidrun, staring out. 'Water on all sides.'

'Hardly a shattering observation, darling.' Ögi's voice emerged from the cloud of his cigar-smoke. He had used the opportunity to get changed, and was now wearing a steel-blue shirt with an old-fashioned matching cravat.

'As you wish, jerk.' Heidrun turned towards him. 'We're standing on a bloody great stone in the Pacific.' She laughed. 'Do you know what that means?'

Ögi blew a spiral galaxy into the approaching night.

'As long as we don't run out of Havanas, it means we're in good hands here.'

As they talked, O'Keefe wandered aimlessly around. The terrace was now half covered by the massive glass dome to which it owed its name. Only a few tables were set for dinner, but Lynn had told him that at peak period there was room for more than three hundred people here. He looked to the east, where the platform stood brightly lit in the sea. It was a fantastic sight. Except that the straight line was absorbed by the dark of the sky.

'Perhaps you'll wish you were standing back on this bloody great stone,' he said.

'Really?' Heidrun flashed her teeth. 'But maybe I'll be holding your little hand – Perry.'

O'Keefe grinned. After plunging lemming-like into the depths of non-commercial film, and choosing his roles in terms of their inappropriateness, he had been more surprised than anyone else when he was awarded an Oscar for his impersonation of Kurt Cobain. *Hyperactive* became the certificate of his ability. No one however could ignore the fact that the famously shy Irishman with the amber gaze, the regular features and sensual lips was already yesterday's man, seen only in unwieldy low-budget and no-budget productions, cryptic *films d'auteur* and blurry Dogme dramas. Box-office poison had become a drug. Cleverly, he had avoided ogling blockbusters and gone on making the sort of things that he liked, except that all of a sudden everybody else liked them too. Azerbaijani directors could still book him for a pittance, if he liked the subject-matter. He cultivated his origins and played James Joyce. He acted out the lives of junkies and homeless people. He did so much both in front of the camera and behind it that his past blurred: born in Galway, mother a journalist, father an operatic tenor. Learned piano and guitar as a boy, acted in theatre to overcome his shyness, bit-parts in TV series and advertisements. Worked his way up from minor to major roles at

Dublin's Abbey Theatre, shone with the Black Sheep in O'Donoghue's pub, wrote poetry and short stories. Even spent a year living with tinkers, Irish gypsies, out of a pure romantic connection with good old Éire. So convincing, finally, as a rebellious farmer's son in the television series *Mo ghrá thú*, that Hollywood called.

Or so they said, and it sounded good, and was somehow true.

That shy Finn had been short-tempered as a child, and had knocked out his fellow pupils' teeth, that he was seen as a slow learner and, unable to decide what to be, had at first done nothing at all, was rarely mentioned. Nor were his fallings-out with his parents, his immoderate alcohol consumption, the drugs. He had no memory at all of his year with the tinkers, because he had spent most of his time pissed, or high, or both. Once he had been successfully socialised in the Abbey Theatre, a German producer had had him in mind for the main role in Süskind's classic *Perfume*, but while Ben Wishaw had auditioned, O'Keefe had fallen noisily asleep on top of a Dublin prostitute and hadn't even turned up for the appointment. Not a word about losing his day job because of similar escapades and being thrown out of the TV series, followed by two more years of neglect among the travelling people, until he had finally been able to effect a reconciliation with his parents and gone into rehab.

It was only then that the myth began. From *Hyperactive* until that remarkable day in January 2017, when an unemployed screenwriter of German origins in Los Angeles got hold of a fifty-year-old pulp novel, that marked the start of an unparalleled literary phenomenon, an intergalactic soap opera that had never been published in America but which could claim to be the most successful sci-fi series of all time. Its hero was a space traveller called Perry Rhodan, whom O'Keefe played as cheerfully as ever, without worrying about success. He interpreted the role in such a way that perfect Perry became a hot-headed fool, who built Terrania, the capital of humanity, more or less by accident in the Gobi Desert, and stumbled out from there into the great expanses of the Milky Way.

The cinema release beat everything that had gone before. Since then O'Keefe had played the space hero in two additional films. He had taken a training course at the Orley Space Centre, and struggled against nausea on board a Boeing 727 converted to take zero-gravity flights. On that occasion he had met and liked Julian Orley, since which time they had formed a loose friendship based on their shared love of cinema.

But perhaps I'll hold your little hand—

Why not, thought O'Keefe, but refrained from replying accordingly to avoid annoying Walo, because he strongly suspected Heidrun of loving the jovial Swiss. You didn't have to know the two of them any better to have a sense that that was the case. It was expressed less in what they said to each other than in the way they looked at and touched each other. Better not to flirt.

For the time being.

In space everything might look very different.

20 May 2025

PARADISE

Shenzhen, Guangdong Province, Southern China

Owen Jericho knew he still had a good chance of entering Paradise today, and he loathed the idea.

Other people loved it. To get there, you needed unbridled lust, the musty sweetness of a misdirected love of children, sadistic tendencies and an ego sufficiently deformed to sentimentalise anything objectionable that you might get up to. Many of those who desired access saw themselves as champions for the sexual liberation of the very ones they were laying their hands on. Control was more important to them than anything else. At the same time most of them considered themselves perfectly normal, and saw the people who got in the way of their self-realisation as the real perverts. Others claimed their legitimate right to be perverted; yet others saw themselves as businessmen. But hardly any of them had endured the shame of being described as sick and weak. It was only once they were up before the courts, when they summoned experts who testified to their inability to resist the call of their own nature, that they turned themselves into pitiably driven individuals in need of sympathy and healing. While still undiscovered, however, and in full possession of their intellectual powers, they were all too happy to withdraw to the playground of their clammy imaginations, the Paradise of the Little Emperors, which was indeed paradise from their vantage point, if not for the little emperors themselves.

For them it was hell.

Owen Jericho hesitated. He knew he shouldn't have followed Animal Ma this far. He saw him, his eyes widened by archaically fat spectacle lenses into an expression of constant astonishment, crossing the square, elliptically swaying his bottom and hips. He owed this duck-like walk to a hip condition which created the false impression that he was easy prey. But Ma Liping, to give him his real name, hadn't been given his nickname by accident. He was considered aggressive and dangerous. In fact he pretended to have been given the name Animal at birth, a bizarre act of showing-off, not least because he also pretended it embarrassed him. Ma was cunning too. He must have been, or else he wouldn't have been able to lull the authorities into the sleepy conviction that he had forsworn paedophilia. As walking proof of the successful reintegration experiment, he worked for the police in the battle against the growing plague of child pornography in China, he provided instructions for the catching of small fry and apparently did everything he could to escape social ostracism.

Five years in jail as a child abuser, he used to say, is like five hundred years in a torture chamber.

This infectiously flourishing suburb of the urban network of Shenzhen in south China, with its boringly functional architecture, had allowed Ma, who was originally from Beijing, the chance to start again. No one knew him here, the local authorities didn't even have a file on him. In the capital they knew where he was living, but the connection had become attenuated, since the paedophile scene was in a state of constant flux, and Ma could credibly suggest that he had lost contact with its inner circle. No one paid him any attention now; there were other things that needed doing. Fresh depths granted nauseating glimpses of worlds of unbelievable human wretchedness.

Worlds like the Paradise of the Little Emperors.

Lost in a morass of mental overload as they tried to protect, check and defraud 1.4 billion individuals all at the same time, the Chinese authorities increasingly resorted to private investigators to give them support. In hock to digitalisation, they relied on cyber-detectives, specialists in all kinds of criminality and dark online practices, and Owen Jericho had the reputation of being extraordinarily gifted in the field. His portfolio was impeccable when it came to cracking web espionage, phishing, cyberterrorism and so on. He penetrated illegal communities, infiltrated blogs, chat-rooms and virtual worlds, tracked down missing people using their digital fingerprints and advised companies on how to protect themselves against electronic attacks, Trojans and malicious software. In England, he had dealt with several cases of child pornography so, when the hell of the 'little emperors' was revealed to a team of shocked investigators, he had been asked for support by Patrice Ho, a high-ranking officer in the Shanghai Police and a friend of his. As a result of this request he was now standing here, watching Animal Ma on his way into the old, abandoned bicycle factory.

He shivered in spite of the heat. Accepting the commission had meant paying a visit to the Paradise of the Little Emperors. An experience that would leave traces in his cerebral cortex for the rest of time, even though he had had a fundamentally clear idea what he was letting himself in for. 'Little emperors' was what the Chinese, with an almost Italian besottedness, called their children. But there had been no way of avoiding the journey to Paradise, he had to log in and put on the hologoggles to understand just *whom* he was looking for.

Animal Ma stepped through the factory door.

After the city planners had, unusually, revealed no inclination to tear down the collection of mouldy brick buildings, artists and freelancers had moved in, including a gay couple who repaired antiquated electrical devices, an ethno-metal band who vied with one another to see who could make the most noise and shake a deserted fitness studio to its foundations, and Ma Liping, with his shop buying and selling all kinds of goods, from cheap imitations of Ming vases to moulting songbirds in portable bamboo cages. The investigator from Shenzhen who was working with Jericho had started observing Ma on 20 May, and had not let the man out of sight for two days. He had followed him from his home to the old factory and back, he had taken photographs, followed every one of his limping steps and drawn up a list of his customers' comings and goings. According to this list, during that time a grand total of four people had wandered into the shop, one of them Ma's wife, an ordinary-looking southern Chinese woman of indeterminable age. What made the small number of customers more surprising was the fact that Ma and his wife lived in a six-storey house, big and nicely presented by local standards, which Ma couldn't possibly have afforded on the small income

that he got from the shop. His wife, as far as anyone knew, didn't do anything at all except cross the street to the shop several times a day and
stay there for some time, perhaps to do office stuff or serve customers
who never came.

Apart from two men.

For a whole series of reasons Jericho had reached the conviction that
Ma, if he wasn't alone, was at least the driving force behind the Paradise
of Little Emperors. Once he'd managed to narrow the circle of suspects
down to a handful of child abusers who were currently rampaging on
the net or had attracted attention there some time before, he had homed
in on Animal Ma Liping. It was here, however, that his ideas and those
of the authorities parted company. While Jericho saw a storm-cloud of
clues over Shenzhen, in the opinion of the police it was a man from the
smoggy hell of Lanzhou who was attracting the most suspicion, and a
raid was being organised there at that very minute. In Jericho's view there
was no doubt that the police would find much of interest in Lanzhou,
just not the thing they were looking for. In the Paradise the beast reigned,
the snake, Animal Ma, he was sure of it, but he had been instructed to
take no further steps for the time being.

An instruction that he basically intended to ignore.

Because apart from the fact that the case bore Ma's trademark, the
fact that he was married gave Jericho food for thought. He had nothing
against reformation and change, but Ma was clearly homosexual; he
was a gay paedophile. It was also striking that the men who came to the
shop only reappeared several hours later. Thirdly, the shop didn't seem
to have anything remotely like fixed opening times, and last of all no one
could have wished for a better place to carry out dark practices than the
abandoned bicycle factory. All the other occupants used side-buildings
with direct access to the street, leaving Ma as the only one with prem-
ises off the internal courtyard and the only one who ever set foot in it,
apart from a few children who trickled in and out.

From Shanghai Jericho had instructed the investigator to pay a visit
to the shop, take a look around and buy something unimportant, if
possible something that Ma stocked in his storeroom. This meant that

Jericho was already familiar with the shop by the time he followed Ma across the square that morning. He waited for a few minutes in the shadow of the factory wall, passed through the gate, crossed the dusty area of the courtyard, climbed a short flight of stairs and stepped inside the crammed shop, which was filled with shelves and tables. Behind the counter the shop's owner was busy with jewellery. A bead curtain separated the sales area from an adjacent room, and a video camera was fixed above the doorway.

'Good morning.'

Ma looked up. The enlarged eyes behind the horn-rimmed glasses studied the visitor with a mixture of suspicion and interest. No one he knew.

'I heard you had something for every occasion,' Jericho explained.

Ma hesitated. He set aside the jewellery, cheap, tarnished stuff, and smiled shyly.

'Who, if I might ask, says that?'

'An acquaintance. It must have been here, yesterday. He needed a birthday present.'

'Yesterday—' Ma mused.

'He bought a make-up set. Art Deco. Green, gold and black. A mirror, a powder compact.'

'Oh, yes!' His suspicion vanished, replaced by eagerness. 'A lovely piece of work, I remember. Was the lady pleased?'

'The lady who received the present was my wife,' said Jericho. 'And yes, she was very pleased.'

'How wonderful. What can I do for you?'

'You remember the design?'

'Of course.'

'She would like more from the same series. If there are any more.'

Ma widened his smile, glad to be of service since, as Jericho knew from the investigator, there were still a matching brush and a comb to buy. With his curious rolling gait he came out from behind the counter, pushed a little stepladder against one of the shelved walls and climbed up it. Comb and brush shared a drawer quite high up, so that Ma was occupied for a few seconds while Jericho scanned his surroundings. The sales room was probably just what it looked like. The counter had a kitschy fake Art Nouveau front, behind which ivory-coloured pearl necklaces dangled. Beyond it, barely visible, lay the second room, perhaps an office. In the midst of all the junk a surprisingly expensive-looking computer adorned the counter, its screen turned towards the wall.

Ma Liping reached up and clumsily brought down the goods. Jericho didn't risk going behind the counter. The danger was too great that the man might turn towards him at that very moment. Instead he walked a little way along the counter until the screen display appeared reflected in a glass case. The glowing surface was divided into three, one part covered with characters, the other half divided into pictures showing two rooms from the perspective of surveillance cameras. Although he couldn't make out any details, Jericho knew that one of the cameras was directed at the sales room, because he saw himself walking around in the window. The other room looked gloomy and it clearly didn't contain very much furniture.

Was it the back room?

'Two very beautiful pieces,' said Ma, as he came down from the ladder and set the comb and brush down in front of him. Jericho lifted both up, one by one, ran his fingers expertly through the bristles and inspected the teeth. Why did Ma need a camera to monitor his back room? Checking the area towards the courtyard made sense, but did he want to watch himself at work? Unlikely. Was there another means of access from outside leading to that room?

'One tooth is broken,' he observed.

'Antiques,' Ma lied. 'The charm of imperfection.'

'What do you want for it?'

Ma quoted a ridiculously high price. Jericho made a no less ridiculous counter-offer, as the situation demanded. At last they agreed upon a sum that allowed both of them to save face.

'While I'm here,' Jericho said, 'there's something else that occurs to me.'

Antennae of alertness grew from Ma's temples.

'She has a necklace,' he went on. 'If only I knew something about jewellery. But I'd like to give her a suitable pair of earrings and, well, I thought—' He pointed rather helplessly to the displays in the counter case.

Ma relaxed. 'I have some things I could show you,' he said.

'Yeah, I'm afraid it won't be much use without the chain.' Jericho pretended he needed to have a think. 'The thing is, I've got some meetings to get to, but this evening would be the ideal time to surprise her with them.'

'If you brought me the chain—'

'Impossible, I have no time. That is, wait a moment. Do you get email?'

'Of course.'

'Then it's all fine!' Jericho acted relieved. 'I'll send you a photograph, and you look for something suitable. Then I'd just have to collect it later. You'd be doing me a big favour.'

'Hmm.' Ma bit his lower lip. 'When would you be coming, round about?'

'Yeah, if only I knew. Late afternoon? Early evening?'

'I've got to go out for a while too. Shall we say from six? I'd be here for another good hour after that.'

Faking gratitude, Jericho left the shop, walked to his hire car two streets away and drove to a better area in search of a jewellery shop. After a short time he found one, had them show him necklaces in the lower price range and asked to be allowed to take a photograph of one with his mobile phone, so that he could send the picture, he said, to his wife for inspection. Back in the car he wrote Ma a brief email and attached the photograph, but not before he had attached a Trojan. As soon as Ma Liping opened the attachment, he would unwittingly load the spy program onto his hard drive, from where it would transmit the drive's contents. Jericho couldn't assume that Ma was stupid enough to store incriminating content on a publicly accessible computer, but that wasn't what he was concerned with in any case.

He drove back to a place near the factory and waited.

Ma had opened the attachment shortly after one o'clock, and the Trojan had started transmitting straight away. Jericho connected his mobile to a roll-out screen and received, sharp and in detail, the impressions from the two surveillance cameras. They captured their surroundings in wide-screen mode, unfortunately without sound. On the other hand, a few moments later he received confirmation that camera two actually was monitoring the back room separated off with beads, when Ma disappeared from one window and appeared again immediately in the other one, shuffled over to a sideboard and fiddled with a tea-maker.

Jericho appraised the furniture. A massive desk with a swivel chair and worn-looking stools in front of it, obliging visitors to assume a petitioner's crouch, some ramshackle shelves, with stacks of paper on the worn plywood, files, wood-carvings and all kinds of horrors like silk flowers and industrially manufactured statues of the Buddha. Nothing to suggest that Ma placed any value on the personal note. No painting interrupted the whitewashed monotony of the walls; there were no discernible signs of that symbiotic connection produced by spouses looking at each other from little frames at work.

Ma Liping, happily married? Ludicrous idea.

Jericho's eye fell on a narrow, closed door opposite the desk. Interesting, but when Ma set down his tea and opened it, he merely revealed a view of tiles, a wash-basin and a piece of mirror. Less than half a minute later the man appeared again with his hands on his flies, and Jericho had to acknowledge that the supposed entrance was probably a toilet.

In that case why was Ma monitoring the damned room? Whom did he hope or fear to see there?

Jericho sighed. He waited patiently for an hour. He watched as Ma, with the photograph of the chain in front of his eyes, assembled an assortment of more or less matching earrings and seized the unexpected appearance of a customer as the opportunity to fob off on her a remarkably ugly set of tableware. He watched Ma polishing glass jugs and ate dried chillies from a bag until his tongue burned. At about three o'clock the so-called wife entered the shop. Supposedly unobserved, in a state of married familiarity, as they both were, one might have expected to see them exchange a kiss, a tiny act of intimacy. But they met as strangers, talked to one another for a few minutes, then Ma closed the front door, turned the open/closed sign around, and they went together into the back room.

What followed needed no soundtrack.

Ma opened the toilet, let his wife step inside, glanced alertly in all directions again and pulled the door closed behind him. Jericho waited tensely, but the couple didn't reappear. Not after two minutes, not after five, not even after ten. Only half an hour later did Ma suddenly come storming out, and into the sales room, where the figure of a man could now be seen outside the glass-panelled entrance. As if frozen, Jericho stared at the half-open toilet door, tried to make out reflections in the mirror, but the bathroom didn't yield up its secrets. Meanwhile Ma had let in the new arrival, a bull-necked, shaven-headed man in a leather jacket, bolted the door again and walked ahead of the new arrival into the back room where they both made for the lavatory and disappeared inside.

Amazing. Either this deadly trio liked to party in a confined space or the toilet was bigger than he thought.

What were the three of them getting up to?

Over an hour and a half went by. At ten past five the guy in the leather jacket and the woman reappeared in the office and came out to the front. This time it was she who opened the sales room, let the bald guy out and followed him, carefully closing the door behind her. Of Ma himself there was no sign. From six o'clock onwards, Jericho guessed, his efforts would be directed at customers and profit, explicitly on complementing a necklace with earrings, but until then, God alone knew what monstrous activities he was pursuing. Meanwhile Jericho thought he had understood the purpose of the second camera monitoring the office. Taking care that no one saw him when he disappeared into the miraculous world of the lavatory, Ma would be equally keen to avoid anyone waiting for him when he came back. The camera probably also supplied a picture to the toilet.

Jericho had seen enough. He would have to catch the bastard unprepared, but was Ma unprepared? Was he ever?

He quickly slipped his phone into his jacket, got out of the car and walked the few minutes back to the factory building as he came up with a battle plan. Perhaps he would have been better off calling the local authorities for support, but they would want to consult further before doing anything. If they obstructed his investigations, he might as well drive back to Shanghai, and Jericho was firmly resolved to get to the bottom of the mystery of the back room. His gun, an ultra-flat Glock, was safely stowed over his heart. He hoped he wouldn't have to use it. He had too many years drenched in sweat and blood behind him, too much active work at the front, in the course of which he, his adversaries or both had needed emergency medical treatment. The cheekbone on the cobblestones, the taste of dirt and haemoglobin in the mouth – all in the past. Jericho didn't want to fight again. He no longer valued the bony grin of his old partner from the hereafter, who up till now had been involved in every shoot-out, who had stormed every house with him, entered every snake-pit with him, without being on anyone's side; who always just reaped the harvest. One last time, in the Paradise of the Little Emperors, he would bring Death into the equation, in the hope of winning him as an ally in spite of his unreliability.

He stepped into the factory courtyard, resolutely crossed it and climbed the steps. As might have been expected, the shop sign said Closed. Jericho rang the bell, long and insistently, excited to see whether Ma would force himself out of the toilet or play dead. In fact he parted the bead curtain after the third ring. Limping elegantly, Ma circled the hideous counter, opened the door and fastened his vision-corrected eyes on the unwelcome guest.

'My mistake, I'm sure,' he said in a pinched voice. 'I thought I said six o'clock, but probably—'

'You did,' Jericho assured him. 'I'm sorry, but I now need the earrings sooner than we agreed. Please forgive my obstinacy. Women.' He spread his arms in a gesture of impotence. 'You understand.'

Ma forced a smile, stepped aside and let him in.

'I'll show you what I've found,' he said. 'I'm sorry you had to wait so long, but—'

'I'm the one who should apologise.'

'No, not at all. My mistake. I was in the toilet. Now, let's have a look.'

Toilet? Jericho registered with amazement that Ma had just given him the password.

'This is very awkward,' he stammered. 'But—'

Ma stared at him.

'Could I use it?'

'Use it?'

'Your toilet?' Jericho added.

The man's hands developed a crawling life of their own, pushed earrings around on the threadbare velvet of the pad. A cough crept up his throat, followed by another. Small, slimy, startled animals. Suddenly Jericho had the horrific vision of a bag in the shape of a humanoid, filled with swarming, chitinous, glittering vermin, stirring Ma Liping's husk from within and imitating humanoid gestures.

Animal Ma.

'Of course. Come with me.'

He held the bead curtain open, and Jericho stepped into the back room. The second camera fastened its dark eye on him.

'But I must—' Ma paused. 'I'm not equipped for this, you know. If you wait a second, I just want to sort out a fresh towel.' He directed Jericho to the desk, and opened the toilet door behind him.

Jericho grabbed the handle and pulled it open.

As if in a flash he took in the scene. A bathroom, sure enough, tall and narrow. The outlines of dead insects in the frosted glass of the ceiling light. The tiles cracked in certain places, mildewed grouting, the mirror stained and tarnished, a rust-yellow back to the wash-basin, the toilet itself little more than a hole in the floor. A wardrobe on the back wall, if you could call it a wall, because it was half open, a disguised door that Ma had neglected to close in his haste to serve Jericho.

And in all this Animal Ma Liping, who seemed at that moment to consist only of his magnified eyes and the sole of a shoe darting out and colliding painfully with Jericho's sternum.

Something cracked. All the air was driven out of his lungs. The kick sent him to the floor. He saw the Chinese man, teeth bared, appear in the doorframe, drew the Glock from its holster and took aim. Ma darted back and turned round. Jericho leapt to his feet, but not quickly enough to prevent his opponent from escaping into the darkness beyond the secret opening. The back wall swung back and forth. Without pausing, he charged through it, stopped at the top of a flight of stairs and hesitated. A curious smell struck him, a mixture of mould and sweetness. Ma's footsteps rang out down below, then everything fell silent.

He mustn't go down there. Whatever lay hidden in that cellar, the secret of the toilet was solved. Ma was in a trap. It was better to call the police, let them take care of whatever horrors lay down there and allow himself a drink.

And what if Ma *wasn't* in a trap?

How many entrances and exits did the cellar have?

Jericho thought of the Paradise. Scattered across the organism of the World Wide Web, the paedophiles' pages were suppurating wounds that sickened society irremediably. The perfidiousness with which the 'goods' were offered was unparalleled, he thought, and just then something from the vaults rose up towards him, ghostly and thin. A whimpering that stopped abruptly. Then nothing more.

He made his mind up.

Gun at the ready, he stepped slowly down. Strangely, with every step, the silence seemed to coagulate; he was moving through a medium enriched with rot and decay, a sound-swallowing ether. The stench grew more intense. The stairs wound round in a curve, led further downwards and opened out into a gloomy vault supported by brick pillars, some connected by wooden slats, crates that had been cobbled together. What they contained was impossible to make out from the foot of the stairs, but at the end of the chamber he glimpsed something that captured his attention.

A film set.

Yes, that was exactly what it was. The more his eyes grew accustomed to the gloom, the clearer it became to him that films were being made there. Phalanxes of unlit floodlights, perched on stands and hanging from the ceiling, peeled from the darkness; folding chairs, a camera on a tripod. The set seemed to be divided into parts, some furnished with equipment, others bare, possibly something like a green-screen so that virtual backgrounds could be added later. Checking in all directions as he walked on, he made out little beds, furniture, toys, an artificial landscape with a children's house, meadows and trees, a dissecting table from a pathology lab. Something on the floor looked unsettlingly like a chainsaw. Cages hung from the ceiling, surrounded by various utensils and something that might have been a small electric chair; tools were mounted on the wall – no, not tools: knives, pincers and hooks – a torture chamber.

Somewhere in all that madness Ma was hiding.

Jericho walked on, heart thumping, putting one foot in front of the other as if crossing ice that might crack at any moment. He reached the crates. Turned his head.

A boy looked at him.

He was naked and dirty, perhaps five years old. His fingers clutched the wire mesh between the slats, but his eyes looked apathetic, almost lifeless, the sort of eyes familiar in people who had withdrawn deep inside themselves. Jericho turned his head in the other direction and saw two girls in the cage opposite, barely clothed. One of them, very small, lay on the ground, clearly sleeping, the other, older, leaned with her back against the wall, hugging a cuddly toy. She lethargically turned a swollen face, and fastened sad eyes upon him. Then she seemed to understand that he was not one of the people who normally came here.

She opened her mouth.

Jericho shook his head and put his finger to his lips. The girl nodded. Holding the gun rigidly out ahead of him, he peered in all directions, checked again and again and ventured further into the hell of the little emperors. Still more children. Only a few who saw him. He gestured to them, the ones who raised their heads, to be silent. From cage to cage it got worse and worse: dirt and degradation, apathy, fear. A baby lay on a grimy blanket. Something dark rattled against a bar and yapped at him, so that he instinctively flinched, turned round and held his breath. The sickly stench seemed to have its source right in front of him. He heard the buzzing of flies, saw something darting across the floor—

His eyes widened and he felt nauseous.

That brief moment of inattention cost him his control. Dragging footsteps echoed, a draught brushed the back of his neck, then someone jumped at him, pulled him back, laid into him, screamed incomprehensible words.

A woman!

Jericho tensed his muscles and jabbed his elbows back again and again. His attacker wailed. As they whirled around he recognised her – Ma's wife or whatever role she might have played in that nightmare – grabbed her, pressed her against one of the columns and held the barrel of the Glock to her temple. How did she get here? He had seen her leave, but he hadn't seen her come back. Was there another entrance to the cellar? Could Ma finally have escaped him?

No, it was his fault! He had been sloppy on the way from the car to the factory. He had neglected to keep an eye on his computer. At some point during that time she must have come back here, to—

The pain!

Her heel had driven itself into his foot. Jericho reached out and slapped her in the face with the back of his hand. The woman struggled like a mad thing in his clutches. He gripped her throat and pushed her harder against the pillar. She kicked out at him and then, surprisingly, she abandoned all resistance and stared at him with hatred.

In her eyes he saw what she saw.

Alarmed, he let go of her and spun round to see Ma sailing through the air in a grotesque posture, coming straight at him, his arm outstretched, swinging a huge knife. He wouldn't have time to shoot him, to run away, he would just have time to—

Jericho ducked.

The knife came down, sliced whistling through the air and through

Mrs Ma's throat, from which a cascade of blood sprayed. Ma staggered, thrown off balance by his own momentum, stared through blood-sprinkled glasses at his collapsing wife and flailed his arms. Jericho hammered the Glock against his wrist and the knife clattered to the floor. He kicked it away, kicked Ma in the belly and again in the shoulder, at which the child-abuser toppled forwards. The man groaned, collapsed on all fours. His glasses slipped from his nose. He felt around, half blind, struggled to his feet, both hands raised, palms outwards.

'I'm unarmed,' he gurgled. 'I'm defenceless.'

'I see a few defenceless people here,' Jericho panted, the Glock aimed at Ma. 'So? Did that help *them* at all?'

'I have my rights.'

'So do the children.'

'That's different. It's something you can't understand.'

'I don't *want* to understand!'

'You can't do anything to me.' Ma shook his head. 'I'm sick, a sick man. You can't shoot a sick man.'

For a moment Jericho was too flabbergasted to reply. He kept Ma in check with the gun and saw the man's lips curling.

'You won't shoot,' said Ma, with a flash of confidence.

Jericho said nothing.

'And you know why not?' His lips pulled into a grin. 'Because you feel it. You feel it too. The fascination. The beauty. If you could feel what I feel, you wouldn't point a gun at me.'

'You kill children,' Jericho said hoarsely.

'The society you represent is so dishonest. *You* are dishonest. Pitifully so. You poor little policeman in your wretched little world. Do you actually realise that you envy people like me? We've attained a degree of freedom of which you can only dream.'

'You swine.'

'We're so far ahead!'

Jericho raised the gun. Ma reacted immediately. Shocked, he threw both hands in the air and shook his head again.

'No, you can't do that. I'm sick. Very sick.'

'Yes, but you shouldn't have made that attempt to escape.'

'What attempt?'

'This one.'

Ma blinked. 'But I'm not escaping.'

'Yes, you're escaping, Ma. You're trying to get away. This very second. So I find myself forced—'

Jericho fired at his left kneecap. Ma screamed, doubled up, rolled on the floor and screeched blue murder. Jericho lowered the Glock and crouched down exhaustedly. He felt miserable. He wanted to throw up. He was dog-tired, and at the same time he had a sense that he would never be able to sleep again.

'You can't do that!' Ma wailed.

'You shouldn't have tried to get away,' Jericho murmured. 'Asshole.'

It took the police a full twenty minutes to find their way to the factory, and when they did they treated him as if he were in cahoots with the child-abuser. He was far too exhausted to get worked up about it, and just told the officers that it would be in the interest of their professional advancement to call a particular number. The duty inspector pulled a sulky face, came back as a different man and handed him the phone with almost childlike timidity.

'Someone would like to speak to you, Mr Jericho.'

It was Patrice Ho, his high-ranking policeman friend from Shanghai. In return for the information that the raid in Lanzhou had thrown up a paedophile ring, although it hadn't been possible to prove a connection with the Paradise of the Little Emperors, Jericho improved his evening with the news that Paradise had been found and the snake defeated.

'What snake?' his friend asked, puzzled.

'Forget it,' Jericho said. 'Christian stuff. Could you make sure that I don't have to put down roots here?'

'We owe you a favour.'

'Fuck the favour. Just get me out of here.'

There was nothing he yearned for so much as the chance to leave the factory and Shenzhen as quickly as possible. He was suddenly enjoying

the deference normally reserved for folk heroes and very popular criminals, but he wasn't allowed to leave until eight. He dropped the hire car
off at the airport, took the next plane for Shanghai, a Mach 1 flying wing,
and checked his messages in the air.

Tu Tian had been trying to contact him.

He called back.

'Oh, nothing in particular,' said Tu. 'I just wanted to tell you your
surveillance was successful. The hostile competitors admitted to data
theft. We had a talk.'

'Brilliant,' said Jericho without any particular enthusiasm. 'And what
came out of the talk?'

'They promised to stop it.'

'That's all?'

'That's a lot. I had to promise to stop it too.'

'Excuse me?' Jericho thought he had misheard. Tu Tian, whose company had proved to have fallen victim to Trojans, had been absolutely
furious. He had spared no expense to get his hands on the, as he put it,
pack of miserable blowflies and cockroaches so presumptuous as to spy
on his company secrets. 'You yourself wanted to—'

'I didn't know who they were.'

'And excuse me, but what difference does that make?'

'You're right, absolutely none at all.' Tu laughed, in great humour
now. 'Are you coming to the golf course the day after tomorrow? You
can be my guest.'

'Very kind of you, Tian, but—' Jericho rubbed his eyes. 'Could I decide
later?'

'What's up? Bad mood?'

Shanghai Chinese were different. More direct, more open. Practically
Italian, and Tu Tian was possibly the most Italian of all them. He could
have performed a convincing version of 'Nessun dorma'.

'Quite honestly,' Jericho said, 'I'm wiped out.'

'You sound it,' Tu agreed. 'Like a wet rag. A rag-man. We'll have to
hang you out to dry. What's up?'

And because fat Tu, for all his egocentricity, was one of the few people who granted Jericho an insight into his own inner state, he told him everything.

'Young man, young man,' Tu said, amazed, after a few seconds of respectful silence. 'How did you do it?'

'I just told you.'

'No, I mean, how did you get wise to him? How did you know it was him?'

'I didn't. It was just that everything pointed in that direction. Ma is vain, you know. The website was more than a catalogue of ready-produced horrors, with men forcing themselves on babies and women forcing little boys to have sex with them before laying into them with a hatchet. There were the usual films and photographs, but you could also put on your hologoggles and be there in 3D, and at various things happening live as well, which gives these guys a special kick.'

'Revolting.'

'But most importantly there was a chat-room, a fan forum where these people swapped information and boasted to each other. Even a second-life sector where you could assume a virtual identity. Ma appeared there as a water spirit. I suspect most paedos aren't familiar with that kind of thing. They tend to be made of more conventional stuff, and they don't much like talking into microphones, even with voice-changer software. They'd rather type out all their bullshit on the keyboard in the old-fashioned way, and of course Ma joined in and there he was. So I got the idea of adding my own contributions.'

'You must have felt like chucking!'

'I've got a switch in the back of my head and another in my belly. I usually manage to turn off at least one of them.'

'And back in the cellar?'

'Tian.' Jericho sighed. 'If I'd managed that, I wouldn't have told you all this crap.'

'I understand. Go on.'

'So, every imaginable visitor to the page is online, and of course Ma, the vain swine, is on there too. He disguises himself as a visitor, but you notice that he knows too much, and he has this huge need to communicate, so that I start suspecting that this guy is at least *one* of the originators, and after a while I'm convinced that it's *him*. A little while ago, I subjected his contributions to a semantic analysis – peculiarities of expression, preferred idioms, grammar – and the computer narrows the field, but there are still about a hundred known internet paedophiles who are possible suspects in this one. So I have the guy analysed while he's online and writing, and his typing rhythms give him away. Just about every time. That leaves four.'

'One of them Ma.'

'Yes.'

'And you're convinced it's him.'

'Unlike the police. They, of course, are convinced that Ma is the only one of the four that it *isn't*.'

'Which is why you went out on your own. Hmm.' Tu paused. 'All due respect to your approach, but didn't you recently tell me the nice thing about i-profiling was that the only fighting you have to do is against computer viruses?'

'I've had it with brawling,' Jericho said wearily. 'I don't want to see any more dead, mutilated, abused people, I don't want to shoot anyone, and I don't want anyone shooting at me. I've had enough, Tian.'

'Are you sure?'

'Completely. That was the last time.'

Back at home – although it wasn't really a home any more, filled as it was with removal boxes that he had spent several weeks packing, making his life look as if it came from a props store and had to be returned in its original packaging – Jericho suddenly had a creeping fear that he'd gone too far.

It was just after ten when the taxi set him down outside the high-rise building in Pudong that he would leave in a few days to move into his dream flat, but every time he closed his eyes he saw the half-decaying baby lying in the shack, the army of organisms that had pounced upon it to consume its flesh; he saw Ma's knife flashing down at him, again he felt the moment of deadly fear, a film that would now be on constant rerun, so that his new home threatened to become a place of nightmare.

Experience alone told him that thoughts were by their nature drifting clouds, and that all images eventually faded, but until that happened it could be a long and painful period of suffering.

He shouldn't have taken on that damned mission!

Wrong, he scolded himself. True despair lurked in the subjunctive, in the spinning-out of alternative plot strands that weren't alternatives because each one had only one path that it could travel down. And you couldn't even tell whether you were travelling voluntarily, or whether someone or something was impelling you – and Christ, what that some-thing might be, there was no way of knowing! Are we just a medium for predetermined processes? Had he had a choice about whether or not to take on the mission? Of course, he could have turned it down, but he hadn't. Didn't that invalidate any idea of choice? Had he had a choice about whether or not to follow Joanna to Shanghai? Whichever path you took, you took it, so there was no choice at all.

A trite acknowledgement of the bitter truth. Perhaps he should write a self-help manual. The airport bookshops were full of self-help man-uals. He himself had even seen some warning against self-help manuals.

How could you be so wide awake and at the same time so tired?

Was there anything else he needed to pack?

He turned on the monitor wall and found a BBC documentary – unlike the bulk of the population, he was able to receive most foreign channels without any difficulty, legal or illegal – and went in search of a box to sit on. At first he could hardly work out what was going on, then the subject started to interest him. Exactly right. Pleasantly far away from everything he had had to deal with over the past few days.

'A year ago today,' the commentator was saying, 'a dramatic wors-ening in Chinese–American relations preoccupied the plenary meeting of the United Nations, one that would become known as:'

The Moon Crisis

Jericho fetched a beer from the fridge and sat cross-legged on the box. The documentary was about the ghost of the previous summer, but began two years earlier, in 2022, a few weeks after the American base on the North Pole of the Moon went into operation. Back then the USA had started quarrying the noble-gas isotope helium-3 in the Mare Imbrium, setting in motion a development that had hitherto occupied the minds only of economic romantics and authors of science-fiction novels. Without a doubt, the Moon had a special part to play in the opening-up of the solar system: as a springboard for Mars, as a place of research, as a telescopic eye reaching the edges of the universe. From a purely economic point of view, compared with Mars Luna was a cheap date. You needed less fuel to get there, you got there quickly and came back quickly too. Philosophers justified moon travel with references to the spiritual sustenance of the enterprise, hoping for proofs or counter-proofs of God's existence and, quite generally, an insight into the status of *Homo sapiens*, as if it took a stone ball 360,000 kilometres away to do it.

Having said this, the distant view of Man's shared, fragile home did seem to encourage the formation of peaceful states of mind. The only questionable aspect was the satellite's economic productivity. There was no gold up there, no diamond mines, no oil. But even if there had been, the cost would have made commercial exploitation absurd. 'We may discover resources on the Moon or Mars that will boggle the imagination, that will test our limits to dream,' George W. Bush had announced in 2004, wearing the face of a founding father, and it had sounded exciting, naïve and adventurous, but then who took Bush seriously? At the time America had been bogged down in wars, and had been about to ruin its economy and its international standing. Hardly anything could have seemed more inappropriate than the idea of the reawakening of a new Eldorado, and besides, NASA had no money.

And yet—

Startled by the announcement by the US that they planned to send astronauts to the Moon again by 2020, the whole world had suddenly been galvanised into frantic activity. Whatever there was to be fetched back from the Moon, the field wasn't to be left open for America again, particularly since this time it seemed to have less to do with the symbolism of flags and footprints than with a tangible policy of economic supremacy. The European Space Agency offered technological support. Germany's DLR fell in love with the idea of having its own moon base. France's ESA carthorse EADS preferred a French solution. China hinted that in a few decades moon-mining would be crucially important to the national economy, explicitly the mining of helium-3. Roskosmos was also flirting with this quarrying idea, and so were the Russian companies Energia Rocket and Space Corporation, which had announced the construction of a moon base by 2015, whereupon India had immediately sent a probe with the beautiful name of Chandrayaan-1 into the polar orbit of the satellite to see how exploitable it was. Given the clear undertone of the Bush doctrine of going it alone, representatives of Russian and Chinese space travel authorities met for discussions about joint ventures, Japan's JAXA entered the game: everyone was in a terrific hurry to court La Luna and make sure they got hold of some of her legendary treasures, as if it were enough simply to go there, dig the stuff up and scatter it over the home territory. Each prognosis outdid the last in terms of boldness until Julian Orley set out his clear conditions.

The richest man in the world had become involved with the Americans.

The result was, to put it mildly, radical. No sooner had international competition for extraterrestrial raw materials begun than it had fizzled out again, as the victor was, thanks to Orley's decision, quite clear: a decision made less for reasons of sympathy than because the notoriously cash-strapped NASA turned out to have more money and a better infrastructure than all the other space-travelling nations put together. Apart from China, perhaps. There, during the nineties, ambitions to soar to cosmic greatness had become apparent, admittedly with a modest self-evaluation and an overall budget that came to a tenth of the USA's, but which were driven by patriotism and claims to world-power status. Then, after one Zheng Pang-Wang had begun financing Chinese space travel in 2014, their budgets and aspirations had become almost equal; there was just a lack of know-how – a shortcoming that Beijing thought it would be able to make up.

Zheng, high priest of a globally active technology company whose greatest ambition lay in putting China on the Moon even before the USA, and making the exploitation of helium-3 a possibility, was often described in the media as the Orley of the East. In fact, like the Englishman he had not only immense wealth but also an army of high-class builders and scientists at his disposal. The Zheng Group went to work feverishly on the realisation of a space elevator, probably in the knowledge that Orley was doing the same thing. But while Orley attained his goal, Zheng didn't solve the problem. Instead, the group managed to build a fusion reactor, but again they fell behind because Orley's model worked more safely and efficiently. China's ruling Communist Party grew nervous. Zheng was urged finally to demonstrate some success, if necessary by making long-nose an offer he couldn't refuse, so old Zheng went for dinner with Orley and told him that Beijing wanted to cooperate in the near future.

Orley said Beijing could kiss his butt. But would Zheng share another bottle of that wonderful Tignanello with him?

Why not share everything? asked Zheng.

Like what?

Well, money, a lot of money. Power, respect and influence.

He had money of his own.

Yes, but China was hungry and extremely highly motivated, far more than slack, overweight America, which was still reeling from the financial crisis of 2009, so that there was something doddery about everything it did. If you asked an American about the future, in seventy per cent of cases he would see something profoundly terrifying about it, while in China everyone faced the coming day with a cheerful heart.

That was all well and good, said Orley, but shouldn't they move on to an Ornellaia?

It was pointless, and certainly all mining plans with traditional rocket technology were economically unproductive, and condemned to throw Chinese space travel into the red. But with the defiance of a foot-stamping child, the Party decided to do just that, trusting in the hope that Zheng and the great minds of the Chinese National Space Administration would soon be back in the running. And because America had shown no scruples about letting its mining machines loose on the very part of the Moon where, according to the general geological view, there was a higher-than-average deposit of helium-3, a border area of the Mare Imbrium, the components for a mobile Chinese base and solar furnaces on caterpillar tracks were transported to that very spot, right next to their unloved competitor, and the Chinese began their own mining operation on 2 March 2023. America acted first amazed, then delighted. China was cordially welcomed to the Moon, there was talk of a global legacy and an international community, and no one worried about the newcomer's touching efforts to squeeze its pathetic portion of helium-3 out of moon dust.

Until 9 May 2024.

Over the past few months both nations had successively stepped up their mining operations. On that day a rather heated discussion took place between the American moon base and Houston. Following immediately on from this, the alarming message reached the White House that Chinese astronauts had deliberately and with unambiguous intentions crossed the mining boundaries and annexed American territory, and that the Americans felt provoked and threatened. The Chinese ambassador was summoned and accused of border violations, and ordered to re-establish the status quo forthwith. The Party asked for an enquiry into what had happened, and on 11 May declared itself unaware of any guilt. Without officially negotiated borders there could be no border violation. Broadly speaking, Washington must know what the world thought of the way that America, in defiance of all clauses in the space treaty in general and the lunar treaty in particular, had invented facts; and how had anyone ever come up with the abstruse idea of crossing that heavenly body – which, according to those treaties, belonged to no one – with borders? And did they really want to have that tiresome discussion all over again, instead of contenting themselves with their own superiority, which was, after all, plainly visible to anyone with eyes to see?

The USA felt snubbed. The Moon was a long way away, no one on Earth could say exactly who was strolling about on whose territory, but on 13 May the moon base announced the arrest of the Chinese astronaut Hua Liwei. The man had been sniffing around on the territory of the American mining station, an automatised facility, which was

why he could hardly have shown up there to talk about the moon weather over tea and cakes. That Hua was also commander of the Chinese
base, a highly decorated officer who was given no opportunity to provide his version of events, did nothing to defuse the situation. Beijing
raged and protested vehemently. At the Ministry for State Security, they
outdid themselves in describing the martyrdom that Hua would have to
endure in the remote polar base, and made demands for his immediate
release which Washington studiously ignored, whereupon Chinese associations, officially this time, invaded American territory with vehicles
and mining robots, or at least that was how it was reported. In fact, only
one unfortunate small robot was involved, which accidentally rammed
an American machine and completely wrote itself off. There could have
been no question of manned vehicles, given the isolated Chinese Rover
roaming around on its own, and on closer inspection the feared associations proved to be the clueless, disorganised remnants of the base staff,
two women who had had to simulate an invasion because of political
arm-twisting, while the American astronauts at the Pole didn't understand why they had had to take poor Hua prisoner, and put all their efforts
into at least giving him a good time.

But no one on Earth was interested in any of that.

Instead, ghosts long thought exorcised tried to scare each other to
death. Imperialism versus the Red Peril. In a sense the excitement was
even justified. It wasn't at all about the few astronauts or a few square
miles of terrain, but who was and would be in charge if more nations
tried to take possession of the Moon. Then Washington promptly
threatened sanctions, froze Chinese bank accounts, prevented Chinese
ships from leaving American ports and expelled the Chinese ambassador, prompting Beijing to threaten massive measures against American
mining, if bank accounts, ships and Hua were not released forthwith.
America insisted on an apology. No one at all would be released before
that. Beijing announced a plan to storm the American station. Bafflingly,
no one asked the question of how the completely overtaxed taikonauts
could take a huge, partly subterranean base at the inaccessible, mountainous North Pole, and once Washington had threatened military strikes

against the Chinese mining station and Chinese facilities on Earth, no one really felt like asking it either.

The world was beginning to get frightened.

Unimpressed, if not actually motivated by this, the aggrieved super-powers continued to tear into each other. Each accused the other of perpetrating a military build-up in space, and of having stationed weapons on the Moon, with the result that the news was full of simulations of lunar nuclear engagements, with dark hints that the conflict might be continued on Earth. While the BBC showed pictures of exploding space stations and, in happy ignorance of physics, gave them an audible bang, the moon-base crews were forbidden to talk to each other. In the end neither party knew what the other was doing and what the whole thing was really about, apart from saving face, until the UN ruled that enough was enough.

That old carthorse, diplomacy, was yoked up to the cart, to drag it out of the dirt. The UN plenary session met on 22 May 2024. China pointed out that because they didn't have their own space elevator they were unable to transport weapons to the Moon, while this was an easy matter for the Americans. Therefore the Americans must be seen as the aggressors, because they had very clearly stationed weapons on the Moon and broken the space treaty yet again, but then what was new? They themselves, incidentally, were not planning to arm, but found them-selves forced by continued provocations to consider a modest contingent for self-defence. The Americans expressed similar intentions. China had been the source of the aggression, and if America were ever to arm itself on the Moon, it would be the consequence of a completely unnecessary border violation.

No border had been violated.

Okay, fine. And we didn't have weapons on the Moon.

Did.

Didn't.

Did.

Didn't.

Did.

The UN General Secretary, with weary rage, condemned both the actions of the Chinese and the imprisonment of the Chinese astronaut by the USA. The world wanted peace. That much was true. Basically, Beijing and Washington wanted nothing more than peace, but face must be saved! It was not until 4 June 2024 that China, teeth gritted, backed down, without reference to the UN resolution, the power of which, once again, seemed to be largely symbolic in character. The truth was that neither of the two nations was either willing or able to engage in open conflict. China withdrew from American territory, which involved the taikonauts carting away the shattered mining machine. Hua was released, along with the Chinese bank accounts and ships, and the ambassadors moved back into their offices. At first the situation was characterised by threats and suspicion. There was a political chill, which meant that the economy froze temporarily as well. Julian Orley, who had wanted to open his Moon hotel as early as 2024, had to suspend its construction for an indefinite period, and helium-3 mining suffered on both sides.

'It took until 10 November 2024,' the commentator said with a serious demeanour, 'for dialogue between the USA and China to resume at the World Economy Summit in Bangkok, for the first time since the outbreak of the dispute, and since then it has been marked by conciliatory tones.' Her voice became more menacing and dramatic. 'The world has escaped an escalation – how narrowly, no one can say.' And again, in a milder tone: 'The USA assured the Chinese of a stronger connection to the infrastructure of the moon base, new agreements for mutual aid in space were signed and existing ones extended, Americans and Chinese reached an understanding on trade agreements that had until then been contentious.' Positive, optimistic, with a sleep-well-little-children smile: 'The waves have been stilled. As ambitiously as they went at each other's throats, gestures of goodwill were now exchanged. For a very simple reason: the economies couldn't do without each other. The integration between the two trading giants, the USA and China, could not withstand a war; each party would only be destroying its own property on hostile territory. There is half-hearted talk about cooperating more strongly in future, while only now is each of the two major world powers able to strive for dominance on the Moon. Meanwhile the space-travelling world is vying for the patents of Julian Orley, who has over the last few days broken into space with an illustrious and suspiciously multinational troop of selected guests, perhaps in order to reconsider his US-exclusive attitude – but perhaps also to show them our small, fragile planet from a distance, and remind them that belligerent disputes would not be won by anyone. On that note: good night.'

Jericho sucked the last bit of foam from the bottle.

Curious race, humanity. Flew to the Moon and abused little children.

He turned off the television, gave the box a kick and went to bed in the hope of being able to sleep.

21 May 2025

THE LIFT

The Cave

'The Stellar Dome was originally planned for the highest point of the island, where the crystal dome with the restaurant is now,' Lynn Orley explained as she walked through the lounge ahead of the group. 'Until, while we were exploring the place, we discovered something that led us to abandon our previous plans. The mountain provided us with an alternative that we could barely have imagined.'

On the evening of the third and last day of their stay on the Isla de las Estrellas the group was waiting for the prelude to their big adventure. Lynn led them to a wide, locked doorway set in the back wall of the lobby.

'It can't have escaped anyone that the Stellar Island Hotel looks like an ocean steamer stranded in the volcano. And *officially* that volcano is extinct.' Here and there she registered unease. In Momoka Omura's imagination in particular, streams of lava seemed to be flowing through the lounge and spoiling the evening once and for all. 'At the summit and along the flank moderate temperatures prevail. Pleasantly cool, ideally suited for storing food and drink, for locating pumps, generators and processing plants, the laundry, janitor's office and various other things. Just behind me' – she turned her head towards the bulkheads – 'offices were planned. We started drilling into the rock, but after only a few metres we found ourselves in a fault that extended into a cave, and at the end of that cave—'

Lynn rested the palm of her hand on a scanner, and the door slid open.

'—lay the Stellar Dome.'

A steeply descending passageway with roughly carved walls stretched beyond the doorway, and turned a corner so that it was impossible to see where it went next. Lynn saw faces filled with curiosity, excitement and anticipation. Only Momoka Omura, once she had been reassured that she would not be burning up in liquid rock, seemed to have lost interest completely, and stared earnestly at the ceiling.

'Any more questions?' Lynn let a mysterious smile play around the corners of her mouth. 'Then let's go.'

A collage of sounds enveloped them, all apparently of natural origin. There were clicks, echoes, whispers and drips, and orchestral surfaces created a timeless atmosphere. Lynn's idea of turning the emotional screw without slipping into the Disneyesque was taking effect: sounds on the boundary edge of perception, as a subtle way of creating moods, which had required the building of a complicated technical installation, but the result exceeded all expectations. The two sides of the door closed behind them, and cut them off from the airy, comfortable atmosphere of the lobby.

'We laid out this section ourselves,' Lynn explained. 'The natural part begins just past the bend. The cave system extends through the whole of the eastern flank of the volcano. You could walk around in it for hours, but we preferred to close the passageways. Otherwise there might be a danger of you getting lost in the heart of the Isla de las Estrellas.'

Past the bend, the corridor stretched out considerably. It grew darker. Shadows flitted over pitted basalt, like the shadows of strange and startled animals escaping to safety from the horde of tourists. The echoes of their footsteps seemed to the group to precede and follow them at the same time.

'How are caves like this formed?' Bernard Tautou threw his head back. 'I've seen a few, but every time I've forgotten to ask.'

'They can have all kinds of possible causes. Tensions in the rock, pockets of water, landslips. Volcanoes are porous structures; when they cool down they often leave cavities. In this case it's most probably lava drainage channels.'

'Oh great,' blustered Donoghue. 'We've landed in the gutter.'

The corridor turned in a curve, narrowed and debouched into an almost circular room. The walls were lined with motifs from the dawn of humanity, some painted, some carved into the rock. Bizarre life-forms stared at the visitors from the penumbra, with fathomlessly dark eyes, horns and tails and helmets with aerial-shaped growths sprouting from them. Some of the clothes looked like spacesuits. They saw creatures that seemed to have merged with complicated machines. A huge, rect-angular relief showed a humanoid creature in a foetal position operating levers and switches. The sound changed, becoming eerie.

'Horrible,' Miranda Winter sighed with relish.

'I hope so,' grinned Lynn. 'After all, we've brought together the most mysterious testimonies of human creativity. Reproductions, obviously. The figures in the striped suits, for example, were discovered in Australia, and according to tradition they represent the two lightning brothers Yag-jagbula and Tabiringl. Some researchers think they are astronauts. Next to them, the so-called Martian God, originally a six-metre cave drawing from the Sahara. The creatures there on the left, the ones who seem to be holding their hands up in greeting, were found in Italy.'

'And this one?' Eva Borelius had stopped in front of the relief and was looking at it with interest.

'The gem of our collection! A Mayan artefact. The gravestone of King Pakal of Palenque, an ancient pyramid city in Chiapas in Mexico. It's supposed to depict the ruler's descent to the underworld, symbol-ised by the open jaws of a giant snake.' Lynn walked over to it. 'What do you recognise?'

'Hard to say, but it looks as if he's sitting in a rocket.'

'Exactly!' cried Ögi, rushing over. 'And you know what? It was a Swiss man who was responsible for that interpretation!'

'Oh?'

'You don't know of Erich von Däniken?'

'Wasn't he a sort of fantasist?' Borelius smiled coldly. 'Someone who saw extraterrestrials everywhere?'

'He was a visionary!' Ögi corrected her. 'A very great one!'

'I'm sorry.' Karla Kramp gave a little cough. 'But your visionary has been regularly contradicted.'

'So?'

'In that case I'd just like to understand what makes him so great.'

'How often do you think, my dear, that the Bible has been

contradicted,' Ögi bellowed again. 'Without fantasists the world would be more boring, more average, more stale. Who cares whether he was right? Do you always have to be right to be great?'

'I'm sorry, I'm a doctor. If I'm wrong, my patients don't generally reach the conclusion that I'm great.'

'Lynn, could you come over here for a moment?' Evelyn Chambers called. 'Where does that come from? It looks as if they're flying.'

Conversations sprouted, a little knowledge blossomed. The motifs were admired and discussed. Lynn provided explanations and hypotheses. This was the first time that a group of visitors had been inside the cave. Her plan to use prehistoric drawings and sculptures to get people in the mood for the mystery to come was a success. At length she drummed the group together and led them from the cave-room to the next stretch of passageway, which grew even steeper, even darker—

And warmer.

'What's that noise?' Miranda Winter wondered. 'Voom, voom! Is that normal?'

And true enough, a dull rumble mingled with the soundtrack, coming from the depths of the mountain, and creating a menacing atmosphere. Reddish wisps of smoke drifted over the rock.

'There's something there,' Aileen Donoghue whispered. 'Some sort of light.'

'God, Lynn,' laughed Marc Edwards. 'Where are you taking us?'

'We must be quite deep already, aren't we?' It was the first time Rebecca Hsu had spoken. Since her arrival she had been constantly on the phone, and nobody had been able to engage her.

'Just over eighty metres,' said Lynn. She stepped briskly on, towards another turn, bathed in flickering firelight.

'Exciting,' O'Keefe observed.

'Oh, come on, it's just theatre,' Warren Locatelli announced from above. 'We're entering a strange world, is what they're trying to suggest. The inside of the Earth, the interior of a strange planet, some waffle like that.'

'Just wait,' said Lynn.

'What's she got for us this time?' Momoka Omura said, striving for disenchantment, while the tone of her voice revealed that streams of lava were starting to flow in her head again. 'A cave, another cave. Brilliant.'

The rumbling and roaring rose in a crescendo.

'So, I think it's—' Evelyn Chambers began, stopped in the middle of the sentence and said, 'Oh, my!'

They had passed the bend. Monstrous heat came roaring at them. The passageway widened, suffused with a pulsating glow. Some of the guests came to an abrupt standstill, others ventured hesitantly forwards. On the right-hand side the rock opened up, providing a glimpse into a huge, adjacent vault, from which the thundering and roaring emanated, drowning out their conversation. A glowing lake half filled the chamber, boiling and bubbling, spitting red and yellow fountains. Basalt spikes jutted from the sluggish surge towards the domed ceiling, which flickered spectrally in the glow. With quiet delight, Lynn studied fear, fascination, astonishment; she saw Heidrun Ögi shielding herself against the heat with her raised hands. Her white hair, her skin seemed to be blazing. As she uncertainly approached, she looked for a moment as if she had just emerged from some inferno.

'What on earth is that?' she asked in disbelief.

'A magma chamber,' Lynn explained calmly. 'A store that keeps the volcano fed with lava and gases. Such chambers form when liquid rock rises from a great depth to the weak areas of the Earth's crust. As soon as pressure in the chamber gets out of control, the lava forces its way up, and the eruption occurs.'

'But didn't you say the volcano was extinct?' Mukesh Nair said in amazement.

'Officially extinct, yes.'

Suddenly everyone was talking at the same time. O'Keefe was the first to voice some suspicion. During the whole excursion he had been strolling thoughtfully along the passageway, absorbed, keeping his distance; now he walked right up to the seething cauldron.

'Hé, mon ami!' called Tautou. 'Don't singe your hair.'

'*Pas de problème*,' O'Keefe turned round and grinned. 'I hardly think there's anything to be afraid of. Isn't that right, Lynn?'

He held out his right hand. His fingers touched a surface. Warm, but not hot. Entirely smooth. He pressed the palm of his hand against it and smiled appreciatively.

'When was the last time it looked like this inside the mountain?'

Lynn smiled.

'According to the geologists, about a hundred thousand years ago. But not as far up. Magma chambers usually lie at a depth of twenty-five to thirty kilometres, and they're much bigger than this one.'

'Anyway, it's the best hologram I've seen in ages.'

'We do our best to please.'

'A hologram?' echoed Sushma.

'More precisely, an interplay of holographic projections with sound, coloured light and thermal panels.'

Sushma stepped up beside O'Keefe and tapped her finger against the surface of the screen, as if there might still be a chance that he was mistaken. 'But it looks perfectly real!'

'Of course. We don't want to bore you, after all.'

Everybody touched the screen now, stepped respectfully back and yielded once more to the illusion. Chuck Donoghue forgot to wisecrack, Locatelli to prattle condescendingly. Even Momoka Omura stared into the digital lava lake and looked almost impressed.

'We're practically at our destination,' said Lynn. 'In a few seconds we'll be able to enter that chamber, only then it will look completely different. You will be travelling from the distant past to the future of our planet, the future of mankind.'

She tapped a switch hidden in the rock. At the end of the passageway a tall, vertical crack appeared. Faint light seeped from it. The music swelled, powerful and mystical, the crack widened and provided a glimpse of the vault beyond. It really did, in appearance and dimensions, look very much like the holographic depiction, except that there was no lava sloshing about. Instead, there was a kind of theatrical arena suspended above the bottomless pit. Steel walkways led to banked rows of comfortable-looking seats, which hovered freely above the abyss. At the centre there arched a transparent surface measuring at least a thousand square metres in area. Its bottom end was lost in the lightless depths, the top reached to just below the domed ceiling, its sides stretched far beyond the rows of seats.

Standing on the gallery was a lone man.

He was of medium height, slightly squat, and youthful in appearance, although his beard and his long, collar-length hair were grey, and the ash-blond colour of earlier years was a thing of the distant past. He wore a T-shirt and jacket, jeans and cowboy boots. There were rings on his fingers. His eyes flashed jauntily, his grin was like a lighthouse beam.

'Here you are at last,' said Julian Orley. 'Okay, then: let's rock 'n' roll!'

Tim stood apart from the others, watching his father greet the guests with handshakes or hugs according to how well he knew them. Julian, the great communicator, laying friendly traps. So keen to meet people that he never doubted for a moment that those people wanted to meet him, and that was exactly what attracted them. The physics of meeting people is based on both attraction and repulsion, but it was practically impossible to escape Julian's gravitational pull. You were introduced to him and you instantly felt warm familiarity. Two, three more times and you were lost in memories of old times together that had never existed. Julian didn't do much, he came out with no quips, he didn't practise speeches in front of the mirror, he just took it for granted that in Newton's two-body system he was the planet and not the satellite.

'Carl, old man! Lovely to have you here!'

'Evelyn, you look fantastic. What idiot ever said the *circle* was the most perfect form?'

'Momoka, Warren. Welcome. Oh, and thank you for last time, I've been meaning to call for ages. To be quite honest, I have no idea how I got home.'

'Olympiada Rogacheva! Oleg Rogachev! Isn't this fantastic? Here we are meeting right now for the first time, and tomorrow we'll be travelling to the Moon together.'

'Chucky, old man, I've got a great joke for you, but we'll have to step aside for a minute if you're to hear it.'

'Where is my Fairy Queen? Heidrun! I've finally met your husband. Did you ever buy that Chagall? – Of course I know about that, I know about all your passions; your wife has been doing nothing but rave about you!'

'Finn, young man, this is where it gets serious. You've got to go up there now. And this *isn't* a movie!'

'Eva Borelius, Karla Kramp. I've been particularly looking forward to . . .'

And so on, and so forth.

Julian found friendly words for everyone, then he came dashing over to Tim and Amber with a furtive grin.

'So? How do you like it?'

'Brilliant,' said Amber, and put an arm around his shoulders. 'The magma chamber's amazing.'

'Lynn's idea.' Julian beamed. He could barely utter his daughter's name without adopting a sickly tone. 'And this is nothing! Wait till you see the show.'

'It'll be perfect, as always,' Tim stammered with barely concealed sarcasm.

'Lynn and I came up with it together.' As usual, Julian pretended not to have noticed Tim's ironic tone. 'The cave is a gift from heaven, I tell you. These rows of seats mightn't look like much, but we can now screen this spectacle for five hundred paying guests, and if it's more—'

'I thought the hotel only had room for three hundred?'

'Sure, but we can basically double our capacity. Put four or five decks on our ocean steamer, either that or Lynn will build a second one. Not a problem either way. The main thing is that we rustle up the cash for another lift.'

'The main thing is that you don't get into difficulties.'

Julian looked at Tim with his light blue eyes.

'And I'm not. Will you excuse me? Enjoy yourselves, see you later. Oh, Madame Tautou!'

Julian darted back and forth between the visitors, a laugh here, a compliment there. Every now and again he drew Lynn to him and kissed her on the temples. Lynn smiled. She looked proud and happy. Amber sipped at her champagne.

'You could be a bit friendlier to him,' she said quietly.

'To Julian?' snorted Tim.

'Who else?'

'What difference does it make if I'm friendly to him? He only sees himself anyway.'

'Perhaps it makes a difference *to me.*'

Tim stared at her uncomprehendingly.

'What's up?' Amber raised her eyebrows. 'Are you slow-witted all of a sudden?'

'No, but—'

'Clearly you are. Then I'll put it a different way. I don't feel like spending the next two weeks constantly staring into your gloomy face, okay? I want to enjoy this trip, and you should too.'

'Amber—'

'Leave your prejudices down here.'

'It's not a matter of prejudices! The thing is, that—'

'It's *always* something.'

'But—'

'No buts. Just be a good boy. I want to hear a yes. Just a simple yes. Do you think you can manage that?'

Tim chewed his bottom lip. Then he shrugged. Lynn walked past them, followed by the Tautous and the Donoghues. She winked at them, lowered her voice and said behind her hand, 'Hey, insider knowledge. This is confidential information for family members only. Row eight, seats thirty-two and thirty-three. Best view.'

'Got it. Over and out.'

Amber linked arms with the group and disappeared without another word towards the auditorium. Tim sauntered along behind her. Someone drew up beside him.

'You're Julian's son, aren't you?'

'Yes.'

'Lovely to meet you. Heidrun Ögi. Your family's completely bonkers. I mean, it's not a problem, it's absolutely fine,' she added when he failed to reply. 'I love people with bees in their bonnets. You're far more interesting than the common run of people.'

Tim stared at her. He would have expected anything from this chalk-white woman with the violet eyes and the white mane of hair: Celtic magic spells, extraterrestrial dialects, just not that kind of misplaced remark.

'Really?' he managed.

'So what sort of madman are you, then? If you take after Julian.'

'You think my father's mad?'

'Of course, he's a genius. So he must be mad.'

Tim said nothing. *What kind of madman are you, then?* Good question. No, he thought, what an idiotic assumption! I'm definitely the only one in the family who *isn't* mad.

'Well—'

'See you.' Heidrun smiled, drew away from him, waving her fingertips, and followed the jovial Swiss chap who was clearly her husband. Slightly startled, he pushed his way to the middle of the eighth row and slumped down next to Amber.

'Who are these Ögis?' he asked.

She looked over her shoulder. 'The guy with the albino wife?'

'Mm-hm.'

'Glittering couple. He runs a company called Swiss Performance. They're involved in all kinds of areas, but mostly he's in the construction business. I think he came up with the first pontoon estates for the flooded areas of Holland. At the moment he's in discussions with Albert over Monaco Two.'

'Monaco Two?'

'Yes, just imagine! A huge floating island. It was on the news a while ago. The thing's only going to cruise in fair-weather zones.'

'Ögi must be the same sort of bonkers as Julian.'

'Could be. He's said to be a philanthropist. He supports needy artists, performers and circus folk, he's started up educational institutions for underprivileged young people, he sponsors museums, he donates money like it was going out of fashion. Last year he donated a considerable part of his fortune to the Bill and Melinda Gates Foundation.'

'How the hell do you know all this?'

'You should read the gossip sheets more often.'

'Don't need to while I've got you. And Heidrun?'

'Yeah . . .' Amber smiled knowingly. 'That's where things get interesting! Ögi's family isn't exactly over the moon about their relationship.'

'Tell me more.'

'She's a photographer. She's talented. She takes pictures of celebrities and ordinary people. She's published picture-books about the, erm . . . red-light scene. In her wild years she's said to have gone so far off the rails that she was thrown out of her house and disinherited. After that she started funding her studies by working as a stripper, and later as an actress in posh porn films. At the start of the millennium she became a cult figure in Switzerland's smart set. I mean, you couldn't exactly claim she's not striking.'

'Good God, no.'

'Eyes straight ahead, Timmy. She gave up the porn films after her studies, but went on stripping. At parties, gallery openings, just for fun. At one of those events she came across Walo, and he helped boost her career as a photographer.'

'Which is why she married him.'

'Apparently she isn't an opportunist.'

'Touching,' said Tim, and was about to add something else when the lights went out. They were immediately sitting in inky blackness. A solo violin started playing. Gentle music wove threads through the dark, shimmering lines that formed elaborate structures. At the same time the space assumed a blue glow, a mysterious, gloomy ocean. From what seemed to be a long distance away – the impressive result of holographic projections on the huge, concave glass wall – something came towards them, pulsating and transparent, something that looked like an organic spaceship with a vague nucleus of alien, shadowy passengers.

'Life,' said a voice, 'began in the sea.'

Tim turned his head. Amber's profile shone like a ghost in the blue light. Enchanted, she watched the cell growing bigger and slowly beginning to rotate. The voice spoke of primal lakes and chemical marriages contracted many years ago. The lonely cell in the infinity of blue divided, and then that division became faster and faster, more and more cells came into being, and all of a sudden something long and serpentine came wriggling towards them.

'Six hundred million years ago, the age of complex, multicellular living creatures began!' the voice announced.

Over the minutes that followed, a speeded-up version of evolution occurred. The realism was so overwhelming that Tim flinched involuntarily when a monster a metre long, with shredder teeth and thorny claws, catapulted towards him, switched direction with a flick of its powerful tail and devoured not him, but a twitching trilobite. The Cambrian age emerged and faded before his eyes, followed by the Ordovician, the Silurian and the Devonian. As if someone had pressed a search button on a geological remote control, life swarmed through the blue and underwent every imaginable metamorphosis. Jellyfish, worms, lancelets and crabs, giant scorpions, octopuses, sharks and reptiles appeared in turn, an amphibian turned into a saurian, everything moved onto land, a radiant, cloud-scattered sky took the place of the depths of the sea, the Mesozoic sun shone down on hadrosaurs, brachiosaurs, tyrannosaurs and raptors, until a huge meteorite came crashing down on the horizon and set off a wave of destruction that swept all life away. In digital perfection the inferno charged onwards, taking the audience's breath away, but when the dust settled it revealed the victory parade of the mammals, and everyone was still sitting unscathed in their rows of seats. Something ape-like swung through a summery green grove, stood upright, turned into a chattering early hominid, armed and clothed itself, changed its build, posture and physiognomy, rode a horse, drove a car, piloted an aeroplane, floated waving through the interior of a space station and out through an opening – but instead of landing in space, it stretched and dived back into the waters of the ocean. Diffuse blue, once again. The human, floating in it, smiled, and they all smiled back.

'They say we are attracted to water because we come from water and we ourselves are over seventy per cent water. But did we originate only in the sea?'

The blue condensed into a sphere and shrank to a tiny drop of water in a black void.

'If we go in search of our origins, we have to look a long way back into the past. Because water, which covers over two-thirds of the Earth, and which we are made of' – the voice paused significantly – 'came from space!'

Silence.

To the deafening sound of an orchestra the droplet exploded into millions of glittering particles, and suddenly everything was full of galaxies, lined up like dewdrops on the threads of a spider's web. As if they were sitting in a spaceship, they approached a single galaxy, flew into it, passed a sun and floated on, towards its third planet, until it hung before them as a fiery sphere, covered with an ocean of boiling lava. Asteroids crashed noisily in as the voice explained how the water had come to Earth on meteorites from the depths of space, bringing organic matter with it. They watched a second ocean of steam settling over the sea of lava. The whole thing reached a climax when a huge planetoid came dashing by, slightly smaller than the young Earth and bearing the name of Theia. The magma chamber shook with the impact, debris flew in all directions, and the Earth survived that too, now richer in mass and water and in possession of a moon that formed from the debris and sped around the planet. The hail of projectiles eased, oceans and continents came into being.

Sitting beside Tim, Julian said quietly, 'Of course the idea that you can have noises in a vacuum is total nonsense. Lynn would rather have stuck to the facts, but I thought we should think about the children.'

'What children?' Tim whispered back. Only now did he notice his father sitting on his other side.

'Well, most of the people making the journey will be parents with their children! To show them the wonders of the universe. The whole show is aimed at children and adolescents. Just imagine how excited they're going to be.'

'So we aren't just drawn back to the sea,' the voice was saying. 'An even older legacy guides our eyes to the stars. We look into the night sky and feel an unsettling closeness, almost something like homesickness, which we can barely explain to ourselves.'

The imaginary spaceship had passed through the planet's new atmosphere, and was now heading towards New York. The Manhattan skyline with the illuminated Freedom Tower lay impressively beneath a fairy-tale night sky.

'And the answer is obvious. Our true home is space. We are island-dwellers. Just as people in every age have pushed their way into the unknown to expand their knowledge and find new places to live, the natural desire to explore is written in our genes. We look up to the stars and ask ourselves why our technological civilisation shouldn't be able to do what the nomads of early times managed using the simplest means, with boats made of animal skins, on peregrinations that lasted for years, defying the wind and weather, impelled only by their curiosity, their endlessly inventive spirit and their yearning for knowledge, the deep desire to understand.'

'And that's where I come in!' squeaked a little rocket, that stomped into the picture and clicked its fingers.

The wonderful panoramic view of New York at night, starry sky and all, disappeared. Some of the audience laughed. The rocket did actually look funny. It was silver and fat with a pointy tip: a spaceship out of a picture-book, with four tailfins on which it marched around, wildly waving arms, and a rather odd-looking face.

'Kids will love this,' Julian whispered with delight. 'Rocky Rocket! We plan comics with this little fellow, cartoons, cuddly toys, the whole shebang.'

Tim was about to reply when he saw his father arriving to stand next to the rocket in the black void. The virtual Julian Orley wore jeans too, an open white shirt and glittering silver trainers. The inevitable rings sparkled on his fingers as he shooed the little rocket off to the side.

'You're not needed here for the time being,' he said, and spread his arms. 'Good evening, ladies and gentlemen, I'm Julian Orley. A warm welcome to the Stellar Dome. Let me take you on a journey to—'

'Yes, with me,' trumpeted the rocket, and came sliding into the foreground in full showbiz style, also with his arms spread, on his knees or whatever rockets called knees. 'Me, the one it all started with, Follow me to—'

Julian shoved the rocket aside again, and it in turn tripped him up. The two of them squabbled for a while about who was going to lead everybody through the history of space travel, until they agreed to do it together. The auditorium was plainly amused, and Chucky's expansive laughter roared out at every trick that Rocky played. What followed was once again accompanied by images, such as a brick-built space station orbiting the Earth which, as Julian informed them, came from the science-fiction story 'The Brick Moon' by the English clergyman Edward Everett Hale. Rocky Rocket dragged a startled-looking dog into orbit and explained that it was the first satellite. The scenery changed again. A huge cannon, its barrel driven into a tropical mountainside. People in old-fashioned clothes climbed onto a kind of projectile and were fired into space by the cannon.

'That was in 1865, eight years after the appearance of "The Brick Moon". In his novels *De la Terre à la Lune* and *Autour de la Lune*, Jules Verne described the beginning of manned space flight with astonishing far-sightedness, even though the cannon, because of the length required, would have been impossible to make. But all the same, the projectile is successfully fired from Tampa in Florida, where, and just think about this, NASA is based today. Unfortunately, over the course of the story the unfortunate dog is thrown overboard at some point and circles the spaceship for a short time, the very first satellite.'

Rocky Rocket threw a bone to the puzzled creature, which tried in vain to catch it, with the result that the bone now went into orbit along with the dog.

'In novels and short stories people started speculating a long time ago about how we could travel to the stars, but it was the Russians who first managed to fire an artificial heavenly body into near-Earth orbit. On 4 October 1957 at 22.29 hours and 34 seconds they fired an aluminium sphere into orbit, just over 84 kilos in weight and with four antennae that broadcast a series of now legendary beeps as a radio signal on 15 and 7.5 metre wavelengths, all across the world: Sputnik 1 took the world's breath away!'

Over the next few minutes the imaginary spaceship turned once again into a time machine, as new objects were constantly fired into space. The dogs Strelka and Belka barked cheerfully on board Sputnik 4. Alexei Leonov ventured out of his capsule and floated like an astral baby on his umbilical cord through space. They met Valentina Vladimirovna Tereshkova, the first woman in space, they saw Neil Armstrong leaving his boot-prints in the Moon's dust on 20 July 1969, and all kinds of space stations circling the Earth. Space Shuttles and Soyuz capsules carried goods and crews to the ISS, China started its first moon probe. A new international space race began, the Space Shuttle was mothballed, Russia revived its Soyuz programme, Ares rockets now headed for the endless construction site that was ISS, the spaceship Orion brought people to the Moon again, the European Space Agency immersed itself in preparations for a flight to Mars, China started to build a space station of its own, almost everyone fantasised about the colonisation of space, via Moon landings, flights to Mars and ventures into galaxies to which no man had ever boldly gone, as a science-fiction series of the early years had so nicely put it.

'But all these plans,' Julian explained, 'shared the problem that space-ships and space stations *couldn't* be built the way they ideally *should* have been built. Which was down to two unavoidable physical givens: air resistance – and gravitation.'

Now Rocky Rocket made his grand entrance again, balancing on a stylised globe, with a distant, friendly lunar face hanging over it. The satellite, unambiguously female, with crater acne but pretty nonetheless, winked at Rocky and flirted so brazenly with the little rocket that he sent sparks into ether from his pointed tip. Tim slipped deeper into his seat and leaned over to Julian.

'Very child-friendly,' he teased quietly.

'What's the problem?'

'The whole thing's a bit phallic. I mean, the Moon is female, so Miss Luna wants to be fucked. Or what?'

'Rockets *are* phallic,' Julian complained. 'What should we have done in your view? Make the Moon masculine? Would you rather have had a gay Moon? I wouldn't.'

'I don't mean that.'

'I don't want a gay Moon. No one wants a gay Moon. Or a gay space-ship with a glowing arse. Forget it.'

'I didn't say I didn't like it. I just—'

'You're a born sceptic.'

Arguing for argument's sake. Tim wondered how they would survive the next two weeks together. Meanwhile Rocky Rocket packed every-thing a rocket might need into his suitcase, cleanly folded a few astronauts in there too, stuffed the case into his belly, and then, blowing kisses, fired off a cute little stream of fire and leapt into the air. Immediately the Earth's surface threw out a dozen extendable arms and pulled him back down again. Rocky, extremely puzzled, tried again, but escaping the planet seemed impossible. High above him, the randy Moon fell into a mild depression.

'If someone jumps in the air, it is one hundred per cent certain that he will fall back to the ground,' screen-Julian explained. 'Matter exerts gravity. The more mass a body contains, the greater is its field of gravity, with which it pulls smaller objects to it.'

Sir Isaac Newton appeared dozing under a tree, until an apple fell on his head and he leapt up with a knowing expression: 'This is exactly,' he said, 'how the heavenly mechanics of all bodies works. Because I am bigger than the apple, you would imagine that the fruit would succumb to my very personal physicality. And in fact I do exert modest forces of gravity. But compared with the mass of the planet, I play a subor-dinate role for the apple, which is ripe for gravitational behaviour. In fact this tiny apple has no chance against Earth's gravity. The more power I summon up in my attempt to throw it back up in the air, the higher it will

FRANK SCHÄTZING · 108

climb, but however hard I try, it will inevitably fall back to the ground.'
As if to prove his remarks, Sir Isaac tried his hand at apple-throwing
and wiped the sweat from his brow. 'You see, the Earth pulls the apple
right back down again. So how much energy would be required to sling
it straight into space?'

'Thank you, Sir Isaac,' Julian said affably. 'That's exactly what's at
issue. If we consider the Earth as a whole, a rocket is not much different
from an apple, even though rockets are, of course, bigger than apples.
In other words, it takes a massive amount of energy for it to be able to
launch at all. And additional energy to balance out the second force that
slows it as it climbs: our atmosphere.'

Rocky Rocket, exhausted by his efforts to reach his celestial beloved,
walked over to an enormous cylinder marked *Fuel* and drank it down,
whereupon he swelled up suddenly and his eyes burst from their sockets.
By now, however, he was finally in a position to produce such a massive
explosion of flame that he took off and became smaller and smaller until
at last he could no longer be seen.

Julian wrote up a calculation. 'Leaving aside the fact that the size
of the fuel tank required for interstellar spaceships becomes a problem
after a certain point, in the twentieth century each new launch cost a
phenomenal sum of money. Energy is expensive. In fact, the amount
of energy required to accelerate a single kilogram to flight velocity sufficient to escape the Earth's gravity was on average fifty thousand US
dollars. Just one kilogram! But the fully crewed Apollo 11 rocket with
Armstrong, Aldrin and Collins on board weighed almost three thousand tonnes! So anything you installed on the ship, anything you took
with you made the costs – *astronomical*. Making spaceships safe enough
against meteorites, space junk and cosmic radiation looked like a wild
fantasy. How could you ever get the heavy armour up there, when every
sip of drinking water, every centimetre of leg-room was already far too
expensive? It was all well and good sharing a sardine-tin for a few days,
but who wanted to fly to Mars in such conditions? The fact that more
and more people were questioning the point of this ruinous endeavour,
while the bulk of the world's population was living on less than a dollar a

day, was another exacerbating factor. Given all these considerations, plans such as the settlement and economic exploitation of the Moon or flights to other planets seemed an impossible dream.' Julian paused. 'When in fact the solution had been sitting on the table all the time! In the form of an essay written by a Russian physicist called Konstantin Tsiolkovsky in 1895, sixty-two years before the launch of Sputnik 1.'

An old man, with cobweb hair, a fuzzy beard and metal-rimmed glasses, stepped onto the virtual stage with all the grace of an ancient Cossack. As he spoke, a bizarre grid construction rose up on the Earth's surface.

'What I had in mind was a tower,' Tsiolkovsky told the audience, hands bobbing. 'Like the Eiffel Tower, but much, much higher. It was to reach all the way to space, a colossal lift-shaft, with a cable hung from the top end that was to reach all the way to the Earth. With such a device, it seemed to me, it would surely be possible to put objects into a stable terrestrial orbit without the need for noisy, stinky, bulky and expensive rockets. During the ascent, these objects, the further they go from the Earth's gravity, would be tangentially accelerated until their energy and velocity are sufficient to remain at their destination, at an altitude of 35,786 kilometres, in perpetuity.'

'Great idea,' cried Rocky Rocket, back from his lunar pleasure-trip, and circled the half-finished tower, which immediately collapsed in on itself. Tsiolkovsky trembled, paled and went back to join his ancestors.

'Yeah.' Julian shrugged regretfully. 'That was the weak point in Tsiolkovsky's plan. No material in the world seemed stable enough for such a construction. The tower would inevitably collapse under its own weight, or be torn apart by the forces exerted upon it. It was only in the fifties that the idea regained popularity, except that now people were thinking about firing a satellite into geostationary orbit and lowering a cable from there to the Earth—'

'Erm – excuse me,' Rocky Rocket cleared his throat.

'Yes? What is it?'

'This is embarrassing, boss, but—' The little rocket blushed and awkwardly scraped its stubby fins. 'What does geostationary mean exactly?'

Julian laughed. 'No problem, Rocky, Sir Isaac, an apple, please.'

'Got it,' said Newton, and slung another apple in the air. This time the fruit sped straight into the air, showing no signs of falling back again.

'If we imagine that the Earth and similar bodies aren't there, no gravity is exerted on the apple. According to the impulse that accelerated its mass when thrown by Sir Isaac Newton's muscles, it will fly and fly without ever coming to a standstill. We know this effect as centrifugal force. Let's put the Earth back where it was, and now gravitation, which we've already mentioned, comes into play, to some extent counteracting centrifugal force. If the apple is far enough away from the Earth, the Earth's field of gravity has become too weak to bring it back, and it will disappear into space. If it's too close, the Earth's gravity will pull it back. Now, geostationary orbit, GEO in short, is found at the exact point where the Earth's force of attraction and centrifugal force balance one another out perfectly, at an altitude of 35,786 kilometres. From there, the apple can neither escape nor fall back down. Instead, it remains for ever in GEO, as long as it circles the Earth synchronously with its rotational velocity, which is why a geostationary object always seems to stand above the same point.'

The Earth spun before their eyes. Newton's apple seemed to stand motionlessly above the equator, fixed to an island in the Pacific. It wasn't really standing still, of course, it was circling the planet at a speed of 11,070 kilometres per hour, while the Earth rotated below it at 1674 kilometres per hour, measured at the equator. The effect was startling. Just as the valve of a bicycle tyre always stands above the same point on the hub when the wheel is turned, the satellite stayed in place, as if nailed up above the island.

'Geostationary orbit is ideal for a space elevator. First for the stable installation of the top floor in a stable position, secondly because of the fixed position of that floor. So once it was clear that you would just need to lower a cable 35,786 kilometres long from that point and anchor it to the ground, the question arose of what loads such a cable would have to support. The greatest tension would arise at the centre of gravity, in the GEO itself, which meant that a cable would have to become either broader or more resilient towards the top.'

Immediately just such a cable stretched between the island and the satellite, into which the apple had suddenly transmuted. Small cabins travelled up and down it.

'In this context a further consideration arose. Why not extend the cable beyond the centre of gravity? To recap: in geostationary orbit gravity and centrifugal force balance one another out. Beyond it, the relationship between the two forces alters in favour of centrifugal force. A vehicle climbing the cable from the Earth needs to use only a tiny fraction of the energy that would be required to catapult it upwards on a rocket. With increasing altitude the influence of gravity declines in favour of centrifugal force, which means that less and less energy is required until hardly any at all is needed in geostationary orbit. Now, if we imagine the cable being extended to an altitude of 143,800 kilometres, the vehicle could go charging beyond the geostationary orbit: it would be continuously accelerated and would actually *gain* in energy. A perfect springboard for interstellar travel, to Mars or anywhere else!'

The cabins were now transporting construction components into orbit, to be assembled into a space station. Rocky Rocket loaded up the cabins and started visibly sweating.

'One way or another the advantages of a space elevator were quite obvious. To carry a kilo of cargo load to an altitude of almost 36,000 kilometres, you no longer needed 50,000 dollars, just 200, and you could also use the lift 365 days a year around the clock. Suddenly the idea of building gigantic space stations and adequately armoured spaceships no longer seemed like a problem. The colonisation of space became a tangible possibility, and inspired the British science-fiction author Arthur C. Clarke to write his novel *The Fountains of Paradise*, in which he describes the construction of space elevators like this.'

'But why does the thing have to be built at the equator, of all places?' asked Rocky Rocket, wiping the sweat from his tip. 'Why not at the North Pole or the South Pole, where it's nice and cool? And why in the middle of the stupid sea and not, for example in' – his eyes gleamed, he took a few dance steps and clicked his fingers – 'Las Vegas?'

'I'm not sure if you seriously want to set off for space surrounded by penguins,' Julian replied sceptically. 'But it wouldn't work anyway. It's only at the equator that you can exploit the Earth's rotation to achieve a maximum of centrifugal force. It's only there that geostationary objects are possible.' He thought for a moment. Then he said, 'Listen, I want to explain something to you. Imagine you're a hammer-thrower.'

The little rocket seemed to like the idea. He threw out his chest and tensed his muscles.

'Where's the hammer?' he crowed. 'Bring it here!'

'It's not a real hammer these days, idiot, that's just its name. These days the hammer is a metal ball on a steel cable.' Julian conjured the object out of nowhere and pressed the handle firmly into both of Rocky's hands. 'Now you have to spin on your axis with your arms outstretched.'

'Why?'

'To speed up the hammer. Let it spin.'

'Heavy, isn't it?' Rocky groaned and pulled on the steel cable. He started to spin around, faster and faster. The cable tightened, the sphere lifted from the ground and reached a horizontal position. 'Can I throw it now?' he panted.

'In a minute. For now you've just got to imagine you're not Rocky, you're the planet Earth. Your head is the North Pole, your feet are the South Pole. In between them is the axis that you're spinning around. If that's the case, what's the middle of your body?'

'Huh? What? The equator, obviously.'

'Well done.'

'Can I throw it now?'

'Wait. From the middle of your body, the equator, the hammer swings out, pulled tight by centrifugal force, just as the cable of the space elevator must be pulled tight.'

'I get it. Can I do it?'

'Just one moment! Your hands are, in a sense, our Pacific islands, the metal sphere is the satellite or the space station in geostationary orbit. That clear?'

'It's clear.'

'Okay. Now raise your hands. Go on spinning, but lift them high above your head.'

Rocky followed the instructions. The steel cable immediately lost its tension and the ball came crashing down on the little rocket. He rolled his eyes, staggered and fell to the ground.

'Do you think you get the principle?' Julian asked sympathetically.

Rocky waved a white flag.

'Then that's all sorted out. Practically every point on the equator is suitable for the space elevator, but there are a few things you have to take into account. The anchor station, the ground floor, so to speak, should be in an area that is free of storms, strong winds and electrical discharges, with no air traffic and a generally clear sky. Most such places are found in the Pacific. One of them lies 550 kilometres to the west of Ecuador, and is the place where we are right now – the Isla de las Estrellas!'

Suddenly Julian was standing on the viewing terrace of the Stellar Island Hotel. Far outside the floating platform could be seen, and the two cables stretching from the inside of the Earth station into the endless blue.

'As you can see, we have built not one, but two lifts. Two cables stretch in parallel into orbit. But even a few years ago it seemed doubtful whether we would ever experience this sight. Without the research work of Orley Enterprises the solution would probably have had to wait for several more years, and all this' – Julian spread his arms out – 'would not exist.'

The illusion vanished; Julian floated in Bible-blackness.

'The problem was to find a material from which a cable 35,786 kilometres long could be manufactured. It had to be ultra-light and at the same time ultra-stable. Steel was out of the question. Even the highest quality steel cable would break under its own weight alone after only thirty or forty kilometres. Some people came up with the idea of spiders' silk, given that it's four times more resilient than steel, but even that wouldn't have given the cable the requisite tensile strength, let alone the fact that for 35,786 kilometres of cable you'd need one hell of a lot of spiders. Frustrating! The anchor station, the space station, the cabins, all of that seemed manageable. But the concept seemed to founder on the cable – until the start of the millennium, when a revolutionary new material was discovered: carbon nanotubes.'

A gleaming, three-dimensional grid structure began to rotate in the black. Its tubal form vaguely resembled the kind of bow net that people use for fishing.

'This object is actually ten thousand times thinner than a human hair. A tiny tube, constructed from carbon atoms in a honeycomb arrangement. The smallest of these tubes has a diameter of less than one nanometre. Its density is one-sixth that of steel, which makes it very light, but at the same time it has a tensile strength of about 45 gigapascals, whereas at 2 gigapascals steel crumbles like a cookie. Over the years ways were found to bundle the tubes together and spin them into threads. In 2004 researchers in Cambridge produced a thread 100 metres long. But it seemed doubtful whether such threads could be woven into larger structures, particularly since experiments showed that the tensile strength of the thread declined dramatically in comparison with individual tubes. A kind of weaving flaw was introduced by missing carbon atoms, and besides, carbon is subject to oxidation. It erodes, so the threads needed to be coated.'

Julian paused.

'For many years Orley Enterprises invested in research into the question of how this flaw could be remedied. Not only were we able to replace the missing atoms, we also managed to enhance the tensile strength of the cables to 65 gigapascals through cross-connections! We found ways to layer them and protect them against meteorites, space junk, natural oscillations and the destructive effect of atomic oxygen. They are just one metre wide but flatter than a human hair, which is why they seem to disappear when you see them from the side. At a distance of 140,000 kilometres from Earth, where they end, we have connected them to a small asteroid, which acts as a counterweight. In future we want to accelerate spaceships along that stretch of ribbon in such a way that they could fly to Mars, or beyond, without any notable outlay of energy.' He smiled. 'In geostationary orbit, however, we have built a space station unlike anything that has ever existed before: the OSS, the Orley Space Station, accessible within three hours by space elevator: research station, space station and port! All manned and unmanned transfer flights to the Moon start from there. In turn, compressed helium-3 from the mining sites comes to OSS, is loaded onto the space elevator and sent to Earth, so that the prospect of ten billion people being provided with unlimited supplies of clean and affordable energy is becoming more and more of a reality every day. We can now say that helium-3 has supplanted the age of fossil fuels, because the necessary fusion reactors required have also been developed to market maturity by Orley Enterprises. The significance of oil and gas has dramatically declined. The plundering of our home planet is coming to an end. Oil wars will be a thing of the past. None of this would have been possible without the development of the space elevator, but we have taken to its conclusion the dream that Konstantin Tsiolkovsky dreamed – and made it reality!'

A moment later everything was back – the viewing terrace, the slope of the Isla de las Estrellas, the floating platform in the sea. Julian Orley, with waving ponytail and sparkling eyes, stretched his arms to the sky as if to receive the eleventh Commandment.

'Twenty years ago, when Orley Enterprises began thinking about the construction of space elevators, I promised the world that I would build it an elevator into the future. Into a future that our parents and grandparents would never have dared to dream of. The best future we have ever had. And we have built it! In a few days you will travel on it to the OSS. You will see the Earth as a whole, our unique and wonderful home – and you will be amazed as you turn your gaze to the stars, to our home of tomorrow.'

To dramatic background music, on columns of red light, two shimmering cabins rose from the cylindrical station building on the sea platform and shot up into the sky. Julian threw back his head and gazed after them.

'Welcome,' he said, 'to the future.'

Anchorage, Alaska, USA

Not again, thought Gerald Palstein. Not the same accusation, the same question, for the fourth time.

'Perhaps it would have been cleverer, Mr Palstein, to keep on the people you are now throwing out of their workplaces and keep them otherwise engaged instead of digging up the last intact ecosystems on Earth in an obsessive quest for oil. Wasn't it a grave mistake by your department to install the facility in the first place, as if energy sources like helium-3 and solar power were an irrelevance?'

Suspicion, incomprehension, malice. The press conference that EMCO was holding to bury the Alaska project had assumed the character of a tribunal, with him as whipping boy. Palstein tried not to let his exhaustion show.

'From the perspective of the time, we acted completely responsibly,' he said. 'In 2015, helium-3 was a crazy dream. The United States of America couldn't base their energy policy purely on the off-chance of a technological stroke of genius—'

'In which you now want to participate,' the journalist interrupted. 'A bit late, don't you think?'

'Of course, but perhaps I could refer you to a few things I thought were familiar to both of us. On the one hand I wasn't yet presiding over the strategy sector of EMCO in 2015—'

'But you were its deputy manager.'

'The final decision for what was to be built was my predecessor's responsibility. But you're right. I supported the Alaska project because there was no way of telling whether either the space elevator or fusion technology would work as predicted. So the project was clearly in the interest of the American nation.'

'Or in the interest of a few profiteers.'

'Let's reconsider the situation. At the start of the millennium our energy policy was aimed at freeing us from dependency on the Middle East. Particularly since we were forced to accept that the one who decides to fight a war doesn't necessarily win the peace. Going into Iraq was madness. The American market couldn't profit from it nearly as much as we had hoped. We had planned to send our people down there and take over the oil business; instead we saw American soldiers coming back in coffins week after week, so we hesitated until other people had divided up the cake between themselves. Except that after even conservative Republicans had reached the conclusion that George W. Bush had been a hugely dangerous fool, who had ruined both our economy and our standing in the world, no one really felt like marching into Iran carrying guns.'

'Do you mean you regret that the option of another war was off the cards?'

'Of course not.' Incredible! The woman just wasn't listening. 'I was always vehemently opposed to war, and still am today. You just have to understand what a jam the United States was in. Asia's hunger for raw materials, Russia's gamble on resources, our disappointing performance in the Middle East, one great big disaster. Then 2015, the uprising in Saudi Arabia. The Stars and Stripes burning in the streets of Riyadh, the whole folklore of the Islamist seizure of power, except that we couldn't just throw those guys out because China had lent them money and arms. An official military intervention in Saudi Arabia would have amounted to a declaration of war on Beijing. You know yourself how things look down there now. Nobody might be interested in it today, but in those days it would have been reckless to depend entirely on Arab oil. We had to take alternatives into consideration. One of those lay in the sea, the other in the exploitation of oil sand and shale, the third in the resources of Alaska.'

Another journalist put her hand up. Loreena Keowa, environmental activist with native American roots, and reporter-in-chief for Greenwatch. Her reports were hugely popular on the net. She was critical, but Palstein knew that under certain circumstances he could see her as an ally.

'I don't think anyone can blame a company for declaring a corpse to be dead,' she said. 'Even if it means a loss of jobs. I just wonder what

EMCO has to offer the people who are now losing their workplaces. Perhaps there's no point crying over spilt milk, but didn't the refusal of ExxonMobil to invest in alternative energies lead to their present disastrous situation?'

'That is correct.'

'I remember Shell pointing out twenty years ago that it was an energy company and not an oil company, while ExxonMobil insisted that it didn't need a foothold in the alternative energies. The end of the oil age, which many saw on the horizon, was, literally, a *widespread misunderstanding*.'

'That assessment was clearly incorrect.'

'And we are feeling the after-effects all the more painfully for that. Perhaps it's true that no one could have predicted a turnaround in the energy market on the present scale. What is clear is that EMCO isn't in a position to employ its people in alternative fields, because there are no alternative fields.'

'That's exactly what we want to change,' said Palstein patiently.

'I know *you* want to change it, Gerald.' Keowa grinned crookedly. 'But your critics see your planned involvement in Orley Enterprises as smoke and mirrors.'

'Incorrect.' Palstein smiled back. 'You see, I don't want to make excuses for anything, but in 2005 I was responsible for drilling projects in Ecuador for Conoco-Phillips, and only switched to strategic management in 2009. At that time the American oil and gas business was dominated by ExxonMobil. Prognoses about alternative energies were pretty much divided on either side of the Atlantic. ExxonMobil invested in the Arabian Gulf and tried to take over Russian oil companies, backed high growth-rates as the result of rising oil prices and disregarded things like ethics and sustainability. In Europe it looked quite different. By the end of the nineties Royal Dutch Shell had created a new commercial division for renewable energies. BP had been a bit shrewder, in opening up deep-sea projects and becoming involved in Russian projects, while at the same time using slogans like "Beyond Petroleum" and diversifying their commercial areas wherever they could.'

Palstein knew that the younger journalists in particular were short of information. He outlined how the process of consolidation had peaked immediately before the seizure of power by the Saudi Islamists, when Royal Dutch Shell was absorbed into BP, producing UK Energies, while in America ExxonMobil had merged with Chevron and ConocoPhillips into EMCO.

'In 2017 I assumed the position of deputy director within the strategic sector of EMCO. On the very first day a press release landed on my table, saying that Orley Enterprises had made a breakthrough in the development of a space elevator. I suggested entering negotiations with Julian Orley for a participation in Orley Energy. I also recommended that we purchase shares in Warren Locatelli's Lightyears or, better still, buy the whole company. Locatelli's market leadership in photovoltaics didn't just come out of the blue; he would still have been open to negotiation in 2015.'

He saw approval on their faces. Keowa nodded.

'I know, Gerald. You tried to steer the EMCO juggernaut in the direction of renewable energies. Everybody knows that you are highly critical about your own sector. But they also know that none of your suggestions has been taken on board.'

'That is regrettably the case. The old Exxon management who still had EMCO in their clutches were only interested in our core products. It was only when the oil market went into free fall, when even the hard-liners had to step aside and the new chairman put me in charge of strategic management, that I was able to act. EMCO has been transformed in the meantime. Since 2020 we have done everything we can to make up for the shortcomings of the past. We have moved into photovoltaics, into wind and water power. Perhaps people aren't generally aware, but we are in a position to transfer our staff into future-oriented commercial sectors. Except that when mistakes have been made for decades, we can't sort them out overnight.'

'Can it still be repaired?'

Palstein leaned back in his chair. Basically he didn't need to reply. Helium-3 was establishing itself as the energy source of the future, there was no doubt about that. Orley's fusion reactors were working reliably around the clock, and in terms of the balance between energy and environment everything was fine; the transport of the element from the Moon to the Earth was no longer a problem. Palstein's sector, however, seemed to be traumatised. The oil companies had reckoned with everything – except the end of the oil age, *without* oil and gas running out! Not even the boldest visionaries of Royal Dutch Shell or BP had been able to imagine that their sector could be wiped out so quickly by an alternative energy source. Only ten years before, UK Energies had calculated the market share of alternative technologies at thirty per cent, nuclear energy included. Equally, it had been clear to everyone that most of those technologies could only be offered at competitive prices by companies operating on a global level. The photovoltaic sector, for example, got a good market share in sunny countries, but it required complex logistical infrastructures. And who was capable of doing that, if not the big multinational oil companies, who only had to make sure that they could make a quick getaway and switch to a different area when it came to the crunch?

That most of the companies weren't even ready to make this shift was down to prognoses about when oil and gas would actually run dry. Like Jehovah's Witnesses constantly changing the date of the end of the world, throughout the 1980s various prophets of doom had predicted that the oil age would come to an end in 2010; in the 1990s it was 2030; at the start of the new millennium, in spite of increased consumption, it was 2050. But now it was clear that the existing reserves would last until 2080, even though production had already peaked, while the resources available suggested an even longer life. There was only one point on which they had all agreed: there would never be cheap oil again. Never again.

But in fact it had become *very* cheap.

So cheap, in fact, that the sector had started to feel like the Incredible Shrinking Man, for whom a house spider represented a deadly threat. The most likely survivors were those who had invested in renewable energies early on. UK Energies had succeeded in reversing their fortunes, the French Total group had diversified enough to survive, even though personnel downsizing was rife. High-efficiency solar technology, as developed by Locatelli's Lightyears, was considered the most trust-worthy fuel, alongside helium-3, and there was also money to be made in wind power. On the other hand the Norwegian association Statoil Norsk Hydro was in its death-throes, while China's CNPC and Russia's Lukoil gazed dispiritedly into an oil-free future, clearly in culpable ignor-ance of the now legendary statement of Ahmed al Jamanis, the former Saudi Arabian oil minister: 'The Stone Age didn't end for want of stones.'

The problem wasn't so much that petrol wasn't needed any more: it was used for plastics, fertilisers and cosmetics, in the textile industry, in food production and pharmaceutical research. Orley's new-fangled fusion reactors were still thin on the ground; most cars ran on combus-tion engines, aeroplanes were fuelled with kerosene. The United States was the chief beneficiary of the new resource. The global switch to a helium-3-based energy economy was still years away, that much was clear.

But not decades away.

The mere fact that the so-called aneutronic fusion of helium-3 with deuterium worked in reactors had sent already sickly oil prices through the floor. At the end of the first decade it had turned out that people were *not* in fact prepared to pay just any sum for oil; if it became too expensive, their ecological conscience sprang to life, they saved electri-city and encouraged the development of alternative energies. The notion popular among speculators that the barrel price might be driven up by panic buying had not become reality. There was also the fact that most countries had set aside strategic reserves, and had not had to make any new purchases, that new generations of cars had batteries with generous storage capacities and filled up at sockets on environmentally friendly electricity which, thanks to helium-3, would soon be available in ample quantities. The United States of America, which had turned a deep dark green in the years after Barack Obama's terms as president, was urging an international agreement on emission reduction, and had discovered the devil in CO_2. A few years after the first helium-3-fuelled fusion reactor had gone live, it was also clear that astronomically high profits could be achieved with environmental-oriented thinking. In the course of these developments, EMCO had slipped in the ranking of the world's biggest mineral-oil companies from first place to third, while the entire sector was threatening to shrink to a microverse. Atrophied by ignorance, EMCO increasingly found itself stumbling, like King Kong just before the fall and, dimly aware that it was doomed to failure, clutching around for something to hold on to, and grasping only air.

Now they'd lost Alaska too.

The drilling plans won through years spent battling against the environmental lobby had to be abandoned because no one was interested in the huge natural gas deposits there any longer. This press conference was barely different from the one they had had to hold in Alberta, Canada a few weeks before, where the exploitation of oil sand was coming to an end, an expensive and environmentally harmful procedure that had given the conservationists nightmares for ages, but which had been feasible as long as the world was still crying out for oil like a baby for milk. What use was it that certain representatives of the Canadian government shared EMCO's concerns, when two-thirds of the world's oil resources were stored in this sand, 180 million barrels on Canadian soil alone? The overwhelming majority of Canadians were glad that it would soon be all over. In Alberta, mining had permanently destroyed rivers and marshes, the northern forest, the complete ecosystem. In view of this, Canada had not been able to stick to its international obligations. Greenhouse emissions had risen, the signed protocols were so much waste paper.

'It can be repaired,' said Palstein firmly. 'We're about to conclude negotiations with Orley Enterprises. I promise you, we will be the first oil company to be involved in the helium-3 business, and we are also in discussion about possible alliances with strategists from other companies.'

'What concrete offers do Orley Enterprises have to make to you?'

'There are a few things.'

The man wouldn't let go. 'The problem with the multinationals is that they haven't a clue about the fusion business. I mean, some of the companies have pounced on photovoltaics, on wind and water power, bioethanol and all that stuff, but fusion technology and space travel – you'll forgive me, but that's not exactly your area of expertise.'

Palstein smiled.

'I can tell you that at present Julian Orley is looking for investors for a second space elevator, not least to develop the infrastructure for the transport of helium-3. Of course we're talking about vast amounts of money here. But we've got that money. The question is how we want to use it. My sector is in a state of shock at the moment. Should have seen it coming, you might say, so what do you think we should do? Go down in flames, feeling sorry for ourselves? EMCO isn't going to achieve supremacy in solar energy, however much we might try to get a foothold in it. Other people are historically ahead of us there. So either we can watch one market after another breaking away until our funds are devoured by social programmes. Or we put the money into a second elevator and organise logistical processes on the Earth. As I have said, discussions are almost concluded, the contracts are about to be signed.'

'When's that due?'

'At the moment Orley is staying with a group of potential investors on the Isla de las Estrellas. From there he will go on to OSS and the opening of Gaia. Yeah.' Palstein shrugged in a gesture somewhere between melancholy and fatalism. 'I was supposed to be there. Julian Orley isn't just our future business partner, he's also a personal friend. I'm sorry not to be able to take this journey with him, but I don't need to remind you what happened in Canada.'

With these words he had rung the bell for round two. Everyone began talking at the same time.

'Have they discovered who shot you?'

'Given the state of your health, how will you get through the coming weeks? Did the injury—'

'What are we to make of conjectures that the attack might have something to do with your decision to put EMCO and Orley Enterprises—'

'Is it true that a furious oil worker—'

'You've made loads of enemies with your criticism of abuses in your sector. Might any of them have—'

'How are you generally, Gerald?' asked Keowa.

'Thanks, Loreena, not bad in the circumstances.' Palstein raised his left hand until silence returned. His right arm had been in a sling for four weeks. 'One at a time. I'll answer all your questions, but I would ask you to show understanding if I avoid speculation. At the moment I can say nothing more except that I myself would love to know who did it. All I know for certain is that I was incredibly lucky. If I hadn't stumbled on the steps up to the podium, the bullet would have got me in the head. It wasn't a warning, as some people thought, it was a botched execution. Without any doubt at all, they wanted to kill me.'

'How are you protecting yourself at the moment?'

'With optimism.' Palstein smiled. 'Optimism and a bullet-proof vest, to tell you the truth. But what use is that against shots to the head? Am I supposed to go into hiding? No! Was it Tschaikovsky who said you can't tiptoe your way through life just because you're afraid of death?'

'To put it another way,' said Keowa, 'who would benefit if you disappeared from the scene?'

'I don't know. If anyone wanted to stop us merging with Orley Enterprises, he would destroy EMCO's biggest and perhaps only chance of a quick recovery.'

'Maybe that's the plan,' a voice called out. 'Destroying EMCO.'

'The market's become too small for the oil companies,' said someone else. 'In fact the company's death would make sense in terms of economic evolution. Someone eliminating the competition in order to—'

'Or else someone wants to get at Orley through you. If EMCO—'

'What's the mood like in your own company? Whose toes did you tread on, Gerald?'

'Nobody's!' Palstein shook his head firmly. 'The board approved every aspect of my restructuring model, and top of the list is our commitment to Orley. You're fumbling around in the dark with assumptions like that. Talk to the authorities. They're following every lead.'

'And what does your gut tell you?'

'About the perpetrator?'

'Yes. Any suspects in mind?'

Palstein was silent for a moment. Then he said, 'Personally I can only imagine it was an act of revenge. Someone who's desperate, who's lost his job, possibly lost everything, and is now projecting his hatred onto me. That I could understand. I'm fully aware of where we are right now. A lot of people are worried about their livelihoods, people who had confidence in us in better years.' He paused. 'But let's be honest, the better times are only just beginning. Perhaps I'm the wrong man to say this, but a world that can satisfy its energy needs with environmentally friendly and renewable resources makes the oil economy look like a thing of the past. I can only stress again and again that we will really do everything we can to secure EMCO's future. And thus the future of our workforce!'

An hour later Gerald Palstein was resting in his suite, his head cradled on his left arm, his legs stretched out as if it would have taken too much effort to cross them. Dog-tired and raddled he lay on the bedspread and stared up at the canopy of the four-poster bed. His delegation was staying in the Sheraton Anchorage, one of the finer addresses in a city not exactly blessed with architectural masterpieces. Anything of any historical substance had fallen victim to the 1964 earthquake. The Good Friday earthquake, as it was known. The most violent hiccup that seismologists had ever recorded on American territory. Now there was just one really beautiful building, and that was the hospital.

After a while he got up, went into the bathroom, splashed cold water into his face with his free hand and looked at himself in the mirror. A droplet hung trembling on the tip of his nose. He flicked it away. Paris, his wife, liked to say she had fallen in love with his eyes, which were a mysterious earthy brown, big and doe-like, with thick eyelashes like a woman's. His gaze was filled with perpetual melancholy. Too beautiful, too intense for his friendly but unremarkable face. His forehead was high and smooth, his hair cut short. Recently his slender body had developed a certain aesthetic quality, the consequence of a lack of sleep, irregular meals and the hospital stay in which the bullet had been removed from his shoulder four weeks previously. Palstein knew he should eat more, except that he barely had an appetite. Most of what was put in front of him he left. He was paralysed by an unsettlingly stubborn feeling of exhaustion, as if a virus had taken hold of him, one that occasional snoozes on the plane weren't enough to shake.

He dried his face, came out of the bathroom and stepped to the window. A pale, cold summer sun glittered on the sea. To the north, the snow-covered peaks of the Alaska chain loomed into the distance. Not far from the hotel he could see the former ConocoPhillips office. Now it bore the EMCO logo, in defiance of the change that was already under way. There were still office spaces to let in the Peak Oilfield Service Company building. UK Energies had put a branch of their solar division in the former BP headquarters and rented out the rest to a travel company, and here too there were many empty spaces. Everything was going down the drain. Some logos had completely disappeared, such as Anadarko Oil, Doyon Drilling and Marathon Oil Company. The place was threatening to lose its position as the most economically successful state in the USA. Since the seventies, more than eighty per cent of all state income had flowed from the fossil fuels business into the Alaska Permanent Fund, which was supposed to benefit all the inhabitants. Support that they would soon have to do without. In the mid-term, the region was left only with metals, fishing, wood and a bit of fur-farming. Oil and gas too, of course, but only on a very limited scale, and at prices so low that the stuff would have been better off left in the ground.

The journalists and activists that he had been dealing with over the past few hours – and who reproached him now for having got involved in the extractions in the first place – certainly weren't representing public opinion when they cheered the end of the oil economy. In fact helium-3 had met with a very muted response in Alaska, just as enthusiasm on the Persian Gulf was notably low-key. The sheikhs imagined themselves being thrown back on the bleak desert existence of former years, their territory returning to the scorpions and sand-beetles. The spectre of impoverishment stripped the potentates of Kuwait, Bahrain and Qatar of their sleep. Hardly anyone seriously wanted to go to Dubai now. Beijing had abandoned its support of the Saudi Arabian Islamists; the USA seemed to have forgotten all about North Africa; in Iraq Sunnis and Shi'ites went on slaughtering each other in time-honoured fashion; Iran provoked unease with its nuclear programmes, bared its teeth in all directions and tried to get close to China, which apart from America was the only nation in the world mining helium-3, albeit in vanishingly small quantities. The Chinese didn't have a space elevator, and didn't know how to build one either. No one apart from the Americans had such a thing, and Julian Orley sat on the patents like a broody hen, which was why China had fallen back entirely on traditional rocket technology, at devastating expense.

Palstein looked at his watch. He had to get over to the EMCO building, a meeting was about to start. It would go on till late as usual. He phoned the business centre and asked to be put through to the Stellar Island Hotel on the Isla de las Estrellas. It was three hours later there, and a good twenty degrees warmer. A better place than Anchorage. Palstein would rather have been anywhere else than Anchorage.

He wanted at least to wish Julian a pleasant journey.

Isla de las Estrellas, Pacific Ocean

Going inside the volcano might have been spectacular, but coming out was a big disappointment. Once the lights had come on, they left the cave via a straight and well-lit corridor which aroused the suspicion that the whole mountain was actually made of scaffolding and papier mâché. It was wide enough to allow a hundred panicking, trampling and thrashing people to escape. After about 150 metres it led to a side wing of the Stellar Island Hotel.

Chuck Donoghue pushed his way through to stand next to Julian.

'My respect,' he bellowed. 'Not bad.'

'Thanks.'

'And this is how you found the cave? Come on! You didn't help a bit? No demolition charges anywhere?'

'Just for the evacuation routes.'

'Incredibly lucky. Of course you realise, my boy, that I'll have to steal this one! Haha! No, don't worry, I still have enough ideas of my own. My God, how many hotels have I built in my life? How many hotels!'

'Thirty-two.'

'You're right,' Donoghue mumbled in amazement.

'Yes, and maybe one day you might be building another one on the Moon.' Julian grinned. 'That's why you're here, old man.'

'I see!' Donoghue laughed even louder. 'And I thought you'd invited me because you liked me.'

At sixty-five the hotel mogul was the oldest member of the group, five years older than Julian, although Julian looked ten years younger. The insignificant age difference didn't keep Donoghue from jovially addressing the richest man in the world as 'my boy'.

'Of course I like you,' Julian said cheerfully as they followed Lynn to the lifts. 'But more than anything else I want to show you *my* hotels so that you'll put *your* money into them. Oh, and by the way, do you know the one about the man doing the survey?'

'Tell me!'

'A guy gets asked, what would you do if you had two possibilities? A: You spend all night having sex with your wife. B:— B, says the man, B!'

It was a crap little joke, and thus exactly right for Chucky, who stayed behind laughing to tell Aileen. Julian didn't have to turn round to see her face, as if she'd just sucked on a lemon. The Donoghues ruled over thirty of the most imposing, expensive and trashy hotels of all time, they had built various casinos, ran an international booking agency through which global stars passed with great regularity – artistes, singers, dancers and animal trainers, and of course you could, if you wished, also book shows in which nothing was left to the imagination. But Aileen, good, fat, cake-baking Aileen, opted for good old southern prudery, as if dozens of showgirls weren't dancing across the stages of Las Vegas every night, breasts bouncing, girls who had contracts that bore her signature. She placed great emphasis on piety, gun ownership, good food, good deeds and the death penalty if all else failed, and sometimes when it didn't. She put morality before everything else. Nonetheless, she would appear for dinner crammed into a little dress so tight it was embarrassing, to collect compliments from the younger men for her laser-firmed cleavage. She would launch her usual nannying campaign and pass on the silly joke with lots of tittering and snorting, before getting drinks for everyone, and her other side would fight its way through, marked by a genuinely felt concern for the welfare of all God's creatures, which made it possible not only to put up with Aileen Donoghue, but even somehow to like her.

The glass lift cabins filled up with people and chatter. After a short trip they discharged the group onto the viewing terrace, beneath a starry sky worthy of a Hollywood movie. With regal dignity an old and beautiful lady in evening dress was directing half a dozen waiters to the guests. Champagne and cocktails were handed out, binoculars distributed. A jazz quartet played 'Fly Me to the Moon'.

'Everyone over here,' Lynn called cheerfully. 'To me! Look to the east.'

The guests happily followed her instructions. Out on the platform yet more lights had been lit, glowing fingers reaching into the night sky. As tiny as ants, people were seen walking around among the structures. A big ship, apparently a freighter, lay massively on a calm sea.

'Dear friends.' Julian stepped forward, a glass in his hand. 'I didn't let you see the whole show earlier. In another version you would also have met the OSS and Gaia, but that one is intended for visitors without the advantage of what you will experience. Relatives of travellers, spending a few days on the island before going back home. To you, however, I wanted to demonstrate the lift. For the rest you won't need films, because you will see it *with your own eyes*! You will never forget the two weeks ahead of you, I promise you that!'

Julian showed his perfect teeth. There was applause, scattered at first, then everyone clapped enthusiastically. Miranda Winter yelled, 'Oh, yeah!' Glowing with pride, Lynn went and joined her father.

'Before we invite everyone to join us for dinner, we have a little taster of your imminent trip.' She glanced at her watch. 'In the next few minutes the two cabins are expected back from orbit. Both will be bringing back to Earth, amongst other things, compressed helium-3 that was loaded onto them on OSS. I think it might be an idea to throw your heads back now, and not just to drink—'

'Although I advise you do that too,' said Julian, raising his glass to everyone.

'Of course,' Lynn laughed. 'What he hasn't yet told you, in fact, is that on OSS we will drastically reduce alcohol consumption.'

'How regrettable.' Bernard Tautou pulled a face, drank his glass down in one and beamed at her. 'So we should make provision.'

'I thought your passion was water?' teased Mukesh Nair.

'Mais oui! Particularly if it's topped up with alcohol.'

'"These vessels here from which we drink / When emptied their appeal does shrink",' declaimed Eva Borelius with a superior smile.

'Pardon?'

'Wilhelm Busch, you wouldn't know him.'

'Can you actually get a hangover in zero gravity?' Olympiada Rogacheva asked timidly, prompting her husband to turn away from her and stare pointedly up at the stars. Miranda Winter snapped her fingers like a schoolgirl:

'And what if you throw up in zero gravity?'

'Then your puke will find you wherever you are,' Evelyn Chambers explained.

'Sphere formation,' nodded Walo Ögi and formed a hypothetical ball of vomit with both hands. 'The puke forms itself into a ball.'

'I'm pretty sure it spreads,' said Karla Kramp.

'Yes, so that we all get some,' Borelius nodded. 'Nice topic, by the way. Perhaps we should—'

'There!' cried Rebecca Hsu. 'Up there!'

All eyes followed her outstretched hand. Two little points of light had started moving in the firmament. For a while they seemed to be heading to the south-east on orbital paths, except that at the same time they were getting bigger and bigger, a sight that contradicted everything that anyone had seen before. Clearly something had gone dimensionally awry. And then, all of a sudden, everyone worked out that the bodies were dropping from space in a perfect vertical. As if the stars were climbing down to them.

'They're coming,' Sushma Nair whispered reverently.

Binoculars were yanked up. After a few minutes, even without magnification, two long structures could be made out, one slightly higher than the other, looking a bit like space shuttles, except that they were both standing upright and their undersides ended in broad, plate-like slabs. The conically pointed tips were brightly illuminated, and navigation lights darted evenly as heartbeats along the sides of the cylindrical bodies. The cabins approached the platform at great speed, and the lower they came the harder the air vibrated, as if stirred by giant dynamos. Julian registered with satisfaction that even his son wasn't immune to the fascination. Amber's eyes were as wide as if she were waiting for her Christmas presents.

'That's wonderful,' she said quietly.

'Yes.' Julian nodded. 'It's technology, and it's still a miracle. "Any sufficiently advanced technology is indistinguishable from magic." Arthur C. Clarke. Great man!'

Tim said nothing.

And suddenly Julian was aware of the bitter taste of repressed rage in his mouth. He simply couldn't work out what was up with the boy. If Tim didn't want to take the job that awaited him at Orley Enterprises, that was his business. Everyone had to go his own way, even if Julian couldn't really understand that there were other paths to take apart from a future in the company, but okay, fine. Except – *what the hell* had he actually done to Tim?

Then everything happened very quickly.

An audible gasp from all the onlookers introduced the final phase. For a moment it looked as if the cabins would crash into the circular terminal like projectiles and pull the whole platform into the sea, then they abruptly slowed down, first one, then the other, and decelerated until they entered the circle of the space terminal and disappeared into it, one after the other. Again there was applause, broken by cries of 'Bravo!' Heidrun came and stood by Finn O'Keefe and whistled on two fingers.

'Still sure you want to get into one of those?' he asked.

She looked at him mockingly. 'And you?'

'Of course.'

'Boaster!'

'Someone will have to stand by your husband when you start clawing the walls.'

'We'll just see who's scared, shall we?'

'If it's me,' O'Keefe grinned, 'remember your promise.'

'When did I ever promise you anything?'

'A little while ago. You were going to hold my hand.'

'Oh yeah.' The corners of Heidrun's mouth twitched with amusement. For a moment she seemed to be thinking seriously about it. 'I'm sorry, Finn. You know, I'm boring and old-fashioned. In my film the woman falls off her horse and lets the man save her from the Indians. Screaming her head off, of course.'

'Shame. I've never acted in that kind of movie.'

'You should have a word with your agent.'

She gracefully raised a hand, ran a finger gently over his cheek and walked away. O'Keefe watched her as she joined Walo. Behind him a voice said:

'Pathetic, Finn. Total knock-back.'

He turned round and found himself looking into the beautiful, haughty face of Momoka Omura. They knew each other from the parties that O'Keefe avoided like the plague. If he did have to go to one, she inevitably bumped into him, as she recently had at Jack Nicholson's eighty-eighth.

'Shouldn't you be filming?' he said.

'I didn't end up in the mass market like you did, if that's what you mean.' She looked at her fingernails. A mischievous smile played around her lips. 'But I could give you some lessons in flirting if you like.'

'Very kind of you.' He smiled back. 'Except you're not supposed to get off with your teacher.'

'Only theoretically, you idiot. Do you seriously think I'd let you anywhere near me?'

'You wouldn't?' He turned away. 'That's reassuring.'

Momoka threw her head back and snorted. The second woman to have walked away from him in the course of only a few minutes, she strutted over to Locatelli, who was noisily talking shop with Marc Edwards and Mimi Parker about fusion reactors, and linked arms with him. O'Keefe shrugged and joined Julian, who was standing with Hanna, Rebecca Hsu, his daughter and the Rogachevs.

'But how do you get the cabin all the way up there?' the Taiwanese woman wanted to know. She looked overexcited and scatterbrained. 'It can hardly *float* up the cable.'

'Didn't you see the presentation?' Rogachev asked ironically.

'We're just introducing a new perfume,' said Rebecca, as if that explained everything. And in fact for half the show she'd been staring at the display on her pocket computer, correcting marketing plans, and had missed the explanation of the principle. At first sight it would look as if the slabs that formed the cabin sterns were sending out bright red beams, but in fact it was the other way round. The undersides of the plates were covered with photovoltaic cells, and the beams were emitted by huge lasers inside the terminal. The energy produced by the impact set the propulsion system in motion, six pairs of interconnected wheels per cabin, with the belt stretched between them. When the wheels on one side were set in motion, those on the other side joined in automatically in the opposite direction, and the lift climbed up the belt.

'It gets faster and faster,' Julian explained. 'After only a hundred metres it reaches—'

There was a beep from his jacket. He frowned and dug out his phone. 'What's up?'

'Forgive the disturbance, sir.' Someone from the switchboard. 'A call for you.'

'Can't it wait?'

'It's Gerald Palstein, sir.'

'Oh. Of course.' Julian smiled apologetically at everybody. 'Could I neglect you for a moment? Rebecca, don't run away. I'll explain the principle to you every hour, or ideally more often, if that'll make you happy.'

He dashed off into a little room behind the bar, stuck his phone into a console and projected the image onto a bigger screen.

'Hi, Julian,' said Palstein.

'Gerald. Where in heaven's name are you?'

'Anchorage. We've buried the Alaska project. Didn't I tell you about that?'

The EMCO manager looked exhausted. They had last seen each other a few weeks before the attempt on his life. Palstein was calling from a hotel room. A window in the background gave a glimpse of snow-covered mountains under a pale, cold sky.

'No, you did,' said Julian. 'But that was before you were shot. Do you really have to do this to yourself?'

'No big deal.' Palstein waved the idea away. 'I have a hole in my shoulder, not my head. That kind of injury lets me travel, although unfortunately not to the Moon. Regrettably.'

'And how did it go?'

'Let's say Alaska's preparing itself with some dignity for the rebirth of the age of the trapper. Of all the union representatives I've met there, most of them would have liked to finish the job that gunman in Canada fluffed.'

'Just don't beat yourself up! Nobody's been as hard on his sector as you have, and from now on they *will* listen to you. Did you tell them about your planned allegiance?'

'The press release is out. So yes, it came up.'

'And? How was it received?'

'As an attempt to get ourselves back in action. At least most people are being kind about it.'

'That's great! As soon as I get back, let's sign the contracts.'

'Other people think it's a smokescreen.' Palstein hesitated. 'Let's not kid ourselves, Julian. It's a great help to us that you're getting us on board—'

'It's a help to *us*!'

'But it's not going to work any miracles. We've been concentrating on petrol for far too long. Well, the main thing for us is to avoid competition. I'd rather have a future as a middle-sized company than go bankrupt as a giant. The consequences would be terrible. There's nothing you can do about your downward slide, but you may be able to prevent the crash. Or cushion it at least.'

'If anyone can do it, you can. God, Gerald! It's a real shame you can't be with us.'

'Next time. Who took my place, by the way?'

'A Canadian investor called Carl Hanna. Heard of him?'

'Hanna?' Palstein frowned. 'To be quite honest—'

'Doesn't matter. I didn't know him either until a few months ago. One of those people who got rich on the quiet.'

'Interested in space travel?'

'That's exactly what makes him so interesting! You don't have to make the subject tempting for him. He wants to invest in space travel anyway. Unfortunately he spent his youth in New Delhi and feels obliged to sponsor India's moon programme because of his old connection.' Julian grinned. 'So I'll have to make a big effort to win the guy over.'

'And the rest of the gang?'

'I'm pretty sure that Locatelli will come up with an eight-figure sum. His megalomania alone dictates that he needs a monument in space, and our facilities are equipped with his systems. Involvement would be only logical. The Donoghues and Marc Edwards have promised me major sums on the quiet, the only issue is how many zeroes there are going to be at the end. There's a really interesting Swiss guy, Walo Ögi. Lynn and I met his wife two years ago in Zermatt; she took some pictures of me. Then we have Eva Borelius on board, perhaps you know her, German stem-cell research—'

'Am I right in thinking that you've simply copied out the Forbes List?'

'It wasn't exactly like that. Borelius Pharmaceuticals was recommended to me by our strategic management team, and so was Bernard Tautou, the water tsar from Suez. Another guy whose ego just needs massaging. Or there's Mukesh Nair—'

'Ah, Mr Tomato.' Palstein raised his eyebrows appreciatively.

'Yes, nice guy. But he has no stake in space travel. It doesn't do us much good that he's rich, so we've had to bring a few extra criteria into play. Wanting to give humanity a more viable future, for example. Even the anti-space-travel brigade stand shoulder to shoulder on that one: Nair with food, Tautou with water, Borelius with medicine, me with energy. That unites us, and it's encouraging the others. And then there are privately wealthy individuals like Finn O'Keefe, Evelyn Chambers and Miranda Winter—'

'Miranda Winter? My God!'

'What, why not? She doesn't know what to do with all her money, bless her, so I'm inviting her to find out. Believe me, the mixture is perfect. Guys like O'Keefe, Evelyn and Miranda really loosen the gang up, it makes it really sexy, and in the end I'll have them all on my side! Rebecca Hsu, with all her luxury brands, isn't that interested in energy, but she goes for space travel as if she'd come up with the idea all by herself. She's completely fixated on the idea that Moët et Chandon will be drunk on the Moon in future. Did you ever look at her portfolio? Kenzo, Dior, Louis Vuitton, L'Oréal, Dolce & Gabbana, Lacroix, Hennessy, not to mention her own brands, Boom Bang and the other stuff. As far as she's concerned we're a unique and inimitable brand. I could fund half of the OSS Grand with the advertising contracts I'm signing with her alone.'

'Didn't you invite that Russian too? Rogachev?'

Julian grinned. 'He's my very personal little challenge. If I manage to get him to put *his* billions into *my* projects, I'll do a cartwheel in zero gravity.'

'Moscow are hardly going to let him go.'

'Wrong! They'll practically force him into it if they think they can do business with me.'

'Which will only be the case if you build them a space elevator. Until that happens, they'll look on Rogachev as if his money's flowing into American space travel through your project.'

'Nonsense. It'll look as if it's flowing into a lucrative business, and that's exactly what it will be doing! I'm not America, Gerald!'

'*I* know that. Rogachev, on the other hand—'

'He knows it too. A guy like that isn't stupid, after all! There isn't a country in the world today that's capable of paying for space travel with its own funds. Do you really think that cheerful community of states that worked so harmoniously to set up the ISS was stirred by a spirit of international fraternity? Bullshit! None of them had the money to do it alone. It was the only way to send anything up into space without E.T. laughing himself sick. To do that they *had* to pull strings and swap information, with the result that they ended up with squat! Funds were short for everything, all kinds of crap was budgeted for, just not space travel. It was private individuals who changed that, after Burt Rutan flew the first commercial sub-orbital flight on Space Ship One in 2004, and who financed that? The United States of America? NASA?'

'I know,' Palstein sighed. 'It was Paul Allen.'

'Exactly! Paul Allen, co-founder of Microsoft. Entrepreneurs showed the politicians how to get things done more quickly and efficiently. Like you, when your sector still meant something. You made presidents and toppled governments. Now it's people like me paying off that pile of bank-breakers, doomsayers and nationalists. We have more money, more know-how, better people, a more creative climate. Without Orley Enterprises there would be no space elevator, no Moon tourism, reactor research wouldn't be where it is today, nothing would. Even though it's not exactly coming down with money, NASA would still have to justify itself to some incompetent regulatory agency or other every time it broke wind. We're not regulated at all, not by any government in the world. And why? Because we're not obliged to any government. Believe me, even Rogachev gets *that* one.'

'Even so, you shouldn't just go handing him the OSS user's handbook. He might get it into his head to copy it.'

Julian chuckled. Then he grew suddenly serious.

'Any news about your assassination attempt?'

'Not really.' Palstein shook his head. 'They're pretty sure where the shot was fired from, but that doesn't really help them much. It was just a public event. There were loads of people there.'

'I still don't quite understand who would want to kill you. Your sector's running out of puff. No one's going to change that by shooting oil managers.'

'People don't think rationally.' Palstein smiled. 'Otherwise they'd have shot *you*. You basically invented helium-3 transport. Your lift finished off my sector.'

'You could shoot me a thousand times, the world would still switch to helium-3.'

'Quite. Actions like that aren't calculated, they're the product of despair. Of blind hatred.'

'Exactly. Hatred has never been used to make things better.'

'But it's created more victims than anything else.'

'Hmm, yes.' Julian fell silent and rubbed his chin. 'I'm not a hater. Hatred is alien to me. I can lose my temper. I can wish someone in hell and send him there, but only if there's a point to it. Hatred is completely pointless.'

'So we're not going to find the murderer by looking for a motive.' Palstein straightened the sling that held his arm. 'Anyway. I just phoned you to wish you a pleasant journey.'

'Next time you'll be there too! Soon as you're better.'

'I'd love to see all that.'

'You will see it!' Julian grinned. 'You'll go walking on the Moon.'

'Good luck, then. Squeeze that cash out of them.'

'Take care, Gerald. I'll call you. From up at the top.'

Palstein smiled. 'You *are* up at the top.'

Julian thoughtfully studied the empty screen. More than a decade ago, while the oil sector had still kept the Monopolies and Mergers Commission busy with their yields and price rises, Palstein had turned up in his London office one day, curious to see what sort of work went on there. The realisation of the lift had just suffered a sharp setback, because the optimistic new material from which the cable was to be made had apparently irreparable crystal structure flaws. The world already knew that moon dust contained huge quantities of an element that could solve all the world's energy problems. But without a plan for mining the stuff and getting it to Earth, along with the lack of appropriate reactors, helium-3 seemed like an irrelevance. Even so, Julian had gone on researching on all fronts, ignored by the oil sector, which had its hands full fighting for alternative trends like wind power and photovoltaics. Hardly anyone really took Julian's efforts seriously. It simply seemed too unlikely that he would be successful.

Palstein, on the other hand, had listened carefully to everything, and recommended to the board of his company – which had just changed its name to EMCO after its marriage to ExxonMobil – that they buy shares in Orley Energy and Orley Space. Notoriously, the company's directors hadn't got on board, but Palstein stayed in contact with Orley Enterprises, and Julian came to like and esteem this melancholy character, who was always gazing into the future. Even though they had barely spent three whole weeks together, usually at spontaneous lunches, now and again at events, rarely in a private context, they were bound together by something like friendship, even though the stubbornness of the one had finally consigned the other to oblivion. Lately Palstein had been forced with increasing frequency to announce the abandonment or limitation of mining projects, as he was doing currently in Alaska and as he had done three weeks previously in Alberta, where he had had to face hundreds of furious people and had promptly been shot.

Julian knew that the manager would prove to be right. A partnership with Orley Enterprises wouldn't save EMCO, but it might be useful to Gerald Palstein. He stood up, left the room behind the bar and returned to his guests.

'—so back here for dinner in three-quarters of an hour,' Lynn was saying. 'You can stay and enjoy the drinks and the view, or freshen up and change. You could even do some work, if that's your drug, conditions here are ideal for that too.'

'And for that you should thank my fantastic daughter,' said Julian, putting his arm around her shoulder. 'She's stunning. She did all this. She's the greatest as far as I'm concerned.' Lynn lowered her head with a smile.

'No false modesty,' Julian whispered to her. 'I'm very proud of you. You can do anything. You're perfect.'

A little later Tim was walking along the corridor on the fourth floor. Everything was antiseptically clean. On the way he met two security men and a cleaning robot insistently searching for the nonexistent leftovers of a world only partially inhabited. There was something profoundly disheartening about the way the machine, buzzing busily, pursued the purpose of its existence. A Sisyphus that had rolled the stone up the mountain and now had nothing left to do.

He stopped in front of her room and rang the bell. A camera transmitted his picture inside, then Lynn's voice said:

'Tim! Come in.'

The door slid open. He entered the suite and saw Lynn, wearing an attractive evening dress, standing at the panoramic window with her back to him. Her hair was loose, and fell in soft waves to her shoulders. When she smiled at him over her shoulder, her pale blue eyes gleamed like aquamarines. With sudden brio she swung round and displayed her cleavage. Tim ignored it, while his sister stared so closely past him that her smile bordered on the idiotic. He walked to a spherical chair, bent down and gave the woman who was lolling in it – scantily clothed in a silk kimono, legs bent and head thrown back – a kiss on the cheek.

'I'm impressed,' he said. 'Really.'

'Thanks.' The thing in the evening dress went on strutting around, twisted and turned, wallowed in its transfigured ego, while the real Lynn's smile started sagging at the corners.

Tim sat down on a stool and pointed at her holographic alter ego.

'Are you planning to wear that tonight?'

'I don't know yet.' Lynn frowned. 'It's a bit too formal, don't you think? I mean, for a Pacific island.'

'Odd idea. You've already thrown the rules of South Sea romanticism to the four winds. It looks great, put it on. Or are there alternatives?'

Lynn's thumbs slid over the remote control. Her avatar's appearance changed without transition. Hologram-Lynn was now wearing an apricot-coloured catsuit, bare at the arms and shoulders, which she presented with the same empty grace as she had the evening dress. Her gaze was directed at imaginary admirers.

'Can you program her to look at you?'

'Absolutely not! Do you think I want to stare at myself the whole time?'

Tim laughed. His own avatar was a character from the days of two-dimensional animations, WALL-E, a battered-looking robot whose winning qualities bore no relation to his external appearance. Tim had seen the film as a child and immediately fallen in love with the character. Perhaps because he himself felt battered in Julian's world of shifting mountains and fetching stars down from the sky.

The avatar's magnificent flowing locks were replaced by a chignon.

'Better,' said Tim.

'Really?' Lynn let her shoulders droop. 'Damn, I've already had it up all day. But you're right. Unless—'

The avatar presented a tight, turquoise blouse with champagne-coloured trousers.

'And this?'

'What on earth kind of clothes are those?' Tim asked.

'Mimi Kri. Mimi Parker's new collection. She brought her entire range with her after I had to promise to wear some of it. Her catalogue is compatible with most of the avatar programs.'

'So mine could wear them too?'

'If they could be restitched to fit caterpillar tracks and bulldozer hands, then sure. Afraid not, Tim, it only works with human avatars. And by the way, the program is ruthless. If you're too fat or too small for Mimi's creation, it won't recalculate. The problem is that most people improve their images so much for the avatar that everything fits the calculator and they look like shit afterwards anyway.'

'Then it's their own fault.' Tim narrowed his eyes. 'Hey, your avatar's bum's far too small! Half the size of your real one. No, a third. And where's your paunch? And your cellulite?'

'Idiot,' Lynn laughed. 'What are you doing here anyway?'

'Oh, nothing.'

'Nothing? Good reason to visit me.'

'Well, yeah.' He hesitated. 'Amber says I'm worrying about you too much.'

'No, it's fine.'

'I didn't want to get on your nerves back there.'

'It's sweet of you to care. Really.'

'Still, perhaps—' He wrung his hands. 'You know, it's just that I suspect Julian of being completely blind to his surroundings. He may be able to locate individual atoms in the space–time continuum, but if you're lying dead in your grave right in front of him, he'll complain that you aren't listening to him properly.'

'You exaggerate.'

'But he completely failed to acknowledge your breakdown. Remember?'

'But that's more than five years ago,' Lynn said softly. 'And he had no experience of anything like that.'

'Nonsense, he denied it! What special experience do you need to recognise a burn-out, complete with anxiety and depression, for what it is? In Julian's world you don't break down, that's the point. He only knows superheroes.'

'Perhaps he lacks the counterbalance. After mother died—'

'Mother died ten years ago, Lynn. Ten years! Since he noticed that at some point she'd given up breathing, talking, eating and thinking, he's been screwing everything that moves and—'

'That's his business. Really, Tim.'

'I'll shut up.' He looked at the ceiling as if searching for clues to the real reason for his visit. 'In fact I only came here to tell you your hotel is fantastic. And that I'm looking forward to the trip.'

'That's sweet.'

'Seriously! You've got everything under control. Everything's brilliantly organised!' He grinned. 'Even the guests are more or less bearable.'

'If one of them doesn't suit you we'll dispose of him in the vacuum.' She rolled her eyes and said in a hollow, sinister voice: 'In space no one can hear you scream!'

'Ha!' Tim laughed.

'I'm glad you're coming,' she added quietly.

'Lynn, I promised to look after you, and that's what I'm doing.' He got to his feet, bent down to her and kissed her again. 'So, see you later. Oh, and wear the trousers and the blouse. And your hair looks great down.'

'That's *exactly* what I wanted to hear, little brother.'

Tim left. Lynn let her avatar go on modelling and trying on jewellery. Traditionally, avatars were virtual assistants, programs made form, who helped organise the networked human being's daily life and created the illusion of a partner, a butler or a playmate. They controlled data, remembered appointments, acquired information, navigated the web and made suggestions that matched their user's personality profile. There were no restrictions on their design, which also included virtually cloning yourself, whether out of pure self-infatuation or simply to spare yourself a trip to the shops. Five minutes later Lynn called Mimi Parker. The avatar shrank and froze, while the Californian appeared on the holoscreen, dripping wet and with a towel around her hips.

'I'm just out of the shower,' she said apologetically. 'Find anything nice?'

'Here,' Lynn said, and sent a jpeg of the avatar, which appeared simultaneously on Mimi's display.

'Hey, good choice. Really suits you.'

'Great. I'll tell the staff. Someone will come and collect the things from you.'

'Fine. See you later, then.'

'Yes, see you later.' Lynn smiled. 'And thank you!'

The projection disappeared. At the same time Lynn's smile went out. Her gaze slipped away. Blank-faced, she stared straight ahead and recapitulated Julian's last remark, before she had left the viewing terrace:

I'm really proud of you. You're the greatest. You're perfect.

Perfect.

So why didn't she feel she was? His admiration weighed down on her like a mortgage on a house with a glorious façade and rotten pipes. Since stepping inside the suite, she had been walking as if on glass, as if the floor might collapse. She pushed herself up, dashed to the bathroom and took two little green tablets that she washed down with hasty sips of water. Then she thought for a moment and took a third.

Breathing, feeling your body. Taking a good deep breath, right into your belly.

After she had stared at her reflection for a while, her gaze wandered to her fingers. They were gripping the edge of the basin, and the sinews stood out on the back of her hands. For a moment she considered wrenching the basin from its base, which of course she wouldn't be able to do, except that it might keep her from screaming.

You're the greatest. You're perfect.

Just fuck off, Julian, she thought.

At that moment a pang of shame ran through her. Heart thumping, she slumped to the floor and performed thirty panting sit-ups. In the bar she found a bottle of champagne and tossed a glass down, even though she never normally drank alcohol. The black hole that had opened up beneath her began to close. She called room service, told them to go to Mimi Parker's suite and went into the shower. When she stepped into the lift a quarter of an hour later, wearing a blouse and trousers and with her hair down, Aileen Donoghue was already waiting there and looked as expected. Christmas baubles dangled from her earlobes. A necklace bit into the big valley of her bosom.

'Oh, Lynn, you look—' Aileen struggled for words. 'Good God, what should I say? Beautiful! Oh, what a beautiful girl you are! Let me give you a hug. Julian is rightly proud of you.'

'Thanks, Aileen,' smiled Lynn, slightly crushed.

'And your hair! It suits you much better down. I mean, not that you should always wear it down, but it brings out your femininity. If only you weren't— Oops.'

'Yes?'

'Nothing.'

'Say it.'

'Oh, you young things are all so thin!'

'Aileen, I weigh fifty-eight kilos.'

'Really?' That plainly wasn't the answer that Aileen wanted to hear. 'So in a minute, once we're upstairs, I'll make you a plate of something. You need to eat, my dear! People have to eat.'

Lynn looked at her and imagined tearing the Christmas balls out of her ears. Zip, zap, so fast that her earlobes ripped and a fine mist of blood sprayed onto the mirrored glass of the lift.

She relaxed. The green pills were starting to work.

'I'm hugely looking forward to tomorrow,' she said brightly. 'When it gets going. It'll be really lovely!'

23 May 2025

THE STATION

Orley Space Station (OSS),
Geostationary Orbit

Evelyn Chambers was dreaming.

She was in an odd room about four metres high and just over five metres deep, and six metres wide. The only level surface was formed by the back wall; ceiling and floor merged into one another, leading her to conclude that she was inside an elliptical tube. In each end of it the architects had set a circular bulkhead at least two metres in diameter. Both bulkheads were sealed, although she didn't feel closed in, quite the opposite. It promised the certainty of being safely accommodated.

When the rooms had been furnished, the plans must have been temporarily upside down. Like a flying carpet, an expansive bed hovered just above the floor; there was a desk with seats, a computer work station, a huge display. Subdued lighting illuminated the room, a frosted glass door hid shower, wash-basin and toilet. The whole thing resembled a futuristically designed ship's cabin, except that the comfortable, red-upholstered sofas hung below the ceiling – and the wrong way up.

But the most remarkable thing was that Evelyn Chambers received all these impressions without touching the room or its furniture with a single cell of her body. Just as naked as the choice combination of Spanish, Indian and North American genes had made her, flattered by nothing but fresh air, set to a pleasant 21 degrees Celsius, she floated above the curved, three-metre panoramic front window, and looked at a starry sky of such ineffable clarity and opulence that it *could* only have been a dream. Shimmering just under 36,000 kilometres below her was the Earth, the work of an Impressionist artist.

It *must* be a dream.

But Evelyn wasn't dreaming.

Since her arrival the previous day she couldn't get enough of her far-away home. There was nothing to obstruct the view, no looming lattice mast, no antenna, no module, not even the space elevator cable running towards the nadir. In a quiet voice she said, 'Lights out,' and the lights went out. There was, indeed, a manual remote control for the service systems, but she didn't want to risk changing her perfect position by waving the thing around. After fifteen hours on board the OSS she had slowly started to get used to weightlessness, even though she was deeply unsettled by the lack of up and down. She was all the more surprised not to have fallen victim to the space sickness people talked about, unlike Olympiada Rogacheva, who lay strapped tightly to her bed, whimpering and wishing she had never been born. Evelyn, on the other hand, felt pure bliss, like the memory of Christmas, pure delight distilled into a drug.

She barely dared breathe.

Staying poised over a single point wasn't easy, she noted. In a state of weightlessness you involuntarily assumed a kind of foetal position, but Evelyn had stretched her legs and crossed her arms in front of her chest like a diver propelling himself over a reef. Any hasty movement might mean that she would start spinning, or drift away from the glass. Now that all the light had gone out and the room, furniture included, had half vanished, every cell of her brain wanted to savour the illusion that there was no protecting shell surrounding her, that she was in fact floating like Kubrick's star-child, naked and alone above this wondrously beautiful planet. And suddenly she saw the tiny, shimmering little ball spinning away and realised that her eyes had filled with tears.

Was this how she had imagined the whole thing? Had she been able to imagine anything at all twenty-four hours ago, when the helicopter came down over the platform in the sea and the travellers got out, the night tugging at their coats and a magnificent sunrise failing to attract anyone's attention?

From a distance the platform looked imposing and mysterious, and even a little scary; now they are actually there it exerts a fascination of a quite different and much deeper kind. First the feeling hits that this isn't Disneyland and there's no going back, that they will soon be swapping this world for a different, alien one. Evelyn isn't surprised to see some members of the group repeatedly looking across at the Isla de las Estrellas. Olympiada Rogacheva, for example, Paulette Tautou – even Momoka Omura casts stolen glances at the ragged cliffs, where the lights of the Stellar Island Hotel are beaming with an unexpectedly cosy radiance, as if warning them to leave this nonsense and come home, to freshly squeezed fruit-juices, sun-cream and the cries of gulls.

Why us? she asks herself irritably. Why is it always the women who get queasy at the idea of getting into the lift? Are we really such cowardy-custards? Forced by evolution into the role of worry-warts because nothing must be allowed to endanger the brood, while males – dispensable once robbed of their sperm – can advance calmly into the unknown and die there? At that moment she notices that Chuck Donoghue is sweating an unusual amount, Walo Ögi is displaying distinct signs of nerves, she sees the tense expectation on Heidrun Ögi's face, Miranda Winter's childlike enthusiasm, the intelligent interest in Eva Borelius' eyes, and is reconciled to her circumstances. Together they walk up to the multi-storey cylinder of the terminal, and all of a sudden she realises why she was getting agitated before.

Embarrassing – but even she is utterly terrified.

'To be perfectly honest,' says Marc Edwards, who is walking along beside her, 'I don't have a very good feeling about this.'

'You don't?' Evelyn smiles. 'I thought you were an adventurer.'

'Hmm.'

'That's what you said on my show, at least. Diving into shipwrecks, diving into caves—'

'I suspect this is going to be different from diving.' Edwards stares pensively at his right index finger, its first joint missing. 'Completely different.'

'Incidentally, you never told me how *that* happened.'

'I didn't? A puffer-fish. I annoyed him, on a reef off Yucatán. If you tap them on the nose they get angry, retreat and inflate themselves. I kept tapping him' – Edwards pesters an imaginary puffer-fish – 'except there was coral everywhere, he couldn't get any further back, so the next time I did it he just opened his mouth. My finger disappeared into it for a moment. Yeah. You should never try to pull your finger out of a fish's mouth, certainly not by force. By the time I pulled it out again, there was just a bone sticking out.'

'You won't have to worry about things like that up there.'

'No.' Edwards laughs. 'It'll probably be the safest holiday of our lives.'

They enter the terminal. It's perfectly circular, and looks even bigger from inside than it seemed from outside. High-powered spotlights illuminate two structures, one in front of the other, identical in every detail but mirror images of one another. At the centre of each the cable stretches vertically upwards from its mooring in the ground, surrounded by three barrel-shaped mechanisms oscillating in appearance between cannons and searchlights, their muzzles pointing to the sky. A double grille runs around each of the structures to head height. Its mesh is wide enough for a person to slip through, but its presence indicates quite clearly that this would be a bad idea.

'And you know why?' Julian calls, in a dazzlingly good mood. 'Because direct contact with the cable can cost you a body-part in a fraction of a second. You must bear in mind that it's thinner than a razor-blade, but incredibly hard. If I ran a screwdriver over the outside edge, I could slice it to shreds. Does anyone want to have a go with a finger? Does anyone want to get rid of their partner?'

Evelyn can't help thinking of what a journalist once said: 'Julian Orley doesn't go on stage, the stage follows him around.' Accurate, but the truth still looks a bit different. You actually *trust* the guy, you believe *every single word* he says, because his confidence is enough on its own to dissolve doubts, ifs and buts, nos and maybes, like sulphuric acid.

Motionless, and about twenty metres above the ground, the two lifts dangle like insects from the cables. From close to they look less like space shuttles, not least because they have no wings or tail-planes. Instead, what you notice is the wide undersides, mounted with photovoltaic cells. Compared with two days ago, when they came back from orbit, their appearance has changed slightly, in that the tanks of liquid helium-3 have been swapped for rounded, windowless passenger modules. Walkways lead from a high balustrade to open entrance hatches in the bellies of the cabins.

'Your technology?' asks Ögi, walking along beside Locatelli, eyes on the lifts' solar panels.

Locatelli stretches, becoming half an inch taller. Evelyn can't help thinking of the late Muammar al-Gaddafi. The similarity is startling, and so is the monarchical posture.

'What else?' he says condescendingly. 'With the traditional junk those boxes wouldn't get ten metres up.'

'They wouldn't?'

'No. Without Lightyears, nothing here would work at all.'

'Are you seriously trying to claim the lift wouldn't work without you?' smiles Heidrun.

Locatelli peers at her as if she is a rare species of beetle. 'What do you know about these things?'

'Nothing. It just looks to me as if you're standing there with an electric guitar around your neck claiming that an acoustic would produce nothing but crap. Who are you again?'

'But, *mein Schatz*' – Ögi's bushy moustache twitches with amusement – 'Warren Locatelli is the Captain America of alternative energies. He's tripled the yield from solar panels.'

'Okay,' murmurs Momoka Omura, who is walking along beside him. 'Don't expect too much of her.'

Ögi raises his eyebrows. 'You may not believe it, my little lotus blossom, but my expectations of Heidrun are exceeded again every day.'

'In what respect?' Momoka gives a mocking grimace.

'You couldn't even imagine. But nice of you to ask.'

'Anyway, with traditional energy those things on the cable would *creep* up at best,' says Locatelli, as if the bickering isn't going on around him. 'It would take us days to get there. I can explain it to you if you're interested.'

'I'm not sure, my dear. Look, we're Swiss, and we do everything very slowly. That's why we built that particle accelerator all those years ago.'

'To produce faster Swiss people?'

'Exactly.'

'Doesn't it keep breaking down?'

'Yes, quite.'

Evelyn stands close behind them, absorbing it all like a bee sucking nectar. She likes this kind of thing. It's always the way: put a lot of birds of paradise in a cage, and the feathers will fly.

The get-up gives a hint of what's to come. First everyone is dressed in silver and orange overalls, the colours of Orley Enterprises, then the whole group heads up to the gallery from which the walkways descend to the lifts. Next they make the acquaintance of a powerfully built black man, whom Julian introduces as Peter Black.

'Easy to remember,' Black says cheerfully, and shakes everyone's hand. 'But just call me Peter.'

'Peter's one of our two pilots and expedition leaders,' Julian explains. 'He and Nina – ah, here she is!'

A blonde woman with a short haircut and a freckled snub nose climbs out of the lift hatch and joins them. Julian puts an arm around her muscular shoulders. Evelyn screws up her eyes and bets that Nina turns up in Julian's bedroom from time to time.

'May I introduce you: Nina Hedegaard from Denmark.'

'Hey!' Nina waves to everybody.

'Same role as Peter: pilot, expedition leader. They will both be by your side over the next two weeks, whenever you're travelling vast distances. They will show you the most beautiful parts of our satellite, and protect you from weird space creatures such as the Chinese. Apologies, Rebecca – the red Chinese of course!'

With a start, Rebecca Hsu looks up from the display of her phone.

'I have no network,' she says pleadingly.

It's cramped inside the lift cabin. You have to climb. Six rows of five seats are arranged vertically, connected by a ladder. The luggage has been stowed in the other lift. Evelyn Chambers sits in the same row as Miranda Winter, Finn O'Keefe and the Rogachevs. She leans back and stretches her legs. In terms of comfort, the seats are easily a match for first class in any airline.

'Ooohh, how nice,' Miranda says, delighted. 'A Dane.'

'You like Denmark?' Rogachev asks with cool politeness, while Olympiada stares straight ahead.

'Excuse me!' Miranda opens her eyes wide. 'I *am* a Dane.'

'You must forgive my ignorance, I work in the steel sector.' Rogachev's mouth curls into a smile. 'Are you an actress?'

'Hmm. Opinions vary on that one.' Miranda gives a loud, dirty laugh. 'What am I, Evelyn?'

'The entertainment factor?' Evelyn suggests.

'Well, okay, I'm actually a model. So I've done pretty much everything. Of course I wasn't always a model, I used to be a salesgirl at the cheese counter, then I was responsible for the fries at McDonald's, but then I was discovered on this kind of casting show? And then Levi's took me on straight away. I caused car accidents! I mean, six foot tall, young, pretty, and boobs, genuine boobs, you understand, the real thing – Hollywood was bound to give me a call sooner or later.'

O'Keefe, slouching in his seat, raises an eyebrow. Olympiada Rogacheva seems to have worked out that you can't deny reality just by looking away.

'So what kinds of parts have you played?' she asks flatly.

'Oh, I had my breakthrough with *Criminal Passion*, an erotic thriller.' Miranda gives a sugary smile. 'I even got a prize, but let's not go into that.'

'Why? That's very— that's great.'

'Not really – they gave me the Golden Raspberry for the worst performance.' Miranda laughs and throws her hands in the air. 'But hey! Then came comedies, but I didn't have much luck with that. No hits, so I just started drinking. Bad stuff! For a while I looked like a Danish pastry with raisins for eyes, until one night there I am careening along Mulholland Drive and I go over this homeless guy, my God, poor man!'

'Terrible.'

'Yeah, but actually not because, between ourselves, he survived and made a lot of money out of it. Not that I'm trying to whitewash any-thing! But I swear, that's what happened, and I had my whole stay in jail filmed from the very first second to the last, they were even able to get into the shower. Prison on prime time! And I was back on top again.' She sighs. 'Then I met Louis Burger. Do you know him?'

'No, I—'

'Oh, right. You're from the steel sector, or your husband is, where you don't know people like that. Although Louis Burger, industrialist, investment magnate—'

'Really not—'

'No, I'm sure I do,' Rogachev says thoughtfully. 'Wasn't there a swim-ming accident?'

'That's right. Our happiness lasted only two years.' Miranda stares straight ahead. Suddenly she sniffs and rubs something from the corner of her eye. 'It happened off the coast of Miami. Heart attack, when swimming, and now can you imagine what his children have done, the revolting brats? Not ours, we didn't have any, the ones from Louis's pre-vious marriage. They only go and sue me! Me, his wife? They're saying I contributed to his death, can you believe it?'

'And did you?' O'Keefe asks innocently.

'Idiot!' For a moment Miranda looks deeply hurt. 'Everybody knows I was acquitted. What can I do about it if he leaves me thirteen billion? I could never harm anyone, I couldn't hurt a fly! You know what?' She looks Olympiada deep in the eyes. 'As a matter of fact I can't do anything at all. But I do it really well! Hahaha! And you?'

'Me?' Olympiada looks as if she's been ambushed.

'Yes. What do you do?'

'I—' She looks pleadingly at Oleg. 'We're—'

'My wife is a member of the Russian Parliament,' says Rogachev without looking at her. 'She's the daughter of Maxim Ginsburg.'

'Hey! Oh, my God! Wooaahh! Ginsburg, wooooww!' Miranda claps her hands, winks conspiratorially at Olympiada, thinks for a moment and asks greedily: 'And who's that?'

'The Russian president,' Rogachev explains. 'Until last year at least. The new one's called Mikhail Manin.'

'Oh, yeah. Hasn't he done it before?'

'He hasn't, in fact.' Rogachev smiles. 'Maybe you mean Putin.'

'No, no, it's longer ago, something with an "a" and "in" at the end.' Miranda trawls through the nursery of her education. 'Nope, it's not coming.'

'Maybe you mean Stalin?' O'Keefe asks slyly.

The PA system puts an end to all their speculation. A soft, dark woman's voice issues safety instructions. Almost everything she says sounds to Evelyn like a perfectly normal aeroplane safety routine. They fasten their belts, like horse harnesses. In front of each row of seats, monitors light up and transmit vivid camera pictures of the outside world, giving the illusion that you're looking through windowpanes. They see the inside of the cylinder, increasingly illuminated by the rising sun. The hatch closes, life-support systems spring to life with a hum, then the seats tip backwards so that they're all lying as if they're at the dentist's.

'Tell me, Miranda,' whispers O'Keefe, turning his head towards Miranda. 'Do you still have names for them?'

'Who?' she asks back, just as quietly. 'Oh, right. Of course.' Her hands become display units. 'This one's Huey. That other one's Dewey.'

'What about Louie?'

She looks at him from under lowered eyelids.

'For Louie we'll have to get to know each other better.'

At that moment a jolt runs through the cabin, a tremor and a vibration. O'Keefe slips lower in his seat. Evelyn holds her breath. Rogachev's face is blank. Olympiada has her eyes shut. Somewhere someone laughs nervously.

What happens next is nothing, but nothing, like the launch of a plane.

The lift accelerates so quickly that Evelyn feels momentarily as if she has merged with her seat. She is pressed into the plump upholstery until arms and armrests seem to have become one. The vehicle shoots vertically out of the cylinder. Below them, from the perspective of a second camera, the Isla de las Estrellas shrinks to a long, dark scrap with a turquoise dot inside it, the pool. Was it really only yesterday that she was lying down there, critically eyeing her belly, bewailing the extra four kilos that had recently driven her from bikini to one-piece, while everyone around her was constantly insisting that her weight increase suited her and stressed her femininity? Forget the four kilos, she thinks. Now she could swear she weighs tonnes. She feels so heavy that she's afraid she might at any moment crash through the floor of the lift and plop down in the sea, causing a medium-sized tsunami.

The ocean becomes an even, finely rippling surface, early sunlight pours in gleaming lakes across the Pacific. The lift climbs the cable at incredible speed. They hurtle through high-altitude fields of vapour, and the sky becomes bluer, dark blue, deep blue. A display on the monitor informs her that they are travelling at three times, no, four times, eight times the speed of sound! The earth curves. Clouds scatter to the west, like fat snowflakes on water. The cabin accelerates further to twelve thousand kilometres an hour. Then, very slowly, the murderous pressure eases. The seat begins to heave Evelyn back up again, and she completes the transformation back from dinosaur to human being, a human being who cares about an extra four kilos.

'Ladies and gentlemen, welcome on board OSS Spacelift One. We have now reached our cruising speed and passed through the Earth's lower orbit, the one in which International Space Station ISS circles. In 2023 operation of the ISS was officially halted, and since then it has served as a museum featuring exhibits from the early days of space travel. Our journey time will be about three hours, the space debris forecast is ideal, so everything suggests that we will arrive at OSS, Orley Space Station, in good time. At present we are starting to pass through a Van Allen radiation belt, a shell of highly charged particles around the Earth, caused by solar eruptions and cosmic radiation. On the Earth's surface we are protected from these particles; above an altitude of one thousand kilometres, however, they are no longer deflected by the Earth's magnetic field, and flow directly into the atmosphere. Around here, or more precisely at an altitude of seven hundred kilometres, the inner belt begins. It essentially consists of high-energy protons, and reaches its highest densities at an altitude of between three thousand and six thousand kilometres. The outer belt extends from altitudes of fifteen to twenty-five thousand kilometres, and is dominated by electrons.'

Evelyn is startled to note that the pressure has completely disappeared. No, more than that! For a brief moment she thinks she's falling, until she realises where she has had this strange feeling of being released from her own body before. She experienced it briefly during the zero-gravity flights. She is weightless. In the main monitor she sees the starry sky, diamond dust on black satin. The voice from the speaker assumes a conspiratorial tone.

'As many of you may have heard, critics of manned space travel see the Van Allen belts as an impassable obstacle on the way to space because of the high concentration of radiation. Conspiracy theorists even see them as proof that man was never on the Moon. Supposedly it would only be possible to pass through them behind steel walls two metres thick. Be assured, none of this is true. The fact is that the intensity of the radiation fluctuates greatly according to variations in solar activity. But even under extreme conditions, the dosage, as long as you are surrounded by aluminium three millimetres thick, is half of what is considered safe under general radiation protection regulations for professional life. Generally it's less than one per cent of that! In order to protect your health to the optimum degree, the passenger cabins of this lift are armoured accordingly, which is, incidentally, the chief reason for the lack of windows. As long as you don't feel an urge to get out, we can guarantee your complete safety as you pass through the Van Allen belt. Now enjoy your trip. In the armrests of your seats you will find headphones and monitors. You have access to eight hundred television channels, video films, books, games—'

The whole caboodle, then. After a while Nina Hedegaard and Peter Black come floating over, handing out drinks in little plastic bottles that you have to suck on to get anything out of them, finger food and refreshment towels.

'Nothing that could spill or crumble,' Hedegaard says, with a

Scandinavian sibilance on the S. Miranda Winter says something to her in Danish, Hedegaard replies, they both grin. Evelyn leans back and grins too, even though she didn't understand a word. She just feels like grinning. She is flying into space, to Julian's far-away city . . .

. . . in which she felt now as if she were alone with the Earth. It lay so far below her, so small, that it looked as if she would just have to reach out and the planet would slip softly into the palm of her hand. Gradually the darkness faded towards the west and the Pacific began to glow. China still slept, while staff in North America were already hurrying to their lunch-breaks, talking on their phones, and Europe was spinning towards the end of the working day. She was astonished to realise that three more earths would have fitted in the space between her and the blue and white sphere, although it would have been a bit of a tight squeeze. Almost 36,000 kilometres above her home, the OSS drifted in space. That in itself stretched her imagination to its limits, and yet to reach the Moon they would have to travel ten times as far.

After a while she pushed herself away from the window and floated over to one of the upside-down sofas. She clambered rather inelegantly into it. Strictly speaking, there was no point in even having furniture in a place like this. Underwater, buoyancy compensated for gravitation to allow you to float, but you were still subject to influences such as water density and current, while in zero gravity no forces at all affected the body. You didn't weigh anything, you didn't tend to move in any particular direction, you didn't need a chair to keep you from falling on your behind, or the comfort of soft cushions, or a bed to stretch out on. Basically you needed only to float in the void with your legs and forearms bent, except that even the tiniest motor impulses, a twitch of a muscle, were enough to set the body drifting, so that you were in constant danger of cracking your head in your sleep. Millions of years of genetic predisposition also required you to lie *on* something, even if it was vertical or stuck to the ceiling. At the same time concepts such as 'vertical' were irrelevant in space, but people were used to systems of reference. Investigations had shown that space travellers found the idea of an earth at their feet more natural than one floating above their heads, which was why psychologists encouraged the so-called gravity-oriented style of construction, to create the illusion of a floor. You just strapped yourself firmly to the bed, in the chair you acted as if you were sitting down, and in the end it felt almost homey.

She stretched, did a somersault and decided to go – float, rather – to breakfast. In the concave wall that seemed to conceal the life-support system, there was a wardrobe from which she chose a pair of dark three-quarter-length trousers and a matching T-shirt and tight-fitting slippers. She paddled over to the bulkhead and said, 'Evelyn Chambers. Open.'

The computer tested pressure, atmosphere and density, then the module opened to reveal a tube several metres across. Many miles of such tubes stretched all the way across the station, connecting the modules to one another and with the central structure, and creating lines of communication and escape routes. Everything was subject to the redundancy principle. There were always at least two possible ways of leaving a module, each computer system had matching mirror systems, there were several copies of the life-support systems. Months before the trip, Evelyn had tried to imagine the massive construction by studying it using models and documents, before establishing, as she had now, that her fantasy had been blinding her to the reality. In the isolation of the cell in which she was staying, she could hardly imagine the colossus that loomed above it, its size, its complex ramifications. The only thing that was certain was that next to it the good old ISS looked like a toy out of a blister pack.

She was on board the biggest structure in space ever created by human beings.

In homage to the concept of the space elevator, the designers had built the OSS on a vertical. Three massive steel masts, each one 280 metres high, arranged at an equal angle to each other, formed the spine, connected at the base and the head, producing a kind of tunnel through which the cables of the lift passed. Like the storeys of a building, ring-shaped elements called tori stretched around the masts, defining the five levels of the facility. At the bottom level lay the OSS Grand, the space hotel. Torus-1 housed comfortable living rooms, a snack and coffee bar, a room with a holographic fireplace, a library and a rather desperate-looking crèche, which Julian stubbornly planned to extend: 'Because children will come, they will love it!' In fact, since its opening two years previously, although the OSS Grand had been well booked, there had so far been no families. Very few people were willing to entrust their offspring to the weightless state, a fact that Julian defiantly dismissed by saying, 'Nothing but prejudice! People are so silly. It's no more dangerous up here than it is in the stupid Bahamas, quite the contrary. There's nothing up here to bite you, you can't drown, you don't get jaundice, the natives are friendly, so what is there to worry about? Space is *paradise* for children!'

Perhaps it was just that people had always had a twisted relationship with paradise.

Like a predatory shark, Evelyn snaked her way along the pipe. You could move incredibly quickly in zero gravity if you put your mind to it. On her way she passed numbered side-tunnels, with suites similar to her own behind them. Every unit consisted of five modules, each divided into two living units and arranged in such a way that all the guests enjoyed an unimpeded view of the Earth. The connection to the torus branched off to the right, but Evelyn fancied breakfast, and continued along the course of the tunnel. It opened out into the Kirk, one of the two most spectacular modules of the OSS. Disc-shaped, these protruded far above the accommodation areas, so that Earth could be seen through the glass floor. The Kirk served as a restaurant; its counterpart to the north, appropriately christened the Picard, alternated between lounge, nightclub and multimedia centre.

'Making this glass floor stretched us to the limits,' Julian never tired of stressing. 'What a struggle! I can still hear the builders' complaints in my ears. So? said I. Since when have we cared about limits? Astronauts have always yearned for windows, lovely great big panoramic windows, except that the walls weren't strong enough on the flying sardine-tins of the past. The problem was solved with the lift. We need mass? Send it up there. We want windows? Let's put some in.' And then, as he always did, he lowered his voice and whispered almost reverently.

'Building them like that was Lynn's idea. Great girl. She's pure rock 'n' roll! I tell you.'

The communication hatch leading to the Kirk was open. Evelyn remembered the hazards of her newly won freedom too late, clutched at the frame of the lock to halt her flight, missed it and flew through, flailing her arms, past a not especially startled waiter. Someone grabbed her ankle.

'Trying to get to the Moon all by yourself?' she heard a familiar voice say.

Evelyn gave a start. The man drew her down to eye-level.

His eyes—

Of course she knew him. Everyone knew him. She'd had him on her show at least a dozen times, but she still couldn't get used to those eyes.

'What are you doing here?' she exclaimed, bewildered.

'I'm the evening entertainment.' He grinned. 'What about you?'

'Morale booster for space grouches. Julian and the media, you know . . .' She shook her head and laughed. 'Incredible. Has anyone seen you?'

'Not yet. Finn's here, I heard.'

'Yeah, he was suitably dismayed to bump into me here. He's become quite trusting now though.'

'No pose is a pose in itself. Finn enjoys playing the part of the outsider. The less you ask him, the more answers you'll get. You up for breakfast?'

'Definitely.'

'Great, me too. And then?'

'To the multimedia centre. Lynn's giving us an introduction to the station. They've divided us up. Some people are having the scientific aspect explained to them, the others are going out to play.'

'And you aren't?'

'No, I am, but later. They can only take six people out at any one time. You fancy coming?'

'I'd love to, but I've got no time. We're shooting a video in Torus-4.'

'Oh, really, you're doing something new? Seriously?'

'Not another word.' He smiled, putting a finger to his lips. His eyes whisked her off to another galaxy. 'Remember, someone has to take care of the old folks.'

Lynn smiled, answered questions, smiled again.

She was proud of the multimedia space, just as she was intensely proud of the whole OSS Grand, of the Stellar Island Hotel and the far-away Gaia. At the same time they all filled her with terrible anxiety, as if she had built Venice on matchstick foundations. Everything she did was affected by that awareness. She tortured herself with apocalyptic scenarios, and catharsis was possible only if her worst fears proved to be well founded. She was trapped in a terrible internal struggle, in which she tirelessly pursued another version of herself. The more arguments she produced to quell her anxieties, the bigger they became, as if she were approaching a Black Hole.

I'm going to lose my mind, she thought. Just like Mom. I'm definitely going insane.

Smile. Smile.

'Lots of people see OSS as a mushroom,' she said. 'Or a parasol, or a tree with a flat crown. A bar table. Other people see a medusa.'

'What's a medusa again, darling?' asked Aileen, as if talking about some kind of fashionable gewgaw that teenagers might be interested in.

'It's a sort of jellyfish thing,' Ed Haskin replied. 'You've got this gooey umbrella thing at the top, with tentacles and other sorts of gooey stuff dangling from the bottom.'

Lynn bit her lips. Haskin, previously a director of the spaceport and for a few months now responsible for the whole technical sector, was a nice man, very competent, and sadly equipped with the sensitivity of a Neanderthal.

'They're also very beautiful creatures,' she added.

They were both orbiting a four-metre-tall holographic model of OSS, projected into the centre of Picard. Drifting in their wake through the virtual space came Walo Ögi, Aileen and Chuck Donoghue, Evelyn Chambers, Tim and some recently arrived French scientists. The Picard had a different design from the Kirk, which was closer to classical restaurant style. Here floating islands of conviviality were arranged on different levels, bathed in muted light and overlooked by a long bar that cried out to be populated by Barbarellas with heavy eyeliner. At the touch of a button, everything could be reconfigured, so that tables and seats grouped themselves into an atrium.

'Jellyfish, table or parasol, such associations are due to the vertical construction and symmetry of the station,' said Haskin. 'We mustn't forget that space stations aren't buildings with fixed foundations. In fact they don't actually need foundations at all, but they are exposed to the constant redistribution of mass and all kinds of possible impact, from joggers on treadmills to moon shuttles attaching themselves to the outer ring. All of these things set the structure vibrating independently, and a symmetrical construction is ideally suited to the redistribution of vibration energies. The vertical alignment contributes to the stabilisation, and matches the principle of the space elevator. As you can see, the smallest moment of inertia is directed towards the Earth.'

Right at the bottom the torus with the hotel in it could be seen, with its outrigger suites, and Kirk and Picard protruding above them. Along the lattice masts, modules containing fitness centres, staff accommodation, storerooms and offices were stacked all the way up to Torus-2, at the centre of which the space elevator came to a halt. Retractable gangways linked the bagel-shaped module with the cabins.

'This is where we arrived yesterday,' Lynn explained. 'Torus-2 serves as the reception area for the OSS Grand, and also as a terminal for passengers and freight. As you see, corridors radiate in a spoke arrangement from there to a larger, surrounding ring.' Her hand passed through a lattice structure that stretched generously around the torus. 'Our spaceport. Those things that look like aeroplanes are evacuation pods, the little tins are moon shuttles. In one of them, the Charon, we'll be heading for the satellite tomorrow.'

'I should have gone on a diet,' Aileen said excitedly to Chuck. 'How am I going to fit in one of those? My bum's the size of Halley's Comet.'

Lynn laughed.

'Oh, no, they're very spacious. Very comfortable. The Charon is over thirty metres long.'

'And that thing there?' Ögi had spotted crane-like structures on the top side of the ring and along the mast. He floated over to them, passed through the projection beam for a moment and looked like a huge cosmic monster attacking the OSS.

'Manipulators,' said Haskin. 'Robot arms on tracks. They unload the arriving cargo shuttles, take out the tanks of condensed helium-3, bring them inside the torus and anchor them to the lifts.'

'What happens exactly when one of those shuttles docks?'

'There's a big bang,' said Haskin.

'But doesn't that mean that the station has too much weight on one side? There isn't always the same number of ships at anchor.'

'That isn't a problem. All the docking sites are transferable, we can always right the balance. Well spotted, by the way.' Haskin looked impressed. 'Are you an architect?'

'An investor. But I've built various things. Residential modules for cities: you click them into already existing structures or put them on high-rise roofs, and when you move, your little house simply goes with you. The Chinese love it. Flood-resistant estates on the North Sea. You know that Holland's being flooded; are they all supposed to move to Belgium? The houses are fixed to jetties and float when the water rises.'

'He's also building a second Monaco,' said Evelyn.

'Why do we need a second Monaco?' asked Tim.

'Because the first one's filled to bursting,' Ögi explained. 'The Monégasques are stacking up like the Alps, so Albert and I flicked through our Jules Verne. Have you heard of Propeller Island?'

'Isn't that the story of the mad captain in that weird underwater boat?' Donoghue asked.

'No, no!' One of the Frenchmen dismissed the idea. 'That was the *Nautilus*! Captain Nemo.'

'Rubbish! I've seen that one. It's by Walt Disney.'

'No! Not Walt Disney! *Mon Dieu!*'

'Propeller Island is a mobile city state,' Ögi explained. 'A floating island. You can't extend Monaco indefinitely, not even with offshore islands, so we hit on the idea of building a second one that will cruise the South Sea.'

'A second Monaco?' Haskin scratched his head. 'You mean a ship?'

'Not a ship. An island. With mountains and coasts, a pretty capital city and a wine cellar for old Prince Ernst August. But artificial.'

'And it works?'

'*You* of all people are asking me that?' Ögi laughed and spread his arms out as if to press the OSS to his heart. 'Where's the problem?'

'There isn't one,' Lynn laughed. 'Or do *we* look as if we've got problems?'

Her eye rested on Tim. Was he actually aware of what was wrong with her? His unease touched and shamed her in equal measure, as he had had every reason to be uneasy since that day, that terrible moment five years before, that was to change their lives, just before six in the evening . . .

. . . Lynn is in the middle of the traffic jam, ten lanes of pumping, overheated metal chugging its way along the M25 to Heathrow with the pace of a glacier, under a ruthless, cold February sun gleaming down from a yellowish, cloudy Chernobyl sky, and suddenly it happens. She has to go to Paris for a meeting, she's always going to some sort of meeting or other, but all of a sudden someone turns off the light in her head, just like that, and everything sinks into a morass of hopelessness. Profound grief sweeps over her, followed by 10,000 volts of pure panic. Later she's unable to say how she got to the airport, but she isn't flying, she's just sitting in the terminal, robbed of all certainties but one, which is that she will not be able to bear her own existence for a second longer, because she doesn't want to go on living with so much sadness and anxiety. But at that point her memory stops till the morning, when she finds herself fully dressed on the floor of her penthouse flat in Notting Hill, mailbox, email and answering machine spilling over with other people's excitement. She walks out onto the terrace, into the icy rain that has started falling diagonally, and wonders whether the twelve storeys will be enough. Then she changes her mind and calls Tim, thus sparing the sensibilities of anyone who might have been passing by.

Henceforth, whenever the topic turns to her illness, Julian invokes various baleful viruses and protracted colds as a way of explaining to himself and others what it is that is so terribly afflicting his daughter, his shining light; Tim, on the other hand, is always talking in terms of therapies and psychiatrists. Her condition is a mystery to Julian, and he represses what he perhaps guesses at, just as he has repressed the memory of Crystal's death. It is ten years since Lynn's and Tim's mother died in a state of mental derangement, but Julian develops a remarkable capacity for denial. Not because he is traumatised, but because he is actually incapable of making a connection between the two.

It's Tim and Amber who come to her rescue. When she feels nothing but naked terror at the loss of all sensation, Tim walks around the block with her, in sunshine and in pouring rain, for hours, he forces her mind back into the present until she is able once again at least to feel the cold and wet, and to become aware of the metallic taste of her fear on her tongue. When she thinks she'll never be able to sleep again, or keep down a bite of food, when seconds stretch into infinities and everything around her – light, colours, smells, music – emits shock-waves of menace, when every house-roof, every parapet, every bridge invites her to leap, when she fears going mad as Crystal did, running amok, killing people, he makes it clear to her that no demon has taken possession of her, that no monsters are after her, that she wouldn't hurt anyone, not even herself, and very gradually she starts to believe him.

Things get better, and Tim bugs her. Forces her to take professional help at last, to lie down on the couch. Lynn refuses, plays down the nightmare. Examining the causes? What for? She isn't even slightly willing to show respect to this miserable phase of her otherwise perfect life. Her nerves have been going haywire, exhaustion, crashing synapses, biochemical mayhem, whatever. Reason to be ashamed, but not to go rummaging for the source of her distress. Why should she? To find what? She is glad and grateful that the company has camouflaged her condition with a series of explanations – flu, very bad flu, bronchitis – now that she's up and smiling and shaking hands again. The crisis has been survived, the broken doll repaired. Again she sees herself as Julian sees her, a perspective that she temporarily lost. Who cares whether she likes herself? Julian loves her! Seeing herself through his eyes solves all her problems. The stale familiarity of self-debasement, she could live with that.

'—are the dining and common rooms for the scientific operations,' she heard herself saying.

She worked her way further up the hologram, from Torus-3 to the sports facilities in Torus-4, to dozens of accommodation and laboratory modules, which Julian had rented out to private and state research establishments from all over the world: NASA, ESA and Roskosmos, his own subsidiaries Orley Space, Orley Travel and Orley Energy. Cheeks aglow, she talked about the vegetable gardens and animal breeding facilities in the domed biospheres above Torus-4, allowed a glimpse into the observatories, workshops, control and meeting rooms of the fifth and final Torus, from which the lift cable led back out and into infinity or what the temporary residents imagined infinity to be. She described the disc-shaped roof, hundreds of metres across, with its wharfs in which moon shuttles and interplanetary spaceships were built, robots dashed busily through the vacuum and solar panels inhaled sunlight, so that the station could feed on the homemade kind during its hours in the Earth's shadow. Laughing on the brink of the abyss, she presented the OSS, the Orley Space Station, whose builder and owner NASA had so yearned to be. But such a proposition would have required political responsibility, and by their nature politicians were voluble, slippery creatures, and tended to criticise the decisions of their predecessors rather than anything else. Hence, in the end, a private investor had taken the dream of the settlement of space that bit further and, *en passant*, established the necessary conditions to set off a landslide in the energy sector, which threw up the question of . . .

'. . . whose interests we are actually subsidising if we decide to join forces with Orley Enterprises.'

'Well, ideally ours,' said Locatelli. 'Don't you think?'

'I completely agree,' Rogachev replied. 'I'd just like to know who else I'm benefiting.'

'As long as Lightyears remains market leader, I couldn't give a rat's ass about anyone else who might be getting anything out of it, if I may be so bold out here in geostationary isolation.'

'*Ryba ishchet gde glubzhe, a chelovek gde luchshe.*' Rogachevo smiled thinly. 'The fish seeks the deepest place, man the best. For my part, I'd prefer a bit more of an overview.'

Locatelli snorted. 'You're not going to get that by looking at everything from outside. Perspective comes from position.'

'Which is?'

'My company's, in my case. I know you're scared of indirectly benefiting Washington and NASA by giving Julian money. But so what? The main thing is that the figures add up at the end of the year.'

'I'm not sure if you can really see it like that,' said Marc Edwards, then realised the vacuousness of his observation and turned his attention to the pairs of boots that Nina was handing out.

'*I* can see it like that. *He* can't.' Locatelli pointed at the Russian with his thumbs outstretched and laughed broadly. 'You see, he's married to politics.'

Finn O'Keefe exchanged a glance with Heidrun Ögi. Rogachev and Locatelli were really getting on his nerves. They were having discussions which, in his opinion, really belonged at the end of the trip. And perhaps he just didn't know enough about how the sector worked, but in any case, he planned to do nothing over the coming days but enjoy himself as best he could, and obediently shoot the little film clip that he had promised Julian he would do: Perry Rhodan on the *real* moon, singing the wonders of the *real* experience. Investor outpourings had no place, he thought, in 'EVA's wardrobe', the dressing area for Extravehicular Activities.

'And what about you?' Locatelli stared at him. 'What's the view like from Holly-wood?'

O'Keefe shrugged. 'Relaxed.'

'He wants your money too.'

'No, he wants my face, so that I can tell moneybags like you that they've absolutely got to get to the Moon. You're right to that extent.' O'Keefe rubbed his index finger and thumb together. 'I get hold of money for him. But not mine.'

'Very clever,' Locatelli observed to Rogachev. 'He probably even gets some for himself as well.'

'Not a cent.'

'And what do you *really* think about it? Space tourism, private flights to the Moon?'

O'Keefe looked around. He had expected to see complete spacesuits hanging here, like limp and motionless astronauts, but the section, with its sterile lighting, felt more like a boutique. Folded overalls of all sizes, helmets, gloves and boots lined up side by side, sections of rigid armour.

'No idea,' he said. 'Ask me again in a fortnight.'

Their little group – Rogachev, Locatelli, Edwards, Mimi, Heidrun Ögi and him-self – had herded around Nina Hedegaard, trying not to spin chaotically away. O'Keefe was mastering the art of space ballet better by the hour, and so was Rogachev, who had allowed himself to be dragged along by the excitement of the evening conversation; in addition to foot-ball, his love of martial arts was now revealed to the world. The Russian now seemed to possess his body only to subject it to reptilian control. His feelings, in so far as he had any, lay hidden beneath the ice of his pale blue eyes. Marc Edwards and Mimi Parker, both passionate divers, held their position tolerably well, Heidrun strove for control, while Locatelli's impetuosity had the potential to injure someone.

'Could I ask you to come closer?' called Nina.

'So, between ourselves' – Mimi Parker lowered her voice – 'there are rumours going around. No idea if there's anything to it, but some people are suggesting that Julian's running out of puff.'

'Meaning?'

'He's as good as broke.'

'That's nothing,' Heidrun whispered. 'You know who really is run-ning out of puff?'

'Sure.' Mimi leaned forward. 'Out with it.'

'You lot, you bunch of chatterboxes. And you'll be running out of puff out there if you don't stop talking nonsense.'

Rogachev studied her with the amusement of a cat being growled at by mice.

'There's something refreshing about you, Mrs Ögi.'

She beamed at him as if he'd just crowned her Miss Moscow. The Russian twitched his eyebrows with amusement and floated closer to Nina. Heidrun followed him clumsily. Her limbs seemed to have grown even longer and more unwieldy in zero gravity. The Dane waited until they had all formed a semicircle around her, then clapped her hands and flashed her perfect teeth to the assembled group.

'So!' A hissed Scandinavian S. 'You're about to embark on your first space-walk. Everyone excited?'

'Sure!' Edwards and Mimi cried simultaneously.

'With reservations,' Rogachev smiled. 'As we are now under your charming care.'

Locatelli flared his nostrils. Excitement was clearly beneath his dignity. Instead he lifted his specially made, vacuum-resistant camera aloft and took a photograph. Nina received the answers and reactions with dimples of delight.

'You should be a bit excited, because Extravehicular Activities are one of the most demanding aspects of manned space travel. Not only will you be entering a vacuum, you will also be exposed to extreme variations in temperature.'

'Oh,' Mimi marvelled. 'I always thought it was just cold in space.'

'From the purely physical point of view, there is no prevalent temperature in space. What we describe as temperature is the degree of energy with which the molecules of a body, a fluid or a gas move. Small example: in boiling water they're charging about all over the place, in ice they're almost motionless, so we experience one as hot and the other as cold. In empty space, on the other hand—'

'Yeah, yeah,' Locatelli murmured impatiently.

'—we find practically no molecules at all. So there's nothing to measure. Theoretically this brings us to zero degrees on the Kelvin scale, or minus two hundred and seventy-three degrees Celsius, absolute zero. However, we record the so-called cosmic background radiation, a kind of afterglow from the time of the Big Bang, when the universe was still unimaginably dense and hot. That comes to just three degrees. Doesn't exactly warm things up. Nonetheless, you can burn up or freeze out there, depending.'

'We all know that already,' Locatelli pressed. 'I'm more interested in where—'

'Well I don't know it.' Heidrun turned her head towards him. 'But I'd *like* to know. As you might imagine, I'm vulnerable to sunburn.'

'But what she's telling us is all general knowledge!'

Heidrun stared at him. Her eyes said, *fuck you, smart-arse.* Nina gave a conciliatory smile.

'So, in empty space any body, whether it's a spaceship, a planet or an astronaut, assumes the temperature that matches its environment. That's based on the factors of solar radiation and reflection into space. That's why spacesuits are white, to reflect as much light as possible, which means they don't heat up as much. Even so, temperatures of over a hundred and twenty degrees Celsius have been measured on spacesuits on the side facing the sun, while the temperature on the shaded side was minus a hundred and one degrees Celsius.'

'Brrr,' said Mimi.

'Don't worry, you won't notice it. Spacesuits are temperature-controlled. Inside they're a bearable twenty-two degrees Celsius. Of course only if the suit has been put on right. Negligence can mean death. Later on the Moon you'll find similar conditions: in the polar regions there are craters which, at minus two hundred and thirty degrees, are amongst the coldest areas in the whole solar system! Light never enters them. On average the daytime temperature on the Moon's surface is a hundred and thirty degrees Celsius; at night it falls to minus a hundred and sixty degrees – which is, incidentally, a reason why the Apollo landings took place in the Moon morning, when the sun is low and it's not quite so hot. Still, when Armstrong passed into the shadow of his moon module, the temperature of his suit dropped all of a sudden from sixty-five to minus one hundred degrees Celsius, in one single step! Any further questions?'

'About the vacuum,' said Rogachev. 'I gather our bodies will explode if we're exposed to an airless space without protection?'

'It's not quite as dramatic as that. But you would die whatever happened, so it's a good idea to keep your helmet on nicely at all times. Most of you are familiar with the old spacesuits in which you looked like a marshmallow. So inflated that the astronauts literally had to go hopping about because their trouser legs didn't bend. For short missions and occasional space outings that was fine. But in continuously inhabited space cities, on the Moon or on Mars, monster suits like that wouldn't make any sense at all.'

Nina pointed to the tight-fitting overall that she herself was wearing. It was made of a thick neoprene-like material and was covered with a network of dark lines. Her elbows and knees were protected by hard shells. Even though she looked as if she'd put on three diving suits one over the other, the ensemble seemed somehow sexy on her.

'That's why they've recently started using suits like these. Bio-suits, developed by a beautiful woman, Professor Dava Newman of MIT. They're pretty, don't you think?' Nina turned slowly on her axis. 'You're going to ask me how the required pressure is created. Very simple. Instead of gas, a huge number of fixed metal braces create a mechanical counter-pressure. It's only where the skin is highly mobile that the material is kept flexible; in all other areas it's rigid, it's practically an exoskeleton.'

Nina took a torso-shaped shell from the nearest shelf.

'All armour and applications fit the basic unit, as this carbon-fibre torso protector reveals. A backpack full of life-support systems is connected to attachment points on the back, and air is pumped into the helmet and guided along pipes to the boots and gloves, the only areas in which there is gas pressure. The traditional, noisy cooling system has been replaced by a temperature-controlling nano-layer. There are additional protectors for the limbs, like the ones you'll know from mediaeval suits of armour, except much lighter and harder. In space you're exposed to cosmic radiation, there are micrometeorites flying about, and on the Moon you'll be exposed to regolith, moon dust. While the movements of your feet in space don't really matter much, on planetary surfaces they're crucially important. To do justice to all that, bio-suits are conceived as construction sets. Dozens of elements can be combined at will, quickly and with only a few rapid manoeuvres. You breathe the same oxygen–nitrogen mixture as you do on Earth and here on board, and now you no longer have to wait for ages in the pressure chamber.'

She started pulling on her boots and gloves, attached the backpack with the life-support systems to the back plate of the suit and linked the connectors to one another.

'Child's play, Dava Newman would say, but be careful. Don't try to do it on your own. Don't make me have to come and pick you up, all dried up and twisted. Okay? Fine! Bio-suits are low-maintenance, and one more thing while we're on the subject: if anyone feels a certain physical need – just let it flow. Your valuable pee is trapped in a thick layer of polyacrylate, so don't worry that it's going to splash down your legs. These' – and Nina pointed to two consoles under the wrist – 'are controls for a total of sixteen thrust nozzles in the shoulder and hip areas. Astronauts no longer dangle like newborn babies from umbilical cords; they navigate by recoil. The blasts are short, and they can be manually released or left up to computer calculation. That option's a new one. When the electronics decide that you've lost control, you're automatically stabilised. Your computers are connected to mine, and remote-controlled as well, so strictly speaking you can't get lost. Here' – her hand slipped over another console along her forearm – 'you'll find thirty little buttons, each one with the option of speaking and receiving. With these you'll decide who you want to communicate with. "Talk to all" means you're talking to everybody, "Listen to all" means you're receiving everybody. To get your declarations of love out of the way, choose the individual connection and switch the rest off.' Nina grinned. 'Anyone worried about me seeing you in your underwear? Nobody? Then off with your clothes! Let's get ready to go out there.'

*   *   *

'What about the chickens?' asked Mukesh Nair.

'A crackpot idea,' Julian objected. 'There are four left. Two are even still laying eggs, little spherical things with the nutritional value of golf balls. The pelvic muscles of the others have regressed so far that they can't push anything out.'

'So much for births in space,' said Eva Borelius. 'Push, push! But what with?'

'And what about the chicken poo?' Karla Kramp seemed weirdly fascinated by the subject.

'Oh, they crap more than we'd like them to,' said Julian. 'We tried to siphon it off, but you have to be careful that you don't suck the feathers off the poor creatures' butts. The whole thing's pretty tricky. Quite honestly, I don't know how to raise chickens in zero gravity. They don't like it. They're always bumping into each other, you have to put them on leashes, they look baffled. Unlike fish, by the way! They don't seem to care, they live in a kind of floating state anyway. We could look into fish-breeding next, if you like.'

'We haven't tried everything yet,' announced Kay Woodthorpe, a squat woman with the face of a Chihuahua, who worked for the bioregenerative systems research group. 'If the worst comes to the worst, we'll try artificial gravity.'

'How would you do that?' asked Carl Hanna. 'By making the OSS rotate?'

'No,' Julian shook his head. 'Just the breeding module, uncoupled and stored a few kilometres away. A structure like OSS isn't suited to spinning. You'd need a wheel for that.'

'Like in science fiction movies?'

'Exactly.'

'But you've got one here,' said Tautou. 'Not a wheel, perhaps, but axial symmetric elements—'

'You're talking about a Bernal sphere, my friend. That's something else. A wheel whose rotational element corresponds to the speed of the Earth's rotation.' Julian frowned. 'Imagine a car tyre or a cylindrical body. When it turns, centrifugal forces arise at the internal wall, opposite the axis. Then something like gravity comes into being. You can walk along a self-enclosed surface, excellent jogging route, by the way, while the gravity decreases towards the axis. Feasible in principle. The problem is the requisite size and stability of such a structure. A wheel with a diameter of – let's say – a hundred metres would have to complete a rotation every fourteen seconds, and the gravity at your feet would probably be stronger than the gravity at your head, because your body accelerates to different degrees. And besides, if you set something like that in motion— You know that from driving: when one of your tyres isn't properly balanced, it lurches like mad; and now imagine a rotating station starting to career. You've got people walking about, how are you going to ensure that they're evenly distributed at all times? You couldn't begin to calculate the vibrations produced, everyone would be nauseous, the thing might explode—'

'But you've left the era of lightweight construction behind,' said Hanna. 'With the lift you can put unlimited mass in orbit. Just build a bigger, more stable one.'

'Would such a thing be possible?' Tautou said in amazement. 'Like the one in 2001?'

'Sure.' Julian nodded. 'I knew Kubrick. The old guy had thought very carefully about that, or let's say he'd had other people think about it for him. I've always dreamed of copying his space station. That massive wheel turning to the sounds of waltz-music, which you can walk around. But it would have to be huge. Four kilometres in diameter. High orbit, highly armoured. So you could fit a whole city inside, with residential areas, parks, maybe a river—'

'I think this is quite fascinating enough,' Sushma Nair said to her husband and, glowing with enthusiasm, touched his arm. 'Look at that, Mukesh. Spinach. Courgettes!'

They were floating along a glass wall several metres high. Behind it all kinds of greenery curled and sprouted, fruits dangled from trees.

'Pioneering work, Julian,' Mukesh agreed. 'You've managed to impress a simple peasant.'

'Just as you have impressed the world.' Julian smiled.

False modesty, Nair, thought Hanna.

While a brave little group explored the vacuum outside, he, Eva Bore-lius, Karla Kramp, Bernard Tautou and the Nairs were, under the expert guidance of Julian and Kay Woodthorpe, viewing the two biospheres, the huge, spherical modules in which the bioregenerative life-support system department was experimenting with agriculture and animal-rearing. Over six floors, Biosphere A brought together courgettes and cabbage, spinach, tomatoes, paprika and broccoli, a real Little Italy of vegetables, as well as kiwi-fruit and strawberries, the whole thing populated by a fauna of bustling robots, constantly planting, fertilising, hoeing, cutting and harvesting. Hanna wouldn't have been surprised to see carbon-fibre-reinforced rabbits with radio-telescope ears gnawing at the lettuce and suddenly floating away at their approach. He threw back his head. One level up, apple-trees stretched knotty branches resplendent with cudgel-hard fruits.

At first, Woodthorpe told them, there had been massive problems. The predecessors of the greenhouses, called salad-machines, had been little more than standard racks in which tomatoes and lettuce flourished in competition. As plants took their bearings from gravity like almost all living creatures, and thus knew where to stretch and in which direction to send their roots, the loss of up and down had led to the formation of terrible thickets – unfortunately at the expense of the fruits, which led a wretched guerrilla lifestyle in the middle of the kraken-like root-monster. Thrown into confusion, even spinach had produced only woody stalks in a desperate bid to cling onto something, until it occurred to someone to subject the fields to artificial tremors, brief shakes as a result of which their fruit and vegetable plants finally sought support down below, where the vibrations came from.

'Since then we've had the rank growth under control, and you can see the quality,' Woodthorpe explained. 'Certainly, it is and will always be greenhouse produce. The strawberries taste a bit watery, you wouldn't necessarily win any prizes with the red peppers—'

'But the courgettes are great,' said Julian.

'Yeah, and so's the broccoli and amazingly the tomatoes too. We don't really know yet why one works better than the other. At any rate the greenhouses give us cause to hope that we may in future be able to close life-support systems that are presently open. On the Moon we've nearly got there.'

'What do you mean "close"?' asked Karla.

'Just like on Earth. Nothing gets lost there. The Earth is a self-enclosed system, everything is constantly being processed. Just look on the space station as a small copy of our planet with proportionately limited resources of water, air and fuel, except that in the past we couldn't rework all those resources. We were constantly forced to maintain supplies. Carbon dioxide, for example, got completely out of hand. Today we can split it in reactors, use the liberated oxygen again to breathe, or combine it with hydrogen to form water, and the remaining carbon can be synthesised with methane to form fuel. Just a bit of sludge gets lost in the process, and it's hardly worth mentioning. The problem is more one of bringing the size and consumption of the reactors into a convincing relationship with their effectiveness. So we try to do that with natural regeneration processes. Plants can also serve that purpose. Our own little rainforest, if you like. On the Moon we have bigger greenhouses, and we're on the brink of completely closing all the cycles.'

'No market for a water-supplier, then,' laughed Tautou.

'No, the OSS is on the way to complete self-reliance.'

'Hmm, self-reliance.' Karla thought for a moment. 'So you could soon be declaring independence, could you? Or the whole Moon. By the way, who does the Moon actually belong to?'

'Nobody,' said Julian. 'According to the lunar treaty.'

'Interesting.' Karla's Modigliani eyebrows raised, arches of amazement, her face an oval full of ovals. 'Given that it doesn't belong to anyone, it's not short of people.'

'That's right. The treaty urgently needs to be rewritten.'

'Perhaps to say that the Moon belongs to everybody?'

'Correct.'

'So the people who got there first. Or who are already up there. America and China.'

'By no means. Anyone else can follow them.'

'*Can* anyone follow them?' she asked slyly.

'That, my dear Karla,' smiled Julian, 'is exactly the point.'

Finn O'Keefe tried to find solace in physics.

The dressing process had gone on for ages, until at last the group hung, packed and helmeted, in the hermetic seclusion of the airlock, a clinically illuminated, empty room with rounded edges. Hand-grips ran along the walls; a display provided information about pressure, temperature and atmospheric composition. Nina explained that this chamber was considerably larger than the other hatches distributed around the OSS. Once Peter Black had joined them, the group now comprised eight people. A hiss, growing quieter and finally fading away, indicated that the air was being sucked out, then the outer bulkheads glided silently open.

O'Keefe gulped.

In thrall to early human fears of plunging into the abyss, and with butterflies in his stomach, he stared outside. Part of the roof extended before his eyes. He didn't know what he had expected: an outlet, a balcony, a gangway, regardless of the fact that none of it made any sense up here. The circular level had no floor – it was an open structure with a diameter of four hundred metres, surrounded by a steel ring, massive enough that railway lines could have passed through it, and fitted with payloads and manipulators. A radial arrangement of supporting constructions led from the torus to the other areas. Beyond that solar park, glittering in the sunlight, radiators circulated and spherical tanks hung from crane-like cantilevers. Batteries of floodlights illuminated huge hangars, the birthplaces of future spaceships. Tiny astronauts floated below the belly of a steel giant, overseeing the installation of rows of seats by robot arms. Bizarre machine-creatures, half man, half insect, criss-crossed the area, carried parts in locust arms, crawled with segmented grasping claws around the scaffolding and girders, carried out soldering work and riveted prefabricated components. Their android faces seemed to have been inspired by the character Boba Fett, the always helmeted contract killer from *Star Wars*, leading inevitably to the conclusion that Julian Orley had been involved in their development – Orley with his enthusiasm for science-fiction films, who always managed to transform quotations into innovations.

Beyond the hatch a chasm yawned.

The vertical structure of the OSS stretched almost three hundred metres below O'Keefe, and below it lay the Earth, an unimaginable distance away. He hesitated, felt his heart thundering. Although he knew about the irrelevance of his weight, it seemed sheer madness to pass beyond the edge, like leaping from a skyscraper.

Physics, he thought. Trust in the law of God.

But he didn't believe in God anyway.

Beside him, Nina Hedegaard and Peter Black sailed sedately outside, turned around and presented the mirrored fronts of their helmets. 'The first time is always a breakthrough,' he heard the Danish woman say. 'But you can't fall. Just try to adjust your way of thinking.'

Got me, thought O'Keefe.

A moment later he was given a push, slipped out over the edge towards the two guides and right past them. Startled, he gasped for air and braced himself as he flew, but there was nothing there to stop him. Dispatched on a journey of no return, he drifted away. The idea of being lost in space, of being slung out into the void, flashed through his mind and he started flailing wildly, which only made him look all the more ridiculous.

'Look,' Laura Lurkin said. 'It's the ladies' programme.'

Amber thought she could physically feel the corrosive effect of the mockery. She knew from Lynn that the fitness trainer, a menacingly sculpted block of humanity with a wrestler's crotch, a troll's arms and a soothing voice, didn't particularly care for space tourists. Her attitude was based on her conviction that private individuals had no business being anywhere higher up than the current passenger flight-paths. Lurkin was a former Navy Seal, hardened in the fire of geopolitical conflicts. When Olympiada, Miranda, Rebecca, Momoka and Amber turned up at the spa area like a delegation of fun-hungry First Ladies, Lurkin's initial reaction had been, quite reasonably, to make fun of them, albeit in a moderately affable tone. After all, it was her job to keep orbital travellers fit, not to depress them.

'You've *got* to go, Amber! Please! We've got the EVA, the guided tour through the scientific area, the multimedia performance: I'd have been happy if we could have distributed the silly women across the three groups, but they wanted their beauty programme. I'm glad we don't have to deal with Paulette, but—'

'I'd actually rather come to your presentation, Lynn.'

'I know. I'm sorry, believe me! But someone has to give those four the feeling that we're making them just as welcome as all the others, who want more from an orbital trip than a bit of sweating and peeling and having their spots squeezed. I'd do the job myself, but I can't!'

'Oh, Lynn. Does it have to be like that? Tim and I—'

'They accept you as a representative, as a hostess.'

'But I'm not the hostess.'

'No, but you are in their eyes. You're an Orley. Please, Amber!'

That pleading tone!

'Okay, fine, whatever. But put me on the second space-walk this afternoon!'

'Oh, Amber, let me kiss you! You can walk all the way to Jupiter, I'll make the sandwiches myself! Thank you!'

So here it was, the ladies' programme.

The fitness centre occupied two modules, elliptically flattened like the accommodation tubes. In the upper part there was a real sauna, without wooden benches, admittedly, but with straps for the hands and feet and generously sized windows, as well as a steam sauna, whose rounded walls copied the stars in the form of hundreds of tiny electric bulbs. In the crystal cave you could drift through droplets of ice-cold water that was sprayed into the room and then sucked back out again, in the quiet zone you could listen to celestial music, read or snooze. A floor further down, various fitness devices, massage rooms and strong hands waited for the stressed-out part-time astronauts.

'—indispensable in space!' Lurkin was saying. 'Zero gravity is all well and good, but it contains a lot of dangers that shouldn't be underestimated, if you're exposed to it over a long period. You'll already have noticed certain changes in yourself. Warming in the head and chest, for example. Immediately after the start of zero gravity, more than half a litre of blood rises from the lower regions of the body to the thorax and head. You'll get apple cheeks and what astronauts call a 'puffy face'. It's a nice effect, by the way, because it compensates for wrinkles and makes you look younger. But not in the long term, unfortunately. Once you get back to Earth, gravity will tug at your tissues just as it always has done, so enjoy the moment.'

'My legs are freezing,' Rebecca Hsu said suspiciously, inflated in her dressing-gown until she looked like a globe made of terry towelling. 'Is that normal?'

'Quite normal. In accordance with the redistribution of your bodily fluids your legs will feel rather cold. You'll get used to that, as you will to your outbreaks of sweating and temporary disorientation. I heard that one of you suffered quite badly from that?'

'Madame Tautou,' Miranda Winter said. 'Wow! The poor woman keeps—' She lowered her voice. 'Well, it's coming out everywhere, in fact.'

'Space sickness.' Lurkin nodded. 'No reason to be ashamed, even experienced astronauts suffer from it. Who else has any other symptoms?'

Olympiada Rogacheva hesitantly raised her hand. After a few seconds Momoka Omura pointed an index finger, before immediately retracting it again.

'Nothing important,' she said.

'Well, with me it's like this,' Rebecca said. 'My sense of balance is a bit confused. Even though I'm actually used to sailing.'

'I'm just happy if I can keep everything down,' Rogacheva sighed.

Lurkin smiled. Of course she had been informed that the oligarch's wife had a breakdown-related alcohol problem. Strictly speaking, Olympiada Rogacheva shouldn't even have been here, but during the two-week training programme she had drunk nothing but tea, confounding all the sceptics. She could clearly manage without vodka and champagne, after all.

'Never mind, ladies. By the day after tomorrow you'll be immune to space sickness. But what affects everybody are physiological long-term changes. In zero gravity your muscle mass declines. Your calves will shrink to chicken legs, your heart and circulation will be overtaxed. That's why daily sport is the chief duty of every astronaut, meaning exercise machine, gymnastics, weight-lifting, all nicely strapped in, of course. On long-term missions a considerable decline in bone substance has also been observed, particularly in the spine and leg areas. The body loses up to ten per cent of its calcium over six months in space, immune disorders appear, wounds heal more slowly, all concomitant effects that *Perry Rhodan* shamefully fails to mention. You'll only be spending a few days in zero gravity, but I urge you to get some exercise. So what shall we start with? Rowing, cycling, jogging?'

Momoka stared at Lurkin as if she had lost her mind.

'No way. I want to go to the steam-room!'

'And you'll get to the steam-room,' said Lurkin, as if talking to a child. 'But first we'll do a spot of fitness training, okay? That's how it is on board space stations. The instructor's word is final.'

'Okay.' Amber stretched. 'I'm going on the exercise machine.'

'And I'm going on the bike,' Miranda cried with delight.

'An exercise machine *is* a bike.' Momoka pulled a face as if being subjected to a serious injustice. 'Can we at least swim here?'

'Of course.' Lurkin spread her muscle-bound arms. 'If you can find a way of keeping water in the pool in zero gravity, we can talk about it.'

'And what about that?' Rebecca looked at a device on the ceiling just above her head. 'It looks like a step machine.'

'Bingo! It trains up your bottom and your thighs.'

'Exactly right.' The Taiwanese woman peeled herself out of her dressing-gown. 'You should never miss an opportunity to fight against physical decay. It's dramatic enough! I feel as if it's only my tight underwear that's keeping me from exploding!'

Amber, who knew Rebecca from the media, raised an eyebrow.

Without a doubt, the queen of luxury had put on a fair bit of weight over the past few years, but her skin looked as smooth and tight as a balloon. What was it that Lurkin had said about 'puffy faces'? Why should the effect be restricted to the face alone? It was obvious that upper arms shouldn't wobble in zero gravity, that breasts were lifted because they weren't being drawn towards the Earth's core, that everything was deliciously rounded and firm. The whole of Rebecca Hsu looked somehow puffy.

'Don't worry,' she said. 'You look great.'

'For your age,' Momoka added smugly.

With Lurkin's help, Rebecca wedged herself onto the step machine, allowed herself to be belted in and smiled down at Amber.

'Thanks, but when the paparazzi need helicopters to get all of you into shot, it's time to face the facts. I'm starting to turn to jelly. I distribute anti-cellulite miracle cures by some of the most famous cosmetic brands in the world, but slap me on the bum and you have to wait for a quarter of an hour until the waves have subsided.'

And she started jogging like a peasant treading grapes, while Miranda Winter doubled up with laughter and Amber joined in. Momoka's gestures passed through various stages of human development, then she laughed as well. Something was dissolved, a deep-seated, unconfessed anxiety, and they all rolled around cackling and panting.

Lurkin waited with an indulgent expression on her face and her arms folded.

'Glad we all agree,' she said.

'Out you go!'

Heidrun's words were followed by a boisterous chortle.

It was the last thing O'Keefe heard before he drifted out of the airlock. Heidrun, that bitch! Frank Poole, the unlucky astronaut from *2001*, had fallen victim to a paranoid computer, now he to a homicidal Swiss woman. His fingers grasped the thruster controls. The first stimulus stopped his flight; the second, intended to turn him back towards the airlock, instead sent him into a spin.

'Very good,' he heard Nina say, as if she were sitting in the corner of his helmet with fairy-wings. 'Wonderful reaction speeds for a beginner.'

'Don't start,' he snarled.

'No, I'm serious. Can you stop the spinning too?'

'Why should he?' laughed Heidrun. 'It looks good. Hey, Finn, you should catch yourself a moon to orbit around you.'

He rotated clockwise. Into the spin.

And it worked. Suddenly he was hanging there motionless, watching the others spin out of the airlock like space debris. The new, close-fitting generation of spacesuits had the advantage of not making everyone who wore them look exactly the same. They let you have an idea of who was in front of you, even if their face was barely recognisable through the mirrored visor. Heidrun, clad like a Star Warrior, was given away by her anorexic, elf-like figure. He longed to give her a good kick.

'I'll get you for that,' he mumbled, but couldn't stop himself grinning.

'Oh, *Perry*! My hero.'

She carried on giggling, then got into difficulties and began to turn upside down. Someone else, it might have been Locatelli, Edwards or Mimi, started to retreat back inside the airlock. A third flailed his arms about. Nothing about the movement suggested it was happening voluntarily. Apart from Nina and Peter, only one member of the group displayed any signs of controlled movement, turning in a neat half circle and coming down to rest next to the two leaders. O'Keefe had no doubt it was Rogachev. Then, suddenly, they all floated back towards each other as if by magic.

'A bit treacherous, isn't it!' laughed Peter. 'Navigating in a vacuum is like nothing else. There's no friction, no current to carry you, no resistance. Once you're in motion you carry on that way until an adequate counter-impulse occurs, either that or you'll drift into the sphere of some celestial body and end up as a meteor or make some pretty little crater. Using a thruster properly takes practice; practice you haven't had. So that's why, from now on, you don't need to do anything. The remote control will take over. For the next twenty minutes we're putting you on control beam, which means you can just sit back and enjoy the view.'

They set off and flew rapidly out over the artificial platform, towards the half-built spaceship. They hovered weightlessly between the flood-light masts.

'We try to limit EVAs to the absolute minimum of course,' Nina explained. 'By now, sunstorm forecasts have become accurate enough for us to take them into account during the planning stages of a mission. And in any case, no astronaut goes outside without a dosimeter. If an unexpected eruption takes place there's still plenty of time to get back inside the station, and there are dozens of armoured storm shelters all around the outer walls of the OSS if it ever gets tight. But then again, even the most high-tech suit doesn't provide long-lasting protection against radiation damage, so we're increasingly reliant on robots.'

'The flying things over there?' said Locatelli in a shaky voice, pointing in the direction of two machines with arms but no legs, crossing their path a short distance away. 'They look like goddamn aliens.'

'Yes, it's astonishing. Now that reality has emancipated itself from science fiction, it's picking up its ideas. We've realised, for example, that humanoid machines accommodate their creators' needs in all kinds of ways.'

'Creation in our own image,' said Mimi Parker. 'Just like the boss did it six thousand years ago.'

Something in those crudely chosen words made O'Keefe stop and think, but he decided to worry about it later. They flew in a wide curve and headed for the spaceship. One of the automatons had anchored itself onto the outer shell like a tick. His two main extremities disappeared inside an open shutter, where they were clearly in the process of installing something; two smaller arms around the machine's upper body were holding components at the ready. The front side of its helmet-like head was adorned with black glassy peepholes.

'Can they think?' asked Heidrun.

'They can count,' said Nina. 'They're Huros-ED series robots, *Humanoid Robotic System for Extravehicular Demands*. Incredibly precise and utterly reliable. So far there's only been one incident involving a Huros-ED, and it wasn't actually caused by it. But after that their circuit board was extended to include a life-saving program. We use them for everything you can think of: servicing, maintenance, construction. If you end up in outer space, you have a very good chance of being picked up by a Huros and brought back safely.'

Their route led them straight up over one of the floodlight masts and over the back of the spaceship.

'It takes two to three days to get to the Moon by shuttle. They're spacious, but just for fun try imagining during the flight that you're on your way to Mars. Six months in a box like that, the sheer horror of it! Human beings aren't machines; they need social contact, private lives, space, music, good food, beautiful design, food for the senses. That's why the spaceship being created here isn't like any conventional ship. Once it's completed it will be an astonishing size; here you're only seeing the main body, almost two hundred metres in length. To put it more precisely, it's constructed from individual elements which are linked up with one another: partly burnt-out tanks from old space shuttles, partly new, larger models. Together they form the working and command area. There will be laboratories and conference rooms, greenhouses and processing plants. The sleep and training modules rotate on centrifugal outriggers around the main body of the ship to allow the presence of a weak artificial gravity, similar to the gravity on Mars. The next construction stage will be to extend it at the front and back, using masts several hundred metres in length.'

'Several hundred metres?' echoed Heidrun. 'Good grief! How long is the ship going to be?'

'About a kilometre, or so I've heard. And that's excluding the sun wings and generators. Around two-thirds of them are situated on the front mast, at the peak of which there will be a nuclear reactor to provide the power. Hence the unconventional design: the living quarters have to be at least seven hundred metres away from the source of radiation.'

'And when will the flight be?' Edwards enquired.

'Realists have their sights set on 2030, but Washington would prefer it to be earlier. After all, it's not just a race to get to the Moon. The USA will do everything they possibly can, even if it means . . .'

'. . . occupying the Red Planet,' completed Rogachev. 'We get the picture. Has Orley rented the entire hangar to the Americans?'

'Part of it,' said Nina. 'Other areas of the station have been rented to the Germans, French, Indian and Japanese. Russians too. They're all running research stations up here.'

'But not the Chinese?'

'No, not the Chinese.'

Rogachev dropped the subject. Their flight led over the hangar towards the outer ring with its work stations and manipulators. Nina pointed out the far ends of the masts, which sprouted spherical objects: 'The site and orbit regulation system. Orb-like tanks feed into the thrusters, which can be used to sink, lift or move the station.'

'But why?' asked O'Keefe. 'I thought it had to stay at exactly this height?'

'In principle, yes. On the other hand, if a meteorite or a particularly big lump of space debris were to come rushing towards us, we would need to be able to adjust the station's position a little. Generally speaking we would know about things like that weeks in advance. A vertical shift would usually suffice, but sometimes it makes more sense to get out of the way by moving slightly to the side.'

'That's why the anchor station is a swimming island!' called Mimi Parker. 'So it can be moved around in synchrony with the OSS!'

'Exactly,' said Nina.

'That's crazy! And does it happen often? That kind of bombardment?'

'Rarely.'

'And you'd know the path of all objects like that?' O'Keefe dug deeper.

'Well.' Peter hesitated. 'The large ones, yes. But small odds and ends pass through here a million times without us needing to know about it: nano-particles, micrometeorites.'

'And what if something like that hits my suit?' Edwards suddenly sounded as if he was longing to be back inside the station.

'Then you'd have one more hole,' said Heidrun, 'and a nicely positioned one, hopefully.'

'No, the suit can take that. The armoured plating absorbs nano-particles, and if a pinprick-sized hole really did appear, it wouldn't have any immediate impact. The fabric is interfaced with a polymer layer; its molecular chains close up as soon as the material reaches its melting point. And the friction heat from the impact of a micrometeorite alone would be enough to do that. You might end up with a small wound, but nothing more than you'd get from stepping on a sea urchin or having a run-in with your cat. The chance of crossing paths with a micrometeorite is far less than, let's say, your chances of getting eaten by a shark.'

'How reassuring,' said Locatelli, his voice sounding strained.

The group had crossed the outer edge of the ring and were now following the course of another pylon. O'Keefe would have liked ideally to turn around and go back. There should have been a fantastic view over the roof to the torus from here. But his spacesuit was like a horse that knew the way and went off all on its own. In front of him the pennons spread like a flock of dark glistening birds with mythical wingspans, keeping watch over these curious patches of civilisation in space. And beyond the solar panels that supplied the station with energy, there was only open space.

'This section should be of particular interest to you, Mr Locatelli. It's your stuff!' said Peter. 'We'd have needed four to five times as many panels using conventional solar technology.'

Locatelli said something along the lines of that being entirely true. Then he added a few other things. O'Keefe thought he picked up the words revolution and humanity, followed by millstone, which was probably supposed to be milestone. Either way, for some reason it all jumbled up and sounded like guttural porridge.

'You should be really proud of it, sir,' said Peter. 'Sir?'

The object of his praise lifted both arms as if he were about to conduct an orchestra. A few syllables escaped from his throat.

'Is everything okay, sir?'

Locatelli groaned. Then they heard eruptive retching.

'B-4, abort,' said Nina calmly. 'Warren Locatelli. I'll accompany him back to the airlock. The group will continue on as planned.'

★ ★ ★

One day, Mukesh Nair told them, back when he was still a boy in the small village of Loni Kalbhor, they had cut his uncle down from the roof beam of his hut, where he had hanged himself. Suicides amongst farmers were a part of daily life back then, the bitter harvest of the Indian agricultural crisis. Mukesh had wandered through the fallow sugarcane fields, wondering what could be done to stem the flood of cheap imports from the so-called developed nations, whose agriculture lounged around in a feather bed of generous subsidies as it deluged the world with dirt cheap fruit and vegetables, while Indian farmers saw no other way out of their debt than to take their own life.

He had realised back then that you couldn't misinterpret globalisation as a process which politicians and companies initiated, accelerated and controlled as they pleased. It wasn't something that could be turned off and on, not a cause, but the symptom of an idea that was as old as humanity itself: the exchange of culture and wares. Rejecting that would have been as naïve as suing the weather for crop failures. From the day human beings had first ventured into other humans' territories to trade or make war, it had always been about doing it in such a way that they could participate and profit from it as much as possible. Nair realised that the farmers' misery couldn't be blamed on some sinister pact between the First World states, but came down to the failure of the rulers in New Delhi to play to India's strengths. And one of those strengths – even though, historically, the country had always been synonymous with hunger – was nourishing the world.

Back then, Nair and a group of others had led the Green Revolution. He went to the villages, encouraging the farmers to switch from sugarcane to chilli, tomatoes, aubergines and courgettes. He provided them with seeds and fertiliser, introduced them to new technologies, secured them cheap credit to relieve their debt, pledged minimum purchases and gave them shares in the profit of his supermarket chain, which he built from scratch by utilising modern refrigeration technology, naming it Tomato after his favourite vegetable. Thanks to sophisticated logistics, the perishable goods found their way so quickly from the fields to the counters of the Tomato supermarkets that all the imported products looked old and rotten in comparison. Desperate farmers, who until recently had been faced with the choice of either going into the city as day labourers or stringing themselves up in the attic, became entrepreneurs. Tomato boomed. More and more branches opened, more and more farmers joined forces with Nair's entourage in the new, emerging India.

'The inhabitants of our hot, microbe-contaminated metropolises loved our air-conditioned, clean fresh-food markets from the word go,' said Nair. 'We had competitors pursuing similar concepts, of course, partly with the support of foreign multi-corporate giants. But I only ever saw my competitors as allies. When it mattered most, we were a hair's breadth ahead of the rest.'

By now, there were branches of Tomato all over the world. Nair had swallowed up most of his competitors. While India's agricultural products were now being exported to the most remote corners of the world, Nair had long since gone on to explore a new field of activity, branching out into genetics and blessing the flood-prone coastal areas of his country with a saltwater-resistant rice.

'And that,' said Julian, 'is the very thing that unites us.'

They watched a small harvest robot plucking cherry tomatoes from the vines with its intricate claws, sucking them up inside itself before they had the chance to roll away.

'We will occupy outer space, colonise the Moon and Mars. Perhaps a little less quickly than we imagined, but it will happen, if only because there are a number of sound reasons why we should. We are standing on the threshold of an era in which the Earth will be only one of the many places where we can live and develop industries.'

Julian paused.

'But you won't be able to make a fortune with fruit and vegetables beyond the Earth just yet, Mukesh. The journey towards establishing Tomato branches on the Moon will be a long one! Bernard, you could supply the Moon with water of course – it's vital for any new development – but you'll barely make a cent in the process. And as far as your work is concerned, Eva: long-term stays in outer space, on the

Moon and on the surface of other planets, will all confront medicine with totally new challenges. And yet research will remain a loss-making business initially, just as I subsidise America's space travel to help promote the most important resource for a clean and lasting energy supply, and the way I subsidised the development of the necessary reactors. If you want to change the world and be a pioneer the first thing you need to do is *spend money*. Carl, you made your fortune through clever investments in oil and gas, then switched sides to solar technology, but in space these new technologies wouldn't yet make any decent turnover. So why should you invest in Orley Enterprises?'

He looked at each of them in turn.

'I'll tell you why. Because we're united by something more than just what we produce, finance and research, and that's our concern for the wellbeing of mankind. Take Eva for example, who has successfully cultivated synthetic skin, nerves and cardiac muscle cells. Incredibly significant work, reliable, highly lucrative, but that's only the half of it, because above all it provides *hope* for coronary-risk patients, cancer patients and burn victims! And Bernard, a man who has provided the poorest of the poor around the globe with access to clean water. Or Mukesh, who opened up a new way of life for India's farmers and fed the world. Carl, whose investment in renewable energies helps to make its actual use possible. And what's my dream? You already know. You know why we're here. Ever since experts began to think about clean, risk-free fusion technology, about how the fuel of the future, helium-3, can be transported from the Moon to Earth, I've been obsessed with the idea of providing our planet with this new, inexhaustible source of energy. I've gone through many years of deficit to develop reactors until they were ready for production and to build the first functioning space elevator so we could give mankind a springboard into outer space. And do you know what?'

He smiled contentedly and paused for several seconds.

'All that idealism has paid off. Now I *want to* and I *will* make money from it! And you should all join me in doing so! In Orley Enterprises, the most important technology experts in the world. It's people like us who move or stop this wonderful planet thirty-six thousand kilometres beneath us. It's down to *us*. It may not increase your sales of vegetables, water or medication if we join forces, but you'll be part of the biggest conglomerate in the world. Tomorrow, Orley Energy will become world market leader in the energy sector with its fusion reactors and environmentally friendly power. With the help of more space elevators and space stations, Orley Space will accelerate the conquest of the solar system for mankind's use, and, together with Orley Travel, expand space tourism too. Believe me, all of that put together will *pay off*! Everyone wants to go into orbit, everyone wants to go to the Moon, to Mars and beyond, both humans and nations. At the beginning of the century we thought the dream was over, but it's only just begun, my friends! And yet only very few countries possess the technologies the whole world needs, and Orley Technologies are way ahead of the game on this one. And everyone, everyone without exception, will pay the price!'

'Yes,' said Nair in awe. 'Yes!'

Hanna smiled and nodded.

Everyone will pay the price—

Everything Julian had said, with his usual eloquence and persuasiveness, reduced down to this last sentence in his ears. He had voiced what had been left behind by rulers retreating from the globalisation process, the attempt for economy to become independent, the privatisation of politics: a vacuum that had been filled with business-men. He defined the future as a product. Even the days ahead wouldn't change that, quite the opposite in fact. The world would be sold yet again.

Just very differently to how Julian Orley imagined.

I'm back,' chirped Heidrun.

'Oh, my darling!' Ögi's moustache bristled with delight. 'Safely and in one piece too, I see. How was it?'

'Great! Locatelli threw up when he saw his solar panels.'

She floated over and gave him a kiss. The action led to repulsion. She slowly retreated again, reached out to grasp the back of a chair and made her way back, hand over hand.

'Did Warren get space sick or something?' asked Lynn.

'Yes, it was great!' Heidrun beamed. 'Nina took him off with her, and after that it was all really nice.'

'I'm not so sure.' Donoghue pursed his lips. Red-cheeked and bloated, he rested grandly back against an imaginary throne like Falstaff, his hair so bouffant it looked as though an animal had died on his scalp. 'It sounds dangerous to me, someone throwing up in their helmet.'

'Well, *you* don't have to go out there,' said Aileen sharply.

'Poppycock! I wasn't saying that . . .'

'You're sixty-five, Chucky. You don't have to join in on everything.'

'I said, it *sounds* dangerous!' blustered Donoghue. 'I didn't say I was scared. I'd still go out there even if I were a hundred. And on the subject of age, have you heard the one about the really old couple and the divorce judge?'

'Divorce judge!' Haskin was starting to laugh already. 'Let's hear it.'

'So they go to the divorce judge, and he looks at the woman and says: "My dear, how old are you?" "Let's see," says the woman, "I'm ninety-five." "Okay, and you?" The man thinks for a second: ninety-eight! "God almighty," says the judge, "I don't believe it. Why on earth would you want to get divorced at your age?" "Well, it's like this, your honour . . ."'

Tim snarled. It was hardly bearable. Chucky had been relentlessly setting off comedy firecrackers, one after the other, for the past two hours.

'". . . we wanted to wait until the children had passed away."'

Haskin did a somersault. Everyone laughed, of course. The joke wasn't that bad, at least not bad enough for Tim to blame Donoghue alone for his apocalyptic mood. But at that moment he noticed Lynn sitting there as if she'd been turned to stone, as if she were somewhere else entirely. She was gazing straight ahead and was clearly clueless of what was going on around her. Then, all of a sudden, she laughed too.

I could be wrong, he thought. It doesn't necessarily mean that it's starting all over again.

'So what did you get up to while we were gone?' Heidrun looked around curiously. 'Have you been to look around the model station?'

'Yes, I could re-create it right now from memory,' bragged Ögi.

'Amazing building. To tell you the truth I was surprised by the safety standards.'

'Why?' asked Lynn.

'Well, the privatisation of space travel adds to the fear that it's all been cobbled together too quickly.'

'But would you be here if you were seriously concerned about that?'

'That's true.' Ögi laughed. 'But in any case, it was quick. Extraordinarily quick. Aileen and Chuck here could certainly tell you a thing or two about building regulations, surveys and restrictions.'

'Just one or two?' growled Chucky. 'I could go on for days.'

'When we were designing the Red Planet, they thought the project would be impossible to complete,' Aileen confirmed. 'What a bunch of cowards! It took a decade to get from the initial design stage to the start of the construction, and even after that they never left us in peace.'

The Red Planet was Donoghue's pièce de résistance, a luxury resort in Hanoi modelled on the landscape of Mars.

'It's now known as the pièce de résistance of structural engineering,' she added triumphantly. 'There's never been an incident with any of our hotels! But what happens? Whenever you start planning something new, they swarm over you like zombies and try to eat you alive, your enthusiasm, your ideas, even the creative power given to you by the almighty Creator himself. You might think that building up a good record over the years would earn you some credit, but it's like they take no notice whatsoever of what you've achieved so far. Their eyes are dead, their skulls stuffed with regulations.'

Oh man, thought Tim.

'Yes, yes.' Ögi rubbed his chin thoughtfully. 'I know exactly what you mean. In this respect, my dear Lynn, I can't help but water down all this adulation with a bit of scepticism. As I said, you made the station into a reality extremely quickly. You might even say suspiciously quickly compared to the ISS, which is smaller yet took a lot longer.'

'Would you like to hear an explanation for that?'

'At the risk of annoying you . . .'

'You're not annoying me in the slightest, Walo. Pressure from competition has always encouraged sloppiness in the race to be first. But Orley Space doesn't have any competitors. So we never needed to be quicker than anyone else.'

'Hmm.'

'The reason we were quick was perfect planning, which ultimately meant the OSS built itself. We didn't need to accommodate dozens of notoriously hard-up space authorities, nor wade through bureaucratic quicksand. We only had one partner, the United States of America, and they would even have sold the Lincoln Memorial to break out of the commodity trap. Our agreement fitted on the back of a petrol receipt. America builds up its moon base and supplies technology for mining helium-3, while we bring in marketable reactors, an inexpensive, quick transport system to the Moon and, last but not least, a great deal of money! Getting authorisation from Congress was a walk in the park! It was a win-win situation! One gets to monopolise the reactor trade, the other returns to the peak of space-travelling nations and gets the solution to all their energy problems. Believe me, Walo, with prospects like those on the table, any other option but *quickly* is completely out of the question.'

'Well, she's certainly right about that!' said Donoghue, his voice like thunder. 'When has it ever been about whether someone *can* build something or not? Now-adays it's always about the damn money.'

'And the zombies,' nodded Aileen vigorously. 'The zombies are everywhere.'

'Sorry.' Evelyn Chambers raised her hand. 'I'm sure you're right, but on the other hand we're not here to inflate each other's egos. This is about investment. And my investment in you is very much linked to trust, so we should put all our cards on the table, don't you think?'

Tim looked at his sister. She looked open and interested, clearly unaware of what Evelyn Chambers was alluding to.

'Of course. What's on your mind?'

'Slip-ups.'

'Such as?'

'Vic Thorn.'

'Of course. That's on the agenda.' Lynn winced, but without batting an eyelid. 'I was planning to talk about him later, but we can bring it forward.'

'Thorn?' Donoghue wrinkled his forehead. 'Who's he?'

'No idea.' Ögi shrugged. 'But I'm happy to hear about slip-ups. Even if only to make my peace with my own.'

'We don't have any secrets,' said Haskin. 'It was all over the news last year. Thorn was part of the first long-term crew on the American moon station. He did an excellent job, so he was recommended for a further six months, as well as being offered a leadership position. He agreed and travelled to the OSS to fly on to the base from there.'

'That's right, it rings a bell,' said Heidrun.

'Same here.' Walo nodded. 'Wasn't there some kind of problem with an EVA?'

'With one of the manipulators to be precise. It was blocking the hatch of the shuttle which was supposed to take Thorn's people to the Moon. It was paralysed mid-movement after being hit by a piece of space debris. So we sent a Huros up . . .'

'A what?' asked Aileen.

'A humanoid robot. It discovered a splinter in one of the joints, which had apparently caused the manipulator to shut itself down.'

'Well, that sounds sensible.'

'Machines don't concern themselves with concepts of reason.' Haskin gave her a look as if she'd just suggested never sending robots outside without warm socks on. 'We agreed to have the joint cleaned, which the Huros wasn't able to do, so that's why we sent Thorn and an astronaut up. Except that the manipulator hadn't turned itself off after all. It had just temporarily fallen into a kind of electro-coma. Suddenly, it woke up and hurled Thorn into space, and it seems his life-support systems were damaged in the process. We lost contact with him.'

'How awful,' whispered Aileen, ashen.

'Well.' Haskin went silent for a moment. 'He probably wouldn't have suffered for long. It's possible that his visor took a lot of the damage.'

'Probably? So you didn't manage to . . . ?'

'Unfortunately not.'

'I always thought you could just dash out after them.' Aileen spread out the thumb and fingers on her right hand to make the shape of aeroplane wings and glided it through the air. 'Like in the movies.'

'Well sure, in the movies,' said Haskin deprecatingly.

'But we should also mention that the new generation of the Huros series would probably have been able to save him,' said Lynn. 'And the spacesuits' remote control has been developed further too. With that, we could at least have got Thorn back.'

'If I remember rightly,' said Evelyn, 'there was an investigation.'

'That's right.' Lynn nodded. 'Which resulted in a case being brought against a Japanese robotics company. They built the manipulator. Clearly it was a case of third-party negligence. Thorn's death was a tragedy, but the operators of the OSS, that is to say, we, were cleared of any responsibility.'

'Thanks, Lynn.' Evelyn looked around at the others. 'That's enough of an explanation for me. Don't you think?'

'Pioneers have to make sacrifices,' grumbled Donoghue. 'The early bird catches the worm, but sometimes he gets eaten by it.'

'Let's look around a little more though,' said Ögi.

'You're not convinced?' asked Lynn.

He hesitated.

'Yes, I think I am.'

And that was it! A barely noticeable twitch in the corner of her mouth, the meltdown of panic in Lynn's gaze as . . .

. . . she feels the pull, just as she had when she was being dragged down into the abyss, and she wonders with horror what she's let herself in for. It started weeks ago: she keeps thinking she saw weaknesses in her work where there definitely weren't any. She's willing to swear an oath that Julian's space station will survive longer than all of foolish mankind put together, but she can't help herself picturing something exploding or falling apart, and only in the lower section. And why?

Because this section is the only one that *she*, not Julian, designed, the only one that was *her* responsibility!

And yet the same designers have been working there; the same architects, engineers, construction teams. There are barely any differences between the modules in her station and the others: identical life-support systems, the same method of construction. And yet Lynn is relentlessly tormented by the idea that they might be faulty. The more Julian praises her work, the more the self-doubt eats into her thoughts. She imagines the worst incessantly. Her otherwise commendable caution has been growing into a paranoia of constant mistrust; she searches obsessively for evidence of her failure, and the less she finds, the more nervous she becomes. The OSS Grand has ballooned into a monster of her arrogance, one that will burst like a bubble, condemning dozens of people to their deaths. Cold riveting, strutting, insulation, electrolysis devices, circulation pumps, airlocks, corridors: in all of it, all she sees is the reflection of her own failings. Just the mere *thought* of the hotel in space and the one on the Moon causes her overwrought brain to erode under the onslaught of adrenalin and cortisol. If, according to theological understanding, fear is the opposite of faith, the separation from the sacred, then Lynn has become the very definition of a heathen. The fear of destroying. The fear of being destroyed. They're one and the same.

At some point in the depths of her despair, the devil has infiltrated her thoughts and whispered to her that the fear of the abyss can only be overcome by entering it there and then. How do you escape the cycle of fear that something horrific *could* happen? How can you find a way out before you completely lose your mind? How can you free yourself?

By it *happening!*

The question, of course, remains what will become of her if her work proves to be transitory. Is she just one of Julian's inventions, a character in a film? What if Julian stops *thinking* her, because she proved herself unworthy of being thought? Will she be condemned to perpetual suffering? Eternal damnation? Disappear without a whimper? Or will she have to disappear to be born again, more vividly than ever? If everything by which she defines herself and by which others define her comes to an end, will she, the real Lynn, finally resurface? If she even exists, that is?

*   *   *

'Miss Orley? Are you unwell?'

'What's wrong, dear?' Aileen's maternal falsetto tones. 'You're as white as a sheet.'

'Lynn?' Tim was next to her. The gentle pressure of his fingers on her shoulder. They slowly began to spin, a twofold sibling star.

Lynn, oh, Lynn. What have you let yourself in for?

'Hey. Lynn!' White, slender fingers stroked her forehead, violet eyes peering at her. 'Is everything okay? Have you smoked something funny?'

'I'm sorry.' She blinked. 'You caught me.'

'Caught you doing what, sweetheart?'

The smile returned to her lips. A horse that knows the way. Tim looked at her searchingly. He wanted to tell her that he knows, but he can't let himself say anything, can't ask her! Lynn pulled herself up straight, freeing herself from the suction. She's won, for now at least.

'Space sickness,' she says. 'Crazy, isn't it? I never thought it would happen to me, but I guess I was wrong. The lights just seemed to go out.'

'Then it's okay for me to admit it.' Ögi grinned. 'I'm feeling a bit queasy too.'

'You?' Heidrun stared at him. 'You're space sick?'

'I am, yes.'

'Why didn't you say anything?'

'Be grateful I didn't. The day will come when I'll have plenty of ailments. Are you feeling better now, Lynn?'

'Yes, thank you.' Lynn shrugged off Tim's hand. 'Let's plan the day ahead.'

Her brother looked at her fixedly. Sure, said his look, you're space sick. And I'm the man in the Moon.

He managed to intercept Julian as he was leaving his suite, an hour before dinner. Tim's father was wearing a fashionably cut shirt with a tie, his usual jeans and elegant slippers adorned with the emblem Mimi Kri.

'You can have a fitting with her if you like,' he said cheerfully. 'Mimi has developed a collection for stays in environments with zero gravity and reduced gravitational pull. Great, don't you think?' He spun around on his axis. 'Fibre-reinforced, so nothing can flap around. Not even the tie.'

'Julian, listen—'

'Oh, before I forget, she brought something along for Amber too. An evening dress. I wanted to surprise her with it, but you can see how much is going on at the moment. I'm not getting a moment's peace with this mob around. Everything okay, my boy?'

'No. I have to—'

'Evening clothes in zero gravity, just think!' Julian grinned. 'Isn't it crazy? Absolutely insane! You could look up all the skirts without these reinforcements. Marilyn Monroe would have stayed just a forgotten orphan, instead of standing on that airshaft with the wind gusting up from below and everything blowing up, you know.'

'No, I don't, actually.'

Julian wrinkled his forehead. He seemed to notice Tim at last, taking in his crumpled overall and flushed face, which didn't seem to bode well.

'You've probably never heard of the film, right?'

'Father, I don't give a toss whose skirt is flying up. Try taking care of your daughter for a change, will you?'

'I do. And have done ever since she was born, to be precise.'

'Lynn isn't well.'

'Oh, that.' Julian looked at the time. 'Yes, she told me. Are you coming along to Kirk with me?'

'Told you about what?' asked Tim, confused.

'That she got space sick.' Julian laughed. 'Although she never has been till now. That would annoy me too!'

'No, wait.' Tim shook his head impatiently. 'You don't understand. Lynn isn't space sick.'

'So what is it then?'

'She's overstretched. On the brink of a nervous breakdown.'

'I can understand that you're concerned, but . . .'

'She shouldn't even be here, Dad! She's falling apart. For God's sake, how often do I need to tell you? Lynn is at the end of her tether. She won't make it. She's never really dealt with what happened five years ago—'

'Hey!' Julian stared at him. 'Are you crazy? This is *her* hotel.'

'And . . . so what?'

'It's *her work*! Good heavens, Tim! Lynn is CEO of Orley Enterprises, she *has* to be here.'

'*Has* to! Exactly.'

'Don't start attacking me! Have I ever forced you to do anything? Did I ever stop you from becoming a teacher and going into your shitty community politics, even though all the doors were open for you at Orley?'

'That's not what this is about.'

'It never is, right? Nor is it ever about the fact that your sister is more successful than you and that, secretly, it annoys the hell out of you.'

'Oh, really?'

'Too right. Lynn has no problems whatsoever. But you do! You try to make her out to be weak because you haven't sorted yourself out.'

'That has to be the most ridiculous nonsense I've ever—' Tim forced himself to calm down and lower his voice. 'As far as I'm concerned you can believe what you like, I don't care. Just look out for her! Don't you remember what happened five years ago?'

'Of course I do. She was exhausted back then. If you had her workload, you'd—'

'No, Julian, she wasn't exhausted. She was burnt out. She was ill, psychologically ill, will you ever get that into your head? Severe depression! A suicide risk!'

Julian looked around as if the walls had ears.

'Now listen to me, Tim,' he whispered. 'Lynn worked hard for all of this. People admire and adore her. This is her *big moment*. I won't allow you to mess everything up for her just because you're seeing ghosts everywhere.'

'God, you don't have a clue what's going on, it's unbelievable! So stupid!'

'No, you're the one who's stupid. Why did you even come?'

'To look after her.'

'Oh.' Julian let out a mocking laugh. 'And I thought it might have had something to do with me, just a tiny bit. My apologies for the descent into sentimentality. I'll speak with her, okay? I'll tell her what a great job she did of everything, that it's perfect, that everyone thinks she's wonderful. Okay?'

Tim stayed silent as Julian, clearly annoyed, floated off towards the airlock. O'Keefe was approaching from the other side.

'Hey, Tim.'

'Finn. All good?'

'Great, thanks. Are you coming to Picard for a drink?'

'No, I'll see you later at dinner.' Tim thought for a moment. 'I need something fibre-reinforced. A fibre-reinforced tie. You can't do anything around here without fibre reinforcement.'

The Soirée

The man with the multicoloured eyes was very interested in the art of cooking steaks 36,000 kilometres above the Earth, so that they were sizzling and brown on the outside and pink on the inside, and all without a single drop of meat juices running out.

And he wanted to know what it was that drew mankind to the Moon.

'Life,' said Julian. 'If we find it there, it will fundamentally change our view of the world. I thought you of all people were fascinated by the idea.'

'And I am. So what do the experts say? Is there life on Mars?'

'Of course,' Julian grinned. 'Spiders.'

'Spiders from Mars.' He grinned back. 'You could do something with that.'

A large number of people from the group, on the other hand, were interested in the man with the multicoloured eyes. Walo Ögi, his greatest admirer, was unfortunately being subjected to a discussion about the economy by Bernard Tautou and Oleg Rogachev, whilst Miranda and Rebecca were deep in discussion, in unfathomable harmony with

Momoka Omura, about the therapeutic effect of luxury on Seasonal Affective Disorder. Warren Locatelli was absent. Like Paulette Tautou, he had fallen victim to the combined forces of nervus vagus and diverse neurotransmitters, which, via the area of his brainstem known as the nausea centre, had led to the torrential emptying of his stomach.

This aside, it was a wonderful dinner.

The lights had been dimmed, allowing the Earth to shine through the glass floor like a huge Chinese lantern. For the first and only time, there was alcohol: champagne from slender goblets topped with sucking teats. Just like the previous evening, the food was of astonishing quality. Julian had flown in a highly decorated Michelin-starred chef for the duration of the trip, a German from Swabia called Johannes King, who had immediately subjected the kitchen to a three-hundred-per-cent increase in efficiency, conjuring up amazing culinary feats such as truffle-infused creamed vegetables, with genuine Périgord truffles, of course, a dish that had gone through endless tests to ensure it could cope with the perils of zero gravity.

'Because, obviously, sauce, or anything liquid or creamy, develops a life of its own in zero gravity.' The chef was just finishing his round of the table. He was an exuberant, lively character with great coordination, and seemed to take to weightlessness like a fish to water. 'Unless its consistency is created in such a way that it sticks to the fish or vegetables. But if it's too concentrated it will impair the taste, so it's a real balancing act.'

Tautou suggested that the *Guide Michelin* should be extended with a chapter on 'Non-Terrestrial Regions'. What could be more apt than awarding their stars *up here*? But he didn't have the effrontery to pour this thin analogy into each person's ear; his enthusiasm for it would gradually tire as the game terrine with cranberries, fillet steaks, potato gratin and an unctuous tiramisu were passed around, one after the other.

'And no garlic, no beans, or anything that causes wind! Escaping bodily gases are a real problem in close conditions like these; people have become violent for far less. Also, what you're eating here would seem over-seasoned on Earth, but in space your taste buds are weakened, on the back burner so to speak. Oh, yes, and make sure you eat nice and slowly. Pick up every bite carefully, lead it to your mouth with intent, put it in quickly and decisively, then chew carefully.'

'Well, the steaks were works of God, anyway!' said Donoghue approvingly.

'Thank you.' King made a bow, which resulted in him tipping over and doing a somersault. 'In actual fact they were sterile synthetic products from the molecular kitchen. We're incredibly proud of them, if I may say so.'

For the next ten minutes, Donoghue fell silent, in a state of deep contemplation.

O'Keefe suckled at the champagne.

He made an effort to maintain his peeved expression. He had noted happily that Heidrun was seated next to him, or rather that her legs were wedged into the braces provided for that purpose. As much as it pleased him, though, he was punishing her with his lack of attention, chatting pointedly with the surprise guest. For her part, she made no attempt to speak to him. It was only once the group began to compare their experiences of the day and the general conversation broke up into individual exchanges that he finally deigned to address her with a hissed remark:

'What the hell were you thinking of this morning?'

She hesitated. 'What are you talking about?'

'Shoving me out of the airlock.'

'Oh.' Heidrun fell silent for a while. 'I get it. You're angry.'

'No, but I'm wondering whether you've taken leave of your senses. That was pretty dangerous.'

'Nonsense, Finn. I may act like a big kid sometimes, but I'm not crazy. Nina had already told me yesterday that the suits were remote-controlled. Do you seriously think they would leave all-inclusive holidaymakers, people whose greatest sporting achievement was getting a badge for swimming two hundred metres, to their own devices out there?'

'So you didn't want to kill me? That's comforting.'

Heidrun smiled mysteriously. 'Sweetheart, I just wanted to find out where Perry Rhodan stops and Finn O'Keefe begins.'

'And?'

'Well, it's quite fitting that you play him as a bit of a dope.'

'Now hang on a minute!' protested O'Keefe. 'A heroic dope.'

'Yes, of course. And it never took you long to work out whether there were any females in the vicinity who might be willing to mate with you. Pleased with yourself?'

He grinned. As he paused, he heard Eva Borelius say: 'But that's not a theological question, Mimi, it's about the origins of our civilisation. Why do people want to cross borders, what are they looking for in space? I sometimes feel inclined to join in the chorus of anger clamouring about the trillions of people who are starving, who have no access to fresh water—'

'By now, sure,' he heard Tautou exclaim from another conversation, only to be put back in his place by a pistol-shot retort of 'No, you haven't!' from Karla Kramp.

'—while all the fun up here devours vast amounts of money. And yet we *have* to research. Our entire culture is based upon exchange and expansion. At the end of the day, what we're looking for in the unknown is ourselves, our meaning, our future, just like Alexander von Humboldt, like Stephen Hawking—'

'I wouldn't be here if I had anything against the spread of the human race,' said Mimi Parker sharply.

'Well, it sure sounded like it just then.'

'No, not at all! I'm just contesting the bigoted desire to discover something that's already obvious. I, for my part, am just here to marvel at His work.'

'Which, according to you, is six thousand years old.'

'Well, it could be ten thousand. Let's say up to ten thousand – after all, we're not dogmatists.'

'But no more than that? Not at least a few little million?'

'Absolutely not. What I expect to find out here—'

Aha, thought O'Keefe. I knew it. *Created in our own image, just as the boss did it six thousand years ago.* Mimi was here to represent the creationists.

'And what do *you* expect to find here?' he asked Heidrun, who was laughing at something Carl Hanna had just said.

'Me?' She turned her head. Her long white ponytail swung softly behind her. 'I'm not here to expect anything.'

'Then why?'

'Because my husband was invited. Whenever that happens, people get me too, whether they like it or not.'

'Okay, fine, but now you're here?'

'Hmm. Regardless. I don't set much store by expectations. Expectations blind people. I prefer to be surprised. And so far it's working out great, in any case.' She hesitated and leaned in a little closer. 'And you?'

'Nothing. I'm just doing my job.'

'I don't understand.'

'What is there to understand? I'm here to do my job, and that's it.'

'Your – job?'

'Yes.'

'You mean you're just letting yourself be used by Julian?'

'That's why I'm here.'

'Good God, Finn.' Heidrun shook her head slowly, in disbelief. He suddenly felt embarrassed, getting the feeling he'd pressed the wrong button. 'You're such a jerk! Every time I'm just starting to like you—'

'Why? What have I done this time?'

'This detachment act of yours! Nothing affects you, right? Hat pulled down over your face, standing aside from the rest. That's exactly what I meant before: Who is O'Keefe?'

'He's sitting right in front of you.'

'Bullshit! You just have this vague notion of who O'Keefe is supposed be, if he wants to make everyone think he's really cool. A rebel, whose problem is that he doesn't actually have anything to rebel against, except boredom perhaps.'

'Hey!' He leaned forward. 'What in God's name gives you the idea I'm like that?'

'This stupid attitude.'

'You said yourself that—'

'I said that I didn't have any expectations, which means I'm open to everything. That's quite a lot to be going on with. You, on the other hand, made out that it was nothing more than a job to you. That you're just buying into the story that Julian's lovely and the Moon is round, and then we'll all hold hands until the cameras get turned off and we can finally go and get pissed. That's lousy, Finn! Are you really that jaded? Do you really intend to tell me, in all seriousness, that you're just in it for the money Julian's throwing your way?'

'Nonsense. I'm not getting paid for it.'

'Okay then, last chance: What are you doing up here? What do you feel when you – well, when you look down at the Earth?'

O'Keefe paused as he gave it some thought. He stared intently through the glass floor below. The problem was, he couldn't think of a convincing answer. The Earth was the Earth.

'Distance,' he said finally.

'Distance.' She seemed to be tasting the word. 'And? Good distance? Bad distance?'

'Oh, Heidrun. Call it attitude if you really want to, but I just want to be left in peace. You think I'm some bored, arrogant type who's lost any interest in getting into a debate. Maybe you're right. Today I'm soft and compliant, the nice Finn. What are you expecting?'

'I don't know. What are *you* expecting?'

'Why are you so interested? We hardly know each other.'

'Because I was – still am – interested in you.'

'Well, I don't know. All I know is that there are directors who make wonderful films on minuscule budgets, against all the odds. Other people play music no one wants to listen to, apart from a few crazy types perhaps, but they're unwavering in what they do, they would die for it. Some people can barely afford the hooch that keeps them writing, but if you happen to stumble upon something of theirs online and download it, you're strangely moved by how humanity and unmarketability seem to come together, and it makes you realise that great emotions always originate in the small, the intimate, the desperate. As soon as an orchestra gets involved, it turns to pathos. If you look at it that way, even the most beautiful woman would be no match for the lousiest hooker. No luxury can give you such a feeling of being alive as getting plastered with the right people, or touching your broken nose when you've picked a fight with the wrong ones. I stay in the best hotels in the world, but being in a mouldy back room with someone who has a dream, in some neighbourhood no sensible person would go of their own accord, well, that moves me much more than flying to the Moon.'

Heidrun thought for a moment.

'It's lovely when you can afford to romanticise poverty,' she commented.

'I know what you mean. But that's not what I'm doing. I don't come from a poor background. I don't have a message, I'm not fuelled by anger at society, I haven't been sent up here by some political party or other. Perhaps that means I'm not committed enough, but it really doesn't seem that way to me. We have a good time when we film *Perry Rhodan*, that's for sure. I'm not about to turn down the money, either. And, recently, I've even started to enjoy being a nice guy, a *rich* nice guy who can fly to the Moon for free. I see all that and think, hey look, that's little Finn. Then I meet women who want to be with me because they think I'm part of their life. Which is true, to some extent. I accompany them through this little, or, as far as I'm concerned, great life, I'm with them the whole time, in the cinema, in magazines, on the internet, in pictures. At night, when they lie awake, they entrust their secrets to me. During times of crisis in their lives, my films are *important* to them. They read interviews with me and after every second sentence they think: Wow, he understands me! He knows exactly what I'm about! Then when they meet me they're convinced they're standing there with a friend, a kindred spirit. They think they know me, but I don't know them. I mean everything to them, but they don't mean anything to me, not in the slightest. Just because my picture was hanging on their wall when they had their first orgasm, just because they may have been thinking about me, it doesn't mean I was there. They're not part of my life. There's no connection between us.' He paused. 'And now tell me, what was it like when you first met Walo? What did you think? Oh, man, interesting, someone I don't know. Who is he, I have to find out. Is that how it was?'

'Yes, pretty much.'

'And he thought the same. You see. The magic of the first impression. I, on the other hand, meet strangers labouring under the delusion that they *know* me. In order to completely let go of this life I would have to stop taking part in it, but it's just too much fun. So I sing and dance along but I keep my distance.'

'Well, that's fame,' said Heidrun. It didn't sound mocking this time, more as if she was surprised by his list of banalities. But that's exactly how things were. Banal. On the whole, there was nothing more banal than fame.

'Yes' he said. 'It sure is.'

'So we haven't managed to come up with anything more original than what the doctor just said. Everyone's looking for themselves in the unknown.'

He hesitated. Then he smiled his famous, shy smile.

'Perhaps we're looking for our soulmates.'

Heidrun's violet eyes lingered on his, but she didn't answer. They looked at each other, entangled in a strange, cocoon-like mood which excited O'Keefe as much as it unsettled him. He felt a twinge of awkwardness. It looked as though he was about to fall head over heels for a cumulative lack of melanin.

He jumped, almost relieved, as Julian clapped his hands.

'Dear friends, I didn't dare hope.'

Silence fell.

'And I swear I didn't ask him to. I merely suggested keeping a guitar handy, *just in case*! And now he's even brought his own along.'

Julian smiled around at them. His gaze wandered over to the man with the multicoloured eyes.

'Back in '69, when I had just turned three years old, he went to the movies and saw *A Space Odyssey*, which would later become my favourite film, and paid immediate tribute to its maker. Almost a quarter of a century later I had my own opportunity to honour Kubrick, modelling my first restaurant on the design of his space station, and I called it Oddity, in honour of the great artist we have with us here. Kubrick lived in Childwickbury Manor at the time, the estate near London that he hardly ever left. He also hated aeroplanes. I suspect that once he moved to the United Kingdom from New York he never put any more than a hop, skip and a jump between himself and English soil. And he was said to be very shy, so I never expected to see *him* in Oddity. But to my surprise, he turned up there one evening, when David was sitting at the bar too. We all talked, and I ended up blurting out the fact that I wanted to take them both to the Moon with me, that all they had to do was say yes and we'd be on our way. Kubrick laughed and said the lack of comfort alone would horrify him. He thought the whole thing was a joke of course. I had the presumption to claim that, by the turn of the millennium, I would have built a spaceship with all comforts and mod cons, of course without the slightest idea of how I would go about achieving such a thing. I had just turned twenty-six, was producing films, more bad ones than good, and was trying my hand at being an actor. I'd brought a new production of Fritz Lang's *Woman in the Moon* to the big screen with David in the lead role, was winning favour with the critics and public alike, and was also just starting to feel my way in the field of gastronomy. Orley Enterprises was still very much in the distant future. I was, however, a passionate flyer and dreamed of the space travel that also fascinated Kubrick. So I finally managed to talk him and David into a bet: *if* I succeeded in building the promised spaceship by the year 2000, the two of them *had* to come on the flight. If not, I would finance one hundred per cent of Kubrick's next film and David's forthcoming album.'

Julian ran his fingers through his beard, transported back to the past.

'Unfortunately, Stanley died before that could happen, and my life changed fundamentally after that evening. I only produce films as a sideline now. Orley Travel was born in a small travel bureau in Soho which I took over at the beginning of the nineties. I owned two airlines and bought an abandoned studio complex to work on the development of space vessels and space stations. With the foundation of Orley Space we pushed into the technology market. Some of the best brains from NASA and ESA worked for us, experts from Russia, Asia and India, engineers from Germany: because we paid higher salaries, created better research conditions, and were more enthusiastic, speedy and efficient than their old employers. By then, no one doubted that state space travel was in urgent need of some live-cell therapy from the private market, but I had set myself the goal of actually taking its place! I wanted to usher in the dawn of the *true* space era, without the hesitancy of the bureaucrats, the chronic lack of money and the dependence on political change. We offered prize money for young designers, had them develop rocket-propelled aircraft, and expanded our tourism range to sub-orbital flights. I've flown machines like that myself many times. And maybe it wasn't yet a proper space flight, but it was a brilliant beginning. Everyone wanted to come! Space tourism promised astronomic yield, that is if we could succeed in reducing the start-up costs.' He laughed softly. 'Well, in spite of that I lost the bet initially. I didn't make it by the year 2000. So I offered to settle my debt with David. But he didn't want me to. All he said was: Keep your money and send me the ticket when it's ready. The only thing I can say today is that his presence on the OSS is a great honour and makes me deeply happy. And whatever one could add about his greatness, his importance to our culture and the lease of life he has given to so many generations, his music can express that much better than I ever could. So now I'll shut up and hand over to – Major Tom.'

The silence that followed was almost sacred. A guitar was passed along. The lights had been dimmed further still during Julian's speech and the Pacific was shimmering as if it had just been polished. Through the oval side window, scattered sugar glowed against a black backdrop.

Looking back later, O'Keefe saw those seconds when David Bowie launched into the opening chords of 'Space Oddity' – alternating between Fmaj7 and Em, soft and muted at first, then swelling powerfully, as if one were nearing the bustle of activity around the launch pad from the indifferent silence of space, right up to the moment when ground control and Major Tom enter into their memorable dialogue – as what may have been the last, and perhaps the *only* really harmonious moment of their journey. In his naïve happiness he forgot what Orley's venture was really about: catapulting people from the globe into a hostile environment, onto a satellite which, despite having spiritualised its previous visitors, had not yet made a single one of them want to return. He was keenly aware that every search for meaning which involved leaving the Earth would only culminate in his looking round at it at every opportunity, and he suddenly pictured himself getting so far away from it that it was completely out of sight, wretched and flooded with fear.

And the stars look very different today—

And when Tom's ballad finally came to an end, and the unlucky Major had been lost to the void of his inflated expectations, he felt, instead of the enchantment he had hoped for, a strange kind of disillusionment, almost like homesickness, although they were *only* 36,000 kilometres away from home. The right-hand side of the planet had begun to darken. He saw Heidrun inhale the moment with her lips half open, her gaze alternating between Bowie and the sea of stars on the other side of the window, while his was drawn over to her as if by magic. He realised that the Swiss woman had arrived in herself a long time ago, that she would happily travel to the very edge of the universe, because she carried her home in and with her, that she had certainly reached a much higher level of freedom than him, and he found himself wishing he were upstairs above some Dublin pub, being held in someone's arms on a threadbare mattress.

It seems quite a few people had the same idea that night.

Perhaps it was the way Amber had comforted him as he'd cried on her shoulder about Julian's ignorance that had stimulated Tim physically as well as emotionally; perhaps it was her kisses, the tautness in her arms, the springy elasticity she'd acquired in the gym; perhaps it was because, after so many years of mundane married life, his fantasies still revolved exclusively around his wife to the extent that he wanted to caress no other behind but hers, glide his hand into no other delta but hers – which meant he was about as suited to infidelity as a steam engine was to leaving the tracks – and even in those moments when he was pleasuring himself, he wanted to imagine no one but her; perhaps it was because her divine looks had not been tainted by the passing of the years – praise to the genes! – and because the buoyancy of zero gravity had returned her breasts to that legendary state which, at the beginning of their relationship, had made him feel as though he were grasping ripe melons; perhaps it was the way his attempt to fumble apart the clasps on her bathrobe had resulted in his being propelled into the opposite corner of the module, which had only turned him on all the more, as she lay there laughing amongst the swinging folds of the open robe, like an angel ready to sin – but whatever the reason was, his body was defying all the adversity of zero gravity, the low supply of blood to the lumbar region, the disorientation and light sense of nausea, by producing a true space rocket of an erection.

He paddled over and grasped hold of her shoulders. Peeling her out of her bathrobe was one thing, but Amber's attempt to free him from his trousers and T-shirt failed as they drifted apart, which they did again and again until he ended up wriggling naked above the bed, heading helplessly for the ceiling. She looked at his galactic erection with visible interest, as helpless as she was amused.

'So what do we do with that now?' she laughed.

'There must be a way.' He was determined. 'People must have thought about this.'

'Hopefully. It'd be a shame if they hadn't.'

Tim did a handstand and ploughed over to her. This time, he managed to get a grip on her hips and buried his head between her legs, which she spread and then immediately closed again to keep his head in place. As a result, the blood rushed to his ears. Circling his tongue, he pressed ahead, capturing the tiny mound beneath the small forest, the density of which threatened to take his breath away as he pressed his nose inside her out of fear of ending up at the other end of the room again, becoming intoxicated by the blend of their lust and countering her first, blissful sighs – provided that his ears, packed tightly between her thighs, weren't deceiving him – with muffled agreement. An overdose of oxygen seemed to mingle with the cabin air – or was it the lack of oxygen that suddenly made him feel as high as a schoolboy? Who cared! Joyfully exhilarated, he made his way deeper inside, panting, grunting, the tip of his tongue flying dedicatedly around. At the moment when the tropical dampness of deep-lying realms opened up to him, believing he heard a declaration of love burst forth, he couldn't hold back and mumbled a 'Me too, oh, me too', but got a puzzling response.

'Ow! Ouch!'

Something had clearly gone wrong. Tim looked up. In doing so, he made the mistake of loosening his grip. Amber flailed around as if she were drowning, kicking him from her. Pushed away, he saw that she was rubbing her head, and that it was in the immediate vicinity of the edge of the desk. Aha. He should have thought of that, that they would drift away in the heat of the moment. Lesson number one: it wasn't enough to clasp on to each other, they needed to fix themselves within the room too. He couldn't help but laugh. Amber wrinkled her nose and frowned, then his gaze fell on something that could offer a solution.

'Look!'

'What?' She dug the fingers of her right hand into his hair and tried to bite his nose, which resulted in her doing a somersault. Tim hopped over to the bed like a frog, pulling Amber, still head over heels, along with him.

'Buckling ourselves in?' she snorted mockingly. 'How unerotic. It'd be like doing it in a car. We'll hardly be able to move—'

'No, silly, not with the sleeping belt. Look!'

Amber's expression brightened. Above the bed were some handles, mounted a little distance apart from one another.

'Wait. I think I saw something that might go with them.'

She hurried over to the cupboard, opened it, rummaged around and unearthed several long bands made from a rubber-like material. They had a red, yellow and green pattern and were adorned with a slogan.

'Love Belt,' she read.

'So there you go,' grinned Tim. 'People did think about it.' For the first time since they'd set off on the journey, he felt carefree and playful, a sensation which just an hour ago he had thought was gone for good. Lynn didn't become entirely insignificant, of course, but just retreated to an insignificant province of his cortex, one that wasn't attending to Amber's scent and the throbbing desire to fuck her. 'It looks like we have to fasten you by the wrists, my darling. No, by the hands and feet. Like in the torture chambers of the Holy Inquisition.'

She started to thread the bands through the handles.

'I think you misunderstood,' she said. 'You're the one getting tied up.'

'Now just a minute! We need to talk about this first.'

'Do you think he wants to talk about it?' she asked, gesturing her head at his royal member. 'I think he wants to do something else, and very quickly too.'

One after the other, she knotted the rubber bands around his wrists and, giggling and snorting, made her way down to fasten his feet, until he was hung in the middle of the room with his extremities stretched out. He wriggled his knees and elbows with curiosity, noticing that the bands were highly elasticated. He could move around, and generously too. It was just stopping him from flying away.

'Do you think this was Julian's idea?' he asked.

'I'd be willing to bet on it.' Amber hovered towards him as if she were on a control beam, clasped his shoulders and slung her legs around his hips. For a moment, her sex balanced on his, like a trapeze artist on the nose of a sea lion.

'In my opinion, sexual positions are the most demanding manoeuvres in the world,' she whispered as she pressed herself against him, lowered herself and drew him inside her.

Seemingly quite a few people had the same idea, but only a few managed to put it into action. Eva Borelius and Karla Kramp also found the straps and figured out what to do with them, as did Mimi Parker and Marc Edwards. However, Edwards found the redistribution of over half a litre of blood from the lower to upper bodily regions a little harder to handle than Tim had, whilst Paulette Tautou would most likely have held Bernard's head down the now-so-familiar toilet bowl if he had come near her with any intentions of that sort.

Wisely, Tautou did no such thing. Instead, in consideration of Paulette's miserable condition, he decided that they should embark on the journey home.

Suite 12 was the scene of similar suffering, the only difference being that Locatelli would never have capitulated to something as mundane as space sickness. Peaceful silence reigned in Suite 38, where the Ögis lay snuggled up to one another like fieldmice in winter. One floor above, Sushma and Mukesh Nair were peacefully enjoying the sight of night falling over the Isla de las Estrellas. In Suite 17, Aileen Donoghue had put in her earplugs, allowing Chuck to snore at the top of his lungs.

On the opposite side of the torus, Oleg Rogachev was staring out of the window while Olympiada Rogacheva stared straight ahead.

'Do you know what I'd like to know?' she murmured after a while.

He shook his head.

'How someone ends up like Miranda Winter.'

'You don't end up like that,' he said, without turning round. 'You're born like it.'

'I don't mean the way she looks,' snorted Olympiada. 'I'm not stupid. I just want to know how someone gets to be so impregnable. So completely pain-free. It's as if she's a walking immune system against every kind of problem, she's like nonchalance personified – I mean, seriously, she's even given names to her breasts!'

Rogachev turned his head slowly.

'No one's stopping you from doing the same.'

'Perhaps a certain amount of it is down to stupidity,' ruminated Olympiada, as if she hadn't heard him. 'You know, I really do believe that Miranda is quite dumb. Oh, what am I saying, she hasn't got two brain cells to rub together. I have no doubt that she's lacking any kind of education, but perhaps that's an advantage. Perhaps it's good to be stupid, desirable even. Dumb and naïve and a little bit calculating. You feel less that way. Miranda loves only herself, whereas it seems to me that every single day I'm pouring all my feelings, all my strength into a vase that's full of holes. Your meanness would be wasted on someone like Miranda, Oleg, like a pinprick in blubber.'

'I'm not mean to you.'

'Oh, no?'

'No. I'm just uninterested. You can't hurt someone you have no interest in.'

'And you suppose that's not mean?'

'It's the truth.' Rogachev glanced at her for a second. Olympiada had burrowed into her sleeping bag and was now belted in and safely out of reach. For a moment he wondered what it might be like if the sack burst open the next morning to reveal a butterfly, an astonishing feat for his rather retarded imagination. But Olympiada wasn't a caterpillar, and he had no intention of weaving her into a cocoon. 'Our marriage was a strategic move. I knew it, your father knew it, and you knew it too. So please stop torturing yourself.'

'One day you'll fall, Oleg,' she hissed. 'You'll end up like a rat. A damn rat in the gutter.'

Rogachev turned to gaze again out of the window, strangely unmoved by the planet darkening below him.

'Just get on with it and take a lover,' he said tonelessly.

Miranda Winter had no intention of heading off to bed any time soon, much to the joy of Rebecca Hsu, who suffered from her inability to cope with being alone. Except that she was alone. A poor, rich woman, as she went to great pains to convince herself, twice divorced, with three daughters of whom she saw shamefully little. A woman who hung around in the company of others until even the last few closed their eyes, after which she would make calls across all the time zones thanks to the world-spanning structure of her group of companies, until even she lost the fight against tiredness. The whole day through, whenever their strictly organised schedule allowed, she had been discussing marketing plans by phone, debating campaign strategies, deliberating purchases, sales and shares. Keeping an eye on her empire: a control freak who was tormented by the thought that she'd driven husbands and daughters away with her manic working habits.

At least she could discuss the lack of husbands with Miranda without falling head first into melancholy afterwards. Besides, some of the beakers of Moët et Chandon had miraculously turned up in Miranda's cabin, which particularly pleased Rebecca, since she had owned the brand for some time now.

Finn O'Keefe didn't know what to think or feel, so he listened to music for a while then fell asleep.

Evelyn Chambers lay awake – if it could be called lying, that is.

She didn't feel the slightest inclination to buckle herself onto the bed like some raving lunatic. She had discovered the rubber bands by chance and anchored herself to the handles near the front of the window, hoping to enjoy the sensation of zero gravity in her sleep too. But when she closed her eyes her body seemed to speed up as if it were on a roller-coaster, trying to loop the loop, and she started to feel sick.

She reached up to free her shackled ankles from the bands, which was no easy task. It was only then that she noticed the inscription: *Love Belt*. Suddenly realising what they were really intended for, a wave of regret washed over her at not being able to appropriately crown the extravagant experience of zero gravity. Intrigued, she wondered whether the others were doing it, and then – rather boldly – whom *she* might be able to do it with! Her thoughts darted from Miranda Winter to Heidrun Ögi and then back again, based on the fact that Heidrun wasn't available, although admittedly neither was Miranda, if only due to lack of inclination.

Rebecca Hsu? Oh, for heaven's sake!

Her desire subsided as quickly as it had risen. And yet she had been so adamant, after her bisexuality had cost her the role of governor, that she was going to enjoy herself properly now. She was still America's most popular and influential chat-show host. In the wake of her polit-ical Waterloo she no longer felt bound to any conservative code. What had remained of her marriage barely justified professing monogamy, especially as her so-called husband was pouring their joint money into his constantly changing acquaintances. Not that that bothered her. Their love had gone down the drain years ago, but she didn't want to go to bed with anyone and everyone, even if she was consumed by lust.

Although perhaps in exceptional circumstances—

Finn O'Keefe. It was worth a try. It would certainly be fun to snare him of all people, but the thought quickly soured.

Julian?

He clearly loved flirting with her. But on the other hand Julian's job meant he flirted with everyone. Still. He was unattached, apart from the affair with Nina Hedegaard, if they were even still having one and it wasn't just her reading too much into it. If she yielded to Julian's advances there would be little danger of hurting anyone else, and they would have fun, she was sure of that. Perhaps something more might even come out of it. And if not, that was fine too.

On the spur of the moment, she dialled the number of his suite.

But no one answered, the screen stayed dark. Feeling foolish all of a sudden, like a sparrow pecking around beneath restaurant tables for food from other people's plates, she crawled hurriedly into her sleeping bag.

'You had them hanging on your every word.'

'But I wasn't even the first.'

Julian raised his eyebrows.

'2013,' said Bowie. 'Chris Hadfield – this ISS astronaut. He was the first person in the world to sing "Space Oddity" in space.'

'Correct, and it wasn't bad at all. But you're the original. You *had* to come up here and sing it!'

Bowie smiled. 'Obviously.'

'And you're quite sure?'

'*Quite* sure.'

'Tautou told me that Madame wants them to come back to earth together. We would have room.' Julian sucked at his bottle. 'Oh, nonsense, forget the Tautous! We'd have room even if they did come. I've always got room for you.'

They were the only ones left in the dimly lit Picard, sucking at their alcohol-free cocktails. Bowie rolled the bottle between his fingers thoughtfully.

'Thanks, Julian. But I'll pass.'

'But why? It's your chance to go to the Moon. You're the star man, you're that guy in *The Man Who Fell to Earth*, you're Ziggy Stardust! Who, if not you? You *have* to go to the Moon.'

'Well, for a start I'm seventy-eight years old.'

'And? You can't tell. You once said you wanted to live to be three hundred. Compared to that you're still a kid.'

Bowie laughed.

'So?' he said, changing the subject. 'Are you going to get the money together for a second lift?'

'Of course,' boomed Julian. 'Shall we bet on it?'

'No more bets. What's going on with the Chinese anyway? I heard they're pestering you with offers.'

'Officially they're doing nothing of the sort, but between ourselves they're kowtowing like mad. Does the name Zheng Pang-Wang mean anything to you?'

'Not off the top of my head.'

'The Zheng Group.'

'Ah!' Bowie wrinkled his brow. 'Yes, I think it does actually. They're a technology company too, right?'

'Zheng is the driving force behind Beijing's space travel. An entrepreneur, bound to the Party, which amounts to the same thing. He never misses a single opportunity to infiltrate my ranks, but I've got my defences up, so he tries to do it by plotting. Obviously the Chinese would love to woo me away and have me all to themselves. They've got money, more than the Americans, but they don't have the patents for the lift, or the brainpower to build fusion reactors that don't immediately shut themselves down again. A few weeks ago I met old Pang-Wang in Paris. A nice guy really. He tried to tempt me with Chinese money, and appealed to my cosmopolitan heart by saying that a clean energy supply would be of benefit to the whole world. He asked whether I didn't think it was indecent that all the money from helium-3 was going to the Americans. So I asked him what the Chinese would think of it if I went on to sell the patents to the Russians, Indians, Germans, French, Japanese and Arabs.'

'I'd be more interested to know what the Americans would think of that.'

'The question is actually a little different: Who has the whip hand? In my opinion, I do, but of course I would create completely new geopolitical relationships. And do I want that? For the most part, I've had a kind of symbiotic relationship with America, to our mutual advantage. Recently, since the Moon crisis, Washington has been haunted by the ghosts of the Little Depression of 2008 to 2010. They're worried things might get out of hand if they give that much power to one single company. Which is ridiculous: *I gave them the power!* The power to stake out their claim up there. Using my means, my know-how! But it seems the desire to have more control over companies is rampant.' Julian snorted. 'Instead of which the governments should be putting their energies into infrastructure, healthcare and education. They should be building streets, schools, houses, old people's homes, but the private economy even has to help them out with that, so what do they have to crow about? Governments have proved incapable of pushing forward global processes, they only know how to squabble, hesitate and make lazy compromises. They didn't manage to get to grips with environmental protection in that laughable treaty, they demand sanctions against corrupt and warfaring states in their shaky voices, despite the fact that no one's bothering to listen, so they just stock up on nuclear arms and impose trading blocks on each other's markets. The Russians don't have any money left for space travel now that Gazprom is hanging in the balance, but it would still be enough to give to me and the Americans for permission to use the next space elevator. Then we'd have another player on the Moon with us, and as far as I'm concerned that's a good thing.'

'But America doesn't agree.'

'Well, no, because they've got me. The fact is, together we don't need anyone else, and in a situation like that Washington thinks they can get away with anything and demand more transparency.'

'So what's your plan? Bringing the Russians over to your side without America's blessing?'

'If America doesn't want to play with them and continues to block my ideas, then yes – as you can see, I've invited some very illustrious guests. Zheng is right, but not in the way he thinks. I've had it up to here with the sponsorship failing to make headway! Competition is invigorating for business. Sure, it would be a bit shabby to run from the Americans to the Chinese now – they're all the same idiots everywhere when it comes down to it – but offering the lift to *all* nations, now that's got a ring to it.'

'And you said as much to Zheng?'

'Yes, and he thought he'd misheard. He certainly never wanted to unleash *that* kind of change in perspective, but he was overestimating his contribution. I'd had the idea for a long time already. He just made me more determined to do it.'

Bowie fell silent for a while.

'Well, I'm sure you know you're playing with fire,' he said.

'With the sun's fire,' said Julian serenely. 'With reactor fire. I'm used to fire.'

'Do your American friends know about your plans?'

'They may have an idea, to a certain extent. It's no secret whom I go trotting off to the Moon with.'

'You sure know how to make enemies.'

'I'll travel with whomever I like. It's my elevator, my space station, my hotel up there. They're far from happy about it of course, but I don't care. They should make me better offers and stop their control games.' Julian suckled noisily at his bottle and licked his lips with his tongue. 'Delicious, isn't it? On the Moon we'll have wine with an alcohol substitute. Totally insane! 1.8 per cent, but it tastes like really hard stuff. Are you sure you want to miss out on that?'

'You don't give up, do you?' Bowie laughed again.

'Never.' Julian grinned.

'But you're too late. Don't get me wrong: I love life, and it's definitely too short, I agree with all that. Three hundred years would be wonderful, especially in times like these! But it's just that I—'

'—ended up being turned from an alien into an earthling after all,' finished Julian with a smile.

'I was never anything else.'

'You were the man who fell to earth.'

'No. I was just someone who tried to get to grips with his difficulties around people by disguising himself, using the line "I'm sorry if the communication between us isn't working, I'm from Mars".' Bowie ran his fingers through his hair. 'You know, my whole life I gleefully absorbed anything that ignited the world, anything that electrified it; I collected fashions and sensitivities like other people collect art or postage stamps. Call it eclecticism, but it may have been my greatest talent. I was never really an innovator, more of a champion of the present, an architect who brought that feeling of being alive and trends together in such a way that it looked like something new. Looking back, I'd say it was my way of communicating: *Hey, people, I understand what moves you, look at me and listen up, I've made a song out of it!* Or something along those lines. But for a long time I couldn't talk to anyone about it. I simply didn't know how to do it, how a simple conversation worked. I was afraid of getting into relationships, incapable of listening to others. For someone like that, the stage, or let's say the world of the arts, is the perfect platform, it's ideally suited to giving monologues. You reach everyone, but no one reaches you. You're the messiah! A puppet of course, an idol, but for that very reason you can't let anyone get close, because then it might get out that you're actually just shy and insecure. And so, with time, you really do become an alien. You don't need to put a costume on to be one, but of course it helps. If you feel as uneasy around people as I did back then, then you just make outer space out to be your home, look for answers from a higher being, or act as though you're one yourself.'

Julian tapped his bottle, let it drift away from him for a moment then grasped it again.

'You sound so terribly grown up,' he said.

'I am terribly grown up,' laughed Bowie, bursting with happiness. 'And it's wonderful! Believe me, this whole spiritual paperchase to find out the connection between humanity and the universe, why we were born and where we go when we die, what gives us and our actions meaning, *if* there even is a meaning – I mean, I love science fiction, Julian, and I love what you've created! But all this space stuff was always just a metaphor for me. It was only ever about the spiritual search. The Churches' maps were always a little too vaguely drawn for me, full of one-way streets and dead ends. I didn't want anyone else to dictate how and where I was supposed to look. You can ritualise God, or you can interpret him. The latter doesn't go down pre-set paths; it demands that you slip away from them. I did that, and I kept on creating new spacesuits for myself in order to explore this empty, endless cosmos, hoping to meet myself, as Starman, Ziggy Stardust, Aladdin Sane, Major Tom. And then, one day, you marry a wonderful woman and move to New York, and suddenly you realise:

Out there, there's nothing, but on the Earth there's everything. You meet people, you talk, communicate, and what seemed difficult before now just happens, with wonderful ease. Your inflated fears shrink to become bog-standard worries; the early flirt with death, the pathos of 'Rock 'n' Roll Suicide' reveals itself to be nothing more than the spectacularly uno-riginal mood of a clueless and inexperienced young boy; you no longer wake up with the fear of going crazy; you no longer think obsessively about the misery of human existence, but about your children's future. And you ask yourself what the devil you were looking for in space! Do you see? I've landed. I've never enjoyed living on Earth so much, amongst other people. And if my health allows I can enjoy it for a few more years. It's bad enough that it will only be another ten or twelve, and not three hundred, so I'm looking forward to every moment. So, give me one good reason why I should fly to the Moon now, now that I've finally found my home and settled in down there.'

Julian thought it over. He could think of a thousand reasons why *he* wanted to fly to the Moon, but suddenly not a single one that would have any relevance for the old man opposite him. And yet Bowie looked any-thing but old, more as though he had just been reborn. His eyes looked as thirsty for knowledge as ever. It wasn't the look of an extraterrestrial observer, though, but that of an earth-dweller.

That's the difference between us, he thought. I was always extremely earthly. Always on the frontier, the great communicator, untouched by fear or self-doubt. And then he wondered what it would be like if one day *he* reached the conclusion that this space opera, of which he was the director and protagonist, had only served to bring him closer to Earth, and whether he would like this realisation or not.

Or was he just an egocentric alien after all, one who didn't even get what was going on with his own children. How had Tim put it?

You don't have a clue what's going on around you!

Julian pulled a face. Then he laughed too, but without any real pleasure, raised his glass and toasted Bowie.

'Cheers, old friend,' he said.

*　　*　　*

A little later, Amber opened her eyes and saw that the Earth had disappeared. Fear shot through her. She had slept straight through the previous night and it had still been there in the morning, half of it in any case. But now she couldn't see even the slightest glimpse of it.

Of course she couldn't. Night had fallen over the Pacific half and the lights of civilisation weren't visible from the height of geostationary orbit. There was no cause for alarm.

She turned her head. Next to her, Tim was staring into the darkness.

'What's wrong, my hero?' she whispered. 'Can't you sleep?'

'Did I wake you?'

'No, I just woke up, that's all.' She crawled nearer to him and rested her head on his shoulder.

'You were wonderful,' he said softly.

'No, *you* were wonderful. Is there something on your mind?'

'I don't know. Perhaps Julian was right after all. Maybe I'm just seeing ghosts.'

'No, I don't think so,' she said after a while. 'It's good that you're keeping an eye on things. It's just that, if you continue to treat him like an enemy, he'll act like one.'

'I'm not treating him like an enemy.'

'Well, you're not exactly the world champion when it comes to diplomacy.'

'No.' He laughed softly. 'I don't know, Amber. For some reason I've just got a bad feeling.'

'That's just the zero gravity,' she murmured, almost asleep again already. 'What could go wrong?'

Tim was silent. She blinked, lifted her head and realised she'd been mistaken. You could still see a narrow blue-white crescent on the right-hand side. Everything was fine. The Earth was still in its place.

Go to sleep, my darling, she wanted to say, but the tiredness overcame her with such force that she could only think it. Before she dozed off, she was overcome by the image of a black cloth spreading out over the two of them. Then, nothing.

*   *   *

Carl Hanna couldn't sleep, but then again he didn't need to. He ran his possessions through his fingers one after another, looking at them searchingly, rotating them, turning them over then packing them carefully away again: the small flacon of aftershave, the bottle filled with shower gel and the one with shampoo, tubes of skin cream, shaving foam, various packages of medication for headaches, sickness, stomach upsets, cotton buds and soft, pliable earplugs, toothbrush and toothpaste. He had even packed dental floss, nail scissors and a file, a hand mirror, his electric hair trimmer and three golf balls. There was a course in the grounds of the Gaia, Lynn had told him, Shepard's Green. Hanna played golf reasonably well, and he also placed a lot of importance on looking well groomed. Apart from that, none of all this junk was what it seemed to be. Just as the guitar wasn't really a guitar, Carl Hanna wasn't the person he pretended to be. It wasn't his real name, nor was his life story anything but complete fabrication.

He thought about Vic Thorn.

They had taken everything into account, everything except the possibility that Thorn might have an accident. The preparation for his mission had been exemplary, everything planned well in advance. Nothing should have gone wrong, but then a tiny speck of space debris had changed everything in a matter of seconds.

Hanna looked out into space.

Thorn was somewhere out there. He had joined the inventory of the cosmos, an asteroid on an unknown path. Many people believed that he must have stayed in the Earth's gravitational field, which would have meant encountering his body cyclically in orbit. But Thorn had still not been found. It was possible that he would crash into the Sun one day in the far future. Plausible that some day in a few million years' time he would turn up in the sphere of a planet inhabited by non-human intelligence and cause a great deal of surprise there.

He held up a roll-on deodorant, pulled off the cap, then put it back on and tucked it away.

This time, it would work.

26 May 2025

THE MISSION

Xintiandi, Shanghai, China

Chen Hongbing bent forward as he entered the room, in that way typical of people whose height is in constant conflict with doorframes and low-hanging ceiling-lights. He was actually extraordinarily tall for a Chinese man. On the other hand, the architect who designed the shikumen could hardly be accused of a lack of consideration for extravagant bodily proportions. The door was a good three metres high, so it hardly required him to hunch his shoulders as he did, or stretch out his chin which, as it approached his breastbone, seemed to linger hesitantly. Despite his size, Chen seemed gaunt and subservient. His gaze had a furtive nature about it, as if he were expecting to be beaten, or worse. Jericho got the impression he had spent his whole life conversing with people who towered over him while he stayed seated.

If indeed this was Chen Hongbing.

The visitor touched the doorframe fleetingly with the tips of his fingers, as if wanting to assure himself of something solid to grasp in case of a sudden collapse. Confused, he looked at the pile of removal boxes, then crossed the threshold with the caution of a tightrope walker. The white midday sun stretched across the room, a sculpture of light, broken into a billion pieces by the whirling dust. In that pale light Chen looked like a ghost narrowing his eyes. He looked younger than Tu Tian had said he was. His skin stretched tautly over his cheekbones, forehead and chin; a face which was deeply carved with lines. Around his eyes, though, a fine macramé pattern branched out, more like cracks than lines. To Jericho, they looked like testimonies to a difficult life.

'*Ta chi le hen duo Ku,*' Tu Tian had said. 'Hongbing has eaten bitterness, Owen, for many long years. Every morning it comes up, he forces it down again, and one day he will choke on it. Help him, *xiongdi*.'

Eaten bitterness. Even misery was available for consumption in China.

Jericho looked indecisively at the box in his hands and wondered if he should heave it onto the desk as planned or back onto the pile. Chen's arrival was ill-timed. He hadn't expected the man to come this early. Tu Tian had said something about an afternoon visit, and it wasn't even twelve yet. His stomach was rumbling, and his brow and upper lip glistened with sweat. The more he ran his hands over his face and hair to mix the dust and sweat, the less he looked like someone who was about to move into the expensive, trendy neighbourhood of Xintiandi. Three days without shaving had taken their toll. Encased in a sticky cloth of a T-shirt, which showed the 37 degrees Celsius and what felt like 99.9 per cent air humidity much more than the colour it had once possessed, and having hardly eaten for twenty-four hours, Jericho wanted nothing more than to put the move behind him as quickly as possible. Just one more box, then off to a food stall in Taicang Lu, carry on unpacking, shower, shave.

That had been the plan.

But when he saw Chen standing there in the dusty light, he knew he couldn't put his visitor off until later. Chen was the kind of person who would stay in your mind if you sent him away, and besides, out of respect to Tu Tian it was completely out of the question. He put the box back on the pile and put on a B-grade smile: warm, but noncommittal.

'Chen Hongbing, I take it.'

The man standing opposite him nodded and looked bewilderedly at the boxes and piled-up pieces of furniture. He coughed slightly, then took a small step back.

'I've come at a bad time.'

'Not at all.'

'It just so happened that I – I was nearby, but if it puts you out I can come back—'

'It's no trouble at all.' Jericho looked around, pulled over a chair and put it in front of the desk. 'Take a seat, honourable Chen, make yourself at home. I'm just moving in, hence the chaos. Can I get you anything?'

You can't, he thought, you would have needed to go shopping for that, but you're a man. When women move house, they make sure they have a full fridge before the first box even leaves the removal van, and if there isn't a fridge, they buy one and plug it in. Then he remembered the half-full bottle of orange juice. It had been on the lounge windowsill since yesterday morning, which meant it had led a two-day-long existence in the glaring sun and intelligent life might even have developed inside it.

'Coffee, tea?' he asked nonetheless.

'No, thank you, but thank you very much.' Chen sank down onto the edge of the chair and stared intently at his knees. If he had come into contact with the surface of the seat, it was by an amount barely meas-urable physically. 'A few minutes of your time is more than I can expect in these circumstances.'

Awkward pride resonated in his words. Jericho pulled a second chair over, placed it next to Chen's and hesitated. There were actually two comfortable armchairs which belonged in front of the desk, and both were in sight, but they had mutated into misshapen clumps of bubble wrap wrapped in packing tape.

'It's my pleasure to be able to assist you,' he said, trying to stop his smile from widening. 'We'll take as much time as we need.'

Chen slid back on his chair and sank cautiously against the backrest. 'You're very friendly.'

'And you're not comfortable. Please accept my apologies. Let me find some more comfortable seating. It's still packed, but—'

Chen lifted his head and squinted up at him. Jericho was confused for a second, then it hit him: essentially, Chen looked good. In his younger years he must have been one of those men women said were beautiful. Until the day when something had ground his well-proportioned features into a mask. Somewhat grotesquely, he now lacked a facial expression, if you didn't count his occasional nervous blinking.

'No, I won't allow you to do that on my account—'

'It would be my pleasure.'

'No, I can't allow you to.'

'They have to be unpacked anyway.'

'Of course, but at a time of your choosing.' Chen shook his head and got up again. His joints clicked. 'Please, I beg of you! I'm much too early, you're in the middle of something and I'm sure you were less than enthusiastic about my arrival.'

'No, that's not the case! I'm pleased you've come to see me.'

'No, I should come back later.'

'My dear Mr Chen, no moment could be better than this one. Please, stay.'

'I couldn't ask that of you. If I had known—'

And so on and so forth.

Theoretically, the game could carry on for ever. It wasn't that either of them harboured any doubt about the other's position. Chen knew only too well that he had caught Jericho at the wrong moment, and no assurances to the contrary would change that. Jericho, in turn, was aware that Chen would have been far more comfortable on a bed of nails than on any of his kitchen chairs. The circumstances were to blame. Chen's presence was down to a system in which favours chased one another like puppies, and he was ashamed to the core at having messed it up. It was because of one of these favours that he was even here in the first place, then he had foolishly arrived too early and stumbled into the middle of a house move, thereby shaming their mediator and putting Jericho, the mediated, into the unpleasant situation of interrupting his work on his account. Because of course Jericho wouldn't ask him to come back later. The ritual of pleasantries allowed for an open-ended succession of 'No, yes, not at all, but of course, it would be an honour, no, I couldn't, yes, no, yes!' A game which, if you wanted to master it, took years of training. If you were a *peng you*, a friend in the sense of a useful go-between, it would be played differently than if you were a *xiongdi*, a close confidant. Social standing, age and gender, the context of the conversation, all of these were factored into the coordinates of decorum.

Tu Tian, for example, had shortened the game when he had rather bluntly requested the aforementioned favour, just by calling him *xiongdi*. The diplomatic walk on eggshells could be dispensed with amongst close friends. Perhaps it was because he was really very fond of Chen, but maybe he just didn't want to interrupt the golf match for such a long-winded process, the outcome of which was already clear either way. In any case, once he had come out with it, the yolk-yellow late afternoon sun broke through the cheerfully dispersing clouds and bathed the surroundings in the tones of an Italian Renaissance landscape painting. Two days of rain came to an end, and Mr Tu, who had begun *comme il faut* with the words: 'Owen, I know you're up to your ears in it with the move, and I wouldn't normally bother you' – looked up to the heavens, picked up his Big Bertha club and ended succinctly – 'but there's a favour you could do for me – *xiongdi*.'

Tu Tian on the Tomson Shanghai Pudong golf course, two days before, deep in concentration.

Jericho waited obediently to find out what the favour might be. Tu was temporarily on another planet as he swung into a powerful drive. The rhythmic momentum came from his back, muscles and joints working in automated harmony. Jericho was talented; for two years now he had enjoyed the honour of playing on the best courses in Shanghai, when people like Tu invited him along, and when they didn't he played in the renowned but affordable Luchao Harbour City Club. The difference between him and Tu Tian was that one of them would never get close to achieving what the other one seemed to have been given genetically. Both of them had decided relatively late to spend time hitting little white balls at over two hundred kilometres per hour in an attempt to guide them into small holes in the ground. But on the day when Tu first walked onto a golf course, he must have felt as if he was coming home. His game was far beyond being described with attributes like accomplished or elegant. From the very beginning, Tu had played the way newborn babies swim. He *was* the game.

Jericho watched respectfully as his friend sent the ball into a perfect trajectory. Tu paused in the teeing position for a few seconds, then let Big Bertha fall with an expression of pure contentment.

'You mentioned a favour,' said Jericho.

'What?' Tu wrinkled his forehead. 'Oh, yes, nothing major. You know.'

He set off, briskly following the journey of his ball. Jericho marched behind him. He didn't know, but he had a good idea what was coming.

'What problem does he have?' he asked, taking a guess. 'Or she?'

'He. A friend. His name is Chen Hongbing.' Tu grinned. 'But that's not the problem you need to help him with.'

Jericho was familiar with the caustic element of his remark. The name was a bad joke, and one at which those it poked fun at were least able to laugh. It was likely that Chen had been born at the end of the sixties in the previous century, when the Red Guards had inflicted terror on the country, and when newborns had been given the most preposterous names in honour of the revolution and the Great Leader Mao: it was quite common for someone of the age where they could not yet control their bladder to be called 'Down with America', 'Honour of the Leader' or 'Long March.'

It was actually fear that had bestowed those names. An attempt to come to terms with things. Before the People's Revolutionary Army brought a bloody end to the Red Guards in 1969, there was uncertainty about who would rule China in the future. Three years before, on the Square of Heavenly Peace in Beijing, Mao Zedong had come down to join the mere mortals, as it were, and had a red armband tied around his sleeve, thereby symbolically becoming the leader of the Guards, a million-strong bunch of predominantly pubescent fanatics, absconding from their schools and universities, who sheared their teachers' heads, beat them and chased them through the streets like donkeys, because anyone who knew the simplest of things and wasn't a farmer or a worker was regarded as an intellectual, and therefore subversive. The chaos didn't end until the spring of 1969 – and only then because the so-called Gang of Four were rattling their chains loudly in the background. But the Red Guards walked the same path as their victims and found themselves back in re-education camps, which, in the opinion of many of the Chinese people, made things even worse. Jiang Qing, Mao's wife, raved about cultural operas and warmed up to some of the worst atrocities in China's history. But the naming of children, at least, slowly normalised.

Chen, Jericho estimated, had come into the world sometime between 1966 and 1969: a time in which his name was about as common as caterpillars in salad. Hongbing literally meant 'Red Soldier'.

Tu looked at the sun.

'Hongbing has a daughter.' The way he said it implied that this alone was worth telling the story for. His eyes lit up, then he got a grip of himself. 'She's very pretty and unfortunately very reckless too. Two days ago, she disappeared without a trace. Generally speaking she trusts me, and I'm tempted to say she trusts me even more than her father. Anyway, it's not the first time she's taken off for a while, but before she has always let someone know, so to speak. Him, me or at least one of her friends.'

'And she forgot this time.'

'Or she didn't have a chance. Hongbing is worried out of his mind, and rightly so. Yoyo has a tendency to annoy the wrong people. Or, shall we say, the right ones.'

Tu had outlined the problem in his own way. Jericho pursed his lips. It was clear what was expected of him. Besides that, the name Yoyo had unleashed something inside him.

'And I'm supposed to look for the girl?'

'You would be doing me a good turn if you met with Chen Hongbing.' Cheerfully Tu spotted his ball and began to pace more briskly. 'Only, of course, if you feel you're able to.'

'What exactly has she done?' asked Jericho. 'Yoyo, I mean.'

Tu stepped over to the white object in the shortly cut grass, looked Jericho in the eyes and smiled. His look said that he wanted to get back to putting now. Jericho smiled back.

'Tell your friend it would be an honour.'

Tu nodded as if he had expected nothing less. He called Jericho *xiongdi* one more time and turned his undivided attention to the putter and ball.

The younger generation in China hardly played the game any more. Their tone of voice had become globalised. If someone wanted something from somebody, they generally came straight to the point without wasting any time. With Chen Hongbing it was clearly a different matter. Everything about him marked him out as a representative of an older China, one in which there were a thousand ways of losing face. Jericho was indecisive for a moment, then had an idea of how he could salvage the situation for Chen. He leaned over, pulled a carpet knife from the toolbox next to the desk and began to briskly cut the chair free from the bubble wrap.

Chen raised both hands in horror.

'I beg you! This is so embarrassing for me—'

'It doesn't have to be.' said Jericho cheerfully. 'To be honest I was hoping for your help. There's a second knife in the toolbox. What would you say to us joining forces and making this place a little more comfortable?'

It was an ambush. At the same time he was offering Chen a way out of the self-inflicted mess. You help me, I'll help you, then you'll be contributing to my move, we'll both be able to sit more comfortably and you can get the dust off your face. Quid pro quo.

Chen seemed uncertain. He scratched his head, rattled himself to his feet, then fished the knife out of the box and took hold of the other chair. As he began to cut through the sticky-tape, he visibly relaxed.

'I appreciate your gesture very much, Mr Jericho. Tian unfortunately didn't have the opportunity to tell me that you were just moving in.'

Which meant the idiot hadn't mentioned it. Jericho shrugged his shoulders and pulled the cover off his armchair.

'He didn't know.'

That was a lie too, but in that way they had both respected Tu and could turn their attention to more important matters. One after the other, they pushed the armchairs in front of the desk.

'It doesn't look so bad after all.' Jericho grinned. 'Now we just need something to refuel. What do you think? I could fetch us some coffee. There's a patisserie downstairs, they do—'

'No, don't worry,' Chen interrupted. 'I'll fetch them.'

Ah yes. The game.

'No, I couldn't let you.'

'Of course you can.'

'No, it's my pleasure. You're my guest.'

'And you're receiving me unexpectedly. As I already said—'

'It's the least I can do for you. How do you like your coffee?'

'How do you like *yours*?'

'That's very kind of you, but—'

'Would you like nutmeg in yours?'

That was the latest thing: nutmeg in coffee. It had allegedly saved Star-bucks from bankruptcy last winter. The whole damn world had started drinking nutmeg coffee and swore that it tasted amazing. It reminded Jericho of the Sichuan Espresso craze which had rolled across the country a few years before, transforming the taste of Italian coffee into an Asian variant of Dante's Inferno. Jericho had taken a little sip from the rim of a cup once, and even days later had still felt as though he could pull the skin from his lips.

He gave in. 'A normal cappuccino would be great. The patisserie is just downstairs on the left.'

Chen nodded.

And, suddenly, he was smiling too. The skin on his face stretched taut, making Jericho fear it might tear off, but it was a thoroughly lovely, friendly smile, and one which disappeared only once it reached the cracked wastelands beneath his eyes.

'Yoyo isn't her real name,' explained Chen, as they sat slurping coffee together. By now the air-conditioning was on and had created a reason-ably bearable temperature. Chen's posture suggested he thought the soft leather seat might throw him off at any second, but compared with the man who had skulked through the doorframe a quarter of an hour before, he made an almost normal impression.

'So what is?'

'Yuyun.'

'Cloud of Jade.' Jericho raised his eyebrows appreciatively. 'A beau-tiful choice.'

'Oh, I gave it a great deal of thought! I wanted it to be a light, fresh name, full of poetry, full of—' Chen's gaze clouded over and wandered off into the distance.

'Harmony,' completed Jericho.

'Yes. Harmony.'

'So why does she call herself Yoyo?'

'I don't know.' Chen sighed. 'I know far too little about her, that's the problem. Just because you have named someone, it doesn't mean you know them. The label doesn't define the content. And what are names anyway? Just rallying calls for the lost. And yet everyone hopes that their own child will be an exception, it's like being anaesthetised. As if names could change anything. As if there has ever been any truth in a name!' He took a noisy gulp of his coffee.

'And Yoyo – Yuyun has disappeared?'

'Let's stick with Yoyo. Apart from me no one calls her Yuyun. Yes, I haven't seen or spoken to her for two days now. Didn't Tu Tian tell you about any of it?'

'Only a little.'

For some unknown reason this seemed to please Chen. Then Jericho realised. The way Tu had said it: *I'm tempted to say that she trusts me more than her father.* Whatever it was that bound Tu and Chen together, and however close this bond was – Yoyo's preference came between them. And that's why Chen had wanted the reassurance that, this time, not even Tu knew anything.

'Well, we were supposed to meet up,' he continued. 'The day before yesterday, for lunch in Lianing Lu. I waited for over an hour, but she didn't show. At first I thought it was because of an argument we'd had, that perhaps she was still angry, but then—'

'You had an argument?'

'We stayed out of each other's way for a while after she confronted me with her reasons for moving out, ten days ago, out of the blue. She didn't consider it necessary to seek my advice, nor did she want my help.'

'You didn't agree with her decision?'

'It seemed too hasty to me, and I told her so. Very plainly! That there wasn't the slightest reason for her to move out. That she was much better off with me than in that robber's den she's been hanging around in for years. That she's not doing herself any favour with those types of people – that it isn't clever—' Chen stared at the cup in his hand. They were silent for a while. Whole universes of dust emerged and disappeared in the sunlight. Jericho's nose was itching, but he repressed the urge to sneeze. Instead, he tried to remember where he had read the name Yoyo Chen.

'Yoyo has many talents,' Chen continued softly. 'Maybe I did hold her back too much. But I didn't have a choice. She incurred the displeasure of prominent circles, and it was getting increasingly dangerous. They caught up with her five years ago – because she didn't follow my advice.'

'What did she do?'

'Do? She completely ignored my warnings.'

'Yes, I know. But that's not a crime. Why was she arrested?'

Chen blinked distrustfully.

'I didn't say that in so many words.'

Jericho frowned. He leaned over, put the tips of his fingers together and looked Chen directly in the eyes.

'Listen to me. I don't want to push you by any means. But we won't get anywhere like this. You wouldn't be here just to say that the Party is giving Yoyo a lifetime achievement award, so let's speak plainly. What did she do?'

'She—' Chen seemed to be looking for a way of formulating it which wouldn't require definitions like 'criticism of the regime'.

'May I voice an assumption?'

Chen hesitated. Then he nodded.

'Yoyo is a dissident.' Jericho knew this to be the case. But where on earth had he read her name? 'She criticises the system, probably on the internet, and has been doing so for years. It drew attention on a number of occasions, but until yesterday she always got off lightly. Now something may have happened. And you're worried that Yoyo may have been imprisoned.'

'She said I was the last person who could reproach her for it,' whispered Chen. 'But I was only trying to protect her. We argued about it, many, many times, and she shouted at me. She said it was pointless, that I don't let anyone get close to me, not even my own daughter, and how I of all people— She said I was a total hypocrite.'

Jericho waited. Chen's expression hardened.

'But I didn't mean to bother you with these stories,' he concluded.

'The main thing is that there hasn't been any sign of life from her in two days.'

'Perhaps it's less serious than you think. It wouldn't be the first time someone's son or daughter has disappeared after an argument. They lie low with friends, play dead for a while, just to teach their parents a lesson.'

Chen shook his head. 'Not Yoyo. She would never use an argument as cause to do something like that.'

'You said yourself that you don't know your daughter well enough—'

'Well, in this respect I know her very well. We are similar in many ways. Yoyo hates that kind of childish nonsense.'

'Have you checked with the authorities?'

Chen balled his hands into fists. His knuckles bulged, white, but his face remained expressionless. Jericho knew they were getting closer to the crux of the matter, the real reason why Tu had sent his friend here.

'You *have* checked, haven't you?'

'No, I haven't!' Chen seemed to chew the words before spitting them out. 'I can't! I can't check with the authorities without risking putting them on Yoyo's trail.'

'So it's not certain that Yoyo has been arrested?'

'Last time I was left in the dark for weeks as to which police station she was in. But the fact that she had been arrested at all, well, I found that out just a few hours after it happened. I should mention that I have managed to build up a few important contacts over the years. There are people who are willing to use their influence for Yoyo and me.'

'Like Tu Tian.'

'Yes, and others too. That's the only reason I knew that Yoyo had been arrested back then. I asked these – friends, but they claimed not to know Yoyo's location. It wouldn't surprise me if she has given the authorities new reasons to hunt her down, but perhaps they haven't even noticed.'

'You mean that perhaps Yoyo just got scared and decided to lie low for a while?'

Chen kneaded his fingers. To Jericho, he looked like a taut bowstring. Then he sighed.

'If I go to the police,' he said, 'I could end up sowing mistrust into a field of ignorance. Yoyo would become a target again, whether she's done anything wrong or not. Any reason would be enough for them. Yoyo avoided provoking them for a while, and it seemed to me that she'd learned her lesson and made her peace with the past, but—' He looked at Jericho with his weary, intensely dark eyes. This time he didn't blink. 'You understand my dilemma, Mr Jericho?'

Jericho looked at him in silence. He leaned back and thought. As long as Chen continued circling the issue like a wolf around a fire, they wouldn't make any progress. So far his guest was only dropping hints. Jericho doubted Chen was even aware he was doing it. He had internalised the sidestepping in such a way that he probably thought he was walking in a straight line.

'I don't want to press you too much, Mr Chen – but could it be that you might be the wrong person to contact the authorities when it comes to dissident activities?'

'How do you mean?'

'I'm just voicing my suspicion that Yoyo isn't only being hunted down for her own actions.'

'I understand.' Chen stared at him. 'You're right, not everything in my past is to Yoyo's advantage. But regardless of that, I'd be doing her a disservice if I went to the police. Can we leave it at that for now?'

Jericho nodded. 'You know the focus of my work?' he asked. 'Did Tu Tian put you in the picture?'

'Yes.'

'My hunting ground is the internet. I imagine he recommended me because Yoyo has become active online.'

'He thinks a great deal of you. He says you're the best.'

'I'm honoured. Do you have a photo of Yoyo?'

'Oh, I have more than that! I have films.' He reached into his jacket and pulled out a mobile phone. It was an older model, one that wasn't compatible with 3D projection. Chen turned his attention to it with his now familiar blinking, pressed a few buttons in succession, but nothing happened.

'May I offer my assistance?' Jericho suggested.

'Yoyo gave it to me, but I hardly ever use it.' A trace of embarrassment crossed Chen's face. He handed the device to Jericho. 'I know, it's laughable. Ask me something about cars. Old cars, vintage. I know all the models, but these things here—'

These things, thought Jericho, are already vintage too, in case you didn't realise.

'You're interested in cars?' he asked.

'I'm an expert! Historical Beauty, in Beijing Donglu. Haven't you been? I manage the Technical Customer Service department. You must do me the honour of a visit; we had a silver Rolls-Royce Corniche in last month, with wood and red leather seats, a splendid specimen. It came from Germany, sold by an old man. Do you like cars?'

'They have their uses.'

'May I ask what you drive?'

'A Toyota.'

'Hybrid?'

'Fuel cell.' Jericho turned the mobile over in his hand and glanced at the connection points. With an adapter he could have projected the contents onto his new holowall, but it wasn't being delivered until the evening. He clicked through to the folder. 'May I?'

'Please. There are only three films on it, all of Yoyo.'

Jericho pointed the device at the wall opposite and activated the integrated beamer. He focused the picture to the size of a standard flat screen so there would be enough clarity despite the penetrating sunlight, and started the first recording.

Tu Tian had been right.

No, he hadn't done her justice! Yoyo wasn't just pretty, she was extraordinarily beautiful. During his time in London Jericho had familiarised himself with the most differing of theories about the existence of beauty: facial symmetry, the shaping of particular features like the eyes or lips, proportioning of bone structure, the amount of childlike characteristics. Studies like these were used in the psychological fight against crime, and they were also used as the basis of tracking down people disguising themselves with virtual personalities. Modern studies concluded that perfect feminine beauty was defined by large, round eyes and a high, lightly curved forehead, while the nose had to be slender and the chin small but clearly defined. If you processed women's faces in a morphing program and added a certain percentage of childlike features, the rate of approval from male viewers soared spontaneously. Full lips trumped narrow ones, eyes which were too close lost against those set at a certain distance. The perfect Venus had high cheekbones, narrow, dark brows, long lashes, glossy hair and an even hairline.

Yoyo was all of this – and yet none of it.

Chen had filmed her during a performance in some badly lit club, flanked by musicians who might or might not have been male. Nowadays, young men cultivated an increasingly androgynous style and wore their hair down to their belts. For anyone who wanted to be someone in the Mando-prog scene, the only other option was to shave their hair off and wear a skull cap. Short hair was out of the question. They could equally have been avatars, leaning over their guitars and bass: holographic simulations, even though that would have been hugely expensive. Only very successful musicians could afford avatars, like the American rapper Eminem who, now over fifty years of age and wanting to relive his heyday, had recently projected numerous versions of himself onto the stage, which played the instruments, danced, and unfortunately displayed much more agility than the master himself.

But all of this – gender, flesh and blood, bits and bytes – all of it lost any meaning next to the singer. Yoyo had combed her hair back tightly and braided it into four ponytails at the nape of her neck, which swung back and forth with each of her sinuous, powerful moves. She was singing a cover version of some ancient Shenggy track. As far as it was possible to deduce from the mobile's mediocre recording quality, she had a good voice, if not a remarkable one. And even though the bad lighting didn't put her sufficiently in the limelight, Jericho still saw enough to know she was perhaps the most beautiful woman he had seen in the thirty-eight years of his life. It was just that Yoyo's particular kind of beauty threw all the theories about what beauty was right out of the window.

The picture blurred for a moment as Chen tried to zoom in on his daughter. Then Yoyo's eyes filled the screen – a gaze like velvet, slender eyelids, curtained by lashes which sank and then quickly lifted again. The camera wobbled, Yoyo disappeared from view, then the recording stopped.

'She sings,' said Chen, as if it were necessary to point that out. Jericho played the next film. It showed Yoyo in a restaurant, sitting opposite Chen, her hair loose. She flicked through a menu, then noticed the camera and smiled.

'What are you doing?'

'Well, I hardly ever see you,' answered Chen's voice. 'So this way I'll at least have you preserved on film.'

'Aha! Bottled Yoyo.'

She laughed. Two horizontal creases formed under her eyes as she did so, which hadn't come up in the psychologists' beauty scenarios, but Jericho found them incredibly exciting.

'And besides, that way I can show you off.'

Yoyo pulled a face at her father. She started to squint.

'No, don't,' said Chen's voice.

The recording ended. The third one showed the restaurant again, apparently at a later date. Music blended into the cacophony of noise. In the background, waiters were hurrying between packed tables. Yoyo took a drag of her cigarette and balanced a drink in her right hand. She opened her lips and let a thin plume of smoke escape. For the duration of the entire clip, she didn't speak a single word. Her gaze rested on her father. It was one of love and noticeable sadness, so much so that Jericho wouldn't have been surprised to see tears flowing from her eyes. But nothing of the sort happened. Yoyo just lowered her eyelids from time to time, as if wanting to wipe away what she saw with her heavy lashes, sipped at her drink, dragged at her cigarette and blew out smoke.

'I'll need these recordings,' said Jericho.

Chen pushed himself out of his chair, his gaze fixed on the now empty wall as if his daughter were still visible on it. His features seemed more rigid than ever. And yet Jericho knew, without knowing the exact circumstances, that there had been times when this face had been contorted with pain. He had seen such faces in London. Victims. Families of victims. Perpetrators who had become victims themselves. Whatever it was that had hardened Chen, he hoped fervently to be far away if this rigidity ever broke down. There was no way in the world he wanted to see what would happen if it did.

'There are more you can have,' said Chen tonelessly. 'Yoyo enjoyed being photographed. But the films are much better. Not these ones though. Yoyo made recordings for Tian as a virtual tour guide. In high resolution, so she told me. And it's true, when you walk through the Museum of Town Planning or through the eye of the World Financial Center with one of those programs, it's as though she's there with you in the flesh. I have some of them at home, but I'm sure Tian can give you better material.' He faltered. 'Assuming, of course, that you're willing to find Yoyo for me.'

Jericho reached for his cup, stared at the remaining puddle of cold coffee and put it back down. Bright sunlight filled the room. He looked at Chen and knew that his visitor wouldn't ask a second time.

'I'm going to need more than the films.'

Jin Mao Tower

Around the same time, a Japanese waitress was approaching Kenny Xin's table, carrying a tray of sushi and sashimi in front of her. Xin, who saw her coming out of the corner of his eye, didn't bother turning round. His gaze was resting on the blue-grey band of the Huangpu three hundred metres below him. The river was busy at this time of day. Chains of barges followed its path like sluggish water-snakes, while heavy cargo-ships headed for the docks to the east of the bend. Ferries, water taxis and excursion boats forced their way between them en route for the Yangpu bridge and the cranes of the unloading bays, past the idyllic Gongqing Park to the estuary, where the oily floods of the Huangpu mixed in a gloomy kaleidoscope with the muddy waters of the Yangtze before dispersing into the East China Sea.

It was thanks to the river's sharp, almost angular bend to the right that Shanghai's financial and economic district, Pudong, seemed like a peninsula, offering panoramic views of the coastal road Zhongshan Lu with its colonial banks, clubs and hotels: relicts from the era after the Opium Wars, when the European trade giants had divided up the country between them and erected monuments of their power on the western bank of the river. A hundred years ago, these structures must have towered over everything around them in splendour and size. Now they looked like toys against the stalagmite-like towers of glass, steel and concrete that stretched out behind them, permeated by highways, magnetic rails and sky trains, surrounded by whirling flying machines, insectoid minicopters and cargo-blimps. Even though the weather was unusually clear, the horizon couldn't be seen. Shanghai went up in smoke, diffused at the edges and became one with the sky. There was nothing to suggest that anything other than yet more development was beyond the development itself.

Xin looked at it all, without granting the woman who was placing the sushi before him the honour of acknowledgement. His concentration was undividable, and right now he was concentrating on the question of where the girl he was looking for might be hiding amidst this twenty-million-strong Moloch. She certainly wasn't at home, he'd checked there. If that student with the ridiculous name of Grand Cherokee Wang hadn't been lying, then there was still the possibility of narrowing down her location. He would have to clutch at this straw, even if the kid seemed dodgy to him: one of Yoyo's two flatmates, clearly in love with the girl and even more so with money, in pursuit of which he made out he had information to offer. And yet he didn't know a thing.

'Yoyo hasn't been living here that long,' he had said. 'She's a real party hen.'

'And we're the cocks,' the other had laughed immediately – showing his swinging uvula – by way of admitting it was a pretty bad joke. Hen was the Chinese term for whore, and the cocks, or cockerels, were the pimps. It seemed he had suddenly pictured what Yoyo might do to him if Xin were to pass on his tasteless little comment.

Could they pass on a message to Yoyo for him?

Xin asked when they had last seen Yoyo.

On the evening of 23 May, they said. The three of them had cooked and knocked back a few bottles of beer together. Afterwards, Yoyo had gone to her room, but then left the house later that same night.

At what time?

Late, Grand Cherokee seemed to remember. Around two or three in the morning. The other guy, Zhang Li, shrugged his shoulders. But since then neither of them had seen her.

Xin thought for a moment.

'Your flatmate could be in trouble,' he said. 'I can't go into it in more detail right now, but her family are very worried.'

'Are you a policeman?' Zhang wanted to know.

'No. I'm someone who was sent to help Yoyo.' He gave each of them a meaningful look. 'And I've also been authorised to show my gratitude for any help in an appropriate manner. Please tell Yoyo that she can reach me on this number at any time.' Xin gave Grand Cherokee a card on which there was nothing but a mobile number. 'And if either of you has any more thoughts about where I might be able to find her—'

'No idea,' said Zhang, clearly uninterested, and disappeared into the next room.

Grand Cherokee watched him go and shuffled from one leg to the other. Xin paused in the doorway to give the boy the chance to take the offensive. Just as he'd expected, he got straight to the point – although in hushed tones – as soon as his pal was out of sight.

'I could find something out for you,' he said. 'For a price, of course.'

'Of course,' echoed Xin, smiling a little.

'Just to cover my costs, you know. I mean . . . there are a few clues, about where she is, and I could—'

Xin slid his right hand into his jacket and pulled it back out with a few notes.

'Could I perhaps take a quick look around her room?'

'I can't do that,' said Grand Cherokee, shocked. 'She would never—'

'It would be for her own safety.' Xin lowered his voice. 'Between you and me, the police could turn up here. I don't want them finding anything that could incriminate Yoyo.'

'Oh, of course. It's just—'

'I understand.' Xin moved to put the notes back in his pocket.

'No, wait – I—'

'Yes?'

Grand Cherokee stared at the money and tried to tell Xin something without using words. It was clear what he wanted. The language of greed doesn't need vocabulary. Xin reached back into his jacket and increased the offer. The boy gnawed on his lower lip, then took the notes and nodded his head towards the corridor.

'Last door on the right. Should I—'

'Thanks. I'll find my way. And as I said – if you should have any clues—'

'I do!' Grand Cherokee's eyes started to glisten. 'I just need to make a few calls, speak to a few people. Hey, I'll take you to Yoyo as soon as I've got things sorted! Although—'

'Yes?'

'I might have to bribe a few people here and there.'

'Are we talking about an advance?'

'Something like that.'

Xin saw the lie in Grand Cherokee's eyes. You don't know a thing, he thought, but it's possible that your greed might lead you to find something out. You'll be in touch sooner or later. You're too sharp not to cash in on this. He pressed two more notes into his hand and left.

*   *   *

That was yesterday.

So far he had heard nothing from the boy, but Xin wasn't worried. He reckoned he would receive a call sometime in the course of the afternoon. He turned his attention to his sushi: just tuna, salmon and mackerel, all of the highest quality. The cuisine of the Japanese restaurant on the fifty-sixth floor of the Jin Mao Tower left little to be desired, that is if you ignored the oversights in how the dishes were presented. The restaurant was part of the Jin Mao Grand Hyatt, which occupied the top thirty-five floors of what had once been China's tallest building. By now, the Jin Mao Tower had been outflanked a dozen times in Shanghai alone – first in 2008 by the neighbouring World Financial Center, which also contained a Hyatt – and yet the aura of excess still clung to its out-dated ambience. It reflected a time when China had begun to seek new self-awareness between communism, Confucius and capital, and had found it just as much in reminiscences of the imperial past as in the Art Deco aesthetic of colonialism. Xin liked that, even if he had to admit that staying in the new place was a more stylish experience. He was drawn here by the idea that he could subject his presence to a concept shaped not by emotions but by cold agreement with the principles of order, ultimately the secret formula of perfection. Kenny Xin was born in 1988, and the Jin Mao Tower surrendered itself to the number eight like the human to the genome. Deng Xiaoping had completed the design of the building at eighty-eight years of age, and the inauguration cere-mony took place on 28 August 1998. Eighty-eight floors were stacked on top of one another and formed a construction in which every seg-ment was an eighth smaller than the base with its sixteen storeys. The steel joists the tower rested on measured 80 metres. The eight could be seen in everything. By 2015 the building had 79 lifts, a flaw which was remedied by creating a lift just for the staff.

There were, of course, a few small imperfections in the otherwise exemplary conception. For example, the fact that the tower only swung a maximum of 75 cm back and forth in a storm or earthquake. Xin won-dered how the constructors could have overlooked that kind of mistake in its mathematical beauty. He was no architect, and perhaps there was no other way, but what were five centimetres against the priority of perfection? Compared with the order of the cosmos, even the Jin Mao Tower looked like a messy child's bedroom.

With one of his manicured fingers, Xin pushed the sushi tray away from him and a little to the left, then placed the bottle of Tsingtao beer and its accompanying glass behind it at an equal distance. It looked better to him already. He was far from subscribing to the obscene order principles of people who put everything at a right angle. Occasionally he even saw the purest order in the appearance of chaos. What could be more perfect than total homogeneity without imperfections, just as a perfectly empty spirit resembles the cosmic ideal, and every thought is a form of contamination, unless you summon it deliberately and dismiss it again at will. To control the mind is to control the world. Xin smiled as he made a few more corrections, shifting the small bowl for the soy sauce, breaking the chopsticks apart and laying them parallel in front of him. In its own way, wasn't Shanghai a wonderful chaos too? Or rather a secret plan, an ordering of capriciousness which only revealed itself to the educated observer?

Xin pushed a few clumps of rice a little further apart on the wooden board until their appearance appealed to him.

He began to eat.

Xintiandi

When Jericho looked back, his life in China seemed like a confused succession of dangerous risks and escapes, all encircled by soundproofed walls and building sites, in the shadow of which he had striven to improve his financial state with the industriousness of an animal burrowing a hole. In the end, the hard slog had shown results. His bank manager began to seem more like a friend. Dossiers about shares in deep-sea vessels, water treatment plants, shopping centres and skyscrapers were presented to him. The whole world seemed intent on making him aware of all the things he could spend his money on. Clasped against the bosom of better society, respected and overworked, Jericho ended up paralysed by his own achievements, too exhausted to add the final chapter to the story of his nomadic life by moving to the kind of area it would be worth growing old in. The step was long overdue, but the thought of packing up yet again made him go cold. So he gave priority to lying wearily on the sofa in the evenings as floodlights and construction noise leaked through the curtains, watching feature films and murmuring the mantra I-have-to-get-out-of-here to himself, then falling asleep in the process.

It was around this time that Jericho began to seriously doubt the point of his existence.

He hadn't doubted it when Joanna had lured him to Shanghai, only to leave him three months later. He hadn't doubted it when he'd realised he didn't have enough money for the flight back, nor to rebuild the life he'd left behind in London. He hadn't doubted in his first Shanghai digs on the edge of a highway, where he'd lived on damp floors and struggled to squeeze a few litres of brown water from the shower every morning, the windows of the two-storey house rattling lightly from the never-relenting traffic.

He had just told himself it could only get better.

And it had.

To start with, Jericho had offered his services to foreign enterprises that had come out to Shanghai to do business. Many felt insecure within the fragile framework of Chinese copyright protection legislation. They felt spied on and cheated. With time, though, the self-service mentality of the dragon had given way to great remorse. While, at the beginning of the century, China had still happily plagiarised everything hackers unearthed from the depths of the global ideas pool, now even Chinese business people were increasingly despairing about their state's inability to protect ideas. They too began to be on the receiving end of the words 'It seemed worthy of imitation to us', which was a polite way of saying 'Of course we stole it, but we admire you for having created it.' For years, the Long-Nose accusations that Chinese companies and institutions had stolen their intellectual property had been indignantly rejected or not even acknowledged, but Jericho found that now it was Chinese companies, above all, who needed web detectives. Native entrepreneurs reacted excitedly to the fact that, during his time with Scotland Yard helping to build up the department for Cyber Crime, he had been fighting *against* them. In their opinion, it could only be advantageous to have their patents protected by someone who had previously done such an excellent job of clobbering them when they crossed the line.

Because the problem – an undulating, proliferating, all-enveloping, truly uncontrollable monster of a problem – was that China's creative elite would go on cannibalising itself so long as a nationally and internationally accepted and implementable system for the protection of intellectual property rights remained elusive. It had always been obvious that capitalism, practically reinvented by China, was *based* upon property rights, and that an economy whose most important asset was know-how couldn't exist without the protection of brands, patents and copyright, but it hadn't really interested anyone – not, that is, until the day when they themselves became victims of the situation. By now, the country suffering the most economic damage at the hands of Chinese espionage was China itself. Everyone was digging around in other people's front gardens, and with electronic spades wherever possible. The hunting ground was the global net, and Owen Jericho was one of the hunters, commissioned by other hunters as soon as they got the impression that they themselves were the quarry.

Once Jericho became part of that network without which no favours would be done and no trade negotiated in China, his career ascended like a rocket. He moved five times in five years, twice of his own free will, the other times because the houses he was living in at the time were to be pulled down for reasons he could no longer remember. He moved to better areas, wider streets, nicer houses, getting ever closer to realising his dream of moving into one of the rebuilt shikumen houses, with stone gateways and peaceful inner courtyards, located in the pulsating heart of Shanghai. Even though he had to make compromises along the way, he had never doubted it would happen at some point.

One day, his bank manager asked him what he was waiting for. Jericho replied that he wasn't quite there yet, but would be someday. The bank manager made him aware of his bank balance and said that 'someday' was, in fact, now. With the revelation that he'd been working so hard he hadn't paid attention to the possibilities now open to him, Jericho left the bank and teetered home in a daze.

He hadn't realised he had come so far.

With the realisation came the doubts. They claimed they'd always been there, but that he had avoided acknowledging them. They whispered: What the devil are you doing here anyway? How did you even get here?

How could this happen to you?

They told him that it had all been for nothing, and that the worst position anyone could ever find themselves in was that of having achieved their goals. Hope blossoms beneath the shelter of provisional arrangements, often for a whole lifetime. Now, suddenly, it had become official. He was to become a Shanghaian, but had he ever wanted that? To settle in a city he would never have moved to without Joanna?

As long as you were on the journey, said the doubts, you didn't have to think about the destination. Welcome to commitment.

In the end – he lived in a fairly prestigious high-rise in the hinterland of Pudong, the financial district, the only drawback of which was the fact that more skyscrapers were being constructed around it, that and the noise and a fine brown dust which settled in the windowsills and airways – it took a further eviction by the city authorities to shake him from his lethargy. Two smiling men paid him a visit, let him serve them tea and then explained that the house he was living in had to give way to an utterly amazing new-build. If he so wished, they would gladly reserve an apartment in it for him. But a further move for the duration of the coming year would, much to their regret, be unavoidable. To which end, the authorities considered themselves overjoyed to be able to offer him an apartment near Luchao Harbour City, a mere sixty kilometres outside Shanghai – which, for a metropolis lovingly embracing other towns in the course of its expansion, wasn't *really* outside at all. Oh, yes, and they wanted to start work in four weeks, so if he could – you know. It wasn't the first time such a thing had happened, and they said they were very sorry, but they weren't really.

Jericho had stared at the delegates as the wonderful certainty of having just awoken from a coma streamed through him. Suddenly, he could smell the world again, taste it, feel it. He shook hands with the baffled men gratefully, assuring them they had done him a great service. And that they could send whomever they wanted to Luchao Harbour City. Then he had phoned Tu Tian and, in keeping with matters of decorum, had asked whether he might know someone who knew someone who knew whether there was a renovated or newly built shikumen house in a lively corner of Shanghai, vacant and which could be moved into at short notice. Mr Tu, who prided himself on being Jericho's most satisfied client as well as his good friend, was the first port of call for questions such as these. He managed a mid-size technology company, was on good terms with the city's powers that be, and happily declared that he would be willing to 'keep an ear to the ground'.

Fourteen days later, Jericho signed the rental contract for a floor in one of the most beautiful shikumen houses, situated in Xintiandi, one of the most popular areas of Shanghai, and which could be moved into right away. It was a new-build of course. There weren't any genuine old shikumen houses left, and there hadn't been for a long time. The last ones had been torn down shortly after the world exhibition of 2010, and yet Xintiandi could still be classified as a stronghold of shikumen architecture just as in similar fashion the old town of Shanghai was anything but old.

Jericho didn't ask who had had to move out to make it vacant. He hoped the apartment really had been empty, put his signature on the document and didn't give any more thought to what favour Tu Tian might ask for in return. He knew he owed Tu. So he prepared for his move and waited humbly for what was to come.

And it came sooner than expected. In the form of Chen Hongbing and an unpleasant commission which there was no way of getting out of without insulting Tu.

Shortly after Chen left, Jericho set up his computer terminal. He washed his face, combed his dishevelled hair into some semblance of order and pulled on a fresh T-shirt. Making himself comfortable in front of the screen, he let the system dial the number. Two T's appeared on the screen, each one melting into the other, the symbol of Tu Technologies. The next moment, an attractive woman in her mid-forties was smiling at him. She was seated in a tastefully decorated room with lounge furniture and floor-to-ceiling windows which offered a glimpse of Pudong's skyline. She was drinking something from a tiny porcelain cup which Jericho knew to be strawberry tea. Naomi Liu would kill for strawberry tea.

'Good afternoon, Naomi.'

'Good afternoon, Owen. How's the move going?'

'Fantastically, thank you.'

'I'm pleased to hear it. Mr Tu told me you're having one of our big new terminals delivered.'

'Yes, this evening, I hope.'

'How exciting.' She put the cup down on a transparent surface which seemed to sway in thin air, and looked at him from beneath her lowered lashes. 'Then I'll soon be able to see you from head to toe.'

'That's nothing compared to the excitement of seeing *you*.' Jericho leaned forward and lowered his voice. 'Anyone would swear that you're sitting right here in front of me.'

'And that's enough for you?'

'Of course not.'

'I'm worried it might be. It will be enough, and you'll see no reason any more to invite me around personally. I think I'll have to convince my boss not to deliver the thing to you after all.'

'No holographic program could compare to you, Naomi.'

'Tell *him* that.' She nodded her head in the direction of Tu's office. 'Otherwise he might come up with the idea of replacing me with one.'

'I would break off all business connections in an instant if he did that. Is he—?'

'Yes, he's here. Take care. I'll put you through.'

Jericho enjoyed their little flirting ritual. Naomi Liu was the conduit for all forms of contact with Tu Tian. Having her on his side could be useful. And Jericho wouldn't have hesitated for a second in inviting her to his apartment, but she would never have taken him up on the offer. She was happily married and the mother of two children.

The shimmering double T rotated again briefly, then Tu's huge head appeared on the screen. The little hair he had left was concentrated just above his ears, where it was grey and bristly. Narrow glasses were balanced on his nose. The left arm looked as if it was held together by transparent sticky-tape. Tu had pushed his sleeves up and was shovelling sticky-looking noodles into his mouth, fishing them out of a paper box with clattering chopsticks. The large desk behind him was full of screens and holo-projectors. In between were piles of hard disks, remote controls, brochures, cardboard boxes and the remains of various packaging.

'No, you're not interrupting,' mumbled Tu with his mouth full, as if Jericho had expressed any concern on the matter.

'I can see that. Have you ever been to your canteen, by the way? They make fresh food there.'

'So?'

'Proper food.'

'This is proper food. I poured boiling water on it and it turned into food.'

'Do you even know what it's supposed to be? Does it say anything on the packaging?'

'It says something or other.' Tu carried on chewing steadily. His rubbery lips moved around like copulating rubber tubes. 'People with your anarchic sense of time management wouldn't understand perhaps, but there are reasons for eating in the office.'

Jericho gave up. As long as he'd known Tu, he'd hardly ever seen him devour a healthy, decent meal. It seemed as though the manager had set himself the task of ruining the Chinese cuisine's reputation as the best, most varied and freshest in the world. He might be a genial inventor and a gifted golf-player – but when it came to culinary matters, he made Kublai Khan look like the father of all gourmets.

'So what were you celebrating?' he asked, with a glance at the chaos in Tu's office.

'We were testing something out.' Tu reached for a bottle of water, washed down the noodles in his mouth and burped audibly. 'Holo-Cops. A commission from the traffic-control authorities. They function excellently in the dark, but sunlight is still giving them problems. It corrodes them.' He chortled with laughter. 'Like vampires.'

'What does the city want with holographic policemen?'

Tu looked at him in amazement.

'To regulate the traffic, what else? Another one of the real ones was run over last week, didn't you read about it? He was standing in the middle of the Siping Lu crossing in Dalian Xilu when one of the furniture transporters raced right into him and distributed him evenly all over the tarmac. It was a huge mess, screaming children, angry letters! No one regulates the traffic voluntarily any more.'

'Since when did the police care whether things are voluntary?'

'They don't, Owen, but it's a question of economics. They're losing too many officers. Being a traffic policeman tops the list of most dangerous jobs right now, and most of them would rather be assigned to tracking down and catching mentally disturbed mass-murderers. And, well, there's the humane aspect too, no one wants dead policemen. It's no problem at all if a Holo-Cop gets run over, it even still manages to file a report about it. The projection sends a signal to the computer, including the car make and number plate.'

'Interesting,' said Jericho. 'And how are the holographic tour guides coming along?'

'Ah!' Tu wiped the corner of his mouth clean with a serviette, one which had clearly had to assist with several other mealtimes too. 'You had a visitor.'

'Yes, I had a visitor.'

'And?'

'Your friend is terribly sad. What happened to him?'

'I told you. He ate bitterness.'

'And beyond that it's none of my business, I get the picture. So let's talk about his daughter.'

'Yoyo!' Tu stroked his hand over his stomach. 'Be honest now, isn't she sensational?'

'Without a doubt.'

Jericho was intrigued as to whether Tu would talk about the girl on a public phone line. It was true that all telephone conversations were recorded by the authorities, but in reality the observation apparatus rarely followed up on the analysis, even though sophisticated programs pre-selected the recordings. As early as the end of the previous century, within the context of their worldwide Ecelon Program, American Secret Services had introduced software which was able to recognise key words, with the result that you could be arrested just for mentioning the word ice-bomb three times in succession when planning Grandma's birthday party. Modern programs by contrast were, to a certain extent, perfectly able to understand the meaning of the conversation and create priority lists. But they were still incapable of recognising irony. Humour and double-meanings were alien to them, which forced the spies themselves to listen in, just like in the old times, as soon as words like dissident or Tiananmen massacre came up. As expected, Tu merely said:

'And now you want a date with the girl, right?'

Jericho grinned cheerlessly. He knew it. There were going to be difficulties.

'If it can be arranged.'

'Well, she has such high standards,' said Tu craftily. 'Perhaps I should give you a few useful pieces of advice, my dear boy. Will you be in the area in the next few hours at all?'

'I have things to do in Bund. I should be free later.'

'Excellent! Take the ferry. The weather's lovely, let's meet in Lujiazui Green.'

Pudong

Lujiazui Green was a picturesque park surrounded by skyscrapers, not far from Jin Mao Tower and the WFC. Tu sat on a bench on the bank of the small lake, basking in the sun. As usual, he was wearing sunglasses over his normal glasses. His crumpled shirt had worked its way almost entirely out of his waistband and was straining at the buttons. Patches of his white belly peeped through the gaps. Jericho sat down next to him and stretched out his legs.

'Yoyo is a dissident,' he said.

Tu turned his head round to him lethargically. His eyes couldn't be seen behind the crooked construction of glasses and sunglasses.

'I thought you would have picked that up from our conversation on the golf course.'

'That's not what I mean. What I mean is that the case is a little different to my normal ones. This time I'm supposed to look for a dissident in order to protect her.'

'A former dissident.'

'Her father sees that differently. Why would Yoyo have gone underground, if not out of fear? Unless she's been arrested. You said yourself that she has a tendency to aggravate the wrong people. Perhaps she crossed someone who was a little too big for her.'

'And what are you planning to do?'

'You know exactly what I'm going to do,' snorted Jericho. 'I'm going to look for Yoyo of course.'

Tu nodded. 'That's very generous of you.'

'No, it goes without saying. The only snag is that I'll have to work without the authorities this time. So I need any information there is about Yoyo and her world, and that's where I'm relying on your help. My impression of Chen Hongbing was that he's extremely honourable and incredibly private. Perhaps he just turns a blind eye; in any case, getting information from him was like trying to get blood from a stone.'

'What did he tell you?'

'He gave me Yoyo's new address. A few films and photos. And dropped a whole load of hints.'

Fumbling, Tu took the sunglasses down from his nose and tried to push the remaining glasses into a reasonably straight position. Jericho noticed that he hadn't been mistaken: the left arm really was bound with sticky-tape. He wondered, not for the first time, why Tu didn't get his eyes lasered or switch to photochromic contact lenses. Hardly anyone wore glasses for the purpose of improving their eyesight any more. They were just eking out an existence as fashion items, and fashion was as alien to Tu Tian as the atomic age was to a Neanderthal.

They were silent for a while. Jericho blinked in the sunlight and watched an aeroplane pass by.

'So' said Tu. 'Ask your questions.'

'There's nothing to ask. Tell me something about Yoyo that I don't know yet.'

'She's actually called Yuyun—'

'Chen told me that much.'

'—and belongs to a group who call themselves Guardians. I bet he didn't tell you that, right?'

'Guardians.' Jericho whistled softly through his teeth.

'You've heard of them?'

'I sure have. Internet guerrillas. Dedicated to human rights, raising the profile of old stories like Tiananmen, attacks on government and industry networks. They're really putting the wind up the Party.'

'And they're right to be nervous. Guardians are of a completely different calibre to our sweet little Titanium Mouse.'

Liu Di, the woman who called herself Titanium Mouse, was one of the pioneers of internet dissidence. At the start of the millennium she had begun to publish edgy little commentaries online about the political elite, initially under the pseudonym of Stainless Steel Mouse. Realising that it wasn't as easy to imprison virtual people as it was those of flesh and blood, Beijing's leadership began to get very nervous. These dissidents showed presence, without being present.

The head of the Beijing secret police remarked that the new threat gave cause for extreme concern and that an enemy without a face was the worst kind, a conclusion that grossly overestimated the first generation of net dissidents – most didn't even contemplate disguising their identity, and even the ones who did made other mistakes sooner or later. The Stainless Steel Mouse, for example, had walked right into their trap when she assured the founder of a new democratic party of her support, not knowing it was an official assigned to her case. As a result of which she was dragged off to a police station and imprisoned for a year without trial. After that, however, the Party learned their next lesson: that it may be possible to make people disappear behind walls, but not on the internet. There, Liu Di's case gained significance, made the rounds in China and attracted the attention of the foreign media. Suddenly, the whole world was aware of this shy, twenty-one-year-old woman, who hadn't even meant any of it that seriously. And that turned out to be the powerful, faceless enemy the Party had cowered so fearfully from.

After her release, Liu Di upgraded from steel to a stronger metal. Titanium Mouse had learned something. She declared war on an apparatus that Mao couldn't have thought up in his wildest dreams: Cypol, the Chinese Internet Police. She routed internet forums via servers abroad and created her blogs with the help of programs that filtered out incriminating words as she wrote. Others followed her example, became increasingly sophisticated in their methods, and by then the Party really *did* have cause to worry. While veterans like Titanium Mouse made no secret of their true identity, Guardians were haunting the net like phantoms. Tracking them down would have required ingenious traps, and although Beijing kept setting them, so far no one had been caught.

'Even today, the Party still has no idea how many of them there actually are. Sometimes they think they're dealing with dozens, sometimes just a few. A cancerous ulcer in any case, one which will eat away at our magnificent, happy and healthy People's Republic from the inside.' Tu hacked up some phlegm and spat it in front of his feet. 'Now, we know what comes out of Beijing, predominantly rumours and very little of anything that makes sense, so how big do you think the organisation really is?'

Jericho thought about it. He couldn't remember ever having heard of a Guardian being imprisoned.

'Oh sure, now and then they arrest someone and claim that person is one of them!' said Tu, as if he had read Jericho's thoughts. 'But I happen to know for certain that they haven't made one successful arrest yet.

Unbelievable, isn't it? I mean, they're hunting an army, so you'd think there'd be prisoners of war.'

'They're hunting something that looks like an army,' said Jericho.

'You're getting close.'

'But the army doesn't exist. There are only a few of them, but they know how to keep slipping through the investigators' nets. So the Party exaggerates them. Makes them seem more dangerous and intelligent than they really are, to distract from the fact that the State still hasn't managed to pull a handful of hackers out of the online traffic.'

'And what do you conclude from that?'

'That for one of Beijing's honourable servants you know a suspicious amount about a bunch of internet dissidents.' Jericho looked at Tu, frowning. 'Is it just my imagination, or are you playing some part in the game too?'

'Why don't you just come out and ask if I'm one of them?'

'I just did.'

'The answer is no. But I can tell you that the entire group consists of six people. There were never more than that.'

'And Yoyo is one of them?'

'Well.' Tu rubbed his neck. 'Yes and no.'

'Which means?'

'She's the brains behind it. Yoyo brought the Guardians to life.'

Jericho smirked. In the distorting mirror of the internet, anything was possible. The Guardians' presence suggested they were a larger group, potentially capable of spying on government secrets. Their actions were well thought out, the background research always exemplary. It all created the illusion of being an extensive network, but in actual fact that was thanks to their multitude of sympathisers, who were neither affiliated to the group nor possessed knowledge about their structure. On closer inspection the Guardians' entire activism boiled down to a small, conspiring hacker community. And yet—

'—they have to be constantly up to date,' murmured Jericho.

Tu jabbed his elbow into his ribs. 'Are you talking to me?'

'What? No. I mean, yes. How old is Yoyo again?'

'Twenty-five.'

'No twenty-five-year-old girl is cunning enough to outmanoeuvre the State Security in the long term.'

'Yoyo is extraordinarily intelligent.'

'That's not what I mean. The State may be limping behind the hackers, but they're not completely stupid. You can't get past the Diamond Shield using conventional methods, so sooner or later you'll have the Internet Police knocking at your door. Yoyo must have access to programs which enable her to always be a step ahead of them.'

Tu shrugged his shoulders.

'Which means that she knows how to use them.' Jericho spun the web further. 'Who are the other members?'

'Some guys. Students like Yoyo.'

'And how do you know all this?'

'Yoyo told me.'

'She told you.' Jericho paused. 'But she didn't tell Chen?'

'Well, she tried. It's just that Chen won't hear any of it. He doesn't listen to her, so she comes to me.'

'Why you?'

'Owen, you don't have to know everything—'

'But I want to *understand*.'

Tu sighed and stroked his bald head.

'Let's just say I help Yoyo to understand her father. Or, that's what she hopes to get from me in any case.' He raised a finger. 'And don't ask what there is to understand. That has nothing whatsoever to do with you!'

'You speak in puzzles just as much as Chen does,' boomed Jericho, aggravated.

'On the contrary. I'm showing you an excessive amount of trust.'

'Then trust me more. If I'm going to find Yoyo, I need to know the names of the other Guardians. I have to find them, question them.'

'Just assume the others have gone underground too.'

'Or were arrested.'

'Hardly. Years ago I had the opportunity to get a close look at the cogs of the State welfare services, the places where they look inside your head and declare you to be infested with all kinds of insanity. I know those types. If they had arrested the Guardians, they would have been boasting about it at the tops of their voices for a while now. It's one thing to make people disappear, but if someone's running rings around you, making you look like a fool in public, then you put their head on a spear as soon as you catch them. Yoyo has caused the Party a great deal of grief. They won't stand for it.'

'How did Yoyo even get into all this?'

'The way young people always get into things like this. She identified with *zi you*, with freedom.' Tu poked around between his shirt buttons and scratched his belly. 'You've been living here for a good while, Owen, and I think you understand my people pretty well by now. Or, let's put it this way, you understand what you see. But a few things are still closed off from you. Everything that takes place in the Middle Kingdom today is the logical consequence of developments and breakthroughs throughout our history. I know, that sounds like something from a travel guide. Europeans always think this whole yin and yang business, this insistence on tradition, is just folklorist nonsense intended to disguise the fact that we're just a band of greedy imitators who want to make their stamp on the world, continually damage human rights and who, since Mao, have no more ideals. But for two thousand years, Europe was like a pot which continually had new things thrown into it; it was a patchwork of clashing identities. You've all overrun each other, made your neighbours' customs and ways your own, even while you were still fighting them. Huge empires came and went as if in time-lapse. For a while it was the Romans having their say, then the French, then the Germans and the Brits. You talk of a united Europe, and yet you speak in more languages than you can possibly understand, and as if that weren't enough, you import Asia, America and the Balkans too. You're incapable of understanding how a nation that for the most part was entirely self-sufficient and self-contained – because it felt the Middle Kingdom didn't need to know what was outside its borders – finds it hard to accept the new, especially when it's brought in from the outside.'

'You guys certainly know how to brush that one under the carpet,' snorted Jericho. 'You drive German, French and Korean cars, wear Italian shoes, watch American films; I can't think of any other nationality that has turned more to the outside in recent years than yours.'

'Turned to the outside?' Tu laughed drily. 'Nicely put, Owen. And what comes to light when you turn to the outside? Whatever's inside. But what is it that you see? What exactly are we turning towards the outside? Only what you recognise. You wanted us to open up? We did that, in the eighties under Deng Xiaoping. You wanted to do business with us? You're doing it. Everything that Chinese emperors didn't want from you over the centuries, we've bought from you in a matter of a few years, and you *sold* it to us willingly. Now we're selling it back to you, and you *buy* it! And on top of all that you have a fancy for a good portion of authentic China. And you get that too, but you don't like it. You get all worked up about us walking all over human rights, but in essence you just don't understand how anyone can be imprisoned for his opinion in a land that drinks Coca-Cola. That doesn't compute to you. Your ethnologists lament the disappearance of the last cannibals and plead for the preservation of their living space, but woe betide them if they start to do business and wear ties. If they did, you'd want them to downgrade back to chicken and vegetables in the blink of an eye.'

'Tian, with the best will in the world, I don't know—'

'Do you realise that the term *zi you* was only exported to China in the middle of the nineteenth century?' Tu continued obstinately. 'Five thousand years of Chinese history weren't enough to create it, nor were they enough for *min zhu*, democracy, or ren quan, human rights. But what does *zi you* mean? To stay true to yourself. To make you and your point of view the starting point for everything you do, not the dogma of how the masses think and feel. You might argue that the demonisation of the individual is a Maoist invention, but you'd be wrong. Mao Zedong was merely a dreadful variant on our age-old fear of being ourselves. Perhaps a just punishment, because we had cooled off in our conviction that all the people outside China were barbarians. When China was forced to open itself up to the Western powers, we were completely ignorant of what every other people with experience of colonialism knew intuitively. We wrongly believed we were the hosts, whereas in reality the guests had long since become the owners. Mao wanted to change that, but he didn't just try to turn back the wheels of history, as the Ayatollahs went on to do in Iran. His efforts were focused on undoing history and isolating China on the summit of his ignorance. That just won't work with a people who think, feel and criticise. That only works with robots. Pu Yi wasn't our last Emperor; Mao was, if you see what I mean. He was the most horrific of them all: he stole everything from us, our language, our culture, our identity. He betrayed every ideal we had and all he left behind was a pile of rubble.'

Tu Tian paused, his fleshy lips twitching. Sweat shimmered on his bald head.

'You asked how Yoyo could have become a dissident? I'll tell you, Owen. Because she doesn't want to live with the trauma that my generation and my parents' generation will never be able to come to terms with. But if she wants to help an entire people find their identity, she can't quote the spirit of the French revolution, nor the foundation of Spanish democracy, nor the end of Mussolini or Hitler, the fall of Napoleon or of the Roman Empire. History may have equipped Europe with the inconceivable eloquence it needs to formulate its demands, but we have long lacked even the simplest words to do so. Oh, sure, China sparkles! China is rich and beautiful and Shanghai is the centre of the world, where everything is permitted and nothing is impossible. We've drawn even with the United States, two economic giants neck to neck, and we're on our way to becoming number one. But amidst all this shine our lives are impoverished on the inside, and we're aware of this poverty. We're not turning to the outside, Owen, it just seems like that. If we did turn to the outside, you would see the emptiness, like a transparent squid. We look to abroad for examples to follow, because the last Chinese example we had betrayed us. Yoyo suffers from being a child of this hollowed-out age more than the self-satisfied critics of globalisation and human rights infringements in Europe and America could ever imagine. You only see our transgressions, not the steps we're taking. Not what we've already achieved. Not the unimaginable toil necessary to stand up for ideals, to even formulate them, without any moral legacy!'

Jericho blinked in the glistening sunlight. He wanted to ask when Chen Hongbing's heart had been torn out, but he didn't say a word. Tu wheezed and swept his hand over his bald head nervously.

'That's what makes people like Yoyo bitter. If someone in England takes to the streets and demands freedom, the most that will happen is that someone might ask them what for. In China we've been labouring under the illusion that our crazy economic upturn would automatically bring freedom along with it, but we had no idea what freedom actually is.

'For over twenty years now, everything in our country has revolved around this word, everyone sings the joys of the individual way of life, but in the end all it means is the freedom to conform. People don't like talking about the other freedom because it questions by implication whether a Communist Party which is no longer communist has any right to absolute rule. The left-wing tyranny has become a right-wing one, Owen, and that in turn has become one without any substance. We live in a consumers' dictatorship, and woe betide anyone who comes and complains that there're still the issues of the farmers and the migrant workers and the executions and the economic support of pariah states and so on.'

Jericho rubbed his chin.

'I consider myself very lucky that you would honour me with all these explanations,' he said. 'But I'd be much happier if you could get back to Yoyo.'

'Forgive an old man, Owen.' Tu looked at him, his face furrowed. 'But I've been talking about Yoyo the whole time.'

'Yes, but without telling me about her *personal* background.'

'Owen, as I already said—'

'I know,' sighed Jericho. His gaze wandered over the glass and steel panels of the Jin Mao Tower. 'It's none of my business.'

Jin Mao Tower

Behind one of the panels, Xin stood staring out at the stifling sauna of the Shanghai afternoon. He had retreated to his spacious Art Deco suite on the seventy-third floor. It had floor-to-ceiling windows on two sides, but even from this exposed viewpoint there was nothing to see but architecture. The higher up one was, the more identical the individual blocks of apartments and offices looked, as if thousands upon thousands of termite tribes had taken up quarters alongside one another.

He dialled a tap-proof number on his mobile.

Someone answered. The screen stayed black.

'What have you found out about the girl?' asked Xin, without wasting any time on pleasantries.

'Very little,' answered the voice in his ear, the time lag barely noticeable. 'Only confirmation of what we already feared. She's an activist.'

'Well known?'

'Yes and no. Some of her files suggest we're dealing with a member of a group of internet dissidents who call themselves Guardians. A faction who are becoming a real nuisance to the Party with their demands for democracy.'

'You mean that Yoyo didn't intentionally seek us out?'

'We can probably rule that out. Pure coincidence. We scanned her hard drives faster than she could switch them off, which suggests the attack surprised her. We didn't manage to destroy her computer though. She must have a highly efficient security system, and unfortunately that doesn't bode well. We're now convinced that fragments – at least – of our transfer data are now in Yuyun – er, Yoyo's computer.'

'She won't be able to do much with it,' said Xin contemptuously. 'The encoding went through the strictest of tests.'

'In any other circumstances I would agree with you. But the way

Yoyo's protection is set up means she could have decoding programs which are much more advanced than the norm. We wouldn't have asked you to come to Shanghai if we weren't seriously concerned about this.'

'I'm as worried as you are. But what concerns me most is how sketchy your information is, if I may be so honest.'

'And what have you found out?' asked the voice, without responding to Xin's comment.

'I went to her apartment. Two flatmates. One knows nothing, and the other says he could take me to her. He wants money of course.'

'Do you trust him?'

'Are you crazy? I have no choice but to follow every lead. He'll be in touch, but I've no idea what will come of it.'

'Did she not mention any relatives to either of the flatmates?'

'Yoyo doesn't exactly seem that communicative. They were having some drinks together on the night of 23 May, then she disappeared some-time between two and three in the morning.'

A short pause followed.

'That could fit,' said the voice thoughtfully. 'The contact materialised just before two, Chinese time.'

'And then she immediately takes off.' Xin smiled thinly. 'Clever kid.'

'Where else have you been?'

'In her room. Nothing. No computer. She did a great job of clearing everything up before she disappeared. There's no trace of her at the uni-versity either, and it wasn't possible to see her file. I could arrange to do so, but I'd prefer it if you took care of that. I'm sure you can get into the university's database.'

'Which university?'

'Shanghai University, Shangda Lu, in the Bao Shan District.'

'Kenny, I don't need to remind you how explosive this thing is. So step up the pace! We need this girl's computer. Without fail!'

'You'll get it, *and* the girl,' said Xin, ending the call.

He stared back out into the urban desert.

The computer. He had no doubt that Yoyo had it with her. Xin wondered what the reasons for her overhasty departure had been. She must have realised that someone had not only noticed her hacking and started a counter-attack on her system, but that they had also downloaded her data, and therefore knew her identity. That was reason enough for concern, but not to flee in panic. Quite a few networks protected themselves by launching a lightning attack to deactivate the computers which had intentionally or unintentionally hacked into theirs and, if possible, they transferred the hacker's data right away. That alone wasn't enough. There must have been something else to make Yoyo think she wasn't safe any more.

There was only one possible explanation.

Yoyo had read something she wasn't supposed to have read.

Which meant the encoding had temporarily failed. An error in the system. A hole had unexpectedly opened up and provided her access. If that was the case, the consequences really could be terrible! The question was how quickly the hole had closed up again. Not quickly enough, that much was clear; just that brief glimpse had been enough to make the girl take flight.

But how much did she really know?

He needed more than the computer. He had to find Yoyo before she had the chance to pass on what she knew. The only hope so far was Grand Cherokee Wang. Quite a poor hope, admittedly. But when had hope ever been more than certainty's pitiful sister? In any case, the guy would sell Yoyo, and her computer included, the second she so much as set foot back in the apartment.

Xin frowned. Something in the way he was standing displeased him. He took a step backwards until he was positioned exactly between two joists, the tips of his shoes at equal distance from where the floor bordered the window.

There, that was better.

Pudong

'I've known Yoyo since the day she was born,' said Tu. 'She was just like any normal teenager while she was growing up, her brain full of romantic ideas. Then she ex-perienced something that changed her. Nothing spectacular, but I think it was one of those crossroads in life when you decide who you're going to be. Have you heard of Mian Mian?'

'The author?'

'Yes, that's the one.'

Jericho thought for a moment. 'It must be an eternity since I read one of her books. She was a figurehead of the scene, right? Quite popular in Europe. I remember being amazed that she made it past the censorship.'

'Oh, her books were banned for a long time! But by now she can do whatever she wants. When Shanghai declared itself to be the nightlife and party capital, she represented the area of conflict between glamour and the gutter, because she knew and could speak convincingly about both. Today, she's a kind of patron saint of the local art scene. In her mid-fifties, established, even the Party uses her as a figurehead. In the summer of 2016 she gave a reading from her new novel, in Guan Di in Fuxing Park shortly before it was torn down, and Yoyo went along. Afterwards, she had the chance to speak with Mian Mian, and they ended up doing a crawl around the clubs and galleries which lasted many hours. After that, it was like she was intoxicated. You have to appreciate the symbolic coincidence, you see. Mian Mian started writing when she was sixteen, as an immediate consequence of her best friend committing suicide, and Yoyo had just turned sixteen.'

'So she decided to become a writer.'

'She decided to change the world. To some extent, it was romantically motivated, but she also had an admirably clear take on reality. At around that time my own star was beginning to rise. I knew Chen Hongbing from the nineties and liked him a great deal. He entrusted his daughter to me because he believed she could learn from me. Yoyo had always been very fond of the virtual world; she practically lived on the internet. She was particularly interested in the vanishing dividing lines between the actual world and the artificial one. In 2018 I was elected onto the board of Dao IT, and Yoyo was just getting to grips with her studies at the time. Chen supported her as much as he could, but she placed a lot of importance on earning her own money. When she heard I was taking over the department for Virtual Environments, she pestered me to find a job for her there.'

'What did she study anyway?'

'Journalism, politics and psychology. The first to learn how to write, the second to know what to write about, and psychology—'

'To understand her father.'

'She wouldn't put it quite like that. The way she sees it, China is like a patient in constant danger of succumbing to insanity. So she looks for diagnoses for our diseased society. And that, of course, is where Chen Hongbing comes into the picture.'

'She got her tools from you,' ruminated Jericho.

'Tools?'

'Of course. When did you found Tu Technologies?'

'2020.'

'And Yoyo was there from the start?'

'Of course.' Tu's expression seemed to clear. 'Ah, I see.'

'She's been looking over your shoulder for years. You develop programs for every-thing under the sun.'

'I already know what role we play in the Guardians, unintentionally of course! But beyond that I can assure you that none of my people would ever dream of technologically arming a dissident.'

'Chen mentioned that she had already been arrested several times.'

'It was actually only during her studies that she realised the true extent to which the authorities censor the internet. For someone who views the net as their natural habitat, closed doors can be incredibly frustrating.'

'So she encountered the Diamond Shield.'

Anyone who tried to accelerate on the Chinese data highway soon found themselves up against virtual roadblocks. At the beginning of the millennium, fearing that the new medium could illuminate explosive topics, the Party had developed a highly armed defence program for net censorship, the Golden Shield, followed in 2020 by the Diamond Shield. With its help, an Internet Police force of over 150,000 rummaged their way though chat-rooms, blogs and forums. While the Golden Shield had been like a tracker dog, snuffling through the most far-flung corners of the web for terms like Tiananmen Massacre, Tibet, student revolts, freedom and human rights, the Diamond Shield was also able to recognise, to a certain extent, contextual meaning in the texts. This was the Party's reaction to the so-called Bodyguard Programs. Titanium Mouse, for example, had figured out after her release how to put critical texts on the net which didn't contain a single word that could be pounced on by the Golden Shield. To do this, she made use of a Bodyguard Program which rapped her on the knuckles, so to speak, while she was typing – if she used any incriminating terms, the Bodyguard would delete them, thus protecting her from herself. As a result the Diamond Shield paid less attention to keywords and instead assessed whole texts, connecting sayings and observations, inspecting the entries for double meanings and coding, and then raised the alarm if subversion was suspected.

Ironically, it was thanks to this very Cerberus that epoch-making advances were made in the hacker scene, enabling dissidents to unleash the maximum criticism with the minimum of risk. Of course, the Diamond Shield also blocked search engines and websites of foreign news agencies. The whole world had experienced the assassination of Kim Jong Un and the collapse of North Korea, but in the Chinese net none of it had ever happened. The bloody uprising against the junta in Burma might have taken place on Planet Earth, but not on Planet China. Anyone who tried to bring up the sites of Reuters or CNN could be sure of reprisal. To the same extent that the Wall of China was crumbling, the wall the Diamond Shield had erected around the country became stronger by the day, and yet so did the authorities' fear. It wasn't just the community of Chinese hackers who seemed to have sworn a solemn oath to shatter the Diamond Wall into a thousand pieces, but activists all around the world were working away on it too, some in the offices of European, Indian and American companies, Secret Services and government bases. The world was caught up in a cyber war, and, as the foremost aggressor, China was the key target for attack.

'Compared with what was going on with hackers,' explained Tu, 'inside China and outside, Yoyo's first steps in the net were kids' stuff. With her big, indignantly wide eyes, she hit out at censorship and signed her name underneath in bold. She pleaded for freedom of opinion and demanded access to the inventories of information provided by Google, Alta Vista and so on. She entered into dialogue with like-minded people who thought chat-rooms could be barricaded against unwanted intruders just as easily as broom cupboards.'

'Was she really that naïve?'

'To start with, yes. It's obvious that she wanted to impress Hongbing. In all seriousness, she really thought she was acting in accordance with his wishes. That he would be proud of his little dissident. But Hongbing was horrified.'

'He tried to stop her from doing it.'

'Yoyo was completely dumbfounded. She just couldn't understand it. Chen became stubborn, and I tell you, he can be as stubborn as a mule! The more Yoyo pushed him to justify his negative reaction, the more he dug his heels in. She argued. She screamed. She cried. But he still wouldn't talk to her. She realised he was worried for her of course, but it wasn't like she'd called for the government to be overthrown, she'd just grumbled a bit.'

'And so she confided in you.'

'She said she thought her father was just a coward. I certainly didn't let her get away with that one easily. I explained that I understood Hongbing's motivations better than she did, which made her bitter at first. Naturally, she wanted to know why Hongbing didn't trust his own daughter. I told her that his silence had nothing to do with lack of trust, but was related to something private. Do you have children, Owen?'

'No.'

'Well, they're little emperors!'

Little Emperors. Jericho stiffened. What an idiot! It was only a few hours since he'd stopped being tormented by the images of that cellar in Shenzhen, and now Tu was starting on about little emperors.

'They're just as wonderful as they are demanding,' Tu continued. 'Yoyo too. Anyway, I made it clear to her that her father had a right to his own life, and that the mere occasion of her birth didn't give her the right to trespass into the secret palaces of his soul, as it were. Children don't understand that. They think their parents are just there to provide a service, existing only to look after them, useful at first, then dumb and ultimately just embarrassing. She defended herself by saying that Hongbing started all of their arguments, that he was trying to control her life, and in that, unfortunately, she was right. Hongbing should have explained to her what it was that had angered him so much.'

'But he didn't. So? Did you?'

'He would never allow me to speak to Yoyo about that. Nor to anyone else, for that matter! So I tried to build a bridge between them. Let her know that her father had once met with a great injustice, and that no one suffered more from his silence than he himself. I asked her to be patient with him. With time, Yoyo began to respect my view, and she became very thoughtful. From that point on she confided in me regularly, which was an honour, although not one I would have actively sought out.'

'And Hongbing became jealous.'

Tu laughed softly, a strange, sad laugh.

'He would never admit it. The bond between him and me goes deep, Owen. But of course he didn't like it. It was inevitable that it would complicate things. Yoyo decided to intensify her tone on the net, to test the authorities' sensitivity threshold. But then again, she was only writing about everyday things: the scene, music, films and travel, and she also wrote poems and short stories. I don't think she was that clear about what she wanted to be: a serious journalist, a dissident or just another Shanghai Baby.'

'*Shanghai Baby* – wasn't that a book by—'

'Mian Mian.' Tu nodded. 'At the beginning of the millennium that's what people called young Shanghai writers. The term has gone out of fashion by now. Well, you've seen Yoyo. She made a name for herself in artists' circles, attracted the interest of the intellectuals, so did that make her an author?' Tu shook his head. 'She never wrote one good novel. And yet I would trust her to single-handedly get to the bottom of the death of John F. Kennedy. She's a brilliant researcher, excellent on the offensive. The censors picked up on that a long time ago. And Hongbing knows it too. That's why he's so worried, because Yoyo is someone others follow. She has charisma, she's believable. All dangerous qualities in the eyes of the Party.'

'When did she first go on their records?'

'To start with, nothing happened. The authorities bided their time. Yoyo was practically part of the furniture at my company; she showed a strong interest in holography and lent a hand in the development of some really fun programs, and the Party can't cope with fun. They just don't know what to make of it. It unsettles them that the Chinese are starting to value fun for the first time in their cultural development.'

'Aristotle wrote a book about laughter,' said Jericho. 'Did you know that?'

'I know my Confucius better.'

'No book ever caused more annoyance to the Church than this one did. They said that he who laughs, laughs also about God, the Pope and the entire clerical apparatus of power.'

'Or the Party. That's true, there are some parallels. On the other hand, anyone who's having fun is less angry and less political. For that reason the Party is on board with fun again, and Yoyo really is a fun-loving character. After a while she shifted her energies to singing and started one of these Mando-prog bands that are springing up everywhere. If Yoyo's not there, there is no party! If you're out and about in the scene, it's very difficult to avoid her. Perhaps back then they thought: The more fun the girl has, the less there'll be to fear from her. I'm sure that, had they left her in peace, it might even have worked.'

Tu pulled a once-white handkerchief from the depths of his trousers and wiped the sweat from his brow.

'But then suddenly, one morning five years ago, all of her blogs were blocked and all entries of her name erased from the net. She was arrested that same day and taken to a police station, where they left her to stew.

They accused her of being a threat to the security of the State and of having goaded the citizens into subversion. She spent a month there before Hongbing even knew where they were holding her. He nearly lost his mind! The whole thing was fatefully reminiscent of the Titanium Mouse case. No charge, no trial, no verdict, nothing. Even Yoyo herself didn't know what she was supposed to have done. She was banged up in a cell with two junkies and a woman who had stabbed her husband. The policemen were friendly to her. In the end they told her why she was there. She was alleged to have shown her support for some rock musician, a friend of hers who was in prison for some impudence or other. It was laughable. According to the constitution, the State prosecutor has six weeks to decide whether to go to trial or release someone. In the end they dropped the case due to lack of evidence, Yoyo received a warning and they let her go home.'

'I guess it goes without saying that Hongbing forbade her to make any more critical comments on the net,' Jericho surmised.

'And achieved exactly the opposite. Which means she acted as innocent as a lamb at first, wrote a few articles for internet magazines, even for Party organs. After a few weeks she stumbled across a case about the dumping of illegal toxic waste in the West Lake. A chemical company near Hangzhou, at the time still under State ownership, had carted over their waste and buried it in the lake, and as a result local residents lost their hair and even worse. The director of the company—'

'—was a cousin of the Minister for Employment and Social Security,' Jericho blurted out. 'Of course! Yoyo knew that, and that's why she wrote about it.'

Tu stared at him in amazement.

'How do you know that?'

'I've finally remembered where I know Yoyo's name from!' He relished the moment as his brain lifted the blockade and released the memory. 'I never saw a picture of her. But I remember the toxic waste scandal. It was all over the net back then, illegal dumping. They told her she was mistaken. Yoyo told them where they could stick it, and was promptly arrested.'

'Once Yoyo dug her feet in, it was just a matter of hours before all her entries in the net were erased again. The security police turned up at her door that same evening, and she found herself back in the cell. Yet, once again, they couldn't accuse her of anything. Her mistake was getting herself tangled up in the web of corruption. The State prosecution demanded to know what was going on. After all, they'd already investigated her the year before and found nothing, but they were put under pressure and had to charge her against their will.'

'I remember. She had to go to prison.'

'It could have been worse. Hongbing has a few contacts, and I have even better ones. So I found Yoyo a lawyer who managed to negotiate her sentence down to six months.'

'But what did they actually charge her with?'

'Passing on State secrets, the same as always.' Tu shrugged and smiled bitterly. 'The chemical company had entered into a joint venture with a British company, and Yoyo had gone to persuade one of its employees to collect evidence about the cloak-and-dagger operation. That was enough. But it was also enough to attract the media's attention to the case. China's journalists aren't as easily intimidated now as they were back in 2005, or even 2010. When one of their own is in the stocks, the dogs start to howl, and the Party is divided when it comes to cases of corruption. The story travelled abroad, Reporters Without Borders took up Yoyo's cause, the British Prime Minister made a few comments in passing during bilateral talks in Beijing. Three months later, Yoyo was released.'

'And the company director went swimming in the lake, right? I heard he killed himself.'

'It was probably more like a case of euthanasia,' smirked Tu. 'The authorities hadn't reckoned with being put under so much public pressure. They were forced to call an investigation. I imagine a lot of names came under question, but after the villain went swimming in his own sewage they could hardly ask him, so to be on the safe side the acting director and plant manager were dismissed and the investigations dropped. In 2022, Yoyo resumed her studies. Have you read her name anywhere since then?'

Jericho thought for a moment. 'Not that I know of.'

'Exactly. She really started to behave herself, at least when her own name was under the texts. She wrote articles on travel and cultural events, tried to spread the new Chinese culture of "fun". On the side, though, she acquired a bunch of pseudonyms and started to adopt different styles. She communicated via foreign servers, kicked the system up the backside whenever she could. She was like' – Tu laughed, spread his arms out and made flapping motions – 'Batgirl! A scene girl on the outside, but secretly embarking on a revenge mission against torture, corruption, the death penalty, legalised crime, environmental sins, the whole shebang. She demanded democracy, but a Chinese form of democracy! Yoyo didn't want to follow the Western path; she wanted the hollow, rotting tooth that called itself the Party to be pulled from the country so real values would have a chance. So we wouldn't be seen as just an economic giant, but also as the representatives of a new humanity.'

'God protect us from missionaries,' murmured Jericho.

'She isn't a missionary,' said Tu. 'She's searching for identity.'

'Something her father can't give her.'

'It's possible that Hongbing is the main motivation, yes. Perhaps all we're dealing with is a child who wants to be picked up and given a hug. But she's not naïve. Not any more! When she called the Guardians into existence, she knew exactly what she wanted. A phantom army. She wanted to be a power in the net which put the fear of God into the Party, and for that she had to uncover their machinations and damage their image in order to save China's. She needed a good year to build up the Guardians technologically.'

Jericho sucked on his cheek. He knew that the discussion had come to an end. Tu wouldn't give away any more than that.

'I need any records of Yoyo you can give me,' he said.

'There are some here.' Tu reached down next to him, opened a battered leather case and took a pair of hologoggles and a holostick from it. The stick was smaller than the current models, the glasses elegantly designed. 'These are prototypes. All the programs for which we used Yoyo as a virtual tour guide are saved on it. You can wander through the clubs with her if you like, visit the Jin Mao Tower and the World Financial Center, roam through the Yu Gardens or go to the MOCA Shanghai.' He grinned. 'You'll have a good time with her. She wrote the texts herself.

The stick also contains her personal files, recordings of conversations, photos and films. That's everything I have.'

'Nice.' Jericho rolled the stick between his fingers and looked at the glasses. 'I've got some hologoggles already.'

'Not like these you haven't. We were convinced the usual suspects would spy on that product development. But you seem to have scared them off with your last mission. Dao IT is still nursing its bruises.'

Jericho smirked. Dao IT, Tu's former employer, had been less than pleased to lose its chief development officer for Virtual Environments when he had decided to set up independently. Since then the company had broken into Tu Technologies' systems multiple times to download trade secrets. Each time, the hackers had hidden their tracks so skilfully that Jericho had had to use all the tricks of his trade to convict them. Tu had presented the evidence to the courts, and Dao IT had had to pay millions in fines.

'By the way, they made me an offer,' he said casually.

'Who?' Tu sat bolt upright. 'Dao?'

'Yes, well, they were impressed. They said if I had managed to track them down, it would be good to have me on their side.'

The manager pushed his construction of glasses up. He smacked his lips together noisily and cleared his throat.

'I guess they've got no shame.'

'I said no of course,' said Jericho slowly. Loyalty was a valuable thing. 'I just thought you might be interested to know.'

'Of course I would.' Tu grinned. Then he laughed and slapped Jericho on the shoulder. 'Get to work then, *xiongdi*.'

World Financial Center

Grand Cherokee Wang moved his body to an inaudible beat. His head nodded with every step, as if confirming his own coolness. Bouncing at the knees, playing imaginary instruments, he skipped along the glass corridor, clicking his tongue loudly, allowing himself the hint of a swing at the hips and baring his teeth. Oh, how he loved himself! Grand Cherokee Wang, the King of the World. He liked it best up here at night, when he could see his reflection in the glass surface that looked out over the sea of light that was Shanghai: it was as if he were towering out of it in the flesh, a giant! There wasn't a single shop window on Nanjing Donglu he forgot to pay homage to himself in: his beautifully structured face with the gold applications on his forehead and cheekbones, his shoulder-length blue-black hair, the white PVC jacket, although it was actually too warm for it at this time of year, but never mind. Wang and reflective surfaces were a match made in heaven.

He was right at the top.

At least, he worked right at the top, on the ninety-seventh floor of the World Financial Center, because Wang's parents had made their financing of his studies dependent on his willingness to contribute to it with earnings of his own. And so that's what he did. With such dedication that his father began to seriously wonder whether his otherwise less than delightful offspring actually loved working. In reality, though, it was thanks to the nature of this job in particular that Grand Cherokee Wang was now spending more time in the World Financial Center than in the lecture theatre, where his presence was more mandatory. On the other hand, it was clear that for a budding electrical and mechanical engineer, there could hardly be a better field trip than to the ninety-seventh floor of the World Financial Center.

Wang had tried to describe it to his grandmother, who had gone blind at the beginning of the millennium before the building had been completed.

'Can you remember the Jin Mao Tower?'

'Of course I can, I'm not stupid. I may be blind, but my memory still works!'

'Then imagine the bottle opener right behind it. You know, don't you, that people call it the bottle opener because—'

'I know they call it that.'

'But do you know why?'

'No. But I doubt I'll be able to stop you from telling me.'

Wang's grandmother often said that going blind had brought with it a series of advantages, the most pleasing of which was no longer having to see the members of her family.

'So, listen, it's a narrow building, with beautifully winding façades. Completely smooth, nothing jutting out, just glass. The sky's reflected in it, all around the building, like with the Jin Mao Tower. Unbelievable! Almost five hundred metres high, a hundred and one floors. How can I describe the shape? It's a quadratic structure at ground level, like a completely normal tower, but as you go higher the two sides level out so it gets narrower and narrower at the top, and the roof is a long ledge.'

'I don't know if I want to know this much detail.'

'You do! You have to be able to picture what they've managed to construct up there. Originally they planned for a circular opening under the ledge, fifty metres in diameter, but then the Party said it was a no go because of the symbolism. If it was round, it would look like Japan's Rising Sun—'

'The Japanese devil!'

'Exactly, so they built a square opening, fifty by fifty metres. A hole in the heavens. With the angular opening, the whole tower looks like a huge, upright bottle opener, and once it was finished in 2008, everyone called it that; there was nothing they could do about it. The lower section of the hole is a viewing platform with a glass pathway leading up above it. And where it cuts off above, there's a glass deck, with a glass floor too.'

'I'll never go up there!'

'Listen, this is where it really gets good: in 2020 someone came up with the absolutely crazy idea of building the highest roller-coaster in the world in the opening, the Silver Dragon. Have you heard of it?'

'No. Yes. I don't know.'

'The hole was too small for a complete roller-coaster of course. I mean, it's huge, but they had something bigger in mind, so they built the roller-coaster station in the opening and laid the track around the building. You climb into the car from the glass corridor, and off it goes, out ten metres beyond the edge of the building, then in a wide arc around the left side column round to the back of the tower. You hang there in the air above Pudong, half a kilometre up in the sky!'

'That's crazy!'

'It's awesome! At the back, the track climbs steeply towards the roof, circles round the right column and then flows into a long horizontal section which goes up onto the roof edge. Isn't that wild? Going for a ride on the roof of the World Financial Center!'

'I'd be dead by the time I got to that bit.'

'That's true, most people end up pissing their pants in the first few metres, but that's nothing yet. On the other side of the edge it suddenly rushes upwards. Into a steep curve! Now the car is really racing! And you know what? It races straight into the hole, into this huge hole, through under the roof axis, then up again, up, up, up, because you're in the god-damn looping section, high out over the roof, then steeply back down again, into the hole, around the right column and back upright and into the station, and three rounds of that. Oh man!'

Every time Grand Cherokee talked about it, he went hot and cold with excitement.

'Shouldn't you be studying?'

Should he be? In the glass corridor, hips swinging, watching the queue as it pushed its way forward at the barrier, faces turned towards him – some derailed between anticipation and the rushing onset of panic, some frozen in shock, others transfigured with the look of addiction – Grand Cherokee felt at an irreconcilable distance from the depressive depths of his studies. The university lay half a kilometre below him. He was far too special for an existence spent in lecture halls. Only the knowledge that all the cramming would ultimately enable him to create something even greater than the Silver Dragon kept him at it. He pushed his way through the queue of people to the glass door which separated the corridor from the platform, opened it and grinned around at them.

'I had to go and pee,' he said jovially.

Some of them pushed their way forward. Others took a step back, as if he had just summoned them for execution. He closed the door behind him, walked into the neighbouring glass-panelled room which housed the computer console, and awoke the dragon. Screens rekindled and lights flickered as the system loaded up. A number of monitors showed the individual sections of the track. The Silver Dragon was easy to operate, idiot-proof to be precise, but the people waiting outside didn't know that. For them, he was the magician in his crystal chamber. *He* was the Silver Dragon! Without Grand Cherokee, there was no ride.

He made the conjoined wagons roll back a little to the only section of the track that was surrounded by bars. They shimmered alluringly in the sun, barely more than silver surfboards on rails. The passengers were safely and securely buckled into their seats, but the ride was designed to be open-plan. No railing to give the illusion that there was anything to hold on to during the loop-the-loop. Nothing to distract you from looking down into the depths. The dragon knew no mercy.

He opened the glass door. Most held their mobile phones or e-tickets in front of the scanner, others had bought a ticket in the foyer. Once two dozen adrenalin-junkies had crossed through to the platform, he closed the door again. A chrome-plated barrier pushed down and opened the way into the dragon. Grand Cherokee helped the passengers into the seats, tested the supports and sent looks of reassurance into each pair of eyes. A female tourist, Scandinavian in appearance, smiled at him shyly.

'Scared?' he asked, in English.

'Excited,' she whispered.

Oh, she was scared all right! How wonderful! Grand Cherokee leaned over to her.

'When the ride's over, I'll show you the control room,' he said. 'Would you like to see the control room?'

'Oh, that would be – that would be great.'

'But only if you're brave.' He grinned, giving her a captivating smile. The blonde woman exhaled and smiled at him gratefully.

'I will be. I promise.'

Grand Cherokee Wang! The King of the Dragon.

Pacing quickly, he was back in the chamber again. His fingers whizzed over the computer table. Rail security on, start train. It was that easy. That's how quickly you could send people on an unforgettable ride between heaven and hell. The dragon left its barred cage and pushed out over the platform edge, speeding up and disappearing from view. Grand Cherokee turned round. Through the glass corridor he could see the powerful side columns, positioned far apart from one another, segmented into penthouse-size floors, and above him the glass-floored observatory which rose to dizzying heights. Visitors were moving about in it as if they were on black ice, looking down to the corridor fifty metres below with its roller-coaster station, where the next group of daredevils was already starting to gather. And everyone was staring at the left tower, from behind which the train was now pushing its way slowly forwards, to climb to the top of the slope, up to the roof, then disappear from view once more.

Grand Cherokee glanced at the monitor.

The wagons were getting closer to the edge of the roof. Beyond it, the track plummeted. He waited. It was the moment he enjoyed the most whenever he had the opportunity to ride along. The first time was the best. The sensation that the rails just suddenly went into the void. To plunge over the edge without anything to grip on to. Thinking the unthinkable, just before the dragon tipped and your gaze rushed ahead into the steep downward curve, before the boiling adrenalin washed every rational thought out of the convolutions of your brain and your lungs expanded into a scream. Tumbling head over heels towards the station, being thrown upside down, finding yourself weightless above the roof and, immediately afterwards, in the racing climb back up to the top.

The cars came back into view.

Fascinated, Grand Cherokee looked up. Time seemed to stand still.

Then the Silver Dragon plunged into the somersault.

He heard the screams even through the glass.

What a moment! What a demonstration of its power over body and spirit, and, in turn, what a triumph to ride the dragon, to *control* it! A feeling of invulnerability overcame Grand Cherokee. He tried to grab a seat on the ride at least once a day, because he was fearless, free from fear of heights, just as he was free of self-doubt, free of shame and scruples, free of the cantankerous voice of reason.

Free of caution.

While two dozen Dragon riders were experiencing their neuro-chemical inferno above him, he pulled his mobile out and dialled a number.

'I've got something,' he said, trying to stretch the words out so he sounded bored.

'You know where the girl is?'

'I think so.'

'Wonderful! That's really wonderful!' The man's voice sounded relieved and grateful. Grand Cherokee curled the corner of his mouth. The guy could try as hard as he liked to play the dear uncle, but it was obvious he wasn't looking for Yoyo so he could take care of her. He was probably Secret Service, or the police. It didn't matter. The fact was, he had money, and he was prepared to part with some of it. For that the guy would get information that Grand Cherokee didn't even have, because in actual fact he didn't have the faintest idea where she was, nor where she might be. Nor did he know who or what had caused the girl to go into hiding, or even whether she really had gone into hiding at all or perhaps had just taken off on holiday without telling anyone. His stock of knowledge on the matter was as empty as his bank account.

On the other hand, he wondered what it would sound like if he told the truth:

'Yoyo works in the World Financial Center with Tu Technologies downstairs. I'm in charge of the roller-coaster station at the top, for everyone who wants to piss their pants up here in zero gravity. That's how I met her. She turned up here because she wanted to ride the Dragon. So I let her have a ride and then afterwards I showed her how you steer the Dragon, and she thought it was – well—'

The truth, Grand Cherokee, the truth!

'—she thought it was a damn sight cooler than I was, even though that usually does the trick, I mean, letting them ride for free, then a trip with me, then a drink afterwards, see? She was crazy about the Dragon, and was looking for a place to crash because she wasn't getting on well with her old man or something, and Li and I happened to have a room free. Although – Li wasn't too happy about it. He says girls disrupt the chemistry, especially when they look like Yoyo, because if they do you end up thinking with your cock instead of your brain and then friendships fall apart, but I insisted, and Yoyo moved in. That was only two weeks ago.'

End of story. Or, perhaps just a little more:

'I thought that if Yoyo stayed with us I'd manage to get her into bed, but no such luck. She's a party girl; she sings and likes everything, which I like about her, even though it's incomprehensible.'

And then:

'Sometimes I saw her hanging around with guys from the real down-and-out neighbourhoods. Biker types. Could be a gang. They have these stickers on their jackets: City Demons, I think. Yeah, City Demons.'

This was the only thing that was worthy of being called information.

But he'd be lucky to get any money for that. So it was time to make something up.

'So where is she now?' the voice on the phone wanted to know.

Cherokee hesitated. 'We shouldn't discuss that on the—'

'Where are you? I can come right away.'

'No, no, I can't right now. Not today. Let's say first thing tomorrow. Around eleven.'

'Eleven isn't first thing.' The other man paused. 'If I understood you correctly, you want to earn some money, right?'

'You did understand me correctly! And *you* want something from *me*, don't you? So who makes the rules?'

'You, my friend.' Was it his imagination, or could he hear the man laughing softly? 'But how about ten regardless?'

Grand Cherokee thought for a moment. He had to tend to the roller-coaster at ten; it opened at half past. But on the other hand, perhaps it was a good idea to speak to Mister Big Money alone. If notes were going to change hands, the fewer onlookers there were the better, and at ten they would be completely alone: him, the man and the dragon.

'That's fine.' Besides, by then he would have thought of something. 'I'll let you know where you need to come.'

'Good.'

'And bring a nice bulging wallet with you.'

'Don't worry. I won't give you cause to complain.'

That sounded good.

Did it sound good? The cars rushed in and braked to a halt. The ride was over. Grand Cherokee looked over at the twenty-four pairs of trembling knees. He mentally prepared himself to provide support to the weakest ones.

Yes, it sounded good all right!

Jericho

Yoyo's shared flat was on Tibet Lu in a neighbourhood of identical-looking concrete towers. Just a few years ago there had been a night market here. Crouched gabled houses had thronged alongside one another in the shadow of the skyscrapers, an island of poverty and decay on just four square kilometres, with insufficient water supply and continual blackouts. Traders used to spread their wares out on the pavements, opening shops and doors so their living space took on the function of a stockroom and salesroom in one, or simply transforming their entire house into a street kitchen. Practically everything was for sale: household goods, medicinal herbs, roots to strengthen the libido, extracts to combat evil spirits, and souvenirs for tourists who had stumbled across the market accidentally and couldn't tell the difference between plastic and antique Buddhas. Pots steamed in every corner, a smell of fried fat and broth filled the narrow passageways. In no way unpleasant, as Jericho remembered from having strolled through there shortly after his arrival. Some of the things which had changed hands in exchange for a few coins had tasted incredibly good.

And yet a life was considered wretched if the people living it were forced to share a chronically blocked-up toilet between ten, assuming, that is, that their building even offered the luxury of a toilet. Logically then, when the real estate companies and representatives of the town planning department rushed in with their offers, one might have expected collective joy. There was talk of light and airy apartments, of electronic hobs and showers. But none of the residents' eyes had reflected the sparkle of sanitary promise. There was neither excitement nor resistance. They just signed the contracts, looked at one another and knew that their time had come. This life would come to an end, but it had still been a life nonetheless. The simple houses had seen better times, back before China's economy had started to accelerate in the early nineties. They were run-down, without a doubt, but with some good will they could still be called home.

Months later, Jericho had gone back there. At first he thought there must have been a bomb attack. A troupe of workers had been busy razing the entire quarter to the ground. His initial surprise had turned into disbelief when it dawned on him that a good half of the inhabitants were still living there, going about their usual business as wrecking balls swung all around, walls collapsed and dumper trucks transported off tonnes of rubble.

He had asked what would happen to the people once the whole quarter had disappeared.

'They'll move,' one of the builders enlightened him.

'And where to?'

The man's answer never came. Jericho, filled with consternation, had wandered around as darkness crept in and the stage was set for an amputated night market, its protagonists seeming to stubbornly deny the destruction taking place around them. Whenever he asked someone about it, they simply assured him, calmly and politely, that it was just the way it was. After a while Jericho became convinced that it couldn't solely be down to the broad Shanghai dialect that he only ever understood that one sentence, and that it must actually be the standardised reaction to every kind of catastrophe and injustice. *Mei you banfa*: There's nothing one can do.

Once night fell, a few people became more talkative. A plump old

woman, preparing delicious little dumplings in broth, told Jericho that
the compensation from the building authorities wasn't anywhere near
enough to buy a new apartment. Nor was it enough to rent one for any
considerable length of time. A second woman who came over said that
each of the inhabitants had been offered a much higher sum to start with,
but that no one had received the amount they had been promised. A
young man was considering making a complaint, but the plump woman
dismissed that with a subdued flick of her hand. Her son had already
complained four times. Every complaint had been rejected, but on the
fourth time they had locked him up in a cell for a week, only showing
him the door after they had administered a number of kicks.

Jericho ended up leaving as clueless as he had come. Now he had
returned for a third time, and there was no indication that there had ever
been anything here but towers with air-conditioning in front of the windows. The blocks were numbered, but in the advancing dusk the numbers
blurred against the background. Some idiot had clearly thought it would
be chic to paint pastel on pastel – in huge numbers, admittedly – but in
poor light they were as hard to make out as snow-white mountain hares
in a snowstorm. Jericho didn't waste time marching up and down the
streets. He pulled out his mobile, entered in the number and let the GPS
figure out his location. A grid-section of the city from satellite perspective appeared on the screen. Jericho projected the map onto the wall of
a nearby house. The beamer was strong enough to generate a brilliantly
clear image measuring two by two metres. The street he was standing
on ran diagonally over the wall, along with a number of side and parallel streets. He zoomed in. One blinking signal pinpointed his current
location down to the nearest metre, another marked out Yoyo's address.

'Please walk straight ahead for thirty-two metres,' said the mobile in
a friendly tone. 'Then turn right—'

He deactivated the voice and set off. He had found out all he needed to
know: that Yoyo's building was just around the corner and easily reached.

Within two minutes he was ringing the doorbell.

It was a surprise visit and therefore an investment of sorts. The relative slimness of the chance he'd find someone at home was cancelled out

by the benefits of the surprise attack. The recipient of the visit, if there were one, had no chance to prepare himself, hide things or rehearse lies. According to Jericho's research, Yoyo's flatmates had never had a criminal record, nor had they ever attracted the attention of the authorities. One of them, Zhang Li, was studying Economics and English, the other was enrolled in Electrical and Mechanical Engineering. As far as the authorities were concerned he was called Wang Jintao, but called himself Grand Cherokee. That was nothing unusual. In the nineties, young Chinese people had begun to put Western names before their family ones, a practice that wasn't always carried out that tastefully. It wasn't uncommon for men, in ignorance of a word's associations, to name themselves after sanitary towels or dog food, whilst on the women's side it wasn't unusual to meet a Pershing Song or White House Liang. Wang, for example, had even selected himself an American four-by-four as a forename.

If Tu was to be believed, neither Wang nor Li was a stay-at-home type, which meant he could have made the journey here in vain. But after he'd rung for the second time, something surprising happened. Without anyone bothering to use the intercom, the buzzer sounded and the door was released. Walking into a bare hallway which stank of cabbage, he took the lift up to the seventh floor and found himself on a whitewashed landing where the neon lighting was flickering nervously. A little further along, a door opened up. A young man came out and looked Jericho up and down coolly.

There was no doubt it was him!

His forehead and cheekbones were adorned with metallic applications, highly fashionable right now. Their arrival had ended the era of piercings and tattoos. Anyone who still dared to have a ring through their eyebrow or silver in their tongue was seen as an embarrassment. Even the hairstyle, smooth and long, fitted in with the trend. It was known as Indian style, as currently worn by the majority of young men around the globe, apart from the Indians themselves of course, who rejected all responsibility for it. A spray-on shirt emphasised Wang's muscles, his wet-look leather trousers gave the impression that they were on duty both day and night. All things considered, the guy didn't look bad, but he didn't look great either. The warlike appearance was lacking about ten centimetres in height, and the edgy quality of his features might be quite pleasing, but they were devoid of any proportional elegance.

'And you are?' he asked, suppressing a yawn.

Jericho held his mobile phone out under Wang's nose and projected a 3D image of his head, along with his police registration number, onto the folded-up display.

'Owen Jericho, web detective.'

Wang squinted.

'So I see,' he said, trying to sound ironic.

'Could I have a moment of your time?'

'What's up?'

'This is the apartment of Chen Yuyun, is that correct? Yoyo for short.'

'Wrong.' The guy seemed to chew the word before spitting it out. 'This apartment belongs to me and Li, and the little one just dumped her books and clothes here.'

'I thought she lived here?'

'Let's get one thing clear, okay? It's not *her* apartment. *I* let her have the room.'

'Then you must be Grand Cherokee.'

'Yeah!' The mention of his forename made its owner suddenly switch into friendly mode. 'You've heard of me?'

'Only good things,' lied Jericho. 'Would you be able to tell me where I can find Yoyo?'

'Where you could find—' Grand Cherokee paused. For some unknown reason the question seemed to take him by surprise. 'That's—' he murmured. 'That's really something!'

'I need to speak to her.'

'You can't.'

'I know Yoyo has disappeared,' Jericho added. 'That's why I'm here. Her father's looking for her, and he's very worried. So if you know anything about where she is—'

Grand Cherokee stared at him. Something about the boy, or rather about his attitude, irritated Jericho.

'As I said,' he repeated, 'if you—'

'Just a moment.' Grand Cherokee raised his hand. For a few seconds he paused like that, then his features seemed to smooth out.

'Yoyo.' He smiled jovially. 'But of course. Don't you want to come in?'

Still confused, Jericho entered the narrow hallway, which branched off into a number of other rooms. Grand Cherokee hurried ahead of him, opened the last door and nodded inside with his head.

'I can show you her room.'

Suddenly, Jericho understood. This much cooperation was bordering on calculation. Slowly, he walked into the room and looked around. It didn't say much. There was hardly anything to suggest who lived here except for a few posters of popular figures from the Mando-prog scene. One of the pictures was of Yoyo herself, posing on a stage. A note fluttered around on a pinboard above a cheap desk. Jericho walked over to it and studied the few symbols.

'Dark sesame oil,' he read. '300 grams of chicken breast—'

Grand Cherokee cleared his throat discreetly.

'Yes?' Jericho turned round to him.

'I could give you some clues about where Yoyo is.'

'Excellent.'

'Well.' Grand Cherokee spread his fingers meaningfully. 'She told me a lot, you know? I mean, the little one likes me. She got quite friendly in the last few days she was here.'

'Were you friendly too?'

'Let's just say I had the opportunity to be.'

'And?'

'Well, come on, that's confidential, man!' Grand Cherokee was clearly making a great effort to look outraged. 'I mean, of course we can discuss everything, but—'

'No, it's fine. If it's confidential.' Jericho turned away and left him standing there. A wise guy, just as he'd feared. One after another, he pulled open the drawers of the desk. Then he went over to the narrow wall cabinet next to the door and opened it. Jeans, a pullover, and a pair of trainers which had seen better days. Two cans of disposable clothing spray. Jericho shook it. Half full. Clearly Yoyo had packed the majority of her things in a great hurry and left the flat in a rush.

'When was the last time you saw your flatmate?'

'The last time?' echoed Grand Cherokee.

'The last time.' Jericho looked at him. 'That's the time after which you didn't see Yoyo any more, so when was that?'

'Ah, yes, er—' Grand Cherokee seemed as though he was just emerging from deep water. 'On the evening of 23 May. We had a little party. Li went off to bed at some point, and Yoyo hung around with me for a while. We chatted and had some drinks, and then she went off to her room. A little later I heard her crashing around and opening drawers. Shortly after that the house door slammed in the lock.'

'When exactly?'

'Between two and three, I guess.'

'You guess?'

'It was before three for sure.'

Given that Grand Cherokee seemed to be making no effort to stop him from doing so, Jericho carried on searching through Yoyo's room. Out of the corner of his eye he saw the student skulking around hesitantly. Jericho's lack of interest in him seemed to be confusing him.

'I could tell you more,' he said after a while. 'If you're interested.'

'Out with it.'

'Tomorrow maybe.'

'Why not now?'

'Because I need to make a few calls to— I mean, I already know where Yoyo hangs out, but before that—' He stretched out his arms and turned his palms to face upwards. 'Let's just say, everything has its price.'

That was clear enough.

Jericho finished his search and walked back into the hall.

'As long as it's worth its price,' he said. 'By the way, where's your flatmate?'

'Li? No idea. He doesn't know anything anyway.'

'Is it just my imagination, or do you not know anything either?'

'Me? Yes, I do.'

'But?'

'No but. I just thought perhaps you might think of how someone might be able to release trapped knowledge?' Grand Cherokee grinned up at him.

'I see.' Jericho smiled back. 'You'd like to negotiate an advance.'

'Let's call it a contribution towards expenses.'

'And for what, Grand Cherokee, or whatever you're called? So that you can mess me about with your garbled imagination? You don't know shit!'

He turned round to go. Grand Cherokee seemed filled with consternation. Obviously he had seen the conversation as going a little differently. He held Jericho back by the shoulder and shook his head.

'I'm not trying to rip anyone off, man!'

'Then don't.'

'Come on! The kind of course I'm on doesn't pay for itself! I'll find out whatever you want to know.'

'Wrong! You have nothing to sell me.'

'I—' The student searched for words. 'Okay, fine. If I tell you something, right here and now, that helps you to make some progress, will you trust me then? That would be my advance, you see?'

'I'm listening.'

'So, there's a biker gang that she hangs out with a lot. She rides a motorcycle too. The City Demons – that's what it says on their jackets at any rate.'

'And where can I find them?'

'That *was* my advance.'

'Now you listen to me,' said Jericho, jabbing a finger at his adversary. 'Here and now I'm paying you nothing. Because you have nothing. Nothing at all. If you should happen to get hold of some real information, driven by the goodness of your heart – and I mean real information! – then we may be able to do business. Is that clear?'

'Perfectly.'

'So when shall I expect your call?'

'Tomorrow afternoon.' Grand Cherokee plucked at the tip of his chin. 'No, earlier. Perhaps.' He gave Jericho a penetrating look. 'But then it's payday, man!'

'Then it's payday.' Jericho smacked him on the shoulder. 'An appropriate amount. Did you want to say anything else?'

Grand Cherokee shook his head silently.

'Then I'll see you tomorrow.'

Then I'll see you tomorrow—

He stood in the hallway as if he were rooted to the spot, even once the detective was already on his way downstairs. As he heard the lift door rattle lightly in the shaft, his thoughts came thick and fast.

Well, this was incredible!

Deep in thought, he went into the kitchen, fetched a beer from the fridge and raised the bottle to his lips. What was going on here? What had Yoyo done to make everyone so interested in her disappearance? First that smart guy and now the detective. And, even more importantly:

How could he profit from it?

It wouldn't be easy, that's for sure. Grand Cherokee was under no illusions: his knowledge of her whereabouts was nonexistent, and the next few hours would do little to change that. On the other hand it would be a real stroke of bad luck if he couldn't come up with a few juicy lies by the next morning. The kind of lies that no one could prove, along the lines of: my information is first-hand, I don't know either, clearly Yoyo got wind of something, it was right under our nose, and so on and so forth.

He would have to push the price right up. Play them off against one another! It was a good thing he hadn't told the detective about Xin's visit. People could say what they wanted about him, but certainly not that he was dumb.

I'm too on the ball for the two of you, he thought.

He was already counting the notes in his mind.

26 May 2025

THE SATELLITE

Arrival

As if there hadn't been dozens of pairs of boots marking the surface of the Moon with the imprint of mankind's heroism since 2018, Eugene Cernan – the commander of Apollo 17 – was still regarded as the last man to have walked on its surface. The years between '69 and '72 were monumental in the landscape of American history: a short but magical epoch of manned missions which were strangely counteracted by Nixon bringing the space programme back down to earth with a bump. As a result, Cernan became the last one up there to turn off the light. He was, and remained, the last of his century. The eleventh Apollo astronaut on the Moon, he walked around the Mare Serenitatis and made hundreds of those small steps that Neil Armstrong had declared to be such a giant leap for mankind. His team collected the biggest sample of lunar rocks and completed more moon surface trips than any other before them. The commander himself even managed to cause the first ever automobile accident on a celestial body, smashing up the rear left wing of his Lunar Rover, before – with a talent for improvisation reminiscent of Robinson Crusoe – patching it back together again. Yet none of this was enough to re-enliven the public's interest. It was the end of an era. Cernan, presented with the opportunity to immortalise himself in encyclopaedias and textbooks with a thunderous obituary, instead offered words of remarkable helplessness:

'We spent most of the trip home,' he said, 'debating the colour of the Moon.'

Incredible. So that was the grand summary of six expensive landings on a rock hundreds of thousands of kilometres away from Earth? That no one even knew what colour it was?

'It looks kind of yellow to me,' said Rebecca Hsu, after gazing silently out of the small porthole for a long while. Hardly any of them were venturing over to the row of windows any more. From there, throughout the two days since their launch, they had watched their home planet get smaller and smaller, a ghostly dwindling of familiarity. It was as if they were dividing their loyalty equally at the midway point between the Earth and Moon before fully succumbing to the fascination of the satellite. From 10,000 kilometres away it could still be seen in its entirety, starkly silhouetted against the blackness of outer space around it. And yet this object of romantic contemplation had billowed to become a sphere with menacing presence, a battlefield, scarred by billions of years of celestial bombardment. In complete silence, unbroken by the soundtrack of civilisation, they raced towards this strange, alien world. Only the tinnitus-like hiss of the life-support systems indicated that there was any technological activity on board at all. Beyond that, the silence made their heartbeats thunder like bush drums and the blood swirl in their veins. It roused lively chatter within the body about the state of its chemical processes and pushed their imaginations to the very limit.

Olympiada Rogacheva paddled up, in awe of her weightlessness. They had advanced another thousand kilometres towards the satellite, and could now see only three-quarters of it.

'It doesn't look yellow,' she murmured. 'To me it seems more mouse-grey.'

'Metallic grey,' Rogachev corrected her coldly.

'I'm not so sure,' Evelyn Chambers looked over from the next window. 'Metallic? Really?'

'Yes, really. Look. Up there to the right, the big, round patch. Dark, like molten iron.'

'You've been in the steel industry for too long, Oleg. You could find something metallic in a chocolate pudding.'

'Of course he could – the spoon! Woohoo!' Miranda Winter did a somersault, cheering gleefully. Most of the others had tired of doing zero-gravity acrobatics. But Miranda couldn't get enough of them and was rapidly getting on the others' nerves. She was incapable of holding a conversation without rolling through the air, squealing and cackling, thumping people in the ribs or whacking them on the chin as she did.

Evelyn, on the receiving end of a kick in the small of her back, snapped: 'You're not a merry-go-round, Miranda. Give it a rest, will you!'

'But I feel like one!'

'Then close yourself down for repairs or something. It's too cramped in here for all that.'

'Hey, Miranda.' O'Keefe looked up from reading his book: 'Why don't you try imagining you're a blue whale instead?'

'What? Why?'

'Blue whales wouldn't act like that. They're content to just hang around, more or less motionless, and eat plankton.'

'They blow water too,' Heidrun commented. 'Do you want to see Miranda blow water?'

'Sure, why not?'

'You're all being silly,' Miranda concluded. 'By the way, I think it's kind of blue. The moon, I mean. It's almost eerie.'

'Uhhh,' O'Keefe shuddered.

'So what colour is it?' Olympiada wanted to know.

'It's every colour, and yet none.' Julian Orley came through the connecting hatch that separated the living quarters of the Charon from the landing module. 'No one knows.'

'How come?' Rogachev wrinkled his forehead. 'I mean, surely we've had enough time to figure that out?'

'Of course. The problem is that no one has seen it through anything other than toned or filtered windows and visors yet. And on top of that, the Moon doesn't have a particularly high albedo—'

'A what?' asked Miranda, rotating like a pig on a spit.

'Reflectivity. The fraction of solar energy which is reflected back to space. The reflection rate of lunar rock is not especially high, particularly not in the maria—'

'I'm not following a word you say.'

'The dry plains on the surface of the Moon,' explained Julian patiently. 'Collectively, they're called maria. The plural of mare. They appear to be even darker than the mountain rings in the craters.'

'So why does the Moon look white when we look at it from Earth?'

'Because it has no atmosphere. Sunlight hits its surface unfiltered, in just the same way it would an astronaut's unprotected retina. The UV rays outside are far more dangerous to our eyes than they would be on Earth, that's why the spaceship's windows are tinted.'

'But loads of lunar samples have been brought back to Earth,' said Rogachev. 'What colour are they?'

'Dark grey. But that doesn't necessarily mean that the whole moon is dark grey. Perhaps some parts of it are brown, or even yellow.'

'Exactly,' said O'Keefe from behind his book.

'Everyone sees it slightly differently. Everyone has their own moon, one might say.' Julian went over to join Evelyn. They were passing over a lone gigantic crater which lay far below them. Molten light seemed to stream from its slopes down to the surface surrounding it. 'That's Copernicus by the way. According to popular opinion it's the most spectacular of all the lunar craters and over eight hundred million years old. It's a good ninety kilometres wide, with slopes that would present a challenge to any mountaineer, but the most impressive thing about it is how deep it is. Do you see that massive shadow inside it? It's almost four kilometres down to the very bottom.'

'There are mountains right in the middle of it,' observed Evelyn.

'How is that possible?' wondered Olympiada. 'I mean, in the middle of the point of impact? Shouldn't it all be flat?'

Julian fell silent for a while.

'Imagine it like this,' he said. 'Picture the surface of the Moon, just as you see it now, but without Copernicus. Okay? Everything is still and peaceful. So far! Then, a boulder eleven kilometres in diameter rushes up from the depths of outer space at a speed of seventy kilometres per second, two hundred times the speed of sound. There's no atmosphere, nothing at all that could slow it down. Imagine what kind of impact it would make crashing into the surface. That alone would happen in just a few thousandths of a second. The meteor would penetrate the surface by about a hundred metres – not particularly deep you might say, and an eleven-kilometre crater like that wouldn't be such a big deal. But there's a little more to it than that. The complex thing about meteorites is that they transform all their kinetic energy into heat at the moment of impact. In other words, they explode! It's this explosion that can create a hole ten to twenty times bigger than the meteorite itself. Millions of tonnes of rock are blasted in all directions and, in a flash, a wall forms around the crater. The whole thing happens at such speed, the displaced layers of lunar basalt can't be restructured as quickly, so the surface gives in to the shock pressure and is compressed many kilometres deep. Meanwhile, huge clouds of debris are collecting overhead. The meteorite, of course, is now fully transformed into heat and no longer exists in its previous form, so the ground rebounds, shooting upwards to form a massive peak in the centre of the crater. The rock clouds continue to spread rapidly and once again the absence of any atmosphere to contain the radius of the cloud makes itself felt. Instead the debris is flung further and further out before descending, hundreds of kilometres away, like billions of missiles. You can still see this ring of fall-out today, known as an ejecta blanket, especially when there's a full moon. It has a different albedo to the darker volcanic rock around it, and seems to glow from within. In actual fact it's just reflecting a little more sunlight. So, that's how you should picture Copernicus coming about. Victor Hugo, by the way, claimed to see an eye within it that looked back at whoever was looking at the Moon.'

'Uh-huh,' said Olympiada dejectedly.

Julian smiled knowingly to himself, relishing the awkward silence that followed his account. All around him cosmic bombs were crashing into their thoughts and converting kinetic energy into questions such as, in the event of a similar impact threatening Earth, whether it would be better to seek refuge in the cellar or to go for one last beer.

'I guess our atmosphere wouldn't be of much help?' Rebecca Hsu suggested.

'Well . . .' Julian pursed his lips. 'Meteorites are always plummeting down to Earth, around forty tonnes of them a day in fact. Most of them are the size of a grain of sand or pebble and end up burning themselves out. Now and again one the size of a fist will come along, and occasionally something bigger will crash into tundra or the sea. In 1908, for example, a sixty-metre-wide fragment of a comet exploded over Siberia and devastated an area the size of New York.'

'I remember hearing about that,' said Rogachev drily. 'We lost some forest, a few sheep and a shepherd.'

'You would have lost a lot more if it had hit Moscow. But yes, in the main, the universe is essentially past the worst. Meteorites like the one that caused Copernicus have become few and far between.'

'How far between exactly?' drawled Heidrun.

Julian pretended to give it some thought. 'The last really significant one came down sixty-five million years ago in the area that's now known as Yucatán. The shock-waves travelled all around the world, causing several years of continuous winter, which led to the loss of considerable amounts of flora and fauna, and unfortunately, almost all the dinosaurs.'

'That doesn't answer my question.'

'You really want to know when the next one will hit?'

'Just for my own planning purposes, yes.'

'Well, according to statistical data there's a global catastrophe every twenty-six million years. How catastrophic exactly depends on the size of the impactor. An asteroid seventy-five metres in diameter has the explosive force of one hundred Hiroshima bombs. Anything exceeding two kilometres can trigger a global winter and would mean the end of mankind.'

'So, according to that we're forty million years overdue,' established O'Keefe. 'How big was the dinosaur-killer again?'

'Ten kilometres.'

'Thank you, Julian, I'm very glad you've brought us up here away from it all.'

'So what can we do about it?' asked Rebecca.

'Very little. The nations with space programmes have avoided dealing with the problem for years, preferring instead to devote their energy to building up an expensive battery of mid-range missiles. But what we really need is a functioning meteorite defence system. When the hammer falls it won't matter whether you're a Muslim, Jew, Hindu or Christian, atheist or fundamentalist, or who you're fighting with, none of that will matter. Crash, and that's it! We don't need weapons against each other. What we really need is one that can save us all.'

'So true.' Rogachev looked at him, expressionless. Then he glided over, took Julian by the arm and pulled him slightly apart from the others.

'But haven't you had that for ages already?' he added, quietly. 'Aren't you in the process of developing weapons against meteorites too?'

'We've created a development team, yes.' Julian nodded.

'You're developing weapons on the OSS?'

'Defence systems.'

'How reassuring for all of us.' The Russian smiled thinly.

'It's a research group, Oleg.'

'Well, I hear the Pentagon are very interested in this research group.'

'Don't worry.' Julian smiled back. 'I know the rumours. Both Russia and China are constantly accusing us of producing space weapons for the Americans. But it's all nonsense! The sole purpose of our research is to be able to act if the laws of probability come into their own. I sure as hell want to be able to shoot if something like that's on a collision course.'

'Weapons can be used against all kinds of things, Julian. You've secured America a position of power in space. You yourself are striving to rule over the energy supply by controlling the technologies. You're wielding a great deal of power, and you're trying to tell me you're not pursuing your own interests?'

'Look out of the window,' said Julian calmly. 'Look at that blue-white jewel.'

'I see it.'

'And? Are you homesick?'

Rogachev hesitated. 'I don't really use terms like that.'

'You can choose whether to believe me on this or not, Oleg, but once this trip is behind you, you'll be a different person. You'll have realised that our planet is a fragile little Christmas tree bauble, covered by a wafer-thin layer of breathable air, *so far* at least. No borders or national states, just land, sea and a few billion people who have to share the bauble because it's the only one they've got. Every decision that's not aimed at keeping our planet together, every aggression for some resource or religious idea will sicken you. Perhaps you'll stand on the peak of some crater and cry, or maybe you'll just ask a few sensible questions, but it *will* change you. There's no way back once you've seen the Earth from space, from the distance of the Moon. There's nothing you can do but fall in love with it. Do you really think I would allow someone to misuse my technologies?'

Rogachev fell silent for a while.

'I don't believe you would *want* to allow it,' he said. 'I'm just asking myself whether you have any choice in the matter.'

'I do, the more friends I get.'

'But you're a world champion in making enemies! I know you have a league of extraordinary gentlemen in mind, a world power of independent investors, but for that you're intruding massively into national interests. How does it fit together? You want my money, Russian money, but on the other hand you don't want anything to do with Moscow.'

'So is it Russian money just because you're Russian?'

'Well, I'm sure they'd prefer it there if I invested my fortune in national space travel.'

'Good luck. Let me know when you've managed to get your own space elevator.'

'You don't think we can?'

'You don't even believe it yourself! I own the patents. But still, I have to admit that I wouldn't have got this far without America. We've both invested astronomical sums in space travel. But Russia is broke. Putin founded his Mafia state on oil and gas, and now no one wants it. You played poker and you lost. Don't forget, Oleg, that Orley Enterprises is ten times the size of Rogamittel. We're the biggest technology company in the world, but my investors and I still need each other nonetheless. But no one in Moscow would do you any favours. It may be a patriotic gesture, sponsoring Russia's ramshackle space travel, but your money would just drain away. You wouldn't last long enough to catch up with me, because your State would have sucked the very last drop out of you before you even had the chance, and without creating any decent results either.'

This time Rogachev was silent for even longer. Then he smiled again.

'Moscow would give you more of a free hand than Washington. Are you sure you don't want to switch sides?'

'I guessed you'd be obliged to ask me that.'

'I was asked to test the waters, see how willing you might be.'

'Firstly, we're not in the Cold War any more. Secondly, Russia can't afford my exclusivity. Thirdly, I'm not on anyone's side. Does that answer your question?'

'Let's put it a different way. With the right conditions, would you be willing to sell your technologies to Russia *too*?'

'Well, would you be prepared to climb on board with me? I mean, you're certainly not here because you're afraid of Moscow.'

Rogachev stroked his chin.

'You know what?' he said. 'I suggest we sleep on it and enjoy a few days of holiday first.'

The Charon was essentially a tube, seven metres in diameter and twenty-eight metres long, segmented into three parts and connected to a landing module. A flying omnibus, divided up into sleeping quarters and command cockpit, bistro and seating area, whose creator had failed to do it the honour of making it aerodynamic given that it would never be required to pass through an atmosphere. The Apollo capsules and the Orion, originally planned as successor to the space shuttle, hadn't exactly met the expectations of design-accustomed cinema-goers either, but they had at least been able to offer a chicly rounded little nose, which began to give off a red glow on entering the thermosphere. Compared with this, the Charon had all the charm of a household appliance. A tonne of white and grey, smooth here, corrugated there, partly filled with fuel, partly with astronauts, and adorned with the O of Orley Enterprises.

'Prepare for braking manoeuvre,' said Peter's voice over the loudspeaker.

Two and a half days in a space shuttle, even if it was incredibly spacious and decorated in a colour scheme developed by psychologists, still brought thoughts of detention centres to mind. The enchantment of the unfamiliar lost its lustre when confronted with the proximity and monotony of their surroundings, and came out in debates about the state of the planet, as well as unexpected chumminess and openly expressed dislike. Sushma and Mukesh Nair, aided by their charismatic shyness, rallied like-minded people around them, including Eva Borelius, Karla Kramp, Marc Edwards and Mimi Parker. They engaged in relaxed conversation, that is until Mimi initiated a discussion about Darwinism: wasn't it just some dead end the natural sciences had ended up in thanks to atheistic arrogance, from which only a creationist world-view could offer the way out? Life, she concluded, was far too complex to have come about by chance in some ancient ocean, and especially not four billion years ago. Karla responded that comments like that questioned the complexity of some of the people present, a riposte which unleashed a series of heated reactions. Aileen Donoghue came to Mimi's aid, saying that although she didn't want to tie herself down to the specifics of a few thousand years more or less, she still questioned any relationship between the species. It was much more likely that all living beings had been created by God in one breath. Karla commented that it was perfectly obvious that Mimi was descended from apes. Besides which, the first two chapters in the Book of Moses each dealt with the creation of mankind differently, so even the Old Testament couldn't offer any unity on the process of creation, in so far as one could base serious scientific knowledge on one single, historically questionable book.

Meanwhile, bonds were formed between Rebecca Hsu, Momoka Omura, Olympiada Rogacheva and Miranda Winter. Evelyn Chambers got on well with everyone, apart from Chuck Donoghue perhaps, who had told Mimi in confidence that he thought Evelyn was godless, a comment which she had immediately passed on to Olympiada and Amber Orley, who, in turn, had told Evelyn. Locatelli, who had now recovered from his space sickness, started showing off again with stories of sailing and motor yachts and how he had won the America's Cup, of his love of running, solar-powered racing cars and the possibility of extracting enough energy even out of a tick that it could make its contribution to the protection of the environment.

'Every single body, even the human one, is a machine,' he said. 'And machines create warmth. All of you here are nothing more than machines, mere heaters. I tell you, people, if we collected everyone around the world into one great big machine, we wouldn't need helium-3.'

'And what about the soul?' asked Mimi indignantly.

'Bah, the soul!' Locatelli threw his arms apart, floated away a little and tapped his finger against his skull. 'The soul is software, my dear lady. Just thinking flesh. But if there were a soul, I would be the first to build a machine out of it. Hahaha!'

'Locatelli was telling us the most amazing things,' said Heidrun to Walo later. 'Do you know what you are?'

'What am I, my love?'

'An oven. Now come here and warm me up.'

Mimi and Karla made their peace with one another, Hanna played guitar – unifying the others at least on a musical level, and winning a fan in Locatelli, who was photographing him constantly – and O'Keefe read screenplays. Each one of them acted as though their noses weren't filled with the steadily intensifying mélange of sweat, intimate odours, flatulence and hair sebum, against which even the high-tech air synthesiser on board was struggling in vain. Space travel might be fascinating, but one of its disadvantages was definitely not being able to open a window to let some fresh air in. Evelyn wondered how it was supposed to work on long-term missions, with all the smells and increasing tension. Hadn't a Russian cosmonaut once said that all the prerequisites for committing murder were there if two men were shut into a narrow cabin and left alone together for two months? But perhaps they would take different people on a mission like that. No individualists, certainly not a load of crazy super-rich people and celebrities. Peter Black, their pilot, certainly seemed well-balanced, one might even say quite boring. A team player without any flamboyant or alarmist characteristics.

'Start braking manoeuvre.'

From a distance of 220 kilometres away they could still see half of the Moon, revealing magnificent detail. It looked so round, on account of its modest proportions, that there seemed good reason to fear they wouldn't be able to get a grip when landing and would just slide down the side. Nina Hedegaard floated over to help them put on their pressure suits, which also contained bladder bags.

'For later, when we land,' she explained with a puzzling smile.

'And who says we'll need to go?' called out Momoka Omura.

'Physics.' Nina's dimples deepened. 'Your bladder could take the onset of gravity as a reason to empty itself without any advance warning. Do you want to soak your pressure suit?'

Momoka looked down at herself as if she already had.

'This whole venture seems to be somewhat lacking in the elegance stakes,' she said, pulling on what she had to wear.

Nina shooed the Moon walkers through the connecting airlock into the landing craft, yet another barrel, this time conically shaped at the top and equipped with four powerful telescopic legs. In comparison with the living module it offered all the movement radius of a sardine-tin. Most of them let the procedure of being strapped in wash over them with the embalmed facial expression of old hands; after all, it was only two and a half days ago that they had sat alongside one another in just the same way, waiting for the shuttle to catapult them from the docking port of the OSS into outer space with an impressive blast of fire. But contrary to all their expectations, the ship had moved away slowly as if it were trying to disappear unnoticed. It was only once they were at a suitable distance from the space city that Peter had ignited the thruster, accelerating to maximum speed then turning off the engines, after which they had raced silently through space towards their pockmarked destination.

The time for relaxing was over, and everyone was happy about it. It was good to finally arrive.

Once again, they were pressed forcefully back into their seats until, at 70 kilometres above the Moon's surface, Peter braked the spaceship down to a speed of 5600 kilometres per hour, rotated 180 degrees and stabilised in orbit. Below them, craters, rock formations and powdery grey plateaux drifted past. Just as in the space elevator, cameras were transmitting all the images from outside onto holographic monitors.

They did a two-hour lap of honour around the satellite, during which Nina Hedegaard explained the sights and particularities of this foreign world to them.

'As you already know from your preparatory training, a Moon day lasts quite a bit longer than an Earth one,' she hissed in her Scandinavian-tinged English. 'Fourteen Earth days, eighteen hours, twenty-two minutes and two seconds to be precise, and the Moon night is just as long. We call the boundary between light and shadow the terminator. It moves at an incredibly slow pace, which means you don't need to be afraid of suddenly being plunged into darkness during a walk. But *when* it gets dark, it really does! The terminator is clear-cut: there's light or shadow, but no dusk. Some of the sights lose their appeal in the dull midday light, so that's why we'll visit the most interesting places in the Moon's morning or evening, when the shadows are long.'

Beneath them they noticed another impressive crater, followed by a bizarrely fissured landscape.

'The Lunar Appenines,' explained Nina. 'The whole area is filled with rimae, groove-like structures. Early astronomers thought they were transport networks made by the Selenites. It's a wonderful landscape! The broad valley winding upwards over there is Rima Hadley; it leads through the Swamp of Laziness, a funny name, because there's neither a swamp there, nor is it lazy. But it's like that all over the Moon, seas which aren't actually seas and so on. Do you see the two mountains to the side of the rima? That's Mons Hadley, and beneath it Mons Hadley Delta. Both of them are well known from photographs, you often see them with a Moon Rover in the foreground. The Apollo 15 landed not far from there. The lunar module's landing gear is still there, along with some other things the astronauts left behind.'

'What other things?' asked Nair, his eyes gleaming.

'Shit,' muttered Locatelli.

'Why do you always have to be so negative?'

'I'm not. They left their shit behind. Everyone knows that, it would have been crazy not to, right? Believe me, wherever there's landing gear like that there'll be astronaut shit lying around somewhere.'

Nair nodded. Even that seemed to fascinate him. The spaceship flew swiftly over more rilles, mountains and craters and finally over the shore of the Sea of Tranquillity. Nina pointed out a small crater, named after Moltke and known for its sprawling cave system, created by flowing lava aeons ago.

'Similar systems have been discovered in the walls and plateaux of the Peary Crater in the northern polar region, where the American moon base was built. We'll visit Moltke at the start of the Moon evening, when the terminator is in the middle of the crater. It's a unique sight! And then there's the museum of course, admittedly a little barren scenically, but an essential visit nonetheless because—'

'Let me guess,' called Ögi. 'Apollo 11.'

'Correct,' beamed Nina. 'It's essential to know that the Apollo missions were dependent on the narrow equatorial belt. Finding a spectacular landing place wasn't the issue, it was just about setting foot on the Moon at all. Of course, it's the symbolic value of the museum that matters most today. By now you'll be able to find evidence of former visits all over the place, and in far more interesting locations, but Armstrong's footprints – well, you can only find them there.'

The flight then took them right across the Mare Crisium, the darkest of the Moon seas, in which, as Nina explained, the highest gravity ever measured on the Moon can be found. For a while they saw nothing but wildly fissured landscapes and ever-increasing shadows which spilled ominously into the valleys and plateaux, forming vast pools and filling the craters until only the highest edges still lay in sunlight. Evelyn shuddered at the thought of having to stumble around in the shapeless darkness, then the very last of the brightly lit islands disappeared and enigmatic darkness covered the monitors, seeping into the arteries and convolutions of the brain and swallowing any peace of mind.

'The Dark Side of the Moon,' sighed Walo Ögi. 'Anybody remember that? Pink Floyd? It was a classic album.'

Lynn, who had felt relatively stable during the journey, was now lost in the darkest depths of her soul. Once again, it seemed as if her courage and vitality had been sucked right out of her. On the far side of the Moon, you couldn't see the Earth, nor, unfortunately, the sun. If there is a hell, she thought, then it wouldn't be hot and fiery, but cold, a nihilistic blackness. It wouldn't need the devil or demons, torture slabs, stakes or boiling cauldrons. The absence of the familiar, the inner and outer world, the end of all feeling; that was hell. It was almost like total blindness. It was the death of all hope, fading into fear.

Take a deep breath, *feel* the body.

She needed to move, she had to get out of here and run, because anyone who ran could make the cold star inside them glimmer again, but she sat there, belted in to her seat as the Charon raced through the darkness. What was Ögi talking about? *The Dark Side of the Moon.* Who was Pink Floyd? Why was Nina blabbering relentless nonsense? Couldn't someone make the stupid goose shut up? Twist her neck, tear out her tongue?

'The far side of the Moon isn't necessarily dark,' she whispered. 'It's just that the same side of it is always facing the Earth.'

Tim, who was sitting next to her, turned his head.

'Did you say something?'

'It's just that the same side of it is always facing the Earth. You don't see the far side, but it's illuminated just as often as the front side.' Breathless, she stumbled over her words. 'The far side isn't dark. Not necessarily. It's just that the same side of it is—'

'Are you afraid, Lynn?'

Tim's concern. Like a rope thrown out for her to catch.

'Nonsense.' She drew air into her lungs. 'I've already flown this route three times. There's no need to be afraid. We'll be back in the light again soon.'

'—can assure you that you're not missing much,' Nina was saying. 'The front side is far more interesting. Remarkably, there are practically no maria on the far side, no seas. It's saturated with craters, rather monotonous, but nonetheless the ideal location for building a space telescope.'

'Why there?' asked Hanna.

'Because the Earth is to the Moon what the Moon is to the Earth, namely a Chinese lantern that intermittently illuminates its surface. Even when it's midnight on the Moon, the surface area is still partially illuminated by the waning residual light of the Earth. The rear side by contrast is, as you can see, as black at night as the cosmos around it: there's no sunlight, no light from the Earth to outshine the view of the stars. Astronomers would love to set up an observation post here, but for now they have to content themselves with a telescope on the Moon's North Pole. It's a compromise at any rate: the sun is low-lying, and you can look at the starry sky on the far side from there.'

Lynn reached for Tim's hand and squeezed it. Her thoughts were circling around murder and destruction.

'I don't know how you're doing,' he said softly, 'but I'm finding this darkness quite oppressive.'

Oh, clever Tim! Playing the ally.

'Me too,' she said gratefully.

'I guess that's normal, right?'

'It won't be for long.'

'And when will we be back in the light?' asked Miranda at the same moment.

'Just another hour,' hissed Nina. *Jussssst*, she said, so affected, so foolish. Julian's stupid little hobby. But feeling Tim's hand pressing against hers, Lynn started to relax, and suddenly remembered that she actually liked the Danish woman. So then why did she react so strongly, so aggressively? What's happening to me? she wondered.

What the hell is happening to me?

Once the surface of the Moon had had nothing to offer for a while, the external cameras began to transmit pictures of the starry sky into the Charon, and O'Keefe felt an unexpected rush of familiarity. Even on the OSS he would have gladly gone back to Earth like a shot. Now he just felt a vague longing. Perhaps because the myriad of lights outside were not unlike the sight of distant, illuminated houses and streets, or because the human being, an aquatic mammal, was by virtue of its own origins a child of the cosmos, built from its elements. The contradictory nature of his emotions confused him, like a child who always wanted to be held by the person who wasn't holding it at that moment. He tried to suppress the thought, but ended up thinking and thinking for an hour, unceasingly, about what he really wanted and where he belonged.

His gaze wandered over to Heidrun. She was two rows in front of him, listening to Ögi tell her something in hushed tones. O'Keefe wrinkled his nose and stared at the monitor. The picture changed. For a moment he couldn't figure out what the light blobs were supposed to be, but then he realised he was looking at sun-illuminated peaks which were rising out of the shadows. A sigh of relief went through the Charon. They were flying in the light again, towards the North Pole.

'We'll detach the landing module now,' said Black. 'The mother ship stays in orbit until we dock back onto it in a week's time. Nina will help you put your helmets on. It may not feel like it, but we're still flying at five times the speed of sound, so prepare yourselves for the next braking manoeuvre.'

'Hey, Momoka,' whispered O'Keefe.

The Japanese woman turned her head around lethargically. 'What's up?'

'Everything okay there?'

'Of course.'

O'Keefe grinned. 'Then don't wet yourself.'

Locatelli let out a hoarse laugh. Before Momoka had time to come up with a rebuke, Nina appeared and pushed the helmet over her head. Within minutes, they were all sitting there with heads like identical golf balls. They heard a hiss as the connection hatch between the mother ship and landing module closed, then a hollow clunk. The landing module freed itself and moved slowly away. So far, there was no sign of the slamming of the brakes they'd been warned about. The landscape changed once more. The shadows became longer again, an indication that they were approaching the polar region. Lava plateaux gave way to craters and mountain ridges. O'Keefe thought he glimpsed a dust cloud in the far distance just over the site, and then the pressure kicked in, the now almost familiar abuse of the thorax and lungs, except that this time the engines were roaring considerably louder than they had been two hours ago. Worried, he wondered whether they might be in difficulties, until he realised that until now it had always been the thrusters far back in the living quarters which were ignited. For the first time, the landing module was manoeuvring by using the engine directly beneath them.

Black's lighting a fire right under our arses, he thought.

With infernal counter-thrust, the landing module reduced its speed again as it rushed quickly, much too quickly, towards the surface of the Moon. A display on the screen counted down the distance kilometre by kilometre. What was happening? If they didn't slow down soon they'd be making their own crater. He thought about Julian's portrayal of the transformation of kinetic energy into heat, felt his ribcage getting tighter, tried to concentrate on the screen. Were his eyeballs shaking? What had they told them in their training? That you weren't cut out to be an astronaut if you couldn't control your eyes, because any shaking in the pupils caused blurriness and double vision. They had to be calmly fixed on the instruments. The *correct* instruments, that's what really mattered! How could you press the right buttons if you were seeing double?

Were Black's eyeballs shaking?

The next moment he felt ashamed, full of scorn at himself. He was such an idiot! The centrifuge at the practice site, the launch of the space elevator, braking in the Moon's orbit; each one had put a lot of pressure on him. Compared with all that, this landing was a walk in the park. He should have been calm personified, but the nerves were reaching out towards him with their electricity-laden fingers, and he had to admit to himself that his inability to breathe properly wasn't down to the pressure, but the sheer fear of smashing into the Moon.

Four kilometres, five.

The second display revealed that they were steadily slowing down, and he breathed out a sigh of relief. All the worry had been in vain. Three kilometres until touchdown. A mountain ridge came into view, a high plateau, lights which segmented a landing field surrounded by protective barriers. Pipes and domes nestled amongst the rock like armoured woodlice, lying in wait for unsuspecting quarry. Solar fields, masts and antennae shimmered in the light of the low-lying sun; a barrel-shaped structure crowned a nearby hilltop. Further in the distance, open, hangar-like structures could be seen; huge machines crawled through a kind of open-cast mine. A rail system connected the habitats to the spaceport, led into a platform, then branched away from it in a wide curve. O'Keefe saw flights of stairs, hydraulic ramps and manipulator arms which were pointed towards a loading bay, then something white with tall, wide wheels drove along the road and stopped on a bridge; possibly manned, possibly a robot. The Charon shook and sank towards the ground. For a moment it was possible to make out a skyline of massive towers with large, bulky flying machines in between them, tanks and containers, unidentified objects. Something that looked like a praying mantis on wheels rolled off across the airfield, the sheer extent of which was now clear: the size of three or four football pitches. The surrounding land and buildings disappeared behind its dam-like borders, then their spaceship touched down carefully with feather-like elegance, teetered impercept-ibly, and came to a standstill.

Something tugged softly at O'Keefe. At first he couldn't place it, but then the realisation amazed him all the more because of the simplicity of the explanation. Gravity! For the first time since they had set off from the Isla de las Estrellas, excluding acceleration and braking manoeuvres, he was no longer weightless. He had a bodyweight again, and even if it was only a sixth of his weight on Earth, it was still wonderful to weigh something again, a relief after all the days of just drifting around! *Hasta la vista*, Miranda, he thought, that's an end to the acrobatics. No more somersaults, no more elbow attacks. A gust of noise ebbed away in his ear canals, a synaptic afterglow; the engines had been turned off long before, but he just couldn't believe it.

'Ladies and gentlemen,' said Black, a little dramatically, 'congratula-tions! You've done it. Nina and I will now help you put on your life-support systems, show you how to regulate the oxygen, cooling and pressure and activate your walkie-talkie systems. After that we'll go through a series of leak tests – you should already be familiar with those from the external expedition on the OSS, and if not, there's no cause for concern. We'll supervise everything. As soon as the checks are done, I'll pump the air out of the cabin, and we'll explain the process of disembarcation. Please don't think I'm being rude if I climb out first, it's only to further the preservation of your heroism, because I'll film you as you leave the Charon and we'll also record your comments for posterity. Does that all make sense? Welcome to the Moon!'

On the Moon.

They were on the Moon.

They had really landed on the goddamn Moon, and the satellite's one-sixth gravity pulled O'Keefe down to it with the tenderness of a lover, his limbs, his head, his inner organs and bodily fluids, oh yes, the fluids, pulled and pulled and pulled something out of him, and it was out before he could clench his butt cheeks. Warm and happy, it flowed into the bag put there for exactly that purpose, a fountain of joy, a high-five to gravity, a gift to the grey, crater-covered guy whose surface they were to inhabit for the next week. He threw a stolen glance at Momoka Omura, as if there were the possibility that she would turn round to him, look him in the eyes and see it, *know* it.

Then he shrugged, thinking of the others who had probably pissed themselves beyond the Earth's orbit. There was worse company to be in.

Peary Base, North Pole, The Moon

Leaving behind footprints was a pioneer's privilege, and one which made life a little easier for those of the custodian type, who were aware of the risks, but without being exposed to them. They were familiar with natural phenomena, the appetite and armoury of the local fauna and flora, knew how to adapt themselves to the defiance of the native inhabitants. Their knowledge was all thanks to the feverish, potentially suicidal curiosity of the discoverer type, who neither could nor wanted to do anything other than spend his life walking the narrow line between victory and death. Even in the days of *Homo erectus*, and the anthroposophists were sure of this, humanity had displayed a tendency to split up into a governing majority alongside a small group which just couldn't stay put. The latter had a special gene, known as the Columbus Gene, Novelty-seeking Gene or just D4DR in the extended version, code for an extraordinary willingness to cross borders and take risks. Naturally, all of these adventurous types were less suited for the cultivation of the conquered regions. They preferred discovering new areas, getting themselves bitten by new species of animals and fulfilling all the prerequisites so that the more conservative types could make advances. They were the eternal scouts, for whom a footprint on terra incognita meant everything. In turn, it was part of the nature of the custodian to subject lime, mud, sand, gravel, silt and whatever other kind of amorphous unspoiled state there was to the dictatorship of smoothed-out surfaces, which meant that when Evelyn Chambers, awestruck, walked down the gangway of the Charon and stepped on to the surface of the Moon for the first time, she left no lasting impression behind her, instead finding herself back on solid concrete.

For a second she was disappointed. The others, too, were looking at their feet as if walking on the Moon were inextricably linked with hall-marking the regolith.

'You'll leave your stamp behind soon enough,' said Julian's voice, switched on in all their helmets.

Some of them laughed. The moment of unmet expectations passed, giving way to amazement and disbelief. Evelyn took a hesitant step, then another, bounced – and was carried over a metre in the air by the force of her thigh muscles.

Unbelievable! Absolutely unbelievable!

After over five days of zero gravity she felt the familiar burden of her weight, and yet she didn't. It was more as though some ominous comic-book radiation had given her superpowers. All around her, the others were leaping wildly around. Black danced attendance amongst them with his camera.

'Where's the star-spangled banner?' boomed Donoghue. 'I want to ram it into the ground!'

'Then you're fifty-six years too late,' laughed Ögi. 'The Swiss flag on the other hand—'

'Imperialists,' sighed Heidrun.

'No chance,' said Julian. 'Unless you're planning to *blast* your flags into the ground.'

'Hey, look at that,' called Rebecca Hsu.

Her ample figure shot past the others' heads, her arms windmilling. If it was Rebecca, that is. It wasn't that easy to tell. You couldn't really make out anyone's face through the mirrored visors; only the printed name on the chest section of the suit betrayed the identity of its wearer.

'Come on then,' laughed Julian. 'Don't be scared!'

Evelyn took a run-up and did a series of clumsy jumps, then sped upwards again and turned on her own axis, drunk on high spirits. Then she lost her balance and sank back down to the ground in a meditative pose. She couldn't help breaking out into silly giggles as she landed softly on her behind. Overcome with delight, she stayed where she was, enjoying the surreal scene that was playing out before her. Within seconds the group of well-established movers and shakers had transformed into a horde of first-graders, playmates going wild. She came back to a standing position without any effort whatsoever.

'Good,' praised Julian, 'very good. The Bolshoi Ballet look like a load of blundering fools compared with you, but I'm afraid we need to interrupt the physical exercise temporarily. You're off to the hotel now, so please turn your attention back to Nina and Peter again.'

It was as though he'd broadcast on the wrong frequency. With the defiance of children who had just been called to the dinner table, they finally trickled over in dribs and drabs to gather around their guides. The image of a bunch of ruffians gave way to one of a secret brotherhood as they stood there, searching for the Holy Grail against the panorama of flying castles. Evelyn let her gaze wander. The base could hardly be seen. Only the station platform loomed imposingly over the landing field, erected on fifteen-metre-high pylons, as Nina explained. Metal staircases and an open elevator led up to the rail tracks, spherical tanks were piled up all around. Two manipulators squatted at the edge of the platform like Jurassic birds, turned to face lobster-like machines with multiple-jointed claws and large loading surfaces. Evelyn guessed their task was probably to receive cargo from the manipulators or to reach it up to them, according to whether goods were being delivered or placed on the rails.

She tried to regulate her breathing. The confinement of the landing module just then had become unbearable for her. She had dreamed feverishly the night before. Higher powers had opened up the Charon using a gigantic tin-opener and exposed its inhabitants to the vacuum, which had turned out to be just a bunch of human-like creatures gaping in at them, and she had been stark naked. Admittedly it was all a bit silly, but still! The iridescent blue-green imprints of Miranda Winter's heels had been immortalised in her hips, and she'd had enough. She was even more amazed at how big the landing module actually was when she saw it in the expanse of the airfield. An imposing tower on powerful telescopic legs, practically a small skyscraper. More spaceships were distributed across the field, some with open hatches and yawningly empty insides, clearly intended for receiving freight goods. Several smaller machines spread their spider legs and stared straight ahead with their glassy eyes. Chambers couldn't help but think of insect spray.

'You'll have to forgive the inhabitants of the base for not coming out to greet you,' said Black. 'You only go outside if it's absolutely necessary here. Unlike you, these people spend six months on the Moon. A week's worth of cosmic radiation won't harm you so long as you don't go out in a solar storm without protection. But long-term stays are a different story. So as we won't be looking around the base until the day of our departure, there's no reception committee today.'

One of the lobster-like robots started up as if by magic, steered over to the Charon and took some large white containers from its cargo hold.

'Your luggage,' Nina explained, 'will be exposed to the vacuum for the first time up here, but don't worry, the containers are pressurised. Otherwise your night cream might turn into a monster and attack your T-shirts. Follow me.'

It was like going underwater, but without the ambient pressure. Excitedly, Evelyn realised that she didn't weigh 66 kilos any more, but just 11, which meant her normal bodily strength would be multiplied by six. As light as a three-year-old, as strong as Superwoman, and carried along by a surge of childlike happiness, she followed Black to the elevator, hopped into the spacious cage and watched the habitats of the base come back into view as they travelled out over the top of the barriers and onto the station platform. Several more rail tracks ran up here. A lit, empty train lay waiting for them, not unlike one of the magnet trains on Earth, but a little less streamlined in shape, which made it look curiously old-fashioned. But why would it have needed to be aerodynamic? There was no wind up here. There wasn't even any air.

She looked into the distance.

A barrage of images confronted her. A great deal of the surrounding area could be seen from up here. A highland. Hills and ridges, the silhouette of long shadows. Craters, like bowls filled with black ink. A glowing white, low-lying sun dissolved the contours of the horizon, the landscape stood out like stage scenery against the backdrop of outer space. There was no mist or atmosphere to diffuse the light; regardless of its actual distance everything was sharply contoured, as though it were close enough to touch. At the other side of the landing field, the track for the magnet train led into a valley filled with blackness, held its own against the darkness for a while thanks to the height of its columns, and then, without warning, was swallowed by it.

'We're just fifteen kilometres away from the Moon's geographical North Pole here,' said Black. 'It's on a plateau at the north-western edge of the Peary Crater, where it borders on its neighbour, Hermite. The area is nicknamed "Mountains of Eternal Light". Can anyone guess why?'

'Just explain, Peter,' said Julian gently.

'Well, at the beginning of the nineties interest in the Pole really grew after it was established that the edges and peaks of some of the craters were in constant sunlight. The main problem with having a manned moon base had always been energy supply, and they wanted to avoid working with nuclear reactors. There was a great deal of resistance to it, even on Earth, because of the fear that a spaceship with a reactor like that on board could crash and fall onto inhabited areas. Back when the station was in the planning stages, helium-3 was still just a vague option, so they backed solar energy as usual. The only thing is, while solar panels are great, unfortunately they're useless at night. A gap of a few hours can be bridged with batteries, but a Moon night lasts fourteen days, and that's how the Pole came into the running. Admittedly the light yield is somewhat less here than at the equator, because the rays of light fall very obliquely, but on the other hand they're constant. If you look over at the hills you'll see entire fields of collectors which are continually aligning their position to face the sun.'

Black paused and let them scan the hills for the collectors.

'And yet even the Poles aren't the ideal position for a base. The rays of sunlight fall obliquely, as I already mentioned, it's quite far away from where the action is up here, and it would have been better to have the lunar telescope on the far side. Some critics also point out that by the time the building work began, the use of helium-3 had become a viable option, so ideally the plans should have been thrown out and the base built in the preferred location, where it could be supplied with energy around the clock by a fusion reactor. It's actually a bit of a paradox that helium-3 wasn't used on the Moon of all places, but they followed the original plans regardless. The Poles also have another advantage: the temperature. By Moon standards it's quite moderate here, a constant forty to sixty degrees in the sun; while on the equator it's well over one hundred degrees in the midday heat but at night the thermometer plummets to minus one hundred and eighty degrees. No building material can handle fluctuations like that on a long-term basis: it would have to expand and contract like crazy, which means it becomes brittle and leaks. And there's one more consideration in favour of the Poles. When the sun creeps in as low over the horizon as it does there, wouldn't that mean there are also areas which are *never* illuminated by it? If that's the case, then there's the chance of finding something there that couldn't actually exist on the Moon: water.'

'Why can't it exist here?' asked Miranda. 'Not even a river or a small lake?'

'Because it would immediately evaporate in the sun and escape into open space. The Moon's gravity isn't enough to hold volatile gases; that's one of the reasons why the Moon has no atmosphere. The only possibility was of frozen water existing in eternal darkness, locked in a molecular bond in moon dust brought here by meteorites. The existence of permanently shadowed chasms like these was quickly proved, for example the impact craters at the base of the Peary Crater, right around the corner from here. And measurements really seemed to confirm the presence of water, which would have enormously favoured the development of a complex infrastructure. The alternative was sending water up here from Earth, which was sheer madness even just from a financial perspective.'

'And have they found water?' asked Rogachev.

'Not so far. A great number of hydrogen deposits of course, but no water. The base was built here regardless because transporting water from Earth turned out to be a lot less complicated and expensive than expected thanks to the space elevator. Now it makes its way to the OSS in tanks, and from that point on mass doesn't matter anyway. But of course people are still searching feverishly for signs of H_2O, and besides' – Black pointed over to the barrel-shaped objects in the distance – 'they've started building a small helium-3 reactor anyway, as a reserve for the base's steadily increasing energy needs.'

'So, if I'm honest,' grumbled Momoka Omura, 'I was expecting the moon base to be a little more impressive.'

'I think it's very impressive,' said Hanna.

'Me too,' called Miranda.

'Absolutely,' Nair added, laughing. 'I still can't believe that I'm on the Moon, that people live here! It's incredible.'

'Wait until you see the Gaia,' said Lynn mysteriously. 'You probably won't ever want to leave again.'

'If it looks like the pile of junk down there then I'll want to leave *immediately*,' snorted Momoka.

'Baby,' said Locatelli, more sharply than usual, 'you're insulting our hosts.'

'How? I only—'

'There are moments when even you should keep your mouth shut, don't you think?'

'I beg your pardon? Shut your own!'

'You'll like the hotel, Momoka,' Lynn interrupted hurriedly. 'Love it, even! And no, it does *not* look like the moon base.'

Evelyn grinned. From a business point of view she enjoyed little spats like these, particularly as Locatelli and his Japanese muse usually joined forces when it came to antagonising others. She had planned to ask Locatelli onto one of her next shows anyway, for which she was contemplating using the title 'War of the World Saviours: How the demise of the oil industry is stirring up power struggles amongst suppliers of alternative energy'. Perhaps one or two private thoughts might punctuate the conversation.

In the best of moods, she followed Black.

Lunar Express

They boarded the train via an airlock and took off their helmets and suits. The air was kept at a constant pleasant temperature and the seats, as Rebecca Hsu said with a heartfelt sigh, were the right size to accommodate even an overweight traveller. The remark was addressed to Amber Orley, whom Evelyn had hardly talked to so far. Amber was friendly towards everyone though, and even Julian's son turned out to be a sociable sort despite his initial reticence – if you could get past his air of leaden concern when it came to looking after his sister. She was visibly spoiling his mood, and Amber's, and on top of all this she seemed to be putting a strain on Tim's relationship with his father. None of this had escaped Evelyn's attention. She reckoned that Lynn had been faking that attack of space sickness in the Picard. Something wasn't right about her, and Evelyn was determined to find out what. Mukesh Nair had latched on to Tim and was letting him know how wonderful life was, so she sat down next to Amber.

'Unless of course you'd rather sit next to your husband—'

'No, no, that's fine!' Amber leaned closer. 'We're on the Moon, isn't that just amazing?'

'It's mind-blowing!' Evelyn agreed.

'And then there's the hotel,' she said, rolling her eyes dramatically.

'You know it then? So far they've made such a huge secret out of it. No pictures, no films—'

'Now and again being in the family has its advantages. Lynn showed us the plans.'

'I'm bursting with curiosity! Hey, look, we're on our way.'

Imperceptibly, the train had started moving. Ethereal music floated through the cabin, light as a breath, languid, as though the orchestra were on drugs.

'That's so beautiful,' said Eva Borelius, sitting behind Evelyn. 'What is it?'

'Aram Khachaturian,' Rogachev answered. 'Adagio for cello and strings, from the *Gayaneh* suite.'

'Bravo, Oleg.' Julian turned round. 'Can you also tell us which recording?'

'I believe it has to be the Leningrad Philharmonic, under Gennady Rozhdestvensky, isn't it?'

'My God, that's connoisseurship.' Borelius seemed stunned. 'You really know your stuff.'

'More than anything else, I know how fond our host is of one particular film,' said Rogachev in an uncharacteristically cheerful tone. 'Let's just say I was well prepared.'

'I had no idea that you were so interested in classical—'

'No,' muttered Olympiada quite audibly, 'you wouldn't think so to look at him.'

Here we go, thought Evelyn. This is getting better and better.

Lynn took up position in the aisle between the seats.

'You may perhaps have noticed,' she said, speaking into a small microphone, 'that it's always down to me to speak when we're talking about the accommodation and facilities. First of all, everything that you see and do on this voyage is a premiere. You were the first guests in the Stellar Island Hotel, and you'll be the first to set foot inside the Gaia. Obviously, you're also the first to enjoy a ride on the Lunar Express, which will take less than two hours to transport us almost thirteen hundred kilometres to the hotel. The station we've just set out from actually functions more as a sort of shipping facility. Helium-3 is mined in the Mare Imbrium, to the north-west. The tanks are brought here by rail, then they're loaded onto spaceships and brought to the OSS. The cargo line runs parallel with our rails for a while and then it turns off to the west a little before we reach our destination, so it's entirely possible that we'll meet a freight train on our way.'

Outside the windows they could see the landing field receding, with its blast walls rearing up around it. The maglev accelerated, drew out from the base along a long, curving downhill path and rushed towards the shadowed valley.

'Our scheduled time of arrival at the hotel is 19.15, and there's no need for you to bother about your luggage. The robots will take it up to your rooms, and meanwhile we'll meet in the lobby, get to know the hotel crew, take a look around, and then you'll have a chance afterwards to freshen up. Dinner will be a little later than usual today, at 20:30. After which I recommend you get some sleep. The journey was fairly strenuous, and you'll be tired, besides which Neil Armstrong reported having slept exceptionally well on his first night on the Moon. So much for the full moon keeping you awake. Any more questions at the moment?'

'Just one.' Donoghue raised a hand. 'Can we get a drink?'

'Beer, wine, whisky,' said Lynn, beaming. 'All alcohol-free.'

'I knew it.'

'It'll do you good,' said Aileen happily, and patted his leg.

Donoghue growled something blasphemous, and as if in punishment, darkness swallowed them up. For a while they could still see the top of the crater walls bathed in harsh sunlight, and then these too were lost to view. Nina Hedegaard brought round some snacks. György Ligeti's Requiem came over the speakers, just the right music for the pitch-black outside, and the downward slope steepened perceptibly while the Lunar Express picked up speed. Black explained that they were in a cleft between Peary and Hermite, then they shot out again into the sunlight, past jagged rock formations and towards a steep-sided hollow. It grew dark again while they passed through a smaller crater. Just a moment ago, Evelyn had been burning to winkle some secrets of family life from Amber, but now all she wanted to do was stare out in wonder at this untouched alien landscape, the archaic brutality of its cliff walls and mountain ridges, the velvet silence that lay over the dust-filled valleys and plains, the complete absence of colour. The cold sunlight fell on the edges of the impact craters, and time itself melted in its glare. Nobody felt like talking any more, and even Chucky stopped short in one of his jokes before the feeble punchline and stared out as though hypnotised. Outside, a blue-white glittering jewel lifted slowly above the horizon, gaining height with every kilometre they travelled south – their home, infinitely far away, and achingly beautiful.

Nina and Black chattered on, informative and enthusiastic. They mentioned the names of further craters, Byrd, Gioja, Main. The peaks dwindled away to hills, the chasms gave way to light-filled plains. After an hour, they reached a long rampart wall, Goldschmidt, its western edge bitten away by the jaws of Anaxagoras, and Nina told them that this was an especially recent impact. A few of them looked upwards, thinking that recent might mean just now, rather than a hundred million years ago, and then coughed or laughed nervously. They crossed Goldschmidt and sped across a desert landscape, this one a darker colour, and Julian stood up and congratulated them on crossing their first lunar sea, the Mare Frigoris.

'And why do they call a dry old desert like this a sea?' Miranda asked, saving her more educated fellow passengers the embarrassment of having to ask the same question.

'Because, earlier, these dark basaltic plains were thought to be seas,' said Julian. 'The assumption was that the Moon had to be shaped in much the same way as the Earth was. As a result, people imagined that they could see seas, lakes, bays and swamps. What's interesting here is how they got their names, for instance why this basin is called the Sea of Cold. There's the Sea of Tranquillity of course, Mare Tranquillitatis, which has gone down in history thanks to Apollo 11, and by the way that's why three tiny little craters near the landing site are called Armstrong, Aldrin and Collins, credit where it's due. Then there's a Sea of Serenity, a Sea of Happiness, a Sea of Clouds and another one of Rain, an Ocean of Storms, the Foaming Sea, the Sea of Waves and so on and so forth.'

'That sounds like the weather forecast,' said Hanna.

'You've hit the nail on the head there.' Julian grinned. 'It's all down to a certain Giovanni Battista Riccioli, a seventeenth-century astronomer and contemporary of Galileo. He had the idea of naming every crater and every mountain chain after a great astronomer or mathematician, but then he ran out of astronomers, as luck would have it. Later the Russians and the Americans took over his system. Now-adays you can find writers, psychologists and polar explorers remembered for all time here on the Moon, and there are lunar Alps, Pyrenees and Andes as well. Anyway, as far as Riccioli was concerned, the dark plains had to be seas. Plutarch had already believed this, and Galileo declared that if the Moon was another Earth, then the light patches were obviously continents and the dark parts must be bodies of water. Naturally Riccioli also wanted to give these seas of his names as well – and that's when he made his big mistake! He reckoned that his observations showed that weather down on the Earth was influenced by the phases of the Moon. For instance, good weather during the waxing moon—'

'And crappy weather during the waning moon.'

'That's it! Since then the seas in the eastern hemisphere on the Moon have had peaceful, harmonious names, while over in the west it never rains but it pours. And a sea up by the North Pole obviously has to be cold, hence Mare Frigoris, the Sea of Cold. Oh, look at that! I do believe there's something coming towards us.'

Evelyn craned her neck. At first she saw nothing but the endless plain and the rails curving away into the distance, then it leapt out at her. A tiny point, hurtling closer, that flew towards them over the rails and became something long and low with blazing headlamps. Then the two trains passed at a speed approaching 1500 kilometres per hour, without the least sound or tremor from where they sat.

'Helium-3,' said Julian reverentially. 'The future.'

And he sat down as though there was nothing further to say.

The Lunar Express flew onward. A little later an enormous mountain range showed on the horizon, becoming taller with amazing speed as though the Mare Frigoris really were a sea and the range were rising from its depths. Evelyn remembered hearing from someone that the effect was down to the Moon's curvature. Black told them that this was the crater Plato, a splendid example with a diameter of more than a hundred kilometres and walls two and a half thousand metres high, another little splinter of information fired into Evelyn's overloaded cerebral cortex that stuck there. The Lunar Express swooped smoothly into the Mare Imbrium, the neighbouring desert plain. The freight tracks branched off, as announced, and vanished off to the west, while they went around Plato and left it behind. More mountains reared up on the horizon, the Lunar Alps, harsh-lit and shot through with veins of shadow. The rails reared boldly upwards into the mountains, where the pillars that held up the maglev track clasped hold of the steep cliffs like claws. The higher they climbed, the more breathtaking the view: stark peaks two thousand metres tall, overhangs like Cubist sculpture, sharp saw-toothed ridges. One last look down at the dusty carpet of the Mare Imbrium, then the tracks curved away into the sea's hinterland, between peaks and plateaux and onward to the edge of a lunar Grand Canyon, and then—

Evelyn couldn't believe her eyes.

A sigh of astonishment shuddered through the train. The barely audible hum of the motor joined in with the bass notes of the *Zarathustra* theme, pregnant with mystery, while the Lunar Express slowed and then the first fanfares burst out brightly. Strauss might have been thinking of Nietzsche's new dawn, while Kubrick used it for the transformation of the human race into something newer, higher, but right at this moment Evelyn was thinking of Edgar Allan Poe, a writer whose depths she had plumbed enthusiastically in her youth, and she remembered one sentence from his work, the terrifying ending of *Arthur Gordon Pym*:

But there arose in our pathway a shrouded human figure, very far larger in
its proportions than any dweller among men. And the hue of the skin of the
figure was of the perfect whiteness of the snow.

She held her breath.

Ten, maybe twelve kilometres away from them, atop a plateau, high
above a promontory that jutted out like a terrace beneath it and then fell
away into a steep canyon, something sat, gazing up at Earth.

A person.

No, it had the shape of a human form. Not a man's shape, but a
woman's, perfectly proportioned. Her head, limbs and body gleamed
gently in front of the endless sea of stars. No expression on that face,
no mouth, eyes or nose, but still there was something soulful, almost
yearning in her posture as she sat there with her legs hanging over the
edge and her arms out to the side, supporting her, elbows straight, her
whole attention focused on that silent, distant planet above her where
she would never walk.

She was at least two hundred metres tall.

Dallas, Texas, USA

If Loreena Keowa hadn't already been the best-known face of Greenwatch, they would have had to invent her.

There was no mistaking her ancestry. She was one hundred per cent
Tlingit, a member of the nation that had inhabited the south-east coast of
Alaska since time immemorial and whose ancestral homeland included
parts of the Yukon Territory and British Columbia. There were about
8000 Tlingit left, with numbers falling. Only a few hundred of the old
people still spoke the melodic Na-Dené tongue perfectly, although these
days more and more young people like Keowa learned it too, seeing
themselves as the standard-bearers of ethnic self-determination in a
newly green America.

Keowa came from a Raven clan in Hoonah, the Village on the Cliffs, a Tlingit settlement on Chichagof Island. Now, if she wasn't spending her time in Vancouver, where Greenwatch was headquartered, she lived forty miles west of Hoonah in Juneau. Her features were unmistakably Indian, but at the same time bore the signs of white ancestry, although to the best of her knowledge no white man had ever married into the clan. Without being good-looking in the classical sense, she had a wild and enticing aura about her that could easily seem romantic. Her long, shining black hair exactly matched what a New York stockbroker might expect Indian hair to look like, whereas her style of dress went dead against all the clichés of the noble savage. As far as she was concerned, you could protect the environment quite as well while dressed in Gucci and Armani. She was clear and factual in her work, and hardly ever launched into polemics. Her reports were known to be well researched, unsparing, but at the same time she managed never to damn a culprit irredeemably. Her enemies called her a walking compromise, the ideal solution for milksop Wall Street eco-activists, while her defenders valued the way she brought people and viewpoints together. Whatever the truth of it, nobody could claim that Greenwatch's success wasn't largely down to Loreena Keowa. In the past couple of years it had grown from a small internet channel to take front place among America's ecologically aware TV stations, and had a remarkably good track record when it came to corrections or retractions – no mean feat, given that the race for a scoop on the internet went hand in hand with a worrying lack of research credibility.

It was typical for Greenwatch to feel a crude sort of sympathy for the chief strategist of EMCO, Gerald Palstein, who should really count as their bad guy. But Palstein argued for various green positions, and he'd been the victim of an attack in Calgary when he put an end to something that had always made environmental activists turn purple with rage. At the beginning of the millennium, companies such as Exxon-Mobil had breathed new life into an area of business that had almost been abandoned, and they had the Bush administration's full, eco-unfriendly support. This was the exploitation of oil sands, a mixture of sand, water and hydrocarbons with huge reserves in Canada, among other places. The reserves in Athabasca, Peace River and Cold Lake alone were estimated at 24 billion tonnes, catapulting the country up in the list of oil-rich nations to place two, behind Saudi Arabia. Mind you, it cost three times as much to extract the black gold from the sands as from conventional sources, making it a losing business as long as the price per barrel hovered between twenty and thirty dollars. But in the end, rapidly climbing prices had justified the intensive investment, thanks also to Canada's proximity to the thirsty primary consumer, the USA, grateful for every oil supplier that wasn't an Arab nation. The oil companies pounced on the slumbering reserves with dollar signs in their eyes, and within a very short time this led to the complete destruction of the boreal forest in Alberta, the moorland biotopes, the rivers and lakes. Additionally, 80 kilos of greenhouse gas were released into the atmosphere for every barrel of this synthetic oil extracted, and four barrels of polluted water flowed out to poison the land.

But the price per barrel collapsed, for ever. Open-cast extraction stopped overnight, leaving the companies that had driven the business unable to repair the damaged ecosystems. All that was left were ravaged tracts of land, increased incidence of cancer in the population – and companies such as Imperial Oil, a traditional business headquartered in Calgary, which for almost 150 years had made its money from extracting and refining oil and natural gas, and, in the end, increasingly from oil sands. Just as it was at the forefront of the industry, the lights went out, and Palstein, strategic director of the majority shareholder EMCO, which owned about two-thirds of Imperial Oil, had to go to Alberta to tell the management and a stunned workforce that they were being let go.

Perhaps because it was more effective to vent anger on one man than on the oh-so-distant Moon, whose resources had led to the disaster, somebody shot at Palstein in Calgary. The deed of a desperate man, at least so most people saw it.

Loreena Keowa thought that there were good grounds for scepticism. Not that she had an answer either. But how long could an embittered, unemployed shooter expect to escape justice? The attempted killing had been one month ago. A great many things about the theory of an enraged lone gunman didn't make sense, and since Keowa was working anyway on a feature about the environmental destruction wreaked by the oil companies, *Trash of the Titans*, it made sense to her that she should look into the case in her own way. Even before helium-3, Palstein had been vocal about the need for his industry to switch direction. He was on record as being no friend of the oil-sands project, and she felt that he had been unfairly treated at the press conference in Anchorage. So she had offered him a TV portrait that would show him in a better light. In exchange, she hoped for some inside information about EMCO, the crumbling giant, and more even than that, she was excited at the thought of being able to help clear up the shooting, in the best tradition of American investigative journalism.

Maybe even solving the case.

Palstein had hesitated a while, and in the end invited her to visit him in Texas, in his house on the shore of Lake Lavon. He was convalescing from his injury here, and recovering from being the bearer of bad news. He made one condition: that for the first conversation, she should turn up without her camera team.

'We'll need pictures though,' Keowa had said. 'We're a TV channel.'

'You'll get some. As long as I feel that I can trust you. But I can only take so many knocks, Loreena. We'll sound one another out for an hour, and then you can fetch your crew. Or maybe not.'

Now, in the taxi bringing them downtown from the airport, Keowa went through her material one more time. Her camera crew and sound technician were lolling on the back seat, wrung out by the humid heat that lay across Texas far too early this year. EMCO was headquartered next door in Irving, but Palstein lived on the other side of town. They had a light lunch in the Dallas Sheraton, then Palstein's driver arrived at the agreed time to fetch Keowa. They left town and drove through the untouched green belt, until the glittering surface of the lake became visible through the trees to the left. It had been a bumpy flight, followed by a plunge into the sauna-like Dallas temperatures, and she enjoyed the ride in an air-conditioned electric van. After a while the driver turned off into a smaller road and then onto a private driveway that led along the water to Palstein's house, which looked, she mused, something like what she had been expecting. Palstein would have stuck out like a sore thumb in a ranch with buffalo horns and a pillared veranda. This was an airy arrangement of Cubist buildings around green open spaces, with glass frontages, soaring slender framework and walls that seemed almost weightless; all this suited his character much better.

The driver let her out. A well-built man in slacks and a T-shirt came towards her and asked politely for some identification. Two more men were patrolling down by the quay. She handed him her ID card, and he held it to the scanner on his phone. He seemed happy with what the screen told him, gave it back to her with a smile and beckoned her to follow him. They hurried through a Japanese garden and past a large swimming-pool, to a jetty where a boat was tied up.

'Do you feel like a ride?'

Palstein was leaning against a bollard, waiting for her in front of a trim, snow-white yacht with a tall mast and furled sails. He was wearing jeans and a polo shirt and looked healthier than last time they had met in Anchorage. The sling on his arm had gone. Keowa pointed to his shoulder.

'Feeling better?'

'Thanks.' He took her hand and shook it briefly. 'It tugs a little sometimes. Did you have a good flight, Shax' saani Keek'?'

Keowa laughed, caught out. 'You know my Indian name?'

'Why not?'

'Hardly anybody does!'

'Etiquette demands that I keep myself informed. Shax' saani Keek' – in Tlingit that means *the younger sister of the girls*, am I right?'

'I'm impressed.'

'And I'm probably an old show-off.' Palstein smiled. 'So, what do you say? I can't offer to take you sailing, that wouldn't work yet with my shoulder, but the outboard works and there are cold drinks on board.'

Under other circumstances Keowa would have been suspicious. But what would have seemed manipulative from anyone else, was just what it seemed coming from Palstein: an invitation from a man who liked his boat and wanted to share a trip.

'Lovely house,' said Keowa, once they had motored out a little way from the shore. The heat stood there like a block over the water, not a whisper of a breeze ruffled the lake surface, but all the same it was more bearable than on land. Palstein looked back and then was silent for a minute, as though considering for the first time whether his homestead could be called beautiful.

'It's based on a design by Mies van der Rohe. Do you know his work?' Keowa shook her head.

'In my view, he's the most important modern architect there was. A German, a great constructivist and a logical thinker. He aimed to tame the chaotic mess that technological civilisation churned out and frame it with order and structure. Mind you, he didn't consider that order neces- sarily meant drawing lines and boundaries – he wanted to create as much open space as possible, a seamless transition between inside and out.'

'And between past and future?'

'Absolutely! His work is timeless, because it gives every age what we need. Van der Rohe will never stop influencing architects.'

'You like clear structures.'

'I like people who can see the whole picture. By the way, I'm sure you know his most famous motto: Less is more.'

'Oh, yes.' Keowa nodded. 'Of course.'

'Do you know what I think? If we could perceive the world the way van der Rohe structured his work, we'd be aware of higher-order con- nections and we'd reach different conclusions. Clarity through reduction. Recognise what's in front of you by clearing away the clutter. A math- ematics of thought.' He paused. 'But you're not here to hear me talking about the beauty of pure number. What would you like to know?'

'Who shot you?'

Palstein nodded, almost a little disappointed, as though he had been expecting something more original.

'The police are looking for one man, someone frustrated, angry.'

'Do you still agree with their profiling?'

'I've said that I do.'

'Would you care to tell me what you really think?'

He put his chin in his hands. 'Let's put it this way: if you want to solve an equation, you need to know the variables. All the same you'll fail if you fall in love with one of the variables and assign it a value that it might not have, and if I'm right, this is exactly what the police are doing. The stupid thing is, though, that I can't offer any better explanation. What do you think?'

'Hey, well. There's an industry going down the drain here, and you stalk the land like a gravedigger, telling people that they're going to lose their jobs, you're shutting down plants, you're letting companies go to the wall; even if the truth of the matter is that you're not a gravedigger, you're the trauma surgeon.'

'It's all a question of perception.'

'Quite. Why couldn't it be some husband and father who just snapped? I'm just surprised that they haven't been able to find someone like that in four weeks. The attack was filmed by several broadcasters, you'd think someone would have seen something. Someone acting suspiciously maybe, drawing a weapon, running away, something like that.'

'Did you know that there's a complex of buildings across from the podium, over the other side of the square—'

' —and the police think that this is where the shot was fired from. Also that nobody remembers having seen anyone going in, or coming out after the attack. There were policemen nearby, all over the place. Doesn't that seem odd to you? Doesn't the whole thing look more like a professional operation, something planned out in advance?'

'Lee Harvey Oswald fired from a building as well.'

'Wait a moment! He fired from where he worked.'

'But not on impulse. He must have planned his action, even if there's nothing to say that he was a professional assassin – whatever millions of conspiracy theorists may prefer to believe.'

'Agreed. All the same, I have to ask who the bullet was meant for here.'

'You mean whether I was being shot as a private individual, as representing EMCO, or maybe as a symbol for the whole system.'

'You're not the symbol for the system, Gerald. Militant environmentalists would look for somebody else, not the only one they can sometimes work with. Perhaps it's the other way about, and you're a thorn in the side of militant *representatives* of the system.'

'They'd have taken the chance to snuff me out while there were still decisions to be made at EMCO,' Palstein said dismissively. 'As you so nicely put it, I'm letting Imperial Oil go to the wall and I'm winding up our involvement in oil sands. If I had done this before helium-3, it might have made sense to get me out of the way so as to be able to keep grubbing around in the muck, but these days? Every unpopular decision I make, the circumstances make for me.'

'Good, then let's consider Palstein the private individual. What about revenge?'

'Personally, against me?'

'Have you been stepping on any toes?'

'Not that I know of.'

'Not at all? Bedded someone's wife? Stolen their job?'

'Believe me, right now nobody wants *my* job, and I don't have time to go bedding other men's wives. But even if there were personal motives involved, why would someone take a shot at me in such difficult terrain, out in public? He could have killed me here at the lake. In peace and quiet.'

'You're well guarded.'

'Only since Calgary.'

'Maybe somebody from your own ranks? Do you stand for something that the powerholders at EMCO don't want at any price, no matter what the situation?'

Palstein laced his fingers together. He had switched off the outboard, and the little yacht sat on its reflection in the water as though glued in place. Behind Keowa's head, the cheerful hum of a bumblebee lost itself in the silence.

'Of course there are some at EMCO who think we should just sit out the whole helium-3 business,' he said. 'They think it's idiotic to buy in with Orley. But that's unrealistic. We're going bankrupt. We can't afford to wait anything out.'

'Would your death have changed anything for Imperial Oil, in particular?'

'It wouldn't have changed anything for anyone. I wouldn't have been able to make a few meetings.' Palstein shrugged. 'Well, as it is, some of them I can't make anyway.'

'You were supposed to fly to the Moon with Orley. He invited you.'

'Truth be told, I asked him whether I could come along. I would have really liked to have flown.' A dreamy look came into Palstein's eyes. 'As well as which, there are a lot of interesting people up there, maybe I could have talked up a joint venture or two. Oleg Rogachev, for instance, he's worth fifty-six billion, the world's biggest steel producer. Plenty of people trying to close a deal with him. Or Warren Locatelli, he's worth nearly as much.'

'EMCO and the world market leader in solar cells,' smiled Keowa. 'Doesn't it make you angry that your industry used to be so powerful, and now you have to court favour with these kinds of people?'

'It makes me angry that EMCO didn't listen to me at the time. I always wanted to work with Locatelli. We should have bought Light-years when the time was right.'

'When you still had something to offer him.'

'Yes.'

'It's absurd, isn't it? Doesn't it seem like history having the last laugh – the oil bosses dictated what happened in the world for nigh on a century, and then, in the end, they weren't in a position to turn new developments to their advantage?'

'Every kind of rule ends in decadence. Anyway, I'm sorry I can't help you with any more reasons for trying to kill me. I'm afraid you'll have to keep looking elsewhere.'

Keowa said nothing. Perhaps it had been naïve of her to hope that out here, on silent Lake Lavon, Palstein would whisper dreadful secrets in her ear. Then she had an idea.

'EMCO still has money, is that right?'

'Absolutely.'

'You see.' She smiled triumphantly. 'So what you did was, you made a decision, where there would have been an alternative.'

'And that would have been?'

'If you're investing in Orley Enterprises, then you must be thinking of considerable amounts of money.'

'Of course. But really, there's no alternative there either.'

'Depends on who's interested, I would say. It needn't necessarily be about keeping EMCO in business.'

'What else?'

'Shutting the place down and taking the money elsewhere. I mean, who might have an interest in actually *speeding up* EMCO's end? Perhaps your rescue plan actually gets in someone's way?'

Palstein looked at her with melancholy in his eyes.

'Interesting question.'

'Think about it! There are thousands out of work who would reckon it makes a lot more sense for EMCO to use the money for their welfare bills, at least for as long as it takes them to get new jobs, and then the ship can go down for all they care. Then there are the creditors who don't want to see their money blast off to the Moon. A government that has dropped you lot without batting an eyelid. Why exactly? EMCO has know-how, after all.'

'We have no know-how. Not on the Moon.'

'But isn't it all resource extraction, even up there?'

Palstein shook his head. 'It's space travel more than it's anything else. Then, Earth-based technologies can't just be mapped onto the Moon one to one, especially not in our line of work. The lower gravity, the lack of atmosphere, it all brings its own problems. A couple of guys from coal-mining are involved, but otherwise they're developing completely new techniques. If you ask me, there's a completely different reason why the government just dropped us. The State wants to control helium-3 extraction, one hundred per cent. So Washington has grabbed the opportunity with both hands, and they're aiming not just to get out of the armlock the Middle East had them in, they want to be free of the oil companies as well.'

'Stick the knife in the kingmaker's ribs,' said Keowa mockingly.

'But of course,' said Palstein, almost cheerfully. 'Oil has made presidents, but no president wants to be a puppet for private business unless he's the biggest fish in that pond. It's just in the nature of things that the new-crowned king wants to get rid of the kingmaker first thing, if he can. Just think of what happened in Russia in the nineties, think of Vladimir Putin – ah, heck, you're too young to remember that.'

'I've studied Russian history,' Keowa said, smiling. 'Putin was supposed to be the oligarchs' puppet, but they underestimated him. Characters like that guy with the unpronounceable name—'

'Khodorkovsky.'

'Right, one of the robber-barons from Yeltsin's day. Putin came onto the scene, a little bit later Khodorkovsky wakes up in a prison camp in Siberia. It happened to a lot of them.'

'In our case, the problem solves itself.' Palstein grinned.

'Nevertheless,' said Keowa insistently, 'during the big crisis sixteen years ago governments all over the world put together packages worth billions to save the banks from sinking. There was talk of pain in the financial markets, as though it were the banks and the board members who were suffering, not the armies of small investors who lost their money and never saw it back from State guarantees. But the states helped the banks. And now they're doing nothing. They're letting the oil giants go to the dogs. It doesn't matter how much they'd like to be free of them, *that* can't be in Washington's interest.'

Palstein looked at her as though at an interesting fish that he hadn't expected to catch in this lake.

'You want a story, no matter what it takes, don't you?'

'If there is one.'

'So you're comparing chalk and cheese just to get one. It was completely different with the banks. Banks are the very essence of the system called capitalism, they hold it up. Do you really believe that back then it was just about individual financial institutions, or about nasty managers and speculators paying themselves performance-related bonuses for no performance at all? It was about keeping the system going that even makes politics *possible*, it was about the temple of capitalism not crashing down, in the final analysis it was about governments' influence on capital which had been lost over time. Let's not kid ourselves, Loreena, the oil companies never played anything like that kind of a role. Our industry was only ever a symptom of the system, it was never part of its structure. You can do without us very well. Those of us who didn't manage to leap aboard the alternative energies bandwagon in time are in our death throes. Why should the State save us? We've nothing to offer it. Back in the day we paid the politicos, which was a comfortable way for them to live, but now you expect them to prop us up? Nobody's interested in that! The State is digging up the helium-3 because it sees the chance to become an investor in its own right again. America now has the once-in-a-lifetime opportunity to secure its energy supply under State control, and this time it won't let the kingmakers appear in the first place.'

'That really sounds like a lot of eyewash,' said Keowa dismissively. 'You name me one capitalist system where capital and private enterprise aren't the real powerbrokers. The USA is switching from EMCO to Orley Enterprises, that's all. Orley will bring Washington to the Moon, build the reactors so that when the stuff gets down to the Earth it does what it has to. The whole project would never have got this far without private sector support. And the new kingmaker is sitting on his patents and laying down the law for his partners. Without him, they'd not be able to build any more elevators, any reactors—'

'Julian Orley isn't a kingmaker in the classic sense. He's an alien, if you like. An out-of-worlder. ExxonMobil, later EMCO, they were Americans, they influenced elections in America and stoked foreign insurrections with their money or by running guns. Orley's not like that, he acts like a state himself, he sees himself as a world power in his own right. That's something that the multinationals always flirted with the idea of doing. Answerable to nobody but himself. Julian Orley would never try to topple an American president he didn't like, he'd even have moral scruples against it. He'd simply break off diplomatic relations with Washington and recall his ambassador.'

'He really thinks that he's a – state?'

'Are you surprised? Julian's rise to power was all plotted out while governments were still rubbing their eyes and demanding a greater say in how the banks were run. It was their own idea to privatise everything they could lay their hands on, and now they saw the welfare state slipping between their fingers. So all of a sudden they wanted more State power, but were forced to concede that if you take capital into State ownership, you rob it of the very strengths that make it grow, and they went back to business as usual. People contented themselves with the idea that the depression of 2008 to 2012 was just a system overheating, that there was nothing wrong with the system itself. They squandered the chance to reinvent capitalism, and with it the chance to strengthen State power in the long term.'

Palstein was gazing off into the distance. He spoke as though giving a lecture, his voice analytical but without empathy.

'That was the moment when private capital took the sceptre from government hands once and for all. Human beings became human resources. The parties in the democratic countries were too busy treading on one another's toes, and the totalitarian powers were wheeling and dealing on their own behalf as always, and meanwhile the big companies forced their way into every aspect of social life and set up shop for modern society. They took over the water supply, medicine, the food chain, they privatised education, built their own universities, hospitals, old folks' homes, graveyards, and it was all bigger, better and more beautiful than what the State had to offer. They formed an anti-war movement, they started aid programmes for the underprivileged, they took up arms against hunger and thirst and torture, against global warming, overfishing and resource depletion, against social division, the gap between the rich and the poor. And as they did so, they were reinfor-cing divisions by deciding who had access and who didn't. They set up generous research budgets, and made the research serve their goals. Planet Earth had been the heritage of all humanity, but now it became an economic asset. They opened up every corner of the planet, every resource. At the same time they put a price on everything, from sources of fresh water all the way to the human genome, they took the world which had been common to all and they drew up a catalogue listing what belonged to which owner, they imposed usage fees, access protocols; if you'll let me coin a rather loaded phrase, they put a turnstile on all Creation. Even free education and drinking water tie people into the commercial ideology once they accept the offer, it's the vision of a brand name.'

'Wasn't it always like that?' said Keowa. 'That the many are rewarded for following the vision of the few, and if they don't, they can expect to be cast out and punished?'

'You're talking about dictators and all their pomp and show. Tutankhamun, Julius Caesar, Napoleon, Hitler, Saddam Hussein.'

'There are other forms of dictatorship, gentler ones.'

'Ancient Rome was a gentle dictatorship.' Palstein smiled. 'The Romans reckoned that they were the freest people on earth. That was something quite different, Loreena, I'm talking about rulers seizing power who don't even have a country, their states aren't shown on the map. The fact that the oil companies look like losing this battle doesn't mean that industry's grip on politics is loosening, quite the opposite. It just shows that influence has shifted. Here on Earth, Incorporated, other departments have become more influential, and to that extent, you're absolutely right: Orley takes EMCO's place. It's just that EMCO acted in America's interests, because our people were in government, but Orley doesn't even want to govern. That's what makes him so unpredictable. That's what the governments are afraid of. And now, please consider the whole long history of state failure, and just ask yourself whether this kind of power transfer is really such a bad thing.'

'Excuse me?' Keowa cocked her head. 'You can't be serious?'

'I'm not trying to sell you anything. I just want you to look at the situation as though it were an equation, look at all the variables, without fear or favour. Can you do that?'

Keowa considered this. Palstein had drawn her into a strange kind of conversation here. She had set out to interview him, and analyse him, and now the tables were turned.

'I believe so,' she said.

'And?'

'There is no ideal state of things. But there are approximations. Some of them have been hard-won. When we abolished slavery, the idea of the free citizen won out, at all levels of society. The citizen of a democratic state is bound by the laws but fundamentally free, isn't that right?'

'*D'accord.*'

'But if you're a member of a company, you're property. That's the change that's happening all over.'

'Also right.'

'It seems to me about as difficult to break out of this pattern as it would be to suspend the laws of nature. The freedom of the individual is nothing but an idea by now. We live on a globe, and globes are closed systems, they offer no chance of escape and the globe is all divided up. At this very moment, while we sit here on this beautiful lake talking the whole thing through, the Moon in its orbit is being divided up, way over our heads, that's the next globe. There's no such thing as uncommercialised space any more.'

'That is so.'

'Well, excuse me, Gerald, yes, I'm a realist – but I'll fight this to the very end!'

'That's your prerogative. I can understand your position, but please, think about it. You can hate the very thought of being property. Or you can make some kind of compromise with it.' Palstein ran a rope through his fingers and laughed. All of a sudden he seemed very relaxed, a Buddha at rest. 'And perhaps compromise is the better choice.'

Gaia, Vallis Alpina, The Moon

The sun was losing mass.

Every minute, sixty million tonnes of material in its mantle was lost, protons, electrons, helium atoms and a few other elements with walk-on roles, the ingredients for that mysterious molecular cloud that supposedly gave birth to all the celestial bodies in our system. The solar wind streamed ceaselessly outward, blowing comets off course, fluorescing in the Earth's atmosphere as the aurorae borealis and australis, sweeping away the accretions of gas in interplanetary space and gusting out, far beyond the orbit of Pluto, to the Oort cloud. Cosmic background radiation joined the mix, weak but omnipresent, a newsfeed at the speed of light, speaking of supernovae, neutron stars, black holes and the birth of the universe.

Ever since the Earth had collided with a proto-planet named Theia and given birth to the Moon, its satellite had been defenceless against all these influences, exposed. The sun's breath blew constantly over the lunar surface. It had no magnetic field to deflect the high-energy particles, and although they only penetrated a few micrometres deep, the lunar dust was saturated with them, and four and a half billion years of meteorite bombardment had turned the whole surface over and over like a ploughed field. Since its creation, the Moon had soaked up so much solar plasma that it held enough to bring mankind up here, hungry for resources, armed with spaceships and mining machinery to rip away the Moon's dowry.

Sometimes there were sunstorms.

Spots formed on the sun's surface, huge arcs of plasma leapt across the raging ocean of fire, hurling umpteen times the usual amount of radiation out into space, and the solar wind became a hurricane, howling through the solar system at twice its usual speed. When this happened, astronauts were well advised to huddle in their habitation modules and not, if at all possible, to be caught in a travelling spaceship. Each ionised particle that passed through a human cell damaged the genetic material irreparably. Every twelve years the solar hurricanes were more frequent: as recently as 2024 they had stopped shuttle traffic for a while and forced the residents at the moon bases underground. Even machines did not cope well with these particle storms, which damaged their outer skin and wiped the data stored in their microchips, caused short-circuits and unwanted chain reactions.

Everyone agreed that sunstorms were the biggest danger of manned space flight.

* * *

On 26 May 2025, the sun was breathing calmly and evenly.

As usual, its breath streamed out into the heliosphere, passed Mercury, mingled with the carbon dioxide on Venus and Mars and with the Earth's atmosphere, blew straight through the gaseous shells of Jupiter, Saturn, Uranus and Neptune, washed up on the shores of all their moons and of course reached the Earth's satellite as well, each particle travelling at 400 kilometres per second. The particles ploughed into the regolith, clinging to the grey dust, spread out across the plains and the crater walls, and a few billions also collided with the female colossus at the edge of the Vallis Alpina in the lunar north, without penetrating her skin, at least in the parts reinforced with mooncrete. Gaia sat there on her cliff edge, unmoved by the cosmic hailstorm, her eyeless face turned towards the Earth.

Julian's woman in the Moon.

Lynn's nightmare.

The stranded ocean liner clinging to the volcanic slopes of the Isla de las Estrellas, the OSS Grand, both of these were products of her imagination. Gaia, though, was from a dream that Julian had had, in which he saw his daughter sitting on the Moon, none other, a figure all of light in front of the black brocade of space sewn with its millions of stars. Typically for him, he saw Lynn exaggerated to the scale of a metaphor, an ideal of humanity, journeying onward, wise and pure, and he woke up and called her there and then from bed and told her about his dream. And of course Lynn enthusiastically took up the idea of a hotel shaped like the human form, congratulated her father and promised to draw up preliminary designs right away, while this sublime vision that was supposed to be her actually turned her stomach so much that she couldn't sleep for a week. Her eating disorders reached a whole new anorexic level, and she began to gobble down little green tablets to help her master her fear of failure, but somehow she managed to place the colossus at the edge of the Vallis Alpina, a giant of a woman, named after Mother Earth in ancient Greek myth.

Gaia.

And she had built this woman! The very last of her energy might have burnt away in the fury of creation, but in return, she could claim a masterpiece. At least, everybody told her that's what it was. She felt no such certainty. The way Julian saw things, she was supposed to recover by working on Gaia; he thought that the project would be a therapy, a countermeasure for the last symptoms of that fearful illness she had just recovered from. He had barely had a clue what the illness was – about as much as if she'd been abducted by aliens and taken to some far-off planet. It was also typical that Julian had convinced himself she was ill because she was short on challenges, stifled by routine, that too much of the same old thing had made her quick blood sluggish. Lynn had been the perfect leader of Orley Travel, the group's tourism arm, for years now. Perhaps she was yearning for something exciting, something new. Perhaps she was understimulated. She made the world run on time, but was the world enough? Back in the late 2010s private sub-orbital space-flight had been part of the portfolio of Orley Space, along with tourist trips to the OSS and to the smaller orbital hotels, but strictly speaking, all these things were tourism as well.

And so Julian decided that it was not Orley Space that was to be entrusted with the greatest adventure in the whole history of hotel-building, but his daughter.

The whole gigantic project was made rather simpler by engineering free-doms, given that everything on the Moon weighed only one-sixth of its weight on Earth. What made it harder was that nobody had any experi-ence at all in lunar high-rise construction. Large parts of the American moon base were underground, the rest was as low-rise as you could get. China had done away completely with the idea of having a site, and its outposts were housed in modular vehicles, built like tanks, that followed along not far behind the mining vehicles by their extraction site. Down at the lunar South Pole, not far from Aitken Crater, a small German moon base shared its little place in the sun with an equivalent French station, each housing two astronauts, while over in the Oceanus Procellarum a lively little automated gizmo surveyed the ideal spot for a Russian base that would never be built. The Mare Serenitatis was home to an inquisitive Indian robot, and Japan had a forlorn uninhabited zone around the corner. Otherwise there was nothing else on the Moon for architectural sightseers. Nevertheless the elevated maglev rails proved that in lunar gravity it was possible to build vaulting filigree frameworks that would have long ago collapsed under their own weight back on Earth.

And Gaia had to be big. This was no bed-and-breakfast operation but a monument to the glory of mankind – and of course a stopover for up to two hundred of the most solvent members of that species.

Lynn had obediently drummed up designers and engineers, and set the plans in motion under the strictest secrecy. It soon became clear that a standing figure would be too tall. So she sketched Gaia seated as an alternative, which met with Julian's especial approval since that was just the way he had dreamed of his hotel. Since there was no question of a detailed depiction of a human body, the first thing the planning team did was fuse the legs together into one massive complex, as though the woman were wearing a narrow skirt that tailed off into a point. The buttocks and thighs were the horizontal base of the building, then below the knee the legs bent downward into the chasm without touching the wall behind them. The daring ambition of this piece of structural engineering was enough in itself to send Lynn clutching the sides of the toilet bowl, where she threw up, half-digested, most of what little food she had been able to choke down. Her tablet consumption rose to compensate, but Julian was in raptures, and the technical team said it could be done.

No need to emphasise that 'it can be done' was Julian's favourite phrase.

Thus the feminine attributes of the building all had to be shown in the torso, basically a high-rise with curved walls rather than straight. It was given a waist, and then lines suggesting a bosom – which was the cause of a great deal of argument. The draughtsmen, being men, drew breasts that were far too large. Lynn declared that she was not interested in tackling the engineering aspects of porn-star-sized boobies just so as to be able to accommodate a few more guests, and she brushed them out of the picture. Suddenly she found the whole idea of a putting a woman on the Moon a hideous platitude. Julian threw in a remark that making the upper body too narrow made the building look like a man, and wasn't it about time to let a woman represent mankind? One of the architects hinted that Lynn might be a prude. Lynn was enraged. She was no flat-chested goody-goody herself, she yelled, but what exactly was Gaia supposed to embody here? A monument to mammaries? Bust expansion? All right then, said Julian, we want curves. No, Lynn retorted, we want as boyish a figure as we can create. But nothing androgynous, protested the head of the team responsible for the façade. Nothing top-heavy either, Lynn insisted. All right then, suggested Julian, *decently* curved, which sounded like the best solution, but what exactly did decent mean here?

An intern scooted past, sat herself down at the computer without a word and drew a curve. Everyone watched her, looked at it. Everyone liked what they saw. Boyish, but not androgynous. The curve united them all, and the point was settled.

The shoulders were feminine but not narrow, atop towers that swept down to the ground, narrowing as they went, with a slight bend halfway and the stylised representation of open palms placed flat on the ground below. A slender neck grew up from the torso and, above that, a head in perfect proportion with the body, hairless, faceless, nothing but the noble contour of a shapely domed cranium, tilted backward a little so that Gaia was looking towards the Earth. As the whole ensemble took shape on the computer, Lynn suffered stomach cramps and cold sweats, but she patiently took on the next challenge: how to use as much glass as possible while keeping the best possible protection against radiation. She declared that Gaia's 'face' should be transparent, that she wanted to put the bars and restaurants in the head, while the back of the head could be clad and reinforced, where the chefs ruled their roost. Glass all over the throat and the curve of the breasts, where the suites were, and the showpiece was to be a huge Gothic window in the belly, four levels housing reception, casino, tennis courts and sauna, then glassed-in shins, and viewing platforms on the outside of the arms. Julian complained that the great window reminded him of having to go to church, back when he couldn't object or resist. Lynn replaced the Gothic point with a Romanesque arch, and the window stayed.

All the rest – back and shoulder, ribs and neck, the top of the thighs and the inside of the arms – was clad with armoured cast-concrete slabs made from regolith, reinforced with sheet-glass sandwiches that held water between the panes to absorb particles and minimise heat loss. If the Americans were agreeable, the concrete was to be manufactured in the existing production facilities at the North Pole, made without water just by heating up the moonrock and casting it into construction-ready components at an automated factory. Mooncrete was said to be ten times more robust than ordinary concrete, resisting erosion, cosmic rays and micro-meteorites, and it was also cheap.

Gaia's skeleton took shape. The spine was a massive main column enclosing all the cables and ducts that the building would need, as well as three high-speed lifts. Steel ribs sprouted from the column to bear the individual floors and the outer skin, and the secondary supports were anchored deep in the rock of the plateau. There didn't seem to be any need for cross-bracing until somebody realised that the structure would be subject to much greater stresses than initial sketches suggested, since it was surrounded by vacuum, with no atmospheric resistance to the pressure of the artificial atmosphere within. Several assumptions had to be rejected, all the parameters frantically recalculated, until the experts declared that the problem had been solved. Since when, Lynn had had a new nightmare scenario to add to her visions of the end: a hotel that would at some moment suddenly go pop.

But Gaia shone.

She glowed from within, and she glowed with the help of the powerful floodlights that bathed her flawless snow-white exterior in white light. After years of struggle, Lynn had managed it. She had finished building the woman of Julian's dream, at least for the most part. Some of the lower-end rooms still lacked plumbing, the multi-religious chapel at the bend of Gaia's knees needed redundant life-support systems if it was to comply with all safety standards, and as for the banal detail of a spaceport, perhaps they would build one later to allow direct connections between Gaia and the OSS. On the other hand, the Lunar Express beat any direct approach hands down. It was undeniably more fun to arrive by train, and apart from that, they had a launch field for point-to-point flights on the Moon itself. It was all fine.

Except inside Lynn's skull.

Gaia had collapsed so often in her nightmares that she had come to long for the day when catastrophe would come. A whole office full of certificates and affidavits swore that it would never happen, but she knew better. The thought that there was something she had overlooked had driven her mad, and madness was destructive.

None of you is safe, she thought, and introduced the woman . . .

'—who will be looking after your comfort and security round the clock, together with her team. My dear friends, I'm delighted to present to you our hotel director, or should I say the manager here at Gaia, Dana Lawrence.'

The Lunar Express had arrived at the hotel's station on schedule. They had run along the edge of the canyon for a while, so that they could enjoy the astonishing view of the building opposite, then crossed over at the further end and approached Gaia in a long, wide curve. Just in front of the hotel the ground sloped upward, so the builders had chosen not to take the rails straight up but to bring them into a tunnel, with the station itself underground. The track ended 300 metres beyond the gigantic figure, in a bare hall. This time there was no vacuum as they disembarked. They walked along gangways and into a wide pressurised corridor, with conveyor bands on the floor which brought them directly under the hotel, then from there to the lifts and up to the lobby, where islands of seating and elegant writing-desks made up one organic landscape. Fish glided behind aquarium panes. Perky little trees bursting with foliage flanked a curving reception desk, and above it holographic projections of the planets circled a bright central star, a model of the solar system with a sun in the middle spewing plasma from its surface. When the guests looked upwards, they could see the great hall vanishing in a nest of criss-crossing glass bridges. Since the reception hall was here in Gaia's glass-fronted belly, with the huge Romanesque window arching in front, there was something cathedral-like about it. They looked out across the canyon to the sunlight on the other side and the pillars of the maglev marching away into the distance. The Earth shone up in the sky, a vision of home.

Dana Lawrence nodded at the group of guests.

She had searching grey-green eyes, an oval face and copper-coloured hair worn shoulder-length. Her high cheekbones and perfectly arched brows gave her an air of British reserve, almost of unapproachability. Even the sensual curve of her lips did little to change that. Only when she took the trouble to smile was the impression dispelled, but Dana was not overly generous with her smiles. She knew exactly what impression she made, and she knew that she came across as brisk, efficient and serious – something that people flying all the way to the Moon appreciated.

'Thank you, Lynn,' she said, and took a step forward. 'I hope you had a pleasant journey. As perhaps you know, in future this hotel will have two hundred guests and a hundred staff. Since you'll have the whole place to yourselves for the coming week, we've taken the liberty of cutting back on staff a little, though you won't feel the lack. Our staff are quite experienced in being able to cater to a guest's wishes before they've even been voiced. Sophie Thiel—'

She turned her head to a knot of young people who stood there wreathed in smiles, all dressed in Orley Group colours. A girlish woman with freckles stepped forward.

'—is my right hand; she leads the housekeeping department and makes sure the life-support systems function without a hitch. Ashwini Anand' – a delicate, Indian-looking woman with a proud gaze nodded her head – 'is responsible for room service and, together with Sophie, takes care of technology and logistics. In the past, astronauts had to endure all sorts of discomforts, first and foremost in their diet. It's been a long road from tube rations to the five-star meal, but you now have the choice between two excellent restaurants under the direction of our head chef, Axel Kokoschka.' A thickset, bashful man with a baby face and bald head lifted his right hand, shifting his weight from one foot to the other. 'He's assisted by our sous-chef, Michio Funaki, who will, among other things, be demonstrating how to make fresh-caught sushi on the Moon.'

Funaki, a wiry man with a buzz-cut, bowed with his whole upper body.

'All four are highly qualified and have trained in some of the best hotels and kitchens in the world, on top of which they have had two years' experience on the Orley Space Station, making each of them a seasoned astronaut, and they know Gaia's systems just as thoroughly as they know all the transport options here-abouts. In future Sophie, Ashwini, Axel and Michio will be the middle management here in Gaia, but for the next few days they are exclusively at your service. The same is true of me. Please don't hesitate to speak to me if you have any concerns. It's an honour to have you here as our guests, and we are extremely pleased to see you.'

A smile, almost infinitely diluted.

'If there are no further questions for the moment, I would like to show you the hotel. In one hour, we will expect you for dinner in the Selene.'

Under the lobby was the casino, a ballroom with a stage, a cocktail bar and gambling tables; one floor below began Gaia's lower belly, and the female shape spread out wider at the hips, so that to everyone's astonishment they found two tennis courts waiting for them.

'There are two more outside,' said Dana. 'For hard-core players. It's no problem playing in spacesuits, but the trouble comes with the balls. Here on the Moon they can fly hundreds of metres at a time, so we've fenced those courts in.'

'How about golf?' Edwards asked.

'Golf on the Moon,' said Mimi, giggling. 'You'd never find the ball.'

'Oh but you do,' said Lynn. 'We've tried it with tracking beacons in the balls. Via LPCS. It works.'

'LP which?'

'Lunar Positioning and Communication System. There are ten satellites orbiting the Moon, letting us communicate and find our way about up here. The golf course is on the other side of the canyon, Shepard's Green. We also call it the "satellite links".'

'And who's it named after?' asked Karla.

'Dear old Alan Shepard,' Julian laughed. 'A real pioneer, he landed with Apollo 14 on the plateau south of Copernicus. The old rascal had actually brought a couple of golf balls along and a six iron head. He hit it and said it went for miles and miles and miles—'

'I most certainly will *not* be playing golf up here,' said Aileen Donoghue, emphatically.

'It's not as bad as all that. He never went looking for his ball, but it can hardly have travelled more than two hundred, four hundred metres. Lunar golf is fun, but the trick of it is not to put too much into your swing.'

'Don't they just sink down into the dust?'

'Too light,' said Dana. 'Try it sometime. We also have holographic tees here in the hotel. Would you like to see the spa?'

The sauna stretched out below the tennis courts, but most impressive of all was the swimming-pool in Gaia's buttocks. It took up almost all the available area. The walls and ceiling simulated the starry sky, a hologram of the Earth glowed with a soft light, while the bottom of the pool and the floor all around were built to look like the lunar regolith, with rugged mountain chains on the horizon. The pool itself was a double crater, as large as a lake and surrounded by recliners. The illusion of bathing on the very surface of the Moon was practically perfect.

Heidrun turned her white face to O'Keefe and smiled. 'So, who's a big hero? Ready for a race?'

'Any time.'

'Careful! You know that I'm better.'

'Just wait and see how things work out in reduced gravity,' Ögi chuckled. 'Could be I'll leave you both behind.'

'All right then, you know we've just *got* to have a swimming race,' Miranda announced, spreading her fingers. 'I lo-o-o-o-ove being in the water.'

'I got it. Huey and Dewey.' O'Keefe lowered his eyes reverently. 'Lord love a duck.'

They visited the floor with the conference rooms, the multi-religious chapel, a meditation centre and a sickbay that gleamed reassuringly like a new pin, then up to Gaia's ribcage. The group all had rooms on floors fourteen to sixteen, in the outer curve of the breasts. The lobby lay almost fifty metres below them. To get to their suites from the lifts, they had to cross the glass bridges. More bridges on the lower floors were set at zigzag angles, obviously placed quite at random. None of them had a railing.

'Anyone suffer from vertigo?' asked Dana. Sushma Nair raised her hand hesitantly. Some of the others looked disconcerted. This time Dana's smile was a little broader.

'Please understand. When you jump from a two-metre-high wall on the Earth, you reach the ground 0.6 of a second later. During that time, your body has accelerated to twenty-two kilometres an hour. On the Moon, the same jump would take three times longer, and your final speed would be less than half. That's to say that you would have to jump from a height of twelve metres to get the same effect as a two-metre jump on the Earth, or in other words, on the Moon you could happily jump from three floors up in an ordinary high-rise. This means that you really don't need to take the lift every time you want to go downstairs. Just jump from bridge to bridge, they're barely four metres apart, which is nothing. Anybody want to try?'

'I will,' said Carl Hanna.

She gave him an appraising look. Tall, muscly, deliberate in his movements.

'The real experts can jump back up again,' she added meaningfully.

Hanna grinned and walked onto the nearest bridge.

'If it turns out she was lying,' he called to the others, 'just throw her after me, okay?'

He sprang from the bridge with Donoghue's cackles of laughter following after. He fell, and landed four metres below without the slightest jar.

'Like jumping down from the kerbstone,' he called up.

In the next moment O'Keefe sailed out from the edge, then Heidrun. They both landed as though they had never moved any other way.

'My goodness,' said Aileen, 'My goodness!' and then looked at each of them in turn, with a 'My goodness!' for everyone.

'C'mon, guys,' Chucky boomed. 'Show us what you're made of! Up you come!'

'You'll have to make room.' Hanna shooed them away with a flap of his hands. They scurried backwards. He looked thoughtfully up at the ledge. When he raised his arms, he was just about two metres fifty tall, so there was still a metre and a half to make up.

'How tall are you?' O'Keefe asked, disconcerted.

'Six foot three.'

'Hmm.' The Irishman rubbed his chin. 'I'm five foot nine.'

'Could be a near thing. Heidrun?'

'One hundred and seventy-eight – five foot ten. Whatever. Whoever doesn't make it has to stand us all a meal.'

'Forget it.' O'Keefe waved the idea away. 'It's all free here anyway.'

'Then back on Earth. Hey, in Zürich! All right with that? A round of schnitzels in the Kronenhalle.'

'Meaning all of us!' called Julian.

'Good, we'll all jump together,' Hanna declared. 'Make room, so we don't get in one another's way. You guys up there, get back! Ready!'

'Yes, sir.' Heidrun grinned. 'Ready.'

'And up we go!'

Hanna sprang powerfully upwards. It looked astonishingly easy. As calmly as a superhero, he flew towards the ledge, grabbed hold, boosted himself up again and landed on his feet. Next to him Heidrun fluttered down, struggling for balance. O'Keefe's hands threatened to slip off the edge of the bridge, then he clambered up, as elegantly as circumstances allowed.

'Sorry about that,' he said. 'Kronenhalle is cancelled.'

'You're all invited anyway,' Ögi called out, in the tones of a man who embraces the whole world. 'This is the first time ever that a Swiss has taken a standing jump of four metres. We'll meet again in Zürich!'

'Optimist,' said Lynn, so quietly that only Dana heard.

The hotel director was stunned. She acted as though she hadn't caught that wan little word with its insidious undertones.

What was the matter with Orley's daughter?

'Please bear in mind,' she said out loud to the group, 'that in reduced gravity your body will be losing muscle mass. There are two guest lifts here in Gaia, the E1 and E2, and a staff lift, but we nevertheless recommend that you work out a lot and take the shortcut via the bridges as often as you can. Now we'll tell you a little more about the facilities and show you the rooms.'

Hanna had Sophie Thiel show him all the secrets of his suite. There was no essential difference between the life-support systems here and those aboard the space station.

'The temperature is set to twenty degrees Celsius, but that's adjustable,' Sophie Thiel explained with a wide-screen smile, pointing out a button by the door; she brushed so close past Hanna as she did so that it was only just within the limits of professionalism. 'Your suite has its own water management system, with wonderfully sterile water—'

'Don't use words like that to the customers,' Hanna said, looking about and at the same time feeling her hungry gaze on his back. No two ways about it, this Thiel woman liked muscular men. 'It sounds as if you're setting out to poison somebody.'

'Well then, let's just call it fresh water. Ha ha.'

He turned to face her. Her eyes were half-moons, their colour barely discernible; on the other hand she looked as if she had a double ration of bright white teeth and inexhaustible reserves of laughter. She was not the least bit beautiful, but very pretty for all that. A grown-up version of Pippi Longstocking, or whatever that Swedish minx was called. He had found the film on a Sunday afternoon at a hotel in Germany, while he was waiting for hours on end for to meet somebody who had been floating dead in the Rhine all the while, and he had watched it all the way through, curiously moved. A childish, clunky old three-reeler, but the childhood it showed him was so amazingly different from his own that it was practically science fiction. He found himself unable to change channels. He'd never watched a kids' movie before, or at least never one like this.

And he'd never watched another one.

Thiel showed him how the lighting was controlled, opened up a respectable mini-bar and told him the numbers to call if he needed anything. The look in her eyes said, *if only things were different. I've worked in the best hotels in the world. Never with guests.* You could hardly say that she put herself forward. She was friendly and professional, it's just that she was also an open book.

But Hanna wasn't here for fun and games.

'If there's anything else you'd like—'

'No, not at the moment. I'll manage.'

'Oh, I almost forgot! You'll find your moon slippers in the bottom of the wardrobe.' She wrinkled her nose. 'We couldn't think of a better name for them. They have lead plates in the soles, in case you want additional weight.'

'Why would I want that?'

'Some people prefer to move on the Moon the way they move on Earth.'

'I see! Very far-sighted of you.'

The look in her eyes said, *unless you take a bit of trouble.*

'Well then – till half past eight, in the Selene.'

'Yes. Thank you.'

He waited until she'd gone. The suite displayed the same discreet, elegant sense of style as the lobby. Hanna didn't know a great deal about design, nothing in fact, but even he could tell that this was the work of experts. After all, he'd had to learn a little about style and appearances to take on this role. Also, he liked clean lines, simple rooms. Much as he loved India, he had always felt rather hemmed in by the local sense of decor, the way they crowded every surface with knick-knacks.

His gaze swept over to the window that took up the whole wall.

They couldn't have found a better place for the hotel, he thought. The plateau below Gaia could be reached by lift, and from here he saw it stretching away towards the canyon, its tennis courts lost and lonely. You must have a fantastic view of the hotel from down there, it would look like a floodlit sculpture. Over on the left, where the cliffs dropped back and the canyon closed, a natural-seeming path curved away to the other side.

What was it that Julian Orley had said just now? Over on the other side of the Lunar Express tracks was the golf course.

A golf course on the Moon!

Suddenly Hanna felt a touch of regret that he wasn't actually here as the person everybody thought he was. He crushed the feeling before it could get to work on him, opened his silver suitcase and delved into it for his computer, a touchscreen device of the usual sort, no bigger than a chocolate bar, and his washbag. He took an electric trimmer from the depths of the bag. With a practised twist, he clicked the trimmer apart and took out a tiny circuit board, which he plugged into the computer. Whistling tunelessly, he booted up and watched as the program uploaded and hooked into the LPCS.

A few seconds later the device alerted him that he had a message.

He opened his mailserver. The message was from a friend, reminding him not to forget Dexter and Stacey's wedding. Unimpressed by the pending nuptials of a couple who didn't exist anyway, he filtered out the white noise that made up the rest of the message and came up with a few more lines of text, nothing more than the addresses of several dozen internet sites. Then he uploaded a symbol – snaking reptilian necks, twisted and knotted together, all growing from a single body – and waited a moment.

Something was happening.

Words and syllables slotted together with lightning speed. The actual message took shape before his eyes. Even while the reconstruction was still under way, he knew there had been trouble. The text was short, but peremptory:

The package has been damaged. It is no longer responding to commands and cannot reach deployment under its own power. This changes your mission. You will repair the package or bring the contents to operational destination yourself. If circumstances permit, you can bring forward insertion. Act swiftly!

Swiftly.

Hanna stared at the display. The implications were quite clear, as present as an unwelcome visitor. Swiftly meant now, or as soon as possible without arousing suspicion. It meant that he would have to leave and then return while everybody was asleep.

Back to Peary Base.

Table Talk

Since they had made love free-floating in orbit, Tim had spared Amber any further speculation about the state of Lynn's mental health, and tried to convince himself that he was showing consideration for his wife, since she was so grimly determined to enjoy the trip; in fact it was because he was quite busy enough grappling with his own dilemmas. More and more he found himself enjoying a trip that he had resolved whole-heartedly to hate: the way the trip had been arranged, Julian's arrogant and high-handed part in it. And the more he was having fun, the more he felt a creeping adolescent sense of betrayal. He was susceptible, he had been corrupted, and by a ticket! He tried to persuade himself that it was only the overwhelming experiences and impressions that somehow, against all expectation, made him like the old snake-charmer. Hadn't he been dead set on hating Julian, the megalomaniac, who couldn't see that he trampled other people underfoot on his march into the future? Who neglected his nearest and dearest, or put them on pedestals, who couldn't understand that they needed a drop of normality in their lives?

It would have been so wonderfully simple just to hate him.

But the Julian he had got to know in the narrow confines of the spaceship unnerved him by *not* being ignorant and egomaniacal, or at least not enough to bear out Tim's sweeping condemnation. Rather, he reminded Tim of his childhood, when he had admired Dad so much. Reminded him of Crystal, who right up to the very moment her sanity had finally crumbled away had insisted that she had never known a more loving man than his father, who had called him her sunbeam, bringing her happiness – all too quickly, before he was gone again. She had praised and admired him, and an hour before she died, he had taken to the skies in a sub-orbital craft of his own design, slipping away into the thermosphere even though he knew how critical her condition was. He had known it – and had forgotten just long enough to break a record, win a prize and earn his son's everlasting enmity.

Lynn had forgiven Julian.

Tim had not.

Instead he had been hard at work demonising the man. And even now he couldn't forgive Julian, even if, or perhaps even because, he could see the pillars that held up his hatred crumbling away. This hotel couldn't have been built solely out of greed and a ruinous sense of self-aggrandisement. There must be more behind it, a dream too overpowering to be shared with only a few family members. Whether he wanted to or not, secretly he was beginning to understand the old guy, the fever in his blood that made him push back all boundaries, his nomadic nature that let him blaze trails where others saw only dead ends, his passionate attachment to progress, innovation, and he began to grow jealous of Julian's great love, the world. And as this change of mind smouldered away below the surface of all he thought he had believed, he felt uncomfortably aware that perhaps he was overreacting where Lynn was concerned, perhaps – without ever intending to! – he was using her as an excuse to get at Julian, that in fact he cared less about her happiness than about Julian's guilt. He flirted with the idea that perhaps she really did feel as fine as she was always claiming, and that he had no reason to feel ashamed of mellowing towards his dad. And suddenly, over dinner in Gaia's nose, or rather where her nose would be if she had one, with the magnificent view of the canyon before his eyes, he wanted nothing more than just to be allowed to have fun, without the ghosts of his past sitting down at table with him, the ghosts that brought out the worst in him.

'It looks like you're enjoying that,' Amber said appreciatively.

They were seated at a long table in Selene, with its black-blue-silver decor, eating red mullet with a saffron risotto. The fish tasted fresh-caught, as though it had just come from the sea.

'Bred in salt water,' Axel Kokoschka, the chef, informed them. 'We've got great big underground tanks.'

'Isn't it rather complicated to re-create ocean conditions up here?' asked Karla Kramp. 'I mean, you don't just tip salt into the water?'

Kokoschka considered the question. 'Not just that, no.'

'Salinity varies from one biotope to the next down on Earth, doesn't it? Doesn't it take a particular chemical composition to make an environment where animal life can thrive? Chloride, sulphate, sodium, traces of calcium, potassium, iodine, and so on.'

'Fish has to feel at home, yes, that's right.'

'I just want to know what's what. Don't a great many fish need a permanent current, a steady oxygen supply, constant temperature, all of that?'

Kokoschka nodded thoughtfully, rubbed his bald head with a shy smile, scratched industriously at his three-day beard. He said, 'Quite,' and vanished. Karla watched him go, flummoxed.

'Thanks for the explanation!' she called after him.

'Not exactly a great talker, is he?' grinned Tim.

She speared a piece of mullet and made it vanish between her Modigliani lips.

'If he can make a fish taste like this up here on the Moon, for all I care he can cut his own tongue out.'

Two restaurants and two bars took up four floors in Gaia's head, their front walls all of glass. The panes curved right the way round to where the temples would be, so that there were wide-screen views all around. Selene and Chang'e, the two restaurants, were in the lower half, with the Luna Bar above them, and right up at the top the Mama Quilla Club for dancing under the stars. From there a glassed-in airlock led to the topmost point of the whole hotel, a viewing terrace which could only be entered in a spacesuit, offering a spectacular 360-degree view. Kokoschka's shyness aside, he served the group of guests with exemplary attention, as did Ashwini Anand, Michio Funaki and Sophie Thiel. Lynn was praised from all sides for her hotel. She let her own food go cold as she cheerfully

FRANK SCHÄTZING · 366

doled out information, answered questions at length, in high spirits and visibly flattered by the attention. For a while there was no other topic of conversation but this strange new world they now walked upon, Gaia, and the quality of the food.

Then the focus of talk shifted.

'Chang'e,' said Mukesh Nair thoughtfully over the main course, venison with truffles, served with wafer-thin slices of toast that gleamed as the foie gras melted on them. 'Isn't that a term from the Chinese space programme?'

'Yes and no.' Rogachev took a swig of the low-alcohol Château Palmer. 'There were a few probes of that name; the Chinese sent them up to explore the Moon at the beginning of the century. But in fact it's a mythological figure.'

'Chang'e, the moon goddess.' Lynn nodded.

'Gaia seems to have a head full of myths then,' smiled Nair. 'Selene was the Greek moon goddess, wasn't she? And Luna was the goddess in ancient Rome—'

'Even I know that,' said Miranda gleefully. 'Luna, and then Sol the sun god, the jerk. Eternal gods, y'know, up, down, round and round, never stopping. One comes home and the other one leaves, like a married couple working different shifts.'

'The sun and moon. Shift workers.' Rogachev twitched his lips in a smile. 'That makes sense.'

'I am so interested in gods and astrology! The stars tell us our future, you know.' She leaned forward, overshadowing the venison scraps on her plate with the great twin stars of her breasts, which she had poured into some shimmering scrap of almost nothing for the evening. 'And do you know what? You want to hear something else?' She stabbed the air with her fork. 'Some of them, the ones that really had a clue what was going on in ancient Rome, they called her Noctiluca, they lit up a temple all for her, at night on the Palatine, that's one of the hills in the city. I've been there, y'know, Rome's like full of hills, not a city up in the hills though, it's a city *on* the hills, if you get me.'

'You should tell us more about your travels,' Nair said amiably. 'What does Noctiluca mean?'

'The one who lights up the night,' Miranda said solemnly, and rewarded herself with an uncommonly large gulp of red wine.

'And Mama Quilla?'

'Somebody's mom, I'd guess. Julian, what's Mama Quilla?'

'Well, we were rather running out of moon goddesses,' said Julian with relish, 'but then Lynn dug up a few more, Ningal, the wife of Sin, the Assyrian god of the moon; Annit, she was Babylonian; Kusra from Arabia, Isis from Egypt—'

'But we liked Mama Quilla most of all,' Lynn spoke across him. 'Mother Moon, an Inca goddess. Even today the heirs of the Inca culture worship her as the protector of married women—'

'Oh, really?' Olympiada Rogacheva pricked up her ears. 'I think the bar might turn out to be my favourite place.'

Rogachev didn't bat an eye.

'I find it surprising that you considered using the Chinese moon goddess,' said Nair, picking up the thread again hastily before the embarrassment could spread.

'Why not?' asked Julian artlessly. 'Are we prejudiced?'

'Well, you are China's greatest competitor!'

'Not me, Mukesh. You mean the USA.'

'Yes, of course. But nevertheless, sitting here at this table I see Americans, Canad-ians, English and Irish, Germans, Swiss, Russians and Indians, and until a while ago we had the pleasure of our French friends' company. But I don't see a single Chinese person.'

'Don't worry, they're here,' said Rogachev equably. 'Unless I'm much mistaken, they're not a thousand kilometres from here, south-west, busy digging away at the regolith.'

'But they're not *here*.'

'No Chinese investor has shown an interest in our project,' said Julian. 'They want their own elevator.'

'Don't we all?' remarked Rogachev.

'Yes, but as you have rightly pointed out, unlike Moscow, Beijing is already mining helium-3.'

'Talking of the elevator.' Ögi scooped up foie gras onto the dark-red meat. 'Is it true that they're just about to make the breakthrough?'

'The Chinese?'

'Mm-hmm.'

'They make that announcement with admirable regularity.' Julian smiled knowingly. 'If it were actually the case, Zheng Pang-Wang would not take every opportunity he can find to drink tea with me.'

'But' – Mukesh Nair propped himself up on his elbows and massaged his imposingly fleshy nose – 'isn't it the case that your American friends would take lasting umbrage if you were to flirt with the Chinese, especially after the Moon crisis last year? I mean to say, are you perhaps not quite so free in your decisions as you would like to be?'

Julian pursed his lips. His face darkened, as always when he set out to explain the extent of his independence of all government power. Then he spread his arms in a fatalistic gesture.

'Just look, what's the reason you're all here? Even though the nation-states all make a big noise about how effective their space programmes are, they would leap at the chance to get in line with the Americans if the offer were ever made. Or let's say, they'd try to deal as equal partners, meaning that they would pump money into NASA's budget and then they'd get to stake their claims. But the offer's never made, and there's a very good reason for that. There's an alternative, though. You can support *me*, and this offer is exclusively reserved for private investors. I'm not selling know-how, but I'm inviting participation. Whoever joins in can earn a great deal of money but can't give away any formulas or blue-prints. That's why my partners in Washington are prepared to put up with this little dinner party of ours. They know that none of your countries are going to be building a space elevator in the foreseeable future, let alone developing the infrastructure to extract helium-3. There's no technological basis, there's no budget, in short, there's nothing at all. Evidently, people such as yourselves would only ever lose money by investing in your own national space programmes at home. Which is why Washington is ready to believe that we're just talking about shares and investment here. It's a different matter with China though. Beijing has *built* the infrastructure! They're *mining* the helium-3! They've laid their groundwork, but they are working with old-fashioned technology, which limits them. That's their dilemma. They've already come too far to hitch themselves to another partner, but they simply don't have the blasted elevator! Believe me, under the circumstances there's not one Chinese politician or investor who would put even a single yuan into my hands, unless of course—'

'They could buy you,' Evelyn Chambers cut in. She was following several conversations at once. 'Which is why Zheng Pang-Wang drinks tea with you.'

'If there were a Chinese dinner guest at the table tonight, he certainly wouldn't be here intending to invest. Washington would conclude that I was taking offers for a transfer of know-how.'

'Don't they already think that, given that you meet with Zheng?' asked Nair.

'People meet all the time in this industry. At congresses, symposia. So what? Zheng's an entertaining old rogue, I like him.'

'But your friends are getting nervous anyway, aren't they?'

'They're always nervous.'

'They're right to be. Anybody who gets up here will start digging.' Ögi wiped his bristling moustache and threw the napkin down by his plate. 'Why don't you do it though, Julian?'

'What? Switch sides?'

'No, no. Nobody's talking about switching sides. I mean, why don't you just sell the space elevator technology to any country that wants to buy, and then you'd be rolling in gold? There'd be healthy competition up here on the Moon, and that would be a real boost to your reactor business. You could secure shares in the extraction side of things worldwide, you could negotiate exclusive contracts for the electricity supply, just as our absent friend Tautou controls fresh water. They sign him over whole aquifers in exchange for treatment plants and supply chain.'

'Meaning that you would not switch from one dependent position to another,' said Rogachev, taking up the idea, 'but everybody would depend on *you*.' He raised his glass to Julian, slightly mocking. 'A true philanthropist.'

'And how is that supposed to work?' Rebecca Hsu broke in.

'Why not?' asked Ögi.

'You want to let China, Japan, Russia, India, Germany, France and who knows else all have access to the elevator technology?'

'Pay for access,' Rogachev corrected her.

'It's a bad plan, Oleg. It wouldn't take long for all of them to be knocking heads up here.'

'It's a big moon.'

'No, it's a small moon. So small that my neighbours in Red China and your American friend, Julian, have nothing better to do with their time than make for the same place to mine in, am I right? It only needed *two* nations,' she said, holding up index finger and middle finger, 'to start a squabble which is euphemistically described as the Moon crisis. The world was on the brink of armed superpower confrontation, and that wasn't much fun.'

'Why did the two of them go to the same place?' Miranda asked ingenuously. 'Accidentally?'

'No.' Julian shook his head. 'Because measurements suggest that the border region between the Oceanus Procellarum and the Mare Imbrium has unusually high concentrations of helium-3, the type you'd usually find only on the dark side of the Moon. There's a bay, the Sinus Iridum, next door and east of the Montes Jura, which seems to be similarly rich in deposits. So obviously everybody claims the right to mine there.'

Rebecca furrowed her brow. 'And how's that going to be any different with more nations?'

'It should be. If we can divide the Moon up before the gold rush starts. But you're right of course, Rebecca. You're all right. I have to admit that I applaud the idea that space travel should be the concern of the whole human race.'

'Perfectly understandable.' Nair smiled. 'You will only profit from the good cause.'

'And us too, of course,' Ögi said emphatically.

'Yes, it's a noble ideal.' Rogachev put down his cutlery. 'There's only one problem, Julian.'

'Which is?'

'How to survive such a shift of opinion.'

Hanna

Small chocolate cakes, served lukewarm, released a gush of heavy, dark sauce when cut open, flooding out into the colourful fruit purees surrounding them. At about ten o'clock a leaden tiredness descended over the table. Julian announced that the next morning was free time, after which everybody could enjoy the hotel facilities to their heart's content or take a look around the lunar surface nearby. There would be no longer excursions until the day after. Dana Lawrence enquired as to whether everything was to their satisfaction. They all had words of praise, Hanna included.

'And I still don't think that Cobain would mean anything to the kids today if we hadn't made that film,' O'Keefe insisted in the lift. 'Just look where grunge has ended up. On the "lousy music" shelves. Nobody's interested in guys like him any more. The kids prefer to listen to the artificial stuff, The Week That Was, Ipanema Party, Overload—'

'You used to play grunge with your own band though,' said Hanna.

'Yes, and I gave up. My God, I think I was ten years old when Cobain died. I wonder what the hell he meant to me.'

'Don't give me that! You played the guy.'

'I could play Napoleon as well, you know, doesn't mean I'm going to try to rule all Europe. It's always been like that, people think that whoever their heroes are at the time, they must be important. *Important!* There are always *important* albums in pop music, then twenty years later not a living soul has heard of them.'

'Great music stays alive.'

'Bullshit. Who knows Prince these days? Who knows Axl Rose? Keith Richards, the only thing we know about him is that he was a mediocre guitar player for a beer-hall band whose songs all sounded the same. Believe you me, the gods of pop are overrated. All stars are overrated. No two ways. We don't go down in history, we just go down to the grave. Unless of course you commit suicide or get shot.'

'And why does everyone these days draw on the works of the seventies and eighties? If what you say is true, then—'

'Okay, it just happens to be in fashion.'

'Has been for a while.'

'And what does that prove? In ten years' time there'll be another nine days' wonder. Nucleosis, for instance, that kind of thing keeps coming around again, two women and a computer, and the computer composes about half their stuff.'

'There's always been computers.'

'Not always as the composer though. I'm telling you, day after tomorrow, all the stars will be machines.'

'Codswallop. They used to say that twenty-five years ago. What came back? Singer-songwriting. Handmade music will never die.'

'Could be. Could be we're just too old. Good night.'

'G'night, Finn.'

Hanna crossed the bridge to his suite and went in. He'd dutifully followed all the conversations as the evening went on, without getting caught up in knotty discussions. For a while he'd tried to share Eva Borelius' passion for horses, and then had steered her towards music, only to find himself bogged down in German Romanticism, about which he knew less than nothing. O'Keefe saved him with a few remarks about the comatose condition of Britpop at the end of the Nineties, about Mandoprog and psychobilly, just the thing to talk about when your thoughts were elsewhere, and Hanna's thoughts really were. Everyone would go off to sleep soon, that much was clear. Back on board the spaceship they had been warned that there'd be a price to pay for the days in zero gravity, the exertions of landing, their bodies adjusting and the flood of new experiences. The bedroom was clad with a mooncrete slab at bed height, so that in an hour at latest, nobody would be looking outside at all, and the staff lived below ground anyway.

Time to wait.

He lay down on the comically thin mattress that was nevertheless enough to support him comfortably here, weighing only sixteen kilos as he did; he put his hands behind his head and shut his eyes for a moment. If he stayed lying here, he'd fall asleep, besides which he still had plenty to do before he set out. Whistling gently, he went back into the living room and stroked his guitar-case. He strummed a brief flamenco, then turned his instrument over on his knees, felt around the edges, pressed here and there, removed the clasp where the strap clipped on and lifted up the whole back.

There was a thin sheet of material fixed to it, exactly the shape of the guitar body, covered with a tracery of fine lines. Orley's security team hadn't examined his luggage, as they would have done with regular tourists, but had just asked a few polite questions. Nobody had even dreamed of doubting that his guitar was just a guitar. Julian's guests were above all suspicion, but nevertheless the organisation had not wanted to take any risks; however, an X-ray would merely have revealed that the instrument had a thicker back than usual. Only an expert would have recognised even this, and certainly wouldn't have known that it was because it was made of two boards lying on top of one another, and that the inner board was made of a special and extremely resistant material.

With both thumbs, he began to press pieces from the sheet. They popped out with a gentle click and fell to the floor, where they lay scattered like the parts of some kind of intelligence test. Next he took the neck of the guitar off the main body and slid out a pipe, forty centimetres long, and snapped this into two equal parts. Several narrower sections of pipe fell out and rolled over the carpet. Hanna swept them together into a heap, opened his suitcase and emptied the contents of his washbag in front of him. He put the shower gel, the shampoo and the kneadable earplugs all within reach, pulled the top off one of his two tubes of moisturiser, squeezed a clear stream of what was inside onto one of the components and then pressed another against it. Straight away the moisturising cream and the plastic panel pieces reacted chemically with one another. Hanna knew that at this stage he couldn't afford the slightest mistake, that there was no way of adjusting what he built. He worked with clarity and concentration, without haste, then unscrewed one of the golf balls, took out tiny electronic components, assembled more parts and slotted them into place. In a few minutes he was holding something flat in his hands, a device with a pipe sticking out from the front like the muzzle of a pistol, which indeed it was. It looked curiously archaic. It had a grip, but instead of a trigger, there was simply a switch. Hanna took the remaining pieces and built an identical device, examined both weapons minutely and then went on to the next stage of his work.

Here he took apart various bits of kit from his washbag and then put them back together in a different order until he had made twenty projectiles, each with chambers that had to be filled separately. Working with the utmost care, he put tiny quantities of the shower gel into the left chambers, and shampoo into the right, and then sealed the capsules. He took the short shells from the neck of the guitar and put into each one a piece of earplug and a small gelatine capsule from a pack of indigestion tablets. Last of all, he put a payload into the tip of each shell, loading five into the handle of the first weapon he had built and then five into the second. Then he put the base of the guitar back onto the body, fastening the neck in place with an expert twist. He collected the last scraps left over from the plastic sheet and shoved them under everything else in his suitcase. He packed the tubes and bottles back into the washbag and then paused as he picked up the aftershave.

Ah yes.

He looked at the bottle thoughtfully. Then he lifted the cap, held it up in front of his throat and pressed the nozzle briefly, firmly.

The aftershave was aftershave.

Nobody crossed his path as he left the suite.

He was wearing spacesuit, harness and survival pack, his helmet clamped under his arm. One of the loaded guns was nestled against his thigh, hidden in a pocket of the same material as the spacesuit so that nobody would notice it. He was also carrying five loose rounds of ammunition. Granted, he hardly expected to need to use the pistol tonight. If everything went as planned, he would never be forced to use it at all, but experience had taught him that errors could creep into the tidiest plan with the persistence of cockroaches. Some time or other the gun could turn out to be very useful indeed. From now on, it would be with him at all times.

With nobody around, Gaia's vast body breathed the atmosphere of a monument that had outlived its builders. Far below lay the deserted lobby. He waited for the doors of E2 to slide apart, entered the cabin and pressed 01. The lift zoomed down to the underground level. He got out in the basement and followed the signs to the wide corridor they had come along just a few hours before, empty here as well, bathed in cold white light and filled with a monotonous hum. Hanna stepped onto one of the conveyor bands. It started up, passing the airlocks that led up to the lunar surface, then the vast hallway that led to the garage – as the hotel's underground landing field was called – then a branch corridor to a narrow tunnel, two kilometres long, leading dead straight to the small helium-3 reactor that supplied Gaia's energy during the lunar night. At the end of the corridor he stepped off the conveyor and looked through a window into the station hall. The Lunar Express was sitting on its tracks, linked to the corridor via gangways. He went inside the train and walked down between the empty seats to the driver's chair. The on-board computer was activated, the display all lit up. Hanna entered a code and waited for authorisation. Then he turned round, took a seat in the first row and stretched out his legs.

He would have been able to do none of this if he had been just a regular guest. But Ebola had got everything ready for him. Ebola made sure that there was nothing Carl Hanna couldn't do here on the Moon, no locked doors, no access forbidden.

Slowly, the Lunar Express drew out.

In his forty-four years of life so far Hanna had grown well used to keeping things clear-cut. In India he had taken part in a whole series of covert operations that would hardly have marked him as a friend of the country if he had been exposed. At the same time he had a circle of local friends and lived with Indian women. He worked against his hosts' interests, undermining the federal democracy's economic and military autonomy, but unlike many of his colleagues he didn't spend his time in cheap bars, seedy joints or expensive clubs that held an alcohol licence. He didn't tip toddy or whisky down his gullet or make racist remarks about the locals when he thought nobody was listening; instead he took care to integrate himself, he rented a neat little flat in the heart of New Delhi and developed a passion for curries and the spice market. He wasn't by nature a man who made friends quickly, but over the years the country's culture and people grew on him, and for a while he even flirted with the idea of settling down on the banks of the Yamuna. His job required a talent to deceive and a steady stream of lies, but if he wasn't actually at work, he tried to live an absolutely normal life out there, following the country's motto *Satyam-eva Jayate*, truth alone shall prevail. He felt no contradiction in such a Janus-faced existence, rather it helped him, Hanna the citizen, break all connections with Hanna the consummate liar, so that they never got in one another's way.

And now too he was enjoying the ride even with the task ahead of him; he enjoyed the unending vistas of the Mare Imbrium, the play of shadows over Plato, the rugged threat of the polar mountains drawing closer, the train's rapid climb. Once more the darkness of the crater's shadow engulfed him as the train raced along the chasm between Peary and Hermite, towards the American moon base, at 700 kilometres an hour.

Then, without warning, it slowed.

And stopped.

The Lunar Express clung to a lonely mountainside amidst the no man's land of the polar craters, less than fifty kilometres from the base. Hanna stood up and went to the middle of the train, where lockers lined the aisle. He rolled up the door of one of these and glanced briefly at the box of kit stored behind it, then studied the assembly plan on the back wall. He heaved down an oval platform with folding telescopic legs and eight little spherical tanks. It had short arms with nozzles that could turn in all directions, and two loaded battery packs. A thick column rising from the platform ended in a crossbar with hand-grips, between which a display gleamed. It was simplicity itself to assemble the thing: after all the grasshopper had been designed for emergencies, when the tour guide might be incapacitated and the guests had to cope for themselves. When it was fully built it stood on coiled legs and had enough room for two astronauts, the one in front steering. Hanna walked it over to the airlock, went back to the locker, took out a toolbox and a device with a readout screen, storing both under a hatch on the grasshopper's floor. Then he put on his helmet and let the suit carry out the usual diagnostics before he started evacuation. A few seconds later the outer bulkhead opened. He climbed onto the hopper, took out his computer, clipped it on at the side of the control panel and opened the outer hatch.

The device with the readout began to sweep and search.

Calmly, he punched coordinates into the grasshopper. The LPCS would help him find the package. He was relieved to see that it was still communicating, for otherwise there would have been no chance of finding it in this wasteland of rifts and chasms. The electronic systems were all working, so the problem must be mechanical. A burst of propulsion, and the grasshopper lifted and accelerated. If he wasn't to lose height he constantly had to create lift, while the nozzles twisted and turned to steer him. A flyer like the grasshopper was by its nature limited to a certain radius, but it was an advantage here that there was no air to provide lift for winged flyers – it meant that there was also no atmospheric pressure to brake the hopper once it got started. It had a top speed of eighty kilometres an hour, and the little round tanks could carry it an astonishing distance.

The signal was reaching him from just six kilometres away. Here in the shadow of the crater wall he was as good as blind, and totally dependent on the weak cones of light from his headlamps, racing ahead as though trying to lose him. Only the hopper's radar system kept him from colliding with cliff edges or overhangs. A good distance away, the sunny expanses of the lowland plain met the sharp black line of the mountain shadow, and high above him blinding sunlight capped the peaks of the crater ridge. The tracks of the Lunar Express had a way back swung off between the cliffs to the next valley and the gentle plain that led up to the heights of Peary. The package should long since have been under way there of its own accord, but its signal called to Hanna from the other direction entirely, deep in the crater base.

He choked back his lift. The grasshopper lost height, its fingers of light showing deeply rutted rock. Huge sharp-edged blocks of stone reared up around him, unnerving indications that an avalanche had thundered down into the valley here not long ago – no, not thundered, had tumbled down in utter silence – then the landscape levelled off and the receiver told him that he had reached his destination. Just a few more metres.

Hanna activated the braking jets and peered about with his headlamps for a place to land. Obviously he hadn't reached the foot of the crater wall here. The surface below was still too rubble-strewn and fissured to set the grasshopper down safely. By the time he had finally found a halfway level stretch, he was forced to hike back, leaping and sliding, a kilometre and a half, constantly at risk of losing his balance and slicing open his spacesuit on the razor-sharp blocks of stone all around. The beam from his helmet lamp wandered aimlessly over heaps of colourless rubble. Several times he had to fight for balance, raising clouds of the fine powdery moon dust, charged with static that made it cling stubbornly to his legs. Gravel leapt out of his path, uncannily alive, and then the ground below him simply stopped and the light was drowned in featureless blackness. He halted where he was, switched off the helmet lamp, opened his eyes wide and waited.

The effect was overwhelming.

A billion points of light in the Milky Way above him. No light pollution from any artificial source. Only the grasshopper far behind, a glowing dot marking its position. Hanna was as alone on the Moon as a human being could ever be. Nothing that he had ever experienced came even close, and for a while he even forgot his mission. That membrane that divides a human being from the experiential universe around him melted away. He became bodiless, at one with the non-dual world. All things were Hanna, all things were at rest within him, and he was within all things. He remembered a sadhu, a monk, telling him years ago that if he wished, he could drink the Indian Ocean dry at one gulp, a claim that Hanna had found cryptic at the time. And now he was standing here – was he standing? – drinking in the whole universe.

He waited.

After a while the hoped-for change set in, and the darkness proved less impenetrable than he had feared. There were photons travelling within it, reflected from the sunlit crater wall opposite that lunged upward from the plain. His surroundings took shape like a photograph in a bath of developing fluid, more a matter of intuition than perception, but it was enough to reveal that what he had thought to be a slope at his feet was only a sinkhole, which he could get round with just a few steps. He switched the headlamp back on. The spell was banished. He had come back to his senses and set out, keeping an eye on the computer display screen, so deep in concentration that he only saw the object when he was practically on top of it.

A heavy rod, rearing upwards!

Hanna tottered, dropping his toolkit and receiver. What was that? The beacon was at least 300 metres out! The thing had almost shattered his visor. Cursing, he began to work his way around it. A little later he knew that it was no fault of the beacon's. This heap of scrap was irrelevant. It was a four-legged transporter crate, its tanks burnt out, lying on its side and partially hidden by rubble. His mission had been to fetch the contents, what the organisation called the package, the part of the delivery that was actually sending the signal, and bring it to the pole.

But the package wasn't here.

It had to be further down.

When he finally found it, jammed in between boulders, it was a sorry sight. Parts of the side panel had opened up and legs and nozzles sprouted from within, some of them twisted or snapped. Fuel tanks clung to the underbelly like fat insect eggs. Obviously the package had begun to unfold and come to life as it had been designed to do, in order to make its way to deployment, when something unforeseen had happened.

And suddenly Hanna knew what that had been.

His eyes drifted over to the brightly lit peaks. He had no doubt that right from the start, the landing unit had set down too close to the crater's edge. Not a problem in itself. The designers had built in extra tolerances, including for the event that the carrier and its package crashed in the crater. The mechanical parts were supposed to be protected for as long as it took for the sensors to report that it was in a stable position, or give any other indication that the landing had been successful. After which the package was supposed to separate from the undercarriage, unfold its legs once it was at rest, and scuttle away. Obviously the sensors had made their report, but at the very moment the limbs were unfolding, parts of the uphill slope had slipped, carrying the robot along with it. The onrushing rocks had shattered its extremities, and the package had lost all mobility.

Moonquake?

Possibly. The Moon was nothing like the calm and placid place that had once been thought. Laymen might not believe it, but there were frequent tremors. Enormous variations in temperature built up tensions which discharged themselves in massive quakes, and the gravitational pull of sun and Earth could tug at deep-lying strata of the moonrock, which was why Gaia had been built to withstand quakes topping 5 on the Richter scale. Hanna inspected the damaged axles and nozzles, wanting to leave no possibility untried. After twenty sweaty minutes of wrestling with the wreck, he had to concede that there was no fixing it. The loss of some of the spider legs might have been overcome, but the unwelcome fact was that one of the jet nozzles was partially torn away, and another was nowhere to be seen.

The best-laid plans of mice and men, thought Hanna. First there had been Thorn's accident, and then this. All this should have been his job. He should have taken care of the package a year ago, but Thorn's corpse was drifting out there somewhere in the universe.

Expecting further disappointments, he unbolted the hatch at the back, opened the container and shone his torch inside, but there at least it all seemed undamaged. Hanna breathed freely again. If the cargo had been lost, that would really have been the end; everything else was mere inconvenience. He took the detector in his hand and checked the seams. Intact. No harm done.

Carefully, he fetched it out.

This simply meant that he would have to take the package across for deployment himself. No problem there. There was enough room on the grasshopper platform. For a moment he considered informing mission control, but time was running short. There was no alternative anyway. He had to act. It was best to be back in the hotel before the others started rubbing the sleep from their eyes.

Best never to have been away.

27 May 2025

GAMES

Xintiandi, Shanghai, China

Jericho woke up on his couch next to two bottles and a glass streaked with drying red wine, and two emptied packets of mango chips. For a moment he didn't know where he was. He sat up, a process which needed two attempts and which raised the question of how the hell this sodden, heavy sponge had got inside his skull. Then he remembered his good fortune. At the same time he felt some indefinable sort of loss. There was something missing that had grown as familiar as his own heartbeat over the years.

Noise.

Never again would he wake up to the hammering sound of high-rises being built around him. Never again would six lanes of early morning traffic rattle his eardrums before the sun had even risen. From now on he was living in Xintiandi, where admittedly there were hordes of tourists, but you could cope perfectly well with them. Generally speaking they never arrived before ten o'clock in the morning and then in the late afternoon they retreated, bathed in sweat and with aching feet, back to their hotels, to gather the strength to go out again in the evening to the restaurants. In the evenings it was mostly Shanghaians in the district's bistros, cafés and clubs, the boutiques and cinemas. In Jericho's new home, you hardly felt either invasion. That was the advantage of a shikumen house. Outside someone could be driving herds of dinosaurs through the streets, but inside all was peace and quiet.

He rubbed his eyes. You couldn't quite say that he lived here, not yet. There were still packed crates scattered through every room in the loft. At least he'd got as far as installing the new media terminal. Tu's customer service team had delivered it the evening before, two cheery and helpful representatives hauling the thing upstairs for him and skilfully fitting it in with the decor so that it was hardly noticeable. Right after that, Jericho had had to set out for his surprise visit to Yoyo. It was only after he got back that he had got around to playing with his new toy, and celebrating his first night in Xintiandi while he did so. He'd gone to town on it, so the two empty bottles told him, though his only company had been Animal Ma Liping and the suffering children in their cages. He wondered whether Joanna would have liked this place, then decided not to even contemplate that.

It was good not to need anyone else.

He went to shower, and switched on his various appliances. Most of all he would have liked to unpack the rest of the crates, but since yesterday Tu Tian and Chen Hongbing had come to join all the other ghosts crowding the back of his mind, and they urged him on in his search for Yoyo. Dutifully, he decided to prioritise the case. He shaved, picked out a pair of light trousers and a shirt jacket, uploaded one of Tu's programs to the datastick in his new hologoggles, and left the house.

He would spend the next hour with Yoyo.

Handily, one of the guided tours went through the French Concession, a colonial relic of the nineteenth century. It was right next door to Xintiandi, separated only by three levels of city highway. Once he had taken the underpass and come back up into the sunlight, he walked along the busy Fuxing Zhong Lu and activated the program's speech recognition protocol.

'Start,' he said.

At first nothing happened. The world on the other side of the lens looked as it always had. People scurried or strolled about. Business types communed with their mobile phones, their eyes fixed on the displays and wireless earbuds firmly in place as they crossed the street, somehow managing not to get run over. Elegantly dressed women came in and out of the chic little boutiques around, chatting to one another or on their phones, while less well-dressed women thronged the Japanese or American department stores. Groups of tourists photographed what they imagined were authentic examples of colonial architecture. Cars, mini-vans and limousines filled the roads, and dozens of the identical CODs, cars on demand, squeezed in among them on the way up to the speedway. Electric scooters and hybrid cruisers wormed their way into gaps in the traffic that were filled before they had ever really opened. Bicycles with rattling mudguards raced futuristic antigrav skates. City buses and vans crept along the packed roads, a formation of police sky-mobiles overflew the Fuxing Zhong Lu, a little further on an ambulance took off, turned in the air and flew west. Gleaming private cars and sky-bikes shot across the sky, following aerial guidance beacons. Everything rumbled, squealed or honked, music blared, advertising slogans and news headlines splashed across the omnipresent video screens.

A quiet day in a calm neighbourhood.

The double T of Tu Technologies appeared in front of Jericho's eyes. The system's projection technology fooled his retina into thinking that the logo was floating, three-dimensional, above the ground several metres away. Then it vanished, and the computer in the arm of the specs projected Yoyo onto the Fuxing Zhong Lu.

It was astonishing.

Jericho had seen plenty of holographic projections in his time. The specs were one continuous curve of glass fibres, and they worked like a 3D cinema that you could carry around on your nose as you walked. The whole system had nothing in common with the early, bulky virtual reality viewscreens. Rather the computer added objects and people into the actual surroundings just by producing them on the glass lens. You could see someone who was not physically present. These could be real people or synthetic avatars, and the program could bring them closer or further away. In electronic environments, they could hardly be told apart from people who were actually there. The problems began out in the real world, when the computer had to combine the avatars' movements and reactions with real-time events. They looked transparent against com-plex backdrops or if there was movement going on behind them. The illusion was broken completely if real people walked through the space where the avatar appeared to be. They simply walked straight through them. Your cheery chatty virtual pal paid no attention if, while they were talking, a truck ran them over. If you moved your head quickly, they would trail behind like ghosts. The system had to continuously scan and upload the real surroundings and synchronise them with the program to bring appearance and reality back together, and so far the attempt had seemed doomed to failure.

Yoyo, though, appeared one simulated metre away from Jericho, on the pavement, showing none of the telltale phantom characteristics of other avatars. She was wearing a close-fitting raspberry catsuit and discreet appliqués, her hair was plaited into a double ponytail and she was lightly made up.

'Good morning, Mr Jericho!' she said, smiling.

Pedestrians hurried past behind her. Yoyo blocked them from view. Nothing about her looked transparent, there were no fuzzy edges. She walked in front of him and looked straight into his eyes.

'Shall we have a look at the French Concession?' The arm of the specs played the sound of her voice into Jericho's ear via the temporal bone.

'A little louder,' he said.

'Of course,' came Yoyo's voice, a touch stronger now. 'Shall we have a look at the French Concession? It's perfect weather, not a cloud in the sky.'

Was that so? Jericho looked upwards. It was so.

'That would be nice.'

'My pleasure. My name's Yoyo.' She hesitated and gave him a look that mixed coquetry with shyness. 'May I call you Owen?'

'No problem.'

Fascinating. The program had automatically linked up with his ID code. It had recognised him, realised what time of day to use in saying hello, and taken a look at the weather at the same time. Already the team at Tu Technologies had topped everything that Jericho had seen in the field.

'Come along,' Yoyo said cheerfully.

Almost with relief, he realised that she no longer seemed so exquisitely beautiful as she had the day before. In flesh and blood, laughing, talking, gesticulating, the ethereal quality that he had thought he saw on Chen's wobbly video was no longer there. What was left was still quite enough to make a pacemaker skip a beat.

Wait a moment. Flesh and blood?

Bits and bytes!

It really was astounding. The computer even calculated the correct angle for the shadow to fall as Yoyo walked in front of him. He no longer wondered how the program had done it but simply concentrated on her walk, her gestures, her movements. His guide turned left, took a place at his side and looked from him to the street and then back again.

'The Si Nan Lu brings together several distinct architectural styles, including those of France, Germany and Spain. In 2018 the last of the original buildings were torn down, with a few exceptions, and then rebuilt. Using the original plans of course. Now everything is much more beautiful and even more authentic than it used to be.' Yoyo smiled a Mona Lisa smile. 'The first residents here included important function-aries of both the Nationalist and the Communist governments. Nobody could resist the quarter's generous charms, everybody wanted to come to the Si Nan Lu. Even Zhou Enlai held court here for a while. This lovely three-storey garden villa on the left was his home. The style is generally called French, although in fact there are elements of Art Deco here as well, with Chinese influences. The villa is one of the very few buildings that has so far escaped the Party's mania for renovation.'

Jericho was taken aback. How had that got past the censors?

Then he recalled that Tu had talked about a prototype. Meaning that the text would be modified later. He wondered whose idea this deviation had been. Had Tu thought up the joke, or had Yoyo suggested it to him?

'Can we visit the villa?' he asked.

'We can go and have a look at it from inside,' Yoyo confirmed. 'The interior is largely untouched. Zhou lived a Spartan sort of life; he felt that it was his duty to the proletariat. Maybe too he simply didn't want the Great Helmsman dropping in to rearrange the furniture.'

Jericho couldn't help grinning.

'I'd rather keep walking.'

'Right you are, Owen. Let the past alone.'

Over the next few minutes Yoyo talked about their surround-ings without barbed remarks. A couple of turnings off the street, they found themselves in a lively little alleyway full of cafés, galleries, ateliers and picturesque little shops selling artworks. Jericho came here often. He loved the quarter, with its wooden benches and palm trees, the neatly renovated shikumen houses with flowerpots in the window.

'Until twenty years ago, Taikang Lu Art Street was an insider tip in the art scene,' Yoyo explained. 'In 1998 a former sweet factory was converted into the International Artists Factory. Advertising agencies and designers moved in, well-known artists opened their studios here, including big names like Huang Yongzheng, Er Dongqiang and Chen Yifei. Despite all that, for a long time the area was still overshadowed by Moganshan Lu north of the Suzhou Canal, where the official art scene met the underground and the avant-garde and they all dominated Shanghai's art market together. It was only when the Taikang Art Foundation was built in 2015 that the centre of balance shifted. It's the complex up there ahead. Locals call it the Jellyfish.'

Yoyo pointed to an enormous glass dome that looked astonishingly delicate and airy despite its massive size. It had been designed to mimic biological structures, along the lines of the larger Medusozoa.

'What was here before?' asked Jericho.

'Originally Taikang Lu Art Street ended in a really lovely fish market. You could buy frogs and snakes here as well.'

'And where did that go?'

'The fish market was torn down. The Party has a giant airbrush which it can use to remove history. Now this is the Taikang Art Foundation.'

'Can we visit the studios?'

'We can visit the studios. Would you like to?'

Yoyo went ahead of him. Taikang Lu Art Street slowly filled up with tourists. It became crowded, but Yoyo looked real and solid as she wormed her way between passers-by. Truth be told, Jericho thought, she actually looked more real than some of the others.

He was brought up short.

Were his eyes playing tricks on him? He concentrated entirely on Yoyo. A group of Japanese tourists approached, shoulder to shoulder, on a collision course, blind to whoever might be coming the other way. He had noticed that the computer had Yoyo step aside whenever there was the chance, but the group blocked the street on both sides. All she could do was drop back before them, or fight her way past. The Japanese, like the Chinese, didn't shrink from barging their way through if they needed to, so Jericho reckoned that if Yoyo were really here she would be using her elbows. Avatars had no elbows, though. Not the sort that others would feel in their ribs.

He watched curiously to see what would happen. A moment later she had passed the group, without it looking as though she had simply walked through. Rather, one of the Japanese seemed to have melted away for a moment to let her by.

Irked, Jericho took off the specs.

Nothing had changed except that Yoyo had vanished. He put them back on again, fought his way through the groups and saw Yoyo a little further on. Standing on the street. She looked across at him and waved.

'What are you waiting for? Come on!'

Jericho took a few steps. Yoyo waited until he drew level with her, and then she set off. Incredible! How did the trick work? He would hardly be able to understand it without an explanation, so he concentrated on trying to catch the program out. From a purely factual perspective, the programmers had done good work. The tour was well researched and thoroughly plotted. So far, everything Yoyo had told him was right.

'Yoyo—' he began.

'Yes?' Her glance showed amiable interest.

'How long have you had this job?'

'This route is completely new,' she answered evasively.

'Not long, then?'

'No.'

'And what are you doing tonight?'

She stopped and gave him a smile, sweet as sugar.

'Is that an offer?'

'I'd like to invite you for a meal.'

'Pardon me for refusing, but I only have a virtual stomach.'

'Would you like to go dancing with me?'

'I would very much like to.'

'Great. Where shall we go?'

'I said I would like to.' She winked. 'Sadly, I can't.'

'May I ask you something else?'

'Go right ahead.'

'Will you go to bed with me?'

She hesitated for a moment. The smile gave way to a look of mocking good humour.

'You'd be disappointed.'

'Why?'

'Because I don't actually exist.'

'Get undressed, Yoyo.'

'I could put something else on.' The smile came back. 'Would you like me to put something else on?'

'I want to sleep with you.'

'You'd be disappointed.'

'I want to have sex with you.'

'You're on your own there, Owen.'

Aha.

This was definitely not the official version.

'Can we visit the studios?' he asked, repeating the earlier question.

'We can visit the studios. Would you like to?'

'Who programmed you, Yoyo?'

'I was programmed by Tu Technologies.'

'Are you a person?'

'I'm a person.'

'I hate you, Yoyo.'

'I'm very sorry to hear that.' She paused. 'Would you like to continue the tour?'

'You're a silly, ugly goose.'

'I do my best to please. Your tone is not appropriate.'

'Pardon me.'

'No need. It was probably my mistake.'

'Slapper.'

'Asshole.'

World Financial Center

'Yoyo is pretty much in demand, isn't she?'

Grand Cherokee gave Xin a knowing wink as his fingers swept across the smooth surface of the steering deck. One by one, he let the computer check the Silver Dragon's systems. It promised to be a perfect day for a roller-coaster ride, sunny and clear, so that despite the omnipresent blanket of smog passengers would still be able to see such distant buildings as the Shanghai Regent or the Portman Ritz Carlton. The skyscraper façades reflected the early morning light. Tiny suns came and went on the bodywork of the skymobiles that swept in graceful curves above the Huangpu. Away from the shore, Shanghai blurred together into the vague suggestion of a city, but on the other side of the river the colonial relics of the Bund stood out all the more clearly in a brightly coloured row of palaces.

Grand Cherokee had met Xin in the Sky Lobby and chattered incessantly in the lift on the way up about what a signal honour it was to be allowed to enter the dragon's lair right at this moment. For all that, he told Xin, the track itself wasn't especially interesting, not considered as a roller-coaster as such: hardly any upside-down stretches, just one classic vertical loop with a heartline roll either side, well, that meant that there were three zero-g points all in all, but basically it was nothing special. Rather, he went on as they walked through the empty glass corridor, the thrill of the thing lay in its speed, combined with the fact of zooming about half a kilometre above the ground. As he opened up the control room and they went in, he kept up his monologue: this masterpiece of adrenalin was one of a kind, worldwide, controlling the ride needed good nerves, just like riding in it, you needed to be a strong personality to tame the dragon.

'Interesting,' Xin had said. 'Show me then. What exactly do you have to do?'

This was when Grand Cherokee stopped for a moment. He was accustomed to seeing reality through the distorting mirror of his own inflated ego, but this last remark got through even to him, and he was suddenly rattled. In fact controlling the ride was perfectly straightforward. Any idiot capable of touching three control boxes on a screen could do it. He stammered out something about irony and hyperbole, and showed Xin the controls, telling him that all he really needed to do was clear the safety checks, which meant knowing the security codes.

'There are three of them,' he told Xin. 'I just put them in one after another – like that – then number two – three – done. System's ready. So now I activate this field on the top right, which unlocks the carriages, this box below starts the catapult, and the program does the rest. This one underneath is the emergency stop. We've never needed it though.'

'And what's this for?' Xin pointed to a menu along the upper edge of the screen.

'That's the check assistant. Before I set the ride in motion, I let the computer run through a set of parameters. Mechanical systems, programs.'

'Simple really.'

'Simple, but clever.'

'Almost a pity that we won't have the chance for a ride, but my time is short. I'd like to—'

'In principle, you could climb in,' said Grand Cherokee and began the check. 'I'll give you such a ride that you won't know which way to stand up when you climb out. I'd have to register it as an unscheduled ride though.'

'Don't bother. Let's talk about Yoyo.'

This was the point when Grand Cherokee grinned at his visitor and made the crack about Yoyo being pretty much in demand. He wanted to add something, but stopped. Something had changed in the other man's face. There was curiosity there now, not just about where Yoyo might be but about Grand Cherokee himself.

'Who else is interested in her?' Xin asked.

'No idea.' Grand Cherokee shrugged. Should he play his trump card already? He had wanted to use the detective to put a little pressure on Xin, but perhaps it was better to play him on the line for a while. 'That's what you said.'

'Said what?'

'Yoyo needed protection because someone was after her.'

'True.' Xin inspected the fingernails on his right hand. Grand Cherokee noticed that they were perfectly manicured, all filed down to exactly the same length, the crescents the colour of mother-of-pearl. 'And you were going to find things out, Wang. Telephone some people, and so on. Bring me to Yoyo. As I remember it, money changed hands. So what do you have for me?'

Pompous arsehole, thought Grand Cherokee. In fact he'd thought up a story the night before. It was all based on a remark that Yoyo had made about the party lifestyle getting on her nerves, that she wanted to go to Hangzhou and the West Lake for a weekend. His grandmother had always spouted clichés and proverbs, and wasn't one of them that Hangzhou was the image of Heaven here on Earth? Grand Cherokee had decided that that was where Yoyo could be found, in some romantic little hotel on the West Lake, and the hotel might be called —

Wait though, he shouldn't be too specific. There were all sorts of places to stay right around the lake shores, for every sort of price. Just to be sure, he had done an internet search and found several named after trees or flowers. He liked that. Yoyo's retreat would be a hotel with a flowery name! Something with a flower, but sadly his contact (who didn't exist anyway) couldn't quite remember what. He hadn't been able to find out more than that for the money, but it was something, wasn't it? Grand Cherokee had laughed out loud at the thought of Xin travelling 170 kilometres to the West Lake to check out every hotel with a botanical name, especially since he planned to send the detective out to the same place. Those two fools wouldn't notice, but they would constantly be crossing paths. For a bit more money, he could also mention the motorbike mob, a completely different lead, since after all the City Demons had little or nothing to do with West Lake. On the other hand, a motorbike trip out to the countryside? Why not?

Xin was lost in contemplation of his fingernails. Grand Cherokee considered. Soon enough he'd be spinning the same line to Jericho, through there he ran the risk that the detective might be less generous.

And there was still a chance.

'You know,' he said slowly and as neutrally as he could manage, 'I've been thinking about it.' He finished the check for the Silver Dragon and looked at Xin. 'And I think you could pay a bit more to find out where Yoyo is.'

Xin didn't look especially surprised. Instead he looked exhausted, as though he'd been waiting for the penny to drop.

'How much?' he asked.

'Ten times.'

Shocked at his own daring, Grand Cherokee felt his heart beat faster. If Xin swallowed *that*—

Wait a moment. It could get even better!

'Ten times,' he repeated, 'and another meeting.'

Xin's expression turned to stone.

'What's this about?'

What's it about? thought Grand Cherokee. Simple enough, you varnished monkey. I'll take the money and run off to Jericho, and give him a choice. Either he tops your offer and gets the exclusive story, or he turns me down, and you get it. But not until I've spoken to Jericho. And if Jericho coughs up twenty times as much, then we'll try you for thirty times.

'Yes or no?' he asked.

The corners of Xin's mouth lifted, almost imperceptibly. 'Which movie have you got this from, Wang?'

'I don't need to watch any movies. You're after Yoyo, I couldn't care less why. I find it much more interesting that the cops want something from her as well. Conclusion: you're obviously not a cop. Meaning that you can't do anything to me. You have to take what you can get, and' – he bowed, and bared his teeth – 'when you can get it.'

Xin looked around, his smile frozen. Then he glanced at the control panel.

'Do you know what I hate?' he asked.

'Me?' said Grand Cherokee, laughing.

'You're vermin, Wang, hatred is too good for you. No, I hate spots. Those greasy fingers of yours have left nasty smears all over the display.'

'So?'

'Clean them up.'

'Do what?'

'Clean up those greasy smears.'

'Listen here, you designer-suited piece of shit, what exactly do you think—'

Something odd happened then, something Grand Cherokee had never experienced before. It was quick as lightning, and when it was over, he was lying on the floor in front of the control panel, and his nose felt as though a grenade had exploded in it. Flashes of colour sparked in front of his eyes.

'Your face wouldn't do very well to keep things clean,' said Xin, then reached down and pulled Grand Cherokee to his feet like a puppet. 'Oh, you look dreadful. What happened to your nose? Shall we talk?'

Grand Cherokee staggered and put a hand on the console to steady himself. He felt his face with the other hand. His forehead appliqué fell into the palm of his hand. He looked at Xin, nonplussed.

Then he swung at him, enraged.

Xin languidly poked him in the sternum.

It was as though somebody had unhooked all systems in the lower half of Grand Cherokee's body. He fell to one knee while a gout of pain shot through his chest. His mouth opened, and he made choking sounds. Xin squatted down and supported him with his right arm before he could collapse.

'It'll pass soon,' he said. 'I know, for a while you think you'll never be able to talk again. Wrong though. Generally speaking, people actually find it easier to talk after they've had that done to them. What did you want to say?'

Grand Cherokee gasped. His lips formed a word.

'Yoyo?' Xin nodded. 'A good start. Try your best, Wang, and above all' – he took him under the arms and heaved him up – 'get to your feet.'

'Yoyo is—' panted Grand Cherokee.

'Where?'

'In Hangzhou.'

'Hangzhou?' Xin raised his eyebrows. 'Mercy me. Do you actually know something? Where in Hangzhou?'

'In – a hotel.'

'Name?'

'No idea.' Grand Cherokee sucked in greedy lungfuls of air. Xin was right. The pain passed, but he didn't feel in the least bit better for it. 'Something with flowers.'

'Don't make things so complicated,' Xin said mildly. 'Something with flowers is about as specific as somewhere in China.'

'Might have been something with trees, even,' Grand Cherokee yelped. 'My informant said flowers.'

'In Hangzhou?'

'On the West Lake.'

'Where on the West Lake? On the city side?'

'Yes, yes!'

'On the western shore then?'

'That's it.'

'Aha! Maybe near the Su dam?'

'The – I think so.' Grand Cherokee felt a glimmer of hope. 'Probably Yes, that's what he said.'

'But the city is on the eastern shore.'

'P-perhaps I didn't quite hear.' The glimmer died away.

'But near the Su dam? Or the Bai dam?

Bai dam? Su dam? It was becoming ever more complicated. Where were these dams anyway? Grand Cherokee hadn't thought about it all that much. Who the hell expected all these questions?

'I don't know,' he said feebly.

'I thought your informant—'

'I just don't know!'

Xin looked at him reproachfully. Then he jabbed his fingers into Grand Cherokee's kidney region.

The effect was indescribable. Grand Cherokee opened and closed his mouth rapidly like a fish snatched from the water, while his eyes opened wide. Xin held him in an iron grip to stop him from collapsing again. For all that the surveillance cameras could see, they were standing side by side like old friends.

'So?'

'I don't know,' Grand Cherokee whimpered, while part of him detachedly observed that pain was orange. 'Really, I don't.'

'What *do* you know, if anything?'

Grand Cherokee lifted his eyes, trembling. There was no mistaking what he could read in Xin's eyes about what would happen to him if he lied one more time.

'Nothing,' he whispered.

Xin laughed contemptuously, shook his head and let go of him.

'Do you want the money back?' Grand Cherokee mumbled, and bent double with the memory of the pain that had shaken his body.

Xin pursed his lips. He looked out at the city shimmering below.

'I keep remembering something you said,' he remarked.

Grand Cherokee gaped at him and waited. The part of him that had floated off detached, pointed out that in fifteen minutes the first visitors would be let in, that it would probably be full because the weather was so exceptionally fine.

'You said that Yoyo is pretty much in demand. I believe those were the words you used, am I right?'

Still fifteen minutes.

'You can make up for lost ground, Wang. Tell the truth this time. Who else was asking about her?'

'A detective,' muttered Grand Cherokee.

'Very interesting. When was this?'

'Last night. I showed him Yoyo's room. He asked the same questions as you.'

'And you gave the same answers. That you'd find something out, but that it would cost a little.'

Grand Cherokee nodded, downcast. If Xin went to Owen Jericho with this information, then he could kiss goodbye to that money. Hurrying to carry out the next order before it was given, he took out Jericho's card and handed it to Xin, who took it with both hands, looked at it curiously and put it away.

'Anything else?'

Of course. He could have told Xin about the motorbike gang. The one trail that might actually lead to Yoyo. But he wouldn't do this fucker any such favour.

'Fuck you,' he said instead.

'Meaning no.'

Xin looked thoughtful. He stepped out of the open door to the control room, to the area between the turnstile and the platform. He paid no further attention to Grand Cherokee, as though he no longer existed. Which would probably be the best thing right now. Just stop existing until the bastard had left this floor. Not give a peep, become about as big as a mouse, less than a fingerprint on a computer display. All this was as clear as anything ever had been, to the detached part of Grand Cherokee Wang, and he spoke a well-meaning word of warning which the other Wang, the Wang blinded by hatred, ignored. Instead he shuffled after Xin and thought about how he could recover his dignity, the dignity of the man who guarded the dragon, which right now was in a fairly shabby state. *You vicious arsehole?* Xin probably knew that he was vicious, and arsehole was too small a word. Grand Cherokee reckoned that insults probably slid straight off Xin anyway.

How could he get at the fucker?

And while the detached part of Grand Cherokee was looking for a mousehole to creep into, he heard Grand Cherokee the big-mouth say:

'Just don't think you're free and clear, you moron!'

Xin, who was just going through the turnstile, stopped.

'First thing I'll do is call Jericho,' yelled Grand Cherokee. 'Then the cops, right after that. Who's going to be more interested, huh? You make sure you get away from here, out of Shanghai if you can, out of China. Off to the Moon, perhaps they've got something for you up there, 'cos down here I'm going to put the boot into you, you can count on that!'

Xin turned around slowly.

'You silly fool,' he said. It sounded almost sympathetic.

'I'll—' Grand Cherokee gulped, and then it dawned on him that he had probably just made the biggest mistake of his life. Xin walked nonchalantly towards him. He didn't look like someone who planned to do much more talking.

Grand Cherokee scuttled backwards.

'This area is under video surveillance,' he said, trying to put a warning note in his voice; it slipped into panic halfway through.

'You're right,' said Xin, nodding. 'I should hurry.'

Grand Cherokee's stomach cramped. He jumped backwards and tried to get a grip on the situation. His foe was standing between him and the passage through to the glass corridor. There was no way past him, and right behind Grand Cherokee was the edge of the platform with the roller-coaster train resting on its rails on the other side. The area where the passengers got on and off was closed off with a transparent wall that curved round underneath, and to the right and left the tracks curved off into empty space.

The look in Xin's eyes left no room for misunderstanding.

With one leap, Grand Cherokee was in the middle car. He glanced towards the head of the dragon. Each car was nothing more than a platform with seats mounted on it, the back of each seat looking like a huge scale or a wing, which made the vehicle vaguely resemble a silver reptile. The only extra detail was up at the front: a projection, something like a long, narrow skull. There was a separate steering system up there which could be used to move the whole train a short distance, in emergencies. Not through the loops, but along the straight sections of track.

Where the track passed around the building's side pillars, just before it began to climb, there was a short bridge from the track into the building, one on each side. Inside the pillars was plant and electronics, and storage rooms. The steel bridges led right into the glass façades of the pillars, and if necessary they could be used to evacuate the train if for some reason it couldn't get to the boarding platform. The bridges led to a separate staircase and lift, not reachable from the glass corridor.

Grand Cherokee ran through all of this in his head as he crouched there, which was his second mistake; he was losing time, instead of acting right away. Xin pounced and landed between him and the dragon's head. There were only two rows of seats between them, and Grand Cherokee realised that he had thrown away his chance of reaching the steering unit. He considered jumping back onto the platform, but it was clear that Xin would be right behind him if he did. Probably he wouldn't even make it as far as the turnstile.

Xin came closer. He clambered through the rows of seating so fast that Grand Cherokee stopped thinking and fled to the end of the train. The glass barrier for the boarding platform ended a little way beyond. Here, the track swung out from the front of the building, curved around a good distance and then about twenty-five metres on, turned the corner that led behind the pillar.

'Very stupid idea,' said Xin, as he approached.

Grand Cherokee stared out at the track, then back to Xin. He had long ago realised that he had gone too far, and the guy meant to kill him. Damn Yoyo! What a dumb bitch, getting him into this kind of trouble.

Wrong, the detached part of Grand Cherokee told him, you're dumb yourself. Ever thought you could climb through thin air? And when big-mouth Wang had no reply, the calm, distant voice added: You do have one great advantage. You don't suffer from vertigo.

Does Xin?

Knowing that the enormous height did nothing to him suddenly freed Grand Cherokee's limbs of their paralysis. His mind made up, he put one foot on the track, took one step, another. Half a kilometre below him he saw the green forecourt in front of the World Financial Center, criss-crossed with footpaths. Cars moved like ants along the two levels of the Shiji Dadao, running from the river to the Pudong hinterland. The sun burned down on him through the enormous hole in the tower as he left the protection of the glassed-in boarding platform and went along the track, one metre at a time. Gusts of warm wind tugged at him. To his left, the glass façade of the tower grew further away with every step, or more exactly, he was getting further away from it. To the right he could see the roof of the Jin Mao Tower. The business high-rises of Pudong grouped themselves around and behind it, with the shimmering curve of Huangpu, and Shanghai stretching all around, unimaginably vast.

His heart beating wildly, he stopped and turned his head. Xin was standing at the end of the train, staring at him.

He wasn't following.

The arsehole didn't have the guts!

Grand Cherokee took another step and slipped between two of the spars.

His heart stopped beating. Like a cat falling, he flung out all four limbs, grabbed hold of the rail and for a hideous moment swung there above the abyss before he managed, using all his strength, to heave himself up. Panting like an engine, he tried to stand. He was halfway between the boarding platform and the curve of the corner, and the track was beginning to tilt. The wind fluttered his coat, which was turning out to be the least practical garment imaginable for a stroll at five hundred metres.

Gasping, he looked round again.

Xin had vanished.

Onward, he thought. How far to the bridge now? Twenty-five metres, thirty? At the most. Get moving! Make sure that you round that corner. Get to safety. Who cares what Xin is doing?

He took heart and walked on, arms stretched for balance, master of himself once more, when he heard the noise.

The noise.

It was something between a rattle and a hum, following a heavy metallic clunk. It drew away in the other direction. It froze the blood in Grand Cherokee's veins, although it was a noise he knew well, a noise he heard every day he spent up here at work.

Xin had woken the Dragon.

He had started the ride!

A scream of fear broke out of him, that was torn away by the warm gusts and scattered over Pudong. Whimpering, he clambered on as fast as he could. His ears told him that the train had just passed the northern pillar, then he saw it climbing the slope through the great gap. At the moment the dragon was still moving slowly, but once it got to the roof it would pick up speed, and then—

He crawled forward like a mad thing in the shadow of the southern pillar. The tilt on the tracks was becoming more pronounced, so that he had no choice but to move ahead on all fours.

Too slow. Too slow!

The fear will burst your heart, thought the detached part of Grand Cherokee. Try cursing.

It helped.

He screamed hell and damnation into the deep blue sky, his voice cracking, grabbed hold of the warm metal of the track and hopped rather than crept forward. The rails had begun to thrum. Twice he nearly lost his balance and fell off the curve, but each time he caught himself and worked his way stubbornly onward. High above him a hollow whistling sound signalled that the carriages had reached their highest point and were now on the flat stretch up above, and he still had not reached his goal. Trying to catch sight of the dragon, he saw only himself reflected in the mirrored glass on the pillar façade, somehow looking damn good, like a movie hero. All in all he should have been having the time of his life here, but there was the nagging question of the happy ending, the fact that the dragon had just passed the catapult.

The rails began to vibrate mightily. Grand Cherokee clambered onward, choking out the word 'Please!' over and over like a mantra, 'Please, please, please—' in sync with the thrumming of the rail.

'Please—' – *Raddangg* – 'Please—' – *Raddangg*—

He came round the pillar. He could see the steel bridge not ten metres in front of him, leading from the rails to the wall of the building.

The dragon swept down from the roof.

'Please—'

The train hurtled down, thunderous, deafening, into the depths, then coiled in on itself in the loop and shot upwards. The whole structure was moving, shaking. The rails seemed to dance to and fro before Grand Cherokee's eyes. He stood up, managed to leap across several spars at once and keep his balance despite the tilt.

Five metres. Four.

The dragon rushed down in the loop.

Three metres.

– shot round the corner—

Two.

– flew towards him.

In the moment that the train crossed the point where the bridge led off, Grand Cherokee did the impossible, a superhuman feat. Howling wildly, he leapt clear, an enormous standing jump. The sharp bow of the front carriage passed below him. He stretched out his arms to grab hold of one of the seats, touched something, lost his grip. His body smashed into the backs of the seats in the next row, was flung high, pirouetted and for a moment seemed to be heading into the deep blue sky, as though he had decided to reach outer space.

Then he fell.

The last thing that went through Grand Cherokee's head was that he had at least tried.

That he hadn't been so bad after all.

Xin craned his head. High above him he could see people going into the glass viewing platform. The corridor would be opened soon as well. Time to get going. He knew how things worked in high-rise surveillance control rooms, he knew that hardly anybody would have glanced at the monitors in the last quarter of an hour. Even if they had, they wouldn't have seen much. Leaving aside the two moments when Wang had suddenly dropped to the control room floor, they had been standing close beside one another most of the time. Two close friends having a chat.

But now he had set the dragon moving. Before the usual time. That would be noticed. He had to get out of here.

Xin hesitated.

Then he quickly wiped his fingerprints from the display with his sleeve, paused, and also wiped the places where Grand Cherokee had fumbled about with his greasy fingers. Otherwise those blasted smears would haunt his dreams. There were some things that tended to cling to the inside of Xin's skull like leeches. Lastly, he hurried along the corridor and left it the way they had come. In the lift he peeled the wig from his head, took off his glasses, tore the moustache from his upper lip and turned his jacket inside out. It had been made specially for him, reversible. The grey jacket became sandy beige, and he stuffed the wig, beard and glasses inside. He decided to change lifts in the Sky Lobby on the twenty-eighth floor, then went down to the basement, through the shopping mall and out into the bright sunshine. Outside he saw people running towards the south side of the building. Cries went up. Somebody shouted that there had been a suicide.

Suicide? All okay then.

As Xin walked onward, faster, under the trees in the park, he took out the detective's card.

27 May 2025

PHANTOMS

Gaia, Vallis Alpina, The Moon

Julian set great store by his inventive genius that generated so many extraordinary ideas, and in particular by the fact that he could simply choose to switch the thinking process on and off. If unsolved problems tried to join him under the covers, he chose to sleep, and was wafted away on the wings of slumber as soon as his head touched the pillow. Sleep was a cornerstone of his mental and physical health, and up until now, he had always slept excellently well on the Moon.

Just not tonight.

The discussion at dinner was going round and round in his head like the horses on a merry-go-round; more precisely, Walo Ögi's remark asking why he didn't simply announce a divorce with Washington and declare that his technologies were up for sale to all comers, offering global access. It was true that there was a difference between taking the *best* offer and taking *every* offer. There was, even, a moral distinction. Playing favourites when it came to the wellbeing of ten billion people laid him open to charges of perfidious profiteering, even if not every one of these ten billion was in a position to build a space elevator in the front garden – charges that were unpalatable to a man who outdid all others in arguing for his autonomy as a businessman, who made speeches about global responsibility and the destructive effects of rivalry.

Tonight Julian lay awake because he saw all his private thoughts and arguments confirmed once more. Especially since, aside from all moral considerations, to make his patents generally available would not only boost economic activity on the Moon, it would also mean better business for him. The Swiss investor had put his finger on it: if another three or four nations had a space elevator, and were mining helium-3, the global switch to aneutronic fusion would be complete within a few years. Orley Enterprises, or more exactly Orley Space, could help the less wealthy countries with finance to build their elevators, which would give Orley Fusion the chance to acquire exclusive concessions for their power network. The reactor business would turn a profit and Orley Energy would become the biggest power provider on the planet. He would just have to deal with the fact that Washington would be less than happy about all this.

But it was a little more complicated than that.

Zheng Pang-Wang had tried several times to woo him for Beijing, which Julian had flatly refused until one occasion when they were having lunch together at Hakkasan, the exclusive Chinese restaurant in London, and Julian realised that he would only be betraying his American partners if he jumped into bed with *one* other trading partner. If on the other hand he offered his goods to *everybody*, this would effectively be the same as offering everybody in the world a Toyota or a Big Mac. Obviously Washington would see things a little differently. They would argue that they had signed a deal based on mutual advantage, a deal where – to continue the fast food metaphor – he supplied the burger while the government provided the bun, since neither could act on their own without the other's support.

In a sudden fit of chattiness, he had shared his thoughts with Zheng. The old fellow nearly dropped his chopsticks.

'No, no, no, honourable friend! You may have a wife and a concubine. Does the concubine want to change anything about the fact that you are married? Not at all. She's happy to share this pleasant way of life with the wife, but she will very quickly lose all taste for this at the thought you may take other mistresses. China has invested too much. We observe regretfully but respectfully that you feel obliged to your lawful partner, but if space elevators were suddenly to sprout up like beanstalks all over, and everybody were to stake a claim on the Moon, that would be a problem of a different magnitude. Beijing would be most concerned.'

Most concerned.

'There's only one problem, Julian. How to stay alive after such a change of direction.'

Rogachev's remark had irked him since it showed once more how arrogant governments and their organs were. Useless mob. What kind of globalisation was this where the players didn't even seem to want to peek at the other guy's hand, where if you tried to give everybody an equal slice of the pie you ran the risk of being murdered? The longer he considered the matter, the higher the flood of biochemical stimulants to his thalamus, until at last, a little after five o'clock, he had had enough of tossing and turning in his bedclothes. He took a shower, and decided to use this unaccustomed attack of sleeplessness to take a stroll out in the canyon. In fact, he was dog-tired, physically at least, but nevertheless he went into the living room, put on shorts and T-shirt, yawned and shoved his feet into some light slippers.

As he raised his head, he thought he saw a movement at the far left of the window, something flitting at the edge of his vision.

He stared out at the canyon.

Nothing there.

He hesitated, indecisive, then shrugged and left the suite. Nobody about. Why would there be? Everybody was exhausted, deep asleep. He went to the locker with the spacesuits and began to dress, wriggled into the narrow, steel-reinforced harness, put on the chestplate and back-pack, held his helmet under his elbow and went down to the basement.

As he went into the corridor, he thought for a moment he was hallucinating.

An astronaut was coming towards him from the train station.

Julian blinked. The other man drew nearer fast, carried along by the conveyor. White light limned his outlines. Suddenly he had the crazy feeling that he was looking at a mirror-world, that he saw himself there at the other end of the corridor, then a familiar face came into focus, oval head with hair cropped short, strong chin, dark eyes.

'Carl,' he called out, astonished.

Hanna seemed no less surprised.

'What are you doing down here?' He stepped off the belt and walked slowly towards Julian, who lifted his eyebrows, unsettled, and peered about as though more early risers might step out of the walls.

'I could ask you the same question.'

'Tchh, well, to be honest—' A furtive look showed in Hanna's eyes, and his smile slipped, becoming foolish. 'I—'

'Just don't tell me that you went outside!'

'I didn't.' Hanna lifted his hands. 'Honestly.'

'But you wanted to.'

'Hmm.'

'Go on, say it.'

'Well, yes. To take a walk. I wanted to go over to the other side of the canyon, look at Gaia from over there.'

'On your own?'

'Of course on my own!' Hanna dropped the schoolboy affectations and put on a grown-up face. 'You know me. I'm not the type for eight hours of sleep, could even be I'm not house-trained for group trips like this. At any rate, I was lying there in bed and I suddenly wondered what it would be like to be the only person on the Moon. How it would feel to walk around out there without the others. Imagine there was no one here but me.'

'That's a half-baked idea.'

'Could be yours, though.' Hanna rolled his eyes. 'C'mon, don't be like that. I mean, over the next few days we're going to be wandering about in herds, aren't we? And that's fine, really. I like the others, I won't go walkabout. But I just wanted to know how it would be.'

Julian ran his fingertips through his beard.

'Well, it looks as though I don't really have to worry,' he grinned. 'You've already got lost before you could even set foot outside.'

'Yes, that was dumb of me, wasn't it?' Hanna laughed. 'I forgot where the darned airlocks are! I know, you guys showed us, but—'

'Here. Right up ahead.'

Hanna turned his head.

'Well, that's great,' he said, downcast. 'It says so in big fat letters.'

'Some lone wolf you are,' Julian said mockingly. 'As it happens, I was about to do just the same.'

'What, just go out on your own?'

'No, you fool, I have a great deal of practical experience which you don't. This isn't just a morning jog! It's dangerous.'

'Sure. Life's dangerous.'

'Seriously.'

'Give me a break, Julian, I know my way around a spacesuit! I had an EVA on the OSS, I had one on the flight here, all of that is more dangerous than taking a hike out here on the regolith.'

'That's true, but—' But I snuck out the same way you did, thought Julian. 'Regulations say that nobody goes out on their own. None of the tourists anyway.'

'Fine and dandy,' said Hanna cheerfully. 'Now there's two of us. Unless of course you'd rather go out alone.'

'Nonsense.' Julian laughed. He went to the airlock and opened the inner door. 'You were found out, so that means you *have* to come along with me, like it or not.'

Hanna followed him. The airlock was built to take twenty people, so they were rather dwarfed by its dimensions as they stood there letting their suits run through diagnostics. Bemused, he worried away at the question of just how unlikely this meeting was, mathematically speaking. If it were true that a person lives in just one of countless parallel universes where every possible course of events is true somewhere: almost identical worlds, radically different worlds with intelligent dinosaurs or where Hitler had won the war, then why did he have to live in the world where Julian had turned up in the corridor at exactly the same time as him? Why not ten minutes later, giving him the chance to get back to his suite unnoticed? The only consolation was that there were other realities where things had turned out even worse, where Julian had actually seen him arrive on the Lunar Express. At least he seemed not to have noticed that at all.

He would have to be more careful, pay more attention.

He, and Ebola.

Xintiandi, Shanghai, China

'Interesting, that program of yours,' said Jericho.

'Ah!' Tu looked pleased. 'I was wondering when you would call. Which one did you try out?'

'French Concession. You're not seriously going to put that on the market, are you?'

'We've drawn its sting.' Tu grinned. 'As I told you, that was a proto-type. Strictly for internal use, so please don't go peddling it. I thought that you would appreciate the jokes, and you also wanted to get to know Yoyo.'

'Was that her idea? Taking swipes at the Party.'

'The whole script is Yoyo's. They're test recordings, she was mostly improvising. Did you try chatting her up?'

'I did. Chatting her up, and calling her names.'

Tu giggled. 'It's impressive, isn't it?'

'A few more responses to choose from wouldn't hurt. Otherwise, very successful.'

'The market-ready version runs on an artificial intelligence. It can generate any response instantly. We didn't even need to film Yoyo to get them, any more than we needed sound recordings. The synthesiser can simulate her voice, her lip movements, gestures, everything really. Your version is very much simpler, but it means you get unadulterated Yoyo.'

'You'll have to explain one thing.'

'As long as you don't go selling it to Dao.'

Idiot, Jericho thought, but he kept it to himself.

'You know I'd never do something like that,' he said instead.

'Just a joke.' Tu dug about with a toothpick, produced a small green scrap of something and flicked it away. Jericho tried not to look. For all that, his eyes were irresistibly drawn to where the scrap, whatever it was, had landed. It was irritating mostly because Tu appeared on his new media screen not just life-size but in perfect perspectival detail, so that it looked as though Jericho's loft apartment had grown an extra room. It wouldn't have surprised him to spot the scrap of food lying on his floor-boards somewhere. Seeing Tu in three dimensions was very much less enjoyable than looking at Naomi Liu.

Now she really did have nice legs.

'Owen?'

Jericho blinked. 'I noticed that the Yoyo avatar is remarkably stable in crowds. How do you do that?'

'Trade secret,' Tu sang happily.

'Tell me. Otherwise I'll have to go and visit my optician.'

'There's nothing wrong with your eyes.'

'Clearly not. I mean, the specs themselves are transparent, just like a window. I'm seeing the real world. Your program can project details in, but it can't change reality.'

'Is that what it does?' Tu asked, grinning.

'You know perfectly well what it does. It makes people blink out of existence.'

'You never thought that perhaps reality is just a projection as well?'

'Could you say that a little less cryptically?'

'Let's say we could do without the lens on the specs.'

'And Yoyo would still appear?'

'Bingo.'

'But what would be the substrate?'

'She'd appear because none of what you see is actual reality. There are tiny cameras hidden in the arms of the specs and in the frame, feeding data on the real world into the computer so that it knows how and where it should fit Yoyo in. What you might have overlooked was the projec-tors on the inside edge.'

'I know that Yoyo is projected onto the lens glass.'

'No, that's just what she's not.' Tu quaked with suppressed laughter. 'The glass is surplus to requirements. The cameras produce a complete image, which is made up of your surroundings, plus Yoyo. Then this image is projected directly onto your retina.'

Jericho stared at Tu.

'You mean none of what I saw—'

'Oh, you definitely saw the real world. Just not first-hand. You see what the cameras film, and the film can be manipulated. In real time, of course. We can make the sky pink, make people disappear or have them grow horns. We turn your eyes into the projection screen.'

'Unbelievable.'

Tu shrugged. 'There are useful applications of virtual reality. Did you know that most cases of blindness are caused by clouding in the lens of the human eye? The retina underneath is healthy and functional, so we project the visible world directly into the retina. We make the blind see again. That's the whole trick.'

'I see.' Jericho rubbed his chin. 'And Yoyo's been working on this.'

'Exactly.'

'You must trust her a lot.'

'She's good. She's full of ideas. A veritable ideas factory.'

'She's an intern!'

'That hardly matters.'

'To me it does. I have to know who I'm dealing with here, Tian. How clued-up is the girl, in truth? Is she really just a—' Dissident, he had been about to say. Stupid mistake. Diamond Shield would have filtered the word out from their conversation in an instant and put it into his file.

'Yoyo knows what's what,' Tu said curtly. 'I never said it would be easy to find her.'

'No,' said Jericho, more to himself than to Tu. 'You didn't.'

'Chin up. I've remembered something else.'

'What?'

'Yoyo seems to have friends in a motorbike gang. She never introduced me, but I remember that she had City Demons on her jackets. That might bring you further forward.'

'I know about that already, thanks. Yoyo didn't happen to mention where they hang out?'

'I think you'll have to find that out on your own.'

'All right then. If anything else comes back to you—'

'I'll let you know. Wait.' Naomi Liu's voice came from the other side of the projection. Tu stood up and disappeared from Jericho's sight. He heard the two of them talking in low tones, then Tu came back.

'Excuse me, Owen, but it looks as though we've had a suicide.' He hesitated. 'Or an accident.'

'What happened?'

'Something awful. Someone fell to his death. The roller-coaster had been set in motion, outside its usual hours. It looks as if whoever it was had been working up there. I'll be back in touch, okay?'

'Okay.'

They hung up. Jericho stayed there, sitting thoughtfully in front of the empty screen. Something about Tu's remark unsettled him. He wondered why. People threw themselves from skyscrapers the whole time. China had the highest suicide rate in the world, higher even than Japan, and skyscrapers were also the most cost-efficient and effective way to leave this life.

It wasn't about the suicide.

What then?

He fished out the stick that Tu had given him, put it on top of the console and let the computer download Yoyo's virtual guided tours, her personnel file, records of conversations and documents. The files also contained her genetic code, voiceprint and eyescan, fingerprints and blood group. He could use the tours to get to know her body language and her gestures, her intonation as well, and the documents and conversation soundfiles would yield all her frequent turns of phrase, figures of speech and even syntactical patterns. This gave him a usable personality profile. A dossier that he could work from.

Perhaps though he should start from what he *didn't* have.

He went online and set his computer looking for the City Demons. It served him up an Australian football club in New South Wales, another in New Zealand, a basketball team from Dodge City, Kansas, and a Vietnamese Goth band.

No demons in Shanghai.

After he had broadened the search mode and told it to allow for spelling errors, he got a hit. Two members of a biker gang called the City Daemons had got into a fight with half a dozen drunken North Koreans in the DKD Club on the Huaihai Zhong Lu; the NKs had been singing an anthem about the murder of their dear departed Supreme Leader. The bikers had got away with a police caution, since the Chinese leadership had declared Kim Jong Un *persona non grata*, posthumously, in recognition of the prevailing mood in reunited Korea. Beijing had several reasons to make sure that they nipped in the bud any cult of nostalgia that might develop around North Korean totalitarianism.

City Daemons. With an 'a'.

Next the computer found a blog where Shanghai hip-hoppers picked up on the incident in the DKD and dwelt on the bravery of two members of the City Demons (with 'e'), who had put their lives on the line to sling the North Koreans out on their ear. A link took Jericho to a biker forum which he browsed through, hoping to find more about the Demons. This confirmed his suspicion that the Demons themselves had posted up the comments. The forum turned out to be an advertising platform for an e-bike and hybrids workshop called Demon Point, whose owner was probably, pretty nearly definitely, a member of the City Demons.

And that was interesting.

The workshop, he learned, lay on the edge of Quyu: a parallel world where hardly anybody had their own computer or a net connection, but there was the black hole of a Cyber Planet on every street corner, sucking in the local youths and never spitting them out again. It was a world ruled by several Triad subclans, sometimes striking deals, mostly at loggerheads, who only really agreed that no kind of crime was off limits. A world of complex hierarchies, outside of which its inhabitants counted for nothing. A world which sent out battalions of cheap factory hands and unskilled labour to the better parts of the city every day, and then drew them back in every evening, a world which offered few sights but which nevertheless drew the well-heeled towards it with some magic charm, offering them something that couldn't be found anywhere else in the Shanghai of urban renewal: the fascinating, iridescent gleam of human decay.

Quyu, the Zone, the forgotten world. The perfect place if you wanted to disappear without trace.

The little bike workshop wasn't in Quyu proper, but it was close enough to function as a gateway in or out. Jericho sighed. He found himself forced to take a step that he didn't like at all. He often worked with the Shanghai police, as he had done just recently. He had good relations with them. The officers would sometimes help him with his own cases, depending on whether they had their own irons in the fire in the cases of corruption or espionage that Jericho was looking into. For all that, they worked shoulder to shoulder when it came to fighting monsters such as Animal Ma Liping. His reputation among the police force was growing, even before he had rooted out the paedophile. When he went out drinking with members of the force, they let it be known that they would like to pass on information if he needed it, and ever since the nightmare in Shenzhen his friend Patrice Ho, a high-ranking officer, owed him a major favour, and had made it clear that this could be a peek into police databases. Jericho would have been all too pleased to call in the favour now, but if the authorities really were after Yoyo, he couldn't even think about it.

And that meant that he had to hack his way in.

He'd dared to do so twice. He'd succeeded twice.

At the time, he had sworn not to chance it a third time. He knew what he'd be in for if they caught wind of him. After Beijing had hacked into European and American government networks in 2007, the West had gone on a counter-offensive, supported by Russian and Arab hackers working off their own grudges. Since then, there was hardly anything China feared more than cyber-attacks. Accordingly, anybody infiltrating Chinese systems was shown no mercy.

With mixed feelings, he set to work.

A little later he had the access he wanted to various archives. Practically every area of the city was decked out with scanners hidden in the walls of houses, in traffic lights and signposts, in door handles and bell-pushes, in advertising hoardings, labels, mirrors, scaffolding and household devices. They scanned retinas, stored biometrics, analysed the way people walked and gestured, recorded voices and sounds. While the phone-tapping system had been brought to the peak of perfection some decades ago, using the American NSA system as a model, retinal analysis was a comparatively new phenomenon. The scanner could recognise individual structures in the human iris from several metres away and thereby identify a person. Microscopically small directional mics filtered the frequencies out of a noisy street crossing till you could hear one voice speaking quite distinctly. The real art of such surveillance lay in evaluating data. The system recognised wanted individuals by the way they moved, could recognise a face even obscured by a false beard. If Yoyo glanced just once into one of the omnipresent scanners, this would be enough to identify her retina, which had been data-captured first as she was born, again on her first day of school, and then at university enrolment. It had also been stored when she was arrested, and when she was released.

Jericho's computer started sifting.

It analysed every twitch of Yoyo's eyes, dived into the crystalline structures of her iris, measured the angle of her lips when she smiled, set up studies for the way her hair moved in the wind, calibrated the sway of her hips, the spread of her fingers as she swung her arms, the line of her wrist as she pointed, her average length of pace. Yoyo became a creature of equations, an algorithm which Jericho sent out into the phantom world of the police surveillance archive, hoping that it would meet its match there. He narrowed down the search window to the time right after she had vanished, but even so the system reported more than two thousand hits. He uploaded the stolen data to his hard drive, stored it under Yoyofiles and withdrew as quickly as he could. His presence had not been noticed. Time to begin evaluation.

Hold on, there was one piece of the puzzle missing. Unlikely though it might seem, this student with the grandiose name might actually have some information to offer. What was the guy called anyway? Grand Cherokee Wang.

Grand Cherokee—

At that moment, Jericho was struck by the realisation.

He had found out in his investigations that Wang had a part-time job at the World Financial Center where Tu's company was headquartered. He handled the Silver Dragon—

And the Silver Dragon was a roller-coaster!

The roller-coaster had been set in motion, outside its usual hours. It looks as if whoever it was had been working up there.

Jericho gazed into empty air. His gut feelings told him that the student hadn't jumped of his own accord, and it hadn't been an accident. Wang was dead because he had known something about Yoyo. No, not even that! Because he had *given the impression* that he knew something about Yoyo.

This put the case in a whole new light.

He paced through the enormous loft, went into the kitchen and said, 'Tea. Lady Grey. One cup, two sugars, milk as usual.'

While the machine attended to his order, he went over what he knew. Perhaps he was seeing ghosts, but his knack for spotting patterns and making connections where others saw only fragments had rarely let him down. It was obvious that there was somebody else after Yoyo, besides himself. This wasn't in itself news. Chen and Tu had both voiced their suspicion that Yoyo was on the run. Both of them had also been doubtful that she was wanted by the police, even if Yoyo herself might believe just that. This time, she hadn't been picked up by police officers as had happened twice before, rather she had vanished at dead of night. Why? The decision seemed to have been taken in great haste. Something must have made Yoyo fear a visit, in the next few minutes or hours, from people who did not have her best interests at heart. So what had she done *before* she took fright?

Had she been warned?

By whom? Against *whom*? If Wang had been telling the truth, she had been alone at the time, so that meant that she might have had a call: Make sure you get out of there. Or an email. Perhaps nothing of the sort. Perhaps she had discovered something on the net, seen something on the news, that frightened her.

A diffident beeping sound from the kitchen let him know that his tea was ready. Jericho picked up the cup, burned his hand, cursed and took a little sip. He decided to call customer service to reprogram the machine. Two sugars was too sweet, one not sweet enough. Lost in thought, he went back to his office area. Shanghai police were not squeamish, but they were hardly in the habit of throwing suspects off the roof. More likely, Grand Cherokee Wang would have come round in a police station. The kid had wanted to play a bluff. A chancer, who hadn't actually had anything to sell, and had tried his act with the wrong customer.

Whose toes had Yoyo been treading on, for heaven's sake?

'Breaking news,' he said. 'Shanghai. World Financial Center.'

Headlines and images grouped themselves together on the wall. Jericho blew on his tea and asked the computer to read him the latest reports.

'Today at around 10.20 local time a man fell to his death from the Shanghai World Financial Center in Pudong,' said a female voice, pleasantly low-pitched. 'Initial reports suggest that he worked in the building, with responsibility for watching and operating the Silver Dragon, the world's highest roller-coaster. At the time he fell, the ride was in motion, outside of usual hours. The Public Prosecutor has opened proceedings against the ride's owners. It has been impossible to establish so far whether this was an accident or suicide, but everything seems to point to—'

'Show filmed reports only,' said Jericho.

A video window opened. A young Chinese woman was standing in front of the Jin Mao Tower with the camera trained on her so that viewers could see the foot of the World Financial Center. Under a veneer of half-hearted distress she was glowing with joy at the thought that some nitwit had given her a headline in the summer silly season by obligingly dying for her.

'It is still a mystery why the roller-coaster ride was even in motion, without passengers and outside of its usual hours,' she was saying, imbuing portent and secrecy into every word. 'An eyewitness video which happened to be filming the tracks when the accident happened has shed some light on the matter. If indeed it was an accident. There is no confirmation as yet of the identity of the dead—'

'Eyewitness video,' Jericho interrupted. 'Identity of victim.'

'The video is sadly not available.' The computer managed to put a note of real regret into the announcement. Jericho had set the system's affective level to twenty per cent. At this setting, the voice didn't sound mechanical, but rather warmly human. The computer also had a personality protocol. 'There are two reports on the dead man's identity.'

'Read, please.'

'Shanghai Satellite writes: The dead man is apparently one Wang Jintao. Wang was a student at—'

'The second.'

'Xinhua agency reports: The dead man has been positively identified as Wang Jintao, also known as Grand Cherokee, who studied—'

'Reports on the precise circumstances of death.'

There were a great many reports, as it turned out, but nobody wanted to commit to a particular story. Nevertheless, they made up an interesting picture. It was certain that somebody had set the Silver Dragon free ten minutes early, before the paying passengers had arrived. Grand Cherokee's job had been to set the system in motion and look after the morning customers, which basically meant working the till and starting the ride. Nobody was supposed to be up there with him at the time of the incident, although there were indications that perhaps somebody had been there after all. Two staff in the Sky Lobby said that they had seen Wang meet a man and go into a lift with him. Further clues came from the eyewitness video, it seemed, which apparently showed Wang moving around on the tracks as the ride was already in motion.

What the hell had Wang been doing out there?

A short article in the Shanghai Satellite speculated that he could have set the ride going without meaning to. Suicide seemed the more likely explanation. On the other hand, why would somebody wanting to commit suicide pick his way along the track when he could have simply leapt from the open stretch of the boarding platform? Especially, another article added, since there were increasing indications that Wang hadn't

FRANK SCHÄTZING · 424

actually jumped but had been run over by the train as it came bearing down on him.

Accident after all? At any rate, nobody was talking about murder, although here and there some commentators speculated about an accident caused by someone other than Wang.

Two minutes later Jericho knew better. Xinhua reported that the surveillance camera footage was now being examined. Wang had apparently been accompanied by a tall man who left the floor right after Wang fell. The two men seemed to have had an argument, Wang had certainly been moving along the track with no safety gear, and the train had run into him level with the southern pillar.

Jericho drank his tea and considered.

Who was the murderer?

'Computer,' he said. 'Open Yoyofiles.'

More than two thousand hits. Where should he begin? He decided to set a profile match of ninety-five per cent, which left 117 files where the surveillance system thought that it had seen Yoyo.

He ordered the computer to select files with direct eye contact.

There was only one, immediately by the block where Yoyo lived, recorded at 02.47. Jericho wouldn't have been able to say exactly where the scanner was, but he suspected it was in a signpost. Exact coordinates were stored in a separate file. There was no doubt that the woman over there on the other side of the street was Yoyo. She was sitting on an unmarked motorbike, no licence plates, her head tilted down, both hands on a crash helmet. Just before she put it on, she lifted her gaze and looked directly into the scanner, then she put down the mirrored faceplate and sped away.

'Gotcha,' muttered Jericho. 'Computer, rewind.'

Yoyo took the helmet briskly off again.

'Stop.'

She looked him straight in the eyes.

'Zoom, two hundred and thirty per cent.'

The new technology of the wall could give him a life-size view of Yoyo. The way she sat there on her bike, every detail clear in three-dimensional surroundings, it was as though he had opened a door out onto the night from his loft. He had judged the zoom quite well. Yoyo looked about three or four centimetres taller now than in real life, and the image was pin-sharp. A system that could recognise the structure of an iris from all the way across the street wasn't nicknamed 'the freckle-counter' for nothing. Jericho knew that this would be his last good look at Yoyo for some time, so he tried to read what he could out of it.

You're frightened, thought Jericho. But you hide it well.

Also, your mind is made up.

He stepped back. Yoyo was wearing pale jeans, knee-boots, a printed T-shirt down over her hips and a short puffy jacket of patent leather that looked as though it might have come from one of the spray cans he had found in her room. Most of the slogan printed on her shirt was in shadow, or under the jacket, and only a little showed where the jacket was open at the front. He would look into that later.

'Find this person in the folder called Yoyofiles,' he said. 'Ninety per cent match.'

Straight away he got the answer, seventy-six hits. He considered having the computer play all the films, but told it instead to plot the recordings' coordinates onto a city map of Shanghai. A moment later the map came up on the wall, showing Yoyo's route, where she had gone on the night she disappeared. The last sighting had been just across from Demon Point, the little e-bike and hybrids workshop. After that, the trail went cold.

She was in the forgotten world.

Yoyo had only remained undiscovered in Quyu because there were hardly any surveillance systems there. Even so, Quyu wasn't a slum in the classic sense, not to be compared with the festering shantytowns that surrounded Calcutta, Mexico City or Bombay and oozed out into the surrounding countryside. As a global city on a par with New York, Shanghai needed Quyu the way the Big Apple needed the Bronx, meaning that the city left the district in peace. It didn't send in the bulldozers, or the riot police. In the years after the turn of the millennium, the historic inner-city areas and slums in the Shanghai interior had been torn down systematically until those boroughs were free of any sort of authentic history. Where the outer district of Baoshan ran up against this new Shanghai core, Quyu had grown up and been allowed to grow, much as a landowner might allow scrubland to grow in order to save the cost of a gardener. Quyu, north-west of Huangpu, now marked the crossover to swathes of makeshift settlements, vestigial villages, run-down small towns and abandoned industrial estates – a Moloch that grabbed more of the surrounding land each year, guzzling down the last remnants of a region that had once been rural.

Quyu was internally autonomous, and externally it was watched as closely as a prison camp; it was one of the most impressive examples of twenty-first-century urban poverty. The population was made up of people displaced from their original homes in the heart of Shanghai, of those who had lived here even before Quyu absorbed their small towns, of migrants from poor provinces lured to the promised land of the global city and living on temporary residence permits that no one ever checked, of battalions of illegal labourers who didn't officially exist. Everybody in Quyu was poor, though some were less poor than others. Most money was made in drugs or in the leisure sector, largely prostitution. The social structure of Quyu's population was unregulated in every way, with not a hint of health insurance, old-age pension or unemployment benefit.

But it was still more than just a horde of beggars.

After all, most of them had work. They manned the assembly lines and the building sites, they cleaned the parks and streets, drove delivery trucks and cleaned the houses of the better-off. They would turn up like ghosts in the regulated world, do their job and then vanish again once they were no longer needed. They were poor because everybody living in Quyu could be replaced at twenty-four hours' notice. They stayed poor because, in the words of the wise old sage Bill Gates, they were part of a global society divided into those who were networked and those who weren't. In Quyu, nobody was networked, even if they owned a mobile phone or a computer. Being networked meant playing the same high-speed game as the rest of the world, not letting your attention lapse for a second. It meant sifting out the relevant information from the irrelevant, grabbing advantages that lapsed as soon as you logged off. It meant being better, faster, leaner, more innovative and more flexible than the competition at every moment, it meant moving home when required, switching jobs.

It meant getting a place at the table.

Gates had said that the future belonged to the networked. Logically, non-networked society therefore had no future. Individuals outside the network were like spiders who didn't spin threads. Nothing got caught in their web. They would starve.

Officially, nobody had starved to death in Quyu yet. Even if the powers-that-be in China had a blind spot when it came to slums or shantytowns, they wouldn't quite so readily allow anyone to die of hunger on the streets of Shanghai. Less from the milk of human kindness, and more because you just couldn't have that sort of thing happening in a world financial centre. On the other hand, official attitudes to Quyu mattered not a jot. What sort of official figures might come out of a district with totally opaque demographics, which was widely seen as ungovernable and uncontrollable, which actually ran its own affairs in some incomprehensible way and where the police hardly dared venture, although they had put a ring of iron around its edge? It was known that there was infrastructure of sorts, houses of sorts, some habitable, others barely more than damp caves. Clean drinking water was scarce, power cuts frequent, there was hardly a flush toilet in the place. There were doctors and ambulances in Quyu, hospitals, schools and kindergartens, snack bars, tea houses, bars, cinemas and kiosks and street markets of the sort that had almost completely vanished from the rest of Shanghai. Nobody knew, though, how life went on in Quyu exactly. Crimes committed there were hardly followed up, and this too was part of the tacit agreement that the district should look after itself, and was to be cut loose from the dynamic of social development. Residents were given no support but they were not held to account either, as long as they didn't break the law outside the borders of their tribal reservation. There was no future here, and that meant no past, or at least not a past one could boast of or build on.

Without a network, they lived outside of time itself, on the dark fringes of a universe whose shining centres were connected by multi-storey freeways and sky trains. Certainly the shortest routes from Shanghai city centre out to the luxurious commuter towns ran through districts like Quyu, but that didn't mean anybody had to pass through the forgotten world and actually take notice of what went on there. The routes simply ran right *overhead*, as though the place were a swamp.

For a while the leadership in Beijing had asked themselves whether this method of running Shanghai might lead to revolt. Nobody doubted that terrorists and criminals had gone to ground there. Nevertheless the necessity of tightening the State's grip in the district was undermined by scepticism that a rabble of migrant farm workers, factory girls, errand boys and building labourers would ever be able to coalesce into anything like a workers' uprising. Large-scale political violence was expected from the bourgeoisie instead, since they had access to the information superhighway and to all kinds of hi-tech. On the other hand, the conventional criminals who haunted Quyu would feel all the safer there, the less danger they were in from outside. When had the Mafia ever called the workers to arms? In the end, the opinion prevailed that every criminal in Quyu was one less in Xaxu, leading Beijing to issue a clear recommendation:

Forget Quyu.

Yoyo had taken shelter in a world which was one of the blank spaces on the map of urbanisation. Jericho wondered whether anyone in Quyu had ever thought that it was also a form of discrimination *not* to be under surveillance.

Probably not.

He had spent the evening looking on the net for texts that Yoyo might have written since she went under. He used the same technology for this that Diamond Shield used in its hectic search for dissidents, or that the American Secret Services used in the unending war on terror, the same he had used himself against Animal Ma Liping. The rhythms of keystrokes on a computer keyboard were just as individual as fingerprints. A suspect could be identified in the very moment that he began to write his text into a browser. Advances in Social Network Analysis were even more interesting: choice of vocabulary, favoured metaphors, everything left grammatical and semantic clues. A computer only needed a few hundred words to identify who was writing with almost one hundred per cent accuracy. Most interesting of all, the system didn't just blindly pile up words, it recognised meaning and context. To a certain extent, it actually understood what the writer was trying to say. It developed an unconscious intelligence, and became capable of tracking down whole networks, world-spanning structures of terrorism or organised crime, where neo-Nazis, bombers, racists and hooligans living thousands of miles apart met in a virtual alliance – though in real life they might well have beaten one another to pulp.

This had helped to track down paedophiles and uncover industrial espionage, but it also proved to be a nightmare for dissidents and human rights activists. It was no surprise that repressive regimes in particular showed great interest in the methods of Social Network Analysis. Nevertheless, Yoyo had always managed to stay one step ahead of the security services' analytical programs, until a few days ago she had been exposed and identified. If indeed that was what had happened. At least Yoyo must have believed that that was the case, and this explained her headlong flight.

What he still couldn't understand was how she noticed.

Jericho yawned.

He was dog-tired. He had had the computer running after clues all night. Obviously he would not be finding Yoyo any time soon. The Internet Police had spent years snapping at her heels, with no success. She probably knew the analytical programs' algorithms inside out and backwards; in such matters, working for Tu Technologies was like sitting in the Jade Temple of Enlightenment. Feeling fairly baffled, he wondered how he could manage something that until just recently not even the government had been able to do; but he had one invaluable advantage.

He knew that Yoyo was one of the Guardians.

While the computer was chasing her virtual shadow, Jericho had unpacked the rest of the crates and turned the loft into something that pretty nearly resembled a flat. When at last the furniture was in place, the pictures were hanging on the walls and his clothes were in the wardrobe, once everything was tidied away and in its place, and Erik Satie's *Trois Gymnopédies* rippled through the room, he felt happy and at peace for the first time in days, free from those images of Shenzhen, and had even lost all interest in Yoyo for the time being.

Owen Jericho, snug in a cocoon of music.

'Match,' announced the computer.

Irksome.

So irksome that he decided there and then to dial up the personality protocol by thirty per cent. At least then the computer would sound like someone you could share a coffee or a glass of wine with.

'There's a blog entry that looks like Yoyo,' said the warm female voice, almost human. 'She posted an entry on Brilliant Shit, a Mando-prog forum. Should I read it out?'

'Are you sure that it's Yoyo?'

'Almost certain. She knows how to cover her tracks. I imagine Yoyo is working with distorters. What do you think?'

Without the personality protocol the remark would have come out as: 'Eighty-four point seven per cent match. Probability that distorter is being used, ninety point two per cent.'

'I think it's very probable that she's working with distorters,' Jericho agreed.

Distorters were programs that go over a text and alter the writer's personal style. They were becoming more and more popular. Some of them rewrote texts using the style of great poets and writers, so that you could dash off a message and have it reach the recipient looking as though it had been written by Thomas Mann, Ernest Hemingway or Jonathan Franzen. Other programs imitated politicians. It became dangerous when malevolent hackers cracked the profiles of other, unsuspecting users and borrowed their style. Many dissidents on the net preferred to use distorters that would rewrite with randomly generated standards, using a variety of styles. The most important thing was that the meaning remain the same.

And that was precisely the weak spot in most programs.

'Elements in the blog post are not stylistically uniform,' said the computer. 'That confirms your theory, Owen.'

A nice touch, using his first name. Polite too to pretend that it had been *his* theory, as though the computer itself hadn't suggested that a distorter was at work. God knows, fifty per cent personality protocol was enough. At eighty per cent the computer would be crawling up his backside. Jericho hesitated. In fact he was fed up with calling the thing 'computer'. What would a girl like this be called? Maybe—

He programs her with a name.

'Diane?'

'Yes, Owen?'

Great. He likes Diane. Diane is his new right-hand woman.

'Please read the entry.'

'Glad to. *Hi all. Back in our galaxy now, have been for a few days. Was really stressed out these last days, is anybody harshing on me? Couldn't help it, really truly. All happened so fast. Shit. Even so quickly you can be forgotten. Only waiting now for the old demons to visit me once more. Yeah, and, I'm busy writing new songs. If any of the band asks: We'll make an appearance once I've got a few euphonious lyrics on the go. Let's prog!'*

Once again Jericho wonders how the program can identify a writer from such a mishmash, but experience has taught him that even less would be enough. Still, he doesn't have to understand it. He's an end-user, not a programmer.

'Give me an analysis,' he says. It's really quite cosy by now, with Satie and this velvet-smooth voice.

'Of course, Owen.'

That's to say, this 'of course' has to go. It reminds him of HAL 9000 from *A Space Odyssey*. Ever since the satnav system was invented, every speaking computer has been doing its best to copy crazy HAL.

'The text is supposed to sound cocky,' the computer said. 'The style is broken though by the terms *even so quickly* and *euphonious. The old demons to visit me once more* seems rather forced – I don't believe that the distorter was at work here. Everything else is just minor detail. *Lyrics on the go* for instance doesn't fit the style of the second and third sentences.'

'What do you make of the content?'

'Hard to say. I might have a couple of suggestions for you. First off, *galaxy*. That might just be loosely meant, or it might be a synonym for something.'

'For instance?'

'Probably for a locality.'

'Go on.'

'*Demons*. You've already been looking for demons. I suspect that Yoyo is referring here to the City Demons, or City Daemons.'

'I'm with you there. By the way, Daemons was a blind alley. Anything else strike you?'

The computer hesitated. The personality protocol once more.

'I don't know enough about Yoyo. I could give you about three hundred and eighty thousand variant interpretations of the other wording and phrases.'

'Put a sock in it,' Jericho murmured.

'I'm sorry, I didn't quite catch that.'

'Doesn't matter. Please search Shanghai for the word galaxy in connection with some place or other.'

This time the computer didn't hesitate. 'No entries.'

'Good. Locate where the text was sent from.'

'Of course.' The computer gave him the coordinates. Jericho is astonished. He hadn't expected it would be so easy to track back the route the message took. He would have thought that Yoyo would lay a few more false trails when communicating.

'Are you sure that you haven't just found an intermediary browser?'

'One hundred per cent sure, Owen. The message was sent from there at 6.24 local time on the morning of 24th May.'

Jericho nods. That's good. That's very good!

And his hope becomes a certainty.

Forgotten World

As Jericho steered his COD along the Huaihai Donglu towards the elway, he went over his conclusions from last night once more.

Hi all. Back in our galaxy now, have been for a few days.

Which could mean, I've been back in Quyu for a few days. Obvious. Not so clear though why Yoyo would call Quyu a galaxy. More likely that she meant one particular place in Quyu.

Was really stressed out these last days, is anybody harshing on me?

Stress. Well, obviously.

And why would anybody be angry at her? That was also fairly easily told. Yoyo wasn't actually asking a question here, she was giving an explanation. That somebody had tracked her down, that this someone was dangerous, and that she didn't know whom she was dealing with.

Couldn't help it, really truly. All happened so fast. Shit.

More difficult. She had taken flight at panic speed. But what did the first part mean? What couldn't she help?

Even so quickly you can be forgotten.

Trivially easy. Quyu, the forgotten world. Almost a platitude. Yoyo must have been in a hurry to get the message out.

Only waiting now for the old demons to visit me once more.

Even easier: City Demons, you know where I am.

Yeah, and, I'm busy writing new songs. If any of the band asks: We'll make an appearance once I've got a few euphonious lyrics on the go. Let's prog!

Which was as much as to say, I'm trying to get the problems under control as fast as I can. Until then, we'll disappear.

And who is *we*?

The Guardians.

The city freeway ran at an angle to Jericho's route. An eight-lane road with enough traffic on it for sixteen, and with several storeys of elevated highway soaring above. Cars, buses and vans crawled through the morning as though through aspic. Hundreds of thousands of commuters flooded into the city from the satellite towns, taxi drivers glowered out at the world around. Not even bikers found a spot where they could squeeze through here. They all wore breathing-masks, but nevertheless you expected to see them turn blue and slump from their saddles. Even though there were more fuel-cell cars in use in the metropolises of China than anywhere else in the world, more hydrogen motors and more electric engines, a blanket of smoggy exhaust fumes lay over the city.

A special traffic track ran high above everything else. It was supported by slender telescopic legs, had only been opened for use a few years ago and was reserved exclusively for CODs. Now COD tracks connected all the most important points in the city and led out to the commuter towns and the coast, some of them at dizzying heights. Jericho threaded his way onto the steep sliproad, waited for his vehicle to click into place on the rails and entered his destination coordinates. From now on he didn't need to steer the COD, which would have been impossible anyway. As soon as CODs were in the system, the driver played no further part.

Jericho's COD climbed up the slope in a row of identical machines. Up on the track, he could see countless numbers of the cabin-like vehicles racing away at more than 300 kilometres per hour, gleaming silver in the sun. One storey down, any sort of movement had ceased.

He leaned back.

The vehicles approaching in the outside lane braked just enough to leave a precisely measured gap for his vehicle to slip into. Jericho loved the moment of rapid acceleration when the COD took off. He was pressed briefly against the back of his seat, then he had reached cruising speed. His phone told him that he had received a message from the computer. The display scanned his iris. An additional voiceprint check wasn't really necessary, but Jericho liked to make assurance doubly sure.

'Owen Jericho,' he said.

'Good morning, Owen.'

'Hello, Diane.'

'I've analysed the writing on Yoyo's shirt. Would you like to see the result?'

He had given the computer this job before he set off. He linked his phone to the interface on the car dashboard.

'What does it say?'

'It's evidently a symbol.'

A large A appeared on the COD monitor. At least, Jericho supposed that it was supposed to be an A. The crossbar was missing, although in its place a ragged ring slanted around the letter instead. Underneath he could read four letters, NDRO.

'Have you looked for similar symbols on the net?'

'Yes. What you see is the result of image enhancement. It's a reconstruction based on high-probability matches. The symbol doesn't turn up anywhere in the data store. The letters might be an abbreviation, or a word fragment. I've found NDRO as an abbreviation several times, just not in China.'

'What word do you reckon it might be?'

'My favourites are androgynous, android, Andromeda.'

'Thank you, Diane.' Jericho thought for a moment. 'Can you see whether I left the bedroom window open?'

'It's open.'

'Shut it, please.'

'Shall do, Owen.'

The COD alerted him that it would leave the track in a few seconds. It had taken only four minutes to travel almost twenty kilometres. Jericho took his phone from the interface. The COD slowed, drew out and threaded into the queue of cars that were leaving the network just before Quyu. He made fairly good speed down the turn-off and onto the main road. Even here, far outside the city centre, the traffic flowed sluggishly, but at least it was moving. Quyu was separated from the city by several storeys of freeway. Streets leading out were bundled together by roadblocks and fed through pinch points, with a police station near every one. There were also army barracks to the east and west. For all that, only a very few people in Quyu could even afford a car or the COD hire fee, so that metro lines and trolley-buses connected the district to the city.

The Demon workshop was just outside Xaxu in a historic quarter, not two kilometres west of here. It was one of the last of the really old quarters. Earlier it had been a village, or a small country town, and sooner or later it would have to give way to the phalanxes of anonymous modern houses. Now that the downtown had been completely remodelled, the planners were having a go at the periphery.

Only Quyu would stay untouched, as ever.

Fast though he had got here on the COD track, it was painfully slow getting to the part of town he wanted to go. It was a typical old-style neighbourhood. Stone buildings, one to three storeys high, with black and dark red gables, lined busy streets where many little alleys branched off, and courtyards opened up. There were open shopfronts and food sellers lurked under colourful awnings, and washing lines stretched between the houses. The Demon Point workshop took up the whole ground floor of a rust-streaked house with a gap-toothed wooden balcony around its first floor. Some windowpanes were missing, others were crazed and blind.

Jericho parked the COD in a side street and strolled across to the workshop. Several handsome hybrids and e-bikes were lined up in front of other, less attractive specimens. There was nobody to be seen until a thin boy in shorts and a baggy T-shirt smeared with oil came out from a tiny office and got to work on one of the e-bikes with a rag and a tin of polish.

'Hello,' said Jericho.

The boy looked up briefly and turned back to his work. Jericho squatted down next to him.

'Very nice bike.'

'Mm-hm.'

'I can see how you're polishing it. Are you one of the ones who cleaned the NKs' clocks as well, in the DKD Club?'

The kid grinned and kept on polishing.

'That was Daxiong.'

'Good work he did.'

'He told the wankers to shut their traps. Even though there were more of them. Said that he didn't feel like listening to their fascist crap.'

'I hope he didn't get any trouble from them.'

'Little bit.' The boy seemed only now to realise that he'd fallen into conversation with somebody he didn't know at all. He put down his rag and looked at Jericho distrustfully. 'Who are you anyway?'

'Ahh, I was just headed for Quyu. Sheer chance that I spotted your workshop here. And given that I'd read that blog post – Well, I thought, since I'm here anyway—'

'Interested in a bike?'

Jericho stood up. He looked where the boy was pointing. Over at the back of the workshop, a burly chopper, an electro, was up on its chocks. The rear wheel was missing.

'Why not?' He walked over to the machine and admired it ostentatiously. 'Been thinking for years of getting a chopper. Lithium-aluminium battery?'

'That's right. It'll give you 280.'

'Range?'

'Four hundred kilometres. Minimum. Are you from downtown?'

'Mm-hm.'

'That's hell for cars. You should think about it.'

'Shall do.' Jericho took out his phone. 'I don't know my way around here, sadly. I'm supposed to meet someone, but you know how Quyu is for addresses. Maybe you can help me.'

The kid shrugged. Jericho projected the A with the hazy ring around it onto the back wall of the workshop. The boy's eyes gave him away – he knew the place.

'That's where you want to go?'

'Is it far?'

'Not really. You just have to—'

'Button your lip,' said somebody behind him.

Jericho turned around and stared at a chest that began somewhere in the south-east and ended further along to the north-east. Way up above the chest there had to be something that the brute used to think. He put his head back and made out a shaven skull, with eyes so narrow that it was hard to believe he could see through them. A blue appliqué on the chin looked vaguely like a pharaoh's beard. The leather jacket was open at the front, and beneath it he could see the City Demons logo.

'It's fine.' The boy looked upwards, uncertain. 'He was just asking where—'

'What?'

'Everything's okay.' Jericho smiled. 'I wanted to know whether—'

'What? What do you want to know?'

The man-mountain made no attempt to bend down to talk to him, which would have made conversation considerably easier. Jericho took a step back and turned his projector to the wall again.

'I'm sorry if I've come at a bad moment. I'm looking for an address.'

'An address?' The other man turned his massive head and looked – as far as Jericho could tell – at the projected image.

'I mean, is that even an address at all?' Jericho asked. 'I've only got—'

'Who gave you that?'

'Someone who didn't have much time to give me directions. Someone from Quyu. Someone I want to help.'

'What with?'

'Social problems.'

'Is there anyone in Quyu who doesn't have those?'

'True enough.' Jericho decided not to take this treatment any longer. 'What now? I don't want to keep this person waiting.'

'He's also interested in the chopper!' added the boy, in a tone that suggested he had already talked Jericho into buying the machine for an enormous sum.

The man-mountain pursed his lips.

Then he smiled.

The suspicion melted sheer away from his features, making way for warm friendship. An enormous paw swooped through space and landed with a playful smack on Jericho's shoulder.

'Why didn't you say so right away?'

That had broken the ice. His suddenly hearty manner didn't yield any more information though, but rather a detailed description of all the chopper's supposed virtues, and he reached a genial crescendo as he named an exorbitant price. The ogre even managed to price the missing rear wheel separately.

Jericho nodded and nodded. At the end, he shook his head.

'No?' said the giant, surprised.

'Not at that price.'

'Fine. Name your price.'

'I'll give you another idea. An A with a frayed ring around it and four mysterious letters beneath. You remember? I go there, I come back. Then we do business.'

The giant wrinkled his brow laboriously. He was thinking, Jericho had to assume. Then he described a route which seemed to run the whole length and breadth of Quyu.

What had the kid said just now? Not really far?

'And what do the letters mean?'

'NDRO?' The giant laughed. 'This friend of yours must really have been in a hurry. It's Andromeda.'

'Ah!'

'It's a live concert venue.'

'Thanks.'

'Your knowledge of Quyu seems to rest on the very slightest acquaintance, if you don't mind my saying so.'

Jericho had to raise his eyebrows. He would never have expected that a man-mountain like this, with such a tough-looking skull, would produce such a refined turn of phrase.

'It's true, I hardly know the place.'

'Then take care of yourself.'

'Of course. I'll see you later, umm – May I ask your name?'

A grin spread across the huge face.

'Daxiong. Just Daxiong.'

Aha. Six Koreans had come away with injuries. Slowly, the story was becoming clearer.

Jericho had never been in Quyu before. He had no idea what was lying in wait for him when he drove through beneath the freeway. But in fact nothing happened. Quyu didn't begin at any clearly marked spot, at least not in this part. It simply just – began. With rows of low-built houses like the ones he had just left. Hardly any shops as such, but instead street vendors cheek by jowl, who had spread out onto their sheets and carpets anything that seemed saleable and couldn't run away. A woman in a rickety rattan chair, dozing in the shadow of a jury-rigged canopy, a basket of aubergines in front of her. A shopper took two of these, put money in her apron and went on without waking her. Old people chatting, some in pyjamas, others bare-chested. Jostling crowds on crumbling pavements. Criss-crossing the street, overhead, the flapping banners of washing hung out to dry, smocks and shirts waving their sleeves at one another whenever the wind found its way between the houses. Murmurs, chatting and shouting, melodic, booming, shrill or low, all woven together into a cacophony. Cheap pedal-bikes everywhere, clawing at the nerves, squeaking and rattling, the thud of hammers and the whine of drills, the sounds of running repairs, maintenance of the make-do-and-mend school. Some traders spotted Jericho's head of blond hair, leapt to their feet and yelled 'Looka, looka!' across the street, waving handbags, watches, sculptures; he ignored them, concentrating on not running anyone over. In Shanghai, downtown Shanghai, traffic was a state of war. Lorries hunted buses, buses chased cars which chased bikes, and all of them together had sworn death to all pedestrians. In Quyu it was less aggressive, but that made it no better. Rather than attacking one another, road users simply ignored one another. Folk who had just now been haggling over chickens or kitchen-ware would hop down into the road, or stand there in little knots, debating the weather, the price of groceries, their families' health.

With every street he went down, Jericho saw fewer traders aiming at the tourist market. The goods offered for sale became poorer. As the number of cars on the street dropped, there were more and more pedestrians and bicycles, and the throng thinned out. More and more often he saw half-demolished houses, their missing walls meagrely patched with cardboard and corrugated iron, all of them inhabited. In between, years and years of rubble. A cluster of grey and dull blue modular blocks appeared at the side of the road as though cast carelessly down like dice, arthritic trees twisted double in front of them, the randomly parked cars dating back to the days when Deng Xiaoping had proclaimed the economic miracle which had never quite taken place in this part of China.

All of a sudden it was dark around him.

The deeper Jericho went into the heart of Quyu, the less clearly structured it became. Every possible style of architecture seemed to have been thrown on the heap here. High-rise blocks abandoned halfway alternated with derelict low-rises and silos several storeys high, their hideousness emphasised by the peeling remains of several colours of paint. Jericho was most moved by the pathetic attempts to make the uninhabitable look like a habitation. There was something almost like an architectural vernacular going on here in the tangle of hand-built shacks, most little more than posts rammed into the ground and covered over with tarpaulin. At least there was life here, while the silos looked like post-atomic tombs.

In the midst of a wasteland of rubbish he stopped and looked at women and children loading whatever they thought they could use onto barrows. Whole swathes here looked as though once-intact city blocks had been pulverised by bombing raids. He tried to remember what he knew about districts like these. A number that he had noticed somewhere flitted through his mind. In 2025, there were one and a half billion people living in slums worldwide. Twenty years before it had been one billion. Every year, twenty or thirty million came to join them. A new arrival in the slums had to fight his way up bizarre hierarchies, where those on the lowest rung collected trash and made from it whatever they could sell or trade. According to Daxiong's description, he would need at least another hour to get to the Andromeda. He drove on, thought of the quarter he had wound up living in years ago, shortly before it had been torn down to make room for the development where Yoyo lived. At the time he hadn't been able to understand why the residents were so attached to their ruins. He understood that they had no choice, except that some of them could have taken up the offer of being relocated in relatively luxurious apartments outside Shanghai, with running water, baths and toilets, lifts and electricity.

'Here, we exist,' they had answered, smiling. 'Outside, we are ghosts.'

It was only later that he realised that the measure of human misery is not in the condition of the housing. Scarce drinking water, overflowing gutters, blocked drains, all these had their place in the annals of hell. But while people were living on the streets, at least they could meet. It was where they sold their wares. It was where they cooked for the labourers who never otherwise had a chance to make a meal. Food preparation alone provided a living for millions of families, and fed them in turn, a livelihood that could only be earned down at street level, just as the street provided social cohesion. People stood by their doorways, deep in conversation. Life at ground level, the openness of houses, all this spread warmth and comfort. Nobody dropped in to buy something on the tenth floor of a high-rise, and if you stepped outside the door, all you could see was a wall. The road took him to a hill. From up here, he could see in every direction, as much as he could see anything through the dirty brown blanket of smog. The COD was air-conditioned, but Jericho thought he could feel the sun on his skin. All around him was a sight he had grown used to by now. Shacks, high-rise blocks, all more or less shabby, poles standing drunkenly festooned with dangling power cables, rubble, dirt.

Should he go on?

Baffled, he told his phone to take bearings. It projected him right in the middle of no man's land. Off the maps. It was only when he zoomed out that it deigned to show him a couple of main roads that ran through Quyu, if the data was still up-to-date.

Was Yoyo really hiding in this desolation?

He entered the coordinates from where the blog post had been uploaded to Brilliant Shit. The computer showed him a spot not far from Demon Point, near the freeway.

Back the other way.

Swearing, he turned round, narrowly avoided a barrow which several kids were pushing across the road, garnered a few choice insults and then drove off fast, back where he had come from. He passed by on his left the area he had driven through at first, got lost in a tangle of streets, blundered through a garment district, spotted a through road between street stalls heaped with clothes and found himself on a wide street with walls each side and remarkably neat-looking houses behind them. It was seething with people and with vehicles of all kinds. The scene was dominated by food stalls, fast food chains, shops and booths. He passed several branches of Cyber Planet. The whole thing looked like a down-at-heel version of London's legendary Camden Town when there had still been a subculture there to speak of, thirty years ago now. Prostitutes leaned in doorways. Groups of men who were definitely not in the peace-and-love business sat around in front of cafés and wok kitchens, or walked about with appraising eyes. Jericho's COD was given many thoughtful looks.

According to the computer his destination was very close, but it seemed there was a curse on him. He kept taking wrong turns. Every attempt to get back to the main road led him deeper into this off-kilter world that was obviously ruled by the triads; this must be where the slumlords lived, the lords of decay. Twice groups of men stopped him and tried to drag him from the car, for whatever reason. At last he found a shortcut, and the quarter was suddenly behind him. The blocky silhouette of a steelworks showed in the distance. He drove over a bulldozed stretch to a gigantic rust-brown complex with chimneys. A group of bikers overtook him, went past and vanished on the other side of the walls. Jericho followed them. The road led to a large open yard, obviously some kind of gathering place. There were bikes parked everywhere, young people sitting together smoking and drinking. Music boomed across the factory yard. Pubs and clubs, brothels and sex-shops had been set up in empty workshops. The inevitable Cyber Planet took up one whole side of the yard, surrounded by stalls offering handmade appliqués. Another shop was flogging second-hand musical instruments. A two-storey brick building stood across from the Cyber Planet. A van was parked in front of the open doors, and martial-looking figures were carrying gear and electronics inside.

Jericho couldn't believe his eyes.

A huge letter A, twice as tall as a man, leapt out at him from above the doors. Underneath, in large letters, a single word:

ANDROMEDA

Tyres squealing, he stopped in front of the van, jumped out and walked back a few paces. All at once he realised what the ragged ring that replaced the crossbar on the A was supposed to be. Diane had done her best with the image that she had, but the whole picture only made sense in the original. The ring was a picture of a galaxy, and Andromeda, or rather the Andromeda nebula, was a spiral galaxy in the Andromeda constellation.

Hi all. Back in our galaxy now, have been for a few days.

Yoyo was here!

Or maybe not. Not any more. Daxiong had sent him on a wild goose chase so as to give her time to disappear. He swore, and squinted up at the sun. The smog smeared its light into a flat film that hurt his eyes. In a foul mood he locked the COD and entered the twilit world of Andromeda. There was this at least: Chen Hongbing had been afraid that his daughter might be sitting in a police cell somewhere with no official charges. Jericho could disabuse him of that worry. On the other hand, Chen hadn't even hired him for this job, at least not in so many words. He could go home. His job was done.

At least, everything *seemed* to say that he had found Yoyo's trail.

And then lost it again.

Irritating, that.

He looked around. A spacious foyer. Later in the evening, this would be where they sold tickets, drinks, cigarettes. The wall across from the cash till was hidden by a flurry of posters, flyers, newsletters and a pin-board bristling with announcements. Obviously some kind of subculture clearing house. Jericho went closer. It was mostly requests for work or for rideshares, for rooms, instruments and software. Second-hand goods of all sorts were offered for sale, some doubtless stolen, and sexual partners for hire – for a night, for longer, for particular tastes. Sometimes the offers matched what other notices sought. Most of the sheets of paper were handwritten, an uncommon sight. He went into the actual concert venue, a bare hall with high windows giving onto the court-yard. Most of the windowpanes were boarded or painted over, so that little light filtered through despite the harsh sun outside. Here and there a sheet of cardboard stood in for missing glass. The far end of the hall was taken up by a stage that could easily have accommodated two full orchestras. Speaker boxes were piled up each side. Two men on lad-ders were adjusting spotlights, others carried crates of kit past him. A steel stair ran up to a balcony along the long side wall across from the windows.

Jericho thought of Chen Hongbing and the suffering in his eyes.

He owed Tu more than just conjecture.

Two men pushed past him with a huge trunk on wheels. One of them lifted the lid and took mic stands from inside, handing them up to the stage. The other went back towards the foyer, paused, turned his head and stared at Jericho.

'Can I help?' he asked in a tone of voice that suggested he should shove off.

'Who's playing tonight?'

'The Pink Asses.'

'The Andromeda was recommended to me,' Jericho said. 'Apparently you have some of the best concerts in Shanghai.'

'Could be.'

'I don't know the Pink Asses. Worth my time?'

The man looked at him derisively. He was well-built, handsome, with regular, almost androgynous features and shoulder-length hair. The orange T-shirt above his shiny leather trousers clung to him like a second skin; it could have come from a spray-can. He wasn't wearing the usual appliqués found in this subculture, or any other jewellery.

'Depends what you like.'

'Anything that's good.'

'Mando-prog?'

'For instance.'

'You're in the wrong place then.' The man grinned. 'The music sounds just like the band's name.'

'It sounds like pink backsides?'

'It sounds like arseholes fucked bloody, you simp. Both genders. Ass Metal, never heard of it? You still want to come?'

Jericho smiled. 'We'll see.'

The other man rolled his eyes and went outside.

Jericho felt stymied for a moment. Should he perhaps have asked the guy about Yoyo? It was easy to be paranoid in a place like this. Everybody here seemed part of a shadow army whose mission was to stop folks like him asking anything about Yoyo.

'Rubbish,' he muttered. 'She's a dissident, not the Queen of Quyu.'

Tu had spoken of six activists. Six, not sixty. Yoyo's blog post had suggested that all six were members of the City Demons. Further, she had to have helping hands here in the Andromeda. It was quite certain that most people here had no idea who Yoyo was nor that she was hiding somewhere in the complex. The real problem was that the locals in a place like Quyu refused on principle to answer questions.

As he watched them putting down cables and lugging instruments up to the stage, he considered his options. Daxiong had warned Yoyo that someone was interested in the Andromeda. He must believe that Jericho was still wandering around in the Quyu hinterland with no clue where he was, out of circulation for the next few hours. Yoyo would think the same.

Time was still on his side.

He glanced all about. The stage was covered over by a kind of alcove, where two windows which used to look out over the factory floor were bricked up. Work went on around him. Nobody was paying him any attention. Unhurried, he climbed the metal steps and went along the balcony. It ended in a door, painted grey. He turned the handle. He had been expecting to find it locked, but it swung silently inwards and showed him a twilit hallway. He slipped in, went through a doorway to the right and found himself in a neon-lit room with a single window that overlooked the yard.

He was right over the stage.

Even though it was cold, barely furnished and unwelcoming, there was something indefinably lived-in about the room, typical of a place vacated just moments before. An energy that lingered on, unconscious memories stored in the molecules, objects that had been moved, recently breathed air. He went to a table with chairs around it, formica seats on rusty legs, under the table a half-full waste-paper basket. A few open shelves, mattresses on the floor, only one of them in use to judge by the tangled sheets and the pillow. Laptops on the shelves, a printer, stacks of paper, some of it printed. More stacks of comics, magazines, books. The centrepiece was a prehistoric stereo with radio and record player. There were vinyl records ranged along the wall, by the look of them survivors from the time when CDs were still rare. Right now of course CDs were a dying species as well. But you could buy records again, in today's download era, new records from new bands.

A few of them really were old, though, as Jericho found out when he squatted down to look. He flicked through the sleeves and read the names on the covers. There were examples of Chinese pop and avant-garde, such as Top Floor Circus, Shen Yin Sui Pian, SondTOY and Dead J, but also albums by Genesis, Van der Graaf Generator, King Crimson, Magma and Jethro Tull. There was scarcely a gap in the collection from the sixties and seventies, the era when prog rock was invented. In the eighties it had been fighting a losing battle against punk and New Wave, in the nineties it was on its last legs, in the first decade of the new millennium it seemed to be dead, and the genre owed its revival not to Europeans but to Chinese DJs who had begun to mix it in with dance beats around 2020. This glittering new mixture of concert rock, dance floor and Beijing Opera had been enjoying a boom ever since, with new bands sprouting daily. Popular artists such as Zhong Tong Xi, third-party, IN3 and B6 made whole new worlds of sound from the complex concept albums of the prog era, and the local superstars Mu Ma and Zuo Xiao Zu Zhou organised all-star projects with grand old men of rock such as Peter Hammill, Robert Fripp, Ian Anderson and Christian Vander, filling clubs and concert arenas.

Yoyo's music.

An omnipresent hum tickled at Jericho's eardrums. He looked up, spotted a fridge at the back of the room, went over and looked in. It was half full of groceries, mostly untouched fast food. Bottles, full or half full, water, juice, beer, a bottle of Chinese whisky. He breathed in the cold air. The fridge made a clicking sound. A breath of air stroked the back of his neck.

Jericho froze.

That click hadn't been from the fridge.

The next moment he was flying through the air, to land on one of the mattresses with a dull thud. The impact drove all the air from his lungs. Fast as lightning, he rolled to one side and raised his knees. His attacker lunged for him. Jericho slammed his feet at him. The man leapt back, grabbed an ankle and twisted him about so that he ended up on his stomach. He tried to get up, felt the other man jump on him and drove an elbow backwards in the blind hope of hitting him somewhere it would hurt.

'Take it easy,' said a voice that seemed familiar. 'Or this mattress will be the last thing you see in your life.'

Jericho wriggled. The other man pushed his face deep into the musty fabric. Suddenly he couldn't breathe. Panic galvanised him. He flailed wildly around, kicked his legs, but the man pressed him mercilessly down into the mattress.

'Do we understand one another?'

'Mmmm,' said Jericho.

'Is that a yes?'

'MMMMMM!'

His tormentor took his hand from the back of his head. The next moment, the weight was gone from his shoulders. Gasping for breath, Jericho rolled onto his back. The good-looking type he had spoken to earlier was leaning above him, and gave him a knife-blade smile.

'This isn't where the Pink Asses are playing, simp.'

'I wouldn't advise them to.'

'What are you looking for up here?'

Well, at least they were on speaking terms now. Jericho sat up and pointed at the shabby furniture.

'You know, I'm a lover of luxury. I was thinking of spending my holidays—'

'Careful, my friend. I don't want to hear anything that might make me angry.'

'Can I show you something?'

'Give it a try.'

'It's on my computer.' Jericho paused. 'That's to say, I'll have to reach into my jacket, and I'm going to produce a device. I don't want you thinking it's a weapon and doing something hasty.'

The man stared at him. Then he grinned.

'Whatever I do, I can assure you I'll have the time of my life doing it.'

Jericho called up Yoyo's image and projected it onto the wall opposite.

'Have you seen her?'

'What do you want with her?'

'I'll tell you when you've answered my question.'

'You've got some nerve, little man.'

'My name's Jericho,' Jericho said patiently. 'Owen Jericho, private detective. I'm five foot eleven, so don't call me that. And drop the mind games, I can't concentrate when someone's trying to kill me. So, do you know the girl or not?'

The man hesitated.

'What do you want from Yoyo?'

'Thank you.' Jericho switched off the projection. 'Yoyo's father, Chen Hongbing, has hired me. He's worried. Truth to tell, he's worried sick.'

'And what makes you think his daughter might be here?'

'Among other things, your friendly and forthcoming manner. Incidentally, who do I have the pleasure of addressing?'

'I ask the questions, friend.'

'All right.' Jericho raised his hands. 'Here's a suggestion. I tell the truth, and you stop the hackneyed dialogue. Can we agree on that?'

'Hmm.'

'Your name's Hmm?'

'My name's Bide. Zhao Bide.'

'Thank you. Yoyo's living here, right?'

'It would be a bit much to call it living.'

'So I see. Look, Chen Hongbing is worried. Yoyo hasn't been in touch for days, she didn't turn up for their meeting, he's a bundle of nerves. My job is to find her.'

'And do what?'

'And do nothing.' Jericho shrugged. 'Well, I'll tell her she really should call her father. Do you work here?'

'In a very loose sense.'

'Are you one of the City Demons?'

'One of—' Something like annoyance flickered in Zhao's eyes. 'No, what makes you think so?'

'It would make sense, wouldn't you say?'

'Do I look like one?'

'Not a clue.'

'That's right. You're clueless.'

'Right now I think that Yoyo's closest friends are the City Demons.'

Zhao looked at him mistrustfully.

'Check my story,' Jericho added. 'You'll find all you need to know about me on the internet. I don't mean Yoyo any harm. I'm not from the police, I'm not Secret Service, I'm nobody she needs to be afraid of.'

Zhao scratched behind his ear. He seemed at a loss. Then he grabbed Jericho by the upper arm and propelled him towards the door.

'Let's go and drink something, little Jericho. If I find out that you've been lying to me, I'll bury you here in Quyu. Alive, just so you know.'

They sat at a café in the sun across from the venue. Zhao ordered, and a girl with so many appliqués stuck onto her shaven scalp that she could have been mistaken for a cyborg brought two bottles of ice-cold beer.

They drank. For a moment, glorious silence reigned.

'It won't be easy to find Yoyo,' Zhao said eventually. He took a long swig at his bottle and belched loudly. 'It's not just her father who's lost sight of her. So have we.'

'Who's we?'

'Us. Yoyo's friends.' Zhao looked at him. 'What do you know about the girl? How much did they tell you?'

'I know that she's on the run.'

'Do you know why?'

'Why do you ask?' Jericho raised his eyebrows. 'Wondering if you can trust me?'

'I don't know.'

'And I don't know if I can trust *you*, Zhao. I only know that this isn't getting us anywhere.'

Zhao seemed to consider this.

'Your knowledge for mine,' he suggested.

'You begin.'

'Fine then. Yoyo's a dissident. She's put the Party in a fine old tizzy these last few years.'

'True.'

'As part of a group calling themselves the Guardians. Criticising the regime, calling for human rights, the odd act of cyber-terrorism. All ideas you can agree with. Until recently, she got away with it.'

'Also true.'

'Your turn.'

'On the night of 25 May, Yoyo left her flat in a hell of a hurry and fled to Quyu.' Jericho took a swig, put down his bottle and wiped his mouth. 'I can only speculate as to why, but I should imagine she saw something online that scared her.'

'All true so far.'

'She was found out. Or at least that's what she thinks. With her previous record, she must be more frightened of being exposed than of anything. She was probably expecting a visit from the police or the Secret Services that same night.'

'Quyu is her fallback position,' said Zhao. 'It's practically free of surveillance, no scanners, no police. Terra incognita.'

'Her first port of call was the City Demons workshop. It's just that it's not safe there for very long. So she came here to the Andromeda, as she has done before.'

'How did you find out that she was at the Andromeda?'

'Because she posted a message to her friends from here.'

'And you read it?'

'It brought me here.'

Zhao narrowed his eyes mistrustfully.

'How did you get hold of the message? Usually only the security services can manage something like that.'

'Take it easy, little Zhao.' Jericho smiled. 'Cryptography is part of my job. I'm a cyber-detective; most of my work has to do with industrial espionage and IP infringement.'

'And how did Yoyo's father get hold of you?'

'That's really none of your concern.' Jericho tipped cold beer down his throat. 'You said that Yoyo has disappeared again.'

'Looks like. She was supposed to be here.'

'When did she vanish?'

'Sometime today. Could be that she's just gone for a walk. Maybe we're worrying unnecessarily, but she usually says if she'll be gone for a while.'

Jericho turned the bottle between his finger and thumb once more. He wondered how to proceed. Zhao Bide had confirmed his suspicions. Yoyo had been here, but that wouldn't be enough to set Chen Hongbing's mind at ease. The man needed certainty.

'Maybe we really don't need to worry,' he said. 'The City Demons let her know I was coming. This time Yoyo disappeared because of me.'

'I understand.' Zhao pointed his bottle at Jericho's silver COD, gleaming in the sun in front of the Andromeda. 'Especially given that you travel fairly ostentatiously, by our standards. CODs don't come to Quyu often.'

'Clearly.'

'Could be that Yoyo was running from the other guy, though.'

Jericho wrinkled his brow. 'What other guy?'

Zhao swept his hand further to the right. Jericho followed the motion and saw another COD parked at the other end of the factory hall. Startled, he tried to remember whether it had already been there as he arrived. He had been distracted by the surprise of reaching the Andromeda, combined with the realisation that Daxiong had been leading him by the nose. He stood, and put his hand up to shade his eyes. As far as he could see, there was nobody in the other car.

Coincidence?

'Did somebody follow you?' asked Zhao.

Jericho shook his head.

'I blundered around half of Quyu before I got here. There was no COD behind me.'

'Are you sure?'

Jericho fell quiet. He knew all too well that a person could be followed without his knowledge. Whoever had parked that car could have already been on his tail in Xintiandi.

Zhao got up as well.

'I'll check you out, Jericho,' he said. 'But my sense for the pure and good tells me that you're clean. We're obviously both concerned for Yoyo's wellbeing, so I suggest that we team up for a while.' He got out a pen, scribbled something down on a scrap of paper and passed it to Jericho. 'My phone number. You give me yours. We'll try to find Yoyo together.'

Jericho nodded. He saved the number and handed over his card in exchange. Zhao was still an unknown quantity, but at the moment his suggestion was the best he had to go on.

'We should make a plan,' he said.

'The plan is that we commit to sharing information. As soon as one of us sees or hears something, we let the other guy know.'

Jericho hesitated. 'Do you mind if I ask you a personal question?'

'Just as long as you don't expect me to answer.'

'What's your relationship with Yoyo?'

'She's got friends here. I'm one of them.'

'I know that she has friends. What I want to know is what *your* relationship with Yoyo is. You're not a City Demon. You know that she's one of the Guardians, but that doesn't mean that you're one yourself.'

Zhao emptied his bottle and belched again.

'In Quyu, we're all in it together,' he said equably.

'Come on now, Zhao.' Jericho shook his head. 'Give me an answer or just drop the thing, but don't try this romance-of-the-slums business on me.'

Zhao looked at him.

'Do you know Yoyo in person?'

'No, just from recordings.'

'Anybody who's met her in person has two choices. He falls in love, or puts his feelings on ice. Since she doesn't want to fall in love with me, I'm working on the second option, but whatever happens, I'll never leave her in the lurch.'

Jericho nodded and asked no more questions. He glanced across to the second car again.

'I'm going to have another look round in the Andromeda,' he said.

'What for?'

'Perhaps I'll find something that might help us.'

'If you like. If you get into trouble, it wasn't me who said you could.'

He clapped Jericho on the shoulder and went across the yard to the rusty delivery van. Jericho saw him speaking to one of the roadies, gesticulating. It looked as though they were talking about where the stage lighting should go. Then the two of them heaved another wheeled trunk from the van. Jericho waited a minute and followed them inside. As he entered the main hall, the sound engineer's desk was just being set up. There was nobody on the balcony. He went up the steel steps, slipped through the grey door, pulled on a pair of disposable surgical gloves and went into Yoyo's shabby den once more. The first thing he did was put a bug under one of the floorboards. Then he quickly scanned the piles of printouts, magazines and books. Nothing there gave him any clues as to where Yoyo might be. Most of it was about music, fashion, design, hip Shanghai, politics, virtual environments and robotics. Specialist literature that Yoyo probably read to keep up with work at Tu Technologies.

He went to the table and sorted through the waste-paper basket underneath: torn packaging, scrunched up and smeared with leftovers. Jericho smoothed them out. Several were from a place called Wong's World, and bore its rather inept logo, a globe on a dish, covered with sauce and served with what was probably supposed to be vegetables. The globe even had a face, and looked visibly depressed.

Jericho took some photos and left the room.

As he went down the steel steps, Zhao looked up at him briefly and then turned back to the mixing desk. Jericho walked past him without a word and went outside. In the foyer, he spotted a poster for the Pink Asses. Unbelievable. They really did use the tagline Ass Metal, promising that their music went 'right up your arse'.

He was fairly sure that he didn't want to hear that.

As he unlocked the COD, he scanned his surroundings. The second car was still parked a little way away. Somebody had been on his tail, it would be naïve to imagine otherwise. He was probably being watched right at this moment.

A student who had promised to get some information about Yoyo, and fell to his death when his own roller-coaster ran him over. A COD that turned up right after he had arrived at the Andromeda. Yoyo's renewed disappearance. How many coincidences did you have to shrug off before dry fear began to fur your tongue? Yoyo hadn't been starting at shadows. She had every reason to hide, and there was still no knowing who was after her. The government, or its representatives the police and the Secret Services, would not shrink from murder if circumstances demanded. But what circumstances could force the Party to go this far? Yoyo might have earned the distinction of being an enemy of the State, but killing her for that wouldn't have been the style of a regime that locked dissidents up these days, rather than killing them as in Mao's times.

Or had Yoyo awoken a quite different sort of monster, one that didn't play by the rules?

It was clear that whoever was hunting her also had Jericho in their sights. Too late to drop the case. He started the COD and dialled a number. It rang three times, and then Zhao's voice spoke.

'I'm getting out of here,' Jericho said. 'In the meantime, you can make yourself useful in this new partnership of ours.'

'What should I do?' asked Zhao.

'Keep an eye on the second COD.'

'Right you are. I'll be in touch.'

Kenny Xin watched him drive away.

Fate was a fickle mistress. It had led him here, from the lofty eyrie atop the World Financial Center to the black crud that accumulated under the fingernails of the world's economic superpower. This was always happening to him. No sooner did he think he had escaped the clutches of that syphilitic whore called humankind, thought that he no longer owed her a glance, would never have to endure her stinking breath again, than she dragged him back to her filthy lair. He'd had to endure the revolting sight of her back in Africa, let her touch him until he feared he was infected all over his body, that he would dissolve into a pool of ichorous pus. Now he had ended up in Quyu, and again the hideous mask of her visage was grinning at him and he couldn't turn away. He felt dizzy, as always when overcome by this disgust. The world seemed to hang skew-whiff, so that he was amazed not to see the houses tumbling down and the people lose their footing.

He pressed finger and thumb against the bridge of his nose until he could think clearly again.

The detective had disappeared. It would have been the easiest thing in the world to bug his COD, but Xin had no doubt that Jericho had left Quyu for the time being and would return the car to the grid soon. He didn't need to follow it. Jericho couldn't get away from him. His gaze wandered over the yard, and he got rid of the disgust he felt by shedding waves of it to every side. How he hated the people in Quyu! How he had hated the underfed, chronically ill, dispirited creatures in Africa! Not that he had anything against them personally. They were anonymous, mere demographic statistics. He hated them because they were poor. Xin hated their poverty so much that it hurt him to see them alive.

High time to get out of here.

Jericho

He was just steering up the slipway onto the high-speed track when he got a call. The display stayed dark.

'The guy who's following you has left the complex,' Zhao told him.

Automatically, Jericho glanced into the mirror. Silly idea. There were only CODs up here on the tracks, all the same shape and the same colour.

'I haven't seen anyone so far,' he said. 'At least he can't have followed me directly.'

'No, he waited a while.'

'Can you describe him?'

'Chinese.'

'I see.'

'About my height. Well dressed, elegant. Somebody who pretty clearly didn't belong in Xuyu.' Zhao paused. 'Even you were less out of place.'

Jericho thought that he heard a grin in his voice. The COD accelerated.

'I went through Yoyo's waste-paper basket,' he said, without responding to Zhao's jab. 'She seems to pick up her food in a place called Wong's World. Heard of it?'

'Maybe. Fast food joint?'

'Could be. Might be a supermarket as well.'

'I'll find out. Can I reach you this evening?'

'You can reach me any time.'

'Thought so. You don't look like a guy who has someone waiting at home.'

'Hey, wait a moment!' Jericho yelped. 'What do you mean by—'

'Talk later.'

Idiot!

Jericho stared ahead into a red cloud of rage, but it soon dissipated. In its place came a feeling of impotence, vulnerability. The worst of it was that Zhao was right. He had nobody waiting for him, not for years now. The man might be a roughneck, but he was right. This, even though Jericho's type was much in demand. He was trim and blond and his eyes were light blue; he was generally taken for a Scandinavian, who were well-liked by Chinese women. He was also well aware that he hardly ever paid attention to the man who looked back at him from the mirror. His clothes were functional, but otherwise nondescript. He groomed himself just enough not to look unkempt. He shaved chin and cheeks every three days, went to the hairdressers every three months to clear the topgrowth, as he liked to say, he bought T-shirts by the dozen without wondering whether they suited him. Fundamentally, even Tu Tian, fat and bald though he was, took more pains in his artlessly messy way.

When the high-speed track spat him out again at Xintiandi, his anger had given way to a brackish sort of defeatism. He tried to visualise his new home, but found no comfort there. Xintiandi seemed further away than ever, a good-time town where he didn't belong, because it wasn't in his nature to have a good time, and others didn't have a good time with him around.

There it was again, the old stigma.

And he had thought he was over it. If there was one thing that Joanna had taught him, it was that he was no longer the kid from his schooldays, the boy who still looked about fifteen when he was eighteen years old. The boy who had never had a girlfriend because every last girl at school was after some other boy. Even that wasn't *quite* true. They had certainly appreciated having him as an understanding male friend, which he reckoned was just an underhanded way of saying a punchbag. They came to him in floods of tears, torturing him with details of their relationships, in endless therapy sessions which they always concluded by telling Jericho that they loved him like a brother, that he was, thank God, the only boy on Earth who didn't want anything from them.

Broken-hearted, he patched up their tattered souls and only ever once tried anything more, with a snub-nosed brunette who had just been dumped by her older boyfriend, a notorious love cheat. More precisely, he had invited her for a meal and tried to flirt with her a bit. It worked like a dream for two hours, although only because the girl hadn't realised what he was doing. Even when he put his hand on hers, she just thought that he was being funny. It was only then that she realised that punchbags had feelings too, and she left the restaurant without a word. Owen Jericho had to turn twenty before a Welsh pub landlord's daughter took pity, and took his virginity. She hadn't been pretty, but she had been through the same sort of hell as he had, and this, along with a few pints of lager, was enough for him.

After that it had gone a little better, or even quite well, and he had his revenge on the pathetic wet blanket who had so stubbornly claimed to be Owen Jericho. With Joanna's help he had buried that boy, although it had been a stupid idea to bury him alive, not suspecting that it would be Joanna too who would bring him back from the grave. The zombie had come back here in Shanghai, where the world was reinventing itself, and taken revenge in turn. The zombie was the boy in his eyes who frightened off the women. He scared them. He scared *himself*.

In a foul mood, he steered his car to the nearest COD point and hooked it back up to the grid. The computer calculated what he had to pay and deducted the amount as he held his phone against the interface. Jericho got out. He had to find out why Grand Cherokee had had to die. He stopped in the middle of the street and called Tu Tian. He only spoke a few words to Naomi Liu. She obviously picked up that he was in a bad mood, smiled encouragingly and put him through.

'I found the girl,' he said without preamble.

Tu raised his eyebrows. 'That was fast.' There was even something like awe in his voice. Then he noticed Jericho's sour look. 'And what's the problem? If there is just one problem.'

'She slipped through my fingers.'

'Ah.' Tu tutted. 'Well then. You'll have done your best, little Owen.'

'I don't particularly want to talk over the details on the phone. Should we fix up a meeting with Chen Hongbing, or would you like to hear about it first?'

'She is his daughter,' Tu said diplomatically.

'I know. I'll say it straight. I'd rather speak to you first.'

Tu looked reassured, as though that was what he had been hoping for. 'I think we'll do that, though it doesn't mean we won't do the other,' he said magnanimously. 'But it would certainly be wise to let me know what's on your mind. When can you be here?'

'In a quarter of an hour, if the roads aren't jammed. Something else, Tian. The fellow who fell from your roof this morning—'

'Yes, a bad business.'

'What do you know about it?'

'The circumstances of his death are somewhat curious, to say the least.' Tu's eyes gleamed. He seemed less distraught than fascinated. 'The guy went for a walk along the tracks, five hundred metres up! I ask you, is that normal behaviour for a student who was just looking to earn a few yuan on the side? What was he doing there?'

'I hear there's a video.'

'An eyewitness video, that's right. It was on the news.'

'Have they released it?'

'Yes, but you can't see very much. Just this what's-his-name, Grand Chevrolet, climbing about like a monkey up there and then trying to jump over the carriages.'

'Grand Cherokee. His name's Grand Cherokee Wang.' Jericho massaged the bridge of his nose. 'Tian, I have to ask you for a favour. In the news it said that the surveillance cameras on the top floor of the World Financial Center showed Wang with a man. Obviously they had an argument. I'd like to have a look at the footage, and—' Jericho hesitated – 'at Wang as well, if possible.'

Tu stared at him. 'I beg your pardon?'

'Well, more specifically—'

'What are you thinking here, Owen? Have you lost your wits? Should I just call up the morgue and say, hey, how are things, could you just take Mr Wang from the drawer, a friend of mine's got a thing for splatted corpses?'

'I want to see his effects, Tian. Whatever he had in his pockets. His phone for instance.'

'How am I supposed to get hold of his phone?'

'You know half of Shanghai.'

'But nobody in the morgue!' Tu snorted and shoved his shabby glasses back up; they had worked their way down the bridge of his nose as they talked. His jowls quivered. 'And as for what the surveillance tapes show, don't get your hopes up.'

'Why not? The footage must be on the system hard drive.'

'I'm not authorised to look at it though. I'm just a tenant here, not the owner. Besides, once the police get involved, that footage will be evidence. You're the one with contacts to the police.'

'In this case it might not be very wise to bother them.'

'Why not?'

'Tell you later.'

'I don't know if I can help you.'

'Yes or no?'

'Unbelievable!' Tu snapped. 'Is that any way to talk to a Chinaman? We don't do "yes or no". We Chinese hate to commit ourselves to anything, you must have learned that by now, Longnose.'

'I know, you chaps prefer an unambiguous "maybe".'

Tu tried to look outraged. Then he grinned and shook his head. 'I must be mad. All right though. I'll do whatever I can. I'm really curious to see what you find so interesting about the jumper.'

In the few minutes that the conversation had lasted, the traffic on the Yan'an Donglu nearby had increased dramatically. The Huaihai Donglu, running parallel, was also suffering from clogged arteries. This heart attack seized hold of the city centre between Huangpu and Luwan twice daily. It was delusional to take your own car, but when Jericho went back to the COD point, he was left standing watching while someone took the last free one. That was the problem with CODs. On the one hand, there were too few of them; on the other hand, every COD that wasn't up on the high-speed track was one car too many on the Shanghai streets.

Jericho's mood plummeted. When he had still lived in Pudong, it had been easier to visit Tu. He walked to Huangpi Nanlu metro station and went down into the brightly lit passages, where hundreds of people were being shoved on board the overcrowded Line 1 by stoical crowd-handlers. Hardly had the carriage doors closed than he was bitterly regretting not having walked the mile to the river bank to catch a ferry. Obviously he still had to learn a few tricks about life in his new neighbourhood. He'd never lived so centrally before. In fact, he couldn't remember ever having taken the metro at this time of day. Even less could he imagine doing it again.

The train picked up speed without any of the passengers even swaying. Almost all the men around were holding their arms up in the air so that their hands were in full view. This habit was based on the fear of being accused of groping. Where twelve people were standing shoulder-to-shoulder on every square metre, it was impossible to say whose hand it was on your crotch. There was sexual molestation every day on the most crowded trains, and often the victims didn't even have the chance to turn around. Once more and more men were also being attacked, women too had got into the habit of raising their hands. A metro trip was a silent agony, and the children suffered most of all in the fug of clothes smell, sweat and genital odour that swirled round their heads.

Jericho was wedged in place right by the doors. As a result, the pressure of the crowd shoved him out onto the platform first at the next stop. He briefly considered going to Houchezhan, where the maglev ran through, connecting Pudong Airport to the town of Suzhou in the west; it ran right past the World Financial Center and offered an invigoratingly luxurious ride, though the price of a ticket was exorbitant, which was why it mostly ran half empty. He'd be at his destination within a minute, but the problem was that getting to the maglev station would take just as long as going on with the metro to Pudong. Nothing would be gained. At the same moment, the mass of humanity pushed him onto the conveyor for Line 2, and he let them carry him on, comforted by the certain knowledge that the bloke who had snapped up the last COD from under his nose wouldn't have got a hundred metres by now.

When he crept out of the air-conditioned passages at Pudong, it felt as though he'd been slapped in the face with a hot towel. The sun hung amidst streaks of high cloud, an unfriendly, glaring dot. Slowly it clouded over. He looked over to the World Financial Center, standing off to one side behind the Jin Mao Tower. Grand Cherokee had been walking along those tracks, as though on a tightrope? Incredible! Either he'd gone mad, or circumstances had left him no choice. He logged on to the internet and loaded up the eyewitness footage on his phone. The shot was very shaky, but zoomed in crisp and clear. It showed a tiny figure up on the tracks.

'Diane,' he said.

'Hello, Owen. What can I do for you?'

'Enhance the video I have open. Get me everything you can with contrast and depth of field. Freeze every three seconds.'

'As you say, Owen.'

He walked over to the bottle-opener, crossed the shopping mall and went up to the Sky Lobby.

Tu Technologies

Tu's company took up floors 74 through 77, with the hotel above and the viewing platform and roller-coaster crowning the lot. A woman smiled warmly at Jericho and wished him good morning. Everyone knew her. Her name was Gong Qing, China's newest female superstar, who had won an Oscar last year and had other things to do with her time than checking who came and went at Tu Technologies. Tu's staff were used to it, they simply returned her greeting and went right on past, while visitors were asked their name and invited to place their palm on the actress's outstretched right hand. Jericho did this too. Briefly he felt the cool surface of Gong Qing's transparent 3D projection box. The system read his fingerprints and the lines on his hand, scanned his iris and stored his voiceprint. Gong Qing confirmed that he was already stored in the system and didn't trouble to ask his name. Instead, a friendly look of recognition flitted across her features.

'Thank you, Mr Jericho. It's a pleasure to see you again. Who would you like to see, please?'

'I have an appointment with Tu Tian,' Jericho said.

'Go up to the seventy-seventh floor. Naomi Liu is waiting for you.'

In the lift, Jericho silently paid tribute to Tu's trick of managing to get a different well-known face for the reception routine every three months. He wondered how much Tu had paid the actress, left the lift and stepped into a vast room that took up the whole floor. All four floors of Tu Technologies were modelled this way. There were no little territories of desks and offices, no empty lifeless corridors. The staff roved around a manifold workscape assisted by their luggage-like lavobots, which carried an interfaced computer in their innards along with storage space for whatever material a staffer might need for that day's work. All the staffers had their own personal lavobot, which they would pick up at reception in the morning and which followed them around from desk to workplace and docked there. There were open workspaces, closed cubicles, team spaces for brainstorming, and glassed-in soundproofed offices fitted with adjustably tinted glass. In the middle of every floor was a lounge oasis with sofas, a bar and a kitchen, harking back to the fireplaces which early man had gathered around two millennia ago.

We don't just give our staff work to do, Tu used to say. We give them a home to come to.

Naomi Liu sat at her desk flanked by a curved conical screen two metres high. The screen, like the surface of her desk, was transparent. Documents, diagrams and film clips ghosted across the surfaces, as Naomi opened or shut them with her fingertips or gave voice commands. When she spotted Jericho, she bared her pearl-white teeth in a smile.

'And? Happy with your new holowall?'

'I'm afraid not, Naomi. The holograms don't carry your scent to me.'

'You exaggerate so elegantly.'

'Not at all. My senses are rather sharper than other people's. Don't forget, I'm a detective.'

'Then of course you'll be able to tell me what perfume I'm wearing today.'

She looked at him half expectantly, half mocking. Jericho didn't even try to guess a brand name. All perfumes smelled the same to him, flowers ground to powder and dissolved in alcohol.

'The best,' he said.

'That answer gets you through to see the boss. He's in the mountains.'

The 'mountains' were a shapeless seating range in the back of the room, its elements ceaselessly adjusting with a life of their own to the bodies which climbed or sprawled over it. You could flop down, climb up or lounge about. The range was stuffed with nanobots which made sure that the range itself constantly shifted position, as did the bodies that had plumped down into it. Experts held that thought came more easily when the body changed posture more often. Practical results bore them out. Most of Tu Technologies' trailblazing ideas had been hatched in the cradling dynamic of the mountains.

Tu was enthroned right at the top, with two project managers, looking like a proud, fat kid up there. When he spotted Jericho, he broke off the conversation, slid down and got to his feet puffing and grunting, making futile attempts to smooth his rumpled trousers. Jericho watched patiently. He was sure that the trousers had already looked like that first thing in the morning.

'An iron would work wonders there,' he said.

'Why?' Tu shrugged. 'These are all right.'

'Aren't you a bit old to go climbing about like that?'

'Really?'

'You came down that slope about as elegantly as an avalanche, if you'll pardon my saying so. You might slip a disc.'

'My discs are not up for discussion. Come along.'

Tu led Jericho to one of the glassed-in offices and shut the door behind them. Then he turned a switch so that the glass tinted itself dark and the ceiling began to glow. In a few seconds, the walls were completely opaque. They took seats at the oval conference table, and Tu settled, an expectant look on his face.

'So, what have you got?'

'I don't believe that the authorities are looking for Yoyo,' Jericho said. 'At least, not the usual security organs.'

'Is she still at large?'

'I imagine so, She's gone to ground in Quyu.'

To his surprise, Tu nodded, as though he had expected nothing less.

Jericho told him everything that had happened since last time they spoke. Afterwards, Tu sat there in silence for a while.

'And what are your suspicions regarding this student who died?'

'My guts tell me he was murdered.'

'Well, hooray for your guts.'

'He lived in Yoyo's flatshare, Tian. He wanted to drum some money out of me for information which he probably didn't even have. Maybe he was playing the same game with somebody else, who was less patient with that sort of thing. Or maybe he really did know something, and was got out of the way before he could tell anybody.'

'You, for instance.'

'Me, for instance.' Jericho gnawed at his lip. 'Well, it's a theory. But it sounds plausible to me. Yoyo clears off, her flatmate makes gnomic remarks about knowing where she is, he wants money and then he falls off the roof. It rather raises the question of who helped him do that. The police? Not on your life! They would have put the kid through the wringer, not tossed him overboard. Apart from which, they would only have one reason to go after Yoyo, and that would be if they had exposed her. Has there been even a single policeman up here to see you?'

Tu shook his head.

'They'd have come here, you can bet your life on that,' Jericho said. 'Yoyo works for you. They'd have been knocking at Chen's door, and squeezing Yoyo's flatmates for information. None of that happened. She must have been stepping on somebody else's toes. Somebody less squeamish.'

Tu pursed his lips. 'Hongbing and I could put a blog entry up on this forum she posted to. We could tell her—'

'Forget it. Yoyo can do without you trying to make contact.'

'I don't understand. Why didn't she at least send Hongbing some message?'

'Because she's frightened of dragging him into it. Right at the moment, she's completely concentrated on just how much she can risk without bringing danger down upon herself *and other people*. How is she to know whether or not Chen's under surveillance, or you? So she's playing dead, and trying to get some information. She was safe in Quyu, for a while, but then she got word that I was on my way. Since then she knows that I've been there. And that someone was following me. With that, the Andromeda was done with as a hiding-place. She had to leave there as well, leaving no more sign than when she left her flat.'

'This Zhao Bide,' Tu said thoughtfully. 'What part do you think he plays in all this?'

'No idea. He was helping to set up the concert, so presumably he's something to do with the Andromeda.'

'A City Demon?'

'He says no.'

'On the other hand, he knows that Yoyo is a Guardian.'

'Yes, but I get the impression that he knew nothing about the message she posted up on Brilliant Shit. It's hard to place him. Definitely some of the Guardians are also City Demons. But not all the Demons are Guardians. Then there are people who help Yoyo without belonging to either group. Such as Zhao.'

'And you think she trusts him?'

'It looks as though he'd very much like her to. Mind you, she hasn't told him where she ran off this time.'

'She didn't tell me or Chen either.'

'Also true. That doesn't get us any further though.' Jericho looked at Tu reproachfully. 'As you well know.'

Tu returned his gaze equably.

'What are you getting at?'

'Every time Yoyo has to run, the number of people she can trust with her whereabouts becomes smaller. But there have to be some who know quite well.'

'And?'

'And with all due respect, I'm wondering whether there's anything you've been keeping from me.'

Tu steepled his fingers.

'You think I know the rest of the Guardians?'

'I think that you're trying to protect Yoyo, and yourself as well. Let's assume that strictly speaking you didn't need my help at all. Neverthe-less, you gave me this investigation to carry out so that you didn't have to take action yourself. Nobody's supposed to know that Tu Tian is unduly interested in a dissident's whereabouts. Chen Hongbing on the other hand is Yoyo's father, there's no problem if he hires a detective.'

Jericho waited to see whether Tu would say anything about that, but all he did was take his crooked glasses off his nose and start polishing them on a corner of his shirt.

'Let's also assume,' Jericho went on, 'that you know where Yoyo ske-daddles to when there's trouble. And now Chen Hongbing comes along, knowing nothing whatsoever of all this, and asks you for help. Should you tell him what his daughter gets up to online, and that you know all about it? More than that, that you approve of what she does and you know where she's hiding? He would go crazy, so you point him towards me and you also slip me the vital clue: the City Demons. By the way, Grand Cherokee Wang told me about them as well. That was how you told me where I should look. Your plan was simple enough: I find the girl, you keep a low profile, you don't need to bare all to Chen, the father is reassured as to where his daughter is, and his friend can sleep soundly.'

Tu looked up briefly and kept on polishing his glasses, not saying a word.

'For all that, what you didn't know and still don't, is who Yoyo's enemies are, and what this whole thing's about. That has unsettled you. Now that Yoyo has left the Andromeda, you're groping around in the dark just like I am. Things have got complicated. You're just as clueless and worried as Chen, and on top of that, someone's dead.'

Breathe on glasses, polish with shirt.

'Meaning that from now on, you *really* need me.' Jericho leaned for-ward. 'And this time it's for a *real* investigation.'

Breathe, polish.

'But to do that, I have to be *able* to investigate!'

With a dry snap, the arm of the glasses, patched already with sticky-tape, broke. Tu cursed under his breath, cleared his throat noisily and tried to put them back on the bridge of his nose, where they balanced like a car about to slip off the edge of a cliff.

'I could recommend you an optician, by the way,' Jericho added drily. 'But first of all you have to tell me what you've been keeping quiet so far. Otherwise I can't help you.'

Otherwise, he found himself thinking, I could fall off a roof myself soon enough.

Tu drummed on the table with the arm of his glasses.

'I knew what I was doing when I hired you. It's just that it wouldn't do you any good if I give you the names of the other five Guardians. They'll have gone to ground as well.'

'For one thing, I have a trail to follow. For another, I have an ally.'

'Zhao Bide?'

'Even if he's not a City Demon, he'll know their faces. I need names and photos.'

'Photos, that will take some time.' Tu dug around in his ear. 'You'll get the names. Anyway, you know one of them already.'

'Really?' Jericho raised his eyebrows. 'Who?'

'His nickname's Daxiong – Great Bear.'

'The man-mountain with the cannonball head?' He tried to imagine Daxiong being politically aware, armed with an intellect that could put the Party in uproar. 'I can hardly believe that. I was convinced that his bike had a higher IQ than him.'

'A lot of people think that,' Tu commented. 'A lot of people think that I'm a fat old coot who doesn't have an optician and eats canned crap. Do you really think that Yoyo got away from you because the Great Bear was that dumb? He sent you off on your tour of the underworld, and you meekly followed his directions.'

Jericho had to admit that he was right.

'Anyway, Tian, now you know why I don't want to trouble my contacts,' he said. 'The police might be somewhat surprised. By now they'll have found out that Wang was Yoyo's flatmate. They'll make inquiries and they'll find out that I'm looking for the girl. Then they'll start putting two and two together: a dead student, possibly murdered, a dissident with a record, a detective asking questions about one who's also looking for the other. They shouldn't be able to draw these conclusions; I want to be able to investigate discreetly. I might end up giving them the idea that they should pay more attention to Yoyo.'

'I understand.' Tu's fingers glided across the tabletop, and the wall across from them became a screen. 'Have a look at this, then.'

He saw the glass corridor and the door to the roller-coaster boarding platform, from the perspective of two security cameras.

'How did you get the footage so quickly?' asked Jericho, surprised.

'Your wish was my command.' Tu giggled. 'The police put an electronic lock on it, but something like that's not a problem for us. Our own surveillance network is linked in with the in-house cameras, apart from which we also hacked into some totally different systems. There would only have been trouble if they'd put a high-security block in place.'

Jericho considered this. Security blocks were commonplace. The fact that the officers in charge hadn't bothered to install one told him something about how important they considered the case to be. Another indication that the police didn't have Yoyo on their radar at all.

Two men appeared in the glass corridor. The shorter man walking in front had long hair and was fashionably dressed, with appliqués on his forehead and cheekbones. It was clearly Grand Cherokee Wang. A tall, slim man in a well-tailored suit walked behind him. There was something dandyish about his combed-back, brilliantined hair, thin moustache and tinted glasses. Jericho watched the way he turned his head about as he walked, scanning the whole corridor and resting his eyes for a fraction of a second on the security camera.

'Smart operator,' he muttered.

The two of them went to the middle of the corridor and disappeared from the corner of one camera's view. The other showed the two of them entering the glass box of the control room with its console.

'They talk for a while.' Tu switched to fast-forward. 'Nothing very much happens here.'

Jericho watched Grand Cherokee gesticulating with jerky speed, obviously showing the other man how the control unit worked. Then the two of them seemed to converse.

'Now watch this,' Tu said.

The film slowed down again to real time. The two men still stood next to one another. Grand Cherokee took a step towards the taller man, who stretched out an arm.

The next moment, the student collapsed, crashed his face into the edge of the console and fell to the ground. The other man took hold of him and pulled him back to his feet. Grand Cherokee staggered. The stranger held him tight. On a cursory examination, it must have looked as though he were holding up a friend who had had a sudden dizzy spell. A few seconds went by, then Grand Cherokee fell to his knees again. The tall man squatted down next to him and talked to him. Grand Cherokee doubled over and then lurched to his feet. A little while later the tall man left the control room, but then stopped and turned back. For the first time since he had stepped into the corridor, he turned his face to the camera.

'Stop,' said Jericho. 'Can you blow him up?'

'No problem.' Tu zoomed the torso and face until they filled the screen. Jericho squinted. The man looked like Ryuichi Sakamoto playing the Japanese occupier in Bertolucci's *The Last Emperor*.

'Does he remind you of anybody?' Tu asked.

Jericho hesitated. The resemblance to the Japanese actor–composer was striking. At the same time he had a creeping feeling that he was barking up the wrong tree. The film was ancient, and Sakamoto was well above seventy.

'Not really. Send the picture over to my computer.'

Tu let the clip play on. Grand Cherokee Wang left the control room and then recoiled from the stranger. The two of them were lost to view for a while, then the tall man came back into sight. He went into the control room and started working at the console.

'I'm wondering why the security guards didn't react to that,' Tu pronounced.

'To what?' Jericho asked.

'What do you mean, to what?' Tu stared at him. 'To what you can see here!'

'What does it look like?'

'Well, the two of them had a spat, didn't they?'

'Did they?' Jericho leaned back. 'Aside from the fact that Wang fell to the ground twice, nothing happened at all. Maybe he's doped up or drunk, or not feeling well. Our oily friend helps him back to his feet, that's all. Also, the guards have a hundred storeys to watch here, you know how it works. They don't spend their whole time staring at the screens. Anyway, is there any exterior footage?'

'Yes, but it's only put through to the Silver Dragon control room.'

'Meaning that we can't—'

'That they can't,' said Tu. 'We certainly can.'

Just at that moment the tall man left the control room, walked along the corridor and vanished into the next part of the building. Tu started another clip. The screen split up into eight smaller pictures, which taken together showed the whole course of the Silver Dragon's track. One of the cameras showed Grand Cherokee standing at the end of the last carriage and looking behind himself again and again.

Then he stepped out onto the track.

'Freeze,' Jericho called. 'I want to see his face.'

There was no doubt about it, Grand Cherokee's face was frozen in a mask of panic. Jericho felt a mixture of fascination and horror.

'Where does he want to go?'

'He's put some thought into it,' Tu said in a low voice, as though talking out loud would make the terrified man on the tracks fall off. Meanwhile, the Silver Dragon left the platform and passed from one camera view to the next. 'There are connections between the track and the building on the way round. With a little luck, he'll reach one.'

'He won't though,' said Jericho.

Tu shook his head silently. Horrified, they watched Grand Cherokee die. For a while neither said a word, until Jericho cleared his throat.

'The time stamps,' he said. 'Once you compare them there's no doubt that it was our friend who started the Silver Dragon. And something else strikes me. We only saw his face twice, and it wasn't clear either time. He knew how to keep his back to the camera as well.'

'And what conclusions do you draw from that?' Tu asked hoarsely.

Jericho looked at him.

'I'm sorry,' he said. 'But you and Chen – you'll have to get used to the idea that Yoyo has a professional killer after her.'

No, he thought, wrong. Not just Yoyo.

Me too.

Tu Technologies was one of the few companies in Shanghai with its own private fleet of skymobiles. In 2016 the World Financial Center had been retro-fitted with a hangar for skycars above the offices on the seventy-eighth floor. It had room for two dozen vehicles, half belonging to the company that owned the building, most of these being huge VTOL craft for evacuation. Since Islamist terrorists had steered two passenger jets into the twin towers of the New York World Trade Center not even a quarter-century ago, there had been growing interest in skymobiles with every passing year, leading to the development of various models. By now nearly every newly built super high rise in China had flight decks. Seven of the vehicles belonged to the Hyatt: four elegant shuttles with steerable jets, two skybikes and a gyrocopter. Tu's fleet consisted of two of the helicopter-like gyros and the Silver Surfer, a gleaming ultra-slim VTOL. Last year Jericho had had the treat of piloting it for a few hours: a reward for a job instead of him billing them. It was a wickedly expensive piece of technology. Now Tu was sitting in the pilot seat. He wanted to visit Chen Hongbing, and then had to meet some people for business in Dongtan City, a satellite city of Shanghai on Chongming Island in the Yangtze, which held the record as the world's most environmentally friendly city. Tu Technologies had developed a virtual canal for the city, which was already threaded with dozens of real canals; their glass tunnel would create the illusion of gliding along through a town in the age of the Three Kingdoms, that beloved cradle of so many stories between the Han and the Jin dynasties.

'We've become the world number-one polluters,' Tu explained

FRANK SCHÄTZING · 474

apropos of Dongtan. 'Nobody poisons the planet as chronically as China does, not even the United States of America. On the other hand, you won't find anyone else as thorough in applying alternative sustainable designs. Whatever we do, we seem to do it to the limit. That's what we understand by yin and yang these days: pushing the very boundaries.'

The huge hangar was brightly lit. The in-house VTOLs rested one next to the other like stranded whales. As Tu steered his manta-flat vehicle over to the starting strip, the glass doors at the front of the hangar slid aside. He swung the machine's four jets to horizontal and accelerated. A howling roar filled the hall, then the Silver Surfer shot out over the edge of the building and fell down towards the Huangpu. Two hundred metres above ground, Hu lifted the machine's nose and steered it over the river in a wide curve.

'I'll give Hongbing a toned-down version,' he said. 'I'll tell him that the police aren't after Yoyo, but that she might believe they are. And that she's still in Quyu.'

'*If* she's still in Quyu,' Jericho threw in.

'Whatever. What will you do next?'

'Sift the net, hoping that Yoyo might have left another message. Take a good close look at a fast food chain called Wong's World.'

'Never heard of it.'

'Probably only exists in Quyu. Yoyo's waste-paper basket was spilling over with Wong's World wrappers. Thirdly, I need information on the Guardians' current projects. Meaning the full picture,' he said with a sideways glance. 'No cosmetic alterations, no cards up your sleeve.'

Tu looked like a deflated balloon. For the first time since Jericho had known him, he looked helpless. The glasses hung uselessly on his nose.

'I'll tell you what I know,' he said penitently.

'That's good.' Jericho pointed to the bridge of his nose. 'Tell me, can you actually see anything with those things?'

Without a word, Tu opened a box in the middle of the instrument panel, took out a completely identical pair of glasses, put them on and threw the old ones behind him. Jericho spent a moment wondering whether his eyes had been playing tricks on him. Were there really a dozen more pairs stored there?

'Why do you repair your glasses with sticky-tape if you've got so many you could just throw them away?' he asked.

'Why not? That pair was all right.'

'It was a long way from – oh, never mind. As far as Hongbing is concerned, I think that sooner or later he'll have to learn the whole truth. What do you say? In the end, he's Yoyo's father. He has a right to know.'

'But not yet.' Tu flew over the Bund, brought the Silver Surfer lower and turned south. 'You have to treat Hongbing with kid gloves – be very careful what you say to him. And something else: this business with Grand Rococo's mortal remains, or whatever the guy was called – well, I reckon there's no chance of getting at his effects, but I'll think a little more about it. You're mostly interested in his phone, is that right?'

'I want to know who he telephoned ever since Yoyo disappeared.'

'Good, I'll do what I can. Where should I drop you?'

'At home.'

Tu bled off some speed and steered towards Luwan Skyport, only a few minutes from Xintiandi on foot. As far as the eye could see, the traffic was jammed solid in the streets, only the cabin cars on the COD track sped along. His fingers manipulated the holographic field with the navigation instruments, and the jets swung down to the vertical. They sank gently down as though in a lift. Jericho looked through the side window. Two city gyrocopters were parked at the edge of the strip, both painted with the markings that identified them as ambulances. Another was just taking off, lifted terrifyingly close to them and roared off towards Huangpu at full power. Jericho felt something in his hip pocket vibrate, took out his phone and saw that somebody was trying to reach him. He picked up the call.

'Hey, little Jericho.'

'Zhao Bide.' Jericho clicked his tongue. 'My new friend and confidant. What can I do for you?'

'Don't you miss Quyu?'

'Give me a reason to miss the place.'

'The crab baozi in Wong's World is excellent.'

'You found the shop, then.'

'I even knew the place. I'd just forgotten what it was called. It's in what you might call the civilised part of Xaxu. You must have driven this way when you came. It's a sort of covered street market. Great big place.'

'Good. I'll have a look at it.'

'Not so fast, Mr Detective. There are two markets. The branches are one block apart.'

'There isn't a third?'

'Just these two.'

The Silver Surfer settled to a halt. Tu shut down the engines.

'I'll be needed in the Andromeda until seven,' Zhao said. 'At least until the Pink Asses have made it onstage, which isn't always so straightforward. After that I'm free.'

Jericho considered. 'Good. Let's take up our posts. One of us watching each branch. Could be that Yoyo and her friends come by.'

'And what's that worth to me?'

'But Zhao, little Zhao!' Jericho expostulated. 'Are those the words of a worried lover?'

'They're the words of a Quyu lover, you hopeless idealist. What about it? Do you want my help or don't you?'

'How much?'

Zhao named a price. Jericho haggled him down to half that, for form's sake.

'And where shall we meet?' he asked.

He gave him directions. 'Half past seven.'

'I hope you understand that this is the most boring job in the world,' Jericho said. 'Sitting still and keeping your eyes peeled without nodding off to sleep.'

'Don't bust my balls about it.'

'I absolutely shan't. See you later.'

Tu gave him a sideways look.

'Are you sure you can trust this guy?' he asked. 'Perhaps he's talking himself up. Perhaps he just wants the money.'

'Perhaps the Pope's a pagan.' Jericho shrugged. 'I can't do much wrong with Zhao Bide. All he has to do is keep his eyes open, nothing else.'

'You know best. Stay available just in case I can find poor Grand Sheraton's phone. Somewhere between his spleen and his liver.'

Quyu

When Jericho travelled back to the forgotten world, the traffic was flowing thick as honey. Pretty brisk by Shanghai standards, then. It meant getting home on time, a hot dinner and children sleepy but still awake so that Mum and Dad could put them to bed together.

On the other hand, if you came from Europe, and were used to things moving a bit faster, every minute on the streets of Shanghai was among the more irksome experiences that life had to offer. Statisticians claimed that the average car-driver spent six months of his urban life sitting at red lights, but that was nothing compared with the amount of life wasted in Shanghai traffic jams. Since CODs had ceased to be appropriate for a visit to Quyu, because they would stand out there like frogs with wings and arouse Yoyo's suspicions, Jericho had no option but to collect his own car from the underground car park. In the afternoon he had sent Diane off in search of Zhao Bide on the net, with no result. There was no one by that name on record. Quyu didn't exist, and neither did its inhabitants.

However, there were the other five Guardians, right there as expected, in the university lists.

Yoyo herself had left no new traces after her piece on Brilliant Shit. Once again Jericho wondered who would send a professional hitman after a dissident who, while she was plainly troublesome, wasn't exactly high risk. Leaving aside the police, State elements were certainly involved. The Party was riddled with secret agents like mould in gorgonzola. No one, probably not even the highest officials, knew the full extent of their interpenetration. Against this background there was a covert operation whose goal lay in preventing the distribution of information that Yoyo should never have been able to get hold of.

Which called for more than killing the girl.

Because if her forbidden knowledge came from the net, it was very probably stored on her computer. A circumstance that didn't do much to improve Yoyo's chances of survival, but made it harder to kill her. As long as the whereabouts of the device was unclear, she couldn't simply be gunned down in the street. The killer had to get hold of the computer, and not only that, he would have to find out whom she had passed her knowledge on to. His task was that of an epidemiologist: to curb the virus, bring all the infected parties together, eliminate them and, last of all, eliminate the first carrier.

The question was where the epidemiologist was at that moment.

Jericho had expected to be pursued. That morning the killer had still been travelling in a COD. He could have swapped vehicles by now, as Jericho had done. Zhao's description of the man matched the video recordings from the World Financial Center, but Jericho doubted that the stranger would show himself to him. On the other hand, the guy didn't know that Jericho had seen his face, thought he was undiscovered and was perhaps becoming reckless. Whatever the truth of the matter, he would have to be careful not to be too successful in his search for Yoyo, and deliver her up for the slaughter.

When he was two kilometres from Quyu, Tu sent him the promised photographs. Apart from 'Daxiong' Guan Guo, they showed two girls called 'Maggie' Xiao Meiqi and Yin Ziyi, and the male Guardians Tony Sung and Jin Jia Wei. Along with the video stills that showed Grand Cherokee's killer, they formed the basis of his search. The hologoggles and scanners that he brought with him would constantly be able to draw on the data, and immediately demonstrate any agreement. Unfortunately the stills were of poor quality, and left barely any hope that the computer might recognise the killer in the crowd. But Jericho was firmly determined to pull out all the stops. With the scanners alone, he and Zhao had half a dozen reliable sleuths at their disposal, who would attack as soon as Yoyo or one of her people developed a craving for Wong's World.

He took the turning for Quyu and stopped at the edge of the road to change the colour of the car. Within seconds, magnetic fields had altered the nano-structure of the paint particles. He'd shelled out a few yuan for his Toyota to have this chameleon-like ability. As he spoke to a client on the phone, the elegant silvery blue turned into a dingy greyish-brown with matt patches. The front part looked as if it had had a rotten paint job. Dark stains defaced the driver's door and created the illusion of dents, with the paint flaking off at the edges. A jagged scratch appeared above the rear left mudguard. By the time Jericho crossed the border separating the realm of the spirits from the world of the living, his car was in a lamentable state – just right if he didn't want to attract attention in the streets of Xaxu.

Zhao had given him a description of the route to the larger of the Wong markets. When he got there, the place was still operating at peak rate. By now he saw this part of Xaxu with different eyes. The largely intact appearance and the busy activity disguised the fact that a fracture in society ran through here, beyond which anyone not in the network lived under the orders of rival triads, whose leaders controlled the turf. In the shadow of the closed-down steelworks to which the district originally owed its existence, the drug trade flourished, money was laundered, prostitution thrived, people dulled their senses in Cyber Planet with virtual wonder-drugs. On the other hand, the triads barely showed the slightest interest in the vast steppes of misery that Jericho had driven through that morning. So Quyu was most honest where it was poorest, and anyone who tried to be honest stayed poor.

Wong's World covered an area the size of a block, and presented itself as a patchwork of steaming cook-shops, piles of preserves on huge walls of shelves, stacked-up cages of clucking, hissing and whining animals, ramshackle stands and curtained-off booths where you could haggle for acid-trips, gambling debts or STDs. Jericho had no doubt that guns were flogged at Wong's as well. It was incredibly cramped in there. Scraps of words and laughter flew in raging swarms above the market, along with the hubbub of Chinese pop music from clapped-out speakers. While he was keeping an eye out for Zhao, the man himself broke away from the crowd and came strolling across the street. Jericho lowered the window and beckoned him over. Zhao wore jeans that had seen better days, and a threadbare windcheater, but he still somehow managed to look neat and tidy. His hair fell silkily as he threw his head back and drank beer from a can that pearled with condensation. He had a battered backpack hung over his shoulder. Without any great haste, he approached Jericho's car and bent down to him.

'Not really your world, is it?'

'I've been in other hells,' Jericho said, nodding towards the interior of the car. 'Come on, get in. There's something I want to show you.'

Zhao walked around the car, opened the door and slumped onto the passenger seat. For a moment his profile shone in the light of a sunbeam battling its way through the billowing brew of clouds. Jericho looked at him and wondered why someone with his looks hadn't ended up in fashion or movies long ago. Or *had* he seen Zhao in the fashion world? On television? In a magazine? Suddenly it seemed more than likely. Zhao, an ex-model, washed up and unwanted in Quyu.

The first raindrops exploded on the windscreen.

'Everything okay?' Zhao asked.

'You?'

'The guys are on-stage. Horrible car you're driving, by the way. Vario-paint?'

Jericho was surprised. 'You know your stuff.'

'A bit. Don't worry. The illusion is perfect.' Zhao bent forwards and wiped a fleck from the instrument-panel with the ball of his hand. 'Anybody would fall for it, as long as they didn't get in and see the gleaming inner life.'

'Tell me about the other market.'

'Just half the size of this one. No chickens, no chicken-heads.'

Jericho reached behind him and handed Zhao a set of hologoggles. 'Ever worn one of these?'

'Of course.' Zhao nodded at the branch of Cyber Planet. 'Everyone in there wears one of these. You know what they call those shops around here?'

'The Cyber Planets? No.'

'Mortuaries. Once you're in there you're as good as dead. I mean, you're breathing, but your existence is reduced to fundamental bodily functions. Eventually they carry you out because you've actually died. People are always dying in Cyber Planet.'

'How many times have you been in there?'

'A few.'

'You don't look that dead to me.'

Zhao looked at him from under lowered eyelids. 'I'm above any kind of addiction, little Jericho. Explain these silly glasses to me.'

'They make a biometric comparison. A hundred-and-eighty-degree panoramic scan. I've loaded photographs of Yoyo and five other Guardians onto the hard drive. If any one of the six comes within range, the goggles turn him red and send you a little beep. Loud enough to wake you up if you've drifted off under the weight of all that responsibility. The control on the left arm of the glasses also makes the outer surface reflective, if you want.' Jericho dropped the goggles in Zhao's lap and held one of the scanners up under his nose. 'I've synchronised three of these things with your specs. You can take them wherever you like, but if possible try to put them somewhere you can't actually see. Here's the focus button, that's how you activate the capture mechanism. They broadcast direct to your specs, and the scanner recordings appear at the bottom of your field of vision.'

'I'm impressed,' said Zhao, and looked as if he really was. 'And how will we communicate?'

'By mobile. Do you know where you're going to be posting yourself?'

'Opposite my branch there's a Cyber Planet. Nice big windows to look out of.'

Jericho's eye wandered to the Cyber Planet on the corner.

'Good idea,' he murmured.

'Of course. Settle yourself in, pay for twenty-four hours, it's more comfortable than sitting in a car. If you sit with the specs on your nose by the window, everyone's going to think you're shagging a hooker from Mars with four tits. There are snacks and drinks, only moderately palatable. You should really try these crab baozis, man. The food in Wong's World is good and cheap.'

'Do you have relatives in there?' Jericho asked derisively.

'No, but I do have taste buds. Would you mind driving me to my stake-out?'

Jericho started the car and had Zhao direct him to his Wong branch. On the way they passed tea-rooms and a Japanese noodle-bar, where the men were playing cards and Chinese chess, or gesticulating wildly as they talked at each other, many of them naked to the waist and with their heads close shaven.

'These gentlemen are the Xaxus,' Zhao said disparagingly. 'They divide the day up between them.'

'No ambition to saw a bit off for yourself?'

'What makes you say that?'

'What's left for someone like you after they've divided the day up among themselves?'

'It doesn't matter.' Zhao shrugged. 'I help stoned idiots onto the stage and back down again. That's a job too.'

'Don't get it.'

'What's not to get?'

'I don't understand what someone like you is doing in Quyu. You could live anywhere else.'

'You think so?' Zhao shook his head. 'No one here can live anywhere else. No one *wants* us to live anywhere else.'

'Quyu isn't a prison.'

'Quyu is a concept, Jericho. Two-thirds of humanity now lives in cities, the countryside's been depopulated. Eventually all the cities will merge into one. They're like carcinomas, sick, proliferating tissue, only the nuclei are healthy, nestling in deserts of despair. The nuclei are sanctuaries, temples of superior development. Human beings live there, real human beings. Guys like you. The rest are cattle, talking animals. Take a look around you. The people here are vegetating at the level of tree-dwellers, they pro-create, demolish the planet's resources, kill each other or die of various illnesses. They're the rejects of creation. The failed part of the experiment.'

'And you're part of it too, aren't you? Or have I misunderstood something?'

'Oh, Jericho.' Zhao smiled smugly. 'The universe has its brightly lit centres, and why? Because darkness prevails in between. Have you ever heard that we must shed light on the darkness of the universe? It's impossible. Any attempt to provide wealth for humanity as a whole is doomed to failure, it just means that everyone's worse off. The superior can't become like the inferior, it must separate itself off if it is to shine. There is no humanity, Jericho, not in the sense of a homogeneous species. There are winners and losers, the ones in the loop and the ones out of it, some on the bright side and most on the dark. The split is complete. No one wants to integrate the Xaxus of this world, break down their boundaries. Oh, and you've got to turn left here.'

Jericho said nothing. The Toyota clattered along a wide, badly paved road, lined with workshops and dirty brick houses. Where Wong's World and the branch of Cyber Planet stood face to face, it opened up into a dusty square and revealed the grounds of the steelworks behind it. The huge blast furnace loomed up above the building.

'You're a mystery to me, Zhao. Who are you really?'

'What do you think?'

'I haven't a clue.' Jericho looked at him. 'You seem to have a weakness for Yoyo, but when it comes to finding her, you let me pay you as if you were some kind of pimp. You live here and despise your own people. Somehow you don't fit with Quyu.'

'Very comforting,' Zhao sneered. 'Like telling a haemorrhoid it's doing a power of good to the arsehole it's grown in.'

'Were you born in Quyu, or did you end up here?'

'The latter.'

'Which means you can leave again.'

'Where to?'

'Hmm.' Jericho thought for a moment. 'There are possibilities. Let's see how our short-term partnership develops.'

Zhao tilted his head and raised an eyebrow.

'Did I understand you correctly? Are you offering me a job?'

'I don't take on any regular employees, but I put teams together as the job requires. You're definitely intelligent, Zhao. I was very impressed by your surprise attack in the Andromeda, you're in good physical condition. I can't exactly claim that I like you, but we don't have to walk down the aisle together. It could be that I need you from time to time.'

Zhao's eyes narrowed.

Then he smiled.

At that moment Jericho had a sudden déjà vu. He saw the familiar in the alien. It spread like a drop of dark ink in a clear liquid, quickly and in all directions, so that a moment later he couldn't have said what the impression related to. Everything around him seemed to be striving for resolution, as in a film he'd once seen, although he couldn't remember the ending. No, not a film, more of a dream, an illusion. A reflection in the water that you destroyed as you tried to capture it.

Quyu. The market. Zhao by his side.

'Everything okay?' Zhao asked again.

'Yes.' Jericho rubbed his eyes. 'We shouldn't waste any time. Let's get started.'

'Why don't you do the job with one of your teams?'

'Because the job consists in protecting a dissident whose identity no one knows, apart from a handful of initiates. The fewer people get involved with Yoyo, the better.'

'Does that mean you haven't talked about the girl to anyone but me?'

'No. I've met her flatmates.'

'And?'

'They don't give much away. Do you know them?'

'I've seen them. Yoyo says they know nothing about her double life. One of them isn't interested in her, the other's pissed off that she isn't interested in him. He's inclined to throw his weight about.'

'You mean Grand Cherokee Wang?'

'I think that's what he calls himself. Ludicrous name. Windbag. What have they told you?'

'Nothing. Wang's not in a position to tell anybody anything. He's dead.'

'Really?' Zhao frowned. 'Last time I saw him he looked very much alive. He was boasting about some kind of roller-coaster he owns.'

'He didn't own anything.' Jericho stared out across the crowded market. 'I won't try to fool you, Zhao. What we're doing here can get dangerous. For everyone involved. Yoyo seems to have crossed some people who walk over corpses. That was why Wang had to die. I thought you should know that.'

'Hmm. Okay.'

'Are you still up for it?'

Zhao let a moment pass. He suddenly looked embarrassed.

'Listen, about the money—'

'It's fine.'

'No, I don't want you to get the wrong impression. I'd help you even if there was nothing in it for me. It's just – I need the money, that's all. I mean, you saw those guys at the edge of the street, right?'

'Dividing up the day?'

'It would be easy to join in with that. Something is always coming up. Most people live by licking those guys' boots. You get me?'

'I think so.'

'And they don't do any of that for nothing, do they?'

'Listen, Zhao, you don't have to apol—'

'I'm not apologising. I'm just setting you straight on a few things.' Zhao stuffed the specs and scanner in his rucksack. 'How long do you plan to keep this stake-out going?'

'As long as necessary. I once spent three weeks outside a single front door.'

'What, and she didn't invite you in?' Zhao opened the car door. 'Well, somehow that fits.'

'What do you mean?'

Zhao shrugged. 'Has anyone ever told you you look like the loneliest man in the world? They haven't? Take care of yourself, first-born!'

A thousand answers collected on the tip of Jericho's tongue, but unfortunately not one that would have made him look as if he was in charge. He watched Zhao strolling unhurriedly across to Wong's World, then turned round and drove back to his branch, where he parked the Toyota so that the scanner below the rear-view mirror captured part of the market. Then he got out, walked around the square and decided on two houses whose positions struck him as right. Each one had plenty of possible locations for the additional scanners. He fixed one under a crumbling window ledge, another in a crack in a wall. The devices, black, gleaming, pea-sized spheres, automatically probed their surroundings, and extended tiny telescopic legs to wedge themselves into the stone.

Wong's World was covered.

A gust of wind ran through the clapped-out canyons of the triad city, tugging at awnings, clothes and nerves. By now it was unbearably sultry, the sky looked like a shroud. A few single, fat drops fell, harbingers of the deluge announced by the far-away rumble. Canopies flapped. Jericho put on his specs and stepped into the foyer of Cyber Planet.

In principle all the branches of the chain looked the same. You were welcomed by standardised machines lined up like terraced houses, with slits for cash and electronic interfaces for remote withdrawals. Two guards chatted behind a counter, never glancing at the monitors. A lot of the guests were regulars, or so it seemed. They didn't spend long at the machines, but looked into eye-scanners, waited till the armoured glass doors opened, and stepped into the area behind with the hesitant gait of the newly blind.

Inside, games consoles and transparent couches were lined up side by side, each fitted with hologoggles. There was a shelf with room for two dozen full-motion suits, rings three metres in diameter, within which you could dangle in a sensor suit, in order to enjoy complete freedom of movement. Far at the back there were lockable cabins, toilets, showers and sleeping-capsules. The rear wall of the huge space was occupied by a kind of supermarket with a bar. Floor-to-ceiling glass windows gave a view of the street and the market. Apart from the guards in the foyer, there was no staff. Everything was automated. Theoretically, you need never leave the Cyber Planet, as long as you were prepared to be satisfied with fast food and soft drinks for the rest of your life. The chain drew you in with special offers of up to a year in which you had to do nothing other than wander through the virtual world wearing a pair of goggles, whether as a passive onlooker or an active designer. You had dreams and nightmares, lived and died.

Jericho paid for twenty-four hours. About half of the couches were occupied when he entered the room, most of them along the big display window. For impenetrable reasons, most of the visitors wanted to be close to the street, even though they were completely cut off from the outside world by goggles and headphones. Jericho spotted an empty berth from which he had a view of Wong's World and the crossroads near where his car was parked, stretched out and tapped the arm of his goggles. The outside glass of the lenses turned into a mirror. He jammed the remote receiver of his phone in his ear and got ready for a long night.

Or several.

It was possible that Yoyo was miles away by now, leaving him and Zhao sitting like idiots in a nightmare delivery station.

He yawned.

All of a sudden it was as if all the light had been sucked from the streets. The storm front drew over Quyu, releasing streams of pitch-black water. Within seconds rubbish was floating down the road, people were running wildly in all directions, shoulders hunched, as if that were any protection against being completely drenched. The onslaught of a quick succession of violent thunder crashes edged closer. Jericho looked into a sky split by electricity.

A foretaste of destruction.

After an hour in which the street turned into a miniature version of the Yangtze and banked-up garbage formed a dinky little model of the Three Gorges Dam, it had passed. As quickly as it had come, the storm moved on. The murky broth drained away, leaving a vista of rubbish and drowned rats against a theatrical background of rising steam. Another hour later a glowing magenta ball had won its battle with the clouds and wasted its fire on streets that were free of tourists. Wong's World welcomed a throng of pale figures, women peeped from tents and shacks, the stale promise of the night, or positioned themselves, scantily dressed, at the crossroads.

At around eleven o'clock a young man on the couch next to Jericho groaned, pulled the goggles from his eyes, sat up and vomited a stream of watery puke between his legs. The couch's self-cleaning systems hummed immediately into action, sucked the stuff away and flooded the surface with disinfectant.

Jericho asked if he could do anything.

The boy, who could hardly have been more than sixteen, considered him with a mumbled curse and staggered to the bar. His body was emaciated, his eyes no longer focused on the presence of things. After a while he came back, chewing something, probably barely aware of what exactly it was. Jericho felt compelled to point out that he was dehydrated, and buy him a bottle of water, which the boy would presumably chuck in his face by way of thanks. If anything at all was left in his eyes, it was the smouldering aggression of those who fear the loss of their last illusions.

The scanners were silent.

Montes Alpes, The Moon

South-east of the basin that marked the start of the Vallis Alpina, a row of striking peaks stretched down to the Promontorium Agassiz, a mountainous cape on the edge of the Mare Imbrium. Overall, the formation looked more like the crusts thrown up by terrestrial subduction zones than the ring range normally found on the Moon. It was only from a great altitude that the weird reality was revealed, that the Mare Imbrium, like all maria, was itself a crater of enormous size, produced in the early days of the satellite more than three billion years ago, when its mantle had still been liquid under its hardening surface. Cataclysmic impacts had torn the young crust open. Lava had risen from the interior, flowed into the basins and created those dark basalt plains which led astronomers like Riccioli to conclude the presence of lunar seas. In reality the complete, 250-kilometre alpine chain marked the tenth part of one of those circular ramparts so colossal that giant craters in the format of a Clavius, Copernicus or Ptolemy shrank to mere pockmarks in comparison.

The mightiest of all these alpine accumulations was Mons Blanc. At a height of three and a half thousand metres, it fell short of its terrestrial counterpart, but that did not detract from its titanic nature. Not only could you see the vast expanse of the south-western Mare Imbrium from its slopes, but once you were up here you felt a bit closer to the stars, almost as if they could suddenly spot you, and greet you appropriately.

And greet you they did. In fact when Julian, in the sudden and inexplicable hope of seeing the glowing trail of a shooting star, raised his eyes to Cassiopeia, billions of indifferent eyes momentarily switched places to unite in cosmic reproach, forming a single, clearly legible word: IDIOT! Subtext: you don't get shooting stars without an atmosphere, if anything just asteroids briefly illuminated by sunlight, so please try to think precisely next time!

Julian paused. Of course the sky formed the word only very briefly, so that it was not noticed by Mimi Parker, Marc Edwards, Eva Borelius or Karla Kramp; nor by Nina Hedegaard, who was leading her little community of mountain climbers – in so far as the conquest of a few hundred metres of gently sloping terrain justified the term mountain-climbing. Resting not far away was the Callisto, which had brought them the forty kilometres from the hotel to here, just below the peak: a clumsy jet shuttle reminiscent of a vastly inflated bumblebee. Julian knew that generations of future tourists would be disappointed by the design of the moon vehicles. But there was no reason for aerodynamics in a vacuum, unless—

Unless you decided to design them aerodynamically anyway, for purely aesthetic reasons.

The thought was enticing, but Julian wasn't in a mood to be seduced. His thought processes were obstructed by shooting stars, even though he wasn't really interested in the stupid things. What had made him think of them? Had he thought of them, in fact, or had he been thinking about transient light phenomena in general? Darting through his brain, leaping from the constant particle-flow of his thoughts, expression of a more complex whole. He tracked down the image, pursued it back through the course of the day to the early hours of the morning, condensed it, forced it into certain coordinates, gave it a place in space and time: very early morning, just before leaving his suite, a glimpse, a flash—

All of a sudden he remembered.

A flash on the outside left edge of the window that took up the wall of the living room facing the gorge. Something darting from right to left, *like* a shooting star, but perhaps you just had to be very tired and sleep-deprived not to work out what it really was. And God knows, he *had* been tired! But Julian's mind was like a film archive, not a scene went missing. In retrospect he saw that the phenomenon was neither virtual in nature nor a product of his imagination, but was extremely real in origin, which meant that he actually had seen something, on the far side of the valley, level with the magnetic rail tracks, even more or less at the height of the rails, where the tracks curved northwards—

He had seen the Lunar Express.

He stopped, dumbfounded.

'—much weirder shapes than we're used to on Earth,' Nina Hedegaard was explaining, as she walked towards a basalt structure that looked like a Cubist statue. 'The reason is that there is no wind to wear away the rock, so nothing erodes. Consequently what is produced—'

He had seen the train! More of an after-image, but it couldn't have been anything else, and it had been on the way to Gaia.

To the hotel.

'Interesting, what every culture has seen in the Moon,' Eva was saying. 'Did you know that many Pacific tribes still worship this great lump of rock as a fertility god?'

'A fertility god?' Hedegaard laughed. 'The tiniest protozoon wouldn't survive up here.'

'I'd have put my money on the Sun,' said Mimi Parker. Her tone contained a certain contempt for all native cultures because their representatives hadn't come into the world as respectable Christians. 'The Sun as a giver of life, I mean.'

'In tropical regions it's hard to see it that way,' Eva replied. 'Or in the desert. The sun beats down ruthlessly upon you, twelve months without a break; it scorches harvests, dries up rivers, kills people and animals. But the Moon brings coolness and freshness. The fleeting moisture of the day condenses into dew, you can rest and sleep—'

'With each other,' Karla finished her sentence.

'Exactly. Amongst the Maoris, for example, the man only had the job of holding the woman's vagina open with his penis long enough for the moonbeams to penetrate it. It wasn't the man who got the woman pregnant, it was the Moon.'

'Take a look. The old whore.'

'My God, Karla, how churlish,' Edwards laughed. 'I think that's not incompatible with the idea of immaculate conception.'

'Oh, please!' Mimi fumed. 'Perhaps a primitive version of it.'

'Why primitive?' asked Kramp, waiting to pounce.

'Don't you think that's primitive?'

'That the Moon gets women pregnant? Yeah. As primitive as the idea that some unholy spirit is poking around on Earth and selling the result as an immaculate conception.'

'There's no comparison!'

'Why not?'

'Because – well, because there just isn't. One's a primitive superstition, the other is—'

'I just want to understand.'

'With all due respect, are you seriously doubting—?'

Hang on. *The* Lunar Express? Was that the one they'd arrived on? There was a second one, after all, parked at the Pole, which was only to be used if tourist numbers exceeded the capacity of the first. Had somebody arrived on the replacement train, at a quarter past five in the morning?

And why didn't he know anything about it?

Had Hanna seen anything?

'Plato must be behind that somewhere,' said Edwards, trying to calm things down. 'Is the curvature too big?'

'It's not that,' said Nina. 'You'd be able to make out the top edge of the crater from here, except that the flank facing us is in shadow at the moment. Black against black. But if you turn round, you can make out the Vallis Alpina to the north-east.'

'Oh, yes! Fantastic.'

'It's pretty long,' said Mimi.

'A hundred and thirty-four kilometres. Half a Grand Canyon. Come over this way a bit. Up here. Take a look.'

'Where to?'

'Follow my outstretched finger. That bright dot.'

'Hey! That couldn't possibly be—?'

'Certainly is,' cried Marc. 'Our hotel!'

'What? Where?'

'There.'

'To be perfectly honest, I can see nothing but sun and shade.'

'No, there's something there!'

A babble of words, a confusion of thoughts. It could only have been the second train. On closer reflection, hardly surprising. Lynn and Dana Lawrence were taking care of everything. The hotel was their domain. What did he know? Food, oxygen and fuel had arrived during the night. He was a guest like all the others, he could consider himself lucky that everything was working so smoothly. Be proud! Be proud of Lynn, whatever dire predictions Tim had been gloomily coming up with. Ridiculous, that boy! Did someone stressed build hotels like Gaia?

Or was Lynn another reflection on his retina, whose true nature escaped him?

Unbelievable! Now he was starting to do the same thing himself.

'Julian?'

'What?'

'I suggested that we fly back.' Nina's sweet conspiratorial smile behind her helmet could be heard in every word. 'Marc and Mimi want to get to the tennis court before dinner, and apart from that we'll have plenty of time to freshen up.'

Freshen up. Cute code-words. His right hand rose mechanically to stroke his beard, and instead rubbed against the bottom edge of his visor.

'Yes, of course. Let's go.'

'Maybe you've seen me in more spectacular settings before. And thought they were real, even though your rational mind told you it *couldn't* all be real. But then that's the illusionist's job, tricking your reason. And believe me, modern technology can produce *any* kind of illusion.'

Finn O'Keefe spread his arms as he walked slowly on.

'But illusions can't produce emotions of the kind that I'm feeling right now. Because what you're seeing here *isn't* a trick! It's by some way the most exciting place I've ever been, far more spectacular than any film.'

He stopped and turned towards the camera, with the radiant Gaia in the background.

'Before, when you wanted to fly to the Moon, you had to sit in a cinema seat. Today you can experience what I'm experiencing. You can see the Earth, set in such a wonderful starry sky, as if you were seeing all the way to the edge of the universe. I could spend hours trying to describe my feelings to you, but I,' he smiled, 'am *only* Perry Rhodan. So let me express myself in the words of Edgar Mitchell, the sixth man to set foot on the satellite, in February 1971: *Suddenly, from behind the rim of the Moon, in long, slow-motion moments of immense majesty, there emerges a sparkling blue and white jewel, a light, delicate sky-blue sphere laced with slowly swirling veils of white, rising gradually like a small pearl in a thick sea of black mystery. It takes more than a moment to fully realise this is Earth . . . home. A sight that changed me for ever.'*

'Thanks,' Lynn exclaimed. 'That was great!'

'I don't know.' Finn shook his head. The banal realisation dawned on him that shaking your head in a spacesuit doesn't communicate anything to anybody, because your helmet doesn't shake with it. Peter Black checked the result on the display of his film camera. O'Keefe's face was clearly recognisable through his closed visor. He had taken off the gold metallised UV filter, as the surroundings would otherwise have been reflected in it. In spite of his layered contact lenses he wouldn't be able to walk around in the open for very long. And it certainly wasn't a good idea to look into the Sun.

'No, it's great,' Black agreed.

'I think the quote's too long,' said Finn. 'Far too long. A real sermon – I nearly dozed off.'

'It's sacred.'

'No, it's just too long, that's all.'

'We'll cut in shots of the Earth,' said Lynn. 'But if you like we'll do an alternative shot. There's another quote from James Lovell: *People on Earth don't understand what they have. Maybe because not many of them have the opportunity to leave it and then come back.*'

'Lovell won't do,' said Black. 'He never set foot on the Moon.'

'Is that so important?' asked O'Keefe.

'Yes, and there's another reason why not. He was the commander of Apollo 13. Anybody remember? *Houston, we have a problem.* Lovell and his people nearly snuffed it.'

'Didn't Cernan say something clever?' Lynn asked. 'He was a pretty good talker.'

'Nothing comes to mind.'

'Armstrong?'

'*It's one small step for—*'

'Forget it. Aldrin?'

Black thought for a moment. 'Yeah, something short too. *He who has been to the Moon has no more goals on Earth.*'

'That sounds a bit fatalistic,' Finn complained.

'What happened to the monkeys?' Heidrun's voice joined in. O'Keefe saw her coming down the hill in front of Shepard's Green. Even faceless and armoured her elfin figure was unmistakable.

'What monkeys?' Lynn's laugh was slightly too shrill.

'Didn't you send monkeys up at some point? What did they say?'

'I think they spoke Russian,' said Black.

'What are you doing here?' O'Keefe grinned. 'Don't you fancy golf?'

'I've never fancied golf,' Heidrun announced. 'I just wanted to watch Walo falling in the dirt as he took his swing.'

'I'll tell him.'

'He knows. Didn't you boast about beating me at swimming, big-mouth? You'd have the opportunity.'

'What, now?'

Instead of answering, she waved to him and skipped away on her gazelle-like legs.

'We've got filming to do,' he called after her; it was as superfluous as his headshaking, since radio contact remained constant only while visual contact was maintained.

'Dinner's on me if you win,' she whispered, a small, white snake in his ear. 'Schnitzel and rösti.'

'Hey, Finn?' said Lynn.

'Mm-hm?'

'I think that's a wrap.' Was he wrong, or did she sound nervous? Throughout the whole shoot she'd had a tense expression on her face. 'I think the Mitchell quote is fine.'

O'Keefe saw Heidrun setting off along the other side of the gorge.

'Yes,' he said thoughtfully. 'Me too, as a matter of fact.'

Nina Hedegaard was freshening herself up, and freshening Julian up as well. He lay on his back as she guided him like a joystick. He didn't have to do much more than put his arms around her buttocks and contract his own from time to time, to establish counter-pressure – at least that was normally how things worked, but at the moment her soft, tanned, golden body weighed only nine and a half kilos, and threatened to bounce away whenever he thrust too enthusiastically. On the Moon, taking posses-sion of strategically crucial millimetres called for basic knowledge of applied mechanics: where exactly to grip, what contribution the mus-cles had to make – biceps, triceps, pectoralis major – holding the hip bones like a hinge, drawing them to him, pushing them away at a pre-cisely calculated angle, then bringing them back down . . . It was all frustratingly complicated. They managed to crack the problem at one point, but Julian didn't feel entirely comfortable. As Hedegaard slowly writhed her way towards a G-spot tornado measuring 5 on the Fujita scale, he was lost in idiotic thoughts, like the consequences of sex on the Moon if a few meddlesome beams in New Zealand had been enough to make little Maoris. Could they expect decuplets? Would Nina squat like a termite queen in the rocky seclusion of the Gaia Hotel, her abdomen monstrously swollen, popping out a human child every four seconds, or would she simply burst?

He stared at her glimmering, carefully trimmed, downy thicket and saw tiny trains driving through it, glittering reflections on spun gold, while his own Lunar Express valiantly stoked the engine. Hedegaard started moaning in Danish, usually a good sign, except that today it sounded somehow cryptic to his ears, as if he were to be sacrificed on the altar of her desire, to bring a Julian or a Juliana into the world as quickly as possible, a future Master or Miss Orley, and he started feeling uneasy. She was twenty-eight years younger than him. He hadn't asked her for ages what *she* expected from all this, not least because in the few private moments that they enjoyed together he hadn't had time to ask any questions, so quickly had they leapt out of their clothes, but eventually he would have to ask her. Above all he would have to ask *himself*. Which was much worse, because he already knew the answer, and it wasn't that of a sixty-year-old man.

He tried to hold out, then he reached his orgasm.

The climax peaked in a brief erasure of all thoughts, swept clean the convolutions of his brain and reinforced the certainty that old was still twenty years older than he was. For a moment he felt immersed in the pure, delicious moment. Nina snuggled up to him, and his suspicion immediately welled up again. As if sex were merely the pleasurable preamble to a stack of small print, a magnificent portal leading inevitably to the nursery, the most perfidious kind of ambush. He looked helplessly at the blonde shock of hair on his chest. Not that he wanted rid of her. He actually didn't want her to go. It would have been enough for her simply to turn back into the astronaut whose job it was to entertain his guests without that moist promise in her eyes that she would *never leave him*, that henceforth she would *always* be there for him, for a whole *lifetime*! He ran his pointed fingers through the down on the back of her neck, embarrassed by his own reaction.

'I ought to get back to the control room,' he murmured.

His suggestion met with harsh, muted sounds.

'Okay, in ten minutes,' he agreed. 'Shall we shower?'

In the bathroom the general luxury of the equipment continued. Tropically warm rain sprang from a generously curved shower-head, droplets so light that they floated down rather than falling. Hedegaard insisted on soaping him, and concentrated an excess of foam on a small if expanding area. His concern about her excessive demands made way for fresh arousal; the shower cabin was spacious and resplendent with all kinds of handy grips, Hedegaard pressed herself against him and he into her and – bang! – another thirty minutes had passed.

'I've really got to go now,' he said into his fluffy towel.

'Will we meet up again later?' she asked. 'After dinner?'

He had towel in his eyes, towel in his ears. He didn't hear her, or at least not loudly enough, and when he was about to ask what she'd said she was on the phone to Peter Black about something technical. He slipped quickly into jeans and T-shirt, kissed her quickly on the cheek and disappeared before she could end the call.

Seconds later he stepped into the control room and found Lynn in a hushed conversation with Dana Lawrence. Ashwini Anand was planning routes for the coming day on a three-dimensional map. Half the room was dominated by a holographic wall, whose windows showed the public areas of the hotel from the perspective of surveillance cameras. Only the suites were unobserved. In the pool, Heidrun, Finn and Miranda were having a diving competition, watched by Olympiada Rogacheva, whose husband was having a weight-lifting contest with Evelyn Chambers in the gym. The outside cameras showed Marc Edwards and Mimi Parker playing tennis, or at least Julian assumed that it was Marc and Mimi, while the golf-players on the far side of the gorge were just setting off for home.

'Everything okay with you guys?' he asked in a pointedly cheerful voice.

'Great.' Lynn smiled. Julian noticed that she looked somehow chalky, as if she were the only person in the room being illuminated by a different light source. 'How was your trip?'

'Argumentative. Mimi and Karla were discussing the copulative habits of higher beings. We need a telescope on Mons Blanc.'

'So you can spy on them?' Lawrence asked without a hint of amusement.

'Hell no, just to get a better view of the hotel. God! I thought everyone would be so awestruck up here that they'd be falling into each other's arms, and instead they're banging on about the Holy Ghost.' His eye wandered to the window that showed the station. 'Has the train left again?' he asked casually.

'Which train?'

'The Lunar Express. The LE-2, I mean, the one that came in last night. Has it set off again already?'

Dana stared at him as if he had thrown a pile of syllables at her feet and demanded that she cobble a sentence together.

'The LE-2 hasn't arrived.'

'It hasn't?'

Anand turned round and smiled. 'No, that was the LE-1, the one you arrived on yesterday.'

'I know. And where has it been? In the meantime?'

'In the meantime?'

'What are you actually talking about?' Lynn asked.

'Well, about—' Julian hesitated. The screen really did show only one train. He felt a dark premonition creeping up on him, that it was the same Lunar Express that had brought them here. Which led to the reverse conclusion that—

'A train did pull in this morning,' he insisted defiantly.

His daughter and Dana exchanged a swift glance.

'Which one?' asked Dana, as if walking on glass.

'That one there.' Julian pointed impatiently at the screen.

Silence.

'Certainly not,' Anand tried again. 'The LE-1 hasn't left the station since it got here.'

'But I've seen it.'

'Julian—' Lynn began.

'When I was looking out of the window!'

'Dad, you can't have seen it!'

If she had told him she'd temporarily lent the train to a dozen aliens, he would have been less concerned. Only a few hours ago he would have put it all down to a hallucination. Not any more.

'It's one thing after another,' he sighed. 'Today I met Carl Hanna, okay? At half past five in the corridor, and then—'

'I'm sorry, but what were you doing in the corridor at half past five?'

'Neither here nor there! Earlier, anyway—'

Hanna? Exactly, Hanna! He would have to ask Hanna. Perhaps he had seen that ominous train. After all, he had been down there before him, exactly at the same time as—

Just a moment. Hanna had come towards him from the station.

'No,' he said to himself. 'No, no.'

'No?' Lynn tilted her head on one side. 'What do you mean, no?'

Mad! Completely absurd. Why would Hanna be taking secret joy-rides on the Lunar Express?

'Is it possible that you've been dreaming?' she continued. 'Hallucinating?'

'I was wide awake.'

'Fine, you were awake. To get back to the question of what you were doing at half past five—'

'Simple insomnia! God almighty, I went for a walk.'

His eye scoured the monitor wall. Where was the Canadian? There, in the Mama Quilla Club. Slouching, sipping cocktails, on a sofa, with the Donoghues, Nairs and Locatellis.

'Maybe Julian's right,' Dana Lawrence said thoughtfully. 'Maybe we really did miss something.'

'Nonsense, Dana, no way.' Lynn shook her head. 'We both know that no train left. Ashwini knows that too.'

'Do we really know?'

'Nothing was delivered, no one went anywhere.'

'Easy to check.' Dana walked to the monitor wall and opened a menu. 'We just have to look at the recording.'

'Ridiculous! Absolutely ridiculous!' Lynn was getting tense. 'We don't need to look at a recording.'

'With the best will in the world, I can't imagine why you're so resistant to the idea,' Julian said, amazed. 'Let's take a look at it. We should have done that straight away.'

'Dad, we've got everything under control.'

'As you wish,' said Lawrence. 'As a matter of fact it's *my* job to keep everything here under control, isn't it, Lynn? That's why you employed me in the first place. I'm ultimately responsible for the security of your hotel and the wellbeing of your guests, and monorails that operate all by themselves are at odds with that.'

Lynn shrugged. Dana waited for a moment, then issued instructions with darting fingers. Another window opened, showed the interior of the station hall. The timecode said 27 May 2025, 05.00.

Should we go further back?'

'No.' Julian shook his head. 'It was between five fifteen and five thirty.'

Dana nodded and ran quickly through the recording.

Nothing happened. The LE-1 didn't leave the station, and the LE-2 didn't pull in either. God in heaven, Julian thought, Lynn's right. I'm hallucinating. He tried to catch her eye and she avoided his, visibly upset that he hadn't simply believed her.

'Hmm,' he murmured. 'Hmm, okay. Sorry.'

'Nothing to be sorry about,' Dana said seriously. 'It was entirely possible.'

'It wasn't,' Lynn snarled. When she looked at him at last, her pupils were flickering with fury. 'Are you actually sure that you didn't dream that stupid walk of yours? Maybe you weren't in the corridor at all. Maybe you were just *in bed.*'

'As I said, I'm sorry.' Taken aback, he wondered why she was so furious with him. He'd just wanted to be doubly sure. 'Let's just forget it, I made a mistake.'

Instead of answering she stepped up to the monitor wall, tapped in a series of orders and opened another set of recordings. Dana watched, arms folded, while Ashwini Anand pretended she wasn't even there. Julian recognised the underground corridor, 05.20.

'That really isn't necessary,' he hissed.

'It isn't?' Lynn raised her eyebrows. 'Why not? You wanted to be doubly sure, after all.'

She launched the sequence before he could start protesting again. After a few seconds Carl Hanna appeared and climbed on one of the moving walkways. He approached the end of the corridor, looked through the window into the station concourse and disappeared into one of the gangways that led to the train, only to reappear, seconds later, and be carried back again. Almost simultaneously, Julian stepped out of the lift.

'Congratulations,' Lynn said frostily. 'You were telling the truth.'

'Lynn—'

She brushed the ash-blonde hair off her forehead and turned to face him. Behind the fury in her eyes he thought he recognised something else. Fear, Julian thought. My God, she's frightened! Then, all of a sudden, his daughter smiled, and her smile seemed to erase her fury as completely as if she knew nothing in life but benevolence and forgiveness. With a swing of her hips she came over to him, gave him a smacking kiss on the cheek and boxed him in the ribs.

'Let me know when a UFO lands,' she grinned, and left headquarters. Julian stared after her. 'I will,' he murmured.

And suddenly the ghostly thought came to him that his daughter was an actress.

And yet!

In an act of childish perseverance he went to the Mama Quilla Club, whose dance floor was mysteriously illuminated under the eternal light show of the starry sky. Michio Funaki was mixing cocktails behind the bar. When he saw him, Warren Locatelli shot to his feet and raised his glass to him, waving his other hand wildly.

'Julian! That was the most brilliant day of any holiday I've ever had!'

'Impressive, really.' Aileen Donoghue laughed in her tinkling soprano. 'Even if we've had to learn golf all over again.'

'Golf, bullshit!' Locatelli pressed Julian to his chest and pulled him over to the seated group. 'Carl and I went charging around in those moon buggies, it was absolutely crazy! You've got to build a racetrack up here, a real fucking Le Mans de la Lune!'

'And he didn't even win,' giggled Momoka Omura. 'He almost flattened his buggy.'

'More to the point, he nearly flattened *me*,' said Rebecca Hsu, placing a single peanut between her lips. 'Warren's company is inspiring, particularly when you think about moon burials.'

'We had a wonderful day,' smiled Sushma Nair. 'Do come and join us.'

'Right away.' Julian smiled. 'Just for a little while. Carl, have you got a minute?'

'Of course.' Hanna swung his legs off his sofa.

'Just don't go missing on me,' Locatelli laughed. Recently he and Hanna had been spending a lot of time together. One chatty, the other taciturn, somehow strange, but plainly a friendship was developing there. They went to the bar, where Julian ordered the most complicated cocktail on the menu, an Alpha Centauri.

'Listen, I feel a bit silly.' He waited till Funaki was busy, and lowered his voice. 'But I've got to ask you something. When we met in the corridor this morning, you were coming from the station.'

Hanna nodded.

'And?' Julian asked.

'And what?'

'Did you take a look inside?'

'Inside the concourse? Once. Through the window.' Hanna thought. 'After that I went into one of the gangways. You remember, I was a bit dozy when it came to looking for the exits.'

'And did you – did you see anything in the concourse?'

'What are you getting at?'

'I mean, the train, was it there? Did it set off, did it pull in?'

'What, the Lunar Express? No.'

'So it was just parked there.'

'Exactly.'

'And you're a hundred per cent sure about that?'

'I didn't see anything else. So why do you feel silly?'

'Because – oh, this really isn't the place.' And he just told Hanna the whole story, simply out of a need to get rid of it.

'Maybe it was one of those flashes we all see up here,' said Hanna.

Julian knew what he was referring to. High-energy particles, protons and heavy atomic nuclei, occasionally broke through the armour of spaceships and space stations, reacted with atoms in the eye and caused brief flashes of light that were perceived on the retina, but only if you had your eyes shut. Over time you got used to it, until you barely noticed them. Behind the regolith plating of the bedroom they hardly ever occurred. But in the living room—

Funaki set the cocktail down in front of him. Julian stared at the glass without really seeing it.

'Yes, perhaps.'

'You just made a mistake,' said Hanna. 'If you want my advice, you should apolo-gise to Lynn and forget the whole thing.'

But Julian couldn't forget it. Something was wrong, something didn't fit. He *knew without question* that he had seen something, just not the train. Something more subtle was bothering him, a crucial detail that proved he wasn't fantasising. There was a second inner movie that would explain everything if he could just drag it out of his unconscious and look at it, look at it very precisely to understand what he had already seen and just hadn't understood, whether he liked the explanation or not.

He *had* to remember.

Remember!

Juneau, Alaska, USA

Loreena Keowa was irritated. On the day of the boat-trip, Palstein had agreed to let the film crew come along, and had delivered a series of powerful quotes, although without giving her that sense of familiarity that she usually developed with her interviewees. By now she knew that Palstein loved the crystalline aesthetic of numbers, with which he rationalised everything and everyone, himself included, although without losing the emotional dimension in his dealings with people. He esteemed the sound-mathematics of a composer like Johann Sebastian Bach, the fractal Minimalism of Steve Reich, and he was also fascinated by the breakdown of all structures and narrative arcs in the music of György Ligeti. He had a Steinway grand, he played well if a bit mechanically, not classics, as Loreena would have expected, but the Beatles, Burt Bacharach, Billy Joel and Elvis Costello. He owned prints by Mondrian, but also an incredibly intense original by Pollock, which looked as if its creator had screamed at the canvas in paint.

Curious to meet Palstein's wife, Loreena had finally shaken the hand of a gracious creature who commandeered her, dragged her through the Japanese garden she had designed herself for a quarter of an hour and laughed like a bell every now and again for no perceptible reason. Mrs Palstein was an architect, she learned, and had laid out most of the grounds herself. Determined to use the currency of her newly acquired training in small talk, Loreena asked her about Mies van der Rohe, receiving a mysterious smile in return. Suddenly Mrs Palstein was treating her as a co-conspirator. Van der Rohe, oh, yes! Did she want to stay to dinner? While she was considering whether or not to agree, the lady's phone rang, and she went off in a conversation about migraine, forgetting Loreena so completely that she found her own way back to the house and, because Palstein had issued no similar invitation, left without dinner.

Afterwards, in Juneau, she had admitted to herself that she liked the oil manager, his kindness, his good manners, his melancholy expression, which made her feel strangely exposed, and at the same time made him seem a little weird – and yet she still found him very alien, for reasons she couldn't quite explain. Instead of devoting herself to her report, she had plunged into research, had flown from Texas to Calgary, Alberta, dropping in unannounced on the police station there. With her Native-American face and her peculiar charm, she managed to get to the office of the police lieutenant, who promised to keep her informed about any progress in investigations. Loreena extended her antennae for under-tones, and established that there had been no progress, thanked him, took the next flight back to Juneau and, on the way, told her editorial team she wanted them to collect all available footage about what had happened in Calgary. After she landed, she called an intern to her office and told him what they had to look for.

'I realise,' she said, 'that the police have viewed and analysed all the pictures a hundred times. So let's look at them another hundred times. Or two hundred if it helps.'

On her desk she spread out a few prints showing the square in front of Imperial Oil headquarters. At the time of the shooting, the complex of buildings opposite had lain empty for months, after the open-cast mining company based there had come to a miserable end.

'The police conclude for a whole host of reasons that the shot was fired from the middle one of the three buildings, which are, incidentally, all interconnected. Probably from one of the upper storeys. The complex has entrances to the front, the sides and the back, so there are several possible ways of getting in and out again.'

'You really think we'll discover something that the cops have missed?'

'Be optimistic,' said Loreena. 'Always look on the bright side.'

'I've taken a look at the material, Loreena. Almost all the cameras were trained on the crowd and the podium. It was only after the shooting that some of them were clever enough to swing around to the complex, but you don't see anyone coming out.'

'So who says we have to concentrate on the complex? The police are doing that. I want us to concentrate on the crowd in the square.'

'You mean the guy who did it went from there into the building?'

'I mean that you're a bit of a male chauvinist. It could have been a girl, couldn't it?'

'A killer chick, huh?' giggled the intern.

'Carry on like that and you'll meet one in person. Look at every indi-vidual figure in the square. I want to know if anyone filmed the building before, during and after the attack.'

'Oh, God! This is slave labour!'

'Stop whining. Jump to it. I'll take care of Youtube, Facebook, Small-world and so on.'

After the intern had started viewing the material, she had set about compiling a list of all significant decisions that Palstein had made or advocated over the past six months. She also recorded his resistance to the interests of others. She logged on to forums and blogs, followed the internet debate about closures, acquiescence on the one hand, help-less rage on the other, along with the desire to give the oilmen a good kicking, ideally to put them up against the wall right away, but none of these entries raised a suspicion that its author was in any way con-nected with the attack. The people involved in open-cast mining were bitter about it, but glad that it was coming to an end, particularly in the Indian communities. It struck her that the Chinese had been taking a great interest in Canadian oil sand over the past two decades, and had put a lot of money into open-cast mining, which they were now losing, and that regardless of the helium-3 revolution they were still, albeit to a waning degree, dependent on oil and gas. On the other hand there was now so much cheap oil available that anything else seemed more sensible than extracting it in the most unprofitable way imaginable. When, in the early hours of the morning, she finally found no more press information and no more postings, she compiled a file about Orley Enterprises, or more precisely about Palstein's attempts to become involved with Orley Energy and Orley Space.

And suddenly she had an idea.

Dog-tired, she set about backing up her newly fledged theory with arguments. They weren't particularly new: someone was trying to undermine Palstein's involvement with Orley. Except that she suddenly realised, clear as day, that the purpose of the attack had been to keep Palstein from travelling to the Moon.

If that was so—

But why? What would Palstein have had to discuss with Julian Orley on the Moon that they couldn't have sorted out on Earth? Or did it have something to do with other people he was supposed to meet there?

She needed the list of participants.

Her eyes stung. Palstein wasn't supposed to fly to the Moon. The thought stayed with her. It continued in confused dreams, the kind you get when you fall asleep in office chairs, it produced visions in her alarmingly cracked brain, of people in spacesuits shooting at each other from designer buildings, with her caught in the middle.

'Hey, Loreena.'

'Mies is very popular on the Moon,' she mumbled.

'Meeces? Love 'em to pieces.' Someone laughed. She'd been talking nonsense. Blinking and stiff-limbed, she came to. The intern was leaning on the edge of the desk and looked as pleased as punch.

'Shit,' she murmured. 'I dozed off.'

'Yeah, you look like a slaughtered animal. All that's missing is the knife-handle sticking out of your chest. Come on, Pocahontas, get a cup of coffee down you. We've got something! I think we've *really* got something!'

28 May 2025

ENEMY CONTACT

Quyu, Shanghai, China

At around one o'clock, Jericho had had his fourth phone conversation with Zhao, who was at that instant watching a mass brawl and assured him that he was enjoying himself enormously.

Net-junkies came and went. Some made the move to the honeycomb sleeping modules. Almost the entire population of the Cyber Planet was male – women were a vanishingly small minority and most of them were pretty long in the tooth. For Jericho, the only halfway healthy-looking people were the users of the full-motion suits and the treadmills, who were forced to take a bit of exercise as they explored virtual universes. Many of them spent their time in parallel worlds like Second Life and Future Earth, or in the Evolutionarium, where they could pretend to be animals, from dinosaurs all the way down to bacteria. Some of the reclining figures moved their sensor-covered hands, drew cryptic patterns in the empty air, a clue that they were attempting to play an active part in something or other. The overwhelming majority didn't lift a finger. They had reached the terminal stage, reduced to being observers of their own extended agonies.

Strangely, the atmosphere had a cathartic effect on Jericho, in which Zhao's defamations melted away to nothing. The net zombies seemed to stir themselves, letting him know it just took an insignificant effort of will to end the status of his loneliness; they pointed at him with desiccated fingers, accused him of flirting with sadness, of having walled himself up in the past and brought about his own misery; they sent him back to life which, so far, hadn't been *nearly* as bad as he thought. He made a thousand resolutions, soap-bubbles on whose surfaces the future iridesced. In a strange way the Cyber Planet brought him comfort. Then, as if on cue, Zhao called, claiming he just wanted to know how Jericho was getting on.

He was getting on just fine, Jericho replied.

And again he waited. Even though he had plenty of experience of staring stoically at a single spot, the comings and goings in the market were starting to bore him. People ate and drank, haggled, hung around, hooked up, laughed or got into arguments. The night belonged to the gangsters, it was here that they brought the day's bounty back into the cycle of greed, albeit quite peacefully. He started to envy Zhao his punch-up, decided to rely entirely on the scanners for a while, connected the hologoggles up to his phone and logged in to Second Life. The market vanished, making way for a boulevard with bistros, shops and a cinema. Using his phone's touchscreen, Jericho guided his avatar down the street. In this world he was dark-skinned, he had long, black hair and he was called Juan Narciso Ucañan, a name he'd read years ago in some disaster novel or other. Three good-looking young women were sitting at a table in the sun, all with transparent wings and filigree antennae above their eyes.

'Hi,' he said to one of them.

She looked up and beamed at him. Jericho's avatar was a master-piece of programming, and even by the high standards of Second Life, unusually attractive.

'My name's Juan,' he said. 'I'm new here.'

'Inara,' she said. 'Inara Gold.'

'You're looking great, Inara. Do you fancy a totally awesome experience?'

The avatar that called itself Inara hesitated. That hesitation was typ-ical of the woman hiding behind it. 'I'm here with my girlfriends,' she said evasively.

'Well, I'd love to,' said one of them.

'Me too,' laughed the other one.

'Okay, let's the four of us all do something.' Jericho Juan put on a wide smile. 'But first I need to discuss something with the most beau-tiful one. Inara.'

'Why me?'

'Because I've got a surprise for you.' He pointed to an empty chair. 'Can I sit down here?'

She nodded. Her big, golden eyes looked at him steadily. He leaned forward and lowered his voice.

'Could we be undisturbed for a moment, beautiful Inara? Just the two of us?'

'It's not up to me, sweetie.'

'We're just going anyway,' one of the girlfriends said and got to her feet. The other sent a snake-tongue darting from between her teeth, fished an insect out of the air, swallowed it and gave an offended hiss. They both spread their wings and disappeared behind a puff of pink clouds. Inara struck a pose and stretched her ribcage. The fabric of the tight top she was wearing started to become transparent.

'I love surprises,' she purred.

'And this is one – Emma.'

Emma Deng was so surprised that she momentarily lost control of her clothes. Her top disappeared completely, revealing perfectly formed breasts. A moment later her torso turned black.

'Don't go, Emma,' Jericho said quickly. 'It would be a mistake.'

'Who are you?' hissed the woman who called herself Inara.

'That doesn't matter.' His avatar crossed his legs. 'You've embezzled two million yuan and passed on company secrets to Microsoft. You can't cope with more problems than that all at once.'

'How – how did you find me?'

'It wasn't hard. Your preferences, your semantics—'

'My what?'

'Forget it. My speciality is hunting down people on the net, that's all. You've been transmitting for so long now that it was easy to locate you.'

Not true, but Jericho knew that Emma Deng didn't have the knowledge to see through his lie. A refined little girl, who had used the fact of her intimate relationship with the senior partner in the company she worked for in order to cheat it for years on end.

'If I want,' Jericho went on, 'the cops will be at your door in ten minutes. You can run away, but they'll find you just like I did. We'll get you sooner or later, so I advise you to listen.'

The woman froze. Outwardly she had as little in common with the real Emma Deng as Owen Jericho had with Juan Narciso Ucañan. If you examined her psychological profile, it was very likely that Emma would opt for a body like Inara Gold's, almost one hundred per cent. Jericho was definitely pleased with himself.

'I'm listening,' she muttered.

'Okay, the honourable Li Shiling is willing to forgive you. That's the information that I'm supposed to pass on to you.'

Emma laughed loudly.

'You're taking the piss.'

'Not at all.'

'Christ, I might be stupid, but I'm not as stupid as that. Shiling wants me to rot in hell.'

'That's not unthinkable.'

'Great.'

'On the other hand Mr Li seems to be missing the delights of your company. Particularly in the genital region, he's been finding life a little dull since you left.'

Inara Gold's beautiful face reflected unconcealed hatred. Jericho assumed that Emma was sitting in front of a full-body scanner that transferred her gestures and facial expressions to her avatar in real time.

'What else did the old fucker have to say for himself?' she hissed.

'You don't want to hear.'

'I do. I want to know what I'm letting myself in for.'

'A refreshing dip in the Huangpu, with your feet encased in lead? I mean, he's furious! Your second-best option is that he'll hand you over to the authorities. But according to his own personal testimony what he'd really like is for you to go on giving him blowjobs.'

'Shiling's disgusting.'

'It doesn't seem to have been that bad.'

'He forced me!'

'To do what? Relieve him of two million? Flog building plans to the competition? Come on to him, to win his trust?'

Emma looked askance. 'And what does he want?'

'Nothing special. He wants you to marry him.'

'Shit.'

'Could be,' Jericho said casually. 'The Huangpu's shit too. The quality of the water has declined dramatically. Mr Li is waiting for your call at the number you know, and he wants to hear a loud, audibly articulated *Yes*. What do you think, could you do that? What shall I tell him?'

'Shit. Shit!'

'That's not what he wants to hear.'

By now Diane had passed on Emma's location via the relevant server. She was in her apartment in Hong Kong. Far away, but not far enough. Nowhere would be far enough, unless she left the solar system.

'He might buy you an apartment in Hong Kong,' he added in a conciliatory tone.

Emma gave up.

'Okay,' she squeaked.

'Mr Li is always available to speak to. I'd like to get a cheerful call from him in an hour at the most, otherwise I'll consider myself forced to blow your cover.' Jericho paused. 'Don't take it personally, Emma. This is how I make my living.'

'Yes,' she whispered. 'We're all whores.'

'You said it.'

He logged out of Second Life. The viewing window of the specs brightened. At the market, the last punters were on their feet. Most of the stands had closed. Jericho keyed in the time.

Four in the morning.

'Diane,' he said into his phone.

'Hi, Owen. You're still awake?'

Jericho smiled. Sympathy from a computer had something going for it if it spoke with Diane's voice. He looked around. Most of the couches were abandoned. Cleaning systems were operating here and there. Even junkies had a vague sense of the time.

'Wake me at seven, Diane.'

'Sure, Owen. Oh, Owen?'

'Yes?'

'I'm just receiving a message for you.'

'Can you read it out?'

'Zhao Bide writes: *Don't want to wake you in case you've dozed off under the burden of responsibility. Pleasant dreams. When it's all over, let's go and raise a glass.*'

Jericho smiled.

'Write back and tell him – no, don't write anything. I'm going to hit the hay.'

'Can I do anything else for you?'

'No thanks, Diane.'

'See you later, Owen. Sleep well.'

See you later, Owen.

Later, Owen.

Owen—

Later and later and later, and she doesn't come back. He lies on his bed and waits. On the bed in the dingy room that he hopes so ardently to be able to leave with her.

But Joanna doesn't come back.

Instead, fat caterpillar-like creatures start creeping up the bed-covers – claws clutching the cotton fibres – the click of segmented legs – alarm-bells – groping feelers brushing the soles of his feet – alarm – alarm—

Wake up, Owen!

Wake up!

'Owen?'

He started awake, his body one big heartbeat.

'Owen?'

The early daylight stung his eyes.

'What time?' he murmured.

'It's only twenty-five past six,' said Diane. 'Sorry if I woke you prematurely. I have a Priority A call for you.'

Yoyo. the idea darted through his head.

No, the scanners were working independently of Diane, they could have woken him with an unnerving noise that was impossible to ignore. And he would have seen red. But among the people who were slowly repopulating the market, there wasn't a single Guardian to be seen.

'Put them through,' he said bluntly.

'What's up? Are you still asleep?'

Tu's square head grinned at him. Behind him, the Serengeti was springing to life. Or something like it: at any rate giraffes and elephants were walking around the landscape. A glowing orange sky hung over pastel-coloured mountains. Jericho pulled himself up. Individual snores rang out through Cyber Planet. Only a young woman sat cross-legged on her stool, with a coffee in her right hand. Plainly not a junkie. Jericho assumed she'd just popped in to see the breakfast news.

'I'm in Quyu,' he said, suppressing a yawn.

'I just thought. Because of your receptionist. A pretty voice, but normally you pick up yourself.'

'Diane is—'

'You call your computer Diane?' Tu asked, interested.

'I'm short-staffed, Tian. You've got Naomi. There was a TV series a long time ago where an FBI agent was always conferring with his secretary, although you never got to see her in person—'

'And her name was Diane?'

'Mm-hm.'

'Nice,' said Tu. 'What's wrong with a real secretary?'

'And where would she stay?'

'If she was pretty, your bed. You've made it now, son. You live in a loft in Xintiandi. It's time for you to arrive in your new life.'

'Thanks. I'm there.'

'You're dealing with people who don't quite get long-term incomers.'

'Anything else, Reverend?' Jericho swung himself off his couch, walked to the bar and chose a cappuccino. 'Don't you want to know how our search is going?'

'You haven't got anything.'

'How do you work that out?'

'If you had anything, you'd have been rubbing my nose in it for ages.'

'Your call is Priority A. Why's that?'

'So that I can boast about being your best member of staff.' Tu giggled. 'You wanted to know who what's-his-name Wang phoned before he died.'

The coffee gurgled into the cardboard cup.

'You mean—?'

'Yes, I do. I'll send you over his telephone traffic. All the conversations he's had since 26 May. You can fall at my feet if you like.'

'How did you manage that?'

'Certainly not by rummaging through his remains. As luck would have it, I play golf with the CEOs of two service providers. The guy was registered with one of them. My acquaintance was kind enough to pass the data on to me, no questions asked.'

'Christ, Tian!' Jericho blew on his coffee. 'Now you owe him all the favours in the world, right?'

'Not at all,' Tu said in a bored voice. 'He owes *me* something.'

'Good. Very good.'

'Where do we go from here?'

'Diane is constantly checking the net for suspicious texts, Zhao and I are keeping an eye on the markets. If no one appears in the course of the next few hours, I'll have to consider extending the circle of investigators and showing photographs around. I'd rather avoid that if we can.' Jericho paused. 'How did your conversation with Chen Hongbing go?'

'So-so. He's worried.'

'Isn't he at least reassured that she's at liberty?'

'Hongbing has turned worrying into an art form. But he trusts you.'

Behind Tu, a big bird of prey flapped into the air. A giraffe came quite close.

'Tell me, where are you?'

'Where do you think?' Tu grinned. 'In my office, of course.'

'And where are you pretending to be?'

'In South Africa. Pretty, isn't it? It's from the autumn collection. We're offering twelve environments. The software places your image in the background as soon as you make your call, and adapts you to the environment. Have you noticed that the sun's shining on my bald head?'

'And the other environments?'

'The Moon's really brilliant!' Tu beamed. 'In the background the American moon base and spaceships landing. The program gives you a spacesuit. One can see your face through the visor of the helmet. Your voice is a bit distorted, like in the moon landings last century.'

'One giant step for mankind,' Jericho teased.

'Let me know if anything new comes up.'

'Will do.'

Jericho took a sip of his coffee. Thin and bitter. He urgently needed fresh air. As he crossed the foyer, Diane told him she had received a data packet from Tu, and passed it on to him. He stepped out into the street, with his eye on the display. Numbers, days and times became visible. Wang's phone traffic. Diane compared the relevant data with information they had already. Of course Jericho didn't expect any matches.

But she told him there was one.

He frowned. The evening before his death, Grand Cherokee Wang had dialled a number that also appeared among Jericho's contacts. Diane had correlated names and numbers, so that there was no doubt about who the student had phoned on the afternoon of 26 May.

Jericho stared at the name.

Suddenly he realised that he'd made a terrible mistake.

Steelworks

He had gone for direct confrontation, which temporarily forced him out of his location. After setting up another scanner near the front door of Cyber Planet, Jericho set off. If the scouts caught one of their target people, he could be back within a few minutes.

The streets were still empty, which meant that he made good headway.

He parked the Toyota behind a soot-black building, straightened his hologoggles and approached Wong's World on foot. The glass façade of this Cyber Planet showed that the market was on the way up. This branch of Wong was decidedly less run down than the other one. As Zhao had described it, it lacked the booths for prostitutes and people running gambling games; everything seemed to be entirely devoted to the preparation of food and the sale of groceries. Vegetables, herbs and spices were displayed in baskets and containers. For one customer, a woman reached into a basket with a grabber and pulled out a snake that went into violent convulsions when the saleswoman routinely cut open its body and pulled off the skin. Jericho turned away and inhaled the smell of fresh wontons and baozis. The stand was busy. Two young men with damply glistening torsos, swathed in the steam that rose from huge pots, swung their ladles, passed bowls of broth and crunchy crab and pork dumplings over the counter. Jericho walked on, ignoring the protests of his stomach. He could eat later. He crossed the street, stepped into Cyber Planet and glanced around. There was no sign of Zhao. There were no sleeping pods, but he might have gone to the toilet. Jericho waited for ten minutes, but Zhao didn't appear.

He stepped outside again.

And suddenly he saw them.

There were two of them. They were both strolling towards the wonton stall and inadvertently looked in his direction as they did so. Their outlines glowed red on the glass of the hologoggles. The boy was wearing jeans and a T-shirt, the girl a mini-skirt for which she was a stone too heavy and a biker's jacket with a massive City Demons logo. They were laden down with Wong's World paper bags. They asked the sweaty wonton cooks to put generous portions of soup in sealable plastic bowls, which they received, chatting and laughing, and put in the bags. Both looked carefree and generally cheerful. They talked to other customers for a while and walked on.

They bought enough breakfast to feed a whole gang.

Jericho followed them while the computer supplied him with details taken from Tu's database: the girl's name was Xiao Meiqi, known as

Maggie, a computer science student. The boy was called Jin Jia Wei, on an electronic technology course. According to Tu, they were part of Yoyo's inner circle. With Daxiong, that meant that Jericho now knew by sight four of the six dissidents. And those two certainly weren't going to be demolishing the contents of those bags all by themselves.

He pushed his way towards them, while at the same time keeping an eye out for Zhao. Maggie Xiao and Jin Jia Wei had their Thermos flasks filled with tea, they bought cigarettes and little cakes with a paste of nuts, honey and red beans that Yoyo loved – so Jericho recalled – then they crossed the street. As soon as he saw their parked e-bikes on the other side, he knew there was no point going on following them on foot. He turned back to his Toyota, started it up and steered it between passers-by and cyclists. The street was too wide for washing-lines, there was nothing to obstruct his view, so he could see the looming silhouette of the blast furnace a few kilometres away. Jin and Maggie dashed towards it on their bikes. Seconds later Jericho too had left the commotion of the market behind him, and now saw a dusty patch of waste ground, with the old steelworks stretching beyond. The bikes raised clouds of dust. He avoided following the two of them in a straight line, instead driving the Toyota into the shadow of a row of low Portakabins.

Yoyo was hiding somewhere in those industrial ruins, he was sure of it.

He watched apprehensively as the bikes headed towards the blast furnace which, standing out against the light of dawn, looked like a launch pad for spaceships, as Jules Verne might have imagined it: a barrel-shaped cylinder, tapering towards the top, a good fifty metres high, encased in a steel girder construction that still gave an idea of the smelter. Levels of scaffolding, bridges and walkable platforms, connected by beams and stairways, overflowing with pumps, generators, floodlights, wiring and other equipment. A conveyor belt ran steeply up from the ground to the filling inlet of the furnace. Above it, a massive pipe stretched into the sky, bent abruptly and ended up in a kind of oversized cooking pot with three huge, upright tanks. Everything in this world seemed to have grown and tangled together. Everything that might have served the exchange of gases and fluids, cables, pipelines and tubes, created the impression of hopelessly tangled intestines, as if the innards of a colossal machine had turned inside out.

Right in front of the furnace a tower of girders grew from the ground, about half as high. As if put there by magic, a little house with a gabled roof and windows stood at the top of it, connected to the furnace construction by a platform. Clearly it had once served as a control room. Unlike the other buildings around it, its windows were intact. Jin and Maggie guided their bikes into an adjoining low-rise building, and a few moments later, swinging their Wong bags, reappeared and began climbing the zigzag stairways of the tower. Jericho slowed his pace, stopped and looked up at the former control room.

Was Yoyo up there?

At that moment he saw something approaching from the market and coming to a standstill on the vacant lot. He turned his head and saw a man sitting on a motorbike. No, not a motorbike. It looked more as though a running machine, a narwhal and a jet engine had been combined into something whose purpose wasn't immediately apparent. Stocky, with a wide saddle, closed side panels and a flattened windscreen, and a gaping hole where its front wheel should have been. Silvery spokes flashed inside it, plainly a turbine. Pivoting jets emerged along the handlebars and the pillion. Apparently the thing slid along on its smooth belly and two tapering fins that pointed to the rear. It was only on closer inspection that you noticed that a nosewheel grew from the belly, and the fins ended in enclosed spheres, which gave it a certain roadworthiness in spite of its flat bottom. But the actual purpose of the machine was quite different. Years ago, when the first models were ready for production, Jericho had applied for a permit, before baulking at the extortionate purchase price. Those things were expensive. Too expensive for Owen Jericho.

Far too expensive for someone from Quyu.

So what was Zhao doing sitting on that thing?

Zhao Bide, who was staring over at the blast furnace, watching Jin and Maggie climb the steps, without noticing Jericho in the shade of the building. Who hadn't called in, in spite of everything they'd agreed, even though he was hot on the heels of two Guardians who would in all likelihood lead him to Yoyo. Whose number Grand Cherokee Wang had dialled the evening before he died, to talk to him for one minute, as Tu's data revealed.

Wang had called Zhao.

Why?

Uneasy and electrified, Jericho was heading across to confront Zhao, who was leaning over right at that moment and wiping something from the dashboard – just as he had polished the display in Jericho's car.

It all fitted.

Cherokee Wang's murderer, just before he fled from the World Financial Center: in an elegant made-to-measure suit, with tinted glasses, a false moustache and wig, which temporarily transformed his even features into the face of Ryuichi Sakamoto, he leaned forward and wiped the controls of the Silver Dragon. But Jericho hadn't been looking carefully enough, because suddenly he reminds him not of a Japanese pop star or a model, but all the time of—

Zhao Bide.

He's the one who's set the hitman on Yoyo's trail.

Just as he puts his foot down on the accelerator, Zhao starts his airbike. A sound of turbines sweeps across the square. The machine swivels its jets into the upright position, balances for a moment on the tips of its fins and shoots steeply upwards, and Jericho realises that there is now hardly a chance of saving Yoyo.

How ridiculously easy everything had been.

And at the same time how excruciating.

Although he had barely been able to conquer his dread over the past few hours when fate had decreed that he go to Quyu, once more having the proof before his eyes that the superiority of the human race was the fevered hallucination of religiously infected Darwinists, a tragic error that called for correction. Sheer revulsion had driven him to speak to Jericho about the failure of creation, the unsuccessful part of the experiment – rashness! What Zhao had by the skin of his teeth managed to turn into sarcasm, now reflected Kenny Xin's genuine outrage. The bulk of his species was a seething parasitic mass, a scandal for any creator, if there had ever been one. Only a few people who felt similarly had taken their insight to its conclusion, like that Roman who had burned his city down, even if he was said to have ruined the moment by singing. But Xin wished he could have seen the purifying fire in which the face of poverty blistered and charred; or even more than that:

He wished he could *be* the fire!

Objectively speaking, an eyesore like Quyu deserved to be reduced to ashes. Worldwide, one and a half billion people lived in slums. One and a half billion upon whom life had been squandered, who breathed in precious air and used up valuable resources, without producing anything but more poverty, still more hunger, still more progeny. One and a half billion who were suffocating the world. Still, Quyu would be a start.

But Xin had learned to rein in his feelings. To declare his independence of the dictates of the emotions. He had furiously set about re-creating, immunising and cleansing himself. So deeply that he would never again be forced to rub his skin off to rid himself of the dirt, the wire-pulling circumstances of his birth, the damp and sticky leavings of daily assaults, the scabs of despair. He had known that he would inevitably perish if he didn't succeed in cleansing himself, and that his own death, the piss-stench of capitulation, would not bring redemption.

So he had acted.

Sometimes, at night, he experienced the day again, over and over. The tribunal of flames. He felt the heat on his cheeks, witnessed the burial of his own sticky corpse, felt the faint amazement of his wonderful, reborn body, his wild joy at the tremendous power that he would now have at his disposal. He was free. Free to do what he felt like. Free to slip into any skin he wished to, such as Zhao Bide's.

How ridiculously simple it had been to latch on to Jericho, to take the man into his service. Grand Cherokee Wang might have been an idiot, but Xin owed him mute thanks for his detective card. Jericho had taken him to Quyu, to the Andromeda, where Xin had decided to take the game to its extreme. No wig this time, no false noses and beards, just appropriate clothing, based on the standard outfit that he carried with him at all times. Perhaps he hadn't looked scruffy enough, he didn't wear appliqués of any kind, but the roadies hadn't minded, they'd just been grateful for someone to help them with the bulky Portakabins, and within a few minutes they'd given him all the information he needed in order to trick Jericho: Ass Metal. The Pink Asses. What could the detective have done but take Xin for one of them?

Jericho had been the mouse, he was the cat. He had come up with his own makeshift plan. Assault, ceasefire, two beers, a pact. Provided by Hydra with sufficient knowledge about the girl to impress the detective. There were some answers he hadn't been able to give. Jericho's question, for example, about whether he was a City Demon had been a complete curve-ball. He had known nothing about any organisation by that name. There was so much he hadn't known that the unsuspecting detective had kindly told him, like where Yoyo and her Guardians liked to go shopping. It had taken him a quarter of an hour to find out the location of the Wong markets. Zhao Bide was a loyal partner, he made every effort to help, which also involved alerting Jericho's attention to his pursuer – Zhao himself.

He had spent the afternoon in the Hyatt, where he had had a long and thorough shower to get rid of the stench of Xaxu at least for a few hours. There had been a message to the effect that the experts had arrived, and that three airbikes were ready, just as he had demanded. He had sent the two men on ahead, and had followed them at a leisurely pace, back into the dirt where he was to meet Jericho.

Owen Jericho and he had been a good team.

Meanwhile, since the scanners had revealed the reappearance of Maggie Xiao Meiqi and Jin Jia Wei, it was time to give up that partnership. Jericho might waste away in Cyber Planet. The airbike rose into the air until Kenny could see the steelworks in all its massive dereliction. Only a few scattered people were in evidence, homeless people and gangs who had found refuge in the factory halls. A little group of bikers crossed the savannahs of the slag-fields, came closer. Meanwhile Xiao Meiqi and Jin Jia Wei had worked their way up the system of steps and climbed the platform on which the former control room of the blast furnace rested. The girl disappeared inside, while Jia Wei turned round and looked out onto the square.

His gaze wandered to the sky.

Kenny spoke into the microphone, issued instructions. Then he swivelled the jets of the airbike to horizontal.

Jin Jia Wei had a reputation for being lazy and truculent, and showed little interest in his studies. On the other hand he was a gifted hacker. No more and no less. He didn't share Yoyo's lofty plans but neither did he challenge them, because they actually didn't interest him. She wanted to improve the world? Fine. More fun, at any rate, than mouldering away in lecture halls, and anyway Jia Wei was head over heels in love with her, as was everybody, in fact. As ideologist in chief, Yoyo found nicely idiotic reasons to break into alien networks, preferably those of the Party, and besides, she supplied the equipment too. For Jia Wei she was a magic toyshop owner, with him as the lucky boy who was allowed to try out all the lovely things she brought along. She had the ideas, and he had the ploys up his sleeve. What did you call that kind of relationship? Symbiosis?

Something like that.

On the positive side, it was worth noting that he would never have betrayed Yoyo. Not least out of self-interest – after all, the group stood and fell with her and her box of tricks filled by Tu Technologies. In return he was even prepared to make her problems his own, particularly because he felt a little responsible for the tense situation. After all, *he* had advised her on this surefire, super-refined matter, and in that he had been successful, unfortunately too successful. Now Yoyo was troubled by worries that robbed her of sleep, so Jia Wei had spent the past two days trying to find out what had actually gone wrong on the night in question. And found something, an incredible coincidence of events. Now, enveloped in a cloud of wonton fragrances rising from Wong's bags, as he looked across the square, he decided to talk to Yoyo about it right after breakfast. Maggie's jabbering emerged from the control centre that they had been using as their headquarters since Andromeda had ceased to be safe; she was chattering cheerfully away into her phone, rounding up the rest of the group.

'Breakfast,' she crowed.

Breakfast, exactly. That was what he needed now.

But all of a sudden his feet felt frozen to the spot. From his elevated observation-point he could see all the way to the far-away coke plant, whose quenching tower loomed sadly into the dawn sky. The factory grounds were enormous, and included the old steel complex. He wondered where the new sound was coming from, the one that he hadn't heard around here for ages, a distant hiss, as if the air over Wong's World were burning.

He narrowed his eyes.

To the left of the quenching tower, something was hanging in the sky.

It took Jin Jia Wei a second to work out that it was the source of the hiss. A moment later he recognised *what* it was. And although he had never heard anyone say that intuition was one of his outstanding qualities, he felt the danger emanating from it as if in waves.

No one in Quyu had an airbike.

He recoiled. Between Wong's World and Cyber Planet, he saw two more of the beefy machines appearing and gliding along not far from the ground. At the same time a car came careening out from behind the surrounding Portakabins and stopped by the blast furnace. The airbike seemed to inflate, a sensory illusion caused by the high speed of its approach.

'Yoyo!' he yelled.

The machine came towards him like a flat flying fish. Reflections of sunlight darted across the flattened windscreen and flashed in the turbine flywheel as the pilot shifted his weight and forced the bike into a curve. Jia Wei staggered back inside, clutching the bags, as the hiss swelled and the mouth of the turbine began to widen as if to suck him into its rotating shredder teeth. A moment later the airbike came down, sweeping Maggie and Yoyo's voices away in a surge of noise, touched the floor of the platform, and he saw something flashing in the pilot's hand—

*　　　*　　　*

Xin fired.

The bullets ploughed through the boy and the bags he was holding. Jia Wei's face exploded, bottles burst, hot soup, cola and coffee, blood, brain matter, wontons and splinters of bone splatted wildly in all directions. While the ruptured body was still tipping backwards, Xin had leapt from the saddle and stepped inside the building.

His glance took in the interior in a fraction of a second, probed, categorised, separated into worth keeping, superfluous, interesting and negligible. Panels with their monitors turned off, covered with dust, suggested a former control centre, equipped with measuring and regulatory technology designed to monitor the blast furnace plant. The room's current purpose was equally obvious. In the middle of the room, tables had been shoved together, with highly modern equipment, transparent displays, computers and keyboards. Plank beds pushed up against the back wall showed that the control centre was inhabited, or sometimes used as a place to sleep.

He brandished his gun. The fat girl, Xiao Meiqi, or was her name Maggie? held her hands up. Whatever. Her mouth was wide open, her eyeballs looked as if they were about to leave their sockets, which made her look rather ugly. Xin shot her down as casually as the powerful shake hands with those less important than themselves, swept aside the bags she had set down on the table with the barrel of his gun and aimed it at Yoyo.

Not a sound came from her lips.

He tilted his head curiously to one side and looked at her.

He didn't know what he'd expected. People showed fear and shock in different ways. For example, in the last second of his life Jin Jia Wei had looked as if you could actually wring the fear out of him. Meiqi's fear, on the other hand, had reminded him of Edvard Munch's *The Scream*, a distorted image of herself. There were people who preserved their dignity and attractiveness even when they were in pain. Meiqi hadn't been one of them. Hardly anyone was.

Yoyo, on the other hand, just stared at him.

She must have leapt up just as Jia Wei called her name, which explained her crouching, cat-like posture. Her eyes were wide, but her face looked strangely unexpressive, regular – *almost* perfect, had a shadow around the corner of her mouth not made her look slightly ordinary. Even so, she was more beautiful than most of the women that Xin had seen in his life. He wondered how much attention such beauty could put up with. Almost a shame they had no time to find out.

Then he saw Yoyo's hands beginning to tremble.

Her resistance was crumbling.

He drew up a chair, sat down on it and lowered his gun.

'I have three questions for you,' he said.

Yoyo said nothing. Kenny let a few seconds pass, waited to see her give in, but apart from the fact that she was trembling nothing in her posture changed. She went on staring at him as before.

'I expect a quick and honest answer to all three questions,' he went on. 'So no excuses.' He smiled the way you smile at women whose favours you are trying to win by being open. They might just as well have been sitting in a smart bar or a cosy restaurant. It struck him that he felt decidedly comfortable in Yoyo's company. Perhaps they did still have a little time left together after all.

'And afterwards,' he said benignly, 'let's go on looking.'

Jericho saw nothing but dust, whirled up by his own car, as he screeched to a halt below the tower of scaffolding. He drew his Glock from its shoulder-holster, pushed the door open and dashed to the steps. They were made of steel, like the rest of the construction, and amplified the sound of his footsteps.

Bonggg, bonggg!

He cursed under his breath. Taking two steps at a time, he tried to walk on tiptoe, slipped and banged his knee painfully against the stair railings.

Idiot! His only advantage was that Zhao hadn't seen him.

That moment shots rang out above him. Jericho hurried on. The closer he got to the platform, the more penetratingly the hiss of the airbike reached his ear. Zhao had not thought it necessary to turn off the engine. Fine. The bike would drown him out. He turned his head and saw movement on the square below him. Motorcyclists. Without paying them any heed, he took the last few steps, paused and peered across the stairhead.

The airbike was parked right in front of him. The door to the control centre was open. He jumped onto the platform, darted over to the building and paused beside the doorway, back to the wall, gun at eye-level. Zhao's voice could be heard, friendly and encouraging:

'First of all, how much do you know? Secondly, who have you told about it? And the third question's very easy to answer.' Pause for effect. 'It's the sixty-four-thousand-dollar question, Yoyo. It is: Where – is – your – computer?'

She was alive. Good.

Less good was the fact that he couldn't see the killer and therefore didn't know what direction he was looking in at that moment. He ran his eye along the façade. Just before the corner of the building he spotted a small window. Ducking down, he crept over to it and peered inside.

Yoyo was standing behind a table full of computers. All he could see of Zhao was legs, a hand and the massive barrel of his gun. He was clearly sitting facing Yoyo, which meant that his back was turned to the door. The window was open a crack, so Jericho could hear Zhao saying, 'It can't be that hard, can it?'

Yoyo mutely shook her head.

'So?'

No reaction. Zhao sighed.

'Right, perhaps I forgot to explain the rules. It's like this: I ask, you answer. Or even better, you just hand the thing over to me.' The gun-barrel came down. 'That's all you have to do. Okay? If you fail to reply, I'll blow your left foot off.'

Jericho had seen enough. A few leaps and he was at the door. He jumped inside and aimed his gun at the back of Zhao's head.

'Sit right where you are! Hands up. No heroics.'

A glance took in the scene. At his feet lay the boy's body, shredded as if bombs had gone off in his head and chest. Maggie crouched a few metres away. She kept her head lowered, mutely contemplating her belly, from which amazing quantities of innards spilled. Floor, chairs and table were sprayed with red. Disheartened, Jericho wondered what Zhao had fired with.

'Flechettes.'

'What?'

'Dart-shaped projectiles,' Zhao repeated calmly, as if Jericho had asked his question out loud. 'Metal Storm, fifty tiny tungsten carbide arrows per round, one and a half thousand kilometres per hour. Pierce steel plates. Opinions are divided. On the one hand you create one hell of a mess, on the other—'

'Shut up! Hands in the air.'

Painfully slowly, Zhao obliged. Jericho caught his breath. He felt helpless and ridiculous. Yoyo's lower lip trembled, her mask slipped, shock took hold of her. At the same time he became aware of a flicker of hope in her eyes. And something else, as if a plan were brewing in her head—

Her body tensed.

'Don't,' Jericho warned, speaking in her direction. 'No chaos. First of all we have to bring this bastard under control.'

Zhao yelled with laughter.

'And how are you going to accomplish that? The way you did in the Andromeda?'

'Shut up.'

'I could have killed you.'

'Set the weapon down on the floor.'

'You owe me a bit of respect, little Jericho.'

'I said, put the gun on the floor!'

'Why don't you just go home and forget the whole thing? I would—'

There was a sharp bang. A few centimetres away from Zhao, Jericho's bullet pierced the tabletop. The hitman sighed. He turned his head slowly so that his profile could be seen. He had a tiny transmitter in his ear.

'Really, Owen, that's too much.'

'For the last time!'

'It's fine.' Zhao shrugged. 'I'll set it down on the ground, okay?'

'No.'

'Meaning not yet?'

'*Drop* it.'

'But—'

'Just let it slip off your knees. Keep your hands in the air. Then kick it over to me.'

'You're making a mistake, Owen.'

'I *have* made a mistake. Do it, right now, or I'll shoot *your* left foot off.'

Zhao gave a thin smile. The gun clattered to the floor. He pushed it with the tip of his boot, so that it slipped a little way towards Jericho and stopped halfway between them.

'Shoot him,' Yoyo said hoarsely.

Jericho looked at her.

'That wouldn't be a—'

'Shoot him!' Tears poured from Yoyo's eyes. Her features distorted with revulsion and fury. 'Shoot him, shoo—'

'No!' Jericho violently shook his head. 'If we want to find out who he's working for, we'll have to—'

He went on talking, but his voice was lost amongst the hisses and wails of the airbike.

They had got louder. Why?

Yoyo cried out and recoiled. A dull blow made the floor shake as something landed outside the control centre. It wasn't Zhao's bike. It was more bikes.

Zhao grinned.

For a paralysing moment Jericho didn't know what to do. If he turned round, the killer would get hold of his gun again. But he had to know what was happening outside.

And then he understood.

The transmitter in Zhao's ear! It had been broadcasting his voice all that time. He'd called for reinforcements. Zhao got up from his chair, his fingers clutching its back. Jericho raised the Glock. His adversary paused, crouching like a beast of prey, ready to spring.

'Drop it,' said a deep voice behind him.

'I'd do what he says, little Owen.'

'I'll shoot you first,' said Jericho.

'Then shoot.' Zhao's dark eyes rested on him, seemed to suck him in. He slowly started to sit up. 'There are two of them, by the way, and it's only thanks to me that you're still alive at all.'

Footsteps rang out behind Jericho. A hand reached over his shoulder and grabbed his gun. Jericho unresistingly allowed it to be pulled from his fingers. His eyes sought Yoyo's. She was pressing herself against the old control-desk, eyes darting back and forth.

A fist pushed him forwards.

Zhao took hold of him, drew back his arm and struck him full in the face with the palm of his hand. His head flew sideways. The next blow hit his solar plexus and forced the air from his ribs. Choking, he fell to his knees. Now he could see the two men, one a thick-set, bearded Asian who had been aiming his gun at Yoyo, the other gaunt, fair and with a Slavic look. They both carried pistols of the same type as their leader's. Zhao laughed quietly. He brushed the silky, black hair off his forehead and drew himself up to his full height. He started walking around Jericho at a measured pace.

'Gentlemen,' he said, 'what you are experiencing here is the triumph of the cerebellum over the belly. The primacy of planning. That's the only possible way of explaining how a man who effectively had me in his power is now cowering at our feet. A detective, note. A professional.' He spat the last word at Jericho. 'And yet I welcome his visit. We now have the opportunity to learn more than before. We can, for example, ask Mr Jericho what he actually wanted to ask *me*.'

Zhao's right hand darted forward, grabbed Jericho's ponytail, pulled him up and to him, so that he could feel the hitman's hot breath on his face.

'The question of the client. Always interesting. Our guest could hardly have hit on the idea of looking for little Yoyo all on his own. So who is *your* client? I'm right, Owen, am I not? Someone threw the stick. Fetch the stick, Owen! Find Yoyo! Woof! – Isn't there anyone else I should be taking care of?'

Even though the situation was anything but funny, Jericho laughed. 'I'd be careful about wasting your time.'

'You're so right.' Zhao snorted, shoved him aside and approached Yoyo, who was no longer trying to hide her fear. Her lower lip trembled, streams of moisture glistened on her cheeks. 'So let's devote ourselves to our lovely do-gooder here, and ask her to help us in answering questions that have been asked once already. Where – is – your – computer?'

Yoyo stepped back. Again her features underwent a change, as if she had just made a surprising discovery. Zhao paused, plainly irritated. At that very moment Jericho heard a faint metallic click.

'You're not going to do anything at all,' a voice said.

Zhao spun round. Two young men and a woman in bikers' leathers had stepped into the room, machine-guns at the ready, aiming at him and his two assistants, who in turn were aiming at the new arrivals. One of them was a giant with a barrel chest, gorilla arms, the top of his head a shaven hemisphere. The point of his chin was extended by a blue prosthesis into an artificial pharaoh's beard. Jericho's breath froze. Daxiong had misled him really badly, but there was no one else that he would rather have seen at that very moment.

Six Koreans, who had all taken a beating—

Daxiong's narrow eyes turned towards Yoyo.

'Come over here,' he roared. 'The rest of you stay where—'

His voice faded away. It was only now that the giant seemed to take in what had happened in the control centre. His gaze wandered from the shredded corpse of Jia Wei to Maggie's grotesquely bent body. His eyes widened very slightly.

'They've killed them,' whimpered the girl by his side. All the colour had fled from her face.

'Shit,' the other guy said. 'Oh, shit!'

Jericho's thoughts went running helter-skelter like a pack of dogs. A thousand possible scenarios flooded his imagination. The hitmen, the City Demons, everyone was aiming at everyone else, while Zhao crouched there, waiting, and Yoyo's eyes wandered from one group to the other. No one dared move for fear of disturbing the fragile equilibrium, which would inevitably have ended in disaster.

It was Yoyo who broke the spell. She walked slowly past Zhao and over to Daxiong. Zhao didn't move. Only his eyes followed her.

'Stop.'

He said it quietly, no more than a sibilant murmur, but it still drowned out the hiss of the airbikes, the dog-like wheezing of the others, the hammering in Jericho's head, and Yoyo stopped.

'No, come here,' Daxiong yelled. 'Don't listen to—'

'You won't survive this,' Zhao interrupted. 'You can't kill us all, so don't even try. Give us what we want to have, tell us what we want to hear and we'll be off. Nothing will happen to anyone.'

'Like nothing happened to Jia Wei?' wept the girl with the gun. 'Or Maggie?'

'That was inev— No, not like that!'

She had swung the gun round slightly; the fat Asian had also swung the barrel of his gun and was aiming it at her head. Daxiong and the other City Demon reacted in similar fashion. The blond guy's jaws worked away. Zhao raised a pleading hand.

'Enough blood has been spilled! – Yoyo, listen, you've seen something you shouldn't have seen. An accident, a stupid accident, but we can wipe this problem out. I want your computer, I have to know who you've entrusted it to. No more people must die, I promise. Survival in exchange for silence.'

You're lying, Jericho thought. Each of your words is pure deceit.

Yoyo turned doubtfully towards Zhao, looked into the beautiful face of the devil.

'Yes, it's fine, Yoyo, all fine!' He nodded. 'I give you my word that nothing will happen to anyone as long as you cooperate.'

'Shit!' yelled the young man next to Daxiong. 'It's all a great big pile of shit! They're going to shoot us all as soon as—'

'You watch yourself!' roared the blond guy.

'Kenny, that won't do any good.' The fat man was quaking with nerves. 'We should kill them.'

'You fat fuck! First we'll take you and—'

'Shut it!'

'One more word! One word and I'll—'

'Stop it! Stop it, all of you!'

Eyes darted back and forth, fingers tightened on triggers. As if the room had filled with an inflammable gas, Jericho thought, and now they were all desperate to click their lighters. But Zhao's authority held them all in check. The explosion hadn't happened. Yet.

'Please – give – me – the computer.'

Yoyo wiped her hand over her face, smearing it with tears and snot. 'Then will you let us go?'

'Answer my questions and give me your computer.'

'I have your word?'

'Yes. Then we'll let you go.'

'You promise that nothing will happen to Daxiong and Ziyi – and Tony? And that guy there?'

How thoughtful, thought Jericho.

'Don't listen to him,' he said. 'Zhao will—'

'I've never broken my word,' Zhao cut in, paying him no attention. It sounded friendly and honest. 'Look, I'm trained to kill people. Like any cop, any soldier, any agent. National security is a higher good than individual human lives, I'm sure you understand that. But I'll keep my promise.'

'If you give him the computer, he'll kill us all,' Jericho announced. He said it as soberly as possible. 'I'm your friend. Your father sent me.'

'He's lying.' Zhao's voice sounded wheedling. 'You know what? You should be far more afraid of him than you are of me. He's playing a game with you, every word he comes out with is a lie.'

'He's going to kill you,' said Jericho.

'Just let him try,' snorted the boy. So his name was Tony. He jutted his chin belligerently, but his voice and his outstretched weapon trembled slightly. Ziyi, the girl, started to sob uncontrollably.

'Just give him that fucking computer!'

'Don't do it,' Jericho insisted. 'As long as he doesn't know where your computer is, he *has* to let you live.'

'Shut up!' Daxiong yelled at him.

'Just give him the damned computer!' Ziyi shouted.

Yoyo walked to the table. Her fingers floated over a device hardly bigger than a bar of chocolate, connected to the keyboard and the screen.

'You're making a mistake,' said Jericho dejectedly. All the strength was oozing from his limbs. 'He'll kill you.'

Zhao looked at him.

'The way you killed Grand Cherokee Wang, Jericho?'

'The way I— *What?*'

Yoyo paused.

'Bullshit!' Jericho shook his head. 'He's lying. He's—'

'Just shut your mouth,' yelled the fat guy, pulled his gun around and aimed it at Jericho, who saw with startling clarity every individual drop of sweat on the killer's forehead, glittering like bubble wrap.

Daxiong aimed at Zhao, whose eyes widened.

'No!' he yelled.

The lighter clicked.

Jericho saw Tony lifting his gun, then there were two shots in quick succession, and the fat guy collapsed. Everything happened at the same time. With a deafening bang the fair-haired man's pistol went off and shot away half of Tony's face. He tipped over and obstructed Daxiong's view, while Ziyi squealed and Yoyo stormed towards the door. Zhao tried to grab her, missed her and fell headlong. Jericho reached for the gun on the floor. He grabbed the barrel, but Zhao was faster, while Ziyi was shooting wildly in all directions, forcing the blond guy to take cover behind the table.

He ducked.

Daxiong dashed forward, slipped in Jia Wei's blood and cracked the back of his head on the floor-tiles, dragging Jericho with him. A burst of fire ploughed up the floor next to him. Jericho rolled away from the unconscious giant and saw Ziyi stride like a vengeful goddess over Tony's corpse, shouting and firing indiscriminately. A moment later a bright red fountain sprouted where her right arm had been. The reports from Zhao's pistol rang out as he ran outside. Ziyi hesitated. Glassy-eyed, she turned round, an expression of mild surprise in her eyes, and sprayed her pumping blood at the blond guy, spurting it into his eyes. The man raised a hand to protect himself, tried to avoid her dying body, lost his balance.

Jericho leapt up. Ziyi's severed arm twitched at his feet, and suddenly he was caught up in the vision of a theatrical performance. He was gratefully aware of something within him stepping aside and something else taking control of his thoughts and his motor abilities. He bent down, fumbled the gun from Ziyi's slack fingers, aimed the muzzle at the stumbling hitman and pulled the trigger.

Empty.

With a yell, the blond guy slung the dead girl away from him, reached for his gun and, still blinded by Ziyi's blood, fired his magazine off into the air. Jericho whirled out of the line of fire and without so much as another glance, he leapt over the prostrate bodies and hurried outside.

Xin briefly imagined how simple things might have been. Tracking down the girl and her computer. Knowing which one it was. Charming information out of her as to who he still had to worry about, which would have taken only a few minutes. Xin was sure that Yoyo was extremely susceptible to pain. She would quickly have told him what he needed to know.

Fast work.

Instead, Owen Jericho had turned up as if pulled out of a hat. Xin hadn't the slightest idea what had sent the detective here. Hadn't his disguise been perfect? Irrelevant for the time being. Dark and massive, the blast furnace loomed above him. Two airbikes were parked down below, between Yoyo and the stairs. In her confusion, she had probably spent a moment too long wondering which way was shorter, and meanwhile Kenny had managed to get outside and block her exit route. The tower of girderwork provided no opportunity for escape. So she had fled across the bridge connecting the control centre and the blast furnace, to the other side, into the middle of the jungle of walkways, equipment and pipes that ran riot around the crucible.

He came after her, in no particular hurry. Each level of the furnace's scaffolding was connected to the next by a flight of steps, but the way down was blocked by broken props. By now Yoyo too was aware of her mistake. She looked alternately upwards and at Kenny, as she pushed her way slowly backwards. Once again he was sure that he was going to win. He stopped.

'This isn't what I wanted,' he called out.

Yoyo's features blurred. For a moment he thought he was about to see her bursting into tears again.

'I never planned to give you the thing,' she cried.

'Yoyo, I'm sorry!'

'Then fuck off!'

'Have *I* broken my word?' He put all the hurt he could muster into his words. 'Did I?'

'Kiss my butt!'

'Why don't you trust me?'

'Anyone who trusts you dies!'

'*Your* people started it, Yoyo. Be sensible, I just want to talk to you.'

Yoyo looked behind her, looked up, and turned her gaze back to Kenny. She had almost reached the steps leading to the next level. He set his pistol down in front of him and showed her the palms of both hands.

'No more violence, Yoyo. No bloodshed. I swear.'

She hesitated.

Come on, he thought. You can't get down. You're in a trap, little mouse. Stupid little mouse.

But suddenly the mouse seemed anything but helpless. He uneasily wondered who was actually playing games with whom here. The girl was in shock, sure, but as she approached the stairs she no longer resembled the tear-drenched Yoyo who had been ready to hand him her computer just a minute before. In her catlike agility he recognised his own alertness, practised over the years and based on stubbornness, suspicion, deviousness and a will to survive. Yoyo was stronger than he'd imagined.

As soon as she leapt onto the steps he knew that any further diplomacy was a waste of time. If there had ever been a chance of coaxing the girl down, it was gone.

He picked up his gun.

The wail of a turbine rose up behind him. Kenny turned round and saw Jericho sitting on the saddle of one of the airbikes, trying to get the vehicle started. He weighed up his options in a flash, but Yoyo took priority. He ignored the detective and hurried after the escaping girl whose footsteps made the passageway above him tremble, and watched through the bars as her silhouette dashed away. A few leaps and he was up there. He found himself in a ravine of struts and pipes, and caught a glimpse of flying hair as Yoyo disappeared behind a rusty pillar; then her footsteps hammered towards the next floor up.

She was slowly turning into a nuisance. High time to bring this matter to a close.

He chased after her, floor after floor, until she had nowhere left to go. A few metres above her the furnace tapered, ending in an inlet through which coke and ore had been funnelled in earlier times. Above it rose an angular, winding structure that culminated in a massive exhaust outlet, making the construction visible even from a distance. Vertical scaffolding-rods led to the highest point, about seventy metres up. Nothing beyond that but open sky. No escape was possible, unless you dared to pick your way about twenty metres along a pipe leading sharply downwards, and jump another ten metres down onto the enormous pot-like tank in which it ended.

He listened. It was surprisingly quiet up here, as if the vague and distant sounds of the city and the background noise of Xaxu were a sea that surged below him. The turbines of large aircraft sang somewhere in the stratosphere.

Xin threw his head back. Yoyo had disappeared.

Then he saw her climbing. She clung to the stanchions like a monkey, pulled herself higher up, and he understood that there probably was a possible escape route. A conveyor belt abutted the inlet. It ran down from the top of the furnace to the ground, steep, but walkable.

The bitch.

Did he actually need her alive? She had reached her hand out to the computer, there was no doubt which one it was. It was still in the control room . . . except he didn't know who she'd talked to about the matter.

Cursing, he began his ascent.

A loud hissing sound came towards him. With one hand clamped to the scaffolding and the other gripping his gun, he turned his head.

The airbike was coming straight at him.

Jericho had stalled the first bike he tried. It was a new model, very different from the ones he was used to. The controls gleamed from a flat user interface, there was nothing mechanical on this one. He slipped from the saddle, jumped onto the second airbike, whose engine was running, and ran his hand over the touchscreen. He was luckier this time. The machine reacted like a goaded bull, bucked and reared and tried to throw him off. His hands gripped the handles. Before, they'd been vertical, now they curved upwards and could be twisted in all directions. The bike circled wildly. The display blinked like the lights on a fruit machine. Just by chance Jericho touched two of them, and the carousel-ride came to an end, but he was carried instead towards the front of the control room; he shifted his body weight, narrowly avoiding collision, and flew in an extended 180-degree turn. His eyes scoured the surroundings.

No trace of Yoyo or Zhao.

He gradually got the knack of turning. He brought the bike up, but neglected to pivot the jets at the same time, which immediately got him into trouble again, because the bike now soared into the sky like a rocket. He felt himself sliding helplessly out of the saddle, and struggled with darting fingers to correct the mistake, regained control, and took another turn with his eyes on the blast furnace.

There they were!

Yoyo had made it to the inlet, where the conveyor belt began, followed by Zhao, who hung two metres below her in the scaffolding. Jericho forced the machine upwards, in the hope that it would react as he wished. He saw the hitman give a start and hunch his shoulders. Less than half a metre away from him, Jericho swung the airbike round, turned a circle and bore down on the furnace once more. On the edge of the conveyor belt, Yoyo was looking charmingly helpless. He understood exactly why as he flew over the belt. Where there should have been rollers and struts, part of the construction had simply broken away. For a long stretch only the side braces remained. Getting down from there would have required the skills of a professional tightrope-walker.

Yoyo was trapped.

He cursed himself under his breath. Why hadn't he taken the blond guy's pistol off him? There had been weapons lying around all over the control centre. He watched furiously as Zhao's head and shoulders appeared over the rim. With one bound the hitman was on the inlet. Yoyo recoiled, went down on all fours and gripped the brace of the conveyor belt. She nimbly let herself down on it until her feet touched a rod further below, tried to find a halfway solid footing, began lowering herself down, hand after hand, inch after inch—

Slipped.

Horrified, Jericho saw her fall. A jolt ran through her body. At the last second her fingers had closed on the rod she had just been standing on, but now she was dangling over an abyss a good seventy metres deep.

Zhao stared down at her.

Then he left the cover of the girderwork.

'Bad mistake,' Jericho snarled. 'Very bad mistake!'

By now his glands were firing considerable salvos of adrenalin, whipping his heartbeat and blood pressure up to heroic levels. With each passing second, he was more in control of the machine. Carried on a wave of rage and euphoria, he sent the airbike shooting forward and took aim at Zhao, who was at that moment crouching, about to climb down to Yoyo.

The hitman saw him coming.

Baffled, he came to a halt. The bike shot over the conveyor belt. Anyone else would have been swept into the depths, but Zhao managed to pirouette himself back onto the edge of the inlet. His gun clattered far below. Jericho turned the bike and saw the blond guy staggering out of the control centre and getting onto one of the remaining airbikes. No time to worry about him too. His fingers twitched in all directions. Where on the display – no, wrong, you did it with the handlebars, right? He just had to bring the right handlebar down a touch—

Too much.

The bike plummeted like a stone. Cursing, he caught it, climbed, put his foot down and then immediately decelerated until he hung, jets hissing, right under the wildly flailing Yoyo.

'Jump!' he shouted.

She looked down at him, her face distorted, as her fingers slipped millimetre by millimetre. Gusts of wind grabbed the bike and carried it away. The girders trembled as Zhao jumped gracefully from the edge of the inlet and landed on the lower part of the scaffolding. The hitman plainly didn't suffer from any kind of vertigo. His right hand came down to clutch her wrist. Jericho corrected his position, and the bike spun back under Yoyo.

'Jump, for God's sake! Jump!'

Her right foot struck his temple, and he couldn't see or hear a thing. Now he was underneath her again, looking up. He saw Zhao's fingers stretching out, touching her ankle.

Yoyo let go.

It was a bit like having a sack of cement dropped on him. If he had imagined she would land elegantly on the pillion, he could think again. Yoyo clutched his jacket, slipped off the bike and dangled from him like a gorilla from a rubber tyre. With both hands he pulled her back up, as the bike hurtled towards the ground.

She shouted something. It sounded like *maybe*.

Maybe?

The turbine noise rose to a scream. Yoyo's fingers were everywhere, in his clothes, his hair, his face. The dusty plain rushed up at them, they would be smashed to pieces.

But they weren't smashed, they didn't die. He had clearly done something right, because at the same moment as her hands closed around his shoulders and she pressed her torso against his back, the bike shot straight upwards again.

'Maybe—'

The words were shredded by the squall. The blond guy was approaching on the left, his face a mask of dried blood, from which hate-filled eyes stared across at them.

'What?' he shouted.

'Maybe,' she yelled back, 'next time you'll learn to fly the thing *first*, you fucking idiot!'

Daxiong floated to the surface.

His first impulse was to ask Maggie for a cappuccino, with plenty of sugar and foam, of course. That was why they were here, after all. To have breakfast together, since Yoyo had appointed Andromeda as her summer residence again, as Daxiong jokingly put it, except that right now it seemed to make more sense to go into hiding in the steelworks for a while.

Maggie only ever brought coffee for him. The others, Tony, Yoyo, Maggie herself, Ziyi and Jia Wei preferred tea, like good Chinese. And like good Chinese they had wontons and baozis for breakfast, they ate pork belly and noodles in broth, swallowed down half-raw shrimps, the whole deal, while for unfathomable reasons his heart still beat for the Grande Nation and was devoted to the buttery, warm smell of freshly baked croissants. By now he was even toying with the possibility that he might have French genes, which anyone who saw his face would strenuously have denied. Daxiong was as Mongolian as a Mongolian could be, and Yoyo was forever rattling off all the wonders of the fun, authentic China that had no need of imported Western culture. Daxiong let her talk. For him, the day began with a proper milk foam moustache. Maggie had called and croaked 'Breakfast!' into the receiver, and Ziyi had yelled and screamed.

Why had she done that?

Oh yes, he'd been dreaming. Something terrible! Why would anyone dream something like that? He, Ziyi and Tony had driven over to the blast furnace, following Maggie's call, when two of those flying motorbikes, which were too expensive for him ever to have afforded one, had landed on the control centre platform, where a third one already stood. Amazing. As he approached, he had tried to get through to Maggie, to ask her what kind of guys these were, but she hadn't replied. So they had decided to take the guns out of their saddle-bags, just in case.

A funny dream. They were having a party.

They were all enjoying themselves, but Jia Wei couldn't really join in, because there wasn't much left of him, and Maggie had a sore stomach. Tony was missing half of his face, oh dear, that seemed to be why Ziyi had started screaming, now everything fitted into place, and what on earth kind of people were these?

Daxiong opened his eyes.

Xin exploded with fury.

With simian agility, he leapt back down over the scaffolding, struts and steps. His airbike was still on the platform, engine running. Far below, the detective was wrestling with the hijacked machine, busy driving himself and Yoyo to their deaths.

Jericho, that thorn in his side!

He's on his way out, Xin thought. I've got the computer, Yoyo. Who can you have spoken to apart from your few friends here, and they're dead. I don't need you any more.

Then he saw Jericho wresting control of the machine, gaining height, moving away from the blast furnace—

And being forced back down again.

The blond guy!

Kenny started waving both arms.

'Kill them all!' he yelled. 'Finish them off!'

He didn't know if the blond guy had heard him. He leapt energetically over the edge of the walkway, landed with a thump on the steel of the platform, and ran to his bike. The turbine was running. Had Jericho been fiddling around with it? Before his eyes, the two bikes set off at great speed, and disappeared into the intricate labyrinth of the steelworks. He pivoted the jets to vertical. The machine hissed and vibrated.

'Come on!' he shouted.

The airbike was slowly lifting off, when something whistled past his head so close that he felt the draught. He turned the machine in the air and saw the bald-headed giant from the control centre, a gun in each hand, firing from both muzzles. Nosediving, Xin attacked him. The giant threw himself to the ground. With a snort of contempt he pulled the airbike back up and flew after the others.

Daxiong sat bolt upright. His heart was thumping, the sun was beating down on him. Across the shimmering fields of slag the vanishing airbikes quickly gained distance, but one of the bikes was unmistakably hounding the other and trying to force it to land.

One of the hitmen was dead in the control room. So who was that on the fleeing bike?

Yoyo?

While he was still thinking about it, he clattered down the zigzag stairs. Apart from him and possibly Yoyo none of the Guardians had survived the massacre. The remaining City Demons knew nothing about the double life of the six of them, even though they might have guessed at various things. Yoyo and he had originally brought the Demons to life as a disguise. A motorbike association aroused no suspicion, it wasn't considered intellectual or subversive. They could meet easily, particularly in Quyu. Three more members had joined the previous year. Perhaps, Daxiong thought, as he lowered his full three hundredweight onto his motorbike, the time had come to initiate them. Strictly speaking, he no longer had that option. Whoever their opponent might have been, it was clear that the Guardians had been busted.

As he drove off he selected a number.

There was a ringing noise. It went on too long, far too long. Then he heard the boy's voice.

'Where were you, damn it?' snorted Daxiong.

Lau Ye yawned and talked at the same time.

Then he asked a question.

'Don't ask, Ye,' Daxiong snorted into the mobile. 'Get Xiao-Tong and Mak over here. Right now! Go to the blast furnace and clear the control room, everything you find there, computer, displays, the lot.'

The boy stammered something which Daxiong took to mean that he didn't know where the others were.

'Then find them!' he shouted. 'I'll explain it later. What? No, don't take the stuff to Andromeda, and not to the workshop. Then think of something. Somewhere they won't connect with us. Oh, and Ye—' He swallowed. 'You will find corpses. Brace yourselves, you hear?'

He rang off before Ye could ask any questions.

Jericho's machine took a blow when the blond guy's airbike collided with its chassis. Time and again he had tried to steer towards the airspace above the steelworkers' housing estate. Every time the blond guy forced him back, stared wildly over at them and tried to take aim. The lunar landscape of the slag-fields sped along beneath them. Once again Jericho tried to turn off to the left. The blond guy speeded up and forced him in the other direction.

'Where are you actually trying to get to?' Yoyo's voice rang in his ears.

'We're outdistancing him!'

'You haven't a hope out in the open! Tempt him into the plant.'

The blond guy's airbike shot upwards and immediately plummeted back down again. Jericho saw the machine's fish belly right above him and then dived. They wobbled along just above ground level.

'Be careful!' Yoyo snapped.

'I know what I'm doing!' Rage welled up in him, but he was actually by no means sure about what he should do. Right in front of him a huge chimney rose out of the ground.

'To the right!' screeched Yoyo. 'The right!'

The blond guy drove them further down. The bike scratched along dried-up slag, started skipping, went into a violent roll, then they were around the chimney, only to find themselves in front of a hangar-sized warehouse. They were too close, far too close. No chance of avoiding it, of turning away, of avoiding a collision.

No! The warehouse door was open a crack.

Just before the threatened impact Jericho pulled the machine to the side and shot through it.

Lau Ye dashed through the gloomy concert hall of the Andromeda. He ran as fast as his lanky legs would carry him.

Don't ask any questions. Just don't ask.

He was used to this from Daxiong, and he had never complained. Lau Ye was a novice in the order of the City Demons: he had been the last to join and he was by far the youngest. He respected Daxiong and Yoyo, Ziyi and Maggie, Tony and Jia Wei. He also respected Ma Mak and Hui Xiao-Tong, even though they had only been admitted to the club subsequently. Subsequently in that the others had set up the association together, with Daxiong as founder and Yoyo in the role of Vice President.

But Ye wasn't blind.

Born on the estate just after the steelworks was closed down, with no school education, but more intimately familiar with Xaxu's peculiar qualities and those of its inhabitants, from the very start he had refused to believe that the Demons were just a bike club. Daxiong was from Quyu, too, but he was seen as operating somewhere between the worlds of the connected and the outsiders. No one doubted that he would wake up on the other side one morning, rub his eyes, drive a smart car to an air-conditioned high-rise skyscraper and pursue some well-paid job there. Yoyo, on the other hand, Maggie, Ziyi, Tony and Jia Wei belonged to Quyu about as much as a string quartet belonged in Andromeda. In the control room they'd set up a kind of Cyber Planet for the privileged, and Yoyo had packed all the super-expensive computers full of brilliant games, but she was from a different world. She went to uni. They all went to uni to study something that parents considered sensible.

Yeah. Not his.

Lau Ye's parents didn't pay him much attention. At the age of sixteen he might as well have been living on the Moon. His job in Daxiong's workshop and the City Demons were all he had, and he loved being part of it. And so he didn't ask questions, either. He didn't ask whether the only purpose his humble self, Xiao-Tong and Mak served was to disguise a conspiratorial little student club as something fit for the slums. He didn't ask what the other six organised at their many meetings in the control centre when he, Xiao-Tong and Mak weren't around. Until a few days before, when Yoyo had turned up at the workshop in a complete state. That time he *had* asked Daxiong.

The answer had been a familiar one.

'Don't ask.'

'I just want to know if there's anything I can do.'

'Yoyo's got problems. Best you stay in the workshop for the time being and avoid the control centre.'

'What kind of problems?'

'Don't ask.'

Don't ask. Except that three days later that guy with the fair hair and the blue eyes had turned up, the one Daxiong had later said looked like a – what was it? Scanavian? Scandinavian! Ye had talked to the man and learned that he wanted to get into Andromeda.

'Cool,' he had said to Daxiong later. 'You may have sent him on a wild goose chase. Why would you do that?'

'Don't—'

'No. I'm asking.'

Daxiong had rubbed his bald head and his chin, had poked around in his ears, tugged on his fake beard and finally snarled:

'It could be that we're about to get an unwanted visit. Nasty people.'

'Like the other guys that time?'

'Exactly.'

'And what do they want from us? I mean, what do they want from *us*? What have you done, you – six?'

Daxiong had looked at him for a long time.

'If I confide something in you, little Ye, you'll keep your trap shut and not tell anyone?'

'Okay.'

'Not even Mak or Xiao-Tong?'

'O-okay.'

'Do I have your word?'

'Of course. Erm – what's going on?'

'Don't ask.'

But even on that odd day the standard rebuff hadn't sounded as desperate and furious as it had just now. It seemed as if the suspicions that Ye had held for a long time were being borne out. The six of them had conspiratorial rituals. His limbs quivered as he crossed the inner room, which was still in a state of complete chaos from the previous night, and barely negotiable for leftover food, bottles, cigarette ends and drug paraphernalia. Alcohol, stale smoke and piss launched a general attack on his chemoreceptors. Mak and Xiao-Tong had been together for four weeks, and had been at the same concert as him. After that they'd had one hell of a party. It was only towards morning that Ye had crept, royally zonked, to Yoyo's 'summer residence'. Even now his head felt like an aquarium that the water sloshed around in every time he moved, but Daxiong trusted him.

You'll find corpses—

Something terrible must have happened. Ye guessed where the other two might be found. Ma Mak slept, with his parents and his brothers and sisters, in the ruin of a half-demolished house on the edge of the estate. The family shared a single room, while Hui Xiao-Tong lived alone in a cave-like shed nearby. That was where he would find them.

He staggered out into the harsh light, narrowed his eyes and ran across the vacant lot to his motorbike.

Inside the warehouse it was gloomy, a vast space, the ceiling somewhere between twenty and thirty metres high, riveted walls, steel joists. Huge racks suggested that cast steel had been stored here in the past.

Shots rang out behind them. Their echo was thrown back by walls and ceilings, acoustic ricochets.

'Oi, watch where you're flying,' shouted Yoyo.

Jericho turned his head and saw the blond-haired guy catching up with him.

'Dive!'

Their pursuer approached. Shots whipped through the hall again. Turbine wailing, they raced between the racks towards the rear wall of the warehouse, another door there, ceiling height, which was fortunately open. On the other side yawned a space even darker than this one.

Something that looked like a crane emerged from the darkness.

'Careful!'

'If you don't keep your trap shut—'

'Higher! Higher!'

Jericho obeyed. The airbike skipped away over the crane in a break-neck parabola. Suddenly it was too near the ceiling. At the last minute he swivelled the jets in the opposite direction. The machine turned at an angle, darted downwards and started spinning on its axis at fantastic speed. Circling madly they wheeled into the next hall. Jericho caught a glimpse of their pursuer, saw him just passing under the lintel and going into a controlled nosedive, then the blond guy steered his bike into theirs and rammed them from the side, but what was intended to throw them off course had the opposite effect. As if by a miracle the bike stabilised itself. Suddenly they were flying straight ahead once more, worryingly close to the wall. Jericho narrowed his eyes. This factory space seemed even bigger and higher than the one before. A line of rollers, in their hundreds, ran along the floor, clearly a kind of conveyor belt leading to a tall, looming structure. Massive and gloomy, it looked like a printing press, except that this one would have been producing books for giants.

A rolling mill, it occurred to Jericho. It was the frame for a roller, to crush iron ingots into sheets. The things you know!

Again the blond guy came down, trying to squash them against the wall. Jericho looked across at him. A triumphant grin flashed in the man's blood-spattered face.

At that he saw red.

'Yoyo?'

'What?'

'Hold on tight!'

As soon as she pressed against him, he threw the handlebars around and gave the attacking bike a mighty thump with the back of his own. Yoyo screamed. Splinters of exploding windscreen sprayed in all directions. The hitman's bike was slung aside, his gun disappeared into the darkness. Jericho didn't give him time to breathe, he rammed his bike again, as they hurtled side by side towards the rolling-mill.

'And with my very warmest wishes,' he yelled, 'have a bit of this!'

The third blow rammed the blond guy's rear. His bike somersaulted in the air, whirled towards the rolling mill. Jericho drew past him, saw the hitman struggling for control and balance, arms flailing, and settled into the curve. They flew just past the colossus, but instead of the ugly noise of a bike's fatal impact they heard a sequence of loud gunshots. Somehow the guy had managed to avoid a collision and lower his bike to the floor. Like a stone on the surface of the water, it skipped over the rollers of the conveyor belt, tipped over and threw its rider off.

The next gaping portal opened up in front of them.

'Yoyo,' he called back. 'How the hell do we get back out of here?'

'We don't.' Her outstretched arm pointed past him into the darkness. 'Once you're through there, you go straight to hell.'

Xin didn't bother about the individual biker who was helplessly trying to follow them. The guy was ridiculous. Huge, clumsy, a joke. Let him empty his magazine into the air. In time he'd wish he'd never been born.

He kept a lookout for the airbikes.

They'd disappeared.

Perplexed, he wheeled above the plant, but it was as if the sky had swallowed up the two machines. The last he had seen of them was when they flew around a complex of factory buildings behind which a single big chimney loomed.

It was there that he had lost track of them.

The grouchy whine of the bike reached him from below. He toyed with the idea of raining a few grenades down on the giant's bald head. His index finger tapped against a spot to the side of the instrument panel, and a cover immediately slid aside just above his right knee. Behind it lay a considerable arsenal of weapons. Xin inspected the contents of the compartment on the other side. All there, hand grenades, sub-machine-gun. Gingerly, almost tenderly, his fingers slipped over the butt of the M-79 launcher with the incendiary rounds. All three airbikes were equipped with the same weapons.

Including Jericho's.

He shoved the thought aside and glanced at the altitude gauge: 188 metres above sea level. He continued his search with reduced thrust. The sky couldn't swallow anyone as quickly as that.

If part of the roof hadn't been open, it would have been pitch-dark. But as it was, spears of white daylight jabbed in at an angle, carving weird details from the walls, casting lattices over walkways, steps, balconies, terraces, pipes, cables, segmented and riveted armour, massive, open bulkheads.

Jericho slowed his bike in the beam of light. Hissing softly, it hovered in the air, which was impregnated with iron, rust and the smell of rancid grease.

He threw back his head.

'Forget it,' called Yoyo. Her voice bounced across walls and ceilings, and was caught between the constructions. 'It's barred up there. We won't get through.'

Jericho cursed and looked round. He couldn't really tell whether this room was any bigger than the one they had flown through before, but at any rate it looked monumental, almost Wagnerian in its dimensions, a Nibelheim of the industrial age. Steel joists a metre thick ran along the ceiling; open baskets hung from them, anchored to massive hinges, so big that he could have fitted his Toyota inside any one of them. A pipe about three metres in diameter grew from the darkness of the vaulted ceiling, led downwards at an angle and finished halfway up the hall. More of the basket-like formations were distributed across the floor, and containers were stacked along the walls.

Yoyo was right. There was something hellish about the whole thing. A chilly hell. Still startled by his unexpected knowledge of the rolling mill, Jericho tried to remember the purpose of this place. Steel was heated here, in colossal containers called converters. Right in front of them gaped their skewed, round mouths, hatches leading to the heart of the volcano, great maws that would normally have glowed red and yellow with molten ore. Now they lay there, black and mysterious, three in all.

A world extinguished.

The hiss of the other airbike came across from beyond the passageway, changed, grew more distinct. It was getting closer.

'Hey, what's with these things?' Yoyo leaned forward and pointed at one of the gaping entrances to the converter. 'He won't be able to find us in there.'

Jericho didn't reply. The bike would fit quite easily in one of the converters, with both of them on it. The maw was big enough, the container was bulbous and several metres deep. And yet he didn't like the idea that they might be trapped down there. He brought the machine up, towards the ceiling.

'If only you hadn't brought us in here,' Yoyo complained.

'If only you'd brought your computer with you,' Jericho snarled back. 'Then we wouldn't be making targets of ourselves.'

Between two joists, right below the ceiling, there was a platform from which you had a vantage point over most of the hall. The converters yawned far below them, separated from one another by large armoured bulkheads. Sunbeams stroked their bike, explored its shape, let it go. With extreme concentration Jericho fiddled with the controls, and the jets produced a small amount of reverse thrust, just enough for the machine to move slowly backwards over the edge of the platform.

'He's coming,' hissed Yoyo.

A beam of light crept into the hall from the neighbouring space. The blond guy had turned on the headlight. Jericho silently settled the airbike on the platform and turned off the engine. The hiss faded to a faint hum. He almost felt something like pride at his navigational abilities. The blond guy wouldn't hear them above the noise of his own machine, and the gloom up here would swallow them up. They clung to the ceiling like a fat, lurking insect.

'And by the way I *did* bring my computer,' Yoyo whispered.

Puzzled, Jericho turned round to look at her.

'I thought—'

'That *wasn't* my computer. I just wanted him to think it was. I wear mine on my belt.'

He raised his hand and hushed her. Far below their pursuer appeared and hovered slowly along underneath them. His bike hissed quietly, and a powerful finger of cold, white light crept around the building. Jericho leaned forwards. The blond guy was craning his head in all directions, looking at the ceiling without seeing them, peering between the containers. His gun lay heavy in his right hand.

Had he lost them?

Jericho hesitated. Highly unlikely that the man had gone looking for his pistol after the crash. The force of the collision had slung it far out into the darkness of the hall where the rolling mills were. There was only one explanation. His bike was fitted with more weapons, and if that was true of all of them, then—

On either side of the tank, he thought. That was the only place where there was room, right in front of his legs.

His fingers ran over the body of the bike.

Yep, no doubt about it, there were chambers there, cavities under the casings. But how did you get them open?

Below them, the hitman curved through the hall. The luminous eye darted between constructions and containers, slid along walkways and balconies. Only now did Jericho notice that their pursuer was creeping towards a tunnel-shaped hatch that opened up to the rear of the arched ceiling. Rails led from it to the inside of the hall. The blond guy stopped his bike and glanced in. He seemed uncertain whether to go inside before scouring the entire hall, then he turned back and climbed higher.

He was coming right towards them.

Jericho thought frantically. In a few seconds the killer would find them in their hiding-place. Like a man possessed, he searched the casings and the instrument panel for a way of opening the weapon compartments. The hissing got closer. He felt Yoyo's breath on the back of his neck, craned his head and ventured to look. The blond guy was two-thirds of the way up the hall.

Less than a metre, and he would see them.

But he got no higher.

Instead, his gaze wandered downwards and fixed on the mouths of the converters, that were turned towards him, lips rounded as if to suck him in, and Jericho realised what he was thinking. The bike stood motionless above one of the gaping maws. There was inky blackness within the steel cooking pot, no way of telling if anyone was hiding inside. The blond guy reached into a compartment on his bike, pulled something long from it and threw it down, then accelerated and got out of the danger zone.

A second went by.

Another, and another.

Then came the inferno.

The grenade went off with a deafening boom. A column of fire shot several metres out of the converter as the pressure of the explosion burst from the opening, bathed the hall in glowing red light, whirled smoke in all directions. Jericho grimaced, so painful was the echo in his ears.

The rumble of the explosion spread, escaped through the light-slit in the roof of the converter hall, its panes of glass shattered long since, vibrated the air molecules above and spread through the sky.

Xin heard the explosion two hundred metres higher up.

Something had gone up. Where exactly he couldn't have said, but he was sure that there had been a bang in one of the halls lined up to the west of the blast furnace.

Daxiong, on the other hand, had no doubt that the explosion originated in the converter hall.

He pulled the motorbike round, spraying up gravel, and at the same moment Xin plunged down from the sky like a hawk.

'Get a move on, damn you!'

Lau Ye was really furious. He was hopping from one leg to the other in Xiao-Tong's shed, watching his friends slowly putting on their shirts and trousers, as if the process of getting dressed contained incalculable risks. Ma Mak revealed the stoicism of a zombie, not embarrassed in the slightest that little Ye had found her and Xiao-Tong naked, in a position that left no doubt about the activity they had been engaged in when they fell asleep. Xiao-Tong blinked hard, trying to banish tiny living creatures from the corners of his eyes.

'Come on, now!' Ye clenched his fists, headed nowhere. 'I promised Daxiong that we'd hurry.'

A duet of grunting was heard, but at least the two of them managed to come shuffling after him. Outside, in the early sunlight, they contorted like vampires.

'I need a cup of tea,' murmured Mak.

'I need a fuck,' grinned Xiao-Tong and grabbed her backside. She shook him off and struggled onto her motorbike.

'You've lost it.'

'You've both lost it,' said Ye, and gave Xiao-Tong a shove that managed to get the guy to swing one leg over the saddle. They didn't have far to go. A few blocks up the street was Wong's World, and behind it, in the early morning mist, stood the silhouette of the blast furnace. Xiao-Tong pointed feebly at the market.

'First couldn't we at least go an'—'

'No,' said Ye. 'Pull yourselves together. Party over.'

That sounded good and very grown up, he thought. Could have come from Daxiong, and it seemed at least to make a big impression on Xiao-Tong and Mak. Abandoning all resistance, they left their bikes where they were, and followed him up the street. The closer they drew to the blast furnace, the tighter the feeling in Ye's guts became, and a terrible fear took hold of him.

Daxiong had said something about corpses.

He avoided mentioning that to Xiao-Tong and Mak. Not now. For the time being he was just glad to have managed to wake them up at all.

Jericho held his breath.

The blond guy had steered the airbike over the second converter, bringing himself a good bit closer to them. Again he drew out a hand grenade, pulled the pin, slung it into the container and got out of range. There was a bang; the converter spat fire and smoke.

'Let's get out of here,' Yoyo whispered in his ear.

'Then he'll get us,' Jericho whispered back. 'We won't get away from him another time.'

They couldn't escape for ever. Eventually they would have to finish off the blond guy, particularly since Jericho had no doubt that they would have to deal with Zhao sooner or later. If that was the man's name. One of the hitmen had called him Kenny.

Kenny Zhao Bide?

His gaze darted around. Right below them gaped the maw of the third converter, wide open as if the steel pot were waiting to be fed. A baby dinosaur, Jericho thought. That was what the pot looked like to him. Little birds crouched in the nest with their beaks wide open, greedily demanding worms and beetles, and what were birds if not miniaturised, feathered dinosaurs? This one was massive. With an appetite for something bigger. For human beings.

A moment later the blond guy's bike approached and obstructed his view of the converter. The machine was hovering right above the smelting pot, so close that Jericho could have touched the killer's head with his outstretched arm. A glance at the ceiling would have been enough for the blond guy to see them, but he seemed to have eyes only for the abyss where he assumed the fugitives were hiding.

He bent forward, reached into his arsenal of weapons and pulled out another hand grenade.

'Hold on tight,' Jericho said as quietly as possible. Yoyo pressed his upper arm to indicate that she had understood.

The blond guy pulled the pin from the grenade.

Jericho turned on the engine.

The airbike jumped forward and plunged down at the hitman. For a heartbeat Jericho saw him as if in a flash from a camera, his arm raised to throw the primed grenade, head thrown back, eyes wide with amazement, frozen.

Then they crashed straight into him.

Both turbines screamed to life. Jericho boosted thrust. He relentlessly smashed his opponent's bike against the converter, wrenched the handlebars around and escaped back into the air. The blond guy's machine plunged still further, somersaulted, crashed against the rim of the opening, was slung up in the air and clattered, dragging its rider with it, into the stygian abyss of the pot. A hollow clank and rattle followed them as they climbed. Desperately trying to get away from the hell that was about to break out, Jericho put his bike at top speed, sending prayers up to the hall ceiling.

Then came the explosion.

A demon rose from the depths of the cauldron, stretched roaring above it and fired out incandescent thermal waves. Its hot breath gripped Jericho and Yoyo and slung the bike through the air. They were dragged upwards, they turned and plunged. A quick sequence of explosions like booming cannons drowned out their cries as the blond guy's whole arsenal went up, one piece after another. The volcano spat fire in all directions, set half the plant ablaze in an instant, while they hurtled spinning towards the ground and Jericho tugged wildly on the handlebars. The bike looped, scraped along a column and crash-landed onto a platform. Jericho was breathless. Yoyo screamed and almost broke his ribs for fear of being thrown off. Raising sparks, they dashed along the platform, straight towards a wall. He braked, went into reverse thrust. The machine careened violently, altered course and clanged against a balustrade, where it hung vertical for a moment as if he had suspended it neatly from a hook, then it gave a groan and tipped over.

Jericho fell on his back. Yoyo rolled over next to him and hauled herself up. Her left thigh didn't look great, her trousers in shreds, the skin beneath it torn and bloody. Jericho crept on all fours to the balustrade, grasped the railings and got unsteadily to his feet. All around him everything was on fire. A smell of tar billowed to the ceiling and began to fog the hall.

They had to get out of there.

Yoyo bent double beside him and moaned with pain. He helped her up, as he stared into the thickening wall of smoke. What was that? Something was vaguely taking shape in the roiling clouds, they were brightening. At first he thought it might be another source of fire, but the light was white, spreading evenly, growing in intensity.

The fishlike rump of an airbike pushed its way out of the smoke.

It was Zhao.

*   *   *

As he set his foot on the bottom step of the zigzag stairs, Ye tried to control the trembling of his knee. His glance wandered along the tower of scaffolding to the platform on which the control room rested. All of a sudden he was afraid of what he might see there, so frightened that his legs threatened to give way.

He looked around.

A battered old car, a Toyota, was parked crookedly just below the girderwork, and two motorbikes a little further along. That surprised him. Normally they rode the machines into the adjacent empty building before going up.

He couldn't take his eyes off the bikes.

One of them was Tony's. And the other? He wasn't sure, but he thought it might be Ziyi's.

Tony – Ziyi—

What were they to expect up there?

Mak was trotting upstairs like a shadow in Xiao-Tong's wake. Ye cleared his throat.

'Wait, I've got to—'

'Let's not hang around,' she growled. 'You've got us out of bed now—'

'Terrible time of day,' Xiao-Tong complained.

'—so you can bloody well come too.'

Ye wrung his hands. He didn't know what to do. It was time to tell them Daxiong had mentioned corpses. That something terrible had happened in the control centre. But his tongue clung to his palate, his throat hurt as he swallowed. He opened his lips, and a croak issued from them.

'I'm coming.'

Daxiong hadn't come via the old rolling mill. There was a shortcut, at least he hoped it was still possible to get through it. Trains had once crisscrossed the grounds of the plant, shunting-engines with torpedo-shaped wagons that were filled with liquid pig iron after the blast furnace was tapped. From there they had driven their 1400-degree cargo to the converter hall, where the iron was poured into huge pans and from there into the steel smelting pots.

Daxiong followed the tracks. They led at least two kilometres across the open field and disappeared into a tunnel, more of a covered passageway, really, that opened right into the converter hall. Shots were ringing out from there now. He put his foot right down, caught his front wheel in one of the tracks, slipped. The motorbike threw him off. He skidded along on the seat of his trousers, dumbfounded by his own stupidity, jumped to his feet, cursed. He had got off lightly, but the accident had cost him time.

His eyes scoured the sky.

No trace of an airbike. He righted his toppled motorbike and tried to start it. After several attempts and encouraging words, the most frequent of which was *Merde!*, the machine finally sprang to life, and Daxiong plunged into the darkness of the passageway. What he saw was less than encouraging. A shunting-engine rested, broad and sedate, on one of the two parallel tracks; another was coupled to two torpedo cars. He wouldn't be able to get by on either side, only the space between the trains was wide enough – but there was something blocking it.

He should have gone through the rolling mill!

Forced to stop, he got off his bike and walked over to the obstruction, which turned out to be a twisted metal frame. Bracing his three-hundred-weight bulk against it, he tried to shift it from its position. Further ahead he could see the dim opening beyond which the hall lay. It couldn't have been more than twenty metres away.

He had to get there.

At that moment there was a third explosion, a salvo this time, much louder than the others. The passageway lit up, something burning flew into it and crashed to the ground. Further explosions followed. As if possessed, Daxiong rattled at the metal frame until at last, with a great creak, it started to give. The thing wasn't heavy, just hopelessly stuck. He tensed his muscles. All hell must have broken loose through there, flames were blazing. Daxiong panted, pulled and tugged, pushed and shoved, and all of a sudden the metal frame yielded and twisted a little to the side.

Still. Just enough of a gap for him to squeeze through.

*   *   *

Xin held a hand in front of his mouth and nose as he rode his airbike through the billows. Acrid smoke brought tears to his eyes. What in hell's name had the blond guy been up to? Hopefully it had been worth it at least. Beyond the deep blackness he saw flames flickering. His right hand reached for the butt of the sub-machine-gun in its holster and let go of it again.

First he had to find a way out.

The smoke cleared, giving him a view of the hall. The whole place was in flames. Not a soul in sight, just a toppled airbike hanging from the balustrade of a gallery, dented and blackened. The windscreen was missing. Xin steered towards it, as a great roll of thunder set the hall trembling. Immediately behind him a column of fire shot into the air, the wave of pressure sending heavy vibrations through his bike. He climbed, then glimpsed a movement at the far end of the hall.

Something came roaring out of the wall. The motorbike rider. The bald giant.

Xin drew the gun from the holster.

A greasy black cloud billowed over and enveloped him, hot and suffocating. He held his breath, brought the bike further up, but the cloud wouldn't let go of him. Of course it wouldn't! Smoke drifted upwards. What sort of an idiot was he? Blinded and disorientated, he brought the bike back down again. He couldn't even see the lights on the instrument panel now. He steered haphazardly to the right and collided with something, then dragged the handlebars around.

Further down. He had to get down there.

Small fires crackled around him, immersing his airbike in a flickering red glow. He thought he could hear voices coming from somewhere, headed straight ahead to avoid any further collisions, and managed to get out of the cloud. Between flickering flames and plumes of smoke he saw the motorbike.

Yoyo was sitting on its pillion.

Xin bellowed with fury. The motorbike disappeared into the wide, low passageway from which it had emerged. With hissing jets he shot after the two of them and followed them into the tunnel. The motorbike dashed between two trains. He tried to estimate the amount of room he had: airbikes were a bit broader than motorbikes, but if he was careful he would fit through.

When he was just about to shoot the girl in the back, he saw something blocking the way.

Iron bars. Bent, wedged.

Beside himself with fury, he was forced to look as Yoyo and the giant ducked their heads and managed by a hair to get under the twisted metal. He himself would have been skewered. Not a chance. His bike was too wide, too high. He pivoted the jets and braked, but his momentum carried him on towards the metal poles. For a moment Xin was filled with a paralysing sense of complete helplessness; he pulled the bike round sideways-on, scraping along against the trains, and metal crunched against metal as he managed to reduce his speed.

He held his breath.

The airbike stopped, just centimetres away from the metal frame.

Seething with rage, he stared through it. Daylight entered at the end of the passageway. The motorbike engine seemed to give him an insolent growl as it disappeared from view. Close to losing his self-control, Xin wrenched the airbike round, flew back into the hall, plunged into the smoke, sped through the rolling mill and the warehouse and back outside. Above the slagheap, he turned in a great circle, grateful for the fresh air, opened the cover of the second weapon chamber and reached inside. When his hand came back out, it was holding something long and heavy. Then, at great speed, he bore down on the blast furnace.

Jericho spat and coughed. The smoke billowed into every corner. He wouldn't survive another fight in this inferno. If he didn't get out of here right away, it would all be too late. Another few minutes, and he might as well just settle down and fill his lungs with tar until they were the colour of liquorice.

He hoped devoutly that Yoyo had made it. Everything had happened at impossible speed. Their escape over the platform, Zhao's bike. Then, all of a sudden, Daxiong. The hitman must have seen him, but something had kept him from reacting straight away, fire, perhaps, welling smoke. They had had time to get to Daxiong, who stopped his bike all of a sudden and paused with the engine running. There had been a flicker of puzzlement in the giant's narrow eyes, as he wondered how he would get them both on his narrow pillion.

'Go, Yoyo,' Jericho had said.

'I can't—'

'Go, damn it! No speeches, just fuck off! I'll be fine.'

She had looked at him, soot-blackened, unkempt and plainly shocked, with a mixture of fury and defiance in her eyes. And all of a sudden he had seen that strange sadness in her, which he knew from Chen's photographs. Then Yoyo had jumped on Daxiong's pillion. At that moment Zhao had spotted them both.

Jericho clung to the hope that they'd got away from the hitman. Visibility was getting worse and worse. With his sleeve pressed to his mouth and nose, he edged his way up to the gallery and inspected the airbike. In poor shape, but the damage seemed to be mainly cosmetic in nature. Hoping the handlebars weren't damaged, he bent down and hoisted the machine upright.

His eye fell on something small.

It lay on the ground next to the airbike, something flat, silvery, gleaming. He picked it up, surprised, looked at it, turned it around in his hand—

Yoyo's computer!

She must have lost it here. When she fell off the bike.

He'd found Yoyo's computer!

He quickly slipped the device into his jacket, swung onto his saddle and started the bike. The familiar hiss.

He had to get out of there.

It had been worse than he had feared. Ma Mak had suddenly thrown up, Xiao-Tong alternately yelled curses and the names of their dead friends, and looked as if he would never recover.

Ye was crying.

He knew he would never be able to get these images out of his head. Never in his life.

Don't ask any questions.

'We've got to pack all the stuff up,' he sniffed.

'I can't,' wailed Mak.

'We promised Daxiong. Something to do with all this stuff. It's all got to go.' He started unplugging computers and disconnecting displays. Xiao-Tong stared at him numbly.

'What on earth's happened here?' he whispered.

'Dunno.'

'Where's Yoyo?'

'No idea. Are you going to help me now?'

Mak wiped her mouth, picked up a keyboard and pulled it from the computer. Eventually Xiao-Tong joined in as well. They stuffed the equipment into cardboard boxes and dragged them outside. They didn't touch the corpses, they tried not to look at them or, even worse, to walk through the still damp pools of blood. Everything was covered with blood, the room, the table, the screens, everything. Mak put her arms around a cardboard box, lifted it and set it down again. Ye saw her shoulders twitching. Her head swung back and forth like a clockwork toy, unable to accept what she saw. He stroked her back, took the box from her hands and pulled it through Tony's blood – or was it Jia Wei's, or Ziyi's – and outside.

He paused for a moment, snorted and looked up at the sky.

What was that?

Something was approaching from out of the air beyond the halls. It was quick, and coming closer. A high-pitched hiss heralded its arrival. A flying device. Like a motorbike, but without wheels. Someone was sitting in the saddle steering the thing, steering it straight at the control room—

Ye blinked, screened his eyes against the sun with his hand.

Daxiong?

He was gradually able to make out details. Not who was driving the machine, but that the driver or pilot or whatever you called him was holding something long that flashed for a second in the sun—

'Hey,' he called out. 'Come and take a look at th—'

Something detached itself from the flying motorbike and came hurtling at him with the speed of a rocket.

It *was* a rocket.

'—is,' he whispered.

His last thought was that he must be dreaming. That it wasn't happening, because it couldn't possibly happen.

Don't ask any questions.

Xin sped away.

The little house resting on the scaffolding seemed to inflate for a second, as if taking a deep breath. Then the front part blew apart in a fiery cloud, slinging rubble in all directions, crashing against the main structure of the blast furnace, the façades of the adjacent buildings, the forecourt. Xin curved round and fired further rockets at the rear façade. What remained of the side walls exploded, and the roof collapsed. The struts of the girderwork tower supporting the blazing ruin snapped. The control room began to topple, raining down flaming fragments, broke apart in the middle and sent a flurry of sparks through the tower.

Xin felt a sudden twinge of satisfaction as he spotted Jericho's Toyota in the midst of the avalanche of rubble. A moment later there was nothing more to be seen of the car. The detritus of the old control centre spilled over the ground until all that remained upright was what was left of the scaffolding, a pyre, testimony to the cathartic power of heavy explosives.

Jericho's heart felt cold and clammy as he left the darkness of the warehouse. He saw people running shouting across the slagheaps, drawn by the roar of the fire, whose black column of smoke, scattered with flying sparks, rose far above the furnace and reached towards the pale, early sun.

Had Yoyo been in the building? Had she and Daxiong gone back there? Had Zhao caught them there in the end?

No, Zhao, Kenny or whatever his name was must have destroyed the building for some other reason. Because Yoyo had left him thinking that the computer was still there. He had wiped out most of the Guardians and now he'd destroyed their meeting point, too, with all the electronics it contained, decapitated the organisation, killed anyone Yoyo might have confided in.

He devoutly hoped that her head start had been enough to let her get away from Zhao.

He flew closer. The airbike was harder to steer now than it had been before the crash in the converter hall. It was possible one of the jets had been twisted and could no longer be precisely adjusted any more. Trying to tilt the bike out of its crooked angle, he didn't immediately understand what it was that he actually saw. The memory of his car came sketchily to mind, parked below the tower of scaffolding. It was only when he was so close to the fire that the heat forced him to turn away that he knew for sure that his Toyota was burning at the bottom of the column of flames.

Fear, exhaustion, everything was swept away by a wave of ungovernable fury. He searched feverishly for the mechanism that would open the side compartments, to shoot Zhao from the sky with his own weapons. But nothing opened, and Zhao was nowhere to be seen.

The forecourt filled with people. They came from all directions, on foot, on bicycles and on motorcycles. The whole of Wong's World was pouring towards the blast furnace. Even Cyber Planet opened its doors, releasing pale and baffled figures, unable to believe what they saw.

Nothing helped. Under such circumstances even the police might have been expected to remember that forgotten world. Jericho climbed. He saw various people pointing at him, thrust his engine and passed over the industrial estate.

Xin saw the airbike getting smaller.

A good way away from the scene, he perched on the top of a chimney like a buzzard. For a moment he had considered finishing Jericho off with a well-aimed bullet as well, but the detective might still prove useful. Xin let him go. Yoyo was more important. She couldn't have got far, and yet he would have to get used to the idea of having lost the girl for the time being. He decided to stay here and keep watch for her at least until the forces of law and order arrived.

In spite of his defeat, he had a clear image of the universe at that moment. Existences that came into being and then exploded, a surging froth of birth and death, while Xin remained immortal, the centre, the point where all lines crossed. The idea reassured him. He had sown chaos and destruction, but he had done it for a higher good. The remains of the girderwork joined the burning ruins on the ground; in the west the flames rose high from the converter hall. Lesser men than he would have called it destruction, but Xin saw nothing but harmony. The cleansing fire spread, healing the world of the infectious afflictions of poverty, cauterising the pus from the organism of the megalopolis.

At the same time, with conscientious precision, he recapitulated his commission, translated into the language of money. Because Xin had learned to navigate safely on the ocean of his thoughts. Without the slightest doubt, he was insane, as his family had always maintained, except that he understood his insanity. Of all the things he liked about himself, this one filled him with special pride, being a self-analyst, able to establish quite objectively: he was a perfect example of a psychopath. What terrible power that realisation contained! Knowing who he was. At one and the same second, being able to be *everything* all at the same time – artist, sadist, empath, higher being, ordinary Joe. Right now it was the careerist who had assumed control of his various personalities, the conventional one who liked to attend to business and then relax in a villa by the sea, surrounded by helpful staff, feeling like the centre of the universe. It was that down-to-earth, predictable Xin who restrained his crazed, pyromaniac alter ego in his place and taught him efficiency.

He was so many people. So many things.

High up on his chimney Xin, the planner, started wondering what he had to do to make Yoyo come to him of her own accord.

Jericho

For a while, Owen Jericho rode his bike under the elevated highway that separated Quyu from the real world. Below him, the traffic headed noisily westwards, counterpointed by the boom and roar of the CODs on the freeway above him. He was trapped in a sandwich of noise. When two police skymobiles came chasing over with their sirens wailing he took refuge between the sand-coloured skyscrapers that typified the urban desert around the central district of Shanghai, and followed the course of the main road to Hongkou. As he did so, he tried to stay as low as possible in the canyon of buildings. He assumed that he was flying below the permitted altitude, but he didn't feel at ease on the battered airbike. And he didn't want to experience a sudden engine failure high above the rooftops. Trying to compensate for the leftward tilt of the vehicle, he wound his way between façades, pillars, traffic-light poles, electric wires and elevated road signs, looking alternately straight ahead, into the rear-view mirror and towards the sky as he waited for Zhao. It was only when he had crossed Hongkou and flown the bike out towards the river that he started to think he might have shaken him off. If Zhao had even *wanted* to follow him. He plunged into the busy shopping streets behind the colonial façade of the Bund, landed to the west of Huaihai Park and dragged the airbike to the Xintiandi underground car park. The left rear wheel got stuck and scraped noisily over the asphalt. For a moment he wondered where to park it, until he remembered what had happened to his car.

At least he had a parking space for this thing now.

The scraping of the damaged wheel echoed angrily against the ramp walls as he steered the airbike towards the space reserved for him. He tried to forget his fury over the loss of his car, and grant priority to Yoyo's wellbeing. In a mood of selflessness he extended his concern to Daxiong, as he hurried through the car park, hoping no one would see him with his soot-blackened face, but there wasn't even anyone in the lift. There was a uniform light on the walls, the unit hummed gently. By the time he finally slammed the door of his loft behind him, he was certain no one had caught sight of him.

He sighed with relief and ran his hands over his face and through his hair.

He closed his eyes.

Immediately he saw the corpses, the boy with his face shot away, the dying, spinning girl with bright red fountains shooting from her shredded shoulder artery, her severed arm, saw himself freeing the gun from her clawed fingers – what was up, what had gone wrong? Hadn't he wanted to lead a peaceful life? And now this. Within a few days. Abused children, mutilated young people, he himself more dead than alive. Reality? A dream, a film?

A film, exactly. And popcorn and something nice and cold. Lean back. What was on next? *Quyu* II, *the Return*?

Impressions came chasing after him like rabid dogs. He mustn't let it all get to him. He would never be able to get rid of it again; from now on the images would visit him on sleepless nights, but at the moment he had to think. Stack up his thoughts like building-blocks. Make a plan.

Scattering T-shirt and trousers carelessly around the sitting room, he went to the bathroom, turned on the shower, washed soot and blood from his skin, took stock. Yoyo and Daxiong had got away. A hypothesis, admittedly, temporarily elevated to the status of fact, but then he had to have *something* to go on. Secondly, Yoyo had been able to save her computer, which was now in his possession. Of course Zhao wouldn't be so naïve as to believe that all the data were on the hard drive of a single, small device. The control room hadn't been destroyed on a whim, it had served the purpose of annihilating the group's infrastructure and possibly all the other devices that Yoyo had transferred the data onto. On the other hand Yoyo's bluff might have achieved the desired effect when she suggested to Zhao that she'd left her computer at the control centre. Zhao must have believed he'd solved that problem at least.

What would he do next?

The answer was obvious. He would of course ask himself the question that had been troubling him ceaselessly for days: Who had Yoyo told about her discovery, and who out of them was still alive?

I know about it, he thought, as the hot streams of water massaged the back of neck. No, wrong! I know that she's found something out, but I don't know what. Zhao, on the other hand, knows that I know precisely nothing. Nice and Socratic. I'm not really an accessory, I'm only a witness to a few regrettable incidents.

Only? Quite enough to get him second place on Zhao's hit list.

On the other hand, what were the chances that Zhao planned to kill him as well? Very high, looking at it realistically, but first he might hope that Jericho, the dewy-eyed twit, would lead him to Yoyo a second time.

Jericho paused, his hair a foam sculpture.

Then why hadn't Zhao followed him here?

Very simple. Because Yoyo had actually been able to get away! Zhao assumed she was still in Quyu. He had preferred to continue with the chase. And in any case he didn't need to follow Jericho, since he knew exactly where he would find him.

Still. He'd gained some time.

How much?

He rinsed his hair. Black trickles ran down his chest and arms, as if new dirt were constantly emerging from his pores. A stinging pain testified to some of the grazes he'd got when he crashed in the converter hall. He wondered how Yoyo was at that moment. Probably traumatised, although her big mouth hadn't seemed to be in a state of shock. She'd still been capable of producing a reliable torrent of insults, suggesting a certain mental balance and, at the very least, a degree of resilience. The girl, he guessed, was as tough as sharkskin.

He turned off the tap.

Zhao would show up sooner or later. It was quite possible that he was already on his way. He reached for a towel, ran, still drying himself, through the sunlit expanse of his loft, which he would have to leave again almost as soon as he'd moved in, slipped into fresh clothes, tidied his hair very slightly. Next on the agenda was the flight of Owen Jericho, Inc., which consisted of Jericho himself, Diane, and all his technical equipment. He disconnected the hard drive, a portable unit the size of a shoe-box, and stuffed it in a rucksack along with the keyboard, a foldable touchscreen surface and a transparent 20-inch display. Along with that he packed his ID card, money, his spare mobile phone, a small hard drive for backups, Yoyo's computer, headphones and Tu's hologoggles. He stuffed underwear and T-shirts in with it, a spare pair of trousers, slippers, shaving materials, some pens and paper. The only things left in the loft were his control console and large screen, a few bits of hardware and various built-in drives, all of which were, without Diane, as useless as prosthetic limbs without anyone to wear them. No one who managed to get in here would find a bit or a byte; they wouldn't be able to reconstruct Jericho's work. The flat was more or less data-free.

Without turning round again, he went outside.

In the underground car park he strapped the rucksack onto the pillion seat of the airbike and examined the bent jet. With both hands he forced it back into its position. The result didn't look very convincing, but at least it could be adjusted now. Then he fiddled around with the tailfin, drove the bike up the ramp and, with a certain satisfaction, noticed that the sound of scraping had gone. The ball wheel was turning again. He had swapped the car for an airbike, not voluntarily, but it was still a swap.

Outside the sun poured its light down like phosphorescent milk. Jericho narrowed his eyes, but Zhao was nowhere to be seen.

Where to now?

He wouldn't have to go far. In a city like Shanghai the best hiding-place was always right around the corner. Instead of heading for the notoriously jammed Huaihai Donglu, he took less frequented alleyways that connected Xintiandi with the Yu Gardens, to the Liuhekou Lu, known for a long time as an authentic residue of the Shanghai that had stirred the imaginations of incorrigible colonial romantics. But what, over the passing centuries, did authenticity consist of? Only what existed, the Party taught. There had been a covered market here, scattered with flower stalls, echoing with the scolding of all kinds of animals, chickens jerking their heads back and forth to demonstrate their edible freshness, crickets tapping away against the walls of jam jars and bringing consolation to their owners, whose lives were not all that different in the end. Then, three years ago, the market had made way for a handsome shikumen complex, full of bistros, internet cafés, boutiques and galleries. Diagonally opposite, a few last market stalls were asserting themselves with the defiance of old gentlemen stopping in the middle of the carriageway and threatening approaching cars with sticks until friendly fellow citizens walked them to the other side and assured them of the utter pointlessness of their actions. They too were still a piece of 'authentic' Shanghai. Tomorrow they would have disappeared, to make way for a new 'authenticity'.

Jericho parked the bike two floors down in the underground car park of the complex and withdrew into the back corner of a bistro, where he ordered coffee. Although he wasn't even slightly hungry, he also asked for a cheese baguette, bit into it, scattered crumbs on his T-shirt and trousers and noted with some satisfaction that it didn't all come right back up again.

How far would Zhao go?

This temporary equilibrium was much more bitter than the coffee that he was gulping down. No car. No loft, because it was uninhabitable for the time being. In the sights of a hitman, with his back to the wall. No option but to run away. Forced to act, except that he didn't think he was capable of action. There was no way back into normality, except by getting to the bottom of things. Understanding how the whole drama played out. Find out who had commissioned Zhao.

Jericho stared straight ahead.

Hang on, though! He wasn't entirely incapable of action. Zhao might have forced him onto the defensive, but he had something the hitman didn't know about. His secret weapon, the key to everything.

Yoyo's computer.

He had to find out what she had discovered.

Then he would track her down again, to take her back to her father.

Chen Hongbing. Was it a good idea to call him? Tu Tian had established the contact, but in point of fact Chen was his client. The man had a right to be informed, but what would he say to him? All fine, Yoyo's in great shape . . . No, honourable Chen, it isn't the police who are after her, just a hardened hitman with a weakness for explosive devices, but hey, don't worry, she's still got both arms and legs and her whole face, haha! Where is she? Well, she's on the run! Me too, see you soon.

What *could* he say, if he didn't want the man to die of a heart attack?

And what if he did get the police involved? Of course he would have to give them a bit of background, not least concerning Yoyo. Which risked drawing attention to the girl. They would ask what part she'd played in the massacre, look at her data, establish that she was on file, even that she had a criminal record. Impossible. The police were out of the question, even though Zhao wasn't a cop, regardless of what he might have told Yoyo in the control centre:

I'm trained to kill people. Like all policemen, like all soldiers, all agents.

All agents?

National security is a higher good than individual human lives.

The Secret Service, on the other hand, had already blown plenty of other things sky high, particularly when they got involved in matters of national security. Zhao could have been bluffing, but what if he actually had the blessing of the authorities?

But what about calling Tu?

That looked pretty pointless too. Jericho forced himself to think clearly. First switch on Diane. He looked around. The bistro was two-thirds full, but the tables around him were free. Here and there young people were writing on their laptops or making phone calls. He set keyboard and screen in front of him and connected both to the hard drive in the rucksack. Then he jammed in the headset earbud and linked the system to Yoyo's computer. A symbol appeared, a crouching wolf threateningly showing its fangs. Below it appeared some text:

I'm inviting you to dinner.

Okay, then, thought Jericho.

'Hi Diane,' he said quietly.

'Hi, Owen.' Diane's velvety timbre. The consolation of the machine. 'How did you get on?'

'Fucking awful.'

'Sorry to hear that.' How honest that sounded. Okay, then, it wasn't *dis*honest. 'Can I help?'

You could be made of flesh and blood, thought Jericho.

'Please open the file "I'm inviting you to dinner". You'll find access data in Yoyofiles.'

Silence fell for two seconds. Then Diane said:

'The file is locked four times. I've been able to use three of the tools successfully. I haven't got the fourth access authorisation.'

'Which tools worked?'

'Iris, voice and fingerprint. All assigned to Chen Yuyun.'

'Which one's missing?'

'A password, by the look of it. Shall I decipher?'

'Do that. Have you any idea how long the decoding's going to take you?'

'Afraid not. At the moment I can only speculate that the coding includes several words. Or one unusually long one. Is there anything else I can do for you?'

'Go online,' said Jericho. 'That's it. See you later, Diane.'

'See you later, Owen.'

He logged on to Brilliant Shit. If his assumption was correct, the Guardians' blog was being used as a dead letter drop, and regularly checked.

Jericho to Demon, he wrote. *I've got your computer.* He added a phone number and an email address, stayed logged in and stored the blog as an icon. As soon as someone saved a message in it, Diane would let him know straight away. By now he felt a little better. He bit into his baguette, topped up his coffee and decided to contact Tu.

A call came in for him.

Jericho stared at the display. No picture, no number.

Yoyo? So quickly?

'Hi, Owen,' said a very familiar voice.

'Zhao.' Everything inside Jericho shrank to a tiny lump. He paused for a moment and tried to sound relaxed. 'Or should I say Kenny?'

'Kenny?'

'Don't pretend to be more stupid than you are! Didn't that fat asshole call you that before he kicked the bucket?'

'Oh, right.' The other man laughed quietly. 'As you wish, then – Kenny.'

'Kenny who? Kenny Zhao Bide?'

'Kenny's just fine.'

'Okay, Kenny.' Jericho took a deep breath. 'Then wash your ears out. Yoyo's slipped through your fingers. I got away from you. You won't get any further as long as one of us has a reason to feel threatened by you.'

A sigh of resignation came through the receiver.

'I'm not threatening anybody.'

'Yes, you are. You're shooting people and blowing up buildings.'

'You've got to look the facts in the face, Owen. You put up a decent fight, you and the girl. Admirable, but not especially clever, I'm afraid to say. If Yoyo had cooperated, everyone might still be alive.'

'Ridiculous.'

'It was your people who started all the shooting.'

'Not at all. They only started shooting because you'd killed Xiao Meiqi and Jin Jia Wei.'

'That was unavoidable.'

'Really?'

'Yoyo would hardly have talked to me otherwise. Later I did everything in my power to avert any further bloodshed.'

'What do you want, Kenny?'

'What do you think I want? Yoyo, of course.'

'To do what?'

'To ask her what she knows and who she's told.'

'You—'

'Don't worry!' Kenny cut in. 'I'm not planning on killing even more people. But I'm under a certain amount of pressure, you know? Pressure to succeed. These are the times we're living in, everyone constantly wants to see results, so what would you do in my place? Come away empty-handed?'

'You've got your hands pretty full. You've destroyed Yoyo's computer, and the complete infrastructure of the Guardians. Do you really think any of them wants to mess with you again?'

'Owen,' said Kenny in the voice of a teacher who needs to explain everything three times, 'I don't know anything. I don't know whether I destroyed Yoyo's infrastructure, how many computers she transferred the data to, whether everyone she confided in died in the control centre. What about that huge bike-riding baby? What about you? Didn't she tell you anything?'

'We won't get any further like this. Where are you anyway?'

Kenny paused for a moment.

'Nice flat. Looks like you've done some house-clearing.'

Jericho gave a sour smile. He felt a kind of satisfaction in being proved right and having got out in good time.

'You'll find a cold beer in the fridge,' he said. 'Take it and go.'

'I can't do that, Owen.'

'Why not?'

'Haven't you had jobs to do, like I do? Aren't you used to taking things to their conclusion?'

'I'll tell you once more—'

'Imagine the inferno if the flames should take hold of other parts of the building.'

Jericho's mouth dried up all of a sudden.

'What flames?'

'The ones from your flat.' Kenny's voice had dropped to a whisper and he suddenly reminded Jericho of a snake: a huge talking snake stuffed into the body of a human being. 'I'm thinking of the people, and also of you. I mean, everything here looks new and expensive. You've probably put all your savings into it. Wouldn't it be terrible to lose all that at one go, just for a matter of principle, out of solidarity with some pig-headed girl?'

Jericho said nothing.

'Can you imagine my situation any better now?'

A host of insults collected on the tip of Jericho's tongue. Instead he said as quietly as possible, 'Yes, I think so.'

'That's a weight off my mind. Really! I mean, we weren't a bad team, Owen. Our interests are marginally different, but basically we want the same thing in the end.'

'And now?'

'Just tell me where Yoyo is.'

'I don't know.'

Kenny seemed to think about it.

'Good. I believe you. So you'll have to track her down for me.'

Track her down—

Good God! What sort of bloody idiot was he? He didn't know what tricks the hitman had up his sleeve, but doubtless everything he said was designed to drag the conversation out. Kenny was trying to track *him* down. To locate him.

Without hesitation, Jericho hung up.

Less than a minute later his phone lit up again.

'I give you two hours,' hissed Kenny. 'Not a minute longer. Then I want to hear something that will put my mind at rest, otherwise I'll consider myself forced to undertake a radical restructuring of the building.'

Two hours.

What was Jericho supposed to do in two hours?

He hastily bundled the display and the keyboard back into his backpack, put a banknote on the table and left the bistro without a backwards glance. He strode towards the lift, took it down to the underground garage, climbed onto his bike and brought it out onto Liuhekou Lu, where he started the engine and flew towards the river. During the short flight a bulky ambulance hovered below him, big enough for him to land on. In the distance he saw an armada of unmanned fire-engines making for the hinterland of Pudong. Private skymobiles crossed his path, pleasure-blimps bobbed above the Huangpu. For a moment he considered flying to the WFC and looking up Tu, but it was too early for that. He would need peace to carry out his plan, and he had to have somewhere to stay, for as long as Kenny robbed him of the warmth and security of Xintiadi.

And he knew where.

Looming over the grand buildings of the Bund was one of the most peculiar hotels in Shanghai. Like a huge lotus blossom, China's symbol of growth and affluence, the roof of the Westin Shanghai Bund Center opened itself up to the sky. It made some people think of an agave, others of an outsize octopus extending its tentacles to filter birds and skymobiles out of the air. Jericho saw it only as a refuge whose manager played in the same golf club as himself and Tu Tian. A casual acquaintance without the bonus of familiarity, but Tu liked the man, and tended to use the hotel as accommodation for business partners too lowly for the WFC and the Jin Mao Tower. Jericho was also granted the indulgence of special conditions, a favour that he had so far never called on. Now, since he felt little desire to wander nomadically from bistro to bistro, he decided to make use of it. After he had landed his bike by the front entrance, he stepped into the lobby and asked for a single room. The cameras set into the wall scanned him and passed the relevant information on to the receptionist. She smilingly greeted him by name, a sign that he was already on their files, and asked him to set his phone down on the touchscreen. The hotel computer compared Jericho's ID with the database, authorised the reservation and uploaded the access code to Jericho's hard drive.

'Would you like us to take your car to the underground car park?' the woman asked, and performed the trick of speaking with a smile even though her lips never met.

'I've come on an airbike,' said Jericho.

'We've got a landing bay, as I'm sure you know,' said the smile fixed to the corners of the receptionist's mouth. 'Do you want us to park your bike there for you?'

'No, I'll do that myself.' He grinned. 'Quite honestly, I need every hour of flying time I can get.'

'Oh, I understand.' The smile switched from routine politeness to routine cordiality. 'Safe journey up there. Don't forget, the hotel façade can take more knocks than you can.'

'I'll bear it in mind.'

He left the lobby and flew his bike up along the glazed outside wall, constantly accompanied by his reflection. For the first time he became aware that he wasn't wearing a helmet, as the regulations for airbikes demanded. Another reason to keep away from the police. If they found out that the bike wasn't registered to him, it was going to be a tough thing to explain.

The landing pad was open and almost empty, aside from the hotel's own shuttles. Nearly all twentieth-century visions of the future had assumed some form of private urban air traffic powered by lightbeams, taking it for granted that aerial traffic would shape the face of cities. In fact, the number of such skymobiles was tiny, and they were restricted to State and city institutions, a few exclusive taxi companies and millionaires like Tu Tian. In purely infrastructural terms, of course, there were good reasons for lightening ground traffic by exploiting the airborne variety, except that all these considerations faced a great Godzilla of a counter-argument: fuel consumption. To counteract the force of gravity you needed powerful turbines and a whole load of energy. The economical alternative, the gyrocopter, spiralled its way into the air by rotor power like a helicopter, but had the disadvantage of excessively massive rotor blades. Financially, the expense of making cars fly was entirely disproportionate to the effect, and airbikes, even though they were more economical and affordable, weren't really an exception to that. They were still expensive enough to make Jericho wonder who could afford to supply a hitman with three – especially customised models. The police, chronically underfunded? Hardly. Secret services? More likely. The army?

Was Kenny a soldier? Was the army behind all this?

With his backpack over his shoulder, Jericho took the lift to his floor and held his phone up to the infrared port beside the door to his room. It swung open, revealing a view of the room behind it. Fussy and staid, was his first impression. All in great condition, but stylistically nowhere. Jericho didn't care. Within a few minutes he had freed Diane from her backpack and connected her up. That made this room his new investigation agency.

Would Kenny set the loft on fire?

Jericho rubbed his temples. He wouldn't be surprised, but on the other hand he doubted that the hitman would wait in Xintiandi until he called. Kenny would try to arrest Yoyo on his own initiative, probably aware that Jericho wasn't automatically prepared for collaboration just because he was waving a box of matches around.

'Diane?'

'I'm here, Owen.'

'How's the search for the password going?'

It was a stupid question. As long as Diane registered no success, he didn't need to worry about where things went from here. But talking to the computer made him feel as if he was in charge of a little team that was doing everything in its power.

'You'll be the first to know,' said Diane.

Jericho gave a start. Was that humour? Not bad. He lay down on the huge bed with its gaudy yellow cover and felt terribly tired and useless. Owen Jericho, cyber-detective. Hilarious. He had been supposed to find Yoyo, and instead he'd put a psychopath on her trail. How in God's name would he explain that to Tu, let alone to Chen Hongbing?

'Owen?'

'Diane?'

'Someone's uploading a post to Brilliant Shit.'

Jericho jolted upright.

'Read it to me.'

At first he was disappointed. It was a list of coordinates, with no sender or any kind of accompanying text. Time, input code, nothing else.

An address in Second Life.

Did it come from Yoyo?

With leaden head and arms, he pulled himself upright, walked over to the little desk where he'd put his screen and keyboard, and took a look at the short text. At length he found a single letter that he'd probably overlooked: a D.

Demon.

Jericho took a look at his watch. Just after eleven. At twelve o'clock Yoyo was waiting for him in the virtual world. As long as the message really did come from her and wasn't another attempt by Kenny to locate him. Had he given away the address of the blog to the hitman? Not as far as he remembered. Kenny surely couldn't be so cunning as to turn up all of a sudden in Brilliant Shit as well, but caution was plainly advised. Jericho decided not to take a risk. From now on he would put any online communication through the anonymiser.

He lay back on the bed and stared at the ceiling.

There was nothing he could do.

After a few minutes the turbulent sea of his nerves was calm once more. He dozed off, but he didn't sink into a relaxing sleep. Just below the surface of his consciousness, he was haunted by images of creeping torsos that weren't human beings, but failed designs of human beings, grotesquely distorted and incomplete, covered with blood and mucus like newborn babies. He saw legless creatures, their faces nothing but smooth, gleaming surfaces, split down the middle by obscenely twitching pink openings. Half-charred lumps teetered towards him like spiders on a thousand legs or more. Eyes and mouths suddenly opened up in a scab of shapeless tissue. Something blind stretched towards him, darting a gnarled tongue between fanged jaws, and yet Jericho felt no fear, just a weary sadness, since he knew that in another life all these monstrosities had been as human as he was himself.

Then he fell, and found himself back on a bed, but it was a different bed from the one on which he had lain down. Dark and damp, lit by feeble moonlight that fell through a dirty window and outlined the bleak, bare room where he had ended up, it seemed to exert a curious power over him. Lucidly dreaming, he realised that he must be in his comfortable, boringly furnished room, but he couldn't sit up and open his eyes. He was bound to this rotting mattress as if by magnetic force, swathed in weird, dry silence.

And in the midst of that silence he suddenly heard the click of chitin-armoured legs.

Jagged feet scratched at the edges of the bedcover, snagged in the fabric and drew fat, segmented bodies up to him. A wave of anxiety washed over him. His horror was due less to the question of what the armoured creatures wanted to do to him, than to the most terrible of all realisations: that a perfidious dream had slung him back into the past, to a phase of his life that he thought he had long since overcome. His rise through society in Shanghai, the peace that he had made with Joanna, his arrival in Xintiandi, it was all revealed as a fantasy, the real dream, from which the invisible insects were now waking him with their rustles and clicks.

Close beside him, someone had begun to whimper, in high, singing tones. Everything sank back into darkness, because the fact that his eyes were closed was starting to defeat the vision of that terrifying room. His mind found its way back to reality, except that nobody seemed to have told his body. It didn't respond, it wouldn't move. He was starting to fight against that weird rigidity by emitting those whimpers, real sounds that anyone who had been in the room could have heard as clearly as he did himself, and finally, by summoning all his powers, he managed to move the little finger of his left hand. He was wide awake by now. He remembered stories about people who – having apparently passed away – had been carried to the grave, while they actually saw every moment with crystal clarity, and without the slightest chance of being able to attract anyone's attention, and he whimpered still louder in his panic and despair.

It was Diane who rescued him.

'Owen, I've cracked Yoyo's password.'

A twitch ran through his paralysed body. Jericho sat up. The computer's voice had broken the spell, dream images gurgled away down the drain of oblivion. He took a few deep breaths before asking:

'What was it?'

'*Eat me and I'll eat you alive.*'

My God, Yoyo, he thought. How overdramatic. At the same time he was grateful that she had clearly chosen the access code in a fit of rebellious romanticism, rather than opting for the more secure variation of a random sequence of letters and digits, which would have been much harder to decode.

'Download the content,' he said.

'I've done it.'

'Save it in Yoyofiles.'

'With pleasure.'

Jericho sighed. How was he going to wean Diane off her habit of saying *With pleasure*? Much as he liked her voice, her tone, the words bothered him more each time. There was something servile about it that he found repulsive. He rubbed his eyes and squatted on the edge of the desk chair, his eyes fixed on the monitor.

'Diane?'

'Yes, Owen?'

'Can you— I mean, would it be possible for you to delete the phrase *With pleasure* from your vocabulary?'

'What do you mean exactly? *With pleasure*? Or *the phrase with pleasure*?'

'With pleasure.'

'I can offer to suppress the phrase for you.'

'Great idea. Do that!'

He almost expected the computer to grant his wish with another *With pleasure*, but Diane just said silkily, 'Done.'

And how amazingly simple. Why hadn't he thought of it years ago? 'Show me all the downloads in Yoyofiles from May of this year, sorted by time of day.'

A short list appeared on the screen, totalling about two dozen entries. Jericho skimmed them and concentrated his attention on the time leading up to Yoyo's escape.

There was something.

His weariness fled instantly. About half an hour before Yoyo left her flatshare, data had been transferred to her computer, two files in different formats. He asked Diane to open one of them. It was a shimmering symbol of intertwined lines. It pulsed as if it were breathing. Jericho took a closer look.

Snakes?

It actually did look like a nest of snakes. Snakes twining into a kind of reptilian eye. It seemed to rest in the centre of a body, from which the snake bodies emerged: a single, surreal-looking creature that somehow reminded Jericho of school visits.

Where did snakes go creeping around all over the place in mythology?

He looked at the second file.

friends-of-iceland.com

en-medio-de-la-suiza-es

Brainlab.de/Quantengravitationstheorie/Planck/uni-kassel/32241/html

instead of

Vanessacraig.com

Hoteconomics.com

Littlewonder.at

Jericho rubbed his chin.

You didn't have to be particularly intelligent to understand what it meant. Three websites were to be exchanged. He wondered how Yoyo had got hold of the data. He asked Diane to open the three pages at the top, one by one, all of which were innocuous and generally accessible pages. *friends-of-iceland* was a blog. In it, Scots emigrants to Iceland swapped experiences, provided useful tips to new arrivals and those who were thinking of emigrating, and put photographs on the net. *en-medio-de-la-suiza* was also devoted to the charms of living abroad. Produced in Spain, the page provided a great deal of visual material about Switzerland, in the form of 3D films. Jericho looked at some of them. They had been filmed from a plane or helicopter. At a low altitude he flew over Zürich, landscapes of the canton of Uri and picturesque collections of houses and barns that lay scattered along a winding river.

Brainlab.de/Quantengravitationstheorie/Planck/uni-kassel/32241/html, finally, came from Germany and consisted of closely typed lines of text, examining over twelve pages a phenomenon that physics described as 'quantum foam'. It described what happened if you applied quantum theory and the General Theory of Relativity to the so-called Planck length, which gave you foaming space–time bubbles and at the same time a scientific dilemma, because those bubbles overrode the calculations of General Relativity. The text was remarkable for its lack of paragraphs, and was plainly written for people whose notion of ecstasy involved a blackboard scribbled all over with formulas.

Scotland, Spain, Germany. The joys of Iceland. The beauty of Switzerland. Quantum physics.

Hardly designed to provoke fear and horror.

Curious, he called up the websites that were supposed to be swapped. Vanessa Craig was revealed as a student of agricultural science from Dallas, Texas, who was spending a few months on an exchange programme in Russia. In her online diary she wrote quite unexcitingly about her little university town near Moscow. She was homesick and lovesick and complained of the low temperatures responsible for the innate melancholy of the Russian soul. Behind *Hoteconomics,* an American website offering up-to-the-minute economy news, was *Littlewonder,* an Austrian portal for handmade toys, specialising in the needs of pre-school children.

What was all this? What did travel reports, toys, quantum physics, the global economy and the notes of a shivering American have in common? Nothing.

And that was precisely the quality required by dead letter drops. You walked by, looked at them without suspecting for a moment that they might contain something other than what they actually contained. Yoyo must have found their common properties. Something you couldn't see, but was still there. Again Jericho opened the Spanish address with the film clips from Switzerland, clicked on the snake symbol and moved it aside.

Nothing happened. As if pulled by elastic bands, it darted back into the empty space of the display.

'Weird,' Jericho murmured. 'I could have sworn—'

That it's a mask.

A mask to reveal hidden content in the apparently harmless context of the pages. A decoding program. Again he dragged it onto the Spanish website, and again it slipped away.

'Okay then, friends of Iceland. Let's see what you have to offer.'

And this time it happened.

The moment he dragged the snake symbol to the blog, an extra window opened. It contained a few apparently unconnected words, but his instinct hadn't failed him.

Jan in business address: Oranienburger Strasse 50, continues a that he statement coup Donner be There are

'I knew it! I knew it!'

Jericho clenched his fists. Excited now, he went to work. The snake icon was a key. Anyone who had concealed messages in the pages was using a special algorithm, and the parameters for that algorithm lay in the mask. He opened the page with the essay about quantum foam and repeated the procedure. Further words were added to the fragment:

> *Jan in Andre runs business address: Oranienburger Strasse 50, 10117 Berlin. continues a grave that he knows all about One way or another statement coup Chinese government implemented of timing and Donner be liquidated. There are*

There are? Whatever there were, this stuff here was far more likely to alarm somebody who was the focus of State surveillance! What looked at first glance like sheer Dadaism was really part of a larger message, the text of which had been sent to an unknown number of mailboxes.

Dead letter drops existed wherever states and institutions spied on one another and agents had to avoid being seen together, Jericho thought. During the Cold War they had been the most common form of message transmission. Almost anything at all could be used: rubbish bins, holes in trees, cracks in masonry, public phone books, magazines in waiting rooms, vases and sugar bowls in restaurants, the cisterns in public lavatories. The drop was a place accessible to anyone, where you left something that anybody might see, but which only the initiated recognised as a message. Transmitter and receiver agreed on a period of time, the transmitter deposited what he wanted to pass on – documents, microfilms, demands for cash, journalistically controversial material – left a sign at an agreed place that something was waiting in the drop, and disappeared. A little later the receiver came along, picked up the transmission, left a sign of his own that it had been collected, and also went on his way. The system worked as long as the physical exchange of hardware was involved. Since encrypted messages were now passed on via the internet, they had fallen out of fashion, and were reserved for cases where the information to be passed on could not, with the best will in the world, be transmitted down a fibre-optic cable.

At least that was what people said.

In fact the drop was celebrating an unparalleled renaissance, particularly where electronic encryption was forbidden or if there was a risk that the net police had been given a spare key. The new drops were harmless files and websites that anyone could access. What they contained was unremarkable as long as the content was suited to the transmission of the message. A sentence consisting of twelve words could be broken down into twelve parts and distributed across twelve websites. Word one, *The*, could appear in the second line of a travel piece, word two in the sixth line of the third paragraph of a specialist scientific article, and where it was absolutely imperative that a word should not appear, it was broken down into individual letters that could be found anywhere.

However, no one could do anything with the files while they weren't in possession of a key that separated the words or letters from their contexts and combined them to form a new, secret meaning, a mask, like the kind used in former times, when the Bible or the works of Tolstoy were made to reveal the most incredible content simply by placing a sheet of variously perforated cardboard over a particular page. The matter that appeared in the holes produced the message. In the world of the World Wide Web that mask was a program. Parts of such a program had clearly made their way onto Yoyo's computer, along with an indication that three drops had been replaced by three different ones. Jericho had no idea how many drops were involved overall. It could be dozens, hundreds. Clearly, other addresses were needed for the meaning of the message to be revealed, but Jericho was beginning to understand why Yoyo must have become convinced that she had kicked a hornets' nest.

Jan in Andre runs business address: Oranienburger Strasse 50, 10117 Berlin.

Who could that be? Someone called Jan or Andre, perhaps even a woman – *Jan in*: Janine? Could you run a business address? Unfortunate choice of words. Something was missing, although the address seemed to be complete.

continues a grave that he knows all about One way or another

Something was continuing, and someone knew about it.

that he knows all about

He? Not a woman, then? *Jan in Andre*. Was that one continuous name? Now the controversial bit:

statement coup Chinese government

Here Yoyo's eyes must have popped out of her head. The Chinese government, mentioned in the same breath as the idea of a coup. A person who had *knowledge* of it, possibly to the cost of the people undertaking the coup. Who or what was to be overthrown? The government in Beijing? Were there plans for a coup in parliament, amongst the military, abroad? Hard to imagine? It was more likely that the statement referred to a coup in another country, and that the Chinese government was involved in it. A coup that had succeeded or failed, or else was still to come.

Was there anyone who could have blown the cover on Beijing's role?

implemented of timing and Donner be liquidated

Gobbledygook apart from one word: liquidated. Liquidate Donner? Donner and Blitzen? Donner kebab? Hardly. As everywhere throughout the fragment, crucial passages were missing here too. The text might have been completed with a few words, but it might equally have been hundreds of pages long, and everything that Jericho thought he was reading into it might prove to be erroneous. But if that wasn't the case, a murder was being reported, announced or at least recommended here.

He studied the text once more.

timing. This was about a sequence of events. A sequence of events that was under threat? Yoyo must have assembled the puzzle just as he had, reached similar conclusions and immediately gone into hiding as if the devil were on her tail. And it was perfectly possible to see the Chinese State security service in that light. And yet her escape didn't really make sense. She had been working with controversial material for years. The fragment should surely have aroused her curiosity, stirred her enthusiasm, and instead it had thrown her into a panic.

Had it? Or had she hurried enthusiastically to Quyu, to round up the Guardians and start doing background research in the shelter of the control centre?

No, that would have been absurd. She wouldn't have left her father without a word. There could have been only one reason, that she was worried about putting him and herself in danger by making too close contact. Because she assumed that she was under surveillance. More than that! That night she must have had cause to worry that her enemies would be outside the door in a few minutes, because she had broken into their secret information channels and been noticed.

They had detected Yoyo.

Jericho called to mind her piece on Brilliant Shit, had Diane load the text and read it again:

'Hi all. Back in our galaxy now, have been for a few days. Was really stressed out these last days, is anybody harshing on me? Couldn't help it, really truly. All happened so fast. Shit. Even so quickly you can be forgotten. Only waiting now for the old demons to visit me once more. Yeah, and, I'm busy writing new songs. If any of the band asks: We'll make an appearance once I've got a few euphonious lyrics on the go. Let's prog!'

No one victorious would write like that. It was a cry for help from someone losing control. When she was uploading the web addresses and the mask, she must have realised that she'd been located. That was why she had left so quickly.

He studied the fragment again.

'Diane, find 50 Oranienburger Strasse, 10117 Berlin.'

The reply came in an instant. Jericho looked at his watch. Two minutes to twelve. He connected the hologoggles to the computer, logged on and chose the coordin-ates entered by Yoyo.

The Second World

Since the middle of the last decade, when Second Life had been restructured after its predictable collapse, there was no longer a central hub, any more than the space–time continuum had a real centre, just an infinite number of observation points, each of which created the *illusion* of being the centre, the way an earth-dweller felt that his location was fixed and the whole cosmos was something spinning around him, moving away from him or towards him. An astronaut on the Moon and every creature in the universe felt exactly the same, wherever they happened to be. In the real universe, the totality of all particles was interlinked, which meant that every particle was able to occupy its relative centre.

Similarly, Second Life had turned into a peer-to-peer network, an almost in-finite, decentralised and self-organising system in which every server – like a planet – formed a hub, which was connected by a random number of interfaces with every other hub. Each participant was automatically a host and a user of the worlds of others. How many planets Second Life comprised, who inhabited or controlled them, was unknown. Of course there were lists, cybernetic maps, well-known travel routes and records that made it possible to realise oneself in the virtual world in the first place, just as the outside universe was subject to physical boundary conditions. Within these standards, avatars travelled to all the places on the web that were known to them, and to which they were granted access. But there was no longer anyone who was familiar with *everything*.

Jericho would have expected to land at such an unknown place, but Yoyo's coord-inates led to a public hub. Almost every metropolis in the real world had been virtually copied by now, so he travelled from Shanghai to Shanghai, to find himself back in the People's Square, or at any rate in a nearly identical copy of it. Unlike the real Shanghai, there were no traffic jams and beyond the city boundaries no districts like Quyu. On the other hand new edifices were constantly going up, staying for a while, changing or disappearing with the speed of a mouse-click.

The builder and owner of Cyber-Shanghai was the Chinese government, and it was financed by both Chinese and foreign companies. The Party also maintained a second Beijing, a second Hong Kong and a virtual Chongqing. Like all net cities based on real models, the charm of the depiction lay in the relationship between authenticity and idealism. It could hardly come as a surprise that more Americans lived in Cyber-Shanghai than Chinese, and that most Chinese-looking avatars were bots, machines disguised as living creatures. In turn, some Chinese had second homes in Cyber-New York, in virtual Paris or Berlin. French and Spanish people tended to live in Marrakech, Istanbul and Baghdad, Germans and the Irish liked Rome, the British were drawn to New Delhi and Cape Town and Indians to London. Anyone who dreamed of living in New York and couldn't afford it found an affordable and entirely authentic Big Apple on the net, only wilder, more progressive and even a bit more interesting than the original. People doing business in virtual Paris didn't seek seclusion, but were interested in as many interfaces with the real world as possible. BMW, Mercedes-Benz and other car manufacturers didn't sell fantasy constructs in the cyber-cities, but prototypes of what they actually planned to build.

Basically net cities were nothing but colossal experimental labs in which no one thought twice of travelling by spaceship rather than by ship, as long as the Statue of Liberty stood where it belonged. The owners, meaning the countries in question, were opening another chapter in globalisation here, but above all they were remodelling the world of human beings in a peculiar way. Crime and terrorism did exist in the virtual New York, buildings were destroyed by data attack, avatars were sexually molested, there were muggings, break-ins, grievous bodily harm and rape, you could be imprisoned or exiled. There was only one thing that didn't exist:

Poverty.

What was produced on the net was by no means an illustration of society. You could fall ill here. Hackers planted cyber-plagues and scattered viruses. You could have an accident or simply not feel so great, or become addicted to something. In times of ultra-thin sensor skins that you slipped into in order to feel the illusion of perfect graphics on your body as well, cyber-sex was a great source of income and expenditure. Compulsive gaming flourished, avatars suffered from morbid fears like claustrophobia, agoraphobia and arachnophobia. But far and wide there was no hint of overpopulation. The poor as a source of all evil had been identified and removed from human perception. Networked people could afford a Mumbai or a Rio de Janeiro that was constantly growing, with no impoverishment involved, because bits and bytes were an abundant resource. Even natural disasters had haunted the cybercities – anyone who lived in Tokyo expected an authentic little earthquake from time to time.

But there were no slums.

The representation of the world as it could be became the world itself, with all the light and shade of real existence – and demonstrated who was responsible for global abuse. Not capitalism, not the industrial societies that supposedly didn't want to share. With empirical ruthlessness the virtual experiment identified the guilty as those who had the least. The army of the poor in Quyu, in the Brazilian favelas, the Turkish gecekondular, the megaslums of Mumbai and Nairobi, billions of people who lived on less than a dollar a day – in cyberspace they weren't isolated and locked away, not exploited in the class-war, not the object of Third World summits, development aid, pangs of conscience and denial, they weren't even hate objects.

They simply didn't exist.

And suddenly everything worked smoothly. So where did the problem lie? Who was responsible for the lack of space, overexploitation, environmental pollution, since the virtual universe worked so wonderfully well without poverty? It was the poor. No point stressing the impossibility of comparing the two systems, the carbon-based and the hard-drive-based. With the naïve cynicism of the philosopher who sees overpopulation as the root of all human evil, and stops listening as soon as consequences are discussed, representatives of the net community pointed out that there were no poor here. Not because someone had cut funds, knocked down slums or even killed millions. They had simply never appeared. Second Life showed what the world looked like without them, and it certainly looked considerably better, *honi soit qui mal y pense*.

Of course there were other things that didn't exist in virtual Shanghai. There was no smog, for example, which always unsettled Jericho. Precisely because simulation took human visual habits into account, the lack of the permanent haze completely altered the overall impression.

He looked around and waited.

Avatars and bots of all kinds were on the move, many flying or floating along above the ground. Hardly anyone was walking. Walking in Second Life enjoyed a certain popularity, but more on short journeys. It was only in rurally programmed worlds that you encountered hikers, who could walk for hours. There was swiftly flowing traffic even above the highest buildings. Here too, the programmed Shanghai differed from the real one. On the net the vision of an air-propelled infrastructure had become reality.

Noisy and gesticulating, a group of extraterrestrial immigrants was heading towards Shanghai Art Museum. Recently reptiloids from Canis Major had been turning up in increasing numbers. No one really had much idea who was in charge of them. They were considered mysterious and uncouth, but they did successful business with new technologies for heightening sensitivity. Cyber-Shanghai was entirely controlled by State security which, with a great deal of trouble and the use of a number of bots, kept the huge cybercities under control. Possibly the reptiloids were just a few tolerated hackers, but they might equally have been disguised officers from Cypol. By now extraterrestrials were staggering around all the net metropolises, which hugely extended the possibilities of trade. As a general rule, software companies lay behind these, taking into account the fact that virtual universes had to offer constantly new attractions. The astral light-forms from Aldebaran, for example, with which you could temporarily merge in order to enjoy unimagined sound experiences, had by now been unmasked as representatives of IBM.

Jericho wondered what form Yoyo would appear in.

After a minute or so he glimpsed an elegant, French-looking woman with big dark eyes and a black pageboy cut crossing the square towards him. She was wearing an emerald-green trouser suit and stilettos. To Jericho she looked like a character out of a Hollywood film from the sixties in which Frenchwomen looked the way American directors imagined them. Jericho, who had several identities in Second Life, had appeared as himself, so that the woman recognised him straight away. She stopped right in front of him, looked at him seriously and held out her open right hand.

'Yoyo?' he asked.

She put her finger to her lips, took his hand and pulled him after her. She stopped by one of the flower stalls near the entrance to the metro, let go of his hand and opened a tiny handkerchief. The head of a lizard, the same emerald green as her outfit, peeped out from it. The creature's golden eyes fastened on Jericho. Then the slender body darted upwards, landed on the ground at their feet and wriggled along the floral carpet, where it paused and looked round at them, as if to check that they were following it.

A moment later a transparent sphere about three metres in diameter was floating closely above her. The lizard turned around and darted a forked tongue.

'Just a moment,' he said. 'Before we—'

The woman drew him to her and gave him a shove. The impetus propelled him straight into the inside of the sphere. He sank into a chair that hadn't been there a moment before, as far as he remembered, or at least the sphere had looked completely empty from outside. She jumped after him, sat down beside him and crossed her legs. Jericho saw the lizard looking up at them through the transparent floor.

Then it had disappeared. In its place an illuminated and apparently bottomless shaft had opened up.

''ave you a strong estomac?' The woman smiled. She sounded so French that a real French person would have been horrified.

Jericho shrugged. 'Depends what—'

'Good.'

The sphere plunged down the shaft like a stone.

The illusion was so real that all of Jericho's skin, muscle and brain vessels suddenly contracted and adrenalin pumped violently into his bloodstream. His pulse and heartbeat quickened. For a moment he was actually glad not to have burdened his stomach with a generous breakfast.

'Just shut you' eyes if you don't bear it,' twittered his companion, as if he had complained about something. Jericho looked at her. She was still smiling, a mischievous smile, he thought.

'Thanks, I like it.'

The surprise effect had fled. From now on he could choose which standpoint to emphasise. That of sitting in a hotel room watching a well-made film, or actually experiencing all this. Had he been wearing a sensor skin the choice would have been difficult, almost impossible. The skins erased all distance from the artificial world, while he was wearing only glasses and gloves. The rest of his equipment had stayed in Xintiandi.

'Some people 'ave an injection,' the Frenchwoman said calmly. "ave you been once in a tank?'

Jericho nodded. In the bigger branches of Cyber Planet, which were visited by the more affluent customers, there were tanks filled with cooking salt solution, in which you floated weightlessly, dressed in a sensor skin. Your eyes were protected by 3D glasses, you breathed through tiny tubes that you were barely aware of. Conditions in which you experienced virtuality in such a way that reality afterwards seemed shabby, artificial and irritating.

'A tiny little injection,' the woman continued, 'into the corners of your eyes. It paralyse the lids. The eyes are moistened, but you cannot any more close them. You have to watch everything. *C'est pour les masochistes.*'

It's far worse having to *listen* to everything, Jericho thought. For instance, your ridiculous accent. He wondered how he knew the woman. She must have come from some film or other.

'Where are we actually going, Yoyo?' he asked, even though he had guessed. This connection was a wormhole: it led out of the monitored world of cybernetic Shanghai into a region that was probably unknown to the Internet Police. Lights darted past, a crazy flickering. The sphere started to turn. Jericho looked between his feet through the transparent floor and saw an end to the shaft, except that it seemed to be widening.

'Yo Yo?' She laughed a tinkling laugh. 'I am not Yo Yo. *Le violà!*'

A moment later they were floating under a pulsating starry sky. Rotating slowly before their eyes was a shimmering structure that looked like a spiral galaxy and yet could have been something completely different. It seemed to Jericho like something alive. He leaned forward, but they spent only a few seconds in this majestic continuum before shooting into the middle of a conduit of light.

And floated again.

This time he knew they had reached their goal.

'Impressed?' asked the woman.

Jericho said nothing. Miles below them stretched a boundless blue-green ocean. Tiny clouds drifted close above the surface, their backs sprinkled with pink and orange. The sphere sank towards something big that drifted high above the clouds, something with a mountain and wooded slopes, waterfalls, meadows and beaches. Jericho glimpsed swarms of flying creatures. Colossal beasts grazed on the banks of a glittering river, which snaked around the volcanic peak and flowed into the sea—

No, not flowed.

Fell!

In a great banner of foam the water plunged over the edge of the flying island and scattered into the bluish green of the ocean. The closer they came, the more it looked to Jericho like a gigantic UFO. He threw his head back and saw two suns shining in the sky, one emitting a white light, the other bathed in a strange, turquoise aura. Their vehicle fell faster, braked and followed the course of the river. Jericho caught a swift glimpse of the enormous animals – they weren't like anything he had ever seen before. Then they darted off over gently undulating fields, beyond which the terrain fell to a snow-white beach.

'You will be picked up once more,' said the Frenchwoman, with a little wave. The sphere disappeared, as did she, and Jericho found himself squatting in the sand.

'I'm here,' said Yoyo.

He raised his head and saw her coming towards him, barefoot, her slender body swathed in a short, shiny tunic. Her avatar was the perfect depiction of her, which somehow relieved him. After that fanciful copy of Irma la Douce he'd worried—

That was it! The Frenchwoman had reminded him of a character in a film, and now he knew at last who it was. She was the perfect re-creation of Shirley MacLaine in her role as Irma la Douce. An ancient flick, sixty or seventy years old. That Jericho knew it at all was down to his passion for twentieth-century cinema.

Yoyo looked at him in silence for a while. Then she said, 'Is it true about Grand Cherokee?'

'What?'

'That you killed him.'

Jericho shook his head.

'It's only true that he's dead. Kenny killed him.'

'Kenny?'

'The man who murdered your friends too.'

'I don't know if I can trust you.'

She came up to him and fixed him with her dark eyes. 'You saved me in the steelworks, but that doesn't necessarily mean anything, or does it?'

'No,' he admitted. 'Not necessarily.'

She nodded. 'Let's walk for a while.'

Jericho looked around. He didn't know what to make of it all. Filigree creatures were landing a little way off, neither birds nor insects. They reminded him of flying plants, if anything. He tore his eyes away and together they strolled along the beach.

'We came across the ocean when we were looking around the net for safe hiding-places,' Yoyo explained. 'Pure chance. Perhaps we should have moved here with the control centre straight away, but I wasn't entirely sure if we'd really be undisturbed here.'

'So you didn't program this world?' asked Jericho.

'The island, yes. Everything else was here. Ocean, sky and clouds, weird animals in the water, which sometimes come right close to the surface. The two suns go up and down, slightly out of sync. There's also land. So far we've only seen some in the distance.'

'Someone must have made all this.'

'You think so?'

'There's a server with the data stored on it.'

'We haven't been able to identify it so far. I'm inclined to think there's a whole network involved.'

'Possibly a government network,' Jericho speculated.

'Hardly.'

'How can you be sure of that? I mean, what's going on here? In whose interest is it to create a world like this? For what purpose?'

'An end in itself, perhaps.' She shrugged. 'Nobody today is capable of grasping Second Life as a whole. Over the past few years tools have been produced in vast numbers, and they're constantly being modified. Everyone builds his own world. Most of it's rubbish, some of it's incredibly brilliant. You can get in here, not there. In general they adhere to the rule that everyone can see what other people see, but I'm not sure even that's true. In some regions they have completely alien algorithms.'

Jericho had stepped close to the edge. Where water should have played on the beach, the strand fell vertiginously away. Far below them the light of the suns scattered on the rippled surface of the ocean.

'You mean, this world was made by bots?'

'I'm not the sort of idiot who makes a new religion out of disk space.' Yoyo stepped up next to him. 'But what I think is that artificial intelligence is starting to penetrate the web in a way that its creators couldn't have imagined. Computers are creating computers. Second Life has reached a stage whereby it's developing out of its own impulses. Adaptation and selection, you understand? No one can say when that started, and no one has any idea where it's going to end. What's happening is the consistent continuation of evolution with other means. Cybernetic Darwinism.'

'How did you get here?'

'What I said. Chance. We were looking for a bugproof corner. I thought it was hopelessly old-fashioned, squatting like migrant workers in the Andromeda or the steelworks, where Cypol could walk through the door at any time. Okay, they can kick in your door on the net as well. If you encrypt, you're finished, you might as well just invite them to arrest you. We communicated via blogs, with data distortion and anonymisation. But even that didn't do it. So I thought, let's move to Second Life. There they can go searching for you like mad, but they don't know what they're looking for. All their ontologies and taxonomies don't work here.'

Jericho nodded. Second Life was an ideal hiding-place, if you wanted to escape State surveillance. Virtual worlds were far more complicated in their construction and more difficult to control than simple blogs or chat-rooms. There was a difference between putting textual building blocks in a suspicious context and drawing conclusions about conspiracies and dodgy attitudes from the gestures, facial expressions, appearance and environments of virtual people. In Second Life everything and everyone can be code, whether friend or foe.

It was only logical that no single organisation in China had as many staff as the State internet surveillance authority. Cypol tried to penetrate every area of the virtual cosmos, and it was no more able to do that than the regular police were able to infiltrate the population in the real world. In spite of their massive apparatus they lacked the human staff required to keep countless millions of users under observation. Cypol relied on destabilisation. Not everyone in Second Life was a government agent by any means, but they could be: the sharp businesswoman, the friendly banker, the stripper, the willing sex partner, the alien and the winged dragon, the robot and the DJ, even a tree, a guitar or a whole building. As an additional consequence of chronic staff shortage, the government worked with great armies of bots, avatars that were guided not by human beings, but by machines pretending to be human beings.

By now there were highly refined bot programs. Every now and again, in the course of his Second Life missions, Jericho allowed Diane to take virtual form, and she appeared as a tiny, fluttering elf, white, androgynous, with insect-like, black eyes and transparent dragonfly wings. She might equally well have appeared as a seductive woman and turned the heads of real guys who didn't notice that they were flirting with a computer. At moments like that Diane became a bot that you could only track down using the Turing test, a procedure that no machine was capable of performing, even in 2025. Anyone could carry out the test. It involved engaging a machine in dialogue long enough for it to reveal its cognitive limitations and out itself as a refined but ultimately stupid program.

And herein lay the problem of bot agents. Without genuine intelligence and capacity for abstraction, they were hardly capable of unmasking the behaviour and appearance of virtual people as codes. Small wonder, then, that Yoyo and her Guardians had focused their attention on Second Life: since the decentralised structure of the peer-to-peer network was ideally suited to the creation of hidden spaces, it was extremely hard to identify senders and receivers of data, and the number of worlds tended towards infinity. In fact, only the itineraries of the data between the servers could be reconstructed.

Servers themselves worked with many electronic doorkeepers. Anyone who visited a server and was allowed in was subject to the control of the webmaster in question, while visitors to the server couldn't check one another if they didn't have the requisite authorisation.

The webmaster of Cyber-Shanghai was Beijing. If Jericho had had an investigation centre in the virtual metropolis, he would have been a tenant of the Chinese government, which meant that the authorities would be able to knock at his door and turn his electronic office on its head with a search warrant (although to do that they would have needed judicial permission, which the Chinese were reluctant to grant). That was the only reason Jericho had never considered moving his office there.

He looked out at the bluish-green expanse.

Was it possible that this world had actually been created by a bot network? If computers developed something like aesthetic aspirations, they were copied from those of human beings, while at the same time being unsettlingly alien.

'And is the island safe?'

Yoyo nodded. 'We've drilled into cyberspace at every available point to build our own planets, in such a way that not everyone can get there. Jia Wei' – she hesitated – 'has calculated millions of simultaneous possibilities. That included modifying the protocol. Not significantly, just in such a way that the uninitiated end up in a jumble of data if they don't have the right key. No idea how many variations we tried out, we generated them at random because we thought it was a new idea. Instead we ended up here.'

'And the protocol is—'

'A little green lizard.'

Yoyo smiled. It was the same sad smile that he knew from Chen Hongbing's photograph.

'Of course Cyber-Shanghai's server records the intervention, but it doesn't raise the alarm. It doesn't register the momentary opening of an electronic wormhole, through which you escape into a kind of parallel universe. As far as it's concerned, all that happens is that someone opens a door and closes it again.'

'I figured it was something like that.' Jericho nodded. 'So who's Irma la Douce?'

'Hey!' Yoyo raised her eyebrows. 'You know Irma la Douce?'

'Of course.'

'Heavens! I hadn't the slightest idea who she was when Daxiong turned up with her.'

'A film. A lovely film.'

'A film about a French *poule*.'

'Perhaps it doesn't necessarily represent the glorious Chinese culture,' said Jeri-cho mildly. 'But there's something else, think about it. The avatar is, incidentally, a perfect copy of Shirley MacLaine.'

'She – erm – was an actress, right? A French one.'

'American.'

Yoyo seemed to think for a second. Then she suddenly laughed out loud.

'Oh, that's going to nettle Daxiong. He thinks he knows everything there is to know.'

'About films?'

'Not at all. Daxiong has this thing about France. As if we didn't have enough culture of our own. He could bang on at you all day about— Oh, it doesn't matter.'

She turned away and ran her hand over her eyes. Jericho left her in peace. When she turned back to face him he saw the smeared remains of a tear on her cheek.

'You've got my computer,' she said. 'So, what do you want? What do you want from me?'

'Nothing,' said Jericho.

'But?'

'Your father sent me. He's terribly worried about you.'

'Don't think I don't care,' she said belligerently.

'I don't.' He shook his head. 'I know you don't want to worry him. You thought your communications were being monitored, and that if you sent him an email they'd pounce on him and give him a going-over. Am I right?'

She stared gloomily ahead.

'Hongbing doesn't know about blogs and virtual worlds,' Jericho went on. 'He's happy to be able to use an antediluvian mobile phone. And he's consoling himself with the idea that his daughter has learned her lesson. He doesn't know what you're doing. Or let's say, he guesses what you're up to and doesn't know. I'm sure he hasn't the faintest idea that Tu Tian is protecting you.'

'Tian!' cried Yoyo. 'He commissioned you, right?'

'He referred your father to me.'

'Sure, because Hongbing never— But why didn't he—?'

'Why didn't he send a message for you to the Andromeda? Even though he knew where you'd fetched up? I mean, you never told him anything about the blast furnace, so in the end he got nervous—'

'How do you know Tian?'

'He's a friend of mine. And, I should think, a kind of unofficial member of the Guardians. At least he supported you as best he could. The stuff in the control centre came from him, didn't it? Tian was just as much of a dissident as you are now.'

'As we were.'

Oh, right, thought Jericho. What a miserable subject. Whatever they were talking about, that was where they would always end up.

'Tian didn't need to send me a message,' said Yoyo. 'He knew it wouldn't change a thing.'

'Exactly. But it changed something when Hongbing hit on the idea of having a search made for you. A risky enterprise. Your father might prefer to act ignorant, but he knew he couldn't get the police involved. I guess he secretly knew that you were going through the

Party's rubbish bins out the back. So he asked Tu Tian, the way you ask somebody with connections like that, and also because he accepted through gritted teeth that Tian might have been closer to you than your own—'

'That's not true,' Yoyo rounded on him. 'You're talking nonsense!'

'But that's how it looks to—'

'That has nothing to do with you! Nothing at all, okay? Keep out of my private life.'

Jericho tilted his head.

'Okay, princess. As far as I can. So what was Tian supposed to do? Slap Hongbing on the shoulder and say, no need to worry? I know something you don't know. But all right, your private life is sacred to me, even if it's cost me my car and possibly my flat, which could go up in flames at any moment. You're causing a lot of stress, Yoyo.'

A wrinkle of fury appeared between her eyebrows. She opened her mouth, but Jericho interrupted: 'Save it for later.'

'But—'

'We can't go on wasting time on your island for ever. Let's see how we're going to get ourselves out of this mess.'

'We?'

'You're not listening, are you?' Jericho showed his teeth. 'I'm in this too, so take a good hard look, young lady! You've lost your friends. Why do you think all this happened? Because you stirred up a bit of dust? The Party is used to stepping in dissident shit. They might send you to jail for it, but they're never going to send someone like Kenny.'

Her eyes filled with tears.

'I couldn't—'

Jericho bit his lip. He was making a mistake. Blaming Yoyo for the deaths of the others was as unfair as it was stupid.

'I'm sorry,' he said hastily.

She sniffed, took a step in one direction, then another, and then sliced the air with her trembling hands.

'Maybe I should have – I should have—'

'No, it's okay. There's nothing you can do about it.'

'If only I hadn't come up with that stupid idea!'

'Tell me about it. What did you do?'

'Nothing would have happened. It's my fault, I—'

'It isn't.'

'It is!'

'No, Yoyo, there's nothing you can do about it. Tell me what you've done. What happened during the night?'

'I didn't want any of that.' Her lips trembled. 'It's my fault they're dead. They're all dead.'

'Yoyo—'

She threw her hands to her face. Jericho walked over, gently took her wrists and tried to draw them down. She pulled back and staggered away from him.

He heard a deep, throaty growl behind him.

What was it this time? He slowly turned round and looked into the golden eyes of an enormous bear.

Very impressive, he thought.

'Daxiong.'

The bear showed its teeth. Jericho didn't move. The beast was pretty much as big as a middle-sized pony. Of course the simulation didn't put him in any danger, but he didn't know what impulses were emitted by the gloves. They produced haptic sensations, meaning that they stimulated the nerves. Would they also emit pain if the monster decided to start chewing his fingers?

'It's okay.' Yoyo had joined him. She stroked the huge animal's fur, then looked at Jericho. Her voice was calm again, almost expressionless.

'We tried something out that night,' she said. 'A way of sending messages.'

'Via email?'

'Yes. The whole thing was my idea. Jia Wei supplied the method.'

She tapped the bear on the nose. It lowered its head and a moment later it was gone.

'We're in touch with a lot of activists,' she went on. 'We wouldn't be able to get hold of the relevant information without them. Of course we can't openly ask Washington what dirty tricks China's up to, and I'm registered as a dissident, okay?'

'Okay.'

'So, Second Life is one way of tricking Cypol. It always involves a lot of effort. Good for a meeting like ours, but I wanted something quick and uncomplicated, just to send through a photograph or a few lines.' Yoyo stared at the spot where the bear had stood. 'And there's a constant traffic of mails. Boring, unsuspicious mails containing nothing that would scare the Politburo. So we've tried to hop other people's freight-trains.'

'Parasite mails?'

'Piggybacks, parasites, stowaways – whatever you want to call it. Jia Wei and I wrote a protocol that lets you encode messages in white noise and decode them again; we used it between Daxiong and me and decided to do a test.'

Jericho was gradually working out what had happened that night. The basic idea was designed to trick even the cleverest surveillance experts. It was based on the fundamental principle of email traffic, which was that mails were primarily a collection of data, little travellers that wanted to be helped on their way. So they were crammed into packets of data like passengers into railway carriages, and like those carriages the packets had a standard length. If one carriage was full, the next one turned up, until there was room for the whole message and it could be sent, with the receiver's web address up at the front as the locomotive.

But the difference in the quantities of data usually meant that the last compartment was only partly occupied. The phrase *end of message* defined where the message ended, but because a packet could only be sent as a whole, there was usually some data-free space left over, what was known as white noise. As it arrived, the receiving computer selected the official data of the message, cut the rest off and threw it away. It didn't occur to anyone to look through the white noise for further content, because there was nothing to be found there.

That was where the idea began. Whoever had it first, it was and remained brilliant. A secret message was coded in such a way that it looked like white noise, was immediately switched for the real white noise and sent on its way like a stowaway. There was only one problem that needed to be solved. You had to send the message yourself, or have access to the sender's computer. There was no reason not to let stowaways travel on their own trains. But once you'd attracted attention, your email traffic would be under constant surveillance. Organisations like Cypol might be overstretched, but they weren't stupid, so it was to be feared that they would also check up on white noise.

But there was a solution, which was to use other people's email traffic. Two dissidents who wanted to pass a conspiratorial message one to the other each needed a router or illegal railway station for passing data-trains, and of course they had to agree on the same train. It might be birthday greetings from Mr Huang in Shenzen to his nephew Yi living in Beijing, both reputable citizens with nothing bad to be said about them as far as the State was concerned. So Mr Huang sent off his birthday greetings without guessing for a moment that his train was about to make an unscheduled stop with Dissident One, who took charge of the white noise, swapped it for the disguised message and sent the train on its way again. But before it reached Yi, it was stopped again, this time by Dissident Two, who received the message, decoded it, replaced it with real white noise, and now at last it went on to the nephew in Beijing, who was assured of Mr Huang's esteem, while neither of them knew what purpose they had served. The whole thing suggested innocent tourists who had drugs secretly smuggled into their luggage at the airport and then taken out again at the other end, with the significant difference that the drugs didn't assume the appearance and consistency of their underwear.

'Of course we weren't so naïve as to assume that we'd invented the trick,' said Yoyo. 'But it's really not that likely that you're going to come across an email that already has a stowaway.'

'And whose official mail did you intercept?'

'It came from some government authority or other.' Yoyo shrugged. 'The Ministry of Energy or something.'

'Where exactly?'

'Wait, it was – it was—' She frowned and looked defiant. 'Okay, don't know.'

'I'm sorry?' Jericho looked at her in disbelief. 'You don't know who—?'

'For the love of heaven! It was only a test! Just to see if I could get into it!'

'And what did you write?'

'Just something.'

'Come on! What was it?'

'I—' She seemed to chew the sentence a number of times before spitting it out at Jericho's feet: '*Catch me if you can.*'

'*Catch me if you can?*'

'Am I talking Mongolian? Yesss!'

'Why that?'

'*Why that?*' she said, copying him. 'Doesn't matter. Because I thought it was cool, that's why.'

'Very cool. In a test—'

'Oh, son-of-a-turtle!' She rolled her eyes. 'No – one – was – supposed – to – read – it!'

Jericho sighed and shook his head.

'All right. Go on?'

'The protocol was set to real time. Stop mail, take out noise, put in own message, encode, pass on, all at the same time. So, I write, and at the same time I notice there's something in it already! That I haven't taken out any white noise at all, but some kind of mysterious stuff.'

'Because someone else was trying to do the same thing as you were.'

'Yes.'

Jericho nodded. In fairness, he had to admit that Yoyo couldn't have anticipated this development.

'But by then the email was already on its way again,' he said. 'To the person that the mysterious stuff was meant for. Except that it never got there, because you'd taken it out and swapped it.'

'Unwittingly.'

'Doesn't matter. Imagine this. They're waiting for some complex, secret information. Instead they read: *Catch me if you can.*' Jericho couldn't help it. He raised his hands in the air and applauded. 'Bravo, Yoyo. Lovely little provocation. My congratulations.'

'Oh, fuck you! Of course they immediately worked out that someone had broken in.'

'And they were prepared.'

'Yes, unlike me.' She pulled a sour face. 'I mean, I don't know if they'd expected something like that *exactly*, but their defences work, you have to give them that. Some kind of watchdog program immediately started barking: woof! An extra hub has appeared in the predetermined route, it shouldn't be there. Grrr, where are our data?'

'And traced you back?'

'Traced me back?' Yoyo gave a short, sharp laugh. 'They attacked me! They attacked my computer, I don't know how, it was absolutely terrifying! While I'm still gawping at what I've pulled out of the water, I see them starting to download my data. I couldn't get online quickly enough as they went through my stuff. They knew exactly who I was – and *where* I was!'

'Does that mean you don't have an anonymiser—'

'I'm not stupid,' she hissed. 'Of course I use an anonymiser. But if you're implementing something completely new and playing around with it, you're forced to open up your system for a moment. Otherwise the protection tools downstairs would get in your way, that's what they're there for.'

'So you turned various things off.'

'I had to take that risk.' Her eyes flashed with fury. 'I had to be sure we could work like that.'

'Well, now you know.'

'Lovely, Mister Brain Box.' She folded her arms. 'What would you have done?'

'One bit at a time,' said Jericho. 'First take out the attachment and check it for land mines. Then put my own thing in there. Leave myself the option of cancelling everything before I send it off. And most importantly, don't put any smug little phrases in there, even if you've encoded it as noise a thousand times over.'

'What's the point of data transfer that doesn't make sense?'

'We're talking about a test. As long as you don't know for sure whether your data transfer is safe or not, you've got to sound like a communication error. They might have wondered where their message ended up, but it wouldn't immediately have occurred to them that someone was tapping off their communication.'

She looked at him as if she was thinking of tearing his throat out. Then she spread her arms and let them fall back helplessly by her side.

'Okay, it was a mistake!'

'A big mistake.'

'Could I have guessed, out of all the billions and billions of mails, I would hit on one that had already been infiltrated?'

Jericho looked at her. His rage had flared up for a moment, less about the mistake than about the fact that someone with Yoyo's experience could have made it. With her complacency, she hadn't just put her own life on the line. Almost the whole of her group had been killed, and Jericho didn't feel exactly safe. Then his fury evaporated. He saw the mixture of fear and dismay on her face and shook his head.

'No. You couldn't.'

'So who's on my case?'

'Our case, Yoyo, if you'll forgive me. If I might just remind you about me and my problems.'

She averted her head, looked out at the sea and back at him.

'Okay. Ours.'

'Doubtless someone with power. People with money and influence, technically advanced. To be quite honest I doubt that their communication is still at the experimental stage. You've tried something out. They've been doing it for ages. Just by chance you're using the same protocol, which allowed each of you to read the other's data. From that point it gets speculative, but I also believe that they're influential enough not to be dependent on other people's emails.'

'You mean—'

'Let's assume they're sending mails from their own servers. Quite officially. They're based in public institutions, they can check incoming and outgoing traffic, and pack anything in there as they see fit.'

'They sound like senior officials.'

'You think it's the Party?'

'Who else? All the Guardians' operations are – were – directed against the Party. And we have no illusions about it, the Guardians are – were—'

'—another word for Yoyo.'

'I was the head. Along with Daxiong.'

'I know. You mouthed off, which got State security on your back. Since then you've tried to find ways of protecting yourself. Second Life, parasite emails. And in the process, without meaning to, you break into a secret data transfer, and your worst fears become reality. There's something about "coup" and "liquidating" in connection with the Chinese government, and a minute later they've tracked you down.'

'What would you have done in my place?'

'What indeed?' Jericho laughed mirthlessly. 'I'd have got the hell out, just like you did.'

'That's comforting.' She hesitated. 'So did you – were you on my computer?'

'Yes.'

Jericho expected another blaze of fury, but she just sighed and looked out at the ocean.

'Don't worry,' he said. 'I haven't been snooping. I've just tried to introduce some clarity into the whole business.'

'Did you get anywhere with the third website?'

'The Swiss films?'

'Mm-hm.'

'Not so far. But there must be something on there. Either you need a separate mask or there's something we've overlooked. At the moment I think it's about a coup in which the Chinese government was – or will be – involved, and that someone knows too much and that his liquidation is being considered.'

'Someone called Jan or Andre.'

'More likely Andre. Did you research the address in Berlin?'

'Yes.'

'Interesting, isn't it? *Donner be liquidated.* Somebody called Andre Donner runs a restaurant specialising in African delicacies at that address.'

'The Muntu. I'd got that far.'

'But what does that tell us?' Jericho reflected. 'Is Andre Donner in danger of being liquidated? I mean, what does a Berlin chef know about Beijing's involvement in some sort of planned coup? And what about the second man?'

'Jan?'

'Yes. Is he the killer?'

Or, is Jan the same as Kenny? Jericho thought, but kept the thought to himself. His imagination was fizzing. Basically the fragment of text was too mutilated to provide any useful conclusions.

'It's an African restaurant,' Yoyo said thoughtfully. 'And it hasn't been around for very long.'

Jericho looked at her in amazement.

'Okay, I've had more time to look into it,' she added. 'There are reviews on the net. Donner opened Muntu in December 2024—'

'Only six months ago?'

'Exactly. You can hardly find any information about the man himself. A Dutchman who lived in Cape Town for a while, perhaps was even born there. That's it. But the African connection is interesting in that—'

'—in that Africa's familiar with coups.' Jericho nodded. 'That means we need to take a closer look at the more recent chronology of any dubious or violent government takeovers. An interesting approach. Except that South Africa is ruled out. They've been stable for a long time.'

They fell silent for a while.

'You wanted to know who we were dealing with,' he said at last. 'To engineer coups you need money and influence, both political and economic. But above all you need to have a capable executive, and one that's willing to engage in violence. So these people have managed to set an expert with reinforcements on your trail. Equipped like an army. So let's assume that certain government circles are behind this. Then I think I can put your mind at rest in one respect.'

Yoyo raised her eyebrows.

'They're not interested in dissidents,' Jericho said finally. 'They don't give a damn about what you're up to. They would have hunted down anyone who got in their way . . .'

'Very reassuring,' Yoyo sneered. 'And instead they have hordes of cops who will, when time's up, give me the pleasant feeling that it's not because of my dissident activities that they're going to kill me. Thanks Jericho. I can sleep again at last.'

He gazed along the beach. Shimmering in the double sunlight, it looked oddly vivid. Patterns formed spontaneously in the sand and immediately blurred again. Some of the flower-like creatures spread their wings, transparent and veined as leaves. Clouds of golden dust puffed up among them, and were carried over the edge of the island, where they scattered in the wind. Yoyo and Daxiong had programmed a world of unsettling beauty.

'Okay,' he said. 'I have a few suggestions. First of all I need your permission to upload your data onto my computer. As far as I can tell, all your backup systems have been destroyed.'

'Apart from one.'

'I know. Can I ask what computer you're connected to at the moment?'

She chewed her lip and looked round, as if there were someone there to advise her.

'It's at Daxiong's,' she said reluctantly.

'Where? In the workshop?'

'Yes. He lives there.'

'And you'll get away straight after the meeting.'

'Daxiong's cellar is safe, we—'

'Kenny fires rockets,' Jericho interrupted her gruffly, 'which means that nothing is safe. The workshop is registered as Demon Point, under the name City Demons. It's only a matter of time until Kenny turns up there or sends someone. Does Daxiong have a complete copy of your data?'

'No.'

'Then let me download it.'

'Okay.'

Jericho thought for a moment and counted the points up on his fingers. 'Secondly, we'll follow the African trail. Thirdly, we'll try to crack the Spanish website with the films of Switzerland. Both down to me. Diane has the relevant programs, she—'

'Diane?'

'My – my—' Suddenly he felt embarrassed. 'Doesn't matter. Fourthly, what do all six pages, valid and invalid, have in common?'

'That's obvious.' Yoyo looked at him uncomprehendingly. 'They contain, or contained—'

'And following on from that?'

'Hey! Can you stop sounding like a bloody headmaster?'

'Someone will have to check them,' Jericho continued, unfazed, 'to make sure that the mask – the decoder program – always fits. In terms of content there doesn't seem to be a connection, all the pages are publicly accessible and registered in various countries. But who initiated them? If we can find a common initiator, we might be able to find out which other pages he controls. The more pages we find that fit our mask, the more we will decode.'

'I don't know how to do that. And neither does Tian.'

'But I do.' Jericho took a deep breath. For a moment he imagined it was the clear air of the ocean planet flowing through his capillaries, but he was only breathing whatever the air-conditioning was blowing into his room. With every word he uttered he felt strength and resolution returning. The certainty that he hadn't been handed over defenceless to Kenny and the people behind him flooded his consciousness like a physical glow. 'Fifth, we assume that Andre Donner is on the hit list same as we are. And that immediately gives us two reasons to get in contact with him. To find out more about our own case, and to warn him.'

'If he needs a warning.'

'So we have nothing to lose. Do we?'

'No.'

'Okay then.' He hesitated. 'Yoyo, I don't want to keep coming back to it, but who else have you told about your discovery? I mean, which of them—'

'Which of them is still alive?' she asked bitterly.

Jericho said nothing.

'Only Daxiong,' she said. 'And you.'

She crouched down and let nacreous sand slip through her fingers. The thin streams formed mysterious patterns on the ground before vanishing in a shimmer of light. Then she raised her head.

'I want to call my father.'

Jericho nodded. 'That would have been my next suggestion.'

He wondered if it mightn't have been more sensible to make contact with Tu first. But that decision was entirely up to the girl at his feet, who was now slowly standing up and looking at him with beautiful, sad eyes.

'Shall I leave you alone?' he asked.

'No.' She gave an unladylike sniff, and turned her back on him. 'Maybe it's better if you're here.'

The fingers of her right hand moved through the void, etching something into it. A moment later a dark field appeared in the clear air. An old-fashioned dial tone was heard, absurdly mundane and out of place in this strange world.

'He hasn't activated picture mode,' she said, as if apologising for Hongbing's backwardness.

'I know, his old phone. You gave it to him.'

'I'm amazed he's still using it,' she snorted. It went on ringing. 'He should really be at the car dealership. If he doesn't pick up, I'll call th —'

The dial tone stopped. There was a quiet rustling sound, along with other background noises. No one spoke.

Yoyo looked uncertainly at Jericho.

'Father?' she whispered.

The answer came quietly. It crept up ominously, a fat, weary snake rearing up to take a closer look at its next victim.

'I'm not your father, Yoyo.'

Jericho didn't know what was going to happen. Yoyo was stricken, her friends were dead. She had to deal with the sort of images that are only bearable in nightmares, whose horror subsides in the morning light. But there was no awaking from this nightmare – Kenny's voice seeped like poison into the island idyll. But when Yoyo spoke, there was nothing but suppressed rage in her words.

'Where is my father?'

Kenny took his time, a long time, before answering. Yoyo in turn said nothing, waiting frostily, so both of them remained silent, a mute test of strength.

'I've given him the day off,' he said at last. He crowned the remark with a smug, quiet chuckle.

'That doesn't answer my question.'

'No one told you to ask questions.'

'Is he well?'

'Very well. He's taking a rest.'

The way Kenny said 'very well' was designed to suggest the precise opposite. Yoyo clenched her fists.

'Listen, you sick fuck. I want to talk to my father right away, you hear? After that you can make your demands, but first give me a sign of life, or else you can go on talking to yourself. Did you get any of that?'

Kenny let the rustling noise continue down the line for a while.

'Yoyo, my jade girl,' he sighed. 'Clearly your world-view is based on a series of misunderstandings. In stories like this the roles are assigned in a different way. Every one of your words that doesn't meet with my absolute approval will cause pain to Hongbing. I'll let you off with the "sick fuck".' He giggled. 'You could even be right.'

Vain as a peacock, thought Jericho. Kenny might be a pretty exotic specimen of a contract killer, but he seemed much closer to the profile of a psychopathic serial killer. Narcissistic, in love with his own words, flirting affectionately with his own obnoxiousness.

'A sign of life,' Yoyo insisted.

All of a sudden the black rectangle changed. Kenny's face filled it almost completely. He hovered above the pearly beach like a spirit in a bottle. Then he vanished from the camera's perspective, and a room became visible, with a wall of windows at the back, bright daylight falling through them. The outlines of some items of furniture could be seen, a chair with someone sitting on it. In front of it, something black, massive and three-legged.

'Father,' whispered Yoyo.

'Please say something, honourable Chen,' said Kenny's voice.

Chen Hongbing sat as motionless on his chair as if he had become a part of it. With the light behind him, it was almost impossible to make out his face. When he spoke he sounded as if someone was walking on dry leaves.

'Yoyo. Are you okay?'

'Father,' she cried. 'It's all fine, everything's going to be fine!'

'It— I'm so sorry.'

'No, I'm the one who's sorry. I really am!' A moment later her eyes filled with tears. With a visible effort of will she forced herself to calm down. Kenny appeared in the picture again.

'Terrible quality, this phone,' he said. 'I'm afraid your father could hardly hear you. Perhaps you could come and see him, what do you think?'

'If you do anything—' Yoyo began unsteadily.

'What I do is entirely up to you,' Kenny replied coolly. 'He's quite comfortable at the moment, except that his mobility is a little restricted. He is sitting in the sights of an automatic rifle. He can speak and blink. If he suddenly feels like jumping in the air or just raising his arm, the gun will go off. Unfortunately it will also do that if he tries to scratch himself. Not quite so cosy, perhaps.'

'Please don't hurt him,' sobbed Yoyo.

'I'm not interested in hurting anyone, believe it or not. So come here, and come quickly.' Kenny paused. When he went on talking, the snake-like tone had left his voice. Suddenly he sounded friendly again, almost matey, the way Zhao Bide had spoken. 'Your father has my word that nothing will happen as long as you cooperate. That involves telling me the names of everyone who knows about the intercepted message, or even what was in it. And you are to give me every, really *every* drive with a download of the message on it.'

'You destroyed my computer,' said Yoyo.

'I destroyed something, yes. But did I destroy *everything*?'

'Don't contradict him,' Jericho whispered to Yoyo.

She said nothing.

'You see.' Kenny smiled as if his assumption had been confirmed. 'Don't worry, I'll keep my word. And bring that shaven-headed giant with you, you remember the one. You will both come in through the front door, it's open.' He paused. Something seemed to go through his head, then he asked, 'By the way, has this guy Owen Jericho been in touch with you?'

'Jericho?' Yoyo echoed.

'The detective?'

Jericho had been keeping out of view of the phone, so that he saw the scene in Chen's flat, but couldn't be seen by Kenny. He gave Yoyo a sign and shook his head violently.

'I have no idea where that idiot is,' she said contemptuously.

'Why so harsh?' Kenny raised his eyebrows in amazement. 'He saved you.'

'He wants to jerk me around the same as you do, doesn't he? You said he killed Grand Cherokee.'

A flicker of amusement played around Kenny's lips.

'Yes. Of course. So, when can you get here?'

'As quick as I can,' sniffed Yoyo. 'Depends on the traffic. Quarter of an hour? Is that okay?'

'Completely okay. You and Daxiong. Unarmed. I see a gun, Chen dies. Anyone else comes through the door, he dies. Anyone tries to disarm the automatic rifle, off it goes. As soon as everything's sorted out, we'll leave the house together. Oh, yes – if reinforcements are waiting outside or anyone tries to play the hero, Chen dies too. He can only leave his chair when I've deactivated the mechanism.'

The line went dead.

The weird calls of big animals reached them from the distance. A breeze rustled the bushes that lined the beach to the meadow, and set clusters of blossom bobbing up and down.

'That bastard,' groaned Yoyo. 'That damned—'

'Whatever he is, he's not omnipotent.'

'He isn't?' she yelled at him. 'You saw what's going on! Do you really think he'll let him live? Or me?'

'Yoyo—'

'So what am I supposed to do?' She shrank back. Her lower lip was trembling. She shook her head, as tears ran down her cheeks. 'What on earth am I supposed to do? What should I do?'

'Hey,' he said. 'We'll get him out of there. I promise you. No one's going to die, you hear?'

'And how are you going to achieve that?'

Jericho started walking up and down. He didn't really know either, yet. Bit by bit, a plan was starting to form in his head. A crazy undertaking that depended on a whole series of very different factors. The glass façade behind Chen Hongbing played a part in it, as did the captured airbike. He needed to talk to Tu Tian as well.

'Forget it,' said Yoyo breathlessly. 'Let's go.'

'Wait.'

'But I can't wait! I have to get to my father. Let's get out of here.' She held her right hand out to him.

'Hang on, Yoyo—'

'Now!'

'Just one minute. I—' He chewed on his bottom lip. 'I know how we're going to do this. I know!'

Hongkou

The house on Siping Lu, number 1276, had retained the monotonous pastel of some of the blocks of flats built in the Shanghai district of Hongkou at the turn of the millennium. When the weather was gloomy it seemed to disappear into the sky. As if to counteract this, emphatically green-tinted panes of glass broke up the façade, another stylistic device of an era that made even skyscrapers look like cheap toys.

Unlike the high-rises a street further on, number 1276 contented itself with six floors, had generously sized balconies and also flaunted what looked a bit like a pagoda roof. On either side of the balconies, the dirty white boxes of the air-conditioning system clung to the plaster. Listlessly flapping in the wind was a tattered banner, on which the inhabitants of the building demanded the immediate suspension of building work on the maglev, another elevated highway that would lead right past their front door, and whose pillars already loomed high above the street. Aside from this pitiful gesture towards revolt, the building was no different from number 1274 or 1278.

The flat, covering an area of thirty-eight square metres, comprised a living room with a wall unit, dining area and sofa-bed, a separate bedroom, a tiny bathroom and a kitchen, only slightly bigger, that opened onto the dining table. There was no hall, and instead a screen at the side masked off the front door, creating a small amount of intimacy.

Until recently at any rate.

Now it leaned folded against the wall, so that the whole of the area around the front door was visible. Xin had made himself comfortable on the sofa-bed, a little way away from the chair on whose edge Chen Hongbing sat as if lost in contemplation, tall, angular, bolt upright. His temples glistened in the light that fell through the glass façade to the rear and dissolved into tiny droplets of sweat that covered his taut skin. Xin weighed the remote control for the automatic rifle in his hand, a flat, feather-light screen. He had told the old man that any sudden movement would lead to his death. But the mechanism had not been activated. Xin didn't want to risk the old man bringing about his own demise through sheer nervousness.

'Maybe you should take me hostage,' Chen said into the silence.

Xin yawned. 'Haven't I done that already?'

'I mean, I – I could put myself at your mercy for longer, until you no longer saw Yoyo as a threat.'

'And where would that get you?'

'My daughter would live,' Chen replied hoarsely. It looked odd, the way he uttered words without any gestures, struggling to keep even the movements of his lips to the barest minimum.

Xin pretended to think for a moment.

'No, she will survive as long as she convinces me.'

'I'm asking you only for my daughter's life.' Chen's breathing was shallow. 'I don't care about anything else.'

'That honours you,' said Xin. 'It brings you close to the martyrs.'

Suddenly he thought he saw the old man smiling. It was barely noticeable, but Xin had an eye for such small things.

'What's cheered you up?'

'The fact that you've misunderstood the situation. You think you can kill me, but there isn't much left to kill. You're too late. I've died already.'

Xin began to answer, then looked at the man with fresh interest. As a rule he didn't set much store by other people's private affairs, particularly when they were eking out their final minutes. But suddenly he craved to know what Chen had meant. He got up and stood behind the tripod on which the rifle stood, so that it looked as if it were actually growing from his belly. 'You'll have to explain that to me.'

'I don't think it will interest you,' said Chen. He looked up and his eyes were like two wounds. All of a sudden Xin had the feeling of being able to see inside that thin body, and glimpse the black mirror of a sea below a moonless sky. In its depths he sensed old suffering, self-hatred and repulsion, he heard screams and pleas, doors rattling and slamming shut. Groans of resignation, echoing faintly down endless, windowless corridors. They had tried to break Chen, for four whole years. Xin knew that, without knowing it. He effortlessly identified the focus point, he could touch the spots where people were most vulnerable, just as a single glance into the detective's eyes had been enough to spot his loneliness.

'You were in jail,' he said.

'Not directly.'

Xin hesitated. Might he have been mistaken?

'At any rate you were robbed of your freedom.'

'Freedom?' Chen made a noise between a croak and a sigh. 'What's that? Are you freer than me right now, when I'm sitting on this chair and you're standing in front of me? Does that thing you're pointing at me give you freedom? Do you lose your freedom if you're locked up?'

Xin pursed his lips. 'You explain it to me.'

'No one needs to explain it to you,' Chen croaked. 'You know better than anyone.'

'What?'

'That anyone who threatens anyone else is frightened. Anyone who points a gun at anyone is frightened.'

'So *I'm* frightened?' Xin laughed.

'Yes,' Chen replied succinctly. 'Repression is always based on fear. Fear of dissident opinions. Fear of being unmasked. Fear of losing power, of rejection, of insignificance. The more weapons you deploy, the higher the walls you build, the more ingenious your forms of torture, the more you are only demonstrating your own impotence. You remember Tiananmen? What happened in the Square of Heavenly Peace?'

'The student unrest?'

'I don't know how old you are. You were probably still a child when that happened. Young people demonstrating for something that had already been fought for by many others: freedom. And lined up against them a State almost paralysed, shaken to its foundations, so much so that it finally sent in the tanks and everything sank into chaos. Who do you think was more frightened then? The students? Or the Party?'

'I was five years old,' said Xin, amazed to find himself talking to a hostage as though they were sitting together in a tea house. 'How the hell should I know?'

'You know. You're pointing a gun at me right now.'

'True. So I would guess that you're the one who should be shit scared right now, old man!'

'You'd think so, wouldn't you?' Again a ghostly smile distorted Chen's features. 'And yet I fear only for the life of my daughter. And the other thing that frightens me is that I might have got everything wrong. Stayed silent when I should have talked. That's all. Your gun there can't scare me. My inner demons are more than a match for your ridiculous gun.

But you're frightened. You're frightened about what might be left if you were robbed of your weapons and other attributes of power. You're afraid of backsliding.'

Xin stared at the old man.

'There's no backsliding – haven't you worked that out? There's only striding ahead in time. Just a permanent Now. The past is cold ashes.'

'I agree with you there. Apart from one thing. The cold ashes are what destroys people. The consequences of destruction, on the other hand, remain.'

'You can even cleanse yourself of those.'

'Cleanse?' Bafflement flickered in Chen's eyes. 'Of what?'

'Of what was. When you consign it to the flames. When you *burn* it! The fire purifies your soul, do you understand? So that you are born a second time.'

Chen's wounded gaze drilled into his own. 'Are you talking about revenge?'

'Revenge?' Xin bared his teeth. 'Revenge only makes an adversary bigger, it gives him meaning. I'm talking about complete extinction! About overcoming your own history. What tormented you, your . . . demons!'

'You mean you can burn those demons?'

'Of course you can!' How stupid did you have to be to deny that fundamental certainty? The whole universe, all being, all becoming, was based on transience.

'But what,' Chen said after thinking for a while, 'if you discover that there are no spirits? No demons. That the past has only shaped you like an image and the spirits are part of yourself. Don't you then try to extinguish yourself? In that case, is your cleansing not self-mutilation?'

Xin lowered his eyelids. The conversation was taking a turn that fascinated him.

'What have *you* burned?' asked Chen.

He wondered how to explain it to Chen, so that he would understand Xin's greatness. But suddenly he heard something. Footsteps in the corridor. 'Another time, honourable Chen,' he whispered.

He walked quickly back to the sofa and turned on the automatic trigger. Now it was happening. One false move from Chen, and his body would be shredded. The footsteps came closer.

Then the door swung open and—

Yoyo saw her father sitting on the chair, facing the muzzle of the rifle. He didn't move, only his eyeballs turned slowly towards her. She sensed the tension in Daxiong's massive body beside her and stepped inside, clutching the little computer in her right hand. In the background the hitman rose from the edge of the sofa. He too held something in his hand, gleaming and flat.

'Hello, Yoyo,' he hissed. 'How lovely to see you again.'

'Father,' she said, ignoring him. 'Are you okay?'

Chen Hongbing attempted a crooked smile. 'In the circumstances, I would say so.'

'He's fine as long as you stick to our agreement,' Kenny said. 'The automatic trigger has been activated. Any movement by Chen will kill him.' He held the remote control in the air. 'Of course I can operate the trigger too. So whatever you were planning, forget it.'

'And where do we go from here?' growled Daxiong.

'First shut the door behind you.'

Daxiong gave the door a shove. It fell silently shut.

'And now?'

Kenny turned his back on them and glanced out of the glass façade at the back. He didn't seem to be in any particular hurry. Yoyo shivered and held up the computer.

'You wanted this,' she said.

The hitman looked outside again for a moment. Then he turned towards them.

'Let's say yes for the time being.'

'Yes or no?'

Yoyo was gradually getting nervous, but she tried not to show it. Something must have gone wrong. Why was it taking so long? Where was Jericho?

'Well?' Kenny nodded encouragingly at her. 'I'm listening.'

'I've got a few things to clear up first.'

'I think I remember that we discussed everything clearly.'

She shook her head. 'Nothing's clear yet. What guarantee do we have that you'll let us live?'

Kenny smiled like someone experiencing an anticipated disappointment 'Spare us this, Yoyo. We're not here to negotiate.'

'True,' snorted Daxiong. 'Do you know what I think? As soon as you have what you want, you'll waste us.'

'Exactly,' nodded Yoyo. 'So why should we tell you anything if you're going to kill us anyway? Maybe we'll take a few secrets with us to the grave.'

'I gave you my word,' Kenny said very quietly. 'That should be enough for you.'

'Your word wasn't worth much this morning.'

'But we can play the game another way too,' he went on, ignoring her remark. 'No one has to die straight away. Look at your father, Yoyo. He's a brave man, who isn't afraid of death. I can't help admiring him. I wonder how much pain he can bear.'

Hongbing uttered a croaking laugh. 'You'd be amazed,' he said.

The hitman grinned.

'Boot up your computer. Get the encrypted file up on the screen and throw it over to me. You have no options left, Yoyo. Just your faith.'

Damn Jericho, she thought. What's going on? We can't keep this bastard hanging on much longer. Where are you?

Jericho cursed. Until a moment ago it had gone smoothly – almost too smoothly. While Yoyo and Daxiong were on their way to Chen, he had spoken to Tu and managed to break open the weapon chambers of the airbike. He had chosen a high-velocity rapid-fire automatic laser rifle that lay heavy and secure in the hand, started the engine and flown the machine unimpeded to the agreed meeting point.

They had met not far from number 1276 for a quick briefing.

*　　*　　*

'It's the eighth building along.' Yoyo had pointed down the street. 'The back yards are all the same, with lawns and trees and a path connecting them. It's the left window side, fourth floor.'

'Good,' Jericho nodded.

'Have you brought my computer?'

'Yes. Daxiong too?'

'Here.' The giant had handed him a rather ancient-looking computer. Jericho transferred the fragment of encrypted text to it.

'Can I have mine back now?' asked Yoyo.

'Of course.' Jericho had put her computer back in his pocket. 'When all this is over. It'll be safer with me until then. Kenny mustn't get the chance to take it from you.'

She said nothing, which he took as a sign of assent. He had looked from her to Daxiong and back again.

'All okay?'

'So far, yes.'

'You go into the flat in five minutes exactly.'

'Okay.'

'And I'll be there straight after, and get his back to the wall. Any more questions?'

They both mutely shook their heads.

'Good.'

In five minutes.

That was now! And he was still standing on the corner of the street, because the airbike had suddenly started behaving like a diva who refused to go on stage, however much you cajoled her.

'Come on,' he snapped.

This part of Hongkou was entirely residential, and Siping Lu was a feeder road, several lanes wide. There were hardly any shops, or restaurants either. The pavements were correspondingly empty, since the Chinese, even forty years after Deng Xiaoping's legendary opening up to the West, showed no real liking for strolling as the French, Germans and Italians did. The traffic flowed quickly along, spanned by pedestrian bridges at regular intervals. Because most commuters had been at their desks since the early hours of the morning, the volume of vehicles remained relatively small. From the central strip separating the lanes the massive pillars of the future maglev elevated highway rose and threw long, menacing shadows. A small park with a lawn, a pond and a little wood occupied the opposite side of the road, where old people, divorced from time, practised qigong. It was like watching two films running at different speeds. Against the backdrop of the slow-motion ballet, the cars looked as though they were travelling faster than they really were.

No one paid Jericho any attention in his audible dispute with the airbike, in which he spoke and the machine remained stubbornly silent.

The seconds flew by.

At last he interrupted his monologue and dealt the vehicle a kick in the side, which the plastic casing absorbed so silently that it amounted to an insult. He feverishly ran through the alternatives. As he did so, he went on mechanically trying to start the airbike, so that he was still brooding when the rotors of the turbine suddenly began to turn and the familiar hiss climbed the scale of frequencies, higher and higher, until it finally invited him to fly as if there had never been a problem.

'Fine,' said Yoyo. 'You've won.'

She crouched down and slid the little computer along the floor towards Kenny. When she stood up again, her eyes met Hongbing's. He seemed to be asking her forgiveness for the fact that he could contribute nothing more towards solving her problems than to sit there frozen. In fact, Kenny's perfidious arrangement even kept him from throwing himself at the man who was threatening his daughter. He wouldn't make the first metre. Nothing would have been gained.

'There's nothing you can do,' she said. And then, trusting that Jericho was still on his way, she added, 'Whatever happens, Father, don't move from the spot, you hear? Not an inch.'

'Touching.' Kenny smiled. 'I could puke.'

He lifted the computer and glanced at the screen for a moment. Then he gave Yoyo a contemptuous look.

'Pretty ancient model, isn't it?'

She shrugged.

'Are you sure you've given me the right one?'

'It's the one for backups.'

'Okay, part two. Who else knows about your little outing to forbidden climes?'

'Daxiong,' said Yoyo, pointing at him. 'And Shi Wanxing.'

Daxiong gave her a quick look of surprise. It wasn't just Kenny who would be wondering who Shi Wanxing was. In fact she'd spontaneously invented the name in the hope that Daxiong might understand her bluff and play along. Now that the hitman had taken her computer, or what he thought was her computer, they were effectively dead. She had to try to keep him at arm's length.

'Wanxing?' Kenny's eyes narrowed. 'Who is that?'

'He—' began Yoyo.

'Shut up.' Kenny nodded to Daxiong. 'I asked him.'

Daxiong let a moment's silence pass, a moment that seemed to stretch into eternity. Then, jutting his pharaoh beard, he said, 'Shi Wanxing is, apart from us, the last person you haven't killed. The last surviving Guardian. I didn't know Yoyo had confided in him.'

Kenny frowned suspiciously. 'Even she doesn't seem to have known that until a minute ago.'

'We don't agree on the subject of Wanxing,' growled Daxiong. 'Yoyo thinks a lot of him, for some reason. I didn't want to have him in the group at all. He talks too much.'

'Wanxing is an outstanding crypto-analyst,' Yoyo replied scornfully.

'That's why you shouldn't have transferred all your data to him straight away,' Daxiong complained.

'Why not? He was supposed to decode the page with the Switzerland films on it.'

'And? Did he?'

'No idea.'

'He did absolutely bugger all, is what he did!'

'Hey, Daxiong!' Yoyo railed at him. 'What's really at issue here? Just the fact that you can't stand him.'

'He's a loudmouth.'

'I trust him.'

'But you can't trust him.'

'Wanxing is no loudmouth.'

'Frogshit!' said Daxiong, getting angry. 'It's all he bloody is!'

Kenny tilted his head. He didn't really seem to know what to make of the argument.

'If Wanxing talked to anyone at all about it, it was because he needed extra tools,' Yoyo roared. 'After *you* completely failed!'

'That's exactly what I'm saying.'

'What?'

'That Sara and Zheiying are in possession of this bloody message.'

'What? Why them?'

'Why? Are you blind? Because he fancies Sara.'

'So do you!'

'Hey,' said Kenny.

'You're off your head,' Daxiong snapped. 'Shall we talk about your relationship with Zheiying? The way you make him look like an idiot just because he—'

'Hey!' Kenny yelled, throwing his computer at Daxiong's feet. 'What the hell's going on? Are you taking the piss? Who's Wanxing? Who are these other people? Who else knows about this? Say something, somebody, or I'll blow the old guy to pieces!'

Yoyo opened her mouth and closed it again. She couldn't take her eyes off the hitman, who seemed to have worked something out. That they were bluffing, keeping him at arm's length. That they were actually staring past him, at the source of the hissing noise that Kenny hadn't noticed because he had allowed himself to be distracted by the staged argument. Kenny, the bomb that had to be defused, like in the old films.

Just another few seconds. The countdown approaching zero, half a dozen wires, all the same colour, but only one that you could cut through.

'You're in the crosshairs,' she said quietly.

Xin looked at his display. It showed him what the scanner of the automatic rifle saw: Chen Hongbing, pressed into his seat. Part of the rear glass façade. A dark outline at the edge of the picture.

Something had appeared behind Chen.

'If my father dies, you're dead,' said Yoyo. 'Same if you attack us or try to escape. So listen. One of your airbikes is hovering outside the window right now. Owen Jericho is sitting on it, and he's pointing something at you. I'm not familiar with these things, but judging by the size of it, I'd say that he could blow *you* to pieces with it, so try to keep your temper under control.'

Xin put his thoughts and feelings in order like an accountant. He'd get annoyed later. He had no doubt that Yoyo was telling the truth. If Chen died that second, he would die too. The girl and her enormous friend were unarmed, while he had a gun tucked into the top of his trousers – not much of an advantage really, because before he had drawn the gun he would be dead too.

'What should I do?' he asked calmly.

'Turn off the trigger. That gun. I want my father to get up and come over to us.'

'Right. To do that I'll have to turn off automatic activation. I'll have to touch it, okay?'

'If this is one of your tricks—' roared Daxiong.

'I'm not about to commit suicide. It's just a remote control.'

'Go on,' nodded Yoyo.

Xin tapped on the touchscreen and switched off the automatic trigger. The gun was no longer programmed to respond to Chen Hongbing's movements. It was entirely under his control again.

'Just a moment.' He quickly keyed in swivel angle, rotation speed and fire frequency. 'All done. Stand up, honourable Chen. Go to your daughter.'

Chen Hongbing seemed to hesitate.

Then he hurried from his chair and to the side.

Xin fell to the ground and pressed *Start*.

Cave-dwellers, savannah-runners: they'd experienced everything by the twenty-first century. They saw the rustling of the grass, heard what the wind carried to them, were astonishingly able simultaneously to respond to and intuitively assess a variety of stimuli. Some people drew more from their ancient inheritance than others, and some had preserved their instincts, developed over six million years of human history, to an extra-ordinary degree.

Owen Jericho was one of those.

He had driven the bike right up to the glass façade, clutching his rapid-fire rifle, held so that the red laser dot was resting on Kenny's back. He hung there like a dragonfly, well aware that the hitman must have heard the hissing of the jets long before, but Kenny had shown no sign of turning round. He wasn't prepared for an attack from that direction. They had him over a barrel.

Yoyo said something and pointed at her father.

The laser dot quivered between Kenny's shoulder blades.

Chen's thin, lanky body tensed, the hitman bent his arms. It was pos-sible that he was holding something in his left hand, which he was using with his right.

Then it happened – and Jericho's ancient legacy took hold. His per-ception sped up so quickly that the world seemed to be heading for a standstill and all sounds dropped to sub-audible levels. There was nothing but a dull background hum. As if he had become weightless, Chen slowly rose from the chair, moved away from the seat, centimetre by centi-metre, left leg braced against the floor, right leg bent as he tipped to the side. It was a preparation for a leap, and even before it had really begun, Kenny showed that he was about to throw himself to the floor. Jericho registered all of this, Chen's escape and Kenny's dive, intuitively made connections between them and centred his attention on the remote-con-trolled gun. Even before it began to turn on its tripod, he knew exactly what was about to happen. Chen was able to escape because the gun was no longer aimed at him. The hitman wasn't running away from Jericho's gun, he was fleeing his own, which he was at that very moment directing to fire at the windows.

The same evolutionary calculation that had saved hunters millions of years before taught Jericho to climb a second before the barrel spat its first bullets. He had changed position by the time they left the muzzle.

Then things speeded up.

The gun on the tripod swung around and rattled off its rounds, then turned further on its axis. All the windows exploded. The burst took in Jericho's bike, but he had managed to climb high enough to avoid being hit himself. Two of the bullets struck the rotating wheels of the engine. There was a sound like a cracking bell. The airbike took a terrible blow.

It dropped.

'Down!' yelled Daxiong and threw himself sideways. Three hundred-weight had to get moving, but almost all of Daxiong's colossal body was muscle, so he managed to shove Yoyo and reach Chen Hongbing with a few long strides, the gun following after him. Bullets drilled into the wall and ceiling. Wood, glass and plaster sprayed from gaping holes. Daxiong saw Yoyo fall. At a frequency of eight rounds per second, the gun shredded the door they had been standing outside just a moment before, kept on turning, pursuing him as he breathlessly tried to flee. He collided with Hongbing and pulled him to the floor.

The wall exploded above their heads.

Jericho fell.

Apparently unconnected factors combined unexpectedly, including the principles of construction of flying machines, the effects of heavy ballistics and the ambitions of the city parks commission. Tokyo, for example, symbolised a people that had always lived in a state of extreme self-confinement, which was why you hardly ever saw a tree there. Shanghai, on the other hand, was bursting with parks and tree-lined streets, which enormously enhanced the quality of life, and was also ideal when it came to considerably softening the fall of an airbike plummeting from about twelve metres in the air. Encouraged by the humid climate, the birch trees in the hinterland of Siping Lu had grown luxuriously rampant. The bike crashed into the dense foliage of a tree-top and threw Jericho off. He toppled into the branches, which grew denser as he fell; he flailed around, fell further, whipped by twigs and thrashed by thickening boughs until at last he managed to cling on to one and dangled from it, legs flailing, four to five metres above the courtyard.

Too high to jump.

Where was the airbike?

A crunching and splintering announced that he had overtaken the machine on his way down. It was raging high above him. He threw his head back and saw something flying at him, tried to get out of its way, too late. A branch crashed against his forehead.

When his eyesight had cleared, the airbike was coming straight at him.

Xin rolled over.

Dense clouds of plaster dust formed before his eyes. Near the shattered door he saw Yoyo creeping over to her father on her elbows. By now the spinning rifle had completed its first circuit, and was moving on, still spitting fire, to its second.

'Yoyo, get out!' he heard Daxiong shouting. 'Get out of here!'

'Father!'

Xin waited till the bullets had passed by him, then jumped up and slipped his index finger over the touchscreen of the remote control, stopped the weapon, pulled his finger down and to the right, and the gun followed his movements, and spat a burst of fire at the very spot where Chen and the giant were just getting back to their feet. The bullets missed them by millimetres. Still crouching, they staggered into the next room. Xin fired into the wall, but the masonry had already survived the first shots.

Whatever. In there they were trapped.

He calmly swung the gun round to the left. In a fierce staccato the gun hammered its rounds into the concrete, ploughed through a half-shattered shelf and brought it crashing down completely. A line of craters appeared in quick succession, tracing a line that continued all the way to the girl on the floor.

Yoyo stared at it. Panicking, she tried to get to her feet, but she was ridiculously slow. Her eyes widened when she realised that she was about to die.

'Bye bye, Yoyo,' he hissed.

Turbine mouth downwards, the airbike crashed through the branches as if to kill Jericho and swallow him up at the same time.

He *had* to jump!

The splintering and crashing came to a stop. The machine's rump had jammed less than half a metre above him and come to a juddering standstill.

Bark, leaves and twigs rattled down on him. He looked into the shattered rotors of the turbine, swung towards the trunk and spotted a branch below him that might support his weight.

Worryingly thin, on closer inspection.

Too thin.

The rain of twigs resumed.

He had no choice. He dropped, climbed back up, felt the wood yielding under his weight and wrapped his arms around the trunk.

Xin heard the scream, which had come not from Yoyo but from the giant, who stormed in from the next room, hurled himself like a demolition ball against the tripod and brought it crashing down. The rifle pointed at the ceiling now, bringing down lumps of brick the size of fists. Xin pressed *Stop* and drew his handgun. He saw Hongbing running over to Yoyo, who leapt to her feet and pulled open what was left of the splintered door to the flat.

As Xin took aim at her, Daxiong pulled his legs away.

Xin collapsed onto his back and nimbly rolled sideways. Daxiong crashed to the floor. Xin raised his pistol, but the giant pushed himself up with amazing dexterity and knocked it from his hand. Xin gave him a kick at the spot where his wardrobe-sized chest met his chin, which must therefore have been something like an Adam's apple. Daxiong's pharaoh beard splintered. The giant staggered backwards and uttered a choking croak. With a racing dive Xin was on the pistol, grabbed hold of its butt, felt himself being grabbed and held aloft like a child. Kicking out in all directions, he struggled in vain to free himself from the man's grasp. Daxiong's great paws gripped him like vices as he carried him to the glass façade.

His plan was obvious.

Xin reached back and fired haphazardly. A muffled groan led him to assume that he had hit his target, although it didn't keep Daxiong from hoisting him higher and violently hurling him through one of the windows. There wasn't much glass left in the frame. Under other circumstances the impact would have meant certain death, but the injury had cost the giant some of his strength. Xin spread his arms and legs like a cat, tried to find something to hold on to and caught hold of a strut that hadn't been shattered in the hail of gunfire. His body swung outside. For a moment he looked down at the green sea of leaves below him, tensed his muscles to get back inside, saw Daxiong's fist flying at him and slipped away.

He fell – a little way.

In an instant he spotted and grabbed the bulky box of the air-conditioning system. A jolt ran through his body, his hands clawed around the box, which scraped sideways. Far below him there was crashing, splintering and rattling as if a huge animal were raging in the tree-tops.

Jericho? That was exactly the spot where the detective had fallen.

No matter. He had to get back into the flat. Using all his strength he pulled himself up, braced his feet against the masonry and started climbing.

Jericho clung desperately to the tree trunk. His feet slipped. No bark to claw on to. Just three metres above the ground he decided to let go, pushed himself away, landed on both feet, lost his balance, fell on his back and saw the airbike plunging down on top of him.

Motorbike falls from tree and kills detective.

There were headlines that you didn't want to imagine in print.

With all his strength he catapulted himself sideways. The airbike struck the ground beside him with such force that he was afraid the arsenal of weapons would go up, but he was spared that disaster at least. The bike lay on its side; two jets and part of the casing had come off. As a result it had ceased to function as a flying machine. He looked up, but the tree-tops obscured the view of Chen's flat. When he staggered to the house wall he thought he saw a foot disappearing over the window ledge and narrowed his eyes.

The foot was gone.

He looked around, discovered a back door, pressed the handle and found it was open. Behind it, the corridor lay in darkness. Cool air drifted towards him. He slipped inside and took a moment to find his bearings, saw a turn in the corridor and followed its course. After a short flight of steps he found himself beside the lift-shaft. Ahead of him, the hall stretched to the front door. A series of loud thumps came from the stair-well. Someone was charging down the stairs like an elephant. Jericho jerked backwards, hid behind the lift-shaft and waited to see who would appear in the hall.

It was Daxiong. The giant staggered and rested his arm against the wall. His jacket was torn and bloodstained over his right shoulder. A few quick steps and Jeri-cho was beside him.

'What's going on? Where are Yoyo and Chen?'

Daxiong spun around, fist ready to strike. Then he recognised Jericho, turned and stumbled towards the front door.

'Outside,' he snorted.

'And Kenny?'

'Outside too.'

His knees gave. Jericho grabbed him under the arms.

'Stand up,' he panted.

'I'm too heavy.'

'Nonsense. I've rocked bigger babies than you before. What do you mean outside?'

Daxiong clawed one of his great hands into Jericho's shoulder and shifted his weight to him. Of course he was too heavy. Far too heavy. Almost like dragging a medium-sized dinosaur around with you. Jericho pulled the door open, and they staggered together into the sunlight.

'I threw him out,' wheezed Daxiong. 'Out of the window. The bastard.'

'I think the bastard's crept back in again.' Jericho quickly scanned the surroundings. A car and a bike were on the move, some way apart.

'They must be here somewhere – there!'

Between the vehicles Yoyo waved at them from the other side of the road. She was on the saddle of one of the two motorbikes on which she and Daxiong had arrived. Beside her, Chen Hongbing shifted nervously from one foot to the other. Yoyo pointed to the second motorbike and shouted something.

'Exactly,' growled Daxiong. He took his hand off Jericho's shoulder and stomped unsteadily off. 'Let's get out of here.'

The pagoda-like roof of the building flattened in the middle section, by the shaft of the stairwell. Xin had parked his airbike next to it when he'd gone down to the fourth floor and now he charged back into the open, gun at the ready, safety-catch released in haste, bleeding from a thousand cuts. He ran to the edge of the roof. The pagoda sloped gently below him and hid most of the street, but he could still make out the struts for the new elevated highway and the park on the other side.

He saw Yoyo and her father standing next to a footbridge.

He took aim and realised that his magazine was empty. With a howl of rage he threw the gun away, ran to his airbike, sat on it, started the engine and climbed until he had a wider view of the whole road. Jericho and Daxiong were running along it. They had crossed the central reservation and were now halfway over the bridge. The traffic surged along below them. From the air they looked like mice in a lab run. One of them was limping.

The giant. He *had* hit him.

Xin reached down into the weapon chamber and brought out a sub-machine-gun. Jets wailing, he plunged.

Jericho saw him coming. He grabbed Daxiong – running in front of him, bent almost double – by the sleeve of his jacket and pointed into the air.

'Shit,' gasped Daxiong. He raised both arms to alert the others to the bike, and groaned. His face was contorted with pain. But Yoyo had also realised the danger she was in. She jumped from her motorbike and started running as fast as she could towards the park, with Hongbing hot on her heels.

'Daxiong,' yelled Jericho. 'We've got to get back.'

'No!'

'We'll never make it.'

He gave the giant a shove and pushed him to the point where the walkway crossed the central reservation, next to one of the massive pillar constructions on which the rails of the maglev were going to run. Prongs jutted out from it at regular intervals. Jericho swung himself over the parapet and started climbing down. He hoped Daxiong would be able to summon the strength to follow him. There was no way he could carry the guy down there.

The airbike shot across the footbridge. Shots rang out loudly. Daxiong lost his grip and landed heavily in the grass of the central reservation. Jericho ran to the fallen man, who sat up and uttered a roar that easily drowned out the sound of the cars. To Jericho's relief Daxiong wasn't shouting with pain, but bawled a cascade of curses all of which concerned Kenny's slow and painful demise.

'Up with you,' Jericho shouted at him.

'I can't!'

'Yes, you can. I'm not particularly responsive to stranded whales.'

Daxiong turned his narrow gaze on him.

'I'll tear his stomach out,' he shouted. 'And his guts! First his large intestine, then the small one—'

'As you wish. On your feet now!'

*   *   *

Xin came around in a circle and took aim at Yoyo.

A moment later they had disappeared under the lush foliage of the trees that surrounded the park. He brought the bike down and swept over the field towards the qigong group. Heads high, shoulders lowered, upper and lower body in harmony, the old people stretched their arms out, turned their palms and brought them slowly upwards, stretched their limbs, craned their arms until it looked as if they were keeping the sky from plummeting down on Siping Lu. He saw the fugitives appear between plane trees and weeping willows and fired, tearing gaping holes in the wood. The front members of the group fell out of sync with the rest. They forgot to clasp their fingers, missed the slow exhalation, turned their heads.

A moment later they scattered, as the airbike swept through them.

Xin slowed the bike and headed towards the little wood into which Yoyo and her father had disappeared. No sign of them. He pulled up the nose of the airbike and quickly gained height. Maybe they wanted to seize the right moment and run out on the other side, to get to their motorbikes. Jets hissing, he aimed for the two machines. Being powered by electricity, they wouldn't explode, but after an intensive bombardment they would no longer be usable.

He saw a movement in the central reservation. Ah! Jericho and the colossus who'd tried to throw him out of the window.

So much the better.

'Here he comes!'

Daxiong nodded feebly. They waited until the last moment, then fled between the pillars as the first shots ploughed through the grass and struck the concrete. The airbike dashed past them and then performed a quick turn.

'To the other side.'

They took cover again, hoping to keep Kenny at bay. They could always take shelter behind one of the columns. At least that was what Jericho hoped.

Daxiong leaned next to him, drenched in sweat, breath rattling. His face was now worryingly pale.

'I'm not going to be able to keep this up for much longer,' he panted.

'You won't need to,' said Jericho, but he was starting to worry that for some reason the last part of his plan mightn't work quite as well as he had hoped. His eyes swept the sky. Vehicles roared past on either side at irregular intervals. The hiss of the turbine moved away. For a moment he allowed himself to believe that the hitman had given up. If he was high enough, the pillar wouldn't be much use to them. They could circle the thing like rabbits, but sooner or later they would be hit.

'—and his appendix, if he's still got one,' croaked Daxiong. 'I'll drag that out of him too. Or first the appendix and then—'

Grass and soil sprayed up at their feet. Jericho circled the pillar. Daxiong came staggering after him, barely capable of keeping on his feet.

'Are you okay?' asked Jericho.

'That son of a bitch hit me somewhere in the back,' Daxiong murmured. He coughed and collapsed. 'I think I'm going to—'

'Daxiong! For God's sake! You can't give in now. Do you hear me? Don't faint!'

'I'm – I'm trying – I—'

'There! Look!'

Something had appeared in the sky in the distance, flat and silvery. It dived and came very quickly towards them.

'Daxiong,' yelled Jericho. 'We're saved!'

The giant smiled. 'That's nice,' he said dreamily and tipped sideways.

Xin had briefly shifted his attention to the little wood, so he didn't see the shimmering flatfish until it was almost too late. Within a few seconds it grew menacingly large, but the pilot showed no sign of veering away from him. He gave a start, then realised that the new arrival planned to ram him into the ground. Startled, he raised his arm and fired off a few rounds that the vehicle dodged elegantly before immediately heading straight back towards him again.

Whoever was steering the skymobile was a master of navigation.

He let the airbike drop like a stone and caught it again right above the traffic. The silver discus went into a nosedive. Xin turned, passed over the woods and the artificial lake, twisted and dodged, and still couldn't shake off his pursuer. The silver discus chased him across the park and back to the road, then suddenly turned off and rose steeply into the sky. Xin watched after him in confusion, slowed his bike down and held it hovering above the flow of traffic.

The strange machine disappeared.

Cursing, he remembered what he had to do. It was humiliating! Yoyo and old Chen were hiding somewhere in the bushes watching everything, an idea that made him boil with fury. He would use the grenade launcher and set the woods ablaze – but first Jericho and Daxiong had to go. No police had turned up yet. Gun at the ready, he was heading towards the pillar with the two idiots hiding behind it, when he saw the silver discus coming back and heading straight for him.

He hid his gun. Below him, antediluvian cars impregnated the air with exhaust and street dust. He was seething with rage. He wouldn't allow himself to be hunted again. He would bring that guy down from the sky. His fingers closed around the butt of the rocket-launcher, but it was stuck. He rattled at it frantically, looked down and lost his concentration for a moment.

There was a loud honking noise.

Louder, closer.

Irritated, Xin raised his head.

The front of a roaring heavy goods vehicle, growing, vast. The airbike had dropped while he was battling with the launcher. With horror, he saw the driver shouting and gesticulating behind the windscreen, pulled the bike back up and missed the roof of the driver's cab by inches, only to see the discus shooting away above him, so close that its shock-wave gripped the airbike and whirled it around like a leaf. He flew from the saddle in a high arc and landed on his back. The impact left him breathless. He instinctively reached his arms up, but nothing drove over him. He was lying on something that was solid yet yielding. Battling for breath, he pulled himself upright and saw rusty planks supporting the pile of whatever he was rolling in.

No. Not planks. Bodywork. Xin reached into the mass and let it trickle through his fingers.

Sand.

He had fallen into a heap of sand.

With a cry of rage he got to his feet, saw houses, masts and traffic-lights drifting past him, lost his balance and landed back in the sand as the huge truck he was lying on turned off, accelerated and drove him out of Hongkou, away from Daxiong, Jericho, Yoyo, Chen and Siping Lu.

On the inside of the four westbound lanes, the traffic started to back up. The airbike had fallen on the central reservation, scattering parts of its shell over the carriageway and forcing some drivers into bold braking manoeuvres. If there were no collisions, this was due only to the compulsory introduction of pre-safe sensors, which even old models had had to adopt. Radar systems with CMOS cameras constantly analysed distance and automatically braked the car if the driver in front came to an abrupt standstill. Only flying objects obviously created problems for the sensors.

Meanwhile the Silver Surfer had landed in the park. Jericho peered between the cars and saw the vehicle's side doors lifting and a familiar, fleshy figure climbing out. Then he saw someone else, and his heart thumped with joy.

Yoyo and Chen came running out of the wood.

'Daxiong!' He bent down to the giant and patted his cheek. 'Get up. Come on.'

Daxiong murmured something unfriendly. Jericho brought his hand back and gave him two loud slaps, and jumped backwards just in case he had underestimated the giant's reflexes. But Daxiong just sat up, sighed and looked as if he were about to sink back again. Jericho took his arm and gripped it tightly for a few seconds, before the massive body slipped away from him.

'Damn it, Daxiong!'

He couldn't let the wounded man fall into a coma. Not here. Further slaps were needed. This time he was more successful.

'Have you lost your mind?' Daxiong yelled.

Jericho pointed at the prongs in the pillar that led up to the footbridge. 'You can go to sleep in a minute. First we've got to get up there.'

Daxiong tried to support himself on his left arm, collapsed, tried again and got to his feet. Jericho felt terribly sorry for him. In the movies people with bullet wounds went on charging around the place doing heroic things, but the reality was very different. The wound on Daxiong's back might just have been a graze, but the very shock of it, caused by the velocity of the dart bullets, was enough to send a person out of his mind. Daxiong had lost a lot of blood, and the wound must be very painful.

The big man's gaze wandered up the ladder. By now his face was ashen.

'I won't get up there, Owen,' he whispered.

Jericho breathed out. Daxiong was right. He didn't even feel all that steady on his feet himself. He estimated the width of the central reservation – just wide enough, he thought, and took out his mobile. Two beeps later he had Tu on the line. Jericho could see him over in the park, while Yoyo and Chen were climbing into the skymobile.

'Tian?'

His voice was suddenly trembling. All of him, and everything around him, had suddenly started trembling.

'My God, Owen!' trumpeted Tu. 'What's up? We're waiting for you.'

'Sorry.' He gulped. 'You were great, but I'm afraid the big challenge still lies ahead of you.'

'What? Which one do you mean?'

'Precision landing. Central reservation. See you soon, old friend.'

Tu's Silver Surfer had been designed as a two-seater with an ejector seat. Under the combined weight of five people, two of them massively obese, it shed some of its agility. It also became horribly cramped. They shifted Daxiong to the passenger seat and squashed in together behind him. Hopelessly overladen, the Silver Surfer took off with all the elegance of an arthritic duck. Jericho was surprised it could fly at all. Tu guided the machine over the uniform red-brown roofs of the residential complexes of Hongkou, crossed the Huangpu and headed for the northern shore of the financial district. Within view of the Yangpu Bridge lay the park-like gardens of the Pudong International Medical Center, a collection of weightless-looking glass cocoons, nestling in spruce gardens with artificial lakes, bamboo glades and secret pavilions. The renowned private clinic had been built only a few years previously. It represented the new, 'natural' Shanghai, based on plans which demonstrated that if you built something shaped like the neck of a brachiosaurus it might provide lovely views, but otherwise it created nothing but problems. (The ultimate example of architectural phallic delusion, the Nakheel Tower, also loomed half-finished above the now bankrupt city of Dubai, as if to confirm the platitude that the biggest guy isn't the one with the longest. The monster had been planned to reach a height of 1400 metres. After just over a kilometre the work had been suspended; the architects, in their bid to climb to heaven, had been defeated by the banality of their concept; the *casa erecta* was ripe for inclusion in the book of heroic failures.) Structures like the interlocking cells of the Pudong International Medical Center came much closer to the demands of a metropolis that saw itself as a gigantic urban protozoon; its metabolism was based on neuronal interconnections rather than unfeasibly vast dimensions.

'I know someone here.'

As ever when anything new happened in Shanghai, Tu was on intimate terms with people at the top, in this instance the head of surgery. After they had handed over Daxiong, the men had had a quiet chat. It ended with the assurance that Daxiong's injury would be treated, with no questions asked. The giant had to be stitched up, and would have to get used to the idea of a nice smart scar. And he would be in pain for a while.

'But there are things we can do about that,' the surgeon said as he left, smiling reassuringly at everyone. 'There are things we can do about everything these days.'

In private clinics, his expression added.

Jericho would have liked to ask what he planned to do about Yoyo's pain over the loss of her friends, about Chen Hongbing's emotional torment, and his own inner movies, but instead he just shook Daxiong's hand and wished him all the best. The giant looked at him expressionlessly. Then he let go of his hand, stretched out his right arm and drew him to him. Jericho groaned. If Daxiong could hug you with a gaping wound in his back, he preferred not to know what declarations of love he was capable of in a state of perfect physical health.

'You're not so bad!' said Daxiong.

'My pleasure,' Jericho grinned. 'Be nice to the nurses.'

'And you look after Yoyo till I'm out.'

'Will do.'

'So, see you tonight.'

Jericho thought he had misheard. Daxiong turned his head to one side as if any further discussion about his release were a simple waste of time.

'Leave it,' said Yoyo as she left. 'I'm just glad he didn't want to come with us straight away.'

'And now?' asked Chen Hongbing as they trotted back to the Silver Surfer. It was the first time he had said anything at all since they had left the park. His blank face, whatever hell had caused it, made him seem strangely uninvolved, almost uninterested.

'I think there are some things I should explain to you.' Yoyo lowered her head. 'Except – perhaps not right now.'

Chen raised his hands in a helpless gesture. 'I don't understand all this.' His gaze wandered to Jericho. 'But you'd—'

'I found her,' Jericho nodded. 'Just like you wanted.'

'Yes,' Chen said slowly. He seemed to be wondering whether this was really what he had wanted.

'I'm sorry about what happened.'

'No, no. I'm the one who should be thanking you!'

That sounded exactly like the man who, two days ago – had it really only been two days ago? – had come into his office, conspicuous for his excessive formality. But lurking in the background there was also the question of how someone might seriously expect thanks for having set off on a simple missing-person job and come back with the Horsemen of the Apocalypse in hot pursuit.

Jericho said nothing. Chen said nothing back. Yoyo had discovered something fascinating in the sky. Tu paced about for a while among ferns, bamboo and black pines, and issued a stream of instructions into his phone.

'So,' he announced when he came back.

'So what?' asked Jericho.

'So someone's going to the Westin to collect your computer and the rest of your stuff and bring them to my place, where you'll be living for the next little while.'

'Oh. Fine.'

'And I've organised two people to keep an eye on your loft in Xintiandi. Two more are on their way to Siping Lu. To clean up and stand watch.' He cleared his throat and put his arm around Chen's shoulders. 'Of course we'll have to ask ourselves, my dear Hongbing, what we will tell the police when they come to examine the state of your sitting room.'

'That means we're flying to your place?' Yoyo concluded.

Tu looked at them all. 'Does anyone have a better idea.'

Silence.

'Anyone rather spend the night at home? No? Then excuse me.'

With a quiet hum, the Silver Surfer lifted its wing doors.

'The highest are the wise,' Jericho whispered as he climbed into the back seat.

Tu glared at him.

'Those who are *born* wise,' he said. 'Get Confucius out of your head. I can do it better than you. Longnose!'

Without Daxiong, who counted as two, the flying machine swiftly gained altitude. Tu lived in a villa in a gated area, a fortress-like guarded compound in the hinterland of Pudong, surrounded by park-like areas of green. They landed right in front of the main building, peeled themselves from their upholstered seats and climbed a flight of steps leading to a porch with double doors.

One of the doors opened. An attractive Chinese woman with red-dyed hair appeared in the doorway. She was the complete opposite of Yoyo. Less beautiful, but more elegant in her appearance and, strangely, more sensual. A person with no gaps in her CV, who was used to having the world rotate around her. Tu greeted her with a hug and marched inside. Jericho followed him. The woman smiled and kissed him fleetingly on both cheeks.

'Hi, Owen,' she said in a sonorous voice.

Jericho returned her smile. 'Hi, Joanna.'

Pudong

Tu had instructed Joanna to focus all her care and attention on Chen as soon as they got back. What he really wanted was for her to distract him for a while, a task which Joanna dedicated herself to fully. Steering the confused Chen into her palatial kitchen with the same uncompromising attitude as someone pushing a shopping trolley in front of them, she demanded to know what tea he preferred, asked whether he would like a sauna, a bath or a hot shower, where it hurt, what had happened, whether he would like some cold chicken from the fridge. He didn't know how it had all ended up like that, the guy just suddenly appeared in the room with the gun, and oh God, how did he even get in, and oh, you've got scratches all over you, they could get inflamed, hold still, don't argue, and so on and so forth. She didn't have a clue what was going on, of course. But Joanna wouldn't have been Joanna if that had been a problem. She exuded the bountiful aromas of her optimism, bathing Chen in confidence until he was ready to believe that everything would be okay, purely because she said so. Jericho had never met any other person with such powers of conviction that things would turn out fine, without having the faintest idea *how*. Joanna bluffed for all she was worth. In her world, the tail wagged the dog. Presumably Chen was convinced that he was having a conversation, or even that he had started it. Joanna had a way of driving a man in front of her in such a manner that he would swear it was *her* following *him*.

'So what should we do?' hissed Tu.

'Notify the police,' said Jericho tersely. 'Before they turn up of their own accord.'

'You want to go on the offensive?'

'What other option do we have? That maniac set half the steelworks on fire. It won't take them long to find the bodies and then some witnesses in Quyu. It looks as if a bomb just went off on Siping Lu – doesn't it, Yoyo—?'

'Yes.'

'—and there's a crashed airbike decomposing in the courtyard, chock-a-block with heavy-duty weapons. And one that brought the traffic to a standstill. They'll be able to piece together some of the puzzle from all that.'

'But how much of it?'

'I'm telling you, it will only be a few hours before they start asking what your friend Hongbing had to do with the massacre in Quyu. They'll think of Yoyo in no time at all. I mean, the thing in the steel factory looks like some campaign of destruction against the City Demons, don't you think? And Yoyo's part of the group.'

'And what about you?' asked Yoyo. 'Do you reckon they'll think of you too?'

'How would they? My car was incinerated in Quyu.'

'But they'll be able to identify it.' Tu pursed his lips. 'And besides, Siping Lu has security cameras. Which means they'll have recordings of all of you meeting up, of Yoyo and Daxiong going into the building, of how that – that—'

'Kenny.'

'—Kenny guy herded the two of you in front of him—'

'Not just us,' said Jericho. 'Think about it. You were just as easily visible, in your state of heavenly wrath. And who is it who works in your company to finance her studies?'

'Yoyo, the girl who just can't keep her mouth shut,' snorted Yoyo.

'Yes, my dear, you really do have a sparkling reputation,' commented Tu, scratching his bald head. With his new glasses on, he looked almost civilised. 'So what are we going to tell them? That Yoyo happened to overhear Kenny, completely by chance, while—'

'Forget it,' Yoyo interrupted him. 'You want me to tell the police that

I'm in possession of secret information? With my record? If that arse-hole is from the government I might as well lock myself up and throw away the key. Or better still, just shoot myself!'

'I don't think the police are in on this,' said Jericho.

'Yes, but you don't know what might happen if they get their hands on me.'

'Hold on a second.' Tu was shaking his head energetically. 'Let's be realistic. We're assuming the Shanghai police force has the same powers of deduction as a quantum computer. They're not going to put all the pieces together *that* quickly.'

'Well, either way, we still need to notify them,' said Jericho.

'But perhaps not straight away.'

'Yes, *straight away*. If someone trashes your apartment and you don't report it, that looks odd. Not to mention that Yoyo, Daxiong and I turned up just beforehand, and that I have a flying machine just like Kenny's.'

'Okay fine, then how about this: someone holds up a motorcycle club in Quyu and causes a bloodbath. He has accomplices, all of them on flying machines. What they don't realise is that Yoyo had a family friend visiting, Owen, and he ends up creating a hell of a problem for them, right? Both Yoyo and Owen get hold of one of the airbikes and are able to flee. Not long after, Yoyo receives a call from Hongbing, telling her that someone's trying to break into his apartment.'

'No way!' Yoyo shook her head. 'You don't call your daughter if some-one's trying to break into your place.'

'Fine, then—'

'I know. Kenny threatened to kill all the members of your family,' Jer-icho suggested. 'So you call your father. He doesn't answer, so you go to see him, enlisting the help of Hongbing's best friend, Tian.'

'And we have no idea what the guys want?' asked Yoyo sceptically. 'You expect them to believe that?'

'That's the plan.'

'God, what a cock and bull story.'

'The most important thing is to keep you out of it,' said Tu. 'No dis-sident background, no Guardians.' He gave Yoyo a reproachful look. 'On that note, you could have told me you were all hanging out in a blast furnace. I only knew about the Andromeda.'

'I'm sorry. You weren't supposed to get dragged that far into it.'

'How do you figure that out? I provided the infrastructure for you and your troop of pests. You can't get much deeper involved than that.' Tu sighed. 'But fine. Point two on the agenda. What do we tell Hongbing?'

Yoyo hesitated. 'The same story?'

'*What?*' barked Jericho.

'Well, I just thought—'

'You want to have your father believing this was all the act of some nut job?' Suddenly he was furious with her. He pictured Hongbing, filled with all that sorrow. And now they wanted to pull the wool over his eyes yet again?

'Owen.' Yoyo raised her hand. 'It's great, everything you've done for us, but this really has nothing to do with you.'

'Your father deserves an explanation!'

'I'm not sure if he really wants one.'

'Exactly. You're not *sure*. My God, he was taken hostage, held at gunpoint, his daughter was threatened, his apartment destroyed. You *have* to tell him the truth! Anything else is pure cowardice.'

'Stay out of it!'

'Yoyo,' said Tu softly but firmly, as if commanding a dog to come to heel.

'What?' she snapped. 'What is it? It has nothing to do with him! You said yourself that it would be a mistake to burden my father with it.'

'The circumstances have changed. Owen's right.'

'Oh yes, I forgot.' Yoyo contorted her face mockingly. 'He's a family friend now.'

'No. He's just right – pure and simple.'

'But why? What does Owen know about my father?'

'Well, what do you know about him?' asked Jericho, antagonised.

Yoyo glared at him. Clearly he'd hit a sore spot.

'Hongbing is embittered, set in his ways, introverted,' said Tu. 'But I know him! I'm waiting for the day when he'll break out of that bitter shell, and I don't know whether I should long for it or dread it. He's had to spend years of his life feeling utterly, terribly helpless. Up until now there was no reason to rub his nose in the fact that you're China's most-wanted dissident, but that just changed. After this morning he knows full bloody well that you have some explaining to do.'

Yoyo shook her head unhappily.

'He'll hate me.'

'He's more likely to hate me for having helped you, but I don't genuinely believe that either. You can't carry on lying to him, Yoyo. For him, the worst possible thing would be you not confiding in him. You'd be taking away his—' Tu seemed to be struggling to find the words, 'his purpose as a father.'

'His purpose as a father?' echoed Yoyo, as if she'd misheard.

'Yes. Everybody needs to feel significant in some way or another. Hongbing tried to do something too, a long time ago, and he was punished for it. His purpose was taken away from him.'

'And now he's punishing me.'

'Punishing you is the last thing he wants to do.'

Yoyo stared at him.

'But he's never spoken to me about his life, Tian! Never! He's never confided in me! And you don't think that's a punishment? In what way have I been significant to him? Okay, he worries about me from morning to night, and I'm sure he'd rather lock me in out of sheer worry, but what's the point? What does he want from me if he won't even talk to me?'

'He's ashamed,' said Tu softly.

'Of what? I'm the one suffering. I have a – a zombie for a father!'

'You can't talk like that.'

'Can't I? What about him explaining something to me for a change?'

'He'll probably have to,' nodded Tu.

'Oh, great! When?'

'It's your turn first.'

'Why me again?' exploded Yoyo. 'Why not him?'

'Because you're the one in a position to reach out to him.'

'Don't come to me with your emotional guilt trip,' she shouted. 'My friends are dead, and my father was nearly killed too. I'm the one who's had the most to deal with here.'

'We've all had a lot to deal with,' Jericho interrupted. He had heard enough. 'So solve your problems, but solve them somewhere else. Tian, when do you think my computer will be here?'

'In a few minutes,' said Tian, grateful for the change of subject.

'Good. I'll get to work on the Swiss films again. Can I use your office?'

'Of course.' Tu hesitated, then shrugged his shoulders submissively. 'So I'll notify the police then. Agreed?'

'Yes, do it.'

'Are we all available for questioning?'

'There's no point hiding, otherwise they'll just pay us personal visits.' Jericho furrowed his brow. 'They may have already started. The first victim in Kenny's dirty game was Grand Cherokee Wang.' He looked at Yoyo. 'Your flatmate. They're going to be all over you like a pack of hungry wolves.'

'They can go ahead,' said Yoyo grimly. 'Let's see them try to eat me.'

'Eat me, and I'll eat you alive.'

'Well remembered,' snorted Yoyo, turning round and walking off to the kitchen.

Jericho was ecstatic to have Diane back again. Without holding out any great hopes, he checked the three websites which were supposed to be interchanged according to the report, and was disappointed. The mask hadn't unearthed anything. It seemed they really had been taken out of circulation.

So that just left him with the Swiss films and a hunch.

He gave Diane a series of directions. With programmed courtesy, she informed him that the analysis would take some time, which meant it could just as easily take five years as five minutes. The computer had no plan on this front. He might as well have asked Alexander Fleming how long he would need to discover penicillin. As the films were three-dimensional, Diane had to go through data cubes rather than data surfaces, which threatened to drag the process out for a long time.

Joanna came in, bringing him some tea and English biscuits.

It was four years now since they had broken up, but Jericho still didn't know how to act around the woman who had lured him to Shanghai and then left him out of the blue. At least, that's how it had seemed to him: that Joanna had ditched him in order to marry someone who was hitting the big time in the Chinese boom, someone who didn't conform in the slightest to what one might assume to be her ideal partner. But it was this very man who had become Jericho's closest friend: a friendship, initiated by Joanna, which had started out within the cocoon of a business relationship, and developed in such a way that neither Tu nor Jericho had really realised it was even happening. It had come down to Joanna to alert them to the fact they had become more deeply attached, at the same time hoping to make Jericho realise it was about time he stopped seeing himself as indebted to everyone.

'I don't,' he had retorted with a baffled expression, as if she had just suggested he shouldn't walk to work on all fours any more.

But Jericho knew exactly what she meant. She had exaggerated a bit of course, which was in her nature, because Joanna went to the other extreme: she hardly ever felt guilt. This might lead to accusations of self-righteousness, but her behaviour was far from amoral. She just lacked the guilt that all children were born into. From the day you first come into the world, you find yourself being constantly admonished, lectured, caught in the act, always in the wrong, subjected to judgement and constant corrections, all of which are intended to make an imperfect human being into a better one. The extent of the improvement is measured by how much you live up to others' expectations, an experiment doomed to failure. It normally leads to failure for all involved. Accompanied by good wishes and silent reproaches, you ultimately end up taking your own path and forget to grant the child within you absolution, a child accustomed to being scolded for running off alone. Rushing through the crossroads of 'I can't, I shouldn't, I'm not allowed', you always find your-self back in the same place you set out from a long time ago, regardless of how old you may have become in the process. Your whole life long, you see yourself through the eyes of others, measure yourself by their standards, judge yourself by their canon of values, condemn yourself with their indignation, and you are never enough.

You are never enough for yourself.

That was what Joanna had meant. She had developed a remarkable talent for freeing herself from the entanglements of her childhood. Her way of looking at things was genuine, as sharp as a knife, her behaviour consistent. She had considered herself fully within her rights to break up with Jericho. She knew that the breakdown of their relationship would cause him pain, but in Joanna's world, this kind of pain was no more the result of culpable behaviour than toothache. She hadn't robbed him, hadn't publicly humiliated him, hadn't continually deceived him. She paid no attention to what others felt she should have done or not done. The only person whose gaze she wanted to be able to meet was the one right opposite her in the mirror.

'How are you?' asked Jericho.

'Well, how do you think?' Joanna sank down into one of the canti-lever chairs scattered around Tu's office. 'Very agitated.'

She didn't look particularly agitated. She looked intrigued, and a little concerned. Jericho drank his tea.

'Did Tian tell you what happened?'

'He gave me an overview in passing, so now I know *his* version.' Joanna took a biscuit and nibbled at it thoughtfully. 'And I've heard Hong-bing's too of course. It sounds dreadful. I wanted to speak to Yoyo, but she's in the middle of battling out her tiresome father–daughter conflict.'

Jericho hesitated. 'Do you actually know what that's about?'

'I'm not stupid.' She jerked her thumb in the direction of the door. 'I also know that Tian is involved.'

'And that's not a problem for you?'

'It's his business. He must know what's he's doing. I'm too shame-fully lacking in ambition myself, as you know. I wouldn't make a very convincing dissident. But I understand. His motivations seem clear to me, so he has my unconditional support.'

Jericho was silent. It was obvious that Chen Hongbing wasn't the only one who had eaten bitterness at some point in his past. Tu's professional status implied all manner of things, but not collaboration with a group of dissidents. There must be something from way back that was influencing his behaviour.

'Maybe he'll tell you about it someday,' Joanna added, eating another biscuit. 'In any case, you've all been hunting, and now I'm coming to gather. And as Yoyo is otherwise engaged, I'm starting with you.'

Jericho briefly explained what had taken place since Chen's visit to Xintiandi. Joanna didn't interrupt him; that is if you didn't count the occasional *ahhs*, *mm-hms* and *ohhs* which were ritually expressed in China as a form of courtesy to assure the other person of your attentiveness. During his report, she also devoured all of the biscuits and drank most of the tea. That was fine by Jericho. He still didn't have even the slightest appetite. After he finished talking, they both fell silent for a while.

'It sounds like you've all got a long-term problem,' she said finally.

'Yes.'

'Tian too?' It sounded like *Me too*? Jericho was just about to tell her that her own wellbeing should be the least of her worries, but stopped himself; perhaps he was reading too much into her question.

'You can work that out for yourself,' he said. 'In any case, even Kenny will have to acknowledge the fact that he's cocked things up. By now he could have confided in anyone under the sun. He missed his opportunity to eliminate everyone who knew about it.'

'You mean he won't keep trying to get Yoyo?'

Jericho pressed his fingers against the bridge of his nose. He could feel a headache coming on. 'It's hard to tell,' he said.

'In what way?'

'Believe me, I've met psychopaths who are bad to the core, ones who tortured their victims, filleted them, canned them, let them die of thirst, cut off this or that, things you wouldn't believe. Their type are motivated purely by obsession. And then there are the professional killers.'

'Who combine business with pleasure.'

'The main thing is that they see it as a job. It brings them money. They don't develop any emotional connection to their victims, they just do their job. Kenny botched his up. Aggravating for him, but usually you'd expect him to leave us in peace from now on and turn his attention to other jobs.'

'But you don't think that's the case?'

'He's a professional *and* a psycho.' Jericho circled his index finger over his temple. 'And those guys are a little harder to classify.'

'Which means?'

'Someone like Kenny could feel offended that we've not all been eliminated as planned. He might think we shouldn't have put up a fight. It's possible that he'll do nothing. But it's just as possible that he'll set my loft on fire, or your house, or lie in wait for us and shoot us down, and all just because he's angry.'

'I see you're full of optimism as usual.'

Jericho glowered at her. 'I thought that was *your* job.'

He knew his retort was unfair, but she had provoked him. It was a shabby, mean little comment with sharp teeth and threadbare fur, which had scurried up in a surprise attack, sank its teeth in and then died with a cackle.

'Jerk.'

'Sorry,' he said.

'Don't be.' She stood up and ruffled his hair. Strangely, Jericho felt both comforted and humiliated by her gesture. A display lit up on Tu's computer console. The guard reported that the police had arrived and wished to question Tu as well as the others present on the incidents in Quyu and Hongkou.

The questioning went as questioning tended to go with citizens of a higher social standing. An investigating civil servant with assistants in tow showed great courtesy, assuring all of those present of her sympathy and describing the incidents in quick succession as 'horrifying' and 'abhorrent', Mr Tu as an 'outstanding member of society',

Chen and Yoyo as 'heroic' and Jericho as a 'valued friend of the authorities'. In between all that, she flung questions around like circus knives. It was clear she didn't believe the story in the very parts where it wasn't true, for example when it came to Kenny's motive. Her gaze resembled that of a butcher, talking encouragingly to a pig as he carved it in his mind's eye.

Chen looked even more hollow-cheeked than normal. Tu's face had a purple tinge to it, while Yoyo's was filled with bitter pride. Clearly the arrival of the police had torn them from a heated discussion. Jericho realised that the inspector had gauged the emotional climate down to the exact degree, but she wasn't commenting on it for the time being. It was only in the course of the individual interrogations that she became more explicit. She was a middle-aged woman with smoothly brushed hair and intelligent eyes, behind what looked like old-fashioned glasses with small lenses and thick frames. But Jericho knew better. It was actually a MindReader, a portable computer which filmed the person opposite, ran their expression through an amplifier and projected the result in real time onto the lenses of the glasses. In this way, the merest hint of a smug smile could become perfectly clear to the wearer. A nervous blink would mimic an earthquake. Tell-tale signals in facial expressions that wouldn't normally be noticed became readable. Jericho guessed that she had also linked an Interpreter to it, which dramatised the tone, accentuation and flow of his voice. The effect was uncanny. If you combined the forces of MindReader and Interpreter, the people being questioned suddenly sounded like bad actors, turning into grimacing, crude robots, despite fully believing they had their reactions under control.

Jericho himself had already worked with both programs. Only very experienced investigators used them. It took years of practice to correctly read the discrepancies between the expression, intonation and content of a statement. He showed no sign of having recognised the device, told his version of the incident stoically and fended off question after question.

'And you're really just a friend of the family?'

'And there was no particular reason why you happened to be in the steel factory today of all days?'

'Those guys arrived at the factory at exactly the same time as you, and you expect me to believe that that's pure coincidence?'

'Did you perhaps have a commission in Quyu?'

'Don't you find it strange that Grand Cherokee Wang was murdered one day after you went looking for him?'

'Did you know that Chen Yuyun was once imprisoned for political agitation and passing on State secrets?'

'Did you also know that Tu Tian has not always behaved in the best interests of the Chinese State and our justified concerns for its internal stability?'

'What do you know about Chen Hongbing's past?'

'Am I really supposed to believe that not one of you – although the actions indicate an act which was planned long in advance! – had the faintest clue who this Kenny is and what he wants?'

'I'll ask you once more: What commission did you have that led you to Quyu?'

And so on and so forth.

Eventually she gave up, leaned back and took the glasses off. She smiled, but her gaze continued to saw away at him, hacking off tiny pieces.

'You've been in Shanghai for four and a half years,' she stated. 'According to what I hear, you have an excellent reputation as an investigator.'

'Thank you, it's an honour to hear that.'

'So how is business going?'

'I can't complain.'

'I'm pleased to hear it.' She put the tips of her fingers together. 'Rest assured that you are highly valued in my field. You have successfully collaborated with us a number of times and each time you have displayed a high level of willingness to cooperate. This is one of the reasons why we would like to extend your work permit' – here, her right hand made a waving motion, illustrating some vague future – 'and then to extend it again and again. Precisely because our relationship is based on reciprocity. Do you understand what I mean?'

'You've expressed it very clearly.'

'Good. Now that's clear, I'd like to ask you an informal question.'

'If I'm able to answer it, I will.'

'I'm sure you can.' She leaned over and sank her voice conspiratorially. 'I would like to know what you would make of all this if you were in my seat. You have experience, intuition, you have a good nose. What would you be thinking?'

Jericho resolved not to get taken in by her.

'I would exert more pressure.'

'Oh?' She looked surprised, as if he had just invited her to torture him with burning cigarettes.

'Pressure on my team,' he added. 'To make sure they put all their energy into getting their hands on the man who is responsible for the attacks, and into investigating his background, instead of getting taken in by the crude idea of making victims into perpetrators and threatening them with deportation. Does my answer suffice?'

'I'll make a note of it.'

As far as Jericho could tell, she didn't seem in the slightest bit taken aback. It was clear that she doubted the substance of his statement, but she knew equally well that she had nothing on him. He was more worried about the others. Practically everyone besides him seemed to have come into conflict with the law in one way or another, which put them at the mercy of the police.

'I would like to express my sympathy once again,' she said, in a different tone now. 'You went through a great deal. We will do everything we can to bring those responsible to justice.'

Jericho nodded. 'Let me know if I can be of any assistance.'

She stood up and held out her hand. 'Rest assured I will.'

'So?'

Tu had come into the room. It was late afternoon by now; the skies were overcast and light drizzle was falling on Pudong. The investigators had retreated.

'Nothing new.' Jericho stretched. 'Diane is keeping herself busy with the Swiss films. We're also trying to trace the six websites back to a common source. So far there's nothing to indicate that there is one, but that doesn't necessarily mean anything.'

'That's not what I meant.' Tu pulled a chair over and sank down into it, panting. Jericho noticed that his shirt sleeves were pushed up to different heights. 'How did the questioning go?'

'How do you think it went? She didn't believe a word I said.'

'She didn't believe me either.' For some unknown reason this seemed to fill Tu with satisfaction. 'Nor Yoyo. Hongbing was the only one she seemed to handle with kid gloves.'

'Of course,' murmured Jericho.

From the very moment Chen had first come into his office in Xintiandi, he had noticed something about him that was hard to define, something in his eyes, in his tautly stretched face, something which gave the impression that his soul had been peeled away. Now he realised what he had seen, and the investigator must have seen it too. The idea that this man could lie was inconceivable. Nothing in Chen's features was capable of even hosting a lie. This left him completely at the mercy of his surroundings. He couldn't bear dishonesty, neither from himself nor from others.

'Tian . . .' Jericho said hesitantly.

'Mm-hm?'

'There may be a problem with regard to how we proceed from here. Don't get me wrong, it's not—' He searched for the words.

'What is it? Out with it.'

'I know too little about you.'

Tu was silent.

'Too little about you and Chen Hongbing. I know it has nothing to do with me. It's just – in order to judge what danger you're in regarding the authorities, I would need to – well – I would need an idea, but—'

Tu pursed his lips. 'I understand.'

'No, I don't think you do,' said Jericho. 'You think I'm being nosy. You're wrong. I couldn't care less. Well, no, that's not it. I mean that I respect your silence. Whatever has happened in your or Chen's past has nothing to do with me. But in that case *you* have to be the one to say where we go from here. You're better placed to judge—'

'It's fine,' mumbled Tu.

'It's your business. I respect—'

'No, you're right.'

'Under no circumstances do I want to be inconsiderate of—'

'Enough, *xiongdi*.' Tu clapped him on the shoulder. 'Consideration is the very foundation of your being; you don't need to explain yourself. In any case, I've often thought about strengthening our friendship by confessing a little of my past to you.' His gaze wandered over to the door. Somewhere in the great expanse of the house, Yoyo and her father were wrestling with the past and future. 'It's just that I fear I have to get back in the ring.'

'To mediate?'

'To take some of the heat. Yoyo and I have decided to clear the air. By the end of the day Hongbing will know the whole truth.'

'And how is he taking it so far?'

'I'm sure he's not exactly over the moon.' Tu belched. 'But I'm not seriously concerned. The more pressing question is how long he proposes to brood in his anger. Sooner or later he has to see that you can't earn trust by denying your child long-overdue answers. He'll have to tell Yoyo his truth too.' Tu sighed. 'What happens then, I really don't know. It's not that Hongbing seriously believes a part of his life didn't happen. He just can't bring himself to tell someone he loves about it. Because he's ashamed. He's just an old crab really. And try telling a crab it should cast off its shell.'

'Well, if he did he would be the first crab to be able to do without it.'

'Oh, they shed them a lot when they're young in order to grow. It's a dangerous undertaking though, because the new shell is very soft for the first few hours. They're very vulnerable for that time, easy targets, without any protection. But if they didn't shed them, there wouldn't be enough space for them to live.' Tu stood up. 'And as I said, Hongbing is a pretty old crab, but his shell has definitely got too small for him. I think he needs to shed it again so he doesn't end up shattering into a thousand pieces from the pressure.'

Tu laid his right hand on Jericho's shoulder for a moment. Then he left the room.

Dusk stole in, stuffy and damp.

Diane was still processing.

Jericho wandered through the house and went to see Joanna in her studio, a glass pagoda temple backing onto the artificial lake which formed the centre of the property. He wasn't surprised to find her working on one of her large-format portraits. Joanna wasn't the type to wander through the house wringing her hands if they could be put to better use. She had turned on bright lamps and was giving depth and contour to two beautiful socialites who were pictured arm in arm in front of a mirror, looking as if they had danced through three days and nights straight.

After Chen had emerged, flushed with anger, and disappeared into the guest rooms on the first floor, Tu had intensified the security around his villa and fled to his office. Yoyo had crossed Jericho's path as he walked through the entrance hall. She looked as though she had been crying, and had waved her hands around as if trying to signal that he shouldn't ask any questions. Just when she was about to climb the stairs, her father had appeared on the landing, heading stormily for the bathroom, which was enough for Yoyo to hastily change direction and wander off into the garden, where Jericho had just been coming in from.

All at once, he had felt terribly out of place.

Tu's butler saw him standing around and rushed to attend to his needs. Jericho turned down hot lavender baths and Thai massages, ordered some tea and unexpectedly felt a craving for the kind of biscuits Joanna had brought him just hours before, only to scoff them all under his nose. The butler offered to make up the salon for him. For want of a better idea, Jericho nodded, paced around in a circle twice and noticed that the feeling of being out of place was accompanied by the quicksand-like sensation of helplessness.

Something had to happen.

And it did.

'Owen? This is Diane.'

He felt a frisson of excitement, pulled out his phone and spoke into it breathlessly. 'Yes, Diane? What is it?'

'I've found something in the films that will interest you. A watermark. There's a film within a film.'

Oh, Diane! thought Jericho. I could kiss you. If you looked only half as good as you sound I would even marry you, but you're just a damn computer. But never mind. Make me happy!

'Wait there,' he called, as if there were some risk she might decide otherwise and leave the house. 'I'm coming.'

Yoyo would have liked to convince herself she was past the worst, but she felt the worst still lay before her, and three times as intense. Hongbing had screamed and shouted. They had argued for over an hour. As a result, her eyes were sore and filled with salty tears, as if she had seen nothing but misery and hardship her whole life. She felt guilty about everything. About the massacre in the steelworks, the destruction of the apartment, her father's despair, and finally about the fact that Hongbing didn't love her. Almost as soon as it had appeared, this last thought entered into sinister alliances with all possible forms of self-loathing and gave birth to a new guilt, namely, having done Hongbing an injustice. Of course he had loved her, how could he not have? How low did you have to sink to assume anything else but love from your own father? But now just that thought alone made her undeserving of love, and Hongbing had taken the only logical step and stopped loving her. So what was she complaining about? She was to blame for the fact that his mask of a face had not melted, but shattered.

She had disappointed everyone.

For a while she hung around silently in Joanna's studio, watching as Tian's beautiful wife conjured up a feverish sparkle in the eyes of the exhausted teenagers, that last glimmer of energy moments before all systems shut down. On the monstrous two and a half by four metre canvas, she portrayed carefree natures through pigments: two ornamental fish in the shallow waters of their sensitivities, whose only worry in life was how not to die from boredom before the next party kicked off. Realising that the worst massacres in the lives of the two beauties were probably the ones they had caused in the hearts of pubescent boys, Yoyo cried a little more.

She was probably doing these girls an injustice too. Was she really any better? She had certainly been no stranger to excess in the last few years. She was more than familiar with the moment when one faded out like a dwindling, bright red dot in the blackness of a charred wick. She had sung incessantly against Hongbing's sadness, danced against it, smoked and fucked against it, without once flagging with a soothing emptiness in her gaze like the princesses of the night on Joanna's canvas. Each time, her last thought had been that the excesses weren't worth dying for, that she would have much rather been sitting at home listening to what her father had to tell her about the time before she was born. But Hongbing hadn't told her one single thing.

Joanna created eyelashes with a flourish, pressed in smatterings of mascara and distributed make-up in the corner of the eyes and onto cheekbones. Yoyo watched, overcome with melancholy. She liked Joanna's flirtation with society, the way she wore its colourful plumage. There was no canvas big enough to depict the way China entertained itself, Joanna always said. After all, China was a big country, and so she explained to her feathered friends, whenever they came to sharpen their beaks and sip at champagne, that lack of content couldn't be portrayed on a small scale. It was a witty and catchy comment, but really incomprehensible in an artistic sense. She pompously celebrated the beauty of emptiness and the emptiness of beauty, sold her fans something they could look at, and neglected to tell them it was actually a mirror.

'Don't forget,' she always said with her most charming Joanna smile, 'I'm in the picture too. In every single one. Including yours.'

Yoyo envied Joanna. She envied the egoism with which she sailed through life, and without picking up any bruises along the way. She envied her ability to be uninterested, and her lack of concern in showing it. Yoyo, on the other hand, was interested in everything, and compulsively so. Could that ever end well? Sure, the Guardians had accomplished quite a lot of things. Under their pressure, imprisoned journalists had been released, corrupt civil servants stripped of office and environmental scandals solved. While Joanna's hands were being manicured, Yoyo had been busy dirtying hers by delving them into painful subjects, never tiring in demanding China's right to its own culture of fun. This had given her the reputation of being a nationalist from time to time. Just as well. She was a hedonistic preacher, a liberal nationalist who got fired up by the injustice in the world. Wonderful! And yet there were so many other things she could do. She was sure she could find something, as long as it meant not having to be Chen Yuyun.

Joanna painted, and was simply Joanna. Self-involved, care-free and rich. Everything that repulsed Yoyo from the bottom of her heart, and yet she yearned for it too. Someone who offered security. Someone who wouldn't step aside, because it was something they never did.

She was crying again.

After a while, Yoyo's supply of tears was exhausted. Joanna cleaned her brushes in turpentine. Over the glass surfaces of the pagoda roof, the sky was working its way through every shade of grey in preparation for the evening.

'So how did it go? Well?'

Yoyo sniffed and shook her head.

'It must have gone well,' Joanna decided. 'You screamed at each other, and you cried. That's good.'

'You think?'

Joanna turned to her and smiled. 'Well, it's certainly better than him swallowing his own tongue and talking to the walls at night.'

'I shouldn't have lied to him like that,' said Yoyo and coughed, her airways blocked from all the crying. 'I hurt him. You should have seen him.'

'Nonsense, sweetheart. You didn't hurt him. You told him the truth.'

'Yes, that's what I mean.'

'No, you're getting confused. You're acting as though speaking frankly were some huge moral issue. If you tell the truth, you're one of the good guys. How it's received is a different matter, but that's what psychiatrists are for. There's nothing more you can do to help your father bite the bullet.'

'To be honest, I've got no idea what I'm supposed to do now.'

'I do.' Joanna stretched out her slim fingers, one after another. 'Run yourself a bath, go a few rounds with the punch bag, go shopping. Spend money. Lots of money.'

Yoyo rubbed her elbows. 'I'm not you, Joanna.'

'No one suggested you take off and buy a Rolls-Royce. I want you to understand the principles of cause and effect. The truth is a good thing, even if it can be unpleasant at times. And if it is unpleasant, it strengthens the body's defences.'

'And did it strengthen Owen's defences?'

Joanna held a thick paintbrush up to the light and fanned the bristles out with her fingernail.

'Tian told me that you were together,' Yoyo added quickly. 'Before you got married.'

'Yes, we were together.'

'Okay. We don't have to talk about it if you don't want to.'

'It's fine.' She put the paintbrush down and gave her a beaming smile. 'We had a great time.'

'So why did you break up? I mean, he's a really nice guy.'

Yoyo was surprised by her own words. Did she think Owen Jericho was nice? So far he had only come up in connection with fire-arms, death and severe bodily harm. On the other hand, he had saved her life. Do you automatically think someone is nice because they save your life?

'Relationships are contracts that can be terminated at any time, my dear,' said Joanna, picking up the second brush. 'Without notice. You don't quit sexual relations six weeks before the end of the quarter. If it's not working any more, you have to go.'

'And what wasn't working?'

'Everything. The Owen who came with me to Shanghai bore no resemblance to the one I had met in London.'

'You were in London?'

'Is this an interview?' Joanna raised her eyebrows. 'If it is I'd like to see the article for authorisation later.'

'No, I'm genuinely interested. I mean, we haven't known each other for that long, right? You and Tian, you've been together now for – how many years?'

'Four.'

'Exactly. And we haven't had much of a chance to talk.'

'Woman to woman, you mean?'

'No, not all that rubbish, it's just, I've known Tian for ever, my whole life, but you—'

'You don't know anything about me.' Joanna smirked mockingly. 'And now you're worried about good old Tian, because you can't imagine what a beautiful and spoilt woman would want from a bald-headed, sloppy, overweight old sack who, despite having money coming out of his ears, still fixes his glasses with sticky-tape and wears the seat of his trousers around the backs of his knees.'

'I didn't say that,' replied Yoyo angrily.

'But you thought it. And so did Owen. Fine, I'll tell you a story. It's a lesson about the economics of love. It begins in London, where I moved in 2017 to study English Literature, Western Art and Painting; something for which you need to be either crazy, an idealist or from a rich background. My father was Pan Zemin—'

'The Environment Minister?'

'Deputy Environment Minister.'

'Hey!' cried Yoyo. 'We always admired your father.'

'He'd have liked that.'

'He publicly addressed a number of problems.' Warming enthusiasm flooded through Yoyo. 'He was really brave. And the way he pushed to put more money into solar research, to increase the energy yield—'

'Yes, generally speaking he was pretty salubrious,' said Joanna drily, 'but it didn't hurt that one of the companies which made the breakthrough belonged to him. As I said, crazy, idealistic or from a rich background. In London, the Chinese community had long since outgrown Gerrard Street by then. There were a lot of good clubs in Soho that were popular with Chinese and Europeans. I met Owen in one of them. That was 2019, and I liked him. Oh, I liked him a lot!'

'Yes, well, he's very good-looking.'

'He's easy on the eye, let's say. But the great thing about him wasn't the way he looked, but the fact that he wasn't afraid of me. It was awful, how all the men were instantly afraid of me: such losers; I used to eat them for breakfast.' She smiled maliciously and twirled another brush through the turpentine. 'But Owen seemed determined not to let himself be influenced by my undeniably dazzling looks or my financial independence, and for two whole hours he managed not to look at my tits. That spoke volumes. He also respected my intelligence; I could tell by the way he contradicted me. He was a cyber-cop at Scotland Yard, where they don't exactly shower you in gold, but then I wasn't interested in money. Owen could have slept under London Bridge and I would have lain down next to him.' She paused. 'Well, let's say I would have bought it and then lain down. We were very much in love.'

'So how could that go wrong?'

'Yes, how?' Joanna gave a melodious little sigh. 'In 2020, my father suffered a stroke and was considerate enough not to wake up again. He left behind a respectable fortune, a wife whose patience had been tested and who endured his passing as unquestioningly as she had endured him, and also three children, of whom I am the eldest. Mum was often lonely, and with the unhoped-for inheritance I'd just received, I felt there was no need for me to keep clogging up the lecture theatres in London. So I decided to go back. I asked Owen what he thought of us moving to Shanghai, and he said, without giving it much thought: Sure, let's move to Shanghai. And you know, that was strange in itself.'

'Why? That was exactly what you wanted.'

'Of course, but he didn't have even the slightest objection. And we'd only been together for half a year. But that's the problem. If men do what you tell them to, they're suspect, and if they oppose us we think they're ridiculous. Back then I thought, well, it's because he loves me so much, which was a good thing in itself, because as long as he loved me, he would only betray himself and not me. But back then I was already beginning to ask myself which one of us loved the other more.'

'And he loved you too much.'

'No, he loved himself too little. But I only realised that after we arrived in Shanghai. To start with, everything was great. He knew his way around, liked the city, and had been there numerous times during bilateral investigations. At New Scotland Yard he was a kind of in-house Sinologist, and I should mention that Owen doesn't learn languages laboriously like other people do; he simply swallows them down and then brings them back up in well-worded formulations. I suggested he take a job with the Shanghai Department for Cybercrime, because they already knew and valued him there—'

'Cypol,' snorted Yoyo.

'Yes, your good friends. We moved into an apartment in Pudong and planned a lifetime of happiness. And that's when it started. Little things. His gaze started to waver when he spoke to me. He started to suck up to me. Sure, we were living in *my* country, meeting *my* people, including politicians, intellectuals and all kinds of representatives of society, every one of whom sucked up to me. In my circle, greatness is the result of the degradation of others, but Owen's knees became weaker and weaker. His wonderful self-confidence melted like butter in the sun, he seemed to degenerate, get pimples again, and after a while he asked me, full of timidity, if I loved him. I was totally gobsmacked! It was like he'd just asked me, right in front of a bright blue sky, if the sun was shining.'

'Perhaps he sensed you didn't love him as much as you had before.'

'It's the other way around, sweetheart. The doubts came with the doubter. Owen didn't have the slightest reason to mistrust me, even though he probably thought he did. He had stopped trusting *himself*; that was the problem! You can only fall in love when you're on an equal standing, but if your partner is bowed over in front of you, you have no choice but to look down on him.'

'Did he get jealous?'

'Jealousy's such an ugly addiction. Nothing makes you smaller or less attractive.' Joanna walked over to an open store cupboard, in which dozens of tubes lay next to one another. 'Yes, he did. He was possessed by some old insecurity. Our relationship lost its equilibrium. I'm a positive person, sweetie, and I don't know how to be any other way, which meant that next to me Owen looked increasingly like a pot plant someone had forgotten to water. My optimism left him to wither. The worse he felt, the more I enjoyed my life, or that's what he thought anyway. That was complete nonsense of course! I had always enjoyed life, but before that we used to enjoy it together.' She took out a tube of vermilion and squeezed a small splodge of it onto a palette. 'I left him so that he could finally find himself.'

'How considerate of you,' scoffed Yoyo.

'I know how you see it.' Joanna paused for a second. 'But you're wrong. I could have grown old with him. But Owen had lost his faith. The world is an illusion; everything is an illusion, love intrinsically so. If you stop believing in it, it disappears. If you stop feeling, the sun becomes just a blob and flowers become brambles. That's the whole story.'

Yoyo padded over to a footstool and sank down onto it.

'You know what?' she said. 'I feel sorry for him.'

'Who?'

'Owen, of course!'

'Tsk, tsk.' Joanna shook her head disapprovingly. 'How rude, I thought you would grant him a little more respect. Owen is talented, intelligent, charming, attractive. He could be anything he wants to be; everyone knows that. Everyone except him.'

'He probably believed it for a while. Back in London.'

'Yes, because of the sheer surprise that things were working out with us he temporarily forgot to be a pathetic little jerk.'

Yoyo stared at her. 'Tell me, are you really this heartless, or are you just pretending to be?'

'I'm honest and I try not to be corny. What do you want? Sentimentality? Then go to the movies.'

'Fine. So what happened next?'

'He moved out right away of course. I offered to support him, but he turned it down. After a few months he chucked his job in, purely because *I* had got it for him.'

'Why didn't he go back to England?'

'You'd have to ask him that yourself.'

'You never spoke about it?'

'We kept in touch, sure. There were just a few weeks when we didn't talk, a time during which I fell in love with Tian, whom I had already met at a number of parties. When Owen found out we were seeing each other his entire world-view collapsed.' Joanna looked at Yoyo. 'And yet I don't care how old, fat or bald a man is. None of that matters. Tian is genuine, honest and straightforward, and I sure as hell value that! A fighter, a rock. Quick-witted, educated, liberal—'

'—rich,' completed Yoyo.

'I was rich already. Of course I liked the fact that Tian was looking for a challenge, that he was achieving success after success. But when it comes down to it there's nothing he can do that Owen wouldn't be able to do too. Except that Tian's existence is shaped by an almost unshakable belief in himself. He thinks he's beautiful and that makes him beautiful. That's why I love him.'

Joanna's story had begun to have a pleasantly numbing effect on Yoyo. She suddenly realised that she could breathe more easily when other people's problems were the topic of conversation. At the very least it was good to know that other people *had* problems. Even if they could have done with being just a little bit bigger to fully distract her from the morning's events.

'And what happened with Owen after that?' she asked.

Joanna turned her attentions to the oily strand on her palette and stirred it into a crème with a pointed paintbrush.

'Ask him,' she said, without looking up. 'I've told my story. I'm not responsible for his.'

Yoyo slid indecisively back and forth in her seat. She didn't like Joanna's unexpected uncommunicativeness. She decided to press her, but just at that moment Tu came into the studio.

'There you are!' he said to Yoyo, as if she were obliged to let him know where she was at all times.

'Has something happened?' she asked.

'Yes. Owen's been working hard. Come with me to the office – it looks like he's found out a whole load of stuff.'

Yoyo got up and looked over to Joanna. 'Are you coming?'

Joanna smiled. Vermilion dripped down from the tip of her paintbrush like old, noble blood. 'No, sweetheart, you go ahead. I'd only ask stupid questions.'

At 19.20 hours, Tu, Jericho and Yoyo immersed themselves in the beauty of the Swiss Alps. A 3D film was playing in large format on Tu's multimedia wall. It showed a cable car rising up from a picturesque little town and heading towards a neat alpine pasture, over ravines and forests of fir trees. A low, classic-looking building came into view. The Spanish commentator lauded it as one of the first designer hotels in the Alps, praising the rooms for their comfort and the kitchen for its dumplings, before heading off to accompany a group of hikers across a meadow. Cows plodded over curiously. A pretty city girl watched them approach with scepticism, started walking quickly then broke into a run towards the valley, where two donkeys came shuffling out of their shed, grey and tired, and herded her back towards the cows. Some of the hikers laughed. The next scene showed a farmer kicking one of the cows up the backside.

'Up here, traditions are still quite coarse and primordial,' explained the Spanish commentator in the tone of some behavioural scientist who has just discovered that chimpanzees aren't that intelligent after all.

'Well, this is great,' said Yoyo.

Neither she nor Tu spoke Spanish, but that didn't matter. Jericho stubbornly let the film play on, champing at the bit for his big moment.

'I don't need to explain to either of you how a film like this is developed,' he said. 'And you both know about watermarks too. So—'

'Excuse me,' said someone from the door.

They turned round. Chen Hongbing had come in. He paused, hesitantly took a step towards them and straightened himself up.

'I don't want to interrupt. I just wanted to—'

'Hongbing,' Tu hurried over to his friend and put his arm around his shoulder. 'How lovely that you're here.'

'Well.' Hongbing cleared his throat. 'I thought, we should make them smart, shouldn't we? Not for my sake, but—' He went over to Yoyo, looked at her and then away again, looked around at the others, massaged the tip of his chin and waved his hands around indecisively. Yoyo stared up at him, confused. 'So, the thing is, I'm afraid I don't know.'

'You don't know what, may I ask?' Jericho asked cautiously. Chen gestured vaguely towards the film playing on the screen.

'How something like that is developed. A, erm – watermark.' He cleared his throat again. 'But I don't want to hold you up, don't worry. I just wanted to be here too.'

'You're not holding us up, Father,' said Yoyo softly.

Chen snuffled, let out a whole cascade of throat-clearing noises, and mumbled something incomprehensible. Then he took Yoyo's hand, gave it a brief, firm squeeze and let it go again.

Yoyo's eyes started to shine.

'No problem, honourable Chen,' said Jericho. 'Have the others brought you up to date with what we know?'

'Chen, just call me Chen. Yes, I know about the – the garbled report.'

'Good. We didn't have much more than that until just now. Just a hunch that there must be something else in the films.' He wondered how he could make all of this comprehensible to Chen. When it came to technology, the man was endearingly clueless. 'You see, it's like this: every data stream is made up of data packages. Try imagining a swarm of bees, several million bees of different colours, who keep rearranging themselves in new ways so that your eyes see moving pictures. And now imagine that some of these bees are encoded. In a way that isn't visible to the viewer. But if you have a special algorithm—'

'Algorithm?'

'A mask, a decoding process. It lets you block out all of the non-encoded bees. Only the encoded ones stay. And suddenly you realise that they represent something too. You see a film within a film. That's called an electronic watermark. It's not a new process: at the beginning of the millennium it was used to encode films and songs when the entertainment industry was fighting against pirate copiers. It was enough to make just a small adjustment in the frequency spectrum of a song. The human ear can't tell the difference, but it enabled the computer to investigate the origin of the CD.' He paused. 'Today, the difference is this: the old internet mapped the data streams two-dimensionally, whereas nowadays the internet is construed for three-dimensional content. These kinds, of data streams have to be pictured cubically, which offers much better opportunities for hosting complex watermarks. Although, admittedly, decoding has become equally complex.'

'And you've decoded one of these watermarks?' asked Chen, awestruck.

'Yes. That is, Diane – erm, my computer – found a way to make it visible.'

By now, the group of hikers had valiantly climbed to a high plateau. The pretty city girl was approaching a sheep. The sheep didn't budge, and stared at the woman, who took this as encouragement to circle round, giving it a wide berth.

'Don't keep us in suspense,' said Yoyo.

'Okay.' Jericho looked back at the wall. 'Diane, start the film again. Decoded and compressed, high resolution.'

The alpine world disappeared. In its place appeared a recording of a car journey, filmed from inside the vehicle. It made its way along a bumpy street. Hilly farmland stretched out on both sides, broken up now and then by bushes and the occasional tree. There were a few huts here and there, most of them very run down. The sky was swollen with rainclouds. As the landscape steepened and became more densely populated with trees, the grey cross-hatchings of downpours stopped.

A truck was being driven a fair way ahead of the car, whirling up dust. There were a number of black men sitting in the back, most clad only in shorts. They looked lethargic, at least as far as you could tell from this distance and through the dirt from the road. Then the camera swung round to the driver, a man with ash-blond hair, a moustache and a strong jawline, wearing sunglasses.

The person holding the camera said something incomprehensible. The blond man glanced over and grinned.

'Of course,' he said in Spanish. 'Praise the President.'

They both laughed.

The picture changed. The same man was shown sitting at a long table in the company of men in uniform, this time dressed in a khaki shirt and light jacket, and without sunglasses. The camera zoomed in on him. His eyebrows and lashes were as pale as the hair on his head, his eyes watery blue, one of them with a fixed gaze, possibly a glass eye. Then the camera panned out and captured the table in its entirety. Two Chinese men in suits and ties were presenting some charts. The target audience of their report seemed to be a brawny figure at the head of the table, bald, bull-necked and as black as polished ebony. He was wearing plain overalls. The uniforms of the other participants, who were also black, seemed more formal, dark with red-gold epaulettes and all kinds of decorations, but the bullish one was clearly the nucleus of the whole meeting, while the blond seemed to be taking on the role of spectator.

This conversation was taking place in Spanish too. The Chinese spokesman was fluent, but had an appalling accent. The topic of discussion was clearly the building of a gas to liquid plant, which was eliciting approving nods from the bullish man. The Chinese man asked his colleague for some files, with a light Beijing accent.

The camera zoomed in on the blond man again. He was making notes and following the presentation attentively.

Lines and whirling shapes suddenly flashed across the multimedia wall. Someone was trying to focus the picture. A street came into view, an inner-city landscape, full of cars. Someone was coming out of a glass building on the other side of the street, where holographic advertisement films were hovering over the façade like ghosts. The camera zoomed in on the person, going hazy many times in the process, then captured the head and upper body. Tall, clean-shaven and with his hair dyed dark, at first glance the blond was hardly recognisable. He looked around then walked off down the street. The camera flickered again, then came back into focus to show him sitting in the sun, flicking through a magazine. Now and then he sipped at a cup, then he looked up and the film ended abruptly.

'That's all there is,' said Jericho.

For a while, they were all silent. Then Yoyo said:

'It's to do with Chinese interests in Africa, right? I mean, that conference, it was obvious.'

'Could be. Did any of them look familiar to you?'

Yoyo hesitated. 'I've seen the bull-necked guy before.'

'And the Chinese men?'

'They look like corporate types. What was it about again? Gas to liquid plants? Oil managers, I'd say. Sinopec or Petrochina.'

'But you don't know them?'

'No.'

'Any other thoughts, anyone?'

He looked around. Tu seemed to want to say something, but shook his head.

'Okay. I haven't had a chance to analyse the film yet, but I can tell you a few things. In my opinion the recordings are purely and simply about the blond guy. Twice we see him in an African country, where he seems to hold a public position, then later, with his appearance changed, in a city somewhere in the world. He's dyed his hair darker and shaved off the moustache. Conclusions?'

'Two,' said Yoyo. 'Either he's on a secret mission, or he had to go underground.'

'Very good. So let's ask ourselves—'

'Owen.' Tu gave him a lenient smile. 'Could you not come straight to the point?'

'Sorry.' Jericho shrugged apologetically. 'So, I instructed Diane to scour the internet in search of the man, and she found him.' He added a dramatic pause, not caring whether Tu liked it or not. 'Our friend's name is Jan Kees Vogelaar.'

Yoyo stared at him. 'There's a Jan in the text fragment!'

'Exactly. So we've got two men who are connected with the incidents of the last few days. One of them being Andre Donner, about whom all we know is that he's running an African restaurant in Berlin, but nonetheless. And Jan Kees Vogelaar, top mercenary and personal security advisor to a certain Juan Alfonso Nguema Mayé, if that rings any bells with any of you.'

'Mayé,' echoed Tu. 'Wait, where have I—'

'In the news. From 2017 to 2024 Juan Mayé was the president and sole dictator of Equatorial Guinea.' Jericho paused. 'Until he was violently removed from office.'

'That's right,' murmured Tu. 'Look! We may have our coup.'

'Possibly. So let's assume it's not about plans to overthrow the Communist Party after all, nor some other crazy conspiracy story. That means the coup being discussed in the text fragment would have taken place a long time ago. Last July, to be precise. And with the *involvement* of the Chinese government no less!'

Chen raised his hand. 'Where is Equatorial Guinea anyway?'

'In West Africa,' Yoyo explained. 'A horrid little coastal state with a hell of a lot of oil. And the guy with the bull-neck—'

'—is Mayé,' confirmed Jericho. 'Or rather, *was*. His ambitions to stay in power didn't do him any good. They blew him and his whole clique up. No one survived. It was all over the news in 2024.'

'I remember. We were planning to do some research about Equatorial Guinea back then. When we were still interested in foreign politics.'

'Why aren't you now?'

Yoyo shrugged. 'What else can you do when the rubbish is piling up in front of your own door? You walk through the streets and see the migrant workers sleeping on the building sites the way they always have, the same place where they fuck, breed and kick the bucket. You see the illegal immigrants without papers, without work permits, without health insurance. The filth in Quyu. The queues in front of the appeal offices, the government-hired thugs who turn up at night and beat them black and blue until they've forgotten what they wanted to complain about. And all the while Reporters Without Borders announces that freedom of opinion has demonstrably improved in China. I know it sounds cynical, but after a while the problems of exploited Africans don't even register on your radar.'

Chen lowered his gaze, painfully moved.

'Let's stick with Vogelaar for now,' decided Tu. 'What else can you tell us about him?'

Jericho projected a chart onto the wall. 'I've investigated him as much as I could. Born in South Africa in 1962 as the son of a Dutch immigrant, he did military service, studied at the military academy, and then in 1983, aged twenty-one, he signed up as an NCO with the notorious Koevoet.'

'I've never heard of them,' said Yoyo.

'Koevoet was a paramilitary unit of the South African police formed to combat SWAPO, a guerrilla troop fighting for the independence of South-West Africa, now Namibia. Back then, the South African Union refused to retreat from the area despite a UN resolution, and instead built up Koevoet, which, by the way, is the Dutch word for crowbar. Quite a rough bunch. Predominantly native tribal warriors and trackers. Exclusively white officers. They hunted down the SWAPO rebels in armoured cars and killed many thousands of people. They were said to have tortured and raped too. Vogelaar even became an officer, but by the end of the eighties the group had come to an end and was disbanded.'

'How do you know all that?' asked Tu in amazement.

'I looked it up. I just wanted to know who we're dealing with here. And it's very interesting by the way. Koevoet is one of the causes of the South African mercenary problem: at any rate, the troop included three thousand men who found themselves unemployed after the end of apartheid. Most of them, including Vogelaar, found jobs with private mercenary firms. After the suppression of Koevoet at the end of the eighties, he got into the arms trade, working as a military advisor in conflict areas. Then, in 1995, he went to Executive Outcomes, a privately run security company and meeting place for a large proportion of the former military elite. By the time Vogelaar joined, the outfit was already playing a leading role in the worldwide mercenary trade, after initially being content with infiltrating the ANC. By the mid-nineties, Executive Outcomes had built up perfect connections. A network of military service companies, oil and mining firms: one which headed lucrative contract wars and was very happy to profit from the petroleum industry. They ended the civil war in Somalia in the interest of American oil companies, and in Sierra Leone they recaptured diamond mines which had fallen into the hands of the rebels. Vogelaar built up excellent contacts there. Four years later he transferred to Outcomes' offshoot Sandline International, but it drew unwanted attention through bodged operations and ended up abandoning all activities in 2004. He eventually founded Mamba, his own security company, which operated predominantly in Nigeria and Kenya. And Kenya is where we lose all trace of him, sometime during the unrest after the 2007 elections.' Jericho looked at them apologetically. 'Or, let's say that's where I lose trace of him. In any case, he appears again in 2017, at Mayé's side, whose security apparatus he led from then on.'

'A gap of ten years,' commented Tu.

'Didn't Mayé take power by military coup himself?' asked Yoyo. 'Vogelaar may have helped him with that.'

'It's possible.' Tu grimaced. 'Africa and its regicides. Stabbing everyone in the back. After a while you lose perspective. It just surprises me that they still have a clue what's going on.'

Chen cleared his throat. 'May I, erm, contribute something?'

'Hongbing, of course! We're all ears. Go ahead.'

'Well.' Chen looked at Jericho. 'You said that the whole clique of this Mayé guy got killed in the coup, right?'

'Correct.'

'And I'm translating clique in the broadest sense of the word as government.'

'Also correct.'

'Well, a coup without any fatalities at all would be unusual, to say the least.' Suddenly, Chen seemed jovial and analytical. 'Or, let's say, when weapons come into play, collateral damage is par for the course. But if the entire government clique was killed – then it can hardly be described as collateral damage, can it?'

'What are you getting at?'

'That the coup wasn't so much about forcing Mayé and his people out of office, but more about exterminating them. Every single one of them. It was planned that way from the start, or that's how it looks to me at any rate. It wasn't just a coup. It was planned mass murder.'

'Oh, Father,' sighed Yoyo softly. 'What a Guardian you would have made.'

'Hongbing is right,' said Tu quickly, before Chen could splutter at Yoyo's observation. 'And as we're clearly not afraid to poke around in the dark, we may as well jump straight to assuming the worst. The dragon has already feasted. Our country brought about this atrocity, or at least helped with it.' He sank his double chin down onto his right palm, where it rested plumply. 'On the other hand, what reason would Beijing have for annihilating an entire West African kleptocracy?'

Yoyo opened her eyes wide in disbelief. 'You don't think they're capable of it? Hey, what's wrong with you?'

'Calm down, child, I think they're capable of anything. I'd just like to know *why*.'

'This' – Chen's right hand made vague grasping motions – 'what was he called again, the mercenary?'

'Vogelaar. Jan Kees Vogelaar.'

'Well, he would know.'

'That's true, he—'

They all looked at one another.

And suddenly it dawned on Jericho: of course! If Chen was right and the Mayé government really had been the victim of an assassination, then there could only be two reasons. One, public anger had boiled over. It wouldn't be the first time an enraged mob had lynched its former tormentors, but something like that usually happened spontaneously, and moreover used different methods of execution: dismembering by machete, a burning car tyre around the neck, clubbing to death. In the short time available, Jericho hadn't been able to find out much about relationships in the crisis-torn West African state, but Mayé's fall still seemed like the result of a perfectly planned, simultaneously realised operation. Within just a few hours, all the members of the close circle around the dictator were dead. As if the plan had been to silence the entire set-up.

Mayé and six of his ministers had died in an explosion caused by a long-range missile, while a further ten ministers and generals had been shot.

But one of them had got away. Jan Kees Vogelaar.

Why? Had Vogelaar been playing both sides? A coup of this calibre was only possible with connections on the inside. Was Mayé's security boss a traitor? Assuming that this was true, then—

'—Andre Donner is a witness,' murmured Jericho.

'Sorry?' asked Tu.

Jericho was staring into space.

—*Donner be liquidated*—

'Could you perhaps let us in on your thoughts?' Yoyo suggested.

'*Donner be liquidated*,' said Jericho. He looked at them each in turn. 'I know it's bold to try to read so much into a few scraps of text. But this part seems clear to me. I've no idea who Donner is, but let's assume he knows the true background to the coup. That he knows who's pulling the strings. Then—'

—*continues a grave*—

A grave what? Risk? A risk that Donner, after having gone underground, might divulge what he knew?

—*that he knows all about*—

—*statement coup Chinese government*—

'Then what?' repeated Yoyo.

'Pay attention!' shouted Jericho, worked up. 'Let's assume Donner knows the Chinese government were involved in the coup. And that he also knows why. He could flee. He's probably not even called Donner yet in Equatorial Guinea, he's somewhere in the – in the government? Yes, in the government! Or he's high up in the military, a general or something. But whatever he is, he needs a new identity. So he becomes Donner, Andre Donner. If we had photos of those formerly in power and one of him, we'd be able to recognise him! He goes to Berlin, far away, and builds up a new existence, a new life. New papers, new background.'

'Opens a restaurant,' says Tu. 'And then he gets tracked down.'

'Yes. Vogelaar is given the commission of coordinating the simultaneous liquidation of the Mayé clan. One of them slips through his fingers, someone who could ruin everything. Think of the fuss they made trying to eliminate Yoyo just because she intercepted some cryptic material. Vogelaar's backers are worried. As long as Donner is still alive he could decide to bust the whole thing open.'

'The fact that a foreign regime brought the coup about, for example.'

'Which wouldn't be anything new,' said Jericho. 'Just look at all the places where the CIA has played a part: 1962, attempted coup in Cuba. Early seventies, Chile. 2018, the collapse in North Korea. No one had any doubt that they were involved in the assassination of Kim Jong Un. There are also some who claim China helped in Saudi Arabia in 2015, so why not in West Africa too?'

'I see. And now Vogelaar has arrived in Berlin to eliminate the miraculously rediscovered Donner.' Tu gave his neck a thorough scratch. 'That really is bold.'

'But conceivable.' Chen gave a slight cough. 'It's perfectly clear to me anyway.'

'So there you go,' whispered Yoyo.

'What?' asked Jericho.

'Well what do you think?' she snapped. 'Like I said! It's the government. I have the Party at my throat!'

'Yes,' said Jericho wearily. 'It looks that way.'

She put her face in her hands. 'We need to know more about this country. More about Vogelaar, more about Donner. The more we know, the better equipped we'll be to defend ourselves. Failing that I'll just have to pack my bags. And so will all of you. I'm sorry.'

Tu studied his fingernails.

'Good idea,' he said.

Yoyo lifted her face from the grave-like shape formed by her hands. 'What?'

'To pack your things, leave the country. It's a good idea. That's exactly what we'll do.'

'I don't understand.'

'What is there to understand? We'll look for this Donner guy. He's in grave danger. We'll warn him, and in return he'll tell us what we need to know.'

'You want to—' Jericho thought he'd misheard. 'Tian, the man lives in Berlin. That's in Germany!'

'If they even let us out at all,' said Yoyo.

'One at a time.' Tu raised his hands. 'You lot have more reservations than a porcupine about to engage in sexual activity. As if I were suggesting fleeing headlong over the border. Think about it for a second, the police were just here in this very house. Do you seriously believe we would still be sitting here if they had wanted to grab us? No, we'll just go on a little trip, all official and above board. In my private jet, if you'll allow me to extend the invitation.'

'And when do you want to set off?'

'Sometime after midnight.'

Jericho stared at him, then Yoyo, then Chen.

'Shouldn't we perhaps—'

'That's the soonest we can do it,' said Tu apologetically. 'I've still got a dinner that I can't put off, not for love nor money. It's in an hour's time.'

'Shouldn't we try calling Donner first? How do you even know for sure that he's still in Berlin? Perhaps he's gone away somewhere. Gone underground.'

'You want to warn him we're coming?'

'I just think—'

'That's a lousy idea, Owen. Let's say he answers the phone and believes you. Then we've lost him. You won't have time to catch your breath and ask questions in the time it would take him to disappear. And besides, what else are you going to do? If you sit around here in Pudong you're just going to be making a dent in all my sofa cushions.'

'So you expect us to go to Berlin,' croaked Hongbing. 'In the middle of the night?'

'I have beds on board.'

'But—'

'You're not coming anyway. Just the rapid response team: Owen, Yoyo and me.'

'Why not me?' asked Chen, suddenly outraged.

'It would be too tiring for you. No, no arguments! A small, agile troop is just right for this kind of thing. Nimble and agile. In the meantime, I'm sure Joanna can drown you in tea and give you foot massages.'

Jericho tried to picture Tu as agile and nimble.

'And if we don't find Donner?' he asked.

'Then we'll wait for him.'

'What if he doesn't come?'

'Then we'll just fly back.'

'And who,' he asked, fuelled by a dark suspicion, 'might the pilot be?'

Tu raised his eyebrows. 'Who do you think? Me.'

A few kilometres away and several metres higher up, Xin looked down on the city at night.

After a traffic jam had finally slowed the blasted dump truck down to a walking pace, he had jumped off, caught the metro to Pudong – given that there was no free COD in sight – put the last few hundred metres to the Jin Mao Tower behind him at a running pace, and then crossed the lobby as if he had taken leave of his senses. He was on a mission to satiate his hunger for something sweet, and there was a chocolate boutique in the foyer boasting pralines for the price of haute couture. Xin had purchased a pack of them, half of which he plundered just during the journey upwards. Chocolate, he had realised, helped him to think. After arriving in his suite he had thrown off his clothes, rushed into the huge marble bathroom, turned the shower on and almost rubbed his skin away in his attempt to cleanse himself of the filth of Xaxu and the stain of his defeat.

Yoyo had got away from him yet again, and this time he didn't have the faintest idea where she might be. The answer machine was on at Jericho's place. Fuelled by a surge of hate, Xin contemplated blowing up the detective agency. Then he discarded the thought. He couldn't afford to be vindictive in his current situation, and besides, after the disaster in Hongkou he didn't have the appropriate weapons. What's more, it was clear to him that there was no real reason to punish someone purely because they had exercised their God-given right to defend themselves.

Cleansed, enveloped in a cocoon of terry towelling and at an agreeable distance from the city, Xin tried to impose some order on the hornet swarm of his thoughts. First, he picked up the clothes lying all around him and dumped them in the washing basket. Then he glanced over at the ravaged box of pralines. Accustomed to subjecting his consumption of any kind of food to a master plan, and one which was intended to maintain the symmetry of what was on offer for as long as possible, Xin shuddered at what he had done. He normally ate from the outside, working his way in. There should be no excessive decimation, and the relationship of the components to one another had to remain constant. Just devouring everything on one side of the packaging was an unthinkable act! But that was exactly what he had done. He'd pounced on it like an animal, like one of those degenerate creatures in Quyu.

He sank down into the sprawling armchair in front of the floor-to-ceiling window and watched as dusk enveloped Shanghai. The city was sprinkled with multicoloured lights, an impressive spectacle despite the lousy weather, but all Xin could see was the betrayal of his aesthetic principles. Jericho, Yoyo, Yoyo, Jericho. The transgressions in the box needed to be corrected. Where was Yoyo? Where was the detective? Who had been driving the silver flying machine? The box, the box! Unless he created order there he would drift right into insanity. He began to rearrange the remaining pralines according to the Rorschach style, starting from scratch again and again until an axis ran through the box, a stable, regulatory element, on either side of which the remaining pralines mirrored each other. After that he felt better, and he began to take stock of things. There was no longer any point in following Yoyo and the detective. In just a few days everything would be over anyway, and then they could talk all they wanted. They were no longer important. The operation was the priority now, and there was only one person who could still endanger the plan. Xin wondered what conclusions Jericho had drawn from the fragments of the message that he, Kenny Xin, had sent to the heads of Hydra after tracking down the Berlin restaurant of a certain Andre Donner, recommending his immediate liquidation. Unfortunately he had attached a modified decoding program to the mail, an improved, quicker version. Every few months, the codes were exchanged for new ones. The fact that Yoyo had intercepted this very email had been the worst possible luck.

And there was nothing that could be done about it.

Andre Donner. Nice name, nice try.

He dialled a number on his mobile.

'Hydra,' he said.

'Have you eliminated the problem?'

As always, their conversation was transmitted in code. In just a few words, Xin reported on what had happened. His conversation partner fell silent for a while. Then he said:

'That's a mess, Kenny. You've done nothing you can be proud of.'

'Those that live in glass houses shouldn't throw stones,' responded Xin ill-temperedly. 'If you'd implemented a safe algorithm, we wouldn't even be in this situation.'

'It *is* safe. And that's not the issue here.'

'The issue is whatever I consider worthy of being the issue.'

'You've got a nerve.'

'Oh really?' Xin roared with laughter. 'You're my contact man, or had you already forgotten that? Just a glorified Dictaphone. If I want to hear a lecture, I'll call him.'

The other man cleared his throat indignantly. 'So what are you suggesting?'

'The same thing I've already suggested. Our friend in Berlin has to be got rid of. Anything less would be irresponsible. And besides, the address of the restaurant is in the goddamn email. If Jericho comes up with the idea of getting in touch with him, then we really have a problem!'

'You want to go to Berlin?'

'As soon as possible. I'm not leaving that to anyone else.'

'Wait.' The line went dead for a moment. Then the voice came back. 'We'll book a night flight for you.'

'What about backup?'

'Already on its way. The specialist is setting off in advance as requested. Try to be more careful with the personnel and equipment this time.'

Xin curled his lip contemptuously. 'Don't worry.'

'No, after all, I'm just the Dictaphone,' said the voice icily. 'But he's worried. So make sure you *finish* the job this time.'

Calgary, Alberta, Canada

On 21 April, Sid Bruford and two of his friends made a pilgrimage to an event in Calgary, where EMCO had proposed to outline a future that no longer existed. No one harboured any illusions that Gerald Palstein would announce anything other than the end of oil-sand mining in Alberta, which meant that all hopes were now focused on strategies for redevelopment, consolidation, or at the very least a social security plan. It was in hope of this that they were standing there, aside from the fact that it was only right and proper to be present at your own burial.

The plaza, a square park in front of the company headquarters, was filling slowly but steadily with people. As if mocking their misery, a bright yellow sun shone down on the crowd from a steel blue sky, creating a climate of new beginnings and confidence. Bruford, unwilling to abandon himself to the general bitterness, had decided to make the best of the situation. It was part of the dance of death to make fatalism look like self-confidence, to stock up on the required quota of beer and to avoid violence wherever possible. They talked about baseball for a while and stayed towards the back of the crowd, where the air was less saturated with sweat. Bruford held up his mobile and circled, trying to capture the atmosphere around them. Two pleasingly scantily clad girls came into sight, noticed him, and then started to pose, giggling. A complex of empty buildings stretched out behind them, the headquarters of a now-bankrupt firm for drilling technology, if he remembered rightly. The girls liked him – that was as sure a bet as the closure of Imperial Oil. He had handsome, almost Italian-looking features, and the sculpture of his body was his incentive for wearing little more than shorts and a muscle shirt, even in frosty temperatures. He lingered on them with the phone's camera and laughed. The girls teased. After a few minutes he turned back to his friends for a second, then when he looked round at the girls again, he realised that they were now filming him. Flattered, he began to play the fool, pulling faces, swaggering around, and even his friends felt encouraged to join in. None of them was behaving particularly maturely, or like people who had just had their sole source of income taken from them. The girls began, amidst fits of laughter, to enact scenes from Hollywood films, prompting the boys to respond to their pantomime repertoire, calling out the solutions to one another boisterously. The day was shaping up to be more fun than expected. Besides, whenever Bruford examined his reflection in the mirror he always thought he would be better placed in the film industry than the Cold Lake open-cast mine. Perhaps he would even be grateful to EMCO one day. His mood soared up to the April sun on the wings of Icarus, with the result that he almost missed the small, bald-headed oil manager climbing up onto the platform.

Someone tapped him on the shoulder. It was time. Bruford turned his head just in time to see Palstein stumble. The man steadied himself, wobbled and then collapsed. Security personnel rushed past, forming a wall against the chanting crowd. Bruford craned his neck. Was it a heart attack, a circulatory collapse, a stroke? He pushed forwards, holding his mobile up above the heads of the agitated crowd. It was an assassination attempt, it was obvious! Hadn't people seen enough of that kind of thing in films! The stumble, a mishap. But something had jerked the manager around before he had fallen to the floor. A shot, what else? Someone must have shot at Palstein – that had to be it!

What Bruford didn't know was that twenty minutes before the incident, while he was filming the girls, one of the security cameras had captured him for just a few seconds, albeit blurred and out of focus.

When the police came to analyse the transmitted material, they simply overlooked him.

But the people from Greenwatch didn't.

He could still hardly believe they had managed to track him down from just that snippet of film, on the snowball principle, as Loreena Keowa, the high-cheekboned, not particularly pretty and yet somehow sweat-inducingly arousing native Indian girl had explained to him. Greenwatch had quickly come to the conclusion that the men next to him, who were easier to make out on the film, must be his friends, and then one of them had said something to an old man in the row in front of them. It was Jack 'pain-in-the-ass' Becker of course, he could still remember that, because Becker had wound him up no end with his sentimentality. Unlike the others, Becker, who had worn his Imperial Oil overalls that day, had been captured sharply on the film, and Keowa clearly had contacts in the human resources department of the company. She had identified him, called him and showed him the recording, upon which 'what's-in-it-for-me' Becker had named both Bruford's friends and Bruford himself.

And now he was sitting here. It was a scary world! Anyone could be tracked down. On the other hand, there were worse things than sitting next to Loreena in her rented Dodge, fifty Canadian dollars richer, watching her as she loaded his blurry videos onto her computer. Loreena in her chic clothes, which didn't seem quite right for an eco-girl. A number of things were going through his head. Whether he should have asked for more money. What Greenwatch intended to do with the films. Why native Indian hair was always so shiny, and what he would need to do to make his that shiny for his career in Hollywood.

'Shouldn't we go to the police?' he heard himself suggest. A sensible question, he thought. Loreena stared at the display, concentrating on the transfer process.

'Rest assured, we will,' she murmured.

'Yes, but when?'

'It doesn't matter when,' grumbled Loreena's companion from the back seat.

'I don't know.' He shook his head and made an expression of genuine concern, proof of his acting talents; he'd always known it, it was what he'd been born to do. 'I don't want to get dragged into anything. We're obligated to tell them really, aren't we?'

'So why didn't you do it?'

'I didn't think of it. But now that we're talking about it—'

'Yes, you're right of course, we should reconsider the deal.' Loreena turned her head towards him. 'Do we know whether the material is worth fifty dollars? Perhaps there's not even anything on there.'

Bruford hesitated. 'But that would be your problem.'

'But then perhaps it's worth a hundred dollars, you see?' She raised an eyebrow. 'Don't you think, Sid? On the condition that a certain someone stops asking questions and worrying about the police?'

Bruford suppressed a grin. That was exactly what he had wanted her to say.

'Sure,' he said thoughtfully. 'I think that could be the case.'

She reached into her jacket and brought out another fifty, as if she had reckoned on this development. Bruford took it and put it with the other one.

'There seems to be quite a nest in your jacket,' he said.

'No, Sid, there were only two. And perhaps they'll have to go back in if I come to the conclusion that you can't be trusted.'

'Then I'll just take something else.' Now he couldn't help but grin. 'You have other good things inside your jacket that come in twos.'

Loreena glanced at her companion, who looked willing to resort to violence.

'Okay,' he muttered. 'I'm sorry.'

'No problem. It was a pleasure meeting you.'

He understood. With a shrug of his shoulders he opened the passenger door.

'Oh, and one more thing, Sid, just in case you do decide to call the police in a sudden passion of loyalty to the law: the money in your pocket constitutes withholding evidence for the purpose of your own personal gain. That's an offence, do you understand?'

Bruford stopped short. He suddenly felt deeply offended. With one leg already on the pavement, he leaned back in towards her.

'Are you trying to threaten me?'

'Now, you listen up, Sid—'

'No, *you* listen up! My job has gone down the crapper. I'm trying to get what I can, but a deal is a deal! Is that clear? I may have a loose tongue, but that doesn't mean I shit all over people. So kiss my ass and look after your own business.'

'What a snitch,' said the intern contemptuously as Bruford set off down the street without looking back at them. 'For another hundred dollars he'd have flogged his own grandmother.'

Loreena watched him go.

'No, he was right. We insulted him. If anyone behaved dubiously then it's us.'

'While we're on the subject – *shouldn't* we hand this footage over to the cops?'

Loreena hesitated. She hated the idea of doing something illegal, but she was a journalist, and journalists thrived on having a head start. Without giving an answer, she connected her computer to the in-car system. The Dodge she had rented at the airport had a large display.

'Come up front,' she said. 'Let's have a look at what good old Sid has to offer first.'

'It's a bit of a blind bargain.'

'Sometimes you have to take risks.'

They saw a blurred panning shot, a crowd of people, food stalls, the headquarters of Imperial Oil, a podium. Then Bruford's friends, grinning broadly into the camera. Bruford had been filming straight ahead initially, then he started to swivel round. Two young women came into shot, noticed that they were being filmed and started fooling around.

'They're having fun,' laughed the intern. 'Pretty hot, too. Especially the blonde.'

'Hey, you're supposed to be paying attention to the background.'

'I can do both.'

'Oh, sure. Men and multi-tasking.'

They fell silent. Bruford had used up a lot of memory space on the two backwater beauties' performance, in the course of which several people walked into shot, three policemen appeared, two of them took off again, and one took up his post in the shadow of the building. The girls contorted themselves into a clumsy performance, the significance of which Loreena couldn't decipher at first, until the intern whistled through his teeth.

'Not bad at all! Do you recognise it?'

'No.'

'That's from *Alien Speedmaster 7*!'

'From what?'

'You don't know *Alien Speedmaster 7*?' His amazement seemed to know no bounds. 'Don't you ever go to the cinema?'

'Yes, but it sounds like I see different films to you.'

'Well, there's a gap in your education there. Look what they're doing now! I think they're re-enacting the scene from *Death Chat*, you know the one, where those small, intelligent creatures go for the woman with the artificial arm and—'

'No, I don't know.'

The girls doubled up with laughter. This was disheartening. They had already looked at half of the material without seeing anything more than pubescent nonsense.

'What are they doing now?' puzzled the intern.

'Would you just keep your eyes on the building?'

'It looks like—'

'*Please!*'

'No, wait! I think that's from the slushy love film that was hyped up so much last year. A bit cheesy if you ask me. That guy's in it, that horny old man – you know the one. God, what's his name? Tell me!'

'Absolutely no idea.'

'Yeah, the old bastard who recently got an honorary Oscar for his life's work!'

'Richard Gere?'

'Yes, exactly! Gere! He plays the grandfather of—'

'Shh!' Loreena silenced him with a hand motion. 'Look.'

From the side exit of the central building, two athletic-looking men in casual clothes came out, strolled over to the patrolling policeman and started speaking to him. Both were wearing sunglasses.

'They don't look like oil workers.'

'No.' Loreena leaned forward, wondering why she had a feeling of déjà vu. She played the section back again and again, zooming in on their faces. A moment later, a slim woman dressed in a trouser suit walked out of the building and positioned herself next to the entrance. The policeman pointed to something, the men looked in the direction of his outstretched hand, one of them holding something under his nose, which might have been a map of the city, and the conversation continued. In the background, a pot-bellied man with long black hair approached, wound his way towards the unguarded side entrance and shuffled inside.

'Look at that,' whispered Loreena.

A few moments later, the athletic-looking men shook the policeman's hand and headed off. The woman in the trouser suit leaned against a tree, her arms folded, and then Bruford's recording jumped. Sequences followed in which the girls continued to get up to mischief, without anything happening in the immediate vicinity of the building, then the crowd of people and the podium came into view. Both uniformed officials and civilians were pushing their way forward, everything was hectic. Images that had clearly been filmed right after the assassination attempt.

'The guy that disappeared into the house—' said the intern.

'Could be anyone. The janitor, the engineer, some tramp.' Loreena paused for breath. 'But if not—'

'Then we just saw the killer.'

'Yes, the man who shot Gerald Palstein.'

They exchanged glances like two scientists who had just discovered an unknown, probably fatal virus and could see a Nobel Prize glimmering against the abyss of horror. Loreena isolated a freeze-frame of the fat man, enlarged it, connected her computer with the base station in Juneau and loaded the Magnifier, a program that could do wonders with even the grainiest of material. Within seconds, the blurred features became more contoured, strands of greasy hair separated from white skin, a straggly moustache corresponded with sparse chin stubble.

'He looks Asian,' said the intern.

Chinese, Loreena thought suddenly. China was involved in the Canadian oil-sand trade. Hadn't they even acquired licences? On the other hand, what would the death of an EMCO manager change about the fact that Alberta was lost? Or was Imperial Oil in Chinese hands? But then EMCO would have belonged to them too. No, it didn't make sense. And killing Palstein certainly didn't. As he himself had said: *Every unpopular decision I make reduces my popularity, but I'm really only the strategic leader.*

She stroked her chin.

The sequence with the fat man alone was enough to justify a report, even if the guy turned out to be harmless. Yet it would make the police look a laughing stock. Greenwatch would have used up all its ammunition at once. A brief triumph that would cost them their decisive head-start in the investigations. The chance of solving the case by themselves would be blown.

Perhaps, thought Loreena, you should be content with what you have.

Indecisive, she rewound the film to the moment when the men with the sunglasses engaged the policeman in conversation. She zoomed in on them and let the Magnifier do its work, extracting details from the blurred image which, with all likelihood, came very close to their actual appearance. But even after that the policeman still looked unidentifiable, just an average policeman. The taller of the two men, however, looked familiar to her. Very familiar, in fact.

The computer informed her that the editorial office in Vancouver wanted to speak to her. The face of Sina, editor for Society and Miscellaneous, appeared on the display. 'You wanted to know whether any other managerial figures from the oil trade have been injured since the beginning of the year.'

'Yes, that's right.'

'Bingo. Three, one of them being Umar a-Hamid.'

'The OPEC Foreign Minister?'

'Correct. He fell off his horse in January and broke his leg. He's recovered now. The nag was suspected of having connections in the Islamist camp. No, I'm just kidding. The next, Prokofi Pavlovich Kiselyev—'

'Who in God's name is that?'

'The former Project Manager of Gazprom in West Siberia. He died in March, a car accident, reported to be his own fault. The man was ninety-four years old and half blind. That's it for this year.'

'You said there were three.'

'I took the liberty of going further back. Which brings it to three. There's always someone of course, one gets sick, another dies, a suicide here and there, nothing unusual. Until you look at the case of Alejandro Ruiz, the strategic second in command of Repsol.'

'Repsol? Weren't they taken over by ENI in 2022?'

'It was discussed, but it never actually happened. In any case, Ruiz was, or is, quite an important figure in strategic management.'

'And now? Which is it: *was* or *is*?'

'That's the problem. We're not sure if he can still be counted as being alive. He disappeared three years ago on an inspection trip to Peru.'

'Just like that?'

'Overnight. He vanished. Lost without a trace in Lima.'

'What else do you know about him?'

'Not much, but if you like I can change that.'

'Please do. And thank you.'

Alejandro Ruiz—

Repsol was a Spanish–Argentine company, trailing at the bottom of the field's top ten. There weren't all that many points of contact between the Spanish and EMCO. Was she risking wasting her time? Did the disappearance of a Spanish oil strategist in Lima in 2022 have anything to do with this?

Palstein was a strategist too.

Her thoughts oscillated between this new information and Bruford's film recordings, trying to make some kind of sense out of them, knotting the ropes of logic together.

And suddenly she knew who one of the men in the sunglasses was.

'Really! I swear to you!'

They were sitting in a small café on the Fifth Avenue Southwest, just a few blocks away from the Imperial Oil Limited headquarters. Loreena was drinking her third cappuccino, and the intern was sucking at a Diet Coke and devouring an awe-inspiring breakfast, composed of porridge, fried potatoes, scrambled eggs, bacon, pancakes and much, much more. Loreena's analytical mind couldn't help wondering why someone would drink Diet Coke in the face of neutron-star-like calorie compression. Fascinated, she watched as he led a spoon of warm gruel, saturated in maple syrup, towards his mouth for processing.

'The Magnifier can't perform miracles,' said the intern. 'The picture isn't that sharp.'

'But I saw the guy just two days ago, and he was *this* close to me.' She held her hand in front of her face. Through the gaps between her fingers, she saw a sausage disappear. '*This close!*'

'Which makes me a little concerned that you may have kissed him.'

'Don't be silly. He wanted to see my ID card. As if Palstein's house were the Pentagon or something.'

The intern put his spoon down and wrinkled his forehead.

'There's nothing unusual about his security people keeping a check on things.'

'And did they? Did they check up on things? What had they lost in the house anyway?'

'As I said.' He picked his spoon back up. 'They were keeping a check that—'

'All that cholesterol has blocked up your synapses!' she said angrily. 'It's obvious that he would have security personnel around him, and police too – I mean, he didn't exactly come bearing Christmas presents. But would you send your private bodyguard into an empty house opposite? After all, Palstein isn't Kennedy. How likely is it that someone would shoot at him from there?'

His answer got lost amidst a struggle with an oversized piece of pancake.

'Let's assume the Asian guy was harmless,' she continued. 'He may have just been looking for a bathroom. That would either mean that Palstein's people overlooked him, or that they weren't interested in the fact that he went in. Both are unlikely.'

'The two guys were talking to the policeman. They couldn't even see him.'

'And the woman?'

'Are you sure she was one of them?'

'She came out immediately after them. And besides, those security types all look the same. So, suppose that the Chinese guy is our killer.'

'What makes you think he's Chinese?'

'Asian. It doesn't matter.' She leaned over. 'Just think, will you, three security people! One standing close to the entrance. Two others chatting with a policeman, just a few metres away. And none of them notices the grotesquely overweight apparition entering a building they were supposed to be guarding?'

'Perhaps the Chinese— the Asian guy was security too. Didn't Palstein tell you that he only started using a security team after Calgary? I find that much more surprising.'

'No, he didn't.' She rolled her cup around, mixing the espresso with foam. 'Just that they've been guarding *his house* since Calgary.'

'Well, it would have been better to take on someone else.'

Loreena stared at the foam and espresso mixture.

Would have been better—

'Damn, you're right.'

'Of course I am,' said the intern, scraping together the remains of the porridge. 'About what?'

'He can't trust them.'

'Because they're a dead loss. Too dumb to—'

'No, they're not.' Unbelievable! Why had she only thought of it now? The secur-ity people let the killer pass! In full knowledge of who he was! More than that, they distracted the policeman and kept their eyes on the surroundings to make sure no one stopped him from entering the house.

'Good God,' she whispered.

Dallas, Texas, USA

'It's not long ago that the ability to secure the necessary fossil fuel resources was crucial to the geopolitical role of a nation state. It was under this premise that we foresaw China leading the economic nations in the medium term, knocking the USA down to a distant second, followed by India.'

Gerald Palstein's guest lectureship at UT Dallas, a state university in the suburb of Richardson, had brought around six hundred students into the lecture theatre, most of them budding managers, economists and information scientists. It was very popular, which was as much down to Palstein's media savvy as to the fact that he was depicting a wide-screen panorama of failure, in which a *Titanic* of an energy industry rammed right into an iceberg called helium-3.

'Russia's role at this time was one of a major power as far as oil and gas were concerned. Gazprom was also referred to as a weapon. And no one used this weapon in the battle for Russia's geostrategic role as ably as the country's former president Vladimir Putin. Does anyone here still remember his nickname?'

'Gasputin,' called a young woman from the front row. There was laughter. Palstein raised his eyebrows approvingly.

'Very good. At the time, the Americans looked on with concern as China openly flirted with Russia regarding its energy requirements, and also strengthened its contacts to OPEC. The latter was pleased of course. They hadn't been courted like that in a long time and were hoping for a renaissance of their former status. And so the oil nations in the Gulf started to invest their money in the accounts of the Industrial and Commercial Bank of China, in Turkey and India instead of in American institutions, and China began to settle the bill for its oil supplies from Iran in euros instead of dollars. The balance of power shifted, along with the motivation for America's efforts to free itself from dependence on Eastern oil supplies. In 2006, representatives from Saudi Arabia travelled to Beijing to sign a number of treaties. Even Kuwait was wooing China, because it was afraid of losing ground to Russia. China knew how to exploit all of that. Although I wouldn't want to encourage any hate-filled stereotypes, one might picture the energy-hungry China of the first decade of our millennium as an octopus whose arms were silently unfurling, largely unnoticed, in the traditional mining regions of the Western oil multinationals. In the White House, they developed scenarios in which radical forces toppled the Saudi ruling dynasties, all based on the expectation that China would be involved and would ultimately station Chinese nuclear missiles in the Saudi desert. This fear was, as we now know, not completely unfounded. The fall of the house of Saud most definitely took place with concealed Chinese participation. And it's certain that if the recent conflict between Islamist and monarchist forces had grown to epic proportions and caused a public clash between China and America, then the dawning potential of helium-3 would not have led Washington's interest in another direction.'

Palstein dabbed sweat from his brow. It was hot in the lecture theatre. He wished he were on board a ship on a lake somewhere or, even better, out on the open sea with invigorating winds all around him.

'We can assume the following: if gas and oil had continued to play the dominant role, the world would look a little different today. China might have overtaken the USA instead of just catching up with them. The Chinese, Russian and Gulf states would have made an energy pact. Iran, relatively recently in possession of nuclear devices, would have more power internally than is the case today, despite its nuclear armament, and would probably have exerted more pressure on New Delhi, who, back in 2006, already had its sights on a pipeline project in partnership with Tehran, through which Caspian oil would flow to India. This pipeline was supposed to end at the Red Sea, but then the oil wouldn't have been able to flow to Israel, so for that reason the US was against it. Not an easy situation for India. A collaboration with Iran ran the risk of angering America, while concessions to Washington would have aggravated Iran. In order to escape this Catch-22, the Indians looked to a third power, to help integrate the existing two, having good contacts with both China and Iran. And so the Russians came back into play in the form of Gazprom, taking every opportunity they had to strengthen their nation, for example by turning off the gas taps to their neighbouring states and blackmailing them. Do you recognise the formation of blocs that this heralded? Russia, China, India, OPEC – that couldn't have been in Washington's interest. Faced with this situation, George W. Bush's successor, Barack Obama, turned to diplomacy. He tried to improve relations with Russia and to take the wind out of Iran's sails, a clever strategy that worked in part. But of course even Obama would have secured the USA's energy requirements by force if he had to, if the technological advancement which Washington achieved through its collaboration with Orley Enterprises hadn't opened up completely new possibilities to the Americans—'

A staff member of the UTD office came into the lecture hall, paced briskly towards him and pressed a note into his hand. Palstein smiled out into the auditorium.

'Please excuse me for a moment. What is it?' he asked softly.

'Someone wants to speak to you on the telephone, a Miss—'

'Can't it wait twenty minutes? I'm in the middle of a lecture.'

'She said it was urgent. *Very* urgent!'

'What was her name again?'

'Keowa. Loreena Keowa, a journalist. I wanted to put her off until later, but . . .'

Palstein thought for a moment. 'No, it's fine. Thank you.'

He excused himself once again, left the auditorium, walked out into the hallway and dialled Loreena's number.

'Shax' saani Keek,' he said, as her face appeared on the display of his mobile. 'How are you?'

'I know I'm interrupting—'

'To be honest, yes. I've got one minute, then I've got to get back to educating the future elite. What can I do for you?'

'I'm hoping it's me that can do something for *you*, Gerald. But for that I need a few more minutes of your time.'

'It's a bit awkward right now.'

'It's in *your* interest.'

'Hmm.' He looked out through the window across the sunlit campus. 'Okay, fine. Give me a quarter of an hour to finish my talk. I'll call you immediately afterwards.'

'Make sure no one's listening in.'

Twenty minutes later, he called her from an isolated bench in the shadow of a chestnut tree, with a view out over the university grounds. Two of his security people were patrolling within sight. All around, students were hurrying towards unknown futures.

'You sure know how to worry a man,' he said.

'Do we have an agreement on reciprocity?'

'What do you mean?'

'We help one another,' said Loreena. 'I get information, you get protection.'

'Sorry?'

'Are we in agreement?'

'Hmm.' Now he was really curious. 'Fine, yes, we are.'

'Good. I'm sending you a few photos on your mobile. Open them while we talk.'

His mobile confirmed the arrival of a multimedia message. One after another, he loaded the pictures. They showed two men in sunglasses, and a woman.

'Which of them do you know?'

'All of them,' he said. 'They work for me. Security staff. You must have met one of them, out on Lavon Lake. Lars Gudmundsson. He has the internal power of command.'

'That's right, I met him. Did you order the three of them to guard the building that you were presumably shot at from on 21 April?'

'Well, that would be a bit of an exaggeration.' Palstein hesitated. 'They were just supposed to keep an eye on the surrounding area. To be honest, I wasn't even sure if I should bring them. Having private security makes you seem like you're putting on airs, like you think you're so incredibly important. But there had been a few threats against EMCO, and against me too—'

'Threats?'

'Oh, stupid things. Nothing that we needed to take seriously. Just resentful people with existential angst.'

'Gerald, are the Chinese involved in any way with EMCO?'

'The Chinese?'

'Yes.'

'Not really. I mean, there were many attempts to take over our subsidiaries. EMCO itself is – was – too tough a nut for them to crack. And of course they had a good old poach in our coalmines.'

'Canadian oil sand?'

'That too.'

'Okay. I'm sending you another photo.'

This time an Asian face appeared on the display. Long, unkempt hair, a straggly beard.

'No' he said.

'You haven't seen him before?'

'Not that I know of. If you could let me in on—'

'Of course. Listen, Gerald, this man entered the empty building just before you took to the podium. Your security team was in the building too. In our view there's very little doubt that Gudmundsson's people not only let the Asian man pass, but also made sure that he *could*.'

Palstein stared at the photo in silence.

'Are you completely sure that you've never seen him before?' pressed Loreena.

'Not consciously, at any rate. I would remember someone like him.'

'Could he be one of your people?'

'My people?'

'I mean, do you know all your bodyguards personally, or does Gudmundsson—'

'Of course I know every single one of them, what do you expect? And besides, there aren't that many. Five in total.'

'Whom you trust.'

'Of course. They are paid by us, and besides, a respected agency for personal security provided them, EMCO has been working with them for years.'

'Then you may have a problem. If this Asian guy really is the man who shot at you, then there's good reason to believe that your own people are in on it. I need to ask you one more question, please excuse my abruptness.'

'No, it's fine.'

'Does the name Alejandro Ruiz mean anything to you?'

'Ruiz?' Palstein was silent for a few seconds. 'Wait a moment. That rings a bell.'

'I'll help you. Repsol. Strategic management.'

'Repsol – yes, I think – yes, for sure, Ruiz. We were on the same flight once. It was a while ago.'

'What do you know about him?'

'Practically nothing. My God, Loreena, we're not talking about some close-knit family here, the oil trade is huge, there are a zillion people working in it. Even now, by the way.'

'It seems Ruiz was an important man.'

'Was?'

'He disappeared. Three years ago in Lima.'

'Under what circumstances?'

'During a business trip. You see, I'm interested to find out whether the attack in Calgary has any precedents. Whether it was perhaps less about you personally and more about what you represent. So I put Ruiz's files together. Happily married, two healthy children, no debts. But he does have opponents in his own field for whom he was too liberal, too environmentally aware; he was a moralist – nicknamed Ruiz El Verde. For example, he spoke out against oil-sand exploitation and pushed for more exploration of the deep sea. Now, I don't need to tell you that the companies always shied away from cost-intensive exploration proposals when oil prices were low, and three years ago the demise was already well under way. Ruiz urged Repsol to strengthen their involvement with alternative energies. Does that remind you of anyone? Yourself perhaps?'

Incredible, thought Palstein.

'It could all be a coincidence,' Loreena continued. 'Ruiz's disappearance. China's engagement in the oil-sand trade. Even the Asian man your people allowed into the house. Perhaps he's just harmless and I'm seeing ghosts, but my gut instinct and common sense are telling me that we're on the right track.'

'And what do you think I should do now?'

'Don't trust Gudmundsson and his people. If it should all turn out to be a mistake, I'll be the first one to eat humble pie. Until then: rack your brains! About Ruiz. About critical overlaps with China. About pitfalls in your own business; and another thing too – have a think about who might have had a vested interest in your *not* going along on the moon flight. You can call me, or we can meet up, at any time. Try to find out who the Asian in the photo is, perhaps he might be on EMCO's internal database. Invest in personal security, throw Gudmundsson and his team out on their ear as far as I'm concerned, but don't go to the police. That's the only thing I'm asking of you.'

'Then you're asking a lot!'

'Just not for the moment.'

'This could all be evidence.'

'Gerald,' said Loreena insistently, 'I promise you, I won't do anything that puts you in danger, nor keep things from the police. It's just for the moment. I need a head start to be able to get an exclusive on the story.'

'Do you realise what you're telling me here? What you're asking of me?'

'We have a deal, Gerald. I may have found your would-be assassin, and that's more than the police managed in four weeks. Give me time. We're working on it under extreme pressure. I'll serve those pigs up to you on a silver platter.'

Palstein fell silent. Then he sighed.

'Fine,' he said. 'Do whatever you think is right.'